THE SPECTACULAR ORIGIN OF THE FIRST ROBOTECH WAR

ROBOTECH

THE MACROSS SAGA

BATTLECRY

Robotech novelizations based upon the animated
science fiction series produced by Harmony Gold
and available from Titan Books.

THE MACROSS SAGA: Battlecry

THE MACROSS SAGA: Doomsday

THE MASTERS SAGA: The Southern Cross

THE SPECTACULAR ORIGIN OF THE FIRST ROBOTECH WAR

ROBOTECH

THE MACROSS SAGA

BATTLECRY

JACK McKINNEY

TITAN BOOKS

Robotech – The Macross Saga: Battlecry, Vols. 1–3
Print edition ISBN: 9781803365688
E-book edition ISBN: 9781803365718

Published by Titan Books
A division of Titan Publishing Group Ltd
144 Southwark Street, London SE1 0UP

First Titan edition: October 2023
10 9 8 7 6 5 4 3 2 1

This is a work of fiction. All of the characters, organizations,
and events portrayed in this novel are either products of the author's
imagination or are used fictitiously. Any resemblance to actual persons,
living or dead (except for satirical purposes), is entirely coincidental.

A CIP catalogue record for this title is available from the British Library.

Printed and bound by CPI Group (UK) Ltd, Croydon, CR0 4YY.

BAPTISM OF FIRE

EIGHT WEEKS OF SPECIAL TRAINING HAD FAILED TO PREPARE HIM for the silent insanity of space warfare. Disintegration and silent death, the pinpoints of distant light that were laser beams locked on to his ship, the stormy marriage of anti-particles, the grotesque beauty of short-lived spherical explosions…

Rick Hunter fired the VT's thrusters as two Battlepods closed in on him from above the relative above, at any rate, for there was no actual up or down out here, no real way to gauge acceleration except by the constant force that kept him pinned to the back of his seat or pushed him forward when the retros were kicked in, no way to judge velocity except in relation to other Veritech fighters or the SDF-1 itself. Just that unvarying starfield, those cool and remote fires that were the backdrop of war.

CONTENTS

VOLUME 01
GENESIS

TO CARL MACEK,
WHO PULLED IT ALL TOGETHER

PROLOGUE

I'VE BROUGHT DEATH AND SUFFERING IN SUCH MAGNITUDE, ZOR thought. *It's only right that I spend the balance of my life bringing life.*

He looked out from the observation bay of his temporary groundside headquarters upon a planetary surface that had been lifeless a mere four days before. He saw before him a plain teeming with thriving vegetation. Already the Flowers of Life were sprouting, reaching their eager, knob-tipped shoots into the sunshine.

Zor, supreme intellect of his race and Lord of the Protoculture, nodded approvingly. At times the memories of his own past deeds, much less those of his species, seemed enough to drive him mad. But when he looked down on a scene like this, he could forget the past and be proud of his handiwork.

And above him, blocking out the light of the nearby primary, his gargantuan starship and super dimensional fortress was escaping, as he had directed. The satisfaction he felt from that and from seeing the germinated Flowers made it much easier to accept the fact that he was about to die.

He was tall and slender, with a lean, ageless face and a thick shock of bright starlight hair. The clothes he wore were graceful, regal, cut tight to his form, covered by a short cloak that he now threw back over one shoulder.

Zor could hear the alarm signals ring behind him, and the booming voice of a Zentraedi announced, "Warning! Warning! Invid troop carriers are preparing to land! All warriors to their Battlepods!"

Zor gazed away from the beauty of the exterior scene, back to the harsh reality of the base, as towering Zentraedi dashed about, preparing for battle. Even though the appearance of the Invid had taken them by surprise, even though they were badly outnumbered and at a disadvantage since the enemy held the high ground, there was a certain eagerness to the Zentraedi; war was their life and their reason for being.

In that, they had met their match and more in the Invid. Zor found bitter irony in how his own poor judgment and the cruelty of the Robotech Masters—*his* masters—had turned a race of peaceful creatures, once content with their single planet and their introspective existence, into the most ferocious species in the known universe.

While subordinates strapped armor and weapons on his great body, Dolza, supreme commander of the Zentraedi, glared down at Zor. His colossal head, with its shaven, heavy-browed skull, gave him the aspect of a stone icon. "We should have departed before the Flowers germinated! I warned you!"

Dolza raised a metal-plated fist big enough to squash Zor. Unafraid, Zor looked up at him, though his faithful aide, Vard, was holding a hand weapon uneasily. Around them the base shook as armored Zentraedi and their massive fighting pods raced to battle stations.

"What of the super dimensional fortress?" Dolza demanded. "What have you done with it?"

"I have sent it away," Zor answered calmly. "To a place far removed from this evil, senseless war. It is already nearing the edge of space, too fast and far too powerful for the Invid to stop."

That much, Dolza knew, was true. The dimensional fortress, Zor's crowning technological achievement, was the mightiest machine in existence. Nearly a mile long, it incorporated virtually everything Zor had discovered about the fantastic forces and powers springing from the Flowers of Life.

"Sent it where?" Dolza demanded. Zor was silent. "If I weren't sworn by my warrior oath to protect you"—Dolza's immense fist hovered close—"*I would kill you!*"

A few pods from the ready-reaction force were already on the scene: looming metal battle vehicles big enough to hold one or two Zentraedi, their form suggested that of a headless ostrich, with long, broad breastplates mounting batteries of primary and secondary cannon.

"I don't expect you to understand," Zor said in carefully measured tones, as explosions and shock waves shook the base. They could hear the Zentraedi communication net crackling with reports of the Invid landing.

"You were created to fight the Invid; *that* is what you must do," Zor told the giant as the headquarters' outer wall heaved and began to crumble. "Go! Fulfill your Zentraedi imperative!"

As Zor spun and ducked for cover, Vard shielded him with his own body. Dolza turned to give battle as the wall shuddered and cracked wide. Through the showering rubble leapt Invid shock troopers, the enemy's heaviest class of *mecha*, advanced war machines. Forged from a superstrong alloy, bulky as walking battleships, the mecha resembled a maniac's vision of biped insect soldiers.

They were every bit as massive as the Zentraedi pods, and even more heavily armored. Concentrated fire from the few pods already on the scene—blue lances of blindingly bright energy—penetrated the armor of the first shock trooper to appear. Even as the Invid returned fire with streams of annihilation discs, the seams and joints of its armor expanded under the overwhelming pressure from the eruptions within. It exploded into bits of wreckage and white-hot shrapnel that bounded noisily off the pods' armor.

But a trio of shock troopers had crowded in behind the first, and a dozen more massed behind them. Annihilation discs and red plasma volleys quartered the air, destroying the headquarters command center and equipment, setting fires, and blasting pods to glowing scraps or driving them back.

Armored Zentraedi warriors, lacking the time to reach their pods, rushed in to fight a desperate holding action, spraying the Invids with hand-held weapons, dodging and ducking, advancing fearlessly and suffering heavy casualties.

A swift warrior ran in under an Invid shock trooper, holding his weapon against a vulnerable joint in its armor and then triggering the entire charge all at once, point-blank. The explosion blew the Invid's leg off, toppling it, but the Zentraedi was obliterated by the detonation.

Elsewhere, an Invid mecha seized a damaged pod that could no longer fire, ripped the pod apart with its superhard metal claws, then dismembered the wounded Zentraedi within.

Scouts, smaller Invid machines, rushed in behind the shock troopers to scour the base.

It took only moments for one to find Zor; the Invid had been searching for him for a *long* time and were eager for revenge.

As the scout lumbered toward them, Vard tried to save his lord by absorbing the first blast himself, firing his little hand weapon uselessly at the Invid monster. He partially succeeded, but only at the cost of his own life—immolated in an instant by a disc. The force of the blast drove Zor back and scorched him.

The rest of the discs in the salvo were ignited by the explosion, but, having been flung aside, Zor was spared most of their fury. Still, he'd suffered terrible injuries—skin burned from his body until bone was exposed, lungs seared by fire, bones broken from the concussion and the fall, tremendous internal hemorrhaging. He knew he would die.

Before the Invid scout could finish the job, Dolza was there, firing at it with his disruptor rifle, ordering the remaining pods to concentrate their fire on it. "Zor is down! Save Zor!" he thundered. Switching to his helmet communicator, he tried to raise his most trusted subordinate.

"Breetai! Breetai! Where are you?"

The scout was blown to fiery bits in the withering fusillade, but its call had gone out; the other scouts and the shock troopers were homing in on their archenemy.

Dolza, with the remaining warriors and pods, formed a desperate defensive ring, unflinchingly ready to die according to their code.

Suddenly there was a massive volley from the right. Then an even more intense one from the left. To Dolza's astonishment, they were directed at the Invid.

Breetai had arrived at the head of reinforcements. Some of them were wearing only body armor like himself, but most were in tactical or heavily armed officers' Battlepods. The Invid line began to collapse before a storm of massed fire. More pods were arriving all the time. Dolza couldn't understand how—an invasion force was descending by the thousands from a moon-size Invid hive ship, its troopers as uncountable as insects. Surely the base must be covered by a living, swarming layer of the enemy.

But the enemy *was* being driven back, and Breetai was leading a countercharge on foot, just as a small wedge of shock troopers threatened to make good on a suicide rush at Dolza and Zor. A disc struck a pod near Breetai even as he was firing left and right with his rifle; blast and shrapnel hit his head and the right side of his face.

Breetai dropped, skull aflame, but the Zentraedi countercharge went on—somehow—to drive the Invid back to the breach in the wall.

Finally Dolza wearily lowered his glowing rifle muzzle. Pursuit of the retreating Invid could be left to the field commanders. He began to take reports from the newcomers, thus learning the details of the unexpected Zentraedi victory.

Most of the Invid had been diverted in an attempt to stop or board the dimensional fortress and had been wiped out. Even now, word of the attack was going back to the Robotech Masters; a punitive raid would have to be mounted. Breetai was being attended to by the healers and would live, though he would be scarred for life.

But all of that was of little moment to Dolza. He looked down on the smoking, broken body of Zor. Healers crowded around the fallen genius with their apparatus and medicines, but Dolza had seen enough combat casualties to know that Zor was beyond help.

...

Zor knew it as well as Dolza. Drifting in a near delirium, feeling surprisingly little pain, he heard exchanges about the dimensional fortress. He smiled to himself, though it hurt his scorched face, thankful that the starship had escaped.

Once more, he had the Vision that had made him decide to dispatch the ship; as the master of the limitless power of Protoculture, with his matchless intellect, he had access to hidden worlds of perception and invisible paths of knowledge.

He saw again an infinitely beautiful, blue-white world floating in space, one blessed with the treasure that was life. He sensed that it was or would be the crux of transcendent events, the crossroads and deciding place of a conflict that raged across galaxies.

A column of pure mind-energy rose from the planet, a pillar of dazzling force a hundred miles in diameter, crackling and swaying, swirling like a whirlwind, throwing out shimmering sheets of brilliance, climbing higher and higher into space all in a matter of moments.

As he had before, Zor felt humbled before the mind-cyclone's force. Then its pinnacle unexpectedly gave shape to a great bird, a phoenix of mental essence. The firebird of transfiguration spread wings wider than the planet, soaring away to another plane of existence, with a cry so magnificent and sad that Zor forgot his impending death. He wept for the dreadful splendor of what was to come, two tears flowing down his burnt cheeks.

But he was buoyed by a renewed conviction that the dimensional fortress must go to that blue-white planet.

The sounds of the last skirmishes came from the distance as Zentraedi rooted out and executed the last of the Invid troops. Dolza stood looking down at Zor's blackened body as its life slipped away despite all that the healers could do. Dolza suspected that Zor did not wish—would not *permit* himself—to be saved.

Whatever Zor's plan, there was no changing it now. The ship *itself*, along with a handful of Zentraedi loyal to Zor alone, had jumped beyond the Robotech Masters' reach—at least for the time being.

It was of little comfort to Dolza that final transmissions from the dimensional fortress, in the moments before transition through a spacefold, indicated that the traitors aboard had been badly wounded during the battle to get past the Invid surprise attack.

"Zor, if you die, the mission is over and I must return in defeat and humiliation," Dolza said.

"I have thwarted the Robotech Masters' plan to control the universe." Zor had to pause to cough and regain his breath, with a rattle in it that spoke of dying. "But a greater, finer mission is only beginning, Dolza…"

Zor coughed again and was still, eyes closed forever.

Dolza stood before a screen that was large even for the Zentraedi. Before him was the image of a Robotech Master. Dolza spoke obsequiously.

"…and so we have no idea where the dimensional fortress is, at least for the moment."

The Master's ax-keen face, with its hawkish nose, flaring brows, and swirling, storm-whipped hair, showed utter fury. Dolza wasn't surprised; Zor, who'd given the Masters the key to their power, *and* the mighty dimensional fortress gone, at a stroke! Dolza wondered if the Invid realized just how much damage they'd inflicted in a raid that would otherwise have been an insignificant skirmish. The Robotech Master's voice was eerily lifeless, like a single-sideband transmission. "The dimensional fortress must be recovered at all costs! Organize a search immediately; we shall commit the closest Zentraedi fleet to the mission at once, and all others will join in the effort if necessary."

Dolza bowed to the image. "And Zor, my lord? Shall I have his remains interred in his beloved garden?"

"No! Freeze them and bring them back to us personally. Guard them well! We may yet extract information from his cellular materials."

With that, the Master's image disappeared from the screen.

"Hail, Dolza! Breetai reporting as ordered."

Dolza looked him over. A day or two of Zentraedi healing had the senior commander looking fit for duty; though he was again the fierce gladiator he'd always been, he was far different.

The damage done by the annihilation discs of the Invid could not be completely reversed. The right half of Breetai's black-haired scalp and nearly half his face were covered by a gleaming alloy prosthesis, a kind of half cowl, his right eye replaced by a glittering crystal lens.

Breetai had always been given to dark moods, but his mutilation at the hands of the enemy had made him distant, cold and wrathful. Dolza approved.

Dolza had summoned Breetai to a spot on the perimeter of the reinforced base where Flowers of Life were sprouting underfoot. The supreme commander quickly outlined the situation. The details of the long struggle between Zor and the Masters, and Zor's secret plan for the future of Protoculture, shocked Breetai, as did certain other information that was Dolza's alone to tell.

"You're my best field commander," Dolza finished. "You will lead the expedition to retake the dimensional fortress."

The sunlight glinted off Breetai's metal skullpiece. "But—it *jumped!*"

Sympathy was not part of the Zentraedi emotional spectrum. Dolza therefore showed none. "You must succeed. You must recover the fortress and its Protoculture factory before the Invid do, or we'll have lost everything we've worked for."

Breetai's features resolved in taut lines of determination. "The dimensional fortress will be ours, on my oath!"

01

I had misgivings like everybody else, but I thought [the appearance of SDF-1] just might be a good thing for the human race after all when I saw how it scared hell outta the politicians.

Remark attributed to Lt. (jg) Roy Fokker in *Prelude to Doomsday: A History of the Global Civil War*, by Malachi Cain

WHEN THE DIMENSIONAL FORTRESS LANDED IN 1999 A.D., THE word "miracle" had been so long overused that it took some time for the human race to realize that a real one had indeed come to pass.

In the late twentieth century, "miracle" had become the commonplace description for home appliances and food additives. Then came the Global Civil War, a rapid spiraling of diverse conflicts that, by 1994, was well on its way to becoming a full-scale worldwide struggle; in the very early days of the war, "miracle" was used by either side to represent any highly encouraging battle news.

The World Unification Alliance came into existence because it seemed the best hope for human survival. But its well-meaning reformers found that a hundred predators rose up to savage them: from supranational conglomerates, religious extremists, and followers of a hundred different ideologies to racists and bigots of every stripe.

The war bogged down, balkanized, dragged on, igniting every corner of the planet. People forgot the word "miracle." The war escalated and escalated—gradually, it's true, but everyone knew what the final escalation would be—until hope began to die.

And in a way nobody seemed to be able to stop, the human race moved along the path to its own utter obliteration, using weapons of its own fashioning. The life of the planet was infinitely precious, but no one could formulate a plan to save it from the sacrificial thermonuclear fire.

Then, almost ten years into the Global Civil War, the thinking of *Homo sapiens* changed forever.

The dimensional fortress's arrival was a coincidence beyond coincidence and, in the beginning, a sobering catastrophe.

Its entry was that of a powered object, and it had appeared from nowhere, from some unfathomable rift in the timespace continuum. Its long descent spread destruction and death as its shock waves and the after-blast of its monumental drive leveled cities, deafened and blinded multitudes, made a furnace of the atmosphere, and somehow awakened tectonic forces. Cities burned and fell, and many, many died.

Its approach rattled the world. The mosques were crowded to capacity and beyond, as were the temples and the churches. Many people committed suicide, and, curiously enough, the three most notable high-casualty-rate categories were, in this order: fundamentalist clergy, certain elected politicians, and major figures in the entertainment world. Speculation about their motives—that the thing they had in common was that they felt diminished by the arrival of the alien spacecraft—remained just that: speculation.

At last the object slowed, obviously damaged but still capable of maneuvering. Its astonishing speed lessened to a mere glide— except that it had little in the way of lifting surfaces and was unthinkably heavy. It came to rest on a gently sloping plain on a small island in the South Pacific, once the site of French atomic tests, called Macross.

The plain was long and broad, especially for such a tiny island, but it was not a great deal longer than the ship itself. A few hundred yards behind its thrusters, waves crashed against the beach. A short distance ahead of its ruined bow were sheer cliffs.

Its outer sheath and first layers of armor, and a great portion of the superstructure, had been damaged in the course of its escape, or in the controlled crash of its landing. It groaned and creaked, cooling, as the combers foamed and bashed the sand on an otherwise idyllic day on Macross Island.

The human race began assessing the damage in a dazed, uncoordinated way. But it didn't take long for opposing forces to convince themselves that the crash was no enemy trick.

For the first few hours, it was called "the Visitor." Leaders of the various factions of the civil war, their presumed importance reduced by the alien vessel's appearance, took hasty steps toward a truce of convenience. The various commanders *had* to move quickly and *had* to sacrifice much of their prestige to accommodate one another; all eyes were turned to the sky and to Macross Island. The Global Civil War looked like a minor, ludicrous squabble compared to the awesome power that had just made itself felt on Earth.

Within hours, preparations were being made for an expedition to explore the wreckage. Necessary alliances were struck, but safety factors were built into the expeditionary force. Enemies at the top had accomplished an uneasy peace.

Now, those who'd *fought* the war would have to do the same.

The flight deck of the Gibraltar-class aircraft carrier *Kenosha* retreated beneath the ascending helicopter, a comforting artificial island of nonskid landing surface. Lieutenant (jg) Roy Fokker watched it unhappily, resigning himself to the mission at hand.

He turned to the man piloting the helo, Colonel T.R. Edwards, who was flying the chopper with consummate skill. Roy Fokker was more used to those occasions when he and Edwards were doing turns-and-burns, trying to shoot each other out of the skies.

Roy Fokker was an Internationalist, right down to his soles. His uniform bore the colors of his carrier aviation unit, a fighter squadron: the Jolly Ranger skull-and-crossbones insignia. The colors were from the old United States Navy, the renowned and justly feared VF-84 squadron of the USS *Nimitz* that had hunted the skies in F-14 Tomcats, then Z-6 Executioners, right up to Roy's own production-line-new Z-9A Peregrine.

Roy wished he was back there in his own jet, in his own cockpit.

For so important a takeoff, it would have been normal to see the *Kenosha*'s skipper on the observation deck under phased-array radar antenna and other tower shrubbery—the deck the aviators called Vulture's Row. Admiral Hayes and the other heavy-hitters were all there, but Captain Henry Gloval wasn't. Today, Captain Henry Gloval was belted in the rear of the helo with a platoon of marines and some techs and more scientific equipment and weapons than Roy had seen packed into a bird before. That the Old Man should actually leave his command and go ashore showed how topsy-turvy this spaceship or whatever it was had turned matters on Earth.

It was as oddball a mission as Roy had ever seen; it made him uncharacteristically nervous, *especially* since the opposition junta had picked Edwards as its representative on the team.

The last time Edwards and Roy had crossed contrails, Edwards had been in the hire of something called the Northeast Asian Co-Prosperity Sphere. There was no telling who he was *really* working for now, except that he was *always*, without exception, out to benefit Colonel T.R. Edwards.

Roy told himself to stop thinking about it and do his job. He fidgeted in his seat a little, uncomfortable in web gear weighted with about a hundred pounds of weapons, ammo, and survival and exploration equipment.

He pushed his unruly mop of blond hair back out of his eyes. He wasn't sure why or when long hairstyles had become the norm among pilots, but now it was practically de rigueur. Some *Samurai* tradition?

He glanced over at Edwards. The mercenary was perhaps thirty, ten years older than Roy, with the same lean height. Edwards had tan good-looks and sun-bleached hair and a killer smile. He seemed to be enjoying himself.

Roy's youth didn't make him Edwards's inferior in combat experience or expertise. The practical philosophy of the old-time Swiss and Israelis and others like them was now the rule: Anyone who could fly well did, and they flew as leaders if they merited it, regardless of age or rank.

All the tea-party proprieties about a flyer needing a college education and years of training had been thrown out as the attrition of the war made them untenable. Roy had heard that kids as young as fourteen were in the new classes at Aerial Combat School.

Edwards had caught the glance. "Want to take over, Fokker? Be my guest."

"No thanks, Colonel. I'm just here to make sure you don't mess up and spike us into the drink."

Edwards laughed. "Fokker, know what your problem is? You take this war stuff too personally."

"Tell me something: D'you *like* flying for a bunch of fascists?"

Edwards snorted derisively. "You think there's that much difference between sides, after ten years of war? Besides, The Neasians pay me more in a week than you make in a year."

Roy wanted to answer that, but his orders were to avoid friction with Edwards. As if to remind him of that, a sudden aroma wafted under his nose. It was pipe tobacco, but to Roy it always smelled like a soap factory on fire.

Gloval was at it again. But how do you tell your commanding officer that he's breaking regs, smoking aboard an aircraft? If you are a wise young lieutenant (jg), you do not.

Roy turned back to study Macross and forgot Gloval, Edwards, and everything else. There lay the blackened remains of a ship like nothing Earth had ever seen before.

"*Great God!*" Roy said slowly, and even Edwards had nothing to add.

The wreck was cool, and radiation readings were about normal. Previous fly-bys hadn't drawn fire or seen any activity. The helo set down a few dozen yards from the scorched, broken ruin. In another few moments the team was offloading itself and its equipment.

Gloval, a tall, rangy man with a soot-black, Stalinesque mustache, captain's hat tilted forward on his brow, was establishing security and getting ready for preliminary external examination of the wreckage. He was square-shouldered and vigorous, looking younger than his fifty-odd years until one saw the lines around his eyes.

But while the preparations were going on, Lance Corporal Murphy, always itching to be on the move, couldn't resist doing a little snooping. "Hey, lookit! I think I found a hatch!"

Gloval's voice still retained its heavy Russian accent. "You jackass! Get away from there!"

Murphy was standing near a tall circular feature in the battered hull, waving them over. With his back to it, he didn't see the middle of the hatch open, the halves sliding apart. He couldn't hear his teammates' shouted warnings, as several long, segmented metal tentacles snaked out.

In another moment, the unlucky marine was caught and lifted off his feet. The service automatic in his hand went off, then fell from his grasp, as he was yanked within. None of the others dared to shoot for fear of hitting him.

The hatch snapped shut. Gloval spread his arms to hold back Roy and some of the others; they would have charged for the hatch. "Stand where you are and hold your fire! Nobody goes any closer until we know what we're dealing with!"

An hour later things *had* changed, although the explorers didn't know much more than they had at the beginning.

At Admiral Hayes's insistence, Doctor Emil Lang had been choppered ashore to supervise. Lang was Earth's premier mind, by decree of Hayes and Senator Russo and the others in the alliance leadership, the final authority on interplanetary etiquette.

Lang ordered everyone into anticontamination suits, then directed a human-size drone robot to make preliminary exploration of the ship. When the robot, essentially a bulbous detector/telemetry package on two legs, stopped dead in front of the hatch as the hatch reopened, Long looked thoughtful.

The robot refused to respond to further commands, the hatch stayed open, and there was no sign of activity within. Lang's eyes narrowed behind his suit's visor as he concentrated.

Lang was a man just under medium height, slight of build, but when it came to puzzling out the unknown, he had the courage of a lion. Disregarding his orders, he directed Gloval to select a party to explore the wreck. Gloval picked himself, Roy, Edwards, and eight of the grunts.

"Get those spotlights on," Lang instructed. "And you may chamber a round in your weapons, but leave the safeties on. If anyone fires without my direct order, I'll see that he's court-martialed and hung."

Unnoticed, T.R. Edwards made a wry face inside his suit helmet and flicked his submachine gun selector over to full auto.

The lights they'd brought—spotlights mounted on the shoulders of their web gear—were powerful but not powerful enough to reach the farthest limits of the compartment in which they found themselves. Lang and Gloval only studied what was before them, but from the others were soft exclamations, curses, obscenities.

It resembled a complex cityscape. The alien equipment and machinery was made of glassy alloys and translucent materials, with conduitlike structures crisscrossing in midair and oddly shaped contrivances in every direction. The spacecraft was built to a monumental scale.

Readings still indicated no danger from radiation, atmospheric, or biological contamination; they removed the suits.

"We will divide into two groups," Gloval decided, still in charge of the tactical divisions. "Roy, you'll take four marines. Dr. Lang, Edwards—you'll be in my group."

They were to work their way forward, following opposite sides of the wreck's inner hull, in an attempt to link up in the bow. Failing that, they would observe as much as possible and fall back to their original point of entry in one hour.

They started off. No one heard the inert probe robot suddenly reactivate and step through the open hatch in their wake, moving more nimbly than it had a few minutes before.

Fifteen minutes later, in a passageway as high and wide as a stadium, Roy paused to shine his shoulder-mounted lights around him. "This place must be playing tricks on my eyes. Does it look to you like the walls're moving?" he asked the gunnery sergeant behind him.

The gunny said slowly, "Yeah, kinda. Like there's a fog or somethin' flowin' through all the nooks and crannies."

Roy was about to get them moving again when he heard someone calling softly, "Caruthers. Hey, *man*, where y' at?"

Caruthers was the man walking drag at the rear of the file; they all turned back to see what was going on. Caruthers had fallen far behind for some reason; but he was rejoining them, his spots getting nearer. But something about the man's movements wasn't normal. Moreover, his head hung limply and he appeared to be moving considerably above them, as if on a catwalk.

They flashed their beams his way and stood rooted in astonishment and stark terror. Caruthers's body hung on a line, like a tiny puppet, held in the hand of a humanoid metal monster seventy feet tall.

The armored behemoth swung its free hand in their direction. They didn't have time for permission to react; they wouldn't have listened if Lang had denied it, anyway.

Roy and the gunny and the other marines opened fire, the chatter of their submachine guns loud in their ears. Their tracers lit up the darkness, as the bullets bounced off the monster's armor as if they were paper clips.

Its right hand loosed a stream of reddish-orange fury. A marine disappeared like a zapped bug, turned to ash in an instant.

02

I suppose, in the back of my mind, I was aware that fate had sent my way a chance to he mentioned in the same breath with Einstein, Newton, and the rest. But to tell the truth, I thought little of that. Before the lure of so much new knowledge, any scientist would've made poor old Faust look like a saint.

Dr. Emil Lang, *Technical Recordings and Notes*

ROY AND THE OTHERS EMPTIED THEIR WEAPONS TO NO AVAIL. The looming weapon hand swung to a new target as they ducked, switching their turned and taped double magazines around to lock and load a fresh one.

A second stream of superheated brilliance blazed, and another marine was incinerated.

Roy realized the radio was useless; it was in Hersch's rucksack, and he'd just been fried. Roy turned, spotted the RPG rocket launcher dropped by the first victim, and made a dive for it.

The gunnery sergeant gave him a look of misgiving but kept his peace. Firing the weapon might be suicidal for a number of reasons, including secondary explosions from their attacker, but Roy saw no other options; their escape was cut off, and there was no cover worthy of the name.

The RPG was already loaded. Roy peered through the sights, centering the reticle, and fired at the thing's midsection, where two segments met. The resulting explosion split the metal monster in half; it toppled, venting raging energy. The secondary blast knocked Roy off his feet.

He lost consciousness for a second but came to, momentarily deafened, with the gunny shaking him. Roy managed to read his lips: *"It's still alive!"*

Blearily Roy followed the pointing finger. It was true: Segments of the shattered behemoth were rocking and jouncing; those that had some articulation were trying to drag themselves toward the intruders. Other pieces were firing occasional beams, most of which splashed off the faraway ceiling.

The gunny got Roy to his feet and began dragging him around the remains in what seemed like the direction from which they'd come. Even though he couldn't hear, Roy could feel heavy vibrations in the deck. He turned and found a second monster approaching. He couldn't figure out how the first one had come upon them so silently, and he didn't wait around to find out.

The thing halted by the smoldering debris of the first as Roy staggered off behind the gunny.

"…remember coming through here," Roy dimly heard the gunny say when they paused after what seemed like a year of tottering along the deck. Evidently, the gunny had covered his ears to avoid the rocket's impact; he was listening as well as looking for more enemies.

"Neither do I," Roy said wearily. "But all our other routes were blocked."

"They could've polished us all off, Lieutenant," the gunny said.

Roy shook his head, just as confused as the marine. "Maybe they're herding us along somewhere; I dunno."

They took up their way again. Roy's hearing was coming back, accompanied by a painful ringing. "Maybe they don't want to kill all of us because—"

The gunny screamed a curse. Roy looked down to see that the deck plates were rippling around their legs like a running stream, engulfing them.

Gloval gripped his automatic resolutely. "Are you getting all this on the video, Dr. Lang?"

Lang put his palm to his forehead. "Yes, but those shapes keep shifting… gets me dizzy just looking…"

"Kinda like… vertigo…" T.R. Edwards added.

Gloval was feeling a little queasy himself. He called a halt for a breather, sending Edwards to peer into the next compartment. Gloval watched Lang worriedly; with the arrival of the alien ship, Lang became the most indispensable man on the planet. Lang must be kept safe at all costs, and the fact that Gloval couldn't raise Roy's party or the outside world on the radio had the captain skittish.

Edwards was back in moments, face as white as his teeth.

"You'd better brace yourselves." Edwards swallowed with difficulty. "I found Murphy, but—it's a little hard to take." He swallowed again to keep from vomiting.

One by one they went to join him at the entrance to the next compartment, from which an intense light shone. Lang caught the edge of the hatch to steady himself when he saw what was there.

In a large translucent tank wired with various life support systems floated the various pieces of Lance Corporal Murphy in a tiny sea of sluggish nutrient fluid.

They drifted lazily, here an arm, there the head—sightless eyes wide open—a severed hand bumping gently against the stripped torso. The fluid was filled with fine strands glowing in incandescent greens. Tiny amoebalike globules flocked to the body parts and away from them again, feeding and providing oxygen and removing wastes.

Gloval turned to the marine behind him. "Establish security! Whoever did this may still be around." The men shook off their paralysis and rushed to obey.

All, that is, but one, who was about to pluck out a leg by a white, wrinkled foot that had bobbed to the surface. "We can't leave 'im like this!" Through the grinding war, the marines had maintained their honor and their high traditions proudly; *esprit de corps* was like the air they breathed. To leave one of their own on the battlefield was to leave a part of themselves.

But Lang pulled the grunt back with surprising strength. "Don't touch him! Who knows what the solution is? You want to end up pickled in there too? No? *Good!* Then just draw a specimen with this device and be careful!"

Gloval, carefully gauging the alien topography to keep his mind—and eyes—off Murphy's parts, determined that his suspicions were true: The internal layout of the place was changing around them. There was no way back.

He quickly formed up his little command and got them moving, grimly satisfied that Edwards wasn't so cocky anymore.

Moments later, as the party moved through a darkened area, he felt a marine tug at his shoulder. "Cap'n! There's a—"

And all hell broke loose as armored behemoths set upon Gloval's group from the rear, blasting and trying to stamp the puny humans into the deck.

One marine gave the beginning of a shriek and then blew into fragments, the moisture in his tissues instantaneously converted to steam, the scraps of flesh vaporized in the alien's beam.

The humans cut loose with all weapons, including a manportable recoilless rifle and a light machine gun whose drum magazine was loaded with Teflon semi-armorpiercers. A second marine was cremated almost instantly.

They had better luck than Roy's team in that the machine gunner and the RR man both happened to aim for the lead monster's firing hand and were lucky enough to find a vulnerable point, blowing it off.

The fortress's guardian staggered and shook as the fire set off secondary explosions. "Gloval! *In here!*" screamed Edwards, standing at the human-size hatch to a side compartment. The survivors dashed to it, crowding in, two of the marines hauling Lang between them while the doctor continued recording the scene as the injured machine-thing shot flame and smoke and flying shrapnel through the air.

"We can hold 'em off from here—for now," Edwards said, throwing aside a spent pair of magazines and inserting a fresh one in his Ingram MAC-35.

"Concentrate fire on anything that approaches that door," Gloval told the marines, and turned to survey the rest of the compartment. It was quite tiny by the standards of the wreck: Perhaps eight paces on a side, with no other exit.

Lang was shaken but in control, *willing* his hands to be steady as he took what videos he could of the scene in the outer compartment. Gloval was about to command him to get back out of the line of fire when the floor began to move.

"Hey! Who pushed the up button?" Edwards shouted, pale again.

"*Security wheel!*" Gloval bellowed. "Doctor Lang in the center!"

Lang was thrust into the middle of the rising elevator platform as the others put their backs against him, weapons pointed out before them. The ceiling was about to crush them, but suddenly it rippled like water, letting them pass through. They came up into a brighter place and heard a familiar voice.

"Well, well. 'Bout time you guys got here."

"Roy!" The lieutenant stood leaning against a stanchion in the most immense chamber they'd seen yet, lit as bright as day.

When stories were exchanged, Gloval said, "All right, then, we've been herded here. But why?"

Lang pointed to a bridgelike structure enclosed by a transparent bowl, high to the stern end of the compartment. It was big but seemingly built to human scale.

"I'm betting that is the ship's nerve center, skipper, and that is the captain's station."

"It's our best shot, so we shall try it," Gloval decided, "but you stay with the main body, my good doctor, and let Roy go first."

"What an honor." Edwards grinned at Roy.

Zor's quarters were as he had left them, so long ago and far away. The sleep module, the work station, and the rest were built to human scale and function. Lang stared around himself as if in a dream.

Despite the many objects and installations that were impossible to identify, there was a certain comprehensibility to the place: here, a desk unit, there, a screen of some kind.

Roy, Gloval, and the others were so fascinated that they didn't notice what Lang was doing until they heard the pop and crisp of static.

"Lang, you fool! Get away from there!"

But before Gloval could tear him away from the console, Lang had somehow discovered how to activate it. Waves of distortion chased each other across the screen, then a face appeared among the wavering lines.

Gloval's grip on Lang's jacket became limp. "Good God... it's *human!*"

"Not quite, perhaps, but close, I would say," Lang conceded calmly.

Zor's face stared out of the screen. The wide, almond eyes seemed to look at each man in the compartment, and the mouth spoke in a melodious, chiming language unlike anything the humans had ever heard before.

"It's a 'greetings' recording," Lang said matter-of-factly. "Like those plates and records on the old Voyagers," Roy murmured.

The alien's voice took on a different tone, and another image flashed on the screen. The humans found themselves looking at an Invid shock trooper in action, firing and rending.

"Some kind of war machine. Nasty," Lang interpreted.

As the others watched the image, Roy touched Gloval's shoulder and said, "Captain, I think we'd better get out of here."

"But *how*? This blasted ship keeps rearranging itself."

"*Look!*" cried Edwards, pointing. The deck rippled as a newcomer rose up through it. All weapons came to bear on it except Lang's; the doctor was dividing his attention between what was going on and the continuing message on the screen.

A familiar form stood before them. "It's the drone robot, the one that broke down," the gunny said.

Edward's eyes narrowed. "Yeah, but how could it have followed us?"

"It appears to be functioning again," Gloval said. "Maybe we can use it to contact the base."

Lang crossed to the robot, which waited patiently. He opened a rear access cowling and went to inspect the internal parts there, then snatched his hands back as if he'd been bitten.

They all crowded around warily, ready to blast the machine to bits. "This isn't the original circuitry," Lang said, sounding interested but not frightened. "The components are reshaping themselves."

As they stared, wires writhed and microchips changed like a miniaturized urban renewal project seen from above by time-lapse photography. Things slid, folded, altered shape and position.

It reminded Roy of an unlikely cross between a blossoming flower and those kids' games where the player slides alphanumeric tiles around into new sequences.

"Perhaps it's been sent here to lead us out," Gloval suggested.

"But why'd the other gizmos attack?" Edwards objected.

Lang shrugged. "Who knows what damage the systems have suffered? Perhaps the attacks are a result of a malfunction. Certainly, the message we just saw was intended as a warning, which implies good intentions."

"But what's it all mean, Doc?" Roy burst out.

Lang looked to him. "It means Earth may be in for more visitors, I think. *Lots* more."

"All right, all of you: Get ready," Gloval said. "If we can get the drone to lead us, we'll take a chance on it. We've no alternative."

While the others readied themselves, dividing up the remaining ammunition, reloading the last two rocket launchers, and listening to Gloval direct their order of march, Lang went back to the screen console.

He had been right; this *was* the ship's nerve center, and the console and its peripherals were the nucleus of it all. Lang began form-function analysis, fearing that he would never get another chance to study it.

Certainly, the ship used no source of power that he could conceive of. Some uncanny alien force coursed through the fallen ship and through the console. Perhaps if he could get some data on it or get access to it…

At Lang's cry they all turned with guns raised, as strobing light threw their shadows tall against the bulkheads. The command center flashed and flowed with power like an unearthly network of electronic blood vessels.

The console was surrounded by a blinding aurora of harsh radiance that pulsed through the spectrum. Lang, body convulsed in agony, holding fast to the console, shone with those same colors as the enigmatic forces flooding into him.

"Don't touch him!" Gloval barked at Roy, who'd been about to attempt a body check to knock Lang clear. Edwards moved to one side, well

out of range of the discharges, to get a line of fire on the console that wouldn't risk hitting Lang. Edwards made sure his selector was on full auto and prepared to empty the magazine into the console.

But before he could, the alien lightning died away. Lang slumped slowly to the deck.

"Captain, the robby's leaving!" The gunny pointed to where the deck was starting to ripple around the drone's feet.

There was no time for caution. Roy slung Lang over his shoulder, hoping the man wasn't radioactive or something else contagious. In another moment they were all ranged around the robot, sinking through the floor.

Air and matter and space seemed to shift around them. Lang was stirring on Roy's shoulder, and Roy was getting a better grip on him, distracted, when one of the marines hollered, "Tell me I'm not seein' this!"

The ship had changed again, or they were in a different place. And they were gazing at the remains of a giant.

It was something straight out of legend. The skeleton was still wearing a uniform that was obviously immune to decay. It also wore a belt and harness affair fitted with various devices and pouches. But for the fact that it would've stood some fifty feet tall, it could have been human.

The jaw was frozen open in an eternal rictus of agony and death; an area the size and shape of a poker table was burned through the back of its uniform, fringed by blackened fabric. Much of the skeletal structure in the wound's line of fire was gone.

"Musta been some scrap," a marine said quietly, knowingly. Lang was struggling, so Roy let him down. "Are you all right, Doc—"

Roy gaped at him. Lang's eyes had changed, become all dark, deep pupil with no iris and no white at all. He had the look of a man in rapture, gazing around himself with measureless approval.

"Yes, yes," Lang said, nodding in comprehension. "I *see*!"

There was no time to find out just what it was he saw, because the robot was in motion again. Roy took Lang in tow, and they moved out, only to round a corner and come face to face with two more of the armored guardians.

The gunny, walking point right behind the robby with one of the RPG launchers, let fly instantly, and the machine gunner and the other RPG man cut loose too as the red lines of tracers arced and rebounded off the bright armor.

INTERLUDE

Listen, take the Bill of Rights, the Boy Scout oath, and the Three Laws of Robotics and stick 'em where there's no direct dialing, jerk! "Good" is anything that helps me stay at the top; "bad" is whatever doesn't, got it?

Senator Russo to his reelection committee treasurer

"AND IN BRIEF," ADMIRAL HAYES FINISHED, "CAPTAIN GLOVAL'S party made it back out of the ship with no further casualties, although they encountered extremely heavy resistance."

Senator Russo puffed on his cigar, considering the report. "And Doctor Lang?"

"Seems to be all right," Hayes said. "They wanted to keep him under observation for a while, but he's absolutely determined to resume research on the alien vessel. And you know Lang."

Indeed. Earth's foremost genius, the man to whom they would all have to look now for crucial answers, made his own rules.

"I should add one more part of the aftermission report that I still find it difficult to credit," Hayes grudged. "Captain Gloval estimates, and his and the others' watches corroborate this, that they were inside the ship for some six hours."

Russo blew a smoke ring. "So?"

Hayes scratched his cheek reflectively. "According to the guards posted outside the ship and *their* watches, Gloval and the others were only gone for approximately fifteen minutes." He sat down again at the conference table.

Russo, at the head of the table, thought that over. He knew

Hayes was too methodical an officer to include a claim like that in his report without having checked it thoroughly.

Senator Russo was a florid-faced, obese little man with a gratingly false-hearty manner and a pencil mustache. He had fat jowls and soft white hands bearing pinkie rings. He also had a brilliant tailor, a marvelous barber, and enough political clout to make him perhaps *the* most important figure in the emerging world government.

Now, he looked around the top-secret conference room aboard the *Kenosha*. "Whoever sent this vessel may come to retrieve it. Or someone else might."

He broke into an unctuous smile. "If something like this hadn't come along, we'd've had to invent it! It's perfect!"

The other power mongers gathered there nodded, sharing the sly smile, their eyes alight with ambition.

The timing of the crash was indeed astounding. Not a month before, these same men had been part of a group that had met to lay the groundwork for one of the most treacherous plots in history. It's true they were confronting the ultimate crisis—the likelihood that the human race would destroy itself. But their solution was not the most benign, just the one that would be most profitable for them.

They'd been intent on creating an artificial crisis, something that would stop the war and unite humanity under their leadership. A number of promising scenarios had been developed, including epidemics, worldwide crop failure, and a much less spectacular version of the very thing that had taken place in Earth's atmosphere and on Macross Island.

Russo's smile was close to a leer. "Gentlemen, I don't believe I'm being presumptuous when I say this is destiny at work! The blindest fool can see that mankind *must* band together."

Under our rule, was the unstated subtext. Russo saw that the true power brokers there understood, while Hayes and a few other idealistic dupes were almost teary-eyed with dedication and courage. Suckers…

It had never really mattered to the power brokers what side they served, of course; the ideologies and historical causes of the Global

Civil War meant little or nothing to them. Russo and others like him had given those mere lip service.

The important thing was to use the opportunity, to gain prestige and power. Russo had joined the Internationalists—the world peace and disarmament movement—because they offered personal opportunity. If they hadn't, he'd have thrown in with the factionalists without a qualm, so long as they promised him a route to power.

Hayes was saying, "We must act with all possible speed, throw every available resource into understanding the science behind that ship, into rebuilding it, and using this amazing 'Robotechnology,' as Doctor Lang insists on calling it."

Absolutely beautiful! Russo thought. An enormous tax-supported defense project, more expensive and more massive than anything in human history! The opportunities for profit would be incalculable. In the meantime, the military could be kept distracted and obedient, and all political power would be consolidated. More, this incredible Robotechnology business would ensure that the new world government would be absolutely unchallengeable.

Russo frowned for a moment, considering Hayes again: good soldier, obedient and conscientious, but a plodding sort of fellow (which was Russo's personal shorthand for someone prone to be honest).

Yes, Hayes might present a problem somewhere down the road—say, once Earth was rebuilt and unified and ready to be brought to heel, when it was time to make sure that those in power stayed there for good.

But there would be ways to deal with that. For example, didn't Hayes have a teenage daughter? Ah, yes. Russo recalled her now: a rather plain, withdrawn little thing, as the senator remembered. *Lisa.*

In any case, there'd be plenty of time to neutralize Hayes and those like him once they'd served their purpose. Have to keep an eye on that Lang, too.

But this Colonel Edwards, now; he seemed to be a bright young fellow—knew which side his bread was buttered on. He was already passing secret information to Russo and keeping tabs on Gloval and the others. Edwards would definitely have his uses.

"Let's have Doctor Lang, eh?" Senator Russo proposed.

Lang came in, lean and pale, emitting an almost tangible energy and purpose. The strange, whiteless eyes were unsettling to look at.

"Well, Doctor," Russo said heartily. "We've had a miracle dropped from heaven, eh? But we want you to give us the straight gospel: Can that ship be rebuilt?"

Lang looked at him as if he were seeing Russo for the first time—as if Russo had interrupted Lang during some higher contemplation, as, of course, he had.

"Rebuild it? But of course we will; what else did you think we would do?" It sounded as though he had doubts about Russo's sanity, which was mutual.

Before Russo could say anything, Lang continued. "But you used the word 'miracle.' I suppose that may be true, but I want to tell all of you something that Captain Gloval said to me when we finally fought our way out of the ship."

He waited a dramatic moment, as his whiteless eyes seemed to take in the whole conference room and look beyond.

"Gloval said, 'This will save the human race from destroying itself, Doctor, and that makes it a kind of miracle. But history and legend tell us that miracles bear a heavy price.'"

03

There's a movie my grandfather loved as a boy, and my father sat me on his knee and showed me when I was a little kid, *The Shape of Things to Come*.

The part that made the biggest impression, naturally, was when the scientist-aviator climbs out of his futuristic plane and looks the local fascist right in the eye and tells him there'll be no more war. Babe, how many times I've wished it was that easy!

Lt. Comdr. Roy Fokker, in a letter to Lt. Claudia Grant

"**F**IREWORKS," LIEUTENANT COMMANDER ROY FOKKER MURMURED to himself, neck arched back so that he could watch the bright flowers of light. The gigantic mass of Super Dimensional Fortress One blocked out much of the sky, but he could still see skyrockets burst into brilliant light above every corner of Macross City. There were banners and flags, band music, and the constant laughter and cheering of thousands upon thousands of people.

"Fireworks instead of bombs; celebrations instead of battles." Roy nodded. "I hope it's always like this: parades and picnics. We've seen enough war!"

Macross Island had changed a lot in ten years—all for the better, in Roy's opinion. After the World Government made rebuilding the alien wreck its first priority, a bright modern city had been erected around the crash site, along with landing strips used to airlift supplies and equipment, construction materials, technicians and workers and their families, and military personnel.

A busy deep-water harbor had been dredged, too. Two colossal aircraft carriers were anchored there, though they were dwarfed by the vessel in whose shadow Roy stood. Flights of helos and jetcraft made their passes overhead, rendering salute to the Earth's new defender, Super Dimensional Fortress One.

Roy glanced up at the SDF-1 again. Even after a decade, he was still awed every time he gazed at it. Its hull and superstructures gleamed, sleek and bright now, painted in blue and white. The vast transparent bubble of the bridge bulged like a spacesuit facebowl, giving the eerie impression that the fortress was keeping watch over the city.

Roy still found himself wondering what the ship had originally looked like before its terrible crash. How close had Lang and his team come to restoring it to its original state?

One thing was certain: Lang and the others had performed the most amazing technical feat in Earth's history. Not all the battle fortress's secrets were theirs, not yet; but that seemed only a matter of time. In the meantime they'd gotten the SDF-1 fully operational, and given the Earth the means to build its Robotech Defense Force—the RDF.

And today, for the first time, the general populace was going to see things that had been classified top-secret.

A flight of Veritech fighters, wings swept back for high speeds, performed a fly-by. They were from Skull Team, Roy's command. "Wait'll we show 'em what we can do," he said, smiling.

Across town, a motorcade made its way with flashing lights and wailing sirens toward the SDF-1's platform, already late for the ship's scheduled launch on its maiden flight. Motorcycle outriders led the way, followed by a *long* stretch limousine. Bunting and pennons hung everywhere.

Not everyone in town was overjoyed with the day's festivities. Macross City's mayor, a small, stocky man who usually showed good humor, scowled in disapproval as the motorcade rolled in his direction. Vern Havers, who ran one of the town's more prosperous appliance stores, stood by his side, watching.

"Now what's wrong, Mr. Mayor? What's all that sighing about?"

Mayor Tommy Luan shrugged. "Aw, after all these years, it's hard to believe we may be looking at the old girl for the last time." Both men gazed at the colossal ship, which dominated the city and the island, its running lights blinking and flashing.

Of course, SDF-1 was only leaving for a test flight, to be followed by a short shakedown cruise if everything checked out well; but the mayor could be right—there was no telling when the fortress might return.

Certainly, Macross would never be the same place again.

"We'll all miss her," Vern conceded. "But aren't you proud to see her launched at last?"

"Of course. But if the test is successful, we'll all be unemployed!" the mayor burst out. Vern wasn't looking forward to closing down his business either, but he remembered the war very well. He had to admit he liked the idea of the battle fortress being out there in space, guarding the planet, a lot better than the mayor seemed to.

Vern sighed. A lot of people had forgotten just why Macross City existed. But Vern kept his opinion to himself.

The motorcycles and limousine roared by. "The big shots making their grand entrance!" The mayor sniffed. It was well known that the mayor hadn't been invited to any of the important ceremonies; the world leaders were keeping the prize honors for themselves.

"Captain Gloval doesn't seem too happy about it," Vern observed, hoping it would make Tommy Luan feel a little better.

Not happy, indeed. As the limo shot along, Russo, sharing the back seat with Gloval, waved tirelessly, flashing his smile to everyone with the bland relentlessness of a career politician.

Without turning from the crowds, he chided, "Don't look so sour, Gloval! It's our big day! Surely you realize all those loyal citizens out there consider you their hero! You could at least wave to them."

Gloval grunted, chin sunk on his chest, arms folded. He was wearing his dress uniform, and some pushy liaison officer had seen to it that every decoration Gloval was entitled to wear was in place. Gloval had certainly won more than his share of medals and "fruit salad" over the years, but he didn't much like being in the spotlight. He was grumpy.

Still, there was something to what Russo had said. The senator might consider it *his* big day, but it was those people out there who'd worked like mad these last ten years, sacrificed and hoped, all in the name of peace and security for future generations.

"All right, I'll wave," said Gloval, hoping the speechmakers' foolishness and the political hacks' patting themselves on the back wouldn't last long. Gloval only wanted to be out in space with his new command.

At SDF-1, all was controlled commotion. The Veritech demonstration was due to begin at any moment, and final preparations to get the fortress under way were still not on schedule. Comcircuits and the ship's intercoms rang with checklist items: engine room and astrogation systems, communications and life support, combat and support squadrons, and more. Literally millions of items had to be double-checked by the SDF-1's thousands of crew members during those final days of preparation.

Up on the bridge, Commander Lisa Hayes arrived to make sure everything would be squared away for launching. Admiral Hayes's daughter had always made it a point of honor to show more merit, more skill at her job, and more dedication to the service than anyone around her so that there could be no question of favoritism when the time came for promotion.

She'd carved out an amazing career for herself. At twenty-four, she'd been made First Officer of SDF-1. A lot of that was due, no doubt, to her familiarity with the ship's systems: With the exception of Doctor Lang, no one had such a complete and comprehensive knowledge of the vessel's every bolt and button.

But there were her endless commendations and top evaluations as well, and two decorations for courage under fire. Some people thought her too severe, too single-minded in her obsession with duty, but no one accused her of not earning her rank.

She paused to survey the bridge, a slim, tall, pale young woman with blond-brown hair that bobbed, confined in graceful locks, against her shoulders. Her subordinates were already at their duty stations.

Claudia Grant seemed to have things well in hand, speaking into an intercom terminal from her position at the Bridge Officer's station. "Roger, engine room; that's affirmative."

Vanessa, Sammie, and Kim, three young female enlisted-rating techs, completed the bridge complement; Gloval liked running things with as little confusion and as few people as possible.

Vanessa was feeding computer projections of fuel consumption to the engine room while Kim finished up the astrogation checklist and Sammie saw to the manual systems. They were all young, like Lisa—like most of SDF's crew. Robotechnology and the weapons and machines it had spawned were a whole new game; taking people while they were young and instilling its strange disciplines in them had proved more workable, in most cases, than trying to get veterans to unlearn what they'd already taken to heart.

Lisa sighed, brushing her hair back with her hand, making her way to her station. "The ceremony starts in fifteen minutes. I hope the captain gets here in time. The scuttlebutt is that he didn't get much sleep last night."

Claudia gave a smile, her brown face creasing, eyes dancing. "Yeah; the flag-rank officers threw a farewell party for him. They probably sat up all night telling each other war stories. You know how they are."

Lisa hid a mischievous smile. "And where were you, Claudia? Hmm?"

Claudia was taken off guard. "What're you talking about?"

"You didn't get back to your quarters until four in the morning, that's what! You must've been partying too."

Claudia stuck her nose in the air and struck a glamorous pose. She was taller than Lisa and several years older, with exotic good looks crowned by a cap of close, coffee-colored curls.

"You jealous? I had a late dinner with Commander Fokker."

Lisa had been joking, assuming Claudia had spent her last groundside leave visiting with her family, but suddenly the First Officer was angry.

"Claudia! You stayed out all night, knowing you and Roy both have flight duty today?" Duty was everything to Lisa; she had trouble understanding how anyone could be so casual about such an important mission.

But there was also something else, something about Claudia's love affair with the handsome, heroic Roy Fokker—not jealousy, but rather a feeling of Lisa's own loneliness. It brought an uncharacteristic confusion to her, a sudden emptiness that made her doubt the principles by which she lived her life. She shied away from it, reasserting control over herself by acting every inch the First Officer.

But Lisa wasn't the only one who was angry. Claudia set her hands on her hips. "So? What's the big fuss about, Lisa? We won't let it affect our performance on duty. After all, we're not children—and you're not our mother!"

Lisa felt her cheeks growing red. "Your responsibilities to the ship come first, Claudia!"

Neither one was backing away from the confrontation, and Claudia looked like she was running out of patience. And given her size and temper and the fact that she was an accomplished hand-to-hand fighter, Claudia was nobody to antagonize unnecessarily.

"My private life is my own business! Nobody else's!" Claudia stopped herself just short of some cutting remark: *Why don't you try loosening up for a change, Lisa?* for example.

But she got hold of herself instead. "Now then, let's get to work, all right?" She pointed toward Lisa's duty station. "Get outta here."

Lisa hesitated, unused to backing away from a fight, and still angry but feeling she'd overstepped her authority. Just then Vanessa said slyly, "Lisa doesn't understand about men, Claudia. She's in love with this spaceship."

Claudia couldn't resist a grin, and Kim threw in, "Yeah, you got that right!"

That stung Lisa terribly, though she'd have died before admitting it. She knew she had a reputation as a cold fish among most of the ship's complement; maybe that was why, against the rules of good discipline, she'd found herself becoming close with the other women with whom she spent so much time on the bridge. Besides, Captain Gloval's informal and even indulgent way of running the bridge—rather fatherly, really—made it easy to make friends.

But now Lisa felt herself flush angrily. "That wasn't funny, Vanessa; we have an important job to do here—"

Claudia, still steaming, interrupted her: "You act like I don't care about our mission at all!"

Sammie, at twenty the youngest of the bridge crew, couldn't bear to hear her friends fight anymore. "Oh, don't argue!" she cried.

She was so plaintive that the danger level lowered a little. "I'm not the one who keeps butting into everybody's business," Claudia pointed out.

Not quite ready to retreat, Lisa let out a growl she'd somehow picked up during her time with Gloval. Even as she began, "I'm warning you—" she was aware of a new sound in the bridge, cutting through her anger.

Claudia wore a haughty look, nose in the air again. "I hate to interrupt, but hadn't you better check your monitor, *Commander*?"

Then Lisa realized that an insistent signal was sounding from her duty station. She crossed to it, trying to put the argument out of her mind as Kim called out, "It's an unidentified incoming aircraft, Lisa!"

Checking her monitors, Lisa saw it was on an approved approach path and signaling for landing instructions. Since none of the many military aircraft flying patrol around Macross Island had challenged or interfered with the new arrival, it could be nothing but a peaceful visitor.

Lisa opened a communication link, resolving to try to smooth things out with her friends. She'd so much wanted the day to be right, to be marked by excellence and top performance! Why couldn't anyone share her drive for perfection? Perhaps she was simply fated to be the outcast, the oddball—

"Attention, aircraft approaching on course one-zero-seven," she said coolly. "Please identify yourself."

A youngish male voice came in response. "This is Rick Hunter. I have an invitation for today's ceremonies, invitation number two-zero-three."

Lisa checked it against another computer display, although she found herself irked by the job. The SDF-1 was set to launch, and she was expected to act as an air traffic tech!

But she responded, "That's confirmed as an invitation from Lieutenant Commander Fokker." *Fokker!* Lisa kept emotion out of her voice and avoided meeting Claudia's eyes, finishing, "Follow course five-seven for landing."

"Roger," the voice said cheerfully, and signed off.

With all the important things I have to worry about, Lisa mumbled to herself, *they also have to saddle me with babysitting the Rick Hunters of this world?*

04

All right, you win, "Big Brother." I'll come to your party. I'll even put up with all those military types you hang around with. But try not to make it too boring, okay?

Rick Hunter's RSVP to Roy Fokker's invitation
to the SDF-1's launch ceremonies

HIGH ABOVE MACROSS ISLAND, AN UNUSUAL AIRCRAFT BEGAN TO descend into the complex flight patterns of Launching Day, following course five-seven for landing, just as Lisa Hayes had instructed.

Rick Hunter whistled as he got a better look at the SDF-1. The descriptions and the newscasts just didn't begin to do justice to the astonishing *size* of the thing! The two supercarriers anchored among the flotilla of ships in the harbor were of the new Thor class—each longer than a 150-story office building resting on its side—yet they were modest in comparison to the battle fortress.

And the sky was full of the sleekest, most advanced-looking fighters Rick had ever seen—Robotech fighters, the newscasts had called them. Whatever that meant. For a moment Rick couldn't blame Roy Fokker for dedicating himself to this Robotech stuff.

After a decade of secrecy, the United Earth Government promised the wonderful new breakthroughs made on Macross would be revealed. To Rick, it simply meant that Roy wouldn't have to be so hush-hush about what he was doing, and perhaps their friendship could get back on its old footing.

Rick maneuvered his ship smoothly through the traffic, relying not on his computers but on his own talent and training—a point of pride. He was the offspring of a proud, daring breed: last of the barnstormers, the stunt fliers and the seat-of-the-pants winged daredevils.

He was eighteen years old and hadn't been outflown since—well, long before his voice had changed from a kid's to a young man's.

His plane was a nimble little racer of his own design. A roomy one-seater, white with red trim, powered primarily by an oversize propfan engine but hiding a few surprises under its sleek fuselage. Rick had named it the *Mockingbird*, a fittingly arrogant name for the undisputed star of the last of the flying circuses.

He tossed a dark forelock of hair back and adjusted his tinted goggles, then went into a pushover and power dive for the SDF-1. This Robotech stuff *looked* impressive… but maybe it was time somebody showed these military flyboys that it was the *pilot* that mattered most, not some pile of mere metal.

Far out beyond the orbit of Earth's moon, a portentous tremble shook the spacetime continuum as if it were a spiderweb. It was only a preliminary disturbance, yet it was exacting and of great extent. A force beyond reckoning was making tentative contact on a day that marked a turning point in the history of the unsuspecting Earth.

On Macross Island, in the shadow of the SDF-1, Roy didn't have time to notice the tiny racing plane making a pass over the ship's bow, thousands of feet above him. The public address system carried an announcement to the tens of thousands gathered there.

"And now we present an amazing display of aerial acrobatics, demonstrating the amazing advances we have made through Robotechnology. Lieutenant Commander Roy Fokker, leader of the Veritech fighters' Skull Team, will describe and explain the action for us."

Roy made his entrance to enthusiastic applause; he was known and well liked by most people on Macross Island. Tall and handsome in his uniform, the blond hair still full and thick, he stopped before the microphone stand. He gave a snappy salute, then fell into parade rest and began his address.

"Today, ladies and gentlemen, you'll see how we've applied human know-how to understanding and harnessing a complex alien technology."

Overhead, a half dozen swift, deadly Veritech fighters peeled off to begin their performance.

"Keep your eyes on planes two and four," Roy went on as two and four lined up for the first maneuver, engines blaring. "Flying at speeds of five hundred miles per hour, only fifty feet above the ground, they will pass within just a few yards of one another. Robotechnology makes such precision possible."

Roy looked out over the crowd with satisfaction. All eyes were gazing up in amazement at the onrushing fighters.

But the show would build from there. Precision flying was nothing compared to the *other* forms of control Robotechnology gave human beings over their new instruments. At long last average citizens would get to see Guardian and Battloid modes in action, Robotechnology applications that until now had been used only in restricted training areas or drills far out at sea, when the Veritechs were launching from the decks of the *Daedalus* and the *Prometheus*.

Those people in the throng, the ordinary citizens of Macross, were the ones who deserved the first live look at what the SDF-1 project had brought forth. They'd earned that right—much more than all the politicians, who had merely voted how much time and work and money would be spent—time and work and money that were invariably *not* the politicians'.

Today, all the rumors and speculations about Robotechnology would be put to rest, and the people of Earth would find out that the reality surpassed them all.

Roy was thinking about that happily as he spoke, waiting for the inevitable gasps from the crowd as the first high-speed pass was executed. It took him a few seconds to realize that the people below the speakers' platform weren't gasping.

They were laughing.

Roy whirled, craning his head to look up. Two and four had

been forced to peel off from their pass by the sudden appearance of an interloper, a gaudy little stunt plane, absurdly out of place among the modem miracle machines.

A circus plane! "Oh no-o-o!" Roy didn't have to guess who it was; he'd arranged for the invitation himself, and he was regretting it already. He grabbed the microphone out of its stand and flipped the switch that would patch him through to the aircom net.

"Rick! Is that you, Hunter?"

The little *Mockingbird* gave a jaunty waggle of its wings in salute as Rick banked slowly overhead. His reply came patched through the PA system.

"Roy! It's good to hear your voice, old buddy! They tell me you're a lieutenant commander now. The army must really be desperate!"

Furious, Roy yelled into the mike. "Are you crazy? Get that junk heap out of here!" He forgot that he was still patched through the PA, so that the whole crowd followed the exchange. Of course, as loud and angry as Roy was, the people up front would've had no trouble hearing him anyway.

The people below thought it was great, and the laughter started again, even louder. Roy was shaking one fist at the little stunt plane, holding the mike stand aloft with the other, like Jove brandishing a lightning bolt. "Hunter, when I get my hands on you, I'm gonna—"

Roy didn't get to elaborate on that; just then the bottom half of the telescoping mike stand dropped, nearly landing on his foot.

Roy caught it just in time—at thirty, he was one of the oldest of the Veritech fighter pilots, yet his reflexes hadn't slowed a bit—but couldn't quite get it to fit back together. Fumbling, forgetting what he'd been about to say, he was ready to explode with frustration.

He abruptly became aware of the laughter all around him. The crowd was roaring, some of them nearly in tears.

One young woman in front caught his eye, though. She looked to be in her mid teens, slender and long-legged, with a charming face and hair black as night. She was standing behind a kid, possibly her brother, who was laughing so hard, he seemed to be having trouble breathing.

At some other time, Roy might have tried to catch her eye and exchange a smile, but he just wasn't in the mood. His face reddened as the laughter washed over him, and he unknowingly echoed Lisa Hayes's sentiments of a few moments before: *Why today, of all days?*

Roy covered the mike with his gloved palm and stage-whispered to one of the techs. "Hey, Ed! Switch this circuit over to radio only, will you?" It was going to be awfully hard to chew out his men about com-procedure discipline after today.

It took only a second or two for Ed to make the change. "What're you trying to do, Rick, make a perfect fool of me?" Roy could hear the laughter in his old friend's voice. "Aw, nobody's *perfect*, Commander!"

Roy was just about grinning in spite of himself. People who didn't watch their step every moment were liable to become Rick Hunter's straight men. Roy decided to give him back a bit of his own. "You haven't changed a bit, have you, kid? Well, this isn't an amateur flying circus; my men are *real* pilots!"

"Amateur, huh?" Rick drawled. He looked off in the distance and saw the Veritech fighters in a diamond formation for a power climb, preparing to do a "bomb-burst" maneuver. "I'm gonna have to make you eat those words, Commander. Comin' in."

"Stop clowning around, Rick—look out!"

Mockingbird swooped down in a hair-raising dive, barely missing the speaker's platform, so low that Roy had to duck to avoid getting his head taken off. A lot of people in the crowd hit the dirt too, and most of them cried out in shock. Roy caught another glimpse of the pretty young thing in the front row; she seemed thrilled and happy, not in the least frightened.

Roy spun as the *Mockingbird* zoomed off, building on the acceleration it had picked up in its dive. Suddenly, as the little aircraft was safely away from the crowd, covers blew free from six booster-jet pods mounted around the turbofan cowling at the rear of the ship, and powerful gusts of flame lifted it into a vertical climb. The crowd went *"Oh!"*

Leaving streamers of rocket exhaust, the *Mockingbird* went ballistic, quickly overtaking the slower-moving formation of Veritechs.

"Get out of there!" Roy yelled up at him, not even bothering with the mike, knowing it was pointless. "Headstrong" was a word they'd *invented* with Rick Hunter in mind.

Rick cut in full power, came up into formation perfectly, becoming part of the display, as the Veritech fighters completed their climb and arced away in different directions, like a huge version of the afternoon's skyrockets.

The crowd was applauding wildly, cheering. Roy shook his fist again, furious—but a part of him was proud of his friend.

Out in space, vast forces were coalescing—nothing Earth's detectors could perceive yet, though that would happen soon. Soon, but too late for Earth.

Contact had been made; an inconceivable gap was about to be bridged, a marvel of science put to hellish use.

As *Mockingbird* floated in for a perfect landing, Roy leaped from the speaker's platform, so eager to get at Rick that he forgot to let go of the mike, yanking the stand over and nearly tripping on the microphone cord. The cord snaked along behind him as he ran.

Rick raised the clear bubble of the cockpit canopy as he taxied to a stop, his forelock of dark hair fluttering in the breeze. He pushed his tinted flying goggles high on his forehead. "Whew! Hi, Roy."

Roy was in no mood for *hi*'s. "Who d' you think you are? What were you trying to do, get yourself killed?"

Rick was nonchalant, pulling off his headset and goggles and tossing them back into the cockpit as he hiked himself up. "Hey, calm down!"

Not a chance. Roy still had the mike in one hand, a few yards of cable attached to it. He flung it down angrily on the hardtop runway surface. "And while we're at it, where'd you learn to do that, anyway?"

Rick had his hands up to hold the much bigger Roy at bay. He gave a quick smile. "It was just a simple booster climb. You taught it to me when I was just a kid!"

"*Ahhh!*" Roy reached out, grabbed Rick by the upper arm, and began dragging him off across the hardtop.

"Hey!" Rick objected, but he could see that he'd taken a lot of the voltage out of Roy's wrath with that reminder of old times.

"I have to admit, those guys up there were pretty good," Rick went on, jerking his arm free, straightening his dapper white silk scarf. "Not as good as *me*, of course."

Roy made a sour expression. "You don't have to brag to me, Rick. I know all about your winning the amateur flying competition last year."

"Not amateur; *civilian*!" Rick bristled. Then he went on with great self-pleasure. "And actually, I've won it eight years in a row. What've *you* been doing?"

"I was busy fighting a war! Combat flying and dogfighting kept me kind of occupied. Hundred 'n' eight enemy kills, so they tell me."

"You're proud of being a killer?"

They'd touched on an old, sore subject. Rick's late father had rejected military service in the Global Civil War, though he would have been the very best. Jack "Pop" Hunter had seen combat before and wanted no more part of that. He had instilled a strong sense of this conviction in his son.

Roy stopped, fists cocked, though Rick continued walking. "*What*?" With anyone else, a serious fistfight would have resulted from this exchange. But this was Rick, who'd been like family. More than family.

Roy swallowed his fury, hurrying after. "There was a war on, and I was a soldier! I just did my duty!"

They made a strange pair, crossing the hardtop side by side: Roy in his black and mauve Veritech uniform and Rick, a head shorter, in the white and blazing orange of his circus uniform.

They stopped by a vending machine unlike any Rick had seen before, which offered something called Petite Cola. Rick fed it some coins while the machine made strange internal noises. He took a can of ice-cold soda for himself, giving Roy the other.

"You promised my dad that as soon as the war was over you'd come back to the air circus. Why'd you go back on that, Roy?"

Roy was suddenly distant. "I really felt guilty about letting your father down, only… this Robotech thing is so important, I just couldn't give it up."

He pulled the tab on his soda, torn by the need to explain to Rick and the knowledge that some parts of the original mission to Macross Island, and of Robotechnology, were still classified and might be for decades more. He felt a debt, too, to the late Pop Hunter.

Roy shrugged. "It gets into your blood or something; I don't know."

Rick scowled, leaning back against the Petite Cola machine. "What *is* Robotech, anyway? Just more modern war machinery!" Somewhere, he could hear a kid raising a ruckus. "And the aliens—*huh?*"

He couldn't figure out how he'd lost his balance, sliding along the vending machine. Then he realized it was moving out from behind him.

The Petite Cola machine was rolling eagerly toward the child, a boy of seven or so who was throwing a terrible tantrum.

"Cola! I wanna *cola*! You promised me you'd buy me a cola, Minmei, and I want one right now!" He was dressed in a junior version of a Veritech pilot's uniform, Rick saw disgustedly. *Teach 'em while they're young!*

Roy looked around to see the commotion. He was suddenly very attentive when he saw the person trying to reason with the kid—"Minmei"—was the young lady who'd been standing at the edge of the speaker's platform.

She was charming in a short red dress, pulling on the boy's arm, trying to keep him from the vending machine that was closing in for the sale. "Cousin Jason, behave yourself! I already bought you one cola; you can't have any more!"

Jason wasn't buying it, stamping his feet and screaming. "Why? *I wanna cola-aaahh!*"

To Rick's amazement, the scene turned into a combination wrestling match and game of keepaway: Minmei was trying to prevent Jason from reaching the machine and was crying, "Cancel the order, please, machine!" while Jason struggled to get past her. In the meantime, the machine, circling and darting, made every effort to reach him short of rolling over Minmei. With its persistence and agility, the vending machine somehow gave the impression that it was alive.

"Never saw anything like *that*." Rick blinked.

Roy gave him an enigmatic smile. "Robotechnology has a way of affecting the things around it, sometimes even non-Robotech machines."

Rick groaned. "Robotech again?"

"Jason, you'll make yourself sick!"

"I don't care!" Jason wailed.

"Maybe you could tie a can of soda to a fishing pole and *lure* him home, miss?" Roy suggested.

Minmei turned to him, still deftly keeping the kid from scoring the Petite Cola. She broke into a winsome smile. She was of Chinese blood, Roy figured, though she had strange, blue eyes—not that he was interested! Claudia would probably take a swing at him (and connect) if she found out he was roving. Still, something about Minmei's smile made her irresistible.

"Oh! You're the officer from the stage! You were very, very funny!" Minmei giggled, then turned to the little boy sternly.

"That's it! We're going home! Come on, Jason; don't make me spank you!" She lugged the boy away as the Petite Cola machine made halfhearted attempts to clinch a sale against all hope.

"Well, Roy," Rick commented, elaborately droll, "I see you're still a big ladies' man."

In deep space, dimensions folded and transition began; death was about to come calling.

05

From the first, there were anomalies about the situation on the target world, things that gave me pause. The second-guessers would have it that I was remiss in not advising caution more strongly. But one did not antagonize great Breetai with too much talk of circumspection, you see—not, at least, without great risk.

Exedore, as quoted in Lapstein's *Interviews*

THE STARS SHIMMERED AND WAVERED AS IF SHIVERING WITH dread. And well they should.

The forces that bound the universe were briefly snarled by a tremendous application of energy. The dimensional warp and woof pulled apart for a moment.

In a precisely chosen zone of space beyond Luna's orbit, it was as if a piece of the primordial fireball that gave birth to the cosmos had been brought back into existence.

Motes bright and hot as novas, infinitesimal bits of the Cosmic String, were spewed out of the rift in spacetime like burning sparks of gunpowder from some unimaginable cannon shot; the burning detritus of nonspace moving at speeds approaching that of light itself, consumed almost as soon as they came in touch with three-dimensional reality.

Larger anomalies, like furious comets, flared here and there in the wash of light. Then there was another explosion beyond any description: the pure emission of unadulterated hell. It pushed outward from a rip in the fabric of the universe, taking on shape and shedding a raging wave of incandescence as if it were water.

The shape became longer, more forceful, menacing.

The Zentraedi had come at last.

First was the great flagship, sheets and wind racks of ravenous light streaming away behind it to reveal its shape: nine miles long, an irregular blunt-nosed cylinder.

A vessel many times the size of SDF-1, the flagship was a seemingly endless span of mighty weapons and invulnerable shields, of combat-ship bays and mountainous armor and incalculable firepower. The pride of the Zentraedi fleet, searching the solar system in an instant and knowing where its prey waited.

The flagship had been built with only military conquest, warfare, and destruction in mind. Manning it was a race of beings bred for that single purpose.

The ship was like a leviathan from the deepest oceans of human nightmares, with superstructure features that might be gills here or titanic eyes there, huge spines that were sensor spars, nubbles of the secondary and lesser weapons batteries, projections like questing fangs. Lighted observation ports, some of them a hundred yards across, suggested bulging, multiple eyes.

Behind it came a fleet surpassing any the Zentraedi had ever assembled before, cascading from the spacefold warp that had been their shortcut past the endless light-years. They were a school of gargantuan armored fish numerous enough to fill all the oceans, plated and scaled in sinister greens and browns and blacks, with pale underbellies in sickly grays and blues.

There were more of them than the visible stars. They were the mightiest Zentraedi armada ever seen, and yet they were cautious. They followed a flagship that knew no equal in any fleet they'd ever encountered, and yet they were wary.

If translated into human terms, their caution would mean something like: *Even wolves can be prey to the tiger.*

Having pursued the single wounded tiger across space and time, the fleet of so many hundred thousand ships formed up around the flagship.

In the transparent bowl of the Supreme Commander's flagship, Breetai, tall and stiff in his dress uniform, gazed down on his operations center. Even for a Zentraedi, he was a mighty tower of bone and muscle, as strong as any trooper under his command and as good a fighter. Like many of his engineered race, his skin was a mauve shade suggestive of clay.

A projecbeam drew a two-dimensional image of the target planet in midair, a puny and an unremarkable blue-white sphere, nothing much to look at. Rather disappointing, really.

Breetai reached up one hand to touch the cold crystal-and-metal half cowl that covered much of his head, thinking back to the day so long ago when Zor had died, and the dimensional fortress had been lost. The failure still burned at him.

He'd accepted that with a warrior's fatalism, and with a warrior's lust for triumph he contemplated the final victory that would be his this day.

Breetai studied the Earth coldly. "The finder beam has locked on this planet. Are you sure this is the source of those emanations?" His voice was huge and deep, with a resonance that shook the bulkheads.

Off to one side, Exedore, Breetai's adviser, kowtowed slightly, showing deference from habit even though he wasn't in Breetai's line of vision. "Yes, sir, I'm positive."

Breetai pursed his lips in thought. "They *could* have executed a refold." The thought of losing his quarry again was almost unbearable, but Breetai allowed no emotion to show.

"It's doubtful, sir," Exedore said quickly. "There was no evidence of a second jump into hyperspace."

Savagely, Breetai thought again of those traitors to his race and their narrow escape. "Hmm. They couldn't have gone far in their condition. And they would have to land in order to repair the ship." He looked to Exedore. "That's a logical conclusion, I think."

Exedore inclined his head respectfully. "I agree. It would seem very likely, sir."

Breetai was used to acting on his own instincts and deductions; but it was reassuring that Exedore, the most brilliant intellect of the Zentraedi race, was in accord.

Breetai considered Exedore for a moment: small, almost a dwarf by the standards of their species, and frail into the bargain. Gaunt, with protruding, seemingly lidless eyes and a wild thatch of odd, rust-red hair, Exedore was still the embodiment of Zentraedi law and tradition—and more valuable to the towering commander than any battlefleet. Yet with all that, he was loyal, almost selfless in his devotion to Breetai.

Breetai gave Exedore a curt nod. "Very well; dispatch a scout team for a preliminary reconnaissance."

In the Zentraedi warrior religion, efficiency was a virtue ranking only behind loyalty and courage in battle. The words were scarcely out of Breetai's mouth when two of the fleet's heavy cruisers detached themselves and advanced on the unwary planet.

At the festivities in the shadow of the SDF-1, Rick was getting his first close look at a Veritech fighter that had been put on display. Because he was accompanied by Roy, Rick was allowed into the roped-off area around the craft and permitted a hands-on examination of the ship.

"Whew, this fighter's a real beauty, all right." He looked at it enviously; he had no desire to fly combat, but that didn't stop him from longing to sit at the controls of the fantastic machine, high in the blue.

He ran his hand along the fuselage. "It looks great. How does it handle?"

Roy thought that one over. "Hmm. Well, why don't you climb aboard and see for yourself?"

"You really mean that?"

"Uh huh. I'll ride piggyback behind you." It was, perhaps, bending the rules a bit, though familiarization flights were scheduled for VIPs later in the day. Still, a little sample of what the Veritech could do might change Rick's attitude about military service, and the service could sure use a flier like Rick Hunter.

Rick was already scrambling up the boarding ladder, peering into the cockpit. "The controls look pretty complicated," Roy called up, "but I'll check you out on them."

Rick looked down and smirked. I'm not worried. If *you* can learn to fly one of these things, I sure can."

Roy snorted, "Don't be so modest!"

When Rick was in the pilot's seat and Roy was in the rear seat, Roy handed Rick a red-visored Robotech flight helmet.

Rick turned it over in his hands, examining the interior. "Whoa, what kind of helmet is this? What's all this stuff inside?"

"Receptors. They pick up electromagnetic activity in your brain. You might say the helmet's a mind reader, in some ways."

The receptors were just like part of the helmet's padding: soft, yielding—no safety hazard. But Rick wasn't so sure he liked the idea of having his head wired. "What're they for?"

"For flying a Veritech, buddy boy. You'll still handle a lot of manual controls, but there are things this baby does that it can only do through advanced control systems."

Rick hiked himself around in his seat and leaned out to look back at Roy. "Look, I saw your guys flying, remember? What's so special about these crates that you have to wear a thinking cap just to steer one?"

Roy told him, "The real secrets aren't supposed to go public until the politicians are through with all their blabbing, but I'll tell you this: The machine you're sitting in isn't like anything humans have ever built—it's as different from *Mockingbird* as *Mockingbird* is from a pair of shoes.

"Because you don't just pilot a Robotech ship, Rick; you *live* it."

On the main reviewing stand high above the crowd, Senator Russo stood at the speaker's rostrum, his voice echoing out over the throngs, amplified so that it reached to the farthest shores of the sea of people. Flags snapped in the wind, and the moment felt like a complete triumph.

"This is the day we've all been looking forward to for ten years! The Robotech project has been a tremendous asset to the economy of Macross City and to the welfare of our people!"

Captain Gloval, standing to one side with a few other dignitaries, tried to keep from yawning or simply throwing up his hands in disgust. So far, all Russo and his cronies had done was take credit for themselves and do some not-too-subtle electioneering.

Gloval cast a critical eye at the weather and gave it his grudging approval. He was impatient to launch; various other Earth military forces were already deployed in space, patrolling and awaiting the start of the SDF-1's first space trials. But the politicos didn't care who they kept waiting or what careful timetables they spoiled when they had the spotlight.

A liaison officer came up the steps at the rear of the reviewing stand and approached Gloval as Russo went on. "More important, though, is the fact that the technology developed here will benefit all mankind, now and in the future. And I need not mention what it means to the defense of our great planet, Earth!"

The liaison cupped his hand to Gloval's ear and said, "Excuse me, sir: urgent message from the space monitoring station. A strange flash of light and an explosion, tremendous radiation readings, accompanied by irregularities in solar gravitational fields."

In spite of the warmth of the day, Gloval suddenly felt cold all over. "The same sort of event occurred ten years ago. You know what happened then, don't you?"

The aide was trying to conceal his fear, nodding. "That's when the alien ship arrived."

Gloval assumed the icy calm of a seasoned captain. "Better check it out. Come with me."

Gloval was descending the platform steps as Russo announced what a great honor it was to introduce the commander of SDF-1, Henry Gloval.

For once, Russo didn't know what to say. "Come back here! You have to make a speech!" he shouted.

Gloval never even looked around. The time for speeches was over.

On the SDF-1 bridge, the women who were the battle fortress's heart worked furiously to make some sense of the sudden chaos around them.

"What's going on here, anyway?" Claudia demanded, trying everything she could think of to interpret her instruments and reassert some control over the ship's systems.

"Claudia, give me a readout!" Lisa called calmly. All around her, the bridge was a din of alarms, flashing indicators, malfunctioning controls, and overloaded computers.

Claudia looked up from her hopeless efforts. "Every system on the ship is starting up without being turned on!"

Unprecedented, impossible-to-interpret mechanisms had self-activated in the ship's power plant—the great, sealed engines that not even Lang had dared open. And the many different kinds of alien apparatus connected to it were doing bewildering things to the SDF-1's structure as well as its systems, making the humans helpless bystanders.

"The defense system is activating the main gun!" Claudia reported, horrified.

Far off at the great starship's bow, gargantuan servomotors hummed and groaned. The huge twin booms that made up the forward portion of the ship moved to either side on colossal camlike devices. The booms locked into place, looking like a fantastic tuning fork. The ship's reconstruction had the bow high up now, pointed out above the end of Macross Island's cliff line at the open sea.

Lisa's mind raced. The main gun had never been fired; no one was even sure how powerful it was. That test was to be reserved for empty space. But if it salvoed now, the ensuing death and destruction might well be greater than that created by the ship's original crash.

At the same time, everyone aboard could feel the supership shifting slightly on the massive keel blocks—the monolithic rests on which it lay. Warning klaxons and horns were deafening.

The SDF-1's aiming its gun, Lisa realized. *But at what target?*

"Shut down all systems!" she ordered Claudia.

Claudia, trying the master cutoff switch several times to no effect, looked at Lisa helplessly. "It doesn't work!"

A sudden glare from the bow lit the bridge with red-orange brilliance, throwing their flickering shadows on the bulkhead behind them.

Around and between the forward booms, tongues of orange starflame were shooting and whirling and arcing back and forth.

The fantastic energy cascade began sluicing up the booms toward their tips, sparks snapping, seemingly eager to be set free.

And still Lisa could think of nothing she could do.

Just then the hatch opened and Gloval hurried in so quickly that he bumped his head on the frame. He didn't spare time or his usual swearing at the people who'd refitted the largest machine ever known for not providing a little more headroom.

"Captain, the main guns are preparing to fire!"

Gloval assessed the situation in seconds, but Lisa could see from his expression that he was as much at a loss as she.

"I can't control them!" Claudia told Gloval. "What'll we *do*?"

Lisa absorbed a terrible lesson in that moment. Despite what they might teach in the Academy and the War College and Advanced Leadership School, sometimes there was nothing you could do.

The energy storm around the booms had built to an Earth-shaking pitch, a noise like a million shrieking demons. Then huge eruptions of destructive energy streaked off the booms.

The bolts streamed off into the distance, thickening into a howling torrent of annihilation, a river of starflame as high and wide as SDF-1 itself, shooting out across the city.

Lisa expected to see everything in the volley's path consumed, including the gathered populace.

But that didn't happen. The superbolt went straight out over the cliffs and over the ocean, turning water to vapor and roiling the swells, raising clouds of steam that wouldn't settle for hours. The shot was direct, the curve of the Earth falling away beneath it as it lanced out into space.

And just as Lisa Hayes was registering the fact that the city still remained, intact and unharmed—that her father was down there somewhere, still alive—new information began pouring in on scopes and monitors.

The Zentraedi heavy cruisers, closing in on the unsuspecting Earth, barely had time to realize that they were about to die. By some unimaginable level of control, the blinding shaft of energy split in two.

The twinned beams holed each heavy cruiser through and through, along their long axes. Armor and weapons and hull, superstructure, and the rest were vaporized as the beams hit, skewering them. They expanded like overheated gas bags, skins peeling off, debris exploding outward, only to disappear, blown to nothingness, an instant later in globes of bright mass-energy conversions.

From his command station, Breetai watched impassively, arms folded across his great chest, as the projecbeam displayed the death of the two heavy cruisers.

"Now we know for sure: The ship is on that planet!" This time he didn't bother soliciting Exedore's advice. "All ships advance, but exercise extreme caution!"

The Zentraedi armada took up proper formation, ships-of-the-line moving to the fore, and closed on the target world.

Clouds of superheated air blew out across the ocean; gulls cried in the aftermath of the SDF-1's single volley.

Gloval was at the bridge's protective bowl—its "windshield"—his face all but pressed against it, scanning through the steam and fog. He breathed a prayer of thanks that the city was unharmed.

"Some sort of magnetic bottling," Sammie reported, focused on her work. "All the force was channeled directly out into space, except for some very marginal eddy currents."

"We have control over all systems, again, sir," Claudia announced calmly. "What happened, sir?"

Gloval suddenly felt old—older than the ship, the island, the sea. He wasn't about to speculate aloud, not even to his trusted bridge gang, but he was just about certain he knew. And if he was right, it put the weight of a planet on his shoulders.

06

While Captain Gloval gets admittedly deserved credit for his handling of the disaster that day, male historians frequently gloss over Gloval's straightforward statement that if it weren't for the women on SDF-1's bridge, their nerve and gallantry and professionalism, the Robotech War would have been over before it had fairly begun.

Betty Greer, *Post-Feminism and the Global War*

THE GROUND HAD STOPPED SHAKING, AND THE SKY WAS clearing, The Veritech fighter stopped its trembling dance, and Rick Hunter caught his breath. The air seemed a little hotter in his lungs, but not terribly so.

He called back to Roy in a subdued voice, "Wow. What were all those fireworks about?"

Fireworks! Roy thought. *'Fraid not!* Aloud, he said, "I dunno. I better go check. Wait here; I'll see what's goin' on."

He put aside his flight helmet—the "thinking cap," as Rick had called it—and hiked himself up out of the fighter cockpit. If what Roy feared the most had come to pass, Rick would be as safe where he was as anywhere else. And he'd also understand why some people could spend their lives preparing for war.

"The space monitor report's coming in," Sammie sang out. "It shows what our gun was firing at."

"I have it here, Sammie," Lisa cut in, studying her monitors. "Two large objects, probably spacecraft, origin unknown, on Earth-approach vector, approx two hundred miles out."

Gloval was nodding to himself without realizing it. The ship could be raised or lowered, the booms traversed for—what, a few insignificant minutes of arc? And the SDF-1 hadn't been moved, except to lift it onto the keel blocks, since it crashed. The range was incredibly long, making for a greater field of fire; but still, such a shot, such a series of events, could only come about with some forewarning, or intuition, or—*We forgot that whoever built this vessel had to some extent mastered time; could, perhaps, see through it. Could see this very moment?*

"Both objects were struck dead center by the beam and were destroyed—disintegrated," Claudia said. "Orbital combat task forces are deploying for defense, with Armor One and Armor Ten—sir? Captain Gloval?"

Sammie, Vanessa, Kim—they exchanged looks with one another as Lisa and Claudia traded facial signals. Gloval was laughing, a deep belly laugh, his shoulders shaking. Claudia and Lisa saw that they were both thinking the same thing: If Gloval, their source of strength and calm, had lost his grip, all was lost.

"Captain, what is it?" Lisa ventured. "What are you laughing about?"

Gloval stopped laughing, crashing his fist against the observation-bowl ledge. "It was so *obvious*! We should have known. A booby trap, of course!"

Claudia and Lisa said it at the same time, "Booby trap, sir?"

"Yes, it's one of the oldest tricks in military history! A retreating enemy leaves behind hidden explosives and such."

He clamped his cold pipe between his teeth. "The automatic firing of the main guns means that enemies have approached close enough to be a threat to us." He drew his tobacco bag out of the breast pocket of his uniform jacket.

"Captain Gloval!" Sammie was up out of her chair. Everyone turned to her, wondering what the new alarm was.

"No smoking on the bridge, sir!" Sammie said. "Strictly against regulations!"

Claudia groaned and clapped a hand to her forehead. Lisa reflected, *Nothing throws Sammie.*

"I was just holding it; I wasn't going to light it," Gloval said defensively. The unreality of the situation retreated with Sammie's interruption. There were both good things and bad things about having one's bridge crew be like family.

But doubts were past now. Gloval barked, "Hot-scramble all fighters and sound general quarters! I'm declaring a red alert!"

Down below, the crowds milled uncertainly as helos and other aircraft veered away to report to battle stations. Suddenly, launch crews were scrambling to get Veritechs into the air. Out on the carriers, all catapults were busy, while the SDF-1's own warcraft rushed up from the ship's interior and groundside runways to establish a protective shield overhead.

Out in the void, armored spacecruisers, human-designed vehicles incorporating some of the principles learned from Robotechnology, moved their interceptors and attack craft out of the bays and into fighting position.

It wasn't long before the swarm of human defenders had sensor contact, then visual sighting, on the aliens; the Zentraedi wouldn't have had it any other way.

A Scorpion interceptor pilot reported back to Armor One over the tac net, "Enemy approaching on bearing niner-zero. We are engaging. Commence firing!"

Scorpions and Tigersharks and a dozen other types of Earthly combat spacecraft, ranging up to the mammoth Armors themselves, rushed to close with the aliens' first attack wave.

Missiles—Stilettos and Piledrivers and Mongooses—were launched at extreme range so that all but the glows of their drives were lost to sight until the blackness blossomed with the spherical explosions characteristic of zero-g, the bursts overlapping one another, thicker than a field of dandelions.

The Zentraedi ships-of-the-line forged through the intense fire with few losses, closing the gap in seconds. The formations broke up to lock in a fierce, pitched battle.

The Armors launched all their missiles. Lasers, kinetic energy weapons-rail—gun autocannon and such—were the other main Terran weapons. The Zentraedi's were far superior; their warcraft simply outclassed the defenders', whose design involved fewer Robotech innovations.

Earth's forces fought with savage determination, but the unevenness in technologies was instantly apparent.

Aboard the alien command ship, Breetai studied the engagement solemnly in the projecbeam images and monitors, listening to his staff's relayed readouts with only a small part of his attention.

"Very heavy resistance, sir," Exedore observed.

"Yes," Breetai allowed. "But why are they using such primitive weapons? Our lead ships have broken through. It's unbelievable, this sacrifice they're making! Some sort of trick, no doubt."

Exedore considered that. "Yes, it is puzzling."

Breetai whirled on him. "It makes no sense, then? Even to you?"

"There has to be a reason, but it's beyond me. Surely, the Robotech Masters—"

He was interrupted by an urgent message from the tech at the threat-prioritization computers. "Commander Breetai! Two enemy cruiser-class vessels are approaching; they could be the ones who launched the missile bombardment."

Breetai smiled, but his single eye was chilly. "Destroy them!" Specially designated main and secondary batteries opened fire: phased particle-beam arrays and molecular disruptors, long-range and fearsomely powerful.

Armor Two was hit on the first volley as hundreds of spears of high-resolution blue fury ranged in on it. It tried to evade the barrage; house-size pieces of armor and superstructure were blown from it. Many of the smaller defending craft were completely disintegrated.

Breetai, waiting for effective counterfire, lost patience. Perhaps the foes' hesitation to use reflex weaponry fit into some strange plan, but to forgo use of *any* advanced technology, to sacrifice troops to this kind of slaughter, was perverse.

Incredulous, Breetai wondered if somehow this victory was going to be far easier than it had seemed when that first mighty bolt rose from Terra. "Those idiots behave as though they don't even know how to use their own weapons! Full barrage, all cannon!"

The Zentraedi command ship cut loose again with all forward gun turrets. Armor Two was instantly holed through in a hundred places, the enemy beams penetrating it like ice picks through a cigar box.

Hull integrity went at once, and internal gravity; hatches and seals blew, and space began sucking the atmosphere from the cruiser, tossing crew and contents around like toys. Still more hits made a sieve of the pride of the orbital defense command and destroyed its power plant. A moment later it disappeared in a horrendous outpouring of energy, while lesser ships all around it met a similar fate.

Lisa, more pallid than ever, kept her voice even as she reported to Gloval: "Armor Two is destroyed and Armor Ten is heavily damaged, sir. Other losses extremely heavy. The Orbital Defense Forces are no longer even marginally effective. Alien fleet is closing on Earth."

Gloval sat in his command chair, fingers steepled, chin resting on pressing thumbs. "I had hoped this moment wouldn't come in my lifetime. SDF-1 kept us from exterminating ourselves and let us achieve worldwide peace, but now it has brought a new danger down upon us. We face extinction at the hands of aliens whose power we can only guess at."

Henry Gloval's mind ranged back across a decade to that first investigation of the wrecked SDF-1. *Miracles have a price. And this one, I think, will be very, very high.*

Claudia and Lisa and the other members of the bridge crew swapped quick, worried looks.

"I had hoped that war was a thing of the past. We all had." Gloval looked up from his distraction like a knight at the end of his prayer vigil, ready to take up a shining sword, a gleaming shield.

"But here we go again, like it or not." He rose to his feet, shoulders back, and a vivid current of electricity that hadn't been there a moment before hummed in the air. Gloval was suddenly strong as an old oak.

"All right. Give the order to move out!"

"Yes, sir." Lisa relayed the command crisply. "All forces, deploy in accordance with Contingency Plan SURTUR."

More Veritechs launched all across the island as Lisa's words reverberated to every corner of it, like the gods' final war song. "We are under attack by alien invaders in sector four-one-two. This is not a drill, I say again: This is not a drill."

Roy Fokker, clambering into his fighter, pulling on his flight helmet, gasped, then hissed. He'd been so busy saddling up Skull Team when word came that there was trouble that he'd forgotten all about Rick!

Then he calmed. The fighter in which Rick was sitting had been seconded from active duty for the public relations events; it wasn't as if some angry pilot would be wrestling him out of the cockpit. So Rick was as safe there as anywhere else for the time being.

Lisa's voice rang across the airfield. Roy didn't mind it, but he couldn't help wishing it were Claudia's.

Then Roy got back to the job at hand, settling the all-important helmet on his head. He switched on the tactical net, trying to sound casual, just about bored. The fighter-pilot tradition; dying was something you sometimes couldn't help, but losing your cool was unforgivable.

"Well, boys, you heard her. This is the real thing." Roy practically yawned.

The sky was filled with climbing flights of fast-moving aircraft, vectoring off to their assigned coverages. Dozens, hundreds had arisen from the carriers and the island. The flattops were making ready to stand out to sea so that the foe couldn't concentrate his attacks; that would take some time. But at least with the combat squadrons aloft, Earth wasn't as vulnerable to a single, concentrated strike.

Lisa's voice came over Roy's flight helmet phones. "Wolf Team has cleared. Skull Team, prepare for takeoff."

"Skull Team ready." Roy knew the men in the other parked Veritechs would be watching him as well as listening over the tac net. He gave a quick thumbs-up. "Awright, boys; this is it."

More fighters were streaking up from the flight decks of the carriers, launched out from the waist catapults or propelled out into the air over the Hurricane-style bows.

"Let's go," drawled Roy Fokker. Robotech engines shrilled.

. . .

"What a disorderly arrangement!" Breetai exclaimed, studying Macross City on long-range scanners. The populace, the military forces—they were so unbelievably concentrated! "These people must be completely ignorant of spacewar tactics!"

The sensor image panned until an image-interpretation computer locked it in. Breetai leaned closer to the fishbowl surface that protected his command post.

"What's this? The battle fortress! But—what's happened to it?"

Exedore took that as leave to speak. "It appears to have been completely redesigned and rebuilt, perhaps by the inhabitants of that planet."

Breetai set his fists on his hips. "Mere primitives couldn't possibly have captured a Robotech ship."

Exedore fixed Breetai with his great, protruding eyes, their eerily pinpoint pupils hypnotic, mystical. "Perhaps it crashed on their planet and they managed to salvage it."

"But what about the crew? Zor's traitors wouldn't just let these creatures have the vessel!"

"Maybe they perished in the fighting with the Invid, or in the crash," Exedore suggested delicately. It was an answer of high probability; Breetai saw that at once, chose not to contest it, and congratulated himself on having a friend and adviser like Exedore.

"Even so…" The commander sidestepped the discomfiting idea that the primitives were antagonists to be feared. "The ship would have been terribly damaged. And these primitives wouldn't have the technology to repair it."

This Zentraedi arrogance of ours gets worse with every generation, Exedore thought, even as he readied his answer. *Someday we may all pay for it.*

"I know, sir, but is there any other explanation? It *is* a Robotech vessel, and we know they have—"

"Reflex weaponry!"

"Precisely. And this makes them very dangerous. So we must exercise extreme caution."

Breetai turned back to the projecbeam displays, uttering a feral growl. The instruments and transparent bowl rang with it.

A command center coordinator's voice came up over the intercom. "Target pinpointed, Commander. We're launching fighters!"

Breetai and Exedore contemplated the image of the dimensional fortress.

07

If there exists on record a stranger familiarization flight than Rick Hunter's VT shakedown, I have been unable to find it.

Zachary Foxx, Jr., VT: *The Men and the Mecha*

ZENTRAEDI COMBAT SHIPS OF EVERY KIND CUT DOWN THROUGH Earth's atmosphere in tight, well-maintained formations, plunging at Macross Island and its surrounding waters. The alien pilots were confident, swelled with their swift and smashing victory against the target world's outer defenses.

The bright streaks of their plummeting drives seemed as numerous as raindrops. They were primed for easy kills and a swift capture of the battle fortress that had to be captured whole and undamaged, as Breetai had ordered. The invaders had had it pretty much their own way so far.

All at once that changed . . . and the rout suddenly became a battle again.

Protective covers had been raised from the SDF-1's missile racks; almost all incoming ordnance was intercepted and exploded in midair. Fighters of types the Zentraedi hadn't encountered be fore boiled up to lock in combat with them. And the elite warrior race found out, to their extreme unhappiness, that the primitives had indeed puzzled out quite a bit of Robotechnology.

In Earth's slaughterhouse skies, the dying began again.

Snoozing comfortably, Rick Hunter began to rouse a bit. If the weather had turned so bad—there was constant thunder—maybe he ought to make sure all the windows were shut. Only, he didn't seem to remember where he was. Besides, there was this bothersome voice in his ear; it had the ring of authority, and that was something that never failed to antagonize him.

"This is SDF-1 control calling VT one-zero-two. You down there, on the exhibition grounds! We're on combat alert! Why haven't you taken off?" Lisa Hayes had a million other things to do; prodding slowpoke fighter jocks was the last problem she needed, and it made her mad to have to take time she couldn't spare to do it.

Rick sighed and stretched, then tilted the strange flight helmet back on his head, leaning forward and blinking groggily at one of the cockpit's tiny display screens. A young woman's face peered angrily out of it: pale and intense, impatient. Rick Hunter was used to being regarded as something pretty special, particularly by the opposite sex; he therefore decided at once that whoever she was, she had a pinched and grumpy look.

"You don't mean *me*, do you, lady?" But just then he became aware of distant explosions—not thunder but the reports of incoming fire. And there were blazes in the city, and smoke and damage. Crewpeople were rushing everywhere, fueling and arming and guiding planes, getting them airborne. Meanwhile, up in the *air*…

What *were* all those intertangled contrails and afterburner glows and explosions and tracers?

"Huh? What?" Rick Hunter asked himself weakly. People were scrambling around the plane in which he sat, readying it.

"Don't waste any more time!" the pale face in the screen scolded. "Take off immediately and join your wingman! The fighter squadron's outnumbered as it is!"

Rick gritted his teeth. "What d'you mean take off? The runway's demolished!"

And so it was, one of the primary Zentraedi targets, one of the few to be hit effectively. The young woman on the screen appeared to be counting to control her temper.

"Runway two is operable. You're fully armed, and your engines will overheat very quickly at high standby, so prepare for immediate takeoff!"

Now that she mentioned it, he could hear the high-pitched whine of an engine, could feel it through his seat, but it was not like any he'd ever heard before—and Rick Hunter had heard 'em all.

Rick leaned out of the cockpit for a look. Sure enough, the Veritech was armed to the teeth, external hardpoints and pylons loaded with ordnance, the jet also carrying odd pods that he couldn't quite figure out.

Then a ground crewman was next to him, standing on the boarding ladder. "All set, sir! Good hunting!" The man did something or other, and the cockpit canopy descended.

Rick was to admit later that that would have been a very good time to come clean and admit that he had no idea what was going on, that he was a noncombatant and needed to be shown to a shelter. But that would have entailed admitting that he didn't know how to fly the aircraft in which he was sitting, that he *couldn't*. That he was, in short, nothing but a bystander, a hick, just like the people who gawked up at him at the flying circus.

And when you regard yourself as the greatest pilot in the world, an admission like that is extremely difficult. Besides, there was that irritating female on the screen.

"Well, okay. If you insist."

Rick drew a deep breath, took the controls, and gave himself a quick run-through, remembering all the stuff Roy had told him. He waggled rudders and played around for a second, then increased throttle, taxied out, and stood the fighter nearly on its tail, like a meteor in reverse.

A late Zentraedi missile blew a hole the size of a city block where he'd been parked a few seconds before. He was hoping the ground crews had all gotten clear as the Veritech responded to his demands for speed.

Wow! The proverbial bat.

He adjusted wing sweep and camber and angle of attack, going ballistic, wingtips leaving wispy lines of contrail like spider's thread. And though he would never have admitted it, he was more than a little intimidated. He was riding a rocket.

He punched a hole in a cloud, then found himself in the middle of a vast, swirling gladiatorial combat, the biggest dogfight since the close of what they called WWII.

"Whoa-ooooooo!"

Robotech craft were everywhere, and planes of some design that made no sense to Rick; not aerodynamic but devilishly fast and mounting unprecedented firepower. Explosions flowered all around him, rocking the ship, just as a lazy, familiar voice came over the tac net.

"Skull Leader to Veritech squadron. Intercept new invader flights at zone four-two-eight. Traffic's pretty heavy out here, boys, so break formation, but *don't leave your wingman!*"

"*Roy!*" He sounded short of breath. Rick looked up, open-mouthed, as a Veritech flying the Jolly Roger insignia bagged an alien recon craft shaped something like a flying bottle.

Debris was raining everywhere; pilots from both sides screamed in agony as they were blown to oblivion up where sky met space.

And, because dogfighting was so incredibly demanding physically, the tac net was loud with gasps and grunting. Dogfighters trained themselves to lock the muscles of their lower bodies—turn their legs to iron; suck their gut to their spine. Anything to keep the blood up high in the head. Up in the brain, where it was needed even more than in the heart.

The pressure on the pilots' diaphragms was fearsome; they could draw only short, hard-won breaths, if they were in high-g maneuvers.

The tac net sounded like eight or ten wrestling teams had been paired off for the championship.

And the trophy was Earth.

"Hey, Fokker! Wouldja mind telling me what's going on around here?"

Roy had just finished dusting a bogie off Skull Eight's tail. He switched a communications screen over to ship-to-ship and was, he admitted, not all that surprised to see Rick Hunter's face.

"How's it feel to be a fighter pilot?"

"What're you talkin' about, Big Brother? I'm not a fighter pilot; in fact, I—uhhhh!"

That last, as a wash of light came through Rick's canopy, and Roy's screen dissolved into a storm of distortion. There had been explosions just before the cutoff; in fighter jocks' lingo: *he tuned out.* Tuning out was terminal.

But Roy cut in maximum thrust, checking his situation displays, heading for his friend's location. "Hold on, Rick; I'm coming."

The Veritech's thrust pushed him back, deep into his seat. Roy felt tremendous relief when he sighted VT one-two-zero flying level and unharmed.

Roy caught up and fell in on Rick's wingtip. "You weren't hit; it was just a close one. You all right?" The alien that had come so close to nailing Rick was coming around for another try.

"*Whew!* Yeah, I'm okay," Rick decided.

Roy moved into the lead just a bit. The enemy fighter was closing fast. "Combat flying's scary for everyone first time out," he said. "You'll get used to it, though; it's not that much different from the good old days at the flying circus."

So saying, Roy thumbed the trigger on his control stick and sent two air-to-air Stilettos zooming to score direct hits on the invader and blow it to flaming bits.

"Yeah, but I never got shot at in the circus, Roy." Funny, but now the flying circus seemed like another life, a million years ago.

"You'll get used to it. Just tag along with me and we'll start your on-the-job training—*if* you can keep up with me."

The old smirk was back on Rick's face. "If? I'll do my best not to leave you in my backwash!"

"Let's go get 'em, Little Brother." Roy increased airspeed, beginning a climb, wings folding back for high-speed dogfighting. Out of nowhere, an enemy fighter came in at Rick from six o'clock high, chopping at him with energy bolts.

He let out a cry as he began to lose control, the fighter shaken and bounced by the near misses.

"Climb and bank!" Roy called out, trying desperately to bring his ship around. "Rick!" He himself was dodging Zentraedi cannon fire a moment later. With Rick's ship out of control and nosediving in a spin, the Zentraedi had broken off his attack and turned on the Skull Team leader. The two fighters joined in a vicious duel.

Rick tried everything he'd ever learned but couldn't regain control of the Veritech. "I think I've had it, Roy. I'm getting no response from the controls at all!" Macross Island pinwheeled up at him.

Just then a voice he recognized came up over the net. "This is SDF-1 control calling VT one-two-zero. Pull out! You're diving straight at us!"

"Lady, don't you think I'd like to? But all the controls have lost power."

"Have you tried switching to configuration B?" Lisa Hayes demanded.

"Huh? B? What're you talking about?"

"You don't know?" *This one must've really lost it—complete panic!* "Listen, pull down the control marked B on the left side of your instrument panel."

The ground was very near. Rick, dizzy and almost unconscious from the g forces, somehow guided his hand to the knob in question, having a little trouble sorting it out from an identical one next to it marked G, moving it down in its slot.

The Veritech abruptly slowed in its tailspin, stabilizing, beginning to level off. At the same time, Rick could feel the entire ship start to shudder and shift, its aerodynamics changing in some way that he couldn't comprehend. He could feel vibrations, as if the fighter was—*changing.*

"What's it doing?" The fighter was still descending, the streets of Macross City looming up before the canopy. Rick had been a pilot long enough to know that since its flight characteristics had changed so dramatically, there was no other answer except that the shape of the Veritech had somehow altered.

What he didn't realize, and couldn't see from the cockpit, was that the ship had begun undergoing a process Doctor Lang had dubbed mechamorphosis. It was no longer configured like a conventional fighter but had, instead, gone to Guardian—G—mode, on its way to B.

In this transitional state it resembled a great metal bird of prey, an eagle, with sturdy metal legs stretched to set down and wings deployed, humanlike arms and hands outstretched.

But before Rick could figure out what had happened or the fighter could complete the shift to B, the Veritech crashed into the upper floors of an office building at an intersection in Macross City.

Fortunately, the alert had the population indoors or underground in the sprawling shelter system, and so no one was killed. The Guardian carved a path of devastation through the upper stories of an entire block, its fantastically strong armor and construction resisting damage.

Bricks, concrete, and girders flew in all directions; clouds of plaster went up like a dust storm. Signs crashed down, and broken plumbing gushed; severed power lines spat and snapped. The Guardian's engines cut out as the machine became aware of its situation and reacted to emergency programming.

Rick Hunter could still feel the plane shifting, changing, all around him. In fact, in some way he couldn't figure out, he could sense it—could actually *feel* it.

Rick sat where he was, realizing that he didn't know how to eject, even if the system was a "zero-zero" type that would let him survive a standstill ground-level ejection, which was far from the case.

It felt as if the crazy Robotech fighter was coming to a stop; he readied himself for a quick escape, not wishing to be in the neighborhood if a few tons of highly volatile jet fuel suddenly took a notion to catch fire. But the Robotech ship had one last surprise for him; the relatively smooth slide became a lurch as the plane snagged on some final obstruction. The fighter heaved, and Rick's helmeted head slammed into the instrument panel.

If he hadn't been wearing the flight helmet, it would have been the end. As it was, he saw stars and nearly lost consciousness.

But the Veritech was unhurt. With a creaking of girders and the racket of tons of rubble being moved, the machine began to extricate itself. The mechamorphosis to B mode was complete, and the fighter was now a Battloid.

It looked for all the world like a man in armor, a super-technological knight sixty feet tall. The electric gatling gun that had been pod-mounted under the Veritech's belly was now aligned along its right arm, the giant right hand gripping it like an outlandish rifle.

The cockpit section was unrecognizable, now incorporated in the turretlike "helmet," the Battloid's head. Its visor swung this way and that, taking in the situation, seeing the explosions of the dogfight continuing high above.

The Battloid knew the enemy was there; it was ready to do what it had been designed to do. It awaited orders.

Rick shook his head groggily. "What d'ya know? I'm alive!" Then he saw that something was wrong with his perspective—that he was high above the street, that there were things about Robotech too astounding to believe. He saw the distant air engagement too.

Somehow Rick knew, deep down, that life was never going to be the way it had been fifteen minutes ago. Things had changed forever.

08

Dear Diary,

Launch day's really been fun, even though Jason's making himself a bit of a pest. I met a couple of really dreamy guys, pilots, I guess—a very tall blond one and a cute little dark-haired one.

I'm going back out this evening to sing at the municipal center picnic. Maybe they'll be there! I might—hey! I think something's going on outside. More later.

From the diary of Lynn-Minmei

I N SDF-1'S BRIDGE, VANESSA STUDIED HER SCREENS AND GAVE Gloval a concise report. "Twenty-four unidentified objects are descending from space, projected landing point twenty to thirty miles west of Macross Island, sir. They're definitely not ours."

"Why didn't we detect them before?"

Vanessa looked to the captain, adjusting her big aviator-style glasses. "When the main guns fired, they sapped so much power, our radars malfunctioned."

Gloval reflected on that. "That first wave of attack ships—it was just a decoy. Very clever strategy. Lisa! Recall Lieutenant Commander Fokker's team immediately!"

Lisa, studying her data displays, said, "They're still engaged in combat with the first attack wave, sir. I doubt they can break away without suffering heavy losses."

Gloval nodded stiffly. "I understand. Thank you."

Vanessa updated, "The unidentified crafts have landed in the ocean twenty-five miles west of us. They seem to have submerged, sir."

Gloval could no longer put off giving Lisa the unpleasant command. "Call *Prometheus* and order them to send out reconnaissance choppers."

"I already have them awaiting your go-ahead, sir. They'll be on station in five minutes."

"Mind reader," Gloval growled, though there was real fondness in his voice.

"Yes, sir," Lisa said, cheeks coloring a bit.

There was only a moment in which to be relieved that Gloval wasn't rankled at her for anticipating him; those recon helicopters racing to confront the new alien arrivals were quite capable in their own way, but they weren't Robotech ships. And that could be very bad for the helo crews.

People had crept forth, very hesitantly, to gawk up at the towering knightlike figure that had been VT one-two-zero. The Battloid stood straddle-legged in the middle of the street. As pieces of sheetrock fell from its shoulders and bits of rubble rained around it, it appeared as if it were waiting for a trumpet to sound the call to arms. It took a few faltering steps, nearly toppling over.

"What is that?" one man breathed.

"A giant robot!" a second misguessed.

"Could be an alien invader!" a third ventured. There were already a thousand rumors abroad as to exactly what had happened to Macross Island and to the human race in general.

A few yards away, Lynn-Minmei crouched with her uncle and aunt in the doorway of their restaurant, the White Dragon, unsure what to do. Jason had been outside playing somewhere when the chaos began, and there was no sign of him.

"It's stopped moving; it's just standing there now," Minmei said, looking up at it. She got ready to make a dash, to go look for her cousin.

Suddenly a small figure in bib overalls and yellow sweatshirt dashed out from behind a crumpled trailer, passing by the metal fighting machine's feet, close enough to touch them.

"Wow! Hey, Minmei! Come lookit what's out here! An honest-to-goodness giant robot!"

She caught him up in a hug, as relieved as her Uncle Max and

Aunt Lena were. "Oh, Jason! What if that thing had stepped on you?"

Jason pushed her away with the unconcern of the very young. "Aw, I can take care of myself." Then he broke loose, heading for the stairs, a compact little whirlwind.

"I want to get a good look at that thing! C'mon; we'll go upstairs and look out the window!"

Minmei hurried after. She yelled, "Jason, wait for me!" as her Aunt Lena called, "Don't let him fall out the window!" then went back to trying to figure out what to do with the shambles that had been a thriving business only minutes before.

The two Barracuda naval attack helicopters from *Prometheus* approached watchfully, encountering only calm sea.

"This is PHP two-zero-two," the flight leader radioed. "We're approaching target area. Negative sightings of alien craft so far."

Lisa's reply came after a burst of static. "Roger that, PHP two zero-two. Maintain maximum surveillance; bogies are suspected to be submerged. Prepare to deploy sonobuoys."

Her transmission was just ending as the blue water broke for one, then another, then half a dozen rounded shapes. They bobbed up, shedding water, bulbous and gleaming metallically, with odd projections—tubes—suggesting old-fashioned magnetic mines.

The floating objects turned, the tubes aligning and sighting. All at once they spat lines of dazzling brilliance up at the Barracudas. More and more of the rounded shapes bobbed to the surface, joining in the barrage.

The flight leader barely blurted out, "We're being fired upon!" when the crisscrossing beams found the second chopper and blew it to pieces in midair.

"Let's get out of here!" the leader screamed, firing a missile and preparing to run even as the beams converged on his ship. The chopper became a fireball. The pilot's scream was cut off in midtransmission.

Back on the bridge, Lisa reported woodenly, "They're gone, sir."

Gloval glared out the forward viewport. "And here I am with an untested ship, an inexperienced crew—*And very little time to make my decisions.*

The hatch slid open, and Russo strode onto the bridge, puffing on his cigar and clutching his expensive lapel, seemingly in control. But he was pale and sweating; Lisa could see that and smell it. Under the hail-fellow-well-met exterior, the senator was so frightened that he was in danger of passing out.

"Well, Captain, it's lucky for us we got this ship finished in time to fight off the invaders. When d' you take off?"

The curious timing had occurred to Gloval, too—that the aliens should arrive at this very moment. His own conclusion was that the final activation of the SDF-1's huge, mysterious sealed power plant had somehow drawn the invaders. But he had no time to think about that now.

In answer to Russo's question, he simply *hmphh*ed.

Russo's eyebrows beetled. "You *are* ready, aren't you? Why haven't you taken off? *What are you waiting for?*" He glared up at the captain.

Gloval's upper lip curled. "You must think I'm out of my mind. I can't take this ship into combat with a crew of raw recruits who've never been in space before! What's more, this ship hasn't even been tested yet; we don't even know if it'll fly."

His commitment to his oath of service made him add, "If you order me to take SDF-1 up, I'll obey. But it'll be against my better judgment."

Claudia and Lisa were standing rigidly at their stations, pretending to take no notice. But Sammie turned to Kim and whispered, "D'you think he's serious?"

"I think he means it." Kim nodded after a moment's thought.

Sammie gave a toss of her long mane of wheat-colored hair. "Wow," she whispered with a tremble.

"I *am* ordering you to take off, Captain. Understand?" Russo was saying.

Kim frowned, "What's the matter, Sammie? I thought you *wanted* to go into space."

Sammie's eyes were big, frightened. "I do… I think." *But all of a sudden, it's real!*

"Let it be your responsibility, then," Gloval came back to Russo, "because I'm telling you, it could be suicide. We don't understand half of SDF-1's systemry yet!"

Russo's lip was quivering, but he bristled, "It sounds to me like you're saying you've no confidence in your crew. Is that what you're telling me, Gloval?"

Gloval looked quickly to Lisa and Claudia, who turned back to their duties to avoid being caught watching the confrontation. "I didn't say that."

"Then what *are* you saying? Earth has spent untold resources on this Robotech ship, and I don't want to see it destroyed on the ground."

"Senator—"

"No, Captain! No more excuses; take off!"

"Very well. As ranking official, you may take that seat over there. We'll be under way in a few moments."

Russo almost swallowed his cigar. Claudia had to stifle her snigger. "What?!" the senator exploded. "No! That is, I have too many other things to do on the ground. You're *not* to take off until I've left this ship, is that clear?" The terror in his voice was unmistakable.

"Whatever you say, Senator." Gloval showed a thin smile.

Pulling himself together, Russo beat a hasty retreat. To the bridge gang he said, "Well, girls, we're all depending on you. So don't let us down!" The hatch closed behind him.

Gloval stared at the hatch. *We aren't ready for combat. We just aren't ready!*

Minmei joined Jason at the top-story window. They were gazing up at the immobile war machine from about the height of its waist. The titanic chest had been holed by enemy fire.

"Wow, look how big it is!" the boy squealed with delight.

"Be careful, Jason," Minmei scolded, holding him back so he wouldn't climb out onto the ledge.

"I wonder where it came from?" Jason yelled happily.

As they watched, the cyclopean head tilted far forward as heavy servomechanisms hummed, leaving the torso uppermost.

Down in the street, people were exclaiming, "Look! It moved its head!" "It just fell out of the sky and wiped out those buildings!" "It's as big as a building itself!"

"See? Its back opened up!" Jason cried, pointing. Minmei gasped.

A co-pilot's seat rose on a support pillar, lifted into sight by some inner mechanism. It was empty.

Jason's brows came together. "There's nobody running it!" Machinery whirred again, and the post moved higher, raising the first seat to reveal a second mounted below it. In that seat was Rick Hunter.

Getting out of his seat, looking down, Rick ignored the furor of the crowd below. "What's going on here? What's happened to me?"

"The pilot looks confused," Jason commented; he'd been hoping for someone a little more impressive.

"Maybe he was injured in the crash," Minmei suggested. But something about the young man was familiar.

"I must be seeing things," Rick muttered. "This *used* to be a fighter plane."

He spotted Minmei and Jason. He recalled the girl from somewhere but couldn't take time to try to place her just now.

"Excuse me, but, uh, what is this?" He indicated the Veritech. "I mean, what does it look like to you?"

Minmei took a moment to absorb the question. "Some kind of robot, I think."

"Oh, great," Rick sighed, relieved. "When I got into this thing, it was an aircraft. I thought I'd gone nuts."

"A convertible airplane?" Minmei and Jason both echoed. "You must be joking," Minmei added. She thought he wasn't bad-looking, however, and wondered how old he was. Not much older than she was, she judged.

"I'm as puzzled as anybody about it."

"You're kidding!" she said. "You're the pilot and you don't even know what it is?"

"No, I'm not a military pilot. I'm just—just an amateur!" *Satisfied, Roy?* "It's all, um, a big mistake. I'm not supposed to have it."

"An enemy spy!" Jason squawked.

Minmei gave him a little shake to quiet him. *"Jason!"*

"Spy?" Rick yelped. "Look, this was the army's idea, not mine!" He shook his head, looking down at the Battloid. "Look at all the damage!"

Helicopters were approaching from the distance, and traffic was venturing forth again. "Will you have to pay for it?" Minmei wondered.

Rick's stomach felt like it was doing somersaults. "Me? I hope not." A truck was insistently blowing its horn down by the Battloid's automobile-size feet. "What?" he yelled angrily.

The driver hollered up, "Get that thing off the road! I have a truckload of military supplies to deliver and I'm in a hurry, Mac! Now, move it!"

Rick stood up, surrendering to the inevitable. "I don't know how it works, but I'll try."

"Good luck!" Minmei called. She'd decided he was kind of cute.

"Thanks." *She has a real nice smile.* He'd have to remember his way back here.

"And please be careful."

He gave her a broad grin and a wave. "Sure. I will." He got back to his seat. As it lowered, he tried to think of something else to say but could only come up with, "So long!"

"I hope I see you again sometime!" Minmei called.

Back in the cockpit, Rick told himself, "Well, all I can do is throw a few switches and hope for the best, I guess." The giant head swung back into place.

Taking the control grips, he panned the screen before him. "At least I can see where I'm going. If I can just figure out how to get there."

But as the Battloid stirred, preparing to walk, he felt a distinct lack of confidence, something he was unused to. The machine seemed to want more of him than the mere pushing of buttons.

The Battloid lifted its foot to step, lost balance when it brought it too high, and swayed, about to topple over backward. The crowd that had gathered to stare at the Battloid panicked and began to bolt, yelling and milling. Rick howled in dismay.

Just as the war machine was about to crash into the buildings behind it, back thrusters flared for a quick, intense burn. The Battloid was pushed back to a precarious balance. Then it went off kilter in the opposite direction, staggering toward the little balcony over the White Dragon from which Minmei and Jason watched, open-mouthed.

The two saw that it wasn't going to stop; with wails of fright, they turned and fled just as the Battloid crashed through the wall where they'd been standing, collapsing that whole portion of the building. It came to rest like a drunk who'd passed out across a bar.

Minmei coughed and spat out plaster, checking Jason, whom she'd shielded under her as she went down. "Please tell me you're okay!"

"I am!" Jason said brightly.

Rick's voice came over the Battloid's PA system. "Are you two all right in there?"

"Yes!" Minmei yelled.

In the cockpit, Rick tilted his helmet back to wipe his brow. "Thank goodness!" He couldn't bear the thought of hurting an innocent bystander.

Besides, the girl was real cute.

09

Clearly, as Gloval said, SDF-1 was in part a booby trap. He was too busy to think of it, and I wasn't a trained military man, so it didn't occur to us until it was too late that that particular sword might cut both ways.

Dr. Emil Lang, Notes on Launch Day

THE MOMENT CAME IN A WAY NO ONE HAD FORSEEN EVEN AN hour before; SDF-1, all running lights flashing, prepared to launch for the first time.

"Gravity control systems through bulkhead forty-eight are green light," Sammie relayed to engineering. "Please confirm, over."

From all over the ship the reports came in; the messages went to every corner of it. It was no longer a question of waiting for a perfect checklist; the dimensional fortress was going—now.

"Priority one transmission from HQ, Captain Gloval," Vanessa announced. "Armor One has completed recovery procedures and is departing now to join Armor Ten at Rendezvous Point Charlie."

Gloval grunted acknowledgment and added, "Thank you, Vanessa. Claudia, check the reflex furnace and see if we've recovered full power yet."

Claudia studied her equipment, listened to a brief intercom message, and said, "Ready condition on furnace power, sir."

Once more, Gloval wondered about those enormous, enigmatic, and unprecedentedly powerful engines. "Reflex power" was a term Lang used; even his closest assistants scratched their heads when Lang scribbled equations and tried to explain why he called it that and what he *thought* was going on inside the power plant.

Not that it mattered; all Gloval wanted was for his ship to function, to be battleworthy, for however long it took. A few days—perhaps.

Or a day. Just give me one day!

"Very good. Antigravity: full thrust."

"Aye aye, sir," Kim sang out. "Full thrust." The mountainous bulk of the SDF-1 trembled and was somehow alive under them. The bridge gang went through individual countdowns and checklists, their voices and those from the intercom overlapping.

Then Claudia's rang out clear as an angel's through the ship, and over Macross Island. "Ten… niner… eight…"

A hundred thousand thoughts and fears and prayers hovered over the island, almost a tangible force in themselves.

"…two… one…"

"Full power," Gloval ordered. "Activate the antigravity control system."

The entire city vibrated slightly, as the hundreds of thousands of tons of SDF-1 rose from the ship's Gibraltarlike keel blocks; their unique absorption system adjusted to the sudden unburdening.

The ship rose smoothly, casting its stupendous shadow across the island. "The gyroscope is level, sir," Lisa reported tersely.

Gloval eased back in his chair, hoping it was a good omen. "Well done."

He'd barely said it when a tremor ran through the great ship. Below, he could see the upper-hull/flight deck actually *quake*.

SDF-1 lurched, then listed hard to port, throwing people from their feet. There was a lot of yelling; the intercom was bedlam.

"What in blazes is going on?" Gloval thundered, grasping the arms of his chair to keep from being thrown across the compartment. "Trim the pitch attitude immediately!"

"It must be the gyroscope," Claudia said, struggling to stay at her station.

"No, look!" Lisa was pointing out at the upper-hull/flight deck. Bulges had appeared, like volcanic domes being thrust up against the hardest armor ever developed; the tearing of metal sounded through the SDF-1 like the death throes of dinosaurs. The convexities of armor broke open like overripe fruit, yielding complex cylinders of advanced-design systemry. The cylinders, each the size of a railroad tank car, rose majestically into the air, trailing power leads and torn support frameworks.

"The gravity pods are breaking away!"

Gloval rushed up behind Lisa to see for himself. "What is it? Oh, no! They're tearing away from the ship instead of lifting it!" Everywhere it was the same; the physics of the disaster was inflexible. Dozens of gravity pods tore lose, continuing their ascent as they'd been charged to do, breaking their way through any structure in their path (or, to put it another way, conventional gravity was dragging the SDF-1 down around them).

"This can't be happening!" Gloval breathed, not so much distraught by the probable outcome the disaster would mean for himself and his command as by the utter catastrophe it meant for Earth.

"The ship is losing altitude, Captain!" Lisa cried.

Gloval groaned. *"Please! Tell me I'm dreaming this!"*

"Pardon, sir?" Lisa said.

He hadn't realized he'd spoken aloud. "It's a nightmare."

SDF-1 fell faster, its few operating thrusters unequal to the task of easing it down. All through the ship, people knew that calamity had occurred and waited with varying attitudes to find out what their fate would be.

With alarms hooting and wailing, the ship crashed back onto its keel blocks. Under the velocity of even a cushioned fall, the titanic weight made the monolithic blocks crack, give way, and collapse or drive themselves down into the Earth.

But the impact-absorption systems built into them saved the ship from greater damage and spared lives, before the blocks were overloaded and defeated. SDF-1 settled down with its hull against the rubble and soil and hardtop, but the ship's back hadn't been broken or its hull breached.

The bridge wasn't so different from any other section: outcries and screams and incoherent yelling. In moments, the noise died away and military discipline reasserted itself. SDF-1 rested at a 15-degree list to port.

"Is anyone hurt?" Gloval's voice cut through the confusion.

Everyone else chimed in that they were uninjured, then shut up; the captain's voice must be heard, uninterrupted, at a time like this; and though the bridge gang was untried in space, they knew their duty and they knew their orders.

Gloval strode back toward his seat. "I want a full damage report. Give me a computer readout on every system onboard!" The SDF-1 was a fish in a barrel for the time being; he had only minutes in which to act.

"*Yessir!*" the five voices responded as one, giving the words a choral sound.

Gloval looked infinitely tired. "They'll never let me forget this."

"You shouldn't blame yourself for this, sir," Lisa said softly. Gloval lowered himself into his chair, shaking his head to contradict Lisa.

"I am the captain," he said simply.

In the street outside the White Dragon, a very peculiar salvage operation was in progress.

The Battloid had been rigged with cables attached to two seafood delivery trucks. The civilian populace had always been sympathetic to the military's mission, and by now news broadcasts had made it apparent to most people that a new and awful war had begun and that, like it or not, everyone was a part of that war for the time being. So the truckers and other bystanders were doing their best to get the Battloid righted.

The big box-jobs gunned their engines, tires spinning and squealing, laying down large black patches of rubber and raising reeking clouds of smoke. The trucks backfired, and their engines labored.

Slowly, the armored mechamorph came away from its resting place, toward a vertical position. Rick, sweating over his controls, sat with hands hovering over them, hesitant to court further misfortune by interfering.

The Battloid was standing again—for the moment. It reached the vertical and slowly began to tilt the other way. Volunteer helpers and onlookers let out a wide assortment of exclamations and yowls and scurried for safety; the drivers leapt from the cabs of their trucks and hotfooted it.

Minmei and Jason hugged each other and shouted, "Oh, no!" at the same instant.

Rick grabbed for the controls desperately. At the very least, he had to try to keep this insane metal berserker from doing more damage to the restaurant.

The Battloid lurched, trying to find its balance. Rick tried his best but couldn't seem to do anything right. Again, it was as if the machine was waiting for him to do something more than merely manipulate controls.

The Battloid took a lurching step, and its legs became entangled in the cables; it twirled clumsily and fell backward toward the opposite side of the street, its back crashing against an empty building that had taken heavy damage from the enemy barrage.

It sank down, crunching the building, until it came to rest with its backside halfway to the street, heels dug into the pavement. When Rick was sure the machine was stable for the time being, he wiped his brow again. "Oh, why me? How come these things don't happen to other people?"

The triumphant Veritech squadron flew in tight formation, making its way back to the *Prometheus* and the dimensional fortress.

Roy was in the lead spot, of course. "This is Skull Leader, Veritech squadron, to SDF-1. Am returning to base. We have met the enemy and pretty much cleaned their clocks. They've withdrawn from Earth's atmosphere."

Lisa's face was on the display screen. "Commendable work, Commander Fokker, I'll—"

She was abruptly moved out of the way by Claudia, who said "Let me talk to him! Roy, how many of them did *you* shoot down?"

"Only ten this time," he said nonchalantly. But the dogfight would be a legend by that night, the hardest rat-racing he'd ever seen. Every millisecond was going to be analyzed and refought a hundred times among the flying officers.

"You're slipping, Roy," Claudia told him, but her tone wasn't critical at all.

"Well, don't worry, Claudia; I'll make it up." *Something tells me I'm going to get plenty of opportunities!* "Do you have any word on the VT one-zero-two?"

Lisa crowded back onto the screen. "That section-eight case! He landed in Macross City in a Battloid, and he's doing more damage than the invaders."

Roy laughed. "Thanks, Lisa."

"Who is he? He's not registered as a fighter pilot."

"Don't worry; I know him."

"Well, he sure needs help." Lisa scowled.

"I'd better go check on him." Roy switched to the tac net. "This is Skull Leader to group. You guys head on back to *Prometheus*. I've got some business to take care of in town. Captain Kramer, you take 'em home."

"Will do, boss."

Roy peeled off from the formation and, increasing his wings' sweep for higher speed, plummeted for Macross City. "I should've known better than to leave him alone," he muttered.

Even in a city that had known a peppering of energy bolts and alien rockets, it wasn't too hard to spot the mess made by an out-of-control Battloid. "Aha! That you, Rick, old son?"

The war machine was resting against a building. "Hi, Roy! It's me!"

"Had a busy day down there, huh?"

Rick sighed. "You might say that, Big Brother."

People in the streets spotted the approaching aircraft. The skull insignia was well known; but things had a way of being unexpectedly dangerous today, and nobody was up for taking any more chances.

Everybody sprinted for cover again. Roy switched his ship to Guardian mode for the descent—the mechanoid/eagle configuration that allowed more control in the tight quarters of a city street. It settled in on the bright blue flare of its foot thrusters, chain-gun cradled in its right arm.

In another moment Roy's ship had mechamorphosed to Battloid. Its shoulder structure gave it a look of immense brute power, like a football player. Rick felt like rubbing his eyes. "I must be dreaming this; I don't believe it!"

Jason, crouched with Minmei behind a fallen cornice, yelped, "That airplane became a robot too!"

"Amazing!" Minmei murmured. It was all so strange and almost magical—it made her wonder what the young pilot's name was.

"A few small repairs and you can take that Battloid back into action," Roy said blithely.

"What're you talking about?" Rick yelled over the net. "I don't even know what this thing is, and if you think I'm qualified to operate it, just take a good look around the neighborhood!"

But he watched his screen in utter fascination as Roy's war machine shifted its weapon from its right arm, drew out a long, thick band as sturdy as a heavy-cargo sling, and settled the weapon over its left shoulder, all as casually as an infantryman going to sling-arms.

Rick gaped. No control system in the world could do that. Maybe a battery of computers, *if* the sequence was worked out precisely in advance. But what Roy had done had more of an on-the-spot look to it.

It brought to mind what Roy had told Rick about the Robotech flight helmet—the thinking cap: "You don't just pilot a Robotech ship; you *live* it."

"If you can fly a jet, you can operate a Battloid," Roy began. "I'll tell you what to do. Gross movements are initiated by manuals— the legs are guided by your foot pedals, for instance."

"*Which* foot pedals, Roy? I've got about fifty controls in here!"

"Fifty-seven, if you want to get technical. But that's not the important part. Just button up and listen; I'll explain while I'm making repairs."

The skull-insignia Battloid extruded metal tentacles, tool-servos, waldos, and a host of other advanced repair apparatus. In moments the one Robotech war machine was repairing the other. Welding sparks jumped, and damaged components were replaced.

"The secret's that helmet," Roy said. "You generate general movements or sequences with your controls, but the Robotechnology takes its real guidance straight from your thoughts. You've got to *think* your ship through the things you want it to do."

Rick couldn't help being skeptical in spite of everything he'd seen. "Now you're gonna tell me these junk heaps are *alive*?"

"Close enough for me," Roy said noncommittally, "although you're going to have to make up your own mind about that. We still don't understand the power source—the same power source that runs SDF-1 but we know that, somehow, it's not just a—a blind physical process. It's involved with life forces somehow; with awareness—with *mind*, if I'm not getting too fancy for you."

"*I* think you're bucking for a medical discharge, mental category."

Roy chuckled. "See for yourself. Just pay attention and I'll tell you how it's done."

10

When it comes to testing new aircraft or determining maximum performance, pilots like to talk about "pushing the envelope."

They're talking about a two-dimensional model: the bottom is zero altitude, the ground; the left is zero speed; the top is max altitude; and the right, maximum velocity, of course. So, the pilots are pushing that upper-right-hand corner of the envelope.

What everybody tries not to dwell on is that that's where the postage gets canceled, too.

The Collected Journals of Admiral Rick Hunter

FOR THE NEXT FEW MINUTES ROY REPAIRED RICK'S DOWNED machine while he briefed his friend on the secrets of operating Robotechnology.

"These Battloids are classified top secret," he finished, as he made the last reconnection. "And you've gotta trust me on this one: There is a reason for it." All the repair tackle had neatly withdrawn itself into the skull Battloid's huge body.

"There, that oughta do it," Roy said. "Now switch on energy and depress those foot pedals slowly, like I told you."

Rick did, and *thought* his way through the maneuver as Roy had instructed. He focused his mind's eye on the act of getting back to his feet; *something* at the other end of the helmet's pickups sensed and understood.

Carefully, Rick Hunter's red-trimmed Battloid levered itself up, gaining its feet to stand shoulder to shoulder with Roy's.

"*That's* it," Roy said. "See how easy it is?"

More than easy; it was exaltation. If felt as if there was a feedback or reciprocation mechanism in the control system; Rick felt as if he *were* the Battloid.

Several stories tall. Indestructible. Armed with the most advanced weapons the human race had developed. With the power of flight in a way that did indeed make the *Mockingbird* seem primitive, and metalshod fists capable of punching their way through a small mountain.

Rick drew a deep breath, dizzy with the feeling.

"That's it!" Roy encouraged. "See how easy it is?"

"Wow, you learn fast, don't you?" said a voice from street level over the Battloid's external pickups.

Rick looked down at Minmei and Jason. He automatically guided the Robotech machine so that it leaned down toward the girl. "Thanks."

A voice from the distance—Minmei's Aunt Lena—called, "Minmei! Jason! Come on!"

Minmei waved up at Rick. "See you later! We're being evacuated!" She trotted off with Jason in tow, long, slim legs moving with unconscious grace.

Off the shore of Macross Island the breakers came in, crashed, and sent up high fountains of foam, and the waters pulled back to regroup yet again for their eternal assault on the beach.

But the next breaker brought a different kind of assault.

Zentraedi Battlepods launched straight up out of the water on their thrusters: scout versions, officer versions, and the standard models configured to carry a variety of heavy weapons and equipment.

Their biped design, the legs articulated backward, resembled that of an ostrich. They landed on the shore and began advancing in long leaps like monstrous kangaroos, sensors swinging for in formation, weapons ready for the kill. They arranged themselves in skirmish formation and covered miles in seconds.

Soon they loomed across a ridgeline, looking down on Macross City.

...

At Breetai's command post, the report was patched through. "The recon and Battlepods have landed, Commander. We're ready to attack."

Exedore's protruding, pinpoint-pupiled eyes swung to regard his lord. Breetai leaned to a communications pickup.

"Attention all gunnery crews! Prepare to give covering fire to the recon assault group."

The command "Ready All Guns" and subsidiary orders rang through the armada. The long muzzles were run out and ranged in. In their sights was Macross City.

"We better get moving, Rick," Roy told his friend. "We still have a war to fight."

"I'm still pretty unsure of myself with all these robot controls! I'm not ready for combat."

"Not robot; *Robotech*!" Roy corrected automatically. "Look, pull the control marked G, and we'll switch to Guardian configuration."

Rick complied, muttering, "What the heck is a Guardian? Here goes!"

As the Veritech shifted and mechamorphosed, converting to a bird of prey/war machine, Roy explained. "The Guardian controls operate almost exactly like those of the fighter plane. You can fly it without any problems."

"I've heard that before," Rick reminded him.

On a hill overlooking the city, the crowds waited to be admitted to the underground shelter system. Because of the dangerous nature of research and experimentation going on in the city and the fact that Macross would be a primary military target for any aggressor, the shelters had always had a high priority in the island's construction projects.

Minmei and her relatives were waiting fretfully with the thousands upon thousands of others. The emergency personnel were working as fast as they could, but moving the huge population underground was time-consuming at best.

The job facing the civil defense crews was overwhelming, and to top it off, many people had stopped in the foothills to try to find friends or relatives before moving below.

But that wasn't what made Minmei halt in midstep.

"My diary!" She had been keeping it since she was old enough to hold a pen, xeroreducing her writing so that each page held weeks of entries in a single, thick little volume. In it were all her thoughts, ideas, memories, stories, the lyrics for her songs, her poetry and secret longings, and the most important letter she'd ever received in her life—Minmei's diary *was* her life.

"I have to go back for it!"

"Don't be foolish, child!" Lena cried. "There is no going back." Jason watched wide-eyed; he was too young to have known Minmei before she'd come to live on Macross Island, but he already adored her.

Minmei ducked away from her aunt's restraining hands and avoided Uncle Max's effort to stop her. Older people just didn't understand!

"It won't take me a minute to get it, don't worry!" Then Minmei was off, gamine legs flying.

"Come back!" Aunt Lena moved to follow, but two CD workers, too late to restrain Minmei, blocked her way. Uncle Max and Jason and the others stood watching as Minmei's fleet figure disappeared down into the city. Over all loomed the fallen SDF-1, blocking the sun.

Breetai studied the fire-mission computer models. He gave a grudging nod of satisfaction.

"All guns standing by for bombardment, Commander Breetai," a tech reported.

"Good. Level everything in the path of the assault forces but be careful not to damage that battle fortress. I want to take it intact!" Once the Battlepods had established a beachhead, his plan could be implemented, and Zor's masterpiece would belong to the Zentraedi.

Then let the Robotech Masters beware! Breetai thought.

Lead elements of the armada opened fire; those farther back in the dense cloud of warships couldn't fire without the risk of hitting another Zentraedi vessel.

A torrent of alien bolts rained down like a hellish spring storm, in a kill-zone that encircled the dimensional fortress. Buildings seemed to melt like candles in a blast furnace, riddled by thousands of narrow, high-intensity beams, collapsing in clouds of plaster and concrete dust.

Death was everywhere among the CD teams, emergency personnel, antilooting squads, and others who'd bravely remained behind. Dying screams and the shrieks of the wounded rose on the bolt-splashed heat waves. Zentraedi Battlepods watched it all impassively from their vantage point: wingless, headless armored ostriches bristling with sensors and heavy weapons. The shelters and the masses waiting to enter them were noted, but those were of no importance; Breetai was only interested in the SDF-1.

"They're invading the city!" Rick yelled from his Guardian's cockpit. It was only by accident, he realized, that he'd crash landed outside the kill-zone.

"Yeah; it looks like it was evacuated just in time," Roy said, surveying the blasted landscape from his higher vantage point in the Battloid.

He also had updates on the refugee situation and the various assembly points. "If you're worried about your girlfriend, we could go check on her."

Roy shifted to Guardian mode and showed Rick how it was done; the two Guardians skimmed away like jet-powered skaters, foot thrusters riding them on a blasting carpet mere inches off the ground, safe from most of the enemy fire.

"Do we have a fix on where that bombardment is coming from?" Gloval snapped.

"A fleet of spaceships, numbers uncertain but very, very high. In lunar orbit," Vanessa told him promptly.

Gloval rubbed his jaw. "Beyond the range of our missiles."

Lisa looked up from her monitors. "Captain, an alien assault force is approaching from the east, range eight miles."

It was her job and her prerogative, so she added, "We need air support, sir."

Gloval gave a quick nod that shook his cap a little. "Call for it."

· · ·

The Zentraedi Battlepods leapt from the cliffs around the city and began their fast assault. They moved with the high speed and precision of advanced Robotechnology, hopping nimbly or skating quickly at ground level on their foot thrusters.

At the outskirts of the city they opened weapons ports and missile rack cover plates, then opened fire. Missiles left scorching, corkscrewing trails in the air, converging on SDF-1. Pulsed laser beams strobed and flicked at targets of opportunity.

The initial barrage met with strong defenses. Most of the missiles were jammed by ECM techs or intercepted by countermissiles; the beams were either repulsed by SDF-1's highly reflective surface or failed to do more than warm the great ship's armor at that range and in those atmospheric conditions. Still, the situation was about to get grim if Gloval couldn't change the tactical equations.

"This is SDF-1," Lisa transmitted calmly. "Attention all strike elements: We are under attack and need immediate assistance. Incoming Veritechs, switch to Battloid mode." The tac nets were silent; the situation seemed hopeless. Lisa considered the fact that, in spite of all the beliefs she'd embraced, perhaps humans *weren't* destined to rule Earth. Just then, Gloval played his hole card.

Through a sky crowded with spherical missile explosions, the Veritechs swooped with supreme confidence, dodging the intense ordnance eruptions all around them.

More VTs formed up on the lead formation. In seconds it was a gathering of vengeful eagles. "Roger, SDF-1," Captain Kramer drawled. "We're comin' in. All Veritechs switch to Guardian mode."

Below, the round-bodied, hopping Zentraedi war machines were laying waste Macross City, shooting indiscriminately and ravaging for the love of it. Kramer disliked net discipline as much as Roy did. So he said:

"Skull Team, area four-one. Vermilion Team, area four-four." Kramer gave the other ground-strike assignments, just as Roy would have done. The two had been wingmates long enough for Kramer to know it by heart.

And long enough for Kramer to know how to send the Veritechs on their way: "Awright, boys; let's get on down there an' wrassle 'em around some."

The ships dived in tight formations; the pilots only *talked* imprecisely.

So used to having their own way, the Zentraedi Battlepods didn't seem to understand that with the arrival of the Veritechs, the odds had changed.

In moments, the Veritechs found, fixed, and fought the enemy, and the aliens began to get an unwelcome message.

Zentraedi Battlepods, headless and ominous, were being blown away right and left by Robotech ships in Battloid mode. The giant mechanical infantrymen had all the skill their human pilots had absorbed; if their close-in weapons were somewhat inferior to the Zentraedi's, it mattered very little in the street-to-street, house-to-house, often eye-to-eye close quarters of urban combat.

Alien Battlepods stalked and stomped through Macross city, cannon muzzles angling and firing at will, rockets twist-trailing everywhere, leaving an inferno behind them.

An elite Zentraedi strike squad had encountered nothing that could impede it. Its members didn't know that a computer-assisted gunsight was zeroing in on the squad leader—until it was too late.

A powered Gatling gun opened up, a thousand times louder than a buzz saw, shell casings flying up in a steady stream. The high-density depleted transuranic slugs used in Terran Robotech bullets were very heavy and delivered devastating amounts of kinetic energy on impact. A generation before, 30-mm autocannon had been capable of blowing tanks apart. A lot of improvements had been made since then.

The Battlepods found that they'd dropped into a very angry wasps' nest and that the stings were deadly. Then the squad leader disappeared in a high-density barrage.

A pod swung its upper and lower plastron cannon muzzles, its operator deciding where to direct his fire next. All at once a Battloid broke through the building next to it, bringing up the muzzle of its Gatling to knock the pod back off balance. The pod was twice the defender's size, three times its mass. But the stroke sent the offworld vehicle reeling back.

The pod staggered, legs flailing, ending up against a metal utility pole, bending it. The Battloid leveled its Gatling and opened fire with a sound like ripping cloth amplified to the point where it was deafening.

The Zentraedi pod abruptly became an expanding sphere of flame, gas, and debris. The Battloid whirled, gun held at high port, looking for more enemies.

All across the city it was the same; as wave after wave of pods descended or leaped ashore, the Battloids engaged and overcame them using tactics distilled from SWAT teams and infantry rifle outfits. The Battloids handled themselves like grunt fireteams in fantastic enlargement.

And the Zentraedi learned that the price of Earth, foot for square foot, promised to be very high indeed.

Rick skimmed along behind Roy, twisting and dodging through the war-torn maze that was Macross City. SDF-1's bow was hanging like a threatening hammer above them as tracers drew lines of light through the air, missiles exploded, and alien blasterbolts hyphened all through the combat zone around the dimensional fortress.

The side of an apartment building was blown loose and collapsed in pieces. Rick zigzagged around it, his Veritech still skating along in Guardian mode as he tried to put together in his mind why that girl Minmei was suddenly so important to him that he'd go through *this* for her.

11

In a Veritech y' got every kinda way a pilot can die and just about every kinda hurt-alert a leg infantry might run into, see: Exceptin' possibly trench foot, though I wouldn't bet on it.

Anonymous Wolf Team pilot,
quoted by Zachary Foxx, Jr., *VT: The Men and the Mecha*

MORE PODS GRASSHOPPERED INTO MACROSS CITY, ALL plastron cannon firing.

A damaged pod, hit on descent by SDF-1 missile crews, blazed like a fiery comet, punching through one building and laying a track of devastation across the roofs of three more before colliding with a last in an inferno that sent rubble in thousand-foot arcs.

Nearby, Battloid gunners swung their muzzles from target to target. The pods were falling back on every front. There was word over the net that some guy in Vermilion, out of ammo, had actually downed one with a Battloid roundhouse, and *worked* it good with the Battloid's feet.

Elsewhere, Minmei ran for her life.

It seemed so easy at first: the diary in her hand, the way back to the shelters unobstructed… until the pods had dropped into the neighborhood on every side.

Minmei didn't know where she'd lost the diary; she'd only thought to save her all-important letter. Now she thought only about living. She raced through the streets, the long legs flying, midnight sheets of hair flying, as the pods closed in. Blasts and rockets demolished the buildings around her, and burning wreckage nearly smashed her flat a dozen times.

But bless them, there were also those fantastic robotlike defenders, like the one who'd nearly caved in her aunt's restaurant. They were everywhere, leaping and charging and firing, giving even better than they got. They were like armored giants, but none of them were around now. And now was when Minmei needed one.

A Battlepod stomped after her, hooflike feet sinking deep into the pavement with every step. Minmei understood then that hers was only a little life, of no significance on the grand scale of things. There were so many things she'd never done and so little time to reflect on the things she had—the harshness of it hit her in an instant: the miracle that was life, the irreplaceability of each moment.

The Battlepod was almost upon her, armorshod hooves pounding the street. The very vibrations of it threw Minmei headlong, scraping her elbows and hands and knees, as explosions crashed all around. She was not quite sixteen years old, but she understood in that moment that war had no eligibility requirements.

Gigantic pod feet crashed behind her. Minmei cringed, hands over head, waiting for death to take her. An enormous hoof descended.

Just then an amplified voice said, "Oh, no, you don't!"

She heard an explosion and a tearing of metal and felt waves of heat scorching her back. There was a rending of armor and a ground-shaking crash. Somehow, none of it hurt her.

Minmei gathered her nerve and opened her eyes. The pod had been knocked back through the air, one leg dangling loose, in flames. She'd been protected by great metal wings.

It was another example of those things people were calling Robotech, this time in the metal eagle form they seemed to take on at will. There was something familiar about this one's voice. "Take it easy, honey; you're okay," Roy said over external speakers. "We'll protect you."

Roy turned to Rick. "Take care of the girl! I'll keep the pods off our backs!"

Minmei struggled to her feet while the skull-and-crossbones machine reared, mechamorphosing and growing taller and manlike in a way that put her in mind of some miraculous origami. The second, the red one she recognized from her aunt's restaurant, stayed in the man-bird mode, objecting, "You can't handle them alone!" in another voice she remembered.

Roy brought his Gatling up, covering the area. "Don't argue with me! I'll draw their fire while you get her out of here."

Rick, using controls and mind-imagery, eased the Guardian over, extending its left hand, until fingers the diameter of telephone poles were ready to grasp her. He raised the cockpit canopy to call down, "Don't move! I'm going to pick you up!"

For a damsel in distress, Minmei showed a certain skepticism. "I thought you were an amateur."

The anthropomorphic hand gently enfolded her; Rick sweated bullets, concentrating, and knew that he would never try anything like this with a mere physical-control system. Only Robotechnology allowed such fine discretion.

Minmei had a fleeting feeling that she ought to be wearing a white gown and wondered if she was to be carried to the top of a skyscraper or dragged into the middle of a fight with dinosaurs. In a way, of course, that had already happened. "Huh? *Oh, no!*" she cried as the fingers closed around her.

"Trust me; I can do it!" Rick called down to her.

"Do I have to? Ohhhh!"

But the grip, though firm and secure, didn't mangle her or crush her into jelly or even hurt—at least, not much. Which was just as well, since there were alien pods releasing flights of missiles high overhead.

"Get outta here, Rick! Fire your jets!" Roy hollered, bringing up his Gatling and sweeping it back and forth at the incoming missiles, hoping to cut into the odds a little.

The Guardian's foot thrusters blared; Minmei howled, and they were airborne, zooming away from the attack.

Roy got a number of the missiles, detonating them, which in turn knocked out quite a few others—"fratricide," as the ordnance people called it—as they either veered into one another or detonated from the force of the first explosions. But survivors got through, bearing down on Rick, who didn't dare go faster with

Minmei in hand for fear that the air blast and maneuver forces would injure or kill her.

He could only duck and dodge, engaging his jamming and countermeasures gear as Roy had taught him, and hope for the best. Missiles sizzled by all around to impact far down the street.

Minmei hid her head in her hands, then looked up to see that Rick was yelling something at her, too distracted to remember the external speakers. "What're you saying? I can't hear you!"

Roy spotted a pod just as his radars and other instruments picked it up; it was making a stand on a ridgeline above the housing project which had been gouged into the side of a hill. The Zentraedi pod launched itself off the ridge at him; Roy brought his muzzle around and trap-shot it in midair. It rained down in fire and broken fragments.

His fields of fire were clear for the moment. He raised Rick on the tac net. "How's it goin'? Everything okay?"

"I'm all right now, Roy—"

"I don't care how *you* are; how's the *girl*?"

"Huh? Um, okay. So far." Rick began a steady, smooth ascent to get above the battle and out of the range of the pods in Macross City.

"She's a taxpayer. If anything happens to her, you answer to me."

Rick grinned at Roy's screen image. "Don't forget, Big Brother: I saw her first."

"That's how it is, huh? We'll discuss this later!"

Roy got back to business at hand, leaving Rick to ponder Minmei, whose hair was being whiplashed in her face by the ship's airspeed. They'd already gained enough altitude for it to be pretty cold out there; she couldn't take much of it, in addition to the strain it would put on her simply to breathe.

"Boy, I've gotta figure a way to get her into the cockpit," he whispered.

It was exactly then that his instruments beeped an urgent warning. "Uh oh ..."

In Macross City, an alien pod fitted for heavy weapons stood up from its concealment behind a demolished mall. It was mounted with two large racks of rockets, like fire-breathing Siamese twins. Missiles came spiking at him, superheating the air with their trails.

He cut in all countermeasures, going into a booster climb, going ballistic. He rammed the stick up for a pushover, losing a few of the seekers, unable to tell if the maneuver forces had simply knocked Minmei out or killed her.

Wishing he had Roy's skill at this sort of thing, Rick dodged, white-faced with the thought that he would fail, would let Minmei down and lose both their lives.

Miraculously, he avoided them all—almost.

A hit at the elbow joint of the arm holding Minmei blew the joint in half. Minmei fell away, screaming, as if in slow motion. It seemed to Rick that he could hear the scream echoing away.

He banked, diving after her, though all the books and experts would have said that there wasn't a thing in the world he could do to save her. He concentrated on those fingers—thought and thought hard.

The telephone pole fingers of the Robotech hand slowly opened in answer to his thinking-cap command, and Minmei found herself floating in midair. The ground, the sky, the wind—nothing seemed to be moving but she and the giant hand.

She realized she was still screaming, and stopped, pushing herself free for whatever good it would do. Then there was some thing next to her, matching speeds and distances. She seemed to be floating—swimming outside the canopy, some dream mermaid, kicking and struggling toward him, her eyes so big and terrified and pleading that the sight of them almost paralyzed him.

Earlier that same day, Rick would have said that no aircraft in existence could do what the Veritech was doing now. It drew close to Minmei, canopy easing open (he would have said that an aircraft canopy would be torn away like a piece of tinfoil if subjected to aerodynamic stresses like those), in close obedience to his commands and images.

Her black hair stood back, stark, around her face; the white legs kicked like a swimmer's. She glided toward him, arms outstretched. In that moment he knew that if he didn't save her, life would cease to have any meaning.

Still there was the buffeting of the air and the slipstreams created by the fighter itself; they tore at him as Rick rose up, safety harness released, to draw her into the fighter. No ship, not even a Robotech ship, had ever been subjected to such exacting demands.

Gripping the windshield frame, he grabbed for her hand, missed, grabbed, and missed again, the whole time *imaging* the Veritech's precise positioning at speeds approaching the blackout point. One-armed, its aerodynamics radically changed, the fighter struggled to comply.

They drifted like zero-gravity dancers; it seemed so silent and slow and yet so high-speed, with the air shrieking past them and death only an instant away.

Then, somehow, their fingers were together. Later, Rick never remembered shaping the image, but the Veritech altered its death dive to come around and *catch* them, Minmei drifting into the rear seat, Rick into the front.

A last ripping air current almost carried him away, but the descending canopy pressed him back in to safety, although he didn't recall giving the command for it to close.

Maybe if the pilot lives the ship, the ship lives the pilot? he speculated.

He grabbed the manual controls and got the Guardian stabilized again. Behind, there was a last grand explosion of several alien missiles committing fratricide. The Guardian's foot thrusters blowtorched; Rick trimmed his craft. He descended through debris and smoke for a shaky landing, trembling and wiping his brow while Minmei at last gave in to sobs in the rear seat.

"We're safe now. Please don't cry." Rick turned toward her.

The Guardian was in a slow, easing descent, its feet only inches above the streets of Macross City. Minmei wiped her nose on the back of her hand.

"I'm all right now. *Oh, no!*"

Her eyes were wide as saucers—such a strange blue, he thought again—focused over his shoulder.

Even as he whirled, an image of what the Guardian should do sprang to mind; its heels caught the pavement, digging in as the thrusters retrofired.

A Battlepod had backed around the corner of a building at an intersection dead ahead—damaged and covering its own retreat, later reports indicated. The Guardian took it from behind, wings hitting the backs of its knees, neatly upending it.

The Guardian slid for nearly a hundred yards, upside down, Rick and Minmei howling as the pavement tore at the canopy, until it came to a rest.

The Guardian got to its feet; so did the pod, which seemed rather unsteady and showed heavy damage.

"You okay? *Oh, no! Minmei!*" She was pale and unmoving, slumped in the rear seat.

And why? Because these creatures, or whatever they are, came across a billion light-years to invade us? For more war? FOR MORE WAR?

"Yahhhhhh!" Furiously Rick gripped the trigger on his control stick, the chain-gun pelting the pod with a hail of high-caliber, high-density slugs.

The invader's armored front disappeared in a welter of explosions, shrapnel, and smoke. There were secondary explosions, and the machine fell to the ground like a dying ostrich, strangely articulated legs rising up behind as the rest of it crashed down.

Rick found that he was still thumbing the trigger on his control stick-to no avail; the Gatling's magazine was empty. He took his hand away, breathing a sigh of relief or despair—he wasn't sure which.

And then he heard a sound of metal creaking and shifting.

In the back of the downed pod, a hatch was thrown open. A hatch three yards across.

A figure emerged, helmeted and armored. It was on the scale of the pods—taller than most of the buildings around it. Its helmet's faceplate was a cold and untelling fish eye of green.

It was human-shaped, and it came Rick's way. And for the first time in his life, he froze. Couldn't leave Minmei, had no ammo left, and besides—the sight of the thing had him completely rattled. It was as big as a Battloid.

The ground reverberated under its feet; just as Rick thought things couldn't get any worse, its arms reached up and wrenched off a helmet the size of the Veritech's cockpit, dropping it tiredly. The face might have been the face of anybody on the streets of

Macross City. The monster made bass-register rumbling noises, unintelligible—not surprising in view of how long and muscled its vocal cords must have been if they followed human form.

It staggered and teetered toward the grounded Veritech. Rick froze in his seat—nothing to fire and unwilling to eject or otherwise abandon Minmei. A terrible basso growling shook the air; one metalshod foot of the giant alien warrior squashed a car.

The titan reached toward the Veritech; he quite clearly knew who his enemy was and what Rick had done to him. Dying, he would still have his revenge. Rick sat frozen.

There was a burst of high-decibel, buzz saw sound from somewhere. The alien, fingers not far from Rick's canopy, suddenly looked blank and vulnerable. He toppled to the ground and didn't move again, his weight bending and collapsing his body armor.

The alien pitched onto his face, his back showing the deep penetrations of Veritech Gatling rounds. He'd nearly made it to his objective; his right hand clutched the Guardian's immobilized left foot. The ground shook at Roy Fokker's approach, his Battloid shouldering its weapon.

Rick couldn't shake off his terror. "What was it? What was that thing, Roy?"

Roy's reply sounded flat, tight. "That's the enemy. Now you know why we built the Battloids, Rick. To fight these giant aliens." Roy's Battloid toed the corpse with an armored foot.

Rick felt like he was losing his grip. Maybe it was a good time to, but he didn't have much experience in the practice. "But—that guy looks just like a human being!"

Roy snorted, "Yeah. If you ever saw a human fifty feet tall."

12

Lisa turned to me and yelled, "I am getting sick of that name!"

And I thought, Mr. Rick Hunter, whoever you are, if you know what's good for you, you'll start thinking along the lines of an alias.

She had no idea what you'd brought us, Roy!

None of us did.

Lt. Claudia Grant, in a note to Lt. Commdr. Roy Fokker

ROY AND RICK LOOKED DOWN AT THE DEAD GOLIATH WHO STILL had one hand clasped around the Guardian's ankle in final rigor. Rick was just starting to get over the shakes but was still numb with the idea that beautiful, innocent Minmei, so full of life, had had that life taken from her in such a meaningless and appalling way.

His panic reassailed him as he realized that there were more aliens like this one that the pods and the ships beyond the atmosphere were crowded with them—that a plague of them had come to obliterate the Earth.

"I guess you understand now why we kept this secret." Roy said.

"Engineering reports backup rockets are fueled and ready for firing," Claudia said. "How's the evacuation progressing, Lisa?"

Lisa was still watching Gloval worriedly. "All civilians have been safely transported to shelters. Macross City is deserted except for combat units."

Gloval squared his shoulders. "Very well. Bring up the booster rockets. We'll be blasting off immediately."

Lisa blurted, "I hope the standby boosters *work*," before she could think better of it.

Gloval gripped her shoulder, calm in the eye of the storm, hiding the fact that he harbored the same misgivings. "They'll work, Lisa; *they* were designed and built on *Earth*."

But they'd never been tested under full power.

Gloval glanced around. "All right? Blast off!"

Tight-lipped, Lisa responded by manning her station; the rest of the bridge crew chimed in, "Yes, sir!"

The boosters rained blue-white fire, then flared to full life like chained supernovas, their fury backwashing against the hardtop, raising mist and debris, setting blazes, raising steam clouds from the leaking water that flowed through the streets, melting nearby metal. SDF-1 rose slowly, for the first time in a decade, sustained on fusion-flame.

"Attention Skull Leader." Lisa's voice came over the tac net. "SDF-1 is taking off. Request air cover."

Roy's Veritech mechamorphosed from Battloid to Guardian mode. "We're on our way. Over."

Roy's ship rose on its foot thrusters, hovering when Roy realized that there was no sign of life in Rick's fighter.

"C'mon, Rick; let's go! Get the lead out! What's the matter with you?" He went ballistic, climbing.

Rick reached out and shut off his comma, blanking Roy's image. He hadn't led a sheltered life, but nothing had prepared him for the kind of carnage he'd seen in the last half hour or the fear and hatred he'd known. Or for the dismay and grief he felt over the lifelessness of the beautiful young girl slumped in the seat behind him.

SDF-1 rose on its thrusters. Rick sat, prepared to see it go without him, unable to touch the controls of an aircraft.

He leaned back, lowering his head, catatonic and lost.

Roy, off to rejoin the other Veritechs and provide cover for the dimensional fortress's withdrawal, suddenly realized that Rick hadn't followed along behind.

"Rick! Come in, Rick!" No use; he couldn't raise his young friend.

Poor kid's had to take on more than he could manage, Roy decided. *Well, I can't just leave him back there.*

He got back on the radio. "Skull Leader to Control. Lisa, I'm going back to pick up something I left down in Macross City. Captain Kramer can run the fighter group till I get back, over."

Lisa frowned out at him from a display screen. "Why are you turning back? Over."

"Rick Hunter in fighter VT one-zero-two is still back on the ground, and I have to get him out of there."

Lisa's expression showed her sense of outrage. "That pilot's an imposter! I've gone through all the rosters and I find no record of such a person."

Roy was bringing his ship through a wide bank. "Easy enough to explain. He's a civilian, so he isn't listed in the military registries."

Lisa's hand flew to her face. "A civilian? But I thought—ohhh…!" *And I ordered him to get his fighter into the air!* She could hear Sammie and the others whispering among themselves: *"What?" "Did he say civilian?" "Who is he?"*

Back in Macross, the firefights flared with even greater fury as more pods entered the battle in long, two-footed hops.

Two pods and a pair of Battloids were squared off at a range of one hundred yards—practically close quarters—the red tracer streams and the blue energy bolts crisscrossing over the devastated cityscape.

Rubble was tossed into the air and whole walls were blasted to bits as large chunks were gouged or vaporized from the pavement. It was a nearly even match, but another pod arrived and opened up just as one of the first two went down in a hail of armor-piercing autocannon fire. Still another Zentraedi showed up, to concentrate its chest cannonfire along with the others'. A Battloid, blown in half at the waist and leaking fire and explosions, crumbled and disappeared in a detonation.

The second Battloid shifted to Guardian mode, skimming away at ground altitude, trying to get clear. The pods leapt after, closing in for the kill. All at once the two pods were split open like bursting fruit by direct hits from a pair of Stiletto missiles launched by a diving Veritech.

Roy did a tight bank and came in again. Another Stiletto tore the lead pod's leg in half, toppling it, and the pod blew open like an overtaxed boiler.

Seeing the Guardian was safely on its way home, Roy did a wingover and went down lower, searching through the drifting smoke, steam, and dust.

Rick was brought out of his shock and torpor by a sound. He discovered that he'd been slumped against the instrument panel, head resting on his arms.

He moaned a little, then realized what had snapped him out of it: The girl was coming around, making little groaning noises.

"Thank heaven she's alive," he said aloud to himself. Those endless moments of the midair rescue came back to him again— the look in her eyes and the thought of how important she'd become to him.

He shook off his grogginess and glanced around to take in his situation. The enormous corpse was the first thing he spotted.

"I've gotta get us away from here. She might panic if she sees that."

He reached for the instrument panel, trying to clear his head and recall how things worked. He punched up a takeoff sequence, muttering, "I hope this thing'll fly."

But instead of taking to the air, the Guardian lurched and slammed into the pavement, held down by the corpse's death grip, the ship's nose hitting the ground so hard that Rick was nearly jolted into unconsciousness.

He lay, pale and panting, feeling cold even though sweat poured from him. His eyes were glassy; he couldn't take them off the terrible sight of the dead alien.

"What happened?" Minmei asked, just having come to. "What's wrong? Why're you trembling like that?"

When Rick didn't answer, she leaned forward. "What are you looking at out there? What's there—"

The thought of how the sight might subject her to more pain brought him out of his paralysis. "No! You mustn't look out there!"

She resisted the temptation to do just that; she'd come to trust him. "Why, what's wrong?"

As she was saying it, the ground began to vibrate to colossal footsteps, the approach of another war machine. Rick, remembering his Veritech was immobilized and out of ammunition, gazed up in dread.

But the swirling clouds of the battle parted to reveal Roy's ship in Battloid mode, shouldering its autocannon. "I hate to interrupt you two, but you can't sit around here forever. C'mon; let's go!"

But he could see there was no question of repairing Rick's battered ship this time and saw that the dead alien's grip wouldn't be easy to release, short of blasting the hand off at the wrist. "That big palooka seems to have formed a permanent attachment to you guys."

Fortunately, there was a quicker and less messy way to handle things. Roy's Battloid extruded a long metal tentacle ending in a special waldo. With it, he opened a small access plate in one of the downed Guardian's nacelles, cutting in the rescue overrides manually.

In another moment Rick and Minmei felt themselves jostled around as the cockpit and nose separated entirely from the rest of the machine. Roy caught it up neatly and tucked it into a special fitting on the underside of his Battloid's right forearm.

"Amazing, isn't it?" Rick got out.

"It's—really incredible" was all Minmei could manage to say.

"How's *that* for convenience?" Roy asked. He never got their answer, because at that moment another alien war machine—a pod armed with heavy missiles—sprang from behind a gutted building and zeroed in on the Battloid.

"Hang on, you two!" Roy leapt his Battloid clear just as the pod fired a volley of energy shots. Bringing up his autocannon, the skull leader peppered the pod and sent it crashing backward, riddled and burning.

But more pods were rising from concealment or springing down from the roofs of adjacent buildings. Roy was already shifting to Guardian configuration and jetting away, the aliens galloping in pursuit, firing and firing.

One pod nearly caught him, the vast torso of it filling the sky to starboard. But Roy completed the mechamorphosis to fighter mode and shot away into the sky while salvos ranged around him, thrusters going full-bore.

Two pods stationed on the cliffs at the edge of town poured intense fire at the Veritech as it climbed directly at them. Rick heard Minmei echo his own moan of fear.

Roy stayed dead on course, releasing more missiles when the time was exactly right. The pods went up like a pair of Roman candles, and Roy zoomed into the clear, headed for SDF-1.

The dimensional fortress, its protecting fighters deployed all around it, had achieved a low orbit.

"Shifting to horizontal propulsion," Lisa's voice rang through the fleet, and the enigmatic main engines sent a river of force through the primary thrusters at the ship's stern. Blue infernos raved, and the SDF-1 gathered speed, moving for a higher orbit. "Stand by for fighter retrieval," Lisa went on. "All planes return to carrier bays. Over."

"This is Sepia Three. Roger, Control, returning for retrieval."

On the flight decks, the crews prepared for the feverish, dangerous work ahead. The fleet was still on combat alert, subject to attack at any time. Every attempted landing must be a "trap"—successful—because there was no time to waste on "bolters" that would have to be repeated.

The teams swarmed to their mother ship; everyone from Gloval on down sweated each second of the retrieval. "Lisa, please report whether we have all fighters safely aboard," Gloval said after an eternity.

"Yes, sir." The answer came quickly. "Those were the last two, sir. All others are accounted for except for Commander Fokker and VT one-zero-two."

"Good. I don't think we have to worry about Commander Fokker." Gloval rose. "Vanessa, show me the current orbital data for Armor One and Armor Ten."

Vanessa punched up the information. "Yes, sir. They're both approaching Rendezvous Point Charlie right on schedule. We should be making contact with them in about two-niner minutes."

"Very good. Claudia, any sign of enemy craft?"

"No, Captain. It's all clear."

"Excuse me, Captain, but isn't that strange?" Lisa asked. "After launching a massive attack from orbit, why isn't the enemy continuing their attack? It doesn't make sense, does it?"

Gloval usually kept his own counsel but admitted now, "That's bothering me too. There has to be a reason they're just playing with us. They have the advantage, but they don't attack. But why?"

The bridge crew exchanged troubled looks with one another.

Roy's fighter climbed smoothly out of the atmosphere, making for the dimensional fortress. Inside, though, things were a little stormier.

"She doesn't *want* to go to the ship, Roy!" Rick insisted. "She wants to go back to Macross Island!"

Roy, lips pulled back in anger, snarled at Rick's image on his screen. "Are you crazy? Macross is crawling with aliens! It'd be suicide for her to go back there! Did she give you any reason?"

Minmei butted in, "I'm worried about my aunt and uncle back in the shelter, with all those invaders around them!"

"They're perfectly safe there," Roy insisted. "The shelters are impregnable; this is what they were built for."

Minmei looked winsome even when she was being stubborn. "But I still want to go back to Macross. It's my home!"

Roy shook his head slowly. "I promise, as soon as this trouble's over, I'll take you back there personally."

"What d'you mean *you'll* take her?" Rick blurted. "*I* will!" He heard Minmei make a little shocked sound and realized how possessive he'd sounded. "Uh, that is …"

"Hold on a second, Rick," Roy said, and switched his attention to the mammoth ship looming before him. "This is Skull Leader to SDF-1, over."

Lisa's tone was vexed. "Did you find him?"

Roy answered wryly, "He was annoying a young lady. I had to rescue her as well."

"You rat!" Rick snapped.

Lisa had both screens up on her board, looking Rick Hunter over and not missing Minmei, who was leaning in over his shoulder. Hunter was obviously a wet-behind-the-ears kid and a discipline problem to boot, she saw. As for the girl—well, she was pretty in a way, Lisa supposed, if you liked that type.

"So *that's* our civilian pilot," Lisa said. "I wondered why he didn't know how to fly his aircraft."

Rick recognized those as fighting words. "Who's that old sourpuss, Roy?"

Lisa drew back as if he'd thrown ice water in her face. *Old sourpuss?* The rest of the bridge gang was very discreet about swapping startled but amused looks.

Roy couldn't help laughing out loud. "That old sourpuss is our Control and the ship's First Officer, Lisa Hayes. And if she looks *old* to you, you're not as grown up as I thought, kid."

Lisa grimaced and cut in, "Now, listen up, Commander Fokker! You'd *better* have a good explanation for turning a Veritech fighter over to an amateur civilian pilot! You could face a court-martial for this, or hadn't you thought about that?"

Luckily for all concerned, she didn't notice that Gloval was stifling his laughter off to one side. He hastily resumed a straight face.

"Ooo, she's mad," Roy said blithely.

"As for you, Rick Hunter," Lisa bore on, "you're in a lot of trouble, whether you know it or not!"

Somehow, gallantry seemed to melt away now that there was no danger and people were talking about legal proceedings. He gestured to Minmei helplessly. "This whole thing's because of her, you see…"

Minmei didn't seem offended, but she confided, "I think you'd better apologize, Rick. Women her age can get awful mean, you know."

Lisa Hayes silently counted to ten, trying to keep from putting her fist through the screen.

"Bridge Control, this is Skull Leader requesting landing instructions," Roy reminded her. "Give us a bay number—you old sourpuss."

This time there was no controlling it, and the rest of Lisa's bridge gang broke up in giggles. She clenched her fists but somehow kept her rage contained.

"Roger. Bring your plane into bay zero-niner." *And I hope it's the last I see of you, Rick Hunter!*

13

It is no exaggeration to say that we found the inhabitants of the planet surprising. Quite tenacious and determined in battle, and yet not as suicidal—not as mindlessly ferocious—as, for example, the Invid.

But if they surprised me, surely, I thought, we would awe them by an overwhelming application of force. The thing upon which I did not count was how very much like us they were.

Exedore, from his Military Intelligence Analysis Report

THE BEACHES OF MACROSS ISLAND WERE NOW A STAGING AREA for the Zentraedi withdrawal. Immense saucer-shaped landing craft pulled themselves along the shoreline, their huge access hatches lowered over the breaking waves.

With the SDF-1 gone, the pods had no further reason to be on the island; the shelters were of no interest to them, and no serious effort had been made to breach the human fortifications. Ironically, the Zentraedi's iron warrior code kept them from realizing the value of hostages; hostages were of no significance at all to them, and it never occurred to them that humans might be different.

Wave after wave of pods bounded into the ships, some trailing damaged parts or showing the effects of Veritech hits. There was plenty of room in the landing ships that would bear them back aloft; the pods' ranks had thinned considerably. The saucers lifted away, shedding seawater.

Breetai received the report in his command post. "Recon force now returning to group orbit."

"It appears only half of them survived," Exedore observed.

"Where is the battle fortress now?" Breetai demanded of his techs. Though the missing pods represented a negligible loss, he seethed over it. That Zentraedi warriors should be thus resisted by mere primitives!

"It has passed through the uppermost atmospheric ranges and achieved orbit," a voice reported. "It is apparently on its way to rendezvous with the other orbital units."

"What is your plan, Breetai?" Exedore asked.

Breetai considered. "It would be a simple matter to shoot them down, but I don't want that ship damaged."

Wisely, Exedore didn't point out that notwithstanding Breetai's preferences, that was the specific order that bound him: To capture the dimensional fortress intact. "Once they're out of Earth's gravitational field, they can execute a hyperspace fold, taking them beyond the range of our weapons—perhaps to escape us completely across spacetime once again."

Breetai nodded. "You have a point there. Perhaps I'd better apply a little restraining force to slow them down a bit."

He turned to give the order in his rumbling basso, his gleaming skullpiece and glittering artificial eye catching the light. "Prepare a laser bombardment!"

The order was repeated all through the fleet, as guns were run out in their turrets and casemates—slender, tapering Zentraedi-style barrels like gargantuan steel icicles.

The order resounded through the fleet, "All gun crews stand by for total bombardment of target area. Stand by for order to fire."

Rick and Minmei were speechless at their first view of the SDF-1's interior.

They raced along in a four-seater troop vehicle driven by Roy, who showed his fondness for high speed and squealing tires. They barreled through holds and compartments so vast that there was no feeling of being inside.

Instead it was like driving through an immense metal metropolis studded with lights of all descriptions, reaching up and up, the levels disappearing into a dim ceiling/sky. Rick couldn't imagine what such stupendous amounts of unoccupied space were for.

"I've got a little surprise for you, Rick." Roy smiled. "Wait'll you see it." He made another turn with two wheels off the deck

At last he brought the jeep to a virtual panic stop, tires screeching, so that Rick and Minmei were thrown off balance. "Well, here we are." He hopped out jauntily. "Come on!"

Rick glared, helping Minmei up. "Was that really necessary? She could've been hurt!"

Roy ignored the comment because, of course, he was confident that he'd never let that happen. He flicked on a bank of overhead spotlights. Sitting in a small hangar bay was the *Mockingbird*.

"Golly, Rick! Look at that!" Minmei exclaimed.

"Somebody left this thing behind," Roy said casually, "so I had it stashed here and serviced."

The little plane's booster rocket covers had been replaced, and the way the ship sat on its landing gear let Rick know that it had been completely refueled.

"My racer!" He jumped out of the carrier, dashing to his beloved *Mockingbird*, all but dancing around it. "I thought I'd never see it again! You saved it!"

He had Roy's hand in his, pumping it, ready to give his friend an exuberant hug. "Oh, thank you, Roy, thank you—"

Roy disengaged himself. "Hey, cut it out, Rick! Take it easy! I just thought you'd be more comfortable flying in this thing than in one of our Veritechs. *Mockingbird* doesn't turn into a Battloid."

"I don't know what to say, Roy!"

"I've seen that plane before," Minmei said, joining them. "It was in the air show this morning, wasn't it?"

Yeah, about a million years ago, Rick thought. But as he was about to explain, Claudia's voice came over the PA. "Attention all hands. We are approaching rendezvous with Armor One and Armor Ten. Report to your docking stations immediately! All hands report to stations!"

Roy was already leaping back behind the wheel of the carrier. "I have to get going now. You two stay here and don't wander around. If you start exploring, you'll get lost."

The tires chirped as he broke traction briefly. "You can't imagine how huge this ship is, so stay put!" Then he was gone.

. . .

The Armors and their tenders and destroyer escorts were coming up quickly, strung out in a line so that they could be mated to the SDF-1 in order.

"We have perfect docking alignment," Vanessa announced.

"The enemy ships are preparing to dock, sir," a Zentraedi tech reported.

"All right," Breetai replied. "Tell our gunners to fire their beams *between* the fortress and the other vessels and at the target ships themselves. I don't care how many of the smaller ones are destroyed, but the large one must not be damaged!"

The command was relayed as the long, slender Zentraedi cannon swiveled and came to bear. Then the order was passed: "Gun commanders may fire when ready!"

The Zentraedi beams seemed to light up the universe.

A quick, orderly docking sequence became a bloodbath as alien beams zeroed in from far away, without warning, punching through hulls and turning ships into flowering explosions.

Destroyers, tenders, and escort ships were hit, and Armor Three went up in a ball of fury that lit the SDF-1's bridge in a harsh glare. Wreckage and debris rode the winds of the explosions as though tornado-driven.

Gloval, knocked from his feet, drew himself back up. "Vanessa, what's the enemy's position?"

The bridge crew calmly went back to work. "The current attack is from the exact same location as the first one: They're about ten thousand miles from here in a higher orbit."

Lisa said, "Reporting: *Miranda*, *Circe*, and Armor Three completely destroyed, as well as numerous smaller vessels and heavy damage throughout the Orbital Force."

"They're tearing our fleet to shreds!" Gloval snarled. "And what about *our* damages?"

"We've taken no direct hits, Captain," Sammie declared, and Kim confirmed, "No damage anywhere, sir."

"What's our position?" Gloval snapped, squaring away his cap. "We're just closing our initial orbit," Vanessa told him. "Approaching our original position over Macross Island, distance approximately one hundred miles."

Gloval made up his mind. "Claudia, take us down over Macross Island. At two thousand feet altitude activate the fold system for a position jump."

Claudia debated whether she should question the order; this was a wartime situation. But at certain critical times allegiance to duty could demand something more than mere obedience. "Are you sure you want to do that, Captain? The fold system hasn't even been tested yet!"

"I am well aware of how risky it is, Claudia, but you can read the situation displays and tactical projections as well as I."

She could, and had, as they all had. The alien fleet had already been deployed in an inescapable net and was drawing the net tighter around SDF-1. "If we stay in this position, we'll be totally defenseless," Gloval added.

"But we're not even sure how the system works!" Lisa reminded him.

"That's why I'm bringing us as close to Macross as I dare," Gloval said calmly. "All Doctor Lang's calculations and preliminary findings are based on experiments conducted at that location."

He looked around at his bridge gang. He wasn't used to explaining orders, but it was important that his reasoning go on the record so that if he didn't survive the engagement, what he'd done might be of use in later decisions.

"We can't just surrender!" he said hotly. "We have to try everything we can first! So ready fold system for a position jump, targeting the area on the far side of the moon, within one lunar diameter of the surface. Get your radar ready for an access check, Lisa."

The bridge gang got to work, speaking into comcircuits, operating their consoles, while Gloval gave orders in a steady voice. "We'll make the jump from precisely two thousand feet above the island."

"Don't we need permission from headquarters?" Claudia asked. He shook his head. "We don't have time for that."

"But Captain, you know the regulations specifically—" His gaze was white-hot now, making her falter. "Sorry, sir …"

Gloval took in a breath. "I know what the regs say, but I appreciate your bringing it to my attention."

"I just wanted to—"

"*Claudia! You've got your orders!*" He turned away, hands clasped behind his back once more.

"Yes sir, Captain," she said through locked teeth, and turned to do as she'd been commanded. "Attention all hands. Priority! Fold system standby! Readying energy at maximum-green at all power sources."

The giant untried fold devices came alight like castles of energy. The crews raced to prepare and make secure for the jump, although there wasn't nearly enough time. The chaos was especially acute in the hangar bays.

Nevertheless, throughout the ship, men and women did their best.

"All hands to emergency stations. All hands, emergency stations. This is not a drill, I say again: This is not a drill! Prepare for fold operation in T minus five minutes and counting—mark!"

In the labyrinth shelter system under the smoking ruins of Macross Island, Jason shifted uncomfortably. It wasn't that he felt crowded; the shelters had been built with a far larger population and supply requirement in mind—against the day when Macross might be the last human refuge.

But Jason missed his cousin. "I'm getting worried about Minmei, aren't you? I wonder where she went."

"Don't worry about Minmei. She'll be fine," his mother reassured him. "She just went to another shelter, that's all."

His father was quick to add, "Sure! Nothing's going to happen to anyone as smart as Minmei! Isn't that right?"

But among the grown-ups there passed looks hidden from the boy. They'd felt the distant concussions of the terrible battle, and now, for a long time, there had been an ominous silence with no all-clear signal from the military.

"Yeah…" Jason conceded, and settled himself down to wait some more, gathering his blanket around him.

"Are you planning on going somewhere?" Minmei asked as Rick ran a final preflight check on *Mockingbird* and made a few last adjustments.

He closed an access panel and turned to her. "I'm gonna take you back to the island like I promised." He knelt to replace his tools in the box and return it to its stowage niche. "You still wanna go back, don't you? Because *I'm* not gonna hang around here one way or the other."

He couldn't bring himself to admit how important it was that she come with him; that wasn't the sort of thing one learned to do working in a flying circus.

The SDF-1 resounded with Sammie's latest announcement: "Attention, all hands. Fold in T minus three minutes and counting."

Minmei offered him part of a chocolate bar that had somehow stayed in her pocket against every conceivable adversity. "Candy?"

"Thanks."

"Rick, what's a fold?"

"Aw, nothing to do with us." He offered her his hand to help her into the cockpit. "Come on; let's go."

She looked into the tiny plane's only passenger space dubiously. "It's so small. Will it hold two people?"

"If they're very friendly, it will." And so, she didn't object when he put his hands on her waist and helped her up into the *Mockingbird*.

Rick handed her his Veritech helmet. "Here; put this on."

She gave the helmet that wide-eyed look he'd come to care so much about. "Ohh!" Then she had it on.

"It's so cute on you, Minmei. You could start a whole new fad."

She snorted in exasperation. "Oh, you!"

He chuckled foolishly and turned to work the bay door. The indicators had already let him know that the SDF-1 was descending, quickly; it was low enough for his plane's turbofan to function. The first thing he saw as the doors parted was Macross Island, far below. It occurred to him that that was the ship's most likely landing spot, but be that as it might, he had no intention of remaining aboard. These military types had gotten him—and Minmei—into enough trouble.

Minmei saw Macross, too. She was still staring at it longingly as Rick crowded into the single pilot's seat next to her and got her into his lap.

The propfan was turning slowly; he brought it up while he lowered the canopy and began to turn *Mockingbird*'s nose. It would be the trickiest takeoff of his career; the slipstream caused by SDF-1's descent could break the tiny stunt plane in half if Rick didn't do things just right.

"Hang on to me, Minmei."

"It's awful close in here." She squirmed forward, trying to rest against the instrument panel.

"Hey! I can't see to fly if you sit there!"

She leaned back, and he decided that he had to take his shot now, before the SDF-1 got into the heavy air currents lower down. He gunned the turbofan, launched. Counterrotating blades spun.

"I'm sorry, Rick," Minmei was apologizing, "But it's so tiii—yiiite!" as the *Mockingbird* was seized and twirled.

14

"Who Dares, Wins."

This motto of the Special Air Service commandos of the Royal Air Force of the United Kingdom (latter twentieth century) was known to have been quoted by Gloval, even though his behavior and accomplishments make it clear that he was far from rash.

Certainly, he proved that he knew what the saying meant that day high above Macross Island.

"Starleap," *History of the First Robotech War*, Vol. VIII

RICK SOMEHOW SUCCEEDED IN KEEPING THEM FROM BEING smashed into a large gun turret as the *Mockingbird* nosedived, spinning round and round.

"There's nothing to worry about, Minmei; I'm an expert pilot," Rick insisted in what he hoped was a composed voice, fighting his controls and expecting to be slammed back against the SDF-1's superstrong hull. Minmei meanwhile sat with her head buried against his chest, moaning and wishing life would slow down again, even for a moment, so she could catch her breath. But somewhat to his own surprise, Rick did manage to pull the ship out of its spin, level off, and gain proper flight altitude. "There, okay?"

She got up the nerve to look, saw that things were under control, and couldn't help laughing for joy, hugging him.

Rick Hunter felt very, very pleased with himself and began to wish that the flight could go on forever.

. . .

Macross Island was clearly defined beneath the dimensional fortress, seeming to draw nearer as SDF-1 descended. "We will enter fold in ten seconds," Claudia intoned over the PA. "Nine…"

Gloval watched the dozens of displays and screens with no outward show of the misgivings he felt. The enigmatic sealed engines made the huge vessel tremble, and the high vibrations of the fold generators seemed to cut through everyone aboard.

The seconds seemed to stretch on endlessly, then he became aware of Claudia saying, "… two… one… zero!"

"Execute hyperspace fold-jump!" Gloval ordered. The bridge gang bent to their duty stations to carry out the command.

It seemed to Gloval that he was seeing the view from the bridge in an altered way, that he was perhaps seeing higher into the ultraviolet or lower into infrared. In any case, the superstructure was outlined with strange hot reds, yellows, and oranges that hadn't been there moments before.

Am I seeing into the thermal part of the spectrum, perhaps?

But even that didn't explain the strange, almost ghostly images, not quite identifiable, that suddenly loomed in the air or the way in which vision suddenly altered so that the world looked like a shifting double exposure.

The SDF-1 appeared to be in the center of a hot gas cloud. From it expanded a white-hot globe of light, the same sort that the Zentraedi armada had produced earlier that day. Sounds like nothing humans had ever heard before toned and swirled in the crew's ears, with no apparent source.

The fold-jump globe expanded, defying Lang's theories and calculations, enveloping Macross and its harbor, making even the supercarriers *Daedalus* and *Prometheus* shift in focus and seem to blur into double exposure as the waters crashed as if storm-tossed.

A vibration like an earthquake, far greater than any the Zentraedi attack had produced, shook the shelters, and the refugees thought the worst had come-the worst as they could conceive of it: the end of their world.

In Macross City sudden eddy currents from the fold swept through the streets, destroying buildings and the remains of downed war machines of both armies. The violent side effects of the space jump maneuver caught the tiny *Mockingbird* too, whirling it like a leaf.

Incandescent motes appeared, growing brighter and brighter, circling like lazy insects or sentient miniature stars. On the bridge, it was impossible to focus on instruments or screens. Lisa sobbed, feeling sick and wrenched from herself, as if she were being torn from life itself.

A globe with the SDF-1 at its center now encompassed the island, the waters around it, and a considerable bubble of sky. The ocean crashed against the force field, without effect.

SDF-1 shifted through the double-exposure changes again, stabilizing at last, then began to fade. In one moment, the spherical force field was immovable in the midst of the furious sea—and in the next, it was gone.

Billions of gallons of water poured in to fill the gap, colliding to send up tidal waves that would race around the planet for days. Air rushed in to take the place of the sudden vacuum, creating a thunderclap like the detonation of a nuclear weapon, only sharper.

Over the rim of the world, where the main Zentraedi elements were forming up for a final attack, the event registered only picoseconds before the glow erupted. It lit the horizon like a "diamond necklace" eclipse. Breetai needed no instruments or tech reports to know what had happened.

"A fold! I don't believe it!"

"Impossible that close to planetary gravity!" Exedore burst out in a rare display of emotion. *These primitives somehow rebuilt the SDF-1 and, with whatever modifications or improvising they did, somehow came up with a superior spacefold process! Or perhaps it's something of Zor's; it doesn't matter. If it still exists, we must have that ship!*

Breetai was uttering his terrible animal growl, fists clenched so tightly that Exedore could hear the squeaking of bones and cartilage under the exertion of those corded muscles.

"I want to know their exact position immediately!"

. . .

Out in the farthest reaches of the solar domain it had been cold and dark since the birth pains of the solar system, almost twenty million years before. Here the great furnace of the sun was only a tiny, cold droplet in the night, and Pluto, the only planetary body, nearly forty times as far from the life-giving primary as Earth, maintained a temperature near absolute zero.

But in an incomparable moment, Pluto and its single loyal satellite, Charon, were joined in their lonely, eccentric orbit.

The fold force field appeared, a stupendous orb in space, holding the SDF-1 suspended over an island with a fishbowl-bottom of ocean underneath it, the smoke of battle still rising from Macross City.

The sphere winked out of existence. By all rights, the waters should have boiled away in the vacuum, all atmosphere not pent up in the battle fortress or the shelters dissipated; and the fragment of Earth that was Macross Island itself should have begun coming apart.

That none of these things happened was proof—reinforcing later evidence—that certain other forces were still at work. The Protoculture-powered globe couldn't be maintained for very long, not even by the dimensional fortress's mighty engines, but secondary effects could; Protoculture-powered phenomena were very different from the raw-power manipulations of the universe that humans had been used to until now.

The ocean waters froze, still adhering to the island fragment, expanding and cracking. Most of the atmosphere began to fall toward the island, frozen air snowing down on it, coating it in seconds with a thickening glacial coat—*despite the fact that instruments indicated no gravity whatsoever beyond the negligible amount such a mass would generate.* Be that as it might, the harbor became a solid mass and the aircraft carriers were rimed with permafrost in moments.

These anomalies have always constituted one of the great mysteries of the Robotech Wars, though subsequent events and discoveries gave the human race some tantalizing hints as to what may have happened that chilly afternoon some three and a half billion miles and more beyond Terra's orbit.

. . .

Already disoriented and dismayed, with Minmei clinging to him, and concealing the terror he *wanted* to show, Rick realized two new and frightening things: His propfan engine was no longer having any effect, and the entire canopy was frosting over—fast. It wasn't as if he needed that; he'd already watched with horror as Macross turned to a polarscape. It was clear that there wasn't much gravity in the dark, empty neighborhood, whatever it was. He'd heard *Mockingbird*'s seals close against low pressure—*no* pressure, he was certain—and that spelled very bad luck.

Rick watched the blanket of white cover the canopy and wondered what he could possibly do next, aside from dying.

"Let's have some light in here!" Gloval ordered; the fold-jump had drained all systems. The emergencies cast a weird red glow over everything. Heating units shouldn't have been needed in the vacuum of space; Gloval wondered what was wrong.

"Switching to backups, Captain," Claudia said crisply, and brought lighting back to normal. The bridge gang blinked a bit but kept to their jobs. Powerful running lights showed a dust storm of wreckage blowing past the ship, pieces impacting constantly.

"Radar shows an extremely large object just—beneath us, sir," Vanessa said. At least, it was "beneath" *relative* to the battle fortress; but the readings looked very peculiar, even though the ship's artificial gravity had cut in automatically during the jump.

"Our jump target was the moon; that's what your large object is," Gloval said.

"No; it's too small to be the moon, sir," she countered. "I'll put it on one of the main screens for you."

Everybody there looked, and everybody drew breath in brief astonishment and fright.

"It's corning straight at us, sir!" Vanessa said.

Gloval took a quick look at the readouts and contradicted, "No! *We're* moving toward *it*!"

"It's Macross Island, Captain Gloval!" Vanessa yelled, but Gloval had already seen that and reached his own conclusions as to the magnitude of the disaster. But there were other things that had to be dealt with instantly; reflection must wait for a later time.

"Retro rockets, Claudia! Maximum thrust!"

Claudia worked, tight-lipped, at her station and spared only a moment to say, "It's no-go; I'm getting no response whatsoever from the computer!"

Damn energy drain! Lisa thought, even as she sounded "collision" over the PA. "Emergency! Emergency! Prepare for impact! Prepare for impact!"

Helpless, the SDF-1 floated kneel-on toward Macross Island. "It's covered with ice," Sammie reported, looking into her scope while everyone else could see that on the screen. Claudia yanked her away from the scope so she wouldn't get her nose broken.

SDF-1 hit the tilted surface and crunched through the buildings as if they were a bunch of potato chips dipped in liquid nitrogen, sliding side-on across the surface of the worldlet that had been a thriving, jubilant city only hours ago.

Down in the shelters, people already dealing with the difficulties of mass null-g sickness and panic had their problems complicated by an impact that sent many of them flying once again across the shelters—toward walls and ceilings and floors that weren't padded and wouldn't make kind landing places.

Jason wailed and grabbed for his mother's hand; Lena pulled him back from an impact with the wall, and together they spun helplessly in midair, wondering if this was the end.

The rime frost on the outside of *Mockingbird*'s canopy was gone in that uncanny pulling-together force exerted in the wake of the fold—a force that wasn't gravity but had many of its attributes. A force that seemed to make *conscious* distinctions.

But the cold of the outer rime had transferred through the canopy to the atmosphere in the cockpit, forming a thick glaze. Now Rick wiped away a large patch to get a look at what was going on.

"Ooo! Look how beautiful it is!" Minmei gasped, her long dark hair floating weightless. Rick was struck again by her innocence, the purity of spirit that saw beauty everywhere and gave so little attention to danger and evil.

A starfield shone against the blackness of space. Chunks of rock and debris floated by. Rick tried his controls, without effect.

I'm getting no response at all from the propfan. As crazy as it seems, there's no other answer: We're out in deep space. And that means we're in deep trouble!

"Oh, my, isn't it romantic?" Minmei sighed.

Rick forced himself to smile. "Yes, it is."

There was an abrupt metal-to-metal collision that jarred the little plane brutally, sending it spinning away. Rick had a split-second glimpse of some kind of large machine casing veering off from its impact with *Mockingbird*.

The two cried out in shock as the plane was spun through the vacuum, to collide with another piece of flotsam. The second hit jolted Rick's nose into the back of Minmei's head, but it also absorbed much of the spinning and brought the ship virtually to rest relative to the junk floating around it.

Rick sneezed mightily from the bump on the nose. Minmei looked startled, then laughed, and Rick joined her.

But she stopped in alarm a moment later. "What's that hissing sound?"

Rick was quick to cover his panic. "Oh, it's perfectly all right. Don't get upset about it."

But the hissing was coming from a hairline crack just under the windshield frame. "You hear all kinds of weird noises in these things." He forced himself to laugh lightly.

I don't dare tell her our air's leaking out into space! The flow wafted the ends of stray strands of Minmei's hair toward the crack.

Rick wadded a handkerchief and tried to push it into the crack. *Maybe this'll hold it temporarily.* It didn't seem to do much good.

Minmei's eyes were enormous with fright. "Let's get out of here, okay?"

"Hey, relax; what's your hurry?" Rick could think of only one slim hope of survival. He put the helmet back on her head, and she snuggled into his lap again as he thought, *If the boosters don't work, we're sunk!* "Comfy?"

"Uh huh," Minmei answered. Rick hit his boosters very gently, bringing them up.

He had a certain amount of independent control over each, but that still made steering a very ticklish problem. Attitude thrusters would have been a tremendous help, but there just hadn't been much need for deep-space maneuvering capability in the air circus.

A tiny burn—a mere cough—got the *Mockingbird* under way, infinitesimal spurts from selected boosters were the only way he had to steer. And there wasn't very much fuel in the little rockets.

He was beginning to see where there were some advantages to those nutty Veritechs after all.

"I guess we'll go find the SDF-1," he said. "Something funny's been goin' on around here." The air leak hissed on. At least the frost was melting off the canopy; he gave up wondering how much time they had and concentrated on piloting and spotting the battle fortress.

"There it is!" Minmei said very shortly. SDF-1 was hard to miss: still lodged in the remains of Macross Island, with explosions, tracers, and energy blasts flashing all around it.

The war had resumed.

15

Well, you're never gonna believe *this*!

From the diary of Lynn-Minmei

"**I**T LOOKS LIKE THEY'RE FIGHTING DOWN THERE!" MINMEI SAID.

It doesn't matter; we've got nowhere else to go. "Don't worry." He cut in the boosters, nursing them along exactingly to line up his vector, praying no debris got in his way because there was no hope of dodging anything.

In the fury of the battle back on Earth, human defenders had overlooked the fact that one of the first Zentraedi landing ships, loaded with Battlepods, had been heavily damaged and forced to set down on Macross once again, unable to fly. And so it, too, had been transported into deep space by the fold maneuver.

While the landing ship was no longer operable, the pods were. They'd immediately resumed their attack on the ship, no doubt in response to their assigned mission but moved, too, by the awareness that they were somewhere far from their fleet and that if they couldn't take the fortress, they wouldn't survive for long out by Pluto's orbit.

The island in space was now complete bedlam, with alien mecha massed in suicidal assault waves, while the ship's guns blazed away. Rick Hunter rocketed into the midst of this with a ship he could barely control

Still, he did the best he could, gradually bringing the little racer in end for end through judicious use of the boosters, his only method of halting being a retrofire. He made microburns, slowing, trying to line up his approached. It seemed hopeless.

Then a bad situation became even worse. All the landing bays were closed, sealed tight. "I forgot, they shut them during combat," Rick said, tight-lipped. Minmei blinked, looking at him as if he'd said it in another language.

A mortally damaged pod went tumbling past them, trailing fire like an erratic meteor, victim of an armor-piercing, discarding-sabot round from SDF-1—so close that it all but singed *Mockingbird*'s wingtip. Rick and Minmei shrank from it in reflex, but it was already impacting the SDF-1.

Rick had to crane around, glancing over the back of the plane, to see what happened. The pod gave up all its destructive power in one great explosion, hitting at the confined area of a recessed maintenance causeway.

It was a million-to-one shot, but the explosion acted as a shaped charge, blowing a gaping hole in the dimensional fortress's armored hide. And it was toward that hole that the plane was going.

Until the explosion's shock wave hit it.

Mockingbird was jarred, stopped in midflight, spun. It ended up with its nose more or less pointed at the SDF-1 but moving away from it.

Rick was already feeling a little light-headed, and breathing was an effort. Moreover, the boosters didn't have very much left to give. "Maybe we can get through the hole the invader made!"

Minmei nodded, too short-winded to answer. Rick cut in the boosters, steering as best he could.

Another pilot would have died then. But Rick knew *Mockingbird* well, even under circumstances as bizarre as these. He nursed the racer along with minute bursts of thrust, knowing there'd be no time to flip and retro, hoping he and Minmei could survive a crash.

But they would have to endure one more bad break to even the balance of the sudden luck that had come their way: A thick curtain of armor was descending over the hole, the reaction of an automatic damage-control system.

Rick cut in all boosters full throttle, seeing his only chance of survival disappearing. He cranked up the propfan in full reverse, hoping that it might stop the ship once it hit atmosphere.

He'd calculated that most of the outsurge of air from the breached compartment would have spent itself by the time he got there. There was no point in thinking otherwise; neither boosters nor propfan could take *Mockingbird* "upstream" against the terrific pressure of such a monster air leak.

He wasn't too far off. In fact, he did a piloting job worthy of a place in the record books until the descending armor curtain sheared the racer's uppermost wing off.

Still, the little plane shot into the vast compartment, more or less intact, aimed at a far area of the ceiling. The propfan howled as the blades got some bite in a very thin atmosphere. The armor patch clanged into place.

And there was gravity. *Mockingbird*'s upward climb topped out and became a crash dive. *We almost made it,* Rick realized. The deck whirled at the canopy.

But they'd happened into an area still strung with hoisting cables, rigging slings, and tackle—a jungle of them. *Mockingbird* was successively snagged, whirled, flipped, and caught in a matter of seconds, with more pieces broken from it.

Rick and Minmei felt themselves blacking out but shook it off a few seconds later to discover themselves hanging upside down, the deck only a yard or two below the cockpit dome. The rumble of life-support equipment pumping air back into the chamber was already loud.

Mockingbird hung ensnared in the lines and cables, upside down but stable for the time being. A last piece of good fortune: None of the lines had caught across the canopy to hold the cockpit shut and imprison them.

Rick had no reserves left to think of elegant solutions. He hit the release, and the canopy swung down. He lowered Minmei with the last of his strength and, resigning himself to a fall, released his safety harness. He landed on the deck at her feet, saying only, "Oof!"

She knelt next to him. They looked themselves over with

wonder, having resigned themselves to being dead. Then they looked at each other and burst out laughing at the same moment.

It was the best, loudest laugh either of them had ever had. Somehow, it was immeasurably important to Rick that he share it with Minmei.

"We just shot down the last enemy Battlepod, sir," Sammie relayed the information.

"Very good." Gloval nodded. "Any contact with headquarters yet?"

That was Claudia's hot potato. "No, Captain. I've tried, sir, but nothing works. We can't raise them."

Sammie broke in, "Are you sure there's no system malfunction?"

"Negative," Claudia shot back tersely.

"None at all," Vanessa said, backing her. "It's operating perfectly."

Gloval didn't want to indulge his fears; he had a pretty good idea what had happened, but if it were to prove true, the consequences would be dire indeed. Still, there was no avoiding the inevitable. "Give me the reading on our position."

Vanessa was prompt and precise in answering. "The planet Pluto's orbit, according to the computer plot."

"The planet Pluto?" So much worse than even he had suspected. Gloval dipped deep into the fortitude that develops when death has been cheated a hundred times and comes back for a rematch. Relentlessly.

The bridge gang was gathering around Vanessa, even rocklike Lisa. "Pluto?" "Impossible!"

"It can't be!" Claudia was proclaiming, knowing very well that it was. "I was against this fold-jump business all along!"

More than just about anyone else alive, Gloval knew when it was time to play martinet (rarely) and when it was time to play patriarch (the manner in which he had won every important citation there was, some several times over).

"Now, now, now. Settle down; don't panic." His voice was calm and sure. It brought order and discipline back to the bridge by its very measured resonance. "All we have to do is refold to get back to where we started."

That made them all exchange looks and get a grip on themselves. Gloval was four steps ahead of everyone, as usual; everything was all right.

Far aft, in the engineering section, Lang stared up and laughed, then doubled over, slapping his knees—a laugh that seesawed between the hysterical and the Olympian. The techs and scientists and crewpeople around him looked at him dubiously.

It had been going on for a half minute or so, and each time he took a fresh look, Lang laughed again. Tears had begun squeezing out of the corners of his strange eyes for what he perceived as a monumental joke.

Before anybody around him could act, Lang forced himself to stop. Cosmic jokes weren't something you could share with everybody; the gift of humor didn't run that deep in some people. Lang straightened and caught his breath, gathering himself, shaking his head.

"Somebody get me Gloval."

"There's absolutely nothing to worry about," Gloval was saying. "I hope not, Captain," Lisa muttered, back at her duty station.

And that was when the hot line rang.

"*Now* what?" Gloval got it, growling like a bear. "Yes? What? Are you absolutely sure? Stand fast; I'll be right there."

Gloval slammed the handset down. He ignored the questioning faces around him and headed for the hatch. Lisa stood rooted, stunned by the idea that the captain would even *think* about leaving the bridge at a time like this. "Captain? What happened?"

Gloval paused at the hatch. "Doctor Lang informs me that the fold system has vanished into thin air."

The bridge gang let out stifled cries and moans; Sammie and Kim hugged each other, fighting back tears. Everyone there knew just as well as Gloval what that meant.

"We'll never get back," Claudia whispered.

Outside the hatch, Gloval stopped to fire up his evil-smelling old briar. There was no point in doubting Lang's news; the man was obsessed with Robotechnology but otherwise quite rational. That left Henry Gloval to calculate matters of current orbital positions, distance, life support, and engine performance profiles.

He blew out a cloud of smoke, considering the tobacco in the pipe's bowl. *I'd better cut down; what I have is going to have to last me quite a while.*

"Hmm. Well now," he said aloud. "Gonna be a long trip."

Fantastic as it seemed, Lang was right: The fold engines were gone.

Gloval returned to the bridge to try to salvage this seemingly hopeless situation as best he could.

"I don't know what happened exactly," Gloval shouted into a handset. "But our first priority is to get the civilians onboard this ship as soon as we can!"

He slammed down the handset and turned to his bridge gang. "Well?"

"Captain, we can't raise the *Daedalus* or *Prometheus*," Lisa told him.

His gaze went to the forward viewport. At a distance of a few hundred yards, the titanic shapes of the two supercarriers could be seen clearly amid the cloud of debris and wreckage, the drifting automobiles and furniture, and the more ghastly remains of human victims of the tragedy.

"They're aircraft carriers; all atmosphere would have bled away at once, as soon as the fold force field disappeared." No one needed to be told what that meant; all hands lost in the wake of the jump, like every other unprotected human being. "What a catastrophe!"

But other matters were too urgent for him to dwell on the horror of what those last few seconds must have been like in the supercarriers. Chances of survival and a safe return to Earth were slim, but it was up to him to make the most of them.

Like a handful of others throughout history, Henry Gloval was uniquely suited for this particular moment and situation. History was to record it as a singular stroke of good fortune for the human race.

"Commander Hayes, order a squadron of rescue vehicles to maneuver the carriers alongside the SDF-1. We will make fast to them and get crews working round the clock to make them airtight and operational once again." He shunted aside the thought of what a grisly job the clean-up would be.

Lisa looked surprised. "Captain, is it more important that we link up with them than with Armor One or Ten?"

"Yes. I believe their onboard weapons will still be functioning, and there are Veritechs onboard both of them."

"I hope it works, Captain," Lisa said.

"It must be done quickly," Gloval added.

Claudia muttered, "That's for sure."

Gloval went to stand by the viewport. *All those lives lost! How could I have been so stupid?* But he knew, deep down, that he was being unfair to himself. He'd taken the only option open to him. If he'd chosen another course of action, the SDF-1 would now be in the hands of the alien invaders, and all would have been lost.

"We will also deploy boarding tubes to the shelters and begin transferring all occupants to the SDF-1," he gave the order over his shoulder. "Instruct Colonel Fielding and his staff to drop everything else and begin making temporary living arrangements for them at once. Detail EVE groups five and six to start salvage operations; tell them to bring in all usable materials, with special emphasis on foodstuffs and any water ice they may be able to find."

The bridge gang hopped to it, taking notes, as the orders went on. Inventories of all resources; requirement and capability projections from all division chiefs; long-range scans for any signs of enemy presence or activity.

There was particular attention to that last item. *They found us once,* Gloval thought. *Heaven help us if they do again.*

16

"SOS"

signal attempted by various means by Rick Hunter

FAR BELOW THE BRIDGE AND SLIGHTLY AFT, RICK HUNTER strained against a hoisting line. Grease-stained and exhausted, he persisted, even though it seemed hopeless. Getting the wing patched back onto *Mockingbird* hadn't proved impossible—though he wasn't sure how long the patch would hold—but straightening the frame and repairing the fuselage had him near the limits of his endurance.

The racer still hung upside down, cables and lines looped under its wings, nose canards, and tail. He loved the ship, had built it by hand virtually from scratch; the idea of not saving it was hard to accept, and more important, he had reached the conclusion that it was the key to his and Minmei's survival.

They'd ended up in a portion of the ship that was completely deserted, unequipped with intercom or other communications gear or any indication as to how to get out. Rick had quickly decided that if he could just get his plane working, he could somehow get the armor patch to move, get back out into space, and reach a landing bay.

Minmei had less faith in the plan, but she'd been silent. Up to now. But she touched his shoulder as he strained against the line.

"Rick, you'll never get it to fly. Why don't we see if we can get some help by using the radio in your plane? It seems like it would be the easiest thing."

He let go of the line tiredly. "The radio got busted up when we landed. There are pieces of it all over the compartment: it'll never work."

"Oh," Minmei said in a small voice.

Rick reconsidered something that had been in the back of his mind. He held up his Heiko aviator's-model watch, switching modes. "But maybe this'll help us get out of here."

She came closer, watching. "What've you got there?"

"An inertial tracker—a kind of a compass."

Minmei looked puzzled. "But I thought a compass had two arms that go back and forth?" She held her forefingers together to show what she meant.

"Huh? *Oh!*" Rick laughed.

Minmei looked hurt. "Well, the only compass I ever saw was for drawing circles."

They set out at once, Rick showing the way with a flashlight from his emergency equipment. "With *this* kind of compass we'll be able to make our way back to *Mockingbird* if we get lost inside this big old tub and can't find a way out."

They quickly found out that they were in a maze, a limitless world of conduits, cables, hull, passageways, ducts, and bulk heads. Their footsteps echoed eerily.

"I wonder what all these pipes are for?" Minmei said, reaching out to touch one.

"Maybe to cool some kind of energy unit." Rick shrugged.

"Oh." Then, "Yow!" yelped Minmei, snatching her hand back, fingertips scalded.

"You okay?"

"Oh, I'm all right. It was just a little hot."

Rick's eyebrows went up. "Well, now, that was pretty dumb."

"Sorry." But as he started off again, Rick put his foot right in a puddle of oil and nearly landed flat on his face, flailing and slipping.

"Um, what was that again?" Minmei asked sweetly. Rick grunted and strode off again.

But they came at last to a big compartment filled with scrap, discarded machine parts. "I think it's a dead end," Rick judged.

"You mean," Minmei said with a tremor in her voice, "we can't get back?"

"You can't go searching for your friend *now*, Roy!" Claudia shouted at the screen.

"But I know Rick's out there somewhere," the Skull Leader insisted. "I can't just abandon him."

As much as Roy meant to her, Claudia couldn't help wishing she could reach through the screen into his cockpit and throttle him. "Listen, you can't just leave your post any time you feel like it! What if—"

Gloval was clearing his throat meaningfully. "Lieutenant Grant, let me talk to him."

She bit her lower lip but answered, "I'll patch you through on channel eight, sir."

Gloval took up his handset. "Commander Fokker, your request is denied. I'm sorry to hear about your friend, but we have over seventy thousand civilian survivors aboard this ship, and we'll need every hand working full-time to ensure their safety."

Roy's eyes narrowed. "Aye-aye, *Captain*. I guess friendship's a little more important to some of us than it is to others. Sorry to bother you, *sir*."

Roy signed off, and Gloval slammed down the handset. "Insolent pup!"

"Hothead," Claudia said under her breath, while Lisa tried to get her mind back on what she was doing, bleary-eyed from lack of sleep. She hoped she never heard Rick Hunter's name again in her life.

"Where are we? What is this place?" Minmei wanted to know.

"I dunno; it's huge," Rick exclaimed. Not that she couldn't see that for herself; the compartment was the size of a hangar, with piles of crates and equipment. But the astonishing thing about it was the cyclopean hatch at the far end.

"Why don't we climb up and get a closer look at it?" Minmei proposed, heading for a nearby hill of boxes. As he helped her make the ascent, she bubbled, "Maybe there's a doorway at the top that's open and leads to a hallway that leads to the outside! Why, I could be home in time for dinner!"

But while she rushed off in one direction, he spotted markings in another. "Hey, that thing is a giant air lock! Built to scale for those giant aliens!" He suddenly felt mouse-size and very vulnerable out there in the open. "I hope they don't come back... Minmei? Minmei! Where are you?"

He dashed off to find her at a viewport, staring out as if hypnotized, into space. The debris and wreckage were much thicker, drifting past the ship.

"Look at that," she said sadly. "What do you think happened?"

"I don't know where all that stuff came from. It looks like a whole city blew up."

Minmei seemed about to burst into tears. "Could... could all that be from home? From Macross?"

The bridge crew was taking its first break in what seemed like years, sipping coffee, while Gloval was off on a personal inspection of the ship's situation.

Lisa was shaking her head. "If the aliens attack us again, we won't have a chance."

Vanessa said, "We should have standard communications working very shortly! Maybe Earth can tell us what's going on."

Lisa was skeptical. "If we use conventional transmissions, we'll be taking a big chance. The aliens might get a fix on us; we could give away our location."

"Commander Hayes," Sammie piped up from her duty station, "resettlement team five leader wishes to speak to you. He says it's urgent."

Lisa put aside the coffee, knowing she wouldn't be finishing it any time soon.

"Well, this one doesn't go anywhere either." Rick frowned, shining his light on the blank bulkhead before him. "How does your leg feel? Any better?"

Minmei rubbed her ankle. "My leg's a lot better; I just twisted it, I guess. But I'm getting kind of thirsty."

Rick considered that. "I've got some emergency rations in my plane, but I haven't got any water."

But suddenly inspiration struck. "There's water all around us! Just wait right here!"

He sprinted away while Minmei murmured, "I wonder what in the world he's talking about?"

He was back in moments with a length of steel bar he'd spotted. "Ta-dum! I believe madam requested some water? Refreshments coming right up!"

He wedged it into the junction of two pipes and began pulling at it to break them apart. "Careful! Don't hurt yourself!" Minmei warned.

"Harder… than I thought," he said through gritted teeth. Minmei kicked off her shoes. "Let me help you!" Together they threw all their strength into the effort, the pipes creaking. It took everything they had, but at length there was a snapping of metal and the gushing of water.

Luckily, it was tepid rather than superheated. Rick and Minmei fell backward to the deck as it fountained high to fall back on them like a downpour. "We got it! It's a geyser!" Rick shouted jubilantly. Minmei laughed, and he joined in.

After a few moments of it she got up, sopping wet, and went to catch the streaming water in her hands. "Wow, this is wonderful! Well, I think I'll take a shower."

"Huh?" was all Rick could think of to say.

"Well, I might as well take advantage of this while it lasts." She began unfastening the back of her dress, then stopped to glance at Rick, whose mouth was a big O. "Ahh, Rick …"

"Oh! Um. I, uh, guess I better go scout around a little, hmm?" She grinned, nodding. "And don't peek. Would you push that over here so I can use it as a shower curtain?" He lugged a big hunk of sheet metal into place across the open passageway hatch as he retreated.

"Thank you!" she called over the splashing water. He noticed a small hole in the sheet metal and bent to inspect it, just checking of course, putting his eye to it.

Minmei shrieked. Rick was back on the other side of the partition in a split second, visions of menacing alien giants daunting him. "Minmei, what's wrong? I'm coming—"

He slid to a halt. She was gazing at him with a mischievous glint in her eyes, long dark hair plastered flat against her by the falling water, arms folded, still wearing her dress. "I *thought* I saw something, there by the shower curtain."

"Your imagination, maybe?" he said weakly. "Su-uure." She nodded sarcastically.

"Yeah." He coughed. "Well. Excuse me, I—" He turned and hurried off.

Minmei lost track of time, singing and humming, luxuriating in the feel and taste of the water. Then she heard a sound, too faint to identify.

She, too, thought of alien giants. "Rick? If that's you, stop playing tricks!" She felt a wave of panic. "Rick, you answer me right now."

A small roll of cloth was tossed through the gap in the makeshift partition. "Brought you some fresh clothes," he called. "It's an extra work shirt I had in the *Mockingbird*."

After Rick grabbed a quick shower, they started back for the plane, guided by his inertial tracker and the markings he'd made at various passageway junctions in the course of their explorations.

Rick tried not to be too obvious about ogling Minmei. The shirt was baggy on her but barely covered the tops of her thighs. Her lovely, coltish legs seemed to go on forever.

She was in high spirits—it seemed to be her natural state. "That was just what I needed! I feel a whole lot better now. And thanks for the shirt, Rick."

"You're welcome—"

"Even if it *is* a bit big." She flopped the empty cuffs around to demonstrate, giggling.

Minmei capered over to a highly polished metal panel, which reflected her image like a dark mirror. She made a comical face, sticking her tongue out and crossing her eyes, waggling the overlong sleeves. "'The Creature with No Hands!' *Nyyah!*" She laughed.

They'd come back to the compartment where the *Mockingbird* hung suspended. Rick went over and sat beneath it, on a pallet improvised from shipping crate padding he'd scavenged. He picked up a couple of flat cans.

"I dug out my emergency rations. Here: This one's for you." He tossed it to her.

"Oh! Thank you!" She looked delighted, as she so often did. Minmei found more delight in life than anyone Rick had ever met.

She watched him detach the fork that came with the can, trigger the lid release, and peel it back. "Let's see if this stuff's any good." He dug into the brownish concentrate paste, making approving sounds.

Minmei didn't follow suit, suddenly looking troubled. "Shouldn't we be conserving these in case we have to make it last?"

"I'm not worried." He shoveled in some more. "We'll be out of here soon."

"Yeah, but what if we're not?"

He tried to sound confident. "I used to be a Junior Nature Scout; I'll get us out of here."

She looked at him archly. "Well, I'll bet you didn't get any merit badges for pathfinding, did you?"

"Now, stop worrying," he told her, around a mouthful of food. He swallowed. "I promise you I'll find a way out of here." He suddenly lowered his fork, looking down despondently at the deck. "But that *was* one badge I didn't get," he confessed.

She made him jump by giggling into his ear. "I *knew* it!"

"Hey, what's so funny?"

She was laughing into her hands, unconcerned with their plight for the moment, making him smile involuntarily.

"I was sick the day they gave the test! At least *I* know what a compass looks like!"

Minmei laughed harder and harder. Rick couldn't resist and joined in.

Later they sat on the padding, backs resting against a crate, under *Mockingbird*. "I'm real worried about my family," she confessed.

"Don't be. I'm sure they're safe in the shelters," he insisted, making it sound as positive as he could.

She was blinking sleepily. "Oh, I hope so. Y'know, there was a shelter right next door to our house."

"Well, there you go; they're all fine."

She yawned against the sleeve-covered back of her hand. "I suppose." Her head settled against his shoulder.

Rick was so surprised that he didn't move or speak for some time. "Um. Are you going to sleep?" She was breathing evenly, eyes closed. She looked more enchanting than ever.

"Wake up. You can't go to sleep like this; you'll get a stiff neck."

He reached around her shoulders from either side, about to ease her down into a more comfortable position. His elbow brushed against something alive that was poised behind him on the crate.

With a shrill chitter, a fat gray mouse bounded across Minmei's shoulder, scampered along her arm, and ran down the length of her bare leg, springing away into the dimness. Minmei awoke with a scream, to find Rick's hands on her shoulders. "Ah. Um."

She gave him an appraising look. "Hmm. Maybe I'd better move. *You* stay here, and *I'll* sleep over there." She rose lithely and went to another pile of padding a few yards away.

"Hey, it was a mouse," Rick protested.

"Mm-hmm." Minmei ignored him. She was young and very, very attractive; she'd learned that she had to be careful. She kneeled to pull aside a fold of the padding and rearrange it more to her liking. As she did, a fat, furry gray form bounded out of hiding and went racing off into the darkness.

"There's a mouse!" Minmei covered the distance back to Rick in a single hysterical leap.

He sniffed. "You don't say. I seem to recall mentioning some thing about that, but you didn't believe me."

She hung her head, then looked at him again. "I'm really sorry, Rick. From now on, I promise I'll believe you."

He struck a noble pose. "In that case, fair lady, I shall defend you from these fearsome creatures!"

"Oh, thank you." Minmei stifled another yawn.

"I think we'll be all right for tonight," he added, looking around the compartment as she rested her head on his shoulder once more. Her eyelids were fluttering tiredly. "They're more scared of us than we are of them."

What's more important, he didn't say out loud, so as not to discourage her hopes of escape or rescue, *if they can survive here, we can.* He tried to fight down the feeling that their situation wasn't very promising.

"So if you want to sleep—" he started to say, then realized she was dozing, snuggled against him.

"I'll be darned. Wish I could fall asleep like that." He made himself comfortable as best he could, leaning back against the crate, concentrating. He considered every option and plan he could think of, certain of only one thing.

He wouldn't let Minmei down.

17

If Breetai and company were confused by human behavior as applied to war, one cannot help but wonder, in light of subsequent events and Zentraedi responses, what they would have thought if they could have looked into the remotest corner of SDF-1 and observed the behavior of two castaways.

Zeitgeist, *Alien Psychology*

RICK WAS BROUGHT OUT OF HIS MUSINGS BY A SCRAPE OF metal—a screech, really—that set his teeth on edge and had him alert for danger.

He'd grown used to the endless dripping of water condensed on or leaking from pipes, not even registering it anymore, and could identify most of the ship's sounds—giant circulation systems and the vibrations of far-off machinery. But this one was something new.

It was Minmei. "Let's see: Yesterday was Thursday. Now Friday…" She held a triangular piece of scrap metal in her hand, one edge sharpened against the deck, finishing the line she was gouging in *Mockingbird*'s upside-down fuselage, under the starboard nose canard.

There were two of them, irregular verticals cut deep into the racer's vulnerable skin. She'd picked a spot where there was room for quite a few marks, he saw.

"Hey! What're you doing?"

She turned to him with a smile, happy to be doing something that yielded tangible results, however slight. "I'm keeping a record of how many days we've been stranded here." She offered him the improvised cutter. "Would you like to help?"

It had obviously never occurred to her that his Heiko had a day/ date function. Rick kept the fact to himself; her personal calendar seemed to lift her morale. "No thanks. You're doing fine. I'm gonna get back to work."

"See ya." Minmei grinned and watched him walk off, slinging his clipboard around his neck for another exploration-survey mission.

That was a brand-new paint job! He blew his breath out. It didn't matter anyway; *Mockingbird* would never fly again. *Some help she is! Well, I don't suppose too much else can go wrong today.*

Which was just when he clunked his forehead against a low-hanging pipe. Recoiling back in pain, he hit another with the back of his skull. Hissing in anger and pent-up frustration, he berated himself for not wearing the Veritech helmet as a hardhat.

But he refused to turn back. Marking off the different routes and possible escape paths available to them had seemed easy at first, until he'd come to realize what a tremendously complicated and far-reaching maze they were trapped in. He'd come to so many dead ends that he constantly saw them in his dreams.

Banging on pipes and bulkheads with the metal bar had produced no results, and even sending shorts and longs over a severed power cable was a failure. Depression was hard to fight off, and he couldn't bear the thought of what would happen if he didn't come up with a solution soon.

There was one long shot he hadn't mentioned to Minmei yet, not so much because it was a life-or-death risk for him but rather because, if he tried and failed, she would be alone. Still, his alter natives were fewer and fewer with every passing hour.

When he finally dragged himself back to the plane after more fruitless searching, he was pleasantly surprised to see that he hadn't been the only one hard at work.

"Well, Rick, how do you like our new home?" Minmei asked him, eyes shining.

Rick broke into a smile for the first time he could recall. "It's great!" was all he could say.

Minmei had somehow figured out how to get the parachute out

of the back of the pilot's seat—maybe after reading the ejection instruction plate, it occurred to him. It couldn't have been easy with *Mockingbird* hung upside down eight or nine feet off the deck.

More than that, she'd draped it over the ship to make a roomy red and white striped tent. And best of all, she'd located the survival gear, set up the tiny camp stove, and put together a meal whose smell had his mouth watering until his jaws hurt.

The compartment lights were going dim according to SDF-1's twenty-four-hour day/night schedule. The two moved in under the tent, Rick sitting tailor-fashion while Minmei knelt by the stove, stirring with a plastic spoon.

"By making stew we can make our supplies last longer," she explained. Rick repented of his earlier thought—that she couldn't pull her own weight.

"That's right; I forgot," he said, determined to make it up to her. "You're in the restaurant business."

She was sprinkling bits of what seemed to be seasoning into the stew, only he couldn't remember spices being listed on the rations contents listings. Whatever she'd done, she'd come up with something that smelled heavenly.

"No, the White Dragon was my Aunt Lena's restaurant," Minmei responded, shrugging. She thought a moment, then added, "Actually, I want to be an entertainer."

Rick cocked his head in surprise. "You're planning on being an actress?"

"Well, I studied acting, singing, and dancing." She'd been dishing up his portion. "Here."

"Thanks." He was silent for a while, taken by the image of Minmei dancing. Then, "That doesn't exactly prepare you for something like this, huh." Ruefully, he looked down at his clipboard and the growing map of dead ends.

Five days went by.

"Can you believe they're rebuilding the city *inside* the ship?" someone was saying as Lisa Hayes entered the officers' wardroom. "It's amazing."

She saw by his insignia that he was a Veritech pilot off the *Daedalus*, one of the few who'd been in the air during the spacefold jump and had thus been spared. He and his kind were like specters these days, watching whole new groups of pilots being crash-trained to fly the fighters that the carriers' dead could no longer man.

His comment about the refugees and their rebuilding was grudging. Open area of any kind in a naval or space vessel was always held dear, and now—

"You can leave the trays, steward," Claudia was saying at the table where she waited for Lisa. "Thank you very much. It smells wonderful."

"Yes, ma'am." The steward served awkwardly, a new recruit; everybody with military training had been tapped for higher-priority work these days, and it was most often serve yourself. But things were tough all over, and complaints were very few. This particular steward, Claudia had found out, was to be posted to a gunnery class next shift.

"So he expects me to volunteer and go out and get this castaway shelter module all alone, and I sez, 'Sir, I'm brave but I ain't crazy!'" the VT pilot continued.

"So you didn't volunteer," his tablemate said. "But did you go?"

The first pilot shrugged unhappily and made a zipping motion with his hand, thumb and pinkie spread to indicate a Veritech's wings. They both laughed tiredly.

Some things never change, Lisa thought. Contrary to what most civilians thought, real combat veterans seldom bragged among themselves of their heroism; it was a mark of high prestige to go on about how scared you were, how fouled up things were, how hairy the situation had gotten, how dumb the brass were. Because among them, everyone *knew;* boasts were for outsiders.

"Oh, *there* you are," Lisa said, collapsing into a chair across from Claudia.

Claudia lowered her coffee cup. "What's the latest on the refugees?"

Lisa pursed her lips, weighing the answer. "We finally have them divided by city blocks and the construction's going on twenty-four hours a day."

Claudia's dark eyes were unfocused with fatigue and with the strangeness of what had happened and what was going on.

She could only manage an understatement. "Really? That's incredible."

Gloval had known at once what must be done. His relentless effort to get the Macross survivors and as much salvageable and recyclable material aboard as was possible had yielded amazing results. It was the only way the humans could make the long voyage home.

Miles-square purse-seine nets had been devised overnight by the engineers to collect what could be collected of the wreckage. There'd been too many acts of individual valor to count or keep track of. Not the least of them was the work of the disposal teams, whose grim job was to remove the dead from the supercarriers and other areas where they were encountered.

Hold after hold in SDF-1 that had been reserved for future missions and future purposes that would never come to be were now filled with wreckage, and there were material stores that could be used as well. Robotech fabrication machines aboard the SDF-1 were the most advanced devices of their kind ever developed—the equivalent of an industrial city packed into a few compartments, minifactories that could replicate a staggering assortment of manufactured goods and materials.

As for blueprints and plans, they would be child's play for the SDF-1's computers, since all records of the city's construction, from the first permanent building constructed ten years earlier to the last, were in the ship's data banks.

More importantly, Gloval understood before anyone else aboard just what the long trip to Earth would entail. The civilians couldn't be expected to simply sit in packed emergency billets and twiddle their thumbs; that invited complete social breakdown, and disaster for the SDF-1.

The secret was well kept in subsequent mission reports and in announcements to the refugees, but it was Gloval's liaison officers who planted the seed of the idea: *Why not rebuild Macross City?*

The gouges of Minmei's calendar had multiplied: four verticals with a crosshatch now, and two more besides.

Now Rick dreaded returning to the small light cast by the

miniature camp stove, dreaded having Minmei pretend she wasn't disappointed by another day of bad news.

She'd begun explorations too, to double their chances, over his strenuous objection at first—but with his unspoken acceptance as things became more and more desperate.

Now he sank wearily onto his pallet, while she stirred the thin soup that was the very last stretching of their rations. He hadn't been able to find out how the mice were subsisting, but it wouldn't be very long before he and Minmei would be forced to start trying to catch them. He doubted that even she could make mouse stew taste very good.

He sat, trying to figure out how to phrase his difficult decision.

"No luck, huh?" Minmei said. "Why don't you rest?"

"Minmei," he began, head lowered on his knees, "I don't know what else to do. This ship is like a big prison maze."

"Yeah," she said without looking up, "a big prison floating somewhere in space."

It was an opening he hadn't expected, a chance to make his plan look hopeful, to make her optimistic. "That's it, of course! We're in space!" He tried to sound as though he'd just realized the implications of that.

She looked startled. "What about it?"

"That's our way out of here! Out that air lock we found and into another, somewhere farther above!"

She didn't understand. "We can't do that; we don't have any spacesuits."

He was already on his feet, the Veritech helmet taken down from its resting place. "My flight helmet will protect me. I'll float out, get help, and come back down here for you. It's simple! It'll work!"

He flipped up his flightsuit collar and ran his fingers along the automatic closure to show her how it formed a pressure seal and a collar ring that could be fitted to the helmet's.

She looked terribly confused. "Yes, but—"

"Now, I'm going to need your help," Rick said as he led the way with the flashlight. "So I'll show you how to use the air lock controls, okay?"

She trailed behind unwillingly, hands clasped behind her, silently accepting his help as they began ascending the mountain of packing crates and boxes again.

They reached the Zentraedi-scaled utility shelf near the power panel; it was the width of a country lane. The control dials were the size of wagon wheels, the buttons as big as her bedroom window. "You sure you understand everything?" he checked again.

"Mm-hmmm." Then she said in a rush, "Without oxygen tanks, though, Rick? *How're you going to breathe?*"

"There's air in the helmet and some in the suit. I don't need much time." But he hurried along before she could pinpoint the problem that he'd already spotted: They'd explored the ship in every direction and found no nearby air locks. From this one, it would strain his scant supply of air to the very limits to reach another, even if one lay just beyond their prison.

He turned and started off before she could say anything more. "Wait!" cried Minmei, running after him. "I'm having second thoughts about all this! Rick?"

She ran after him, back around the turn in the shelf. "Where're we going?"

"I want to show you: You can stand by this big viewport here so we can communicate if we have to." The viewport was bigger than a movie screen.

She gasped and threw both hands up to her mouth, feet going pigeon-toed, eyes enormous.

He prepared his most matter-of-fact voice. "Minmei, what is it now? You've gotta stop this constant worrying—huh?"

She wasn't looking at him. She was gaping over his shoulder at the viewport. He whirled. "Look… at… that!"

"I've never seen anything like it!" Minmei breathed. "What kind is it?"

At first he thought it was some kind of new prototype spacecraft, silvery and sleek, and he was already trying to figure a way to signal it. Then he was afraid it might be an alien ship, although it didn't look anything like a pod. But a second later he calmed down and saw what it really was, which was only slightly more fantastic than possibilities one and two.

"Offhand, I'd say it's a tuna," Rick ventured. "I didn't know they grew that big."

This one was as long as *Mockingbird* and appeared to be intact and whole. Why the forces of explosive decompression and vacuum hadn't turned it into something more like a radar-waved football, he couldn't imagine; he was unacquainted as yet with the very singular peculiarities of a Protoculture-generated force field.

It floated along like a schooner, as if it was keeping pace with them. "That sure is a big tuna fish," Minmei observed, licking her lips.

"*Real* big," Rick conceded. He turned to her, and they both yelled "*Yay-yyy!*" at the same instant, pressing their noses and palms up against the viewport. "I wonder if there's a way I could snag it out there," he said longingly.

They turned to each other, chorusing, "Tuna fish!"

Rick made sure the ring seal was as tight as he could make it. Seals at his wrists and ankles were reinforced with all the tape he'd been able to find and some turns of twine. The collar closure was wound tight with layer upon layer of cloth strips.

He realized he couldn't hear anything and opened the faceplate again. Minmei was yelling down to him, "Be careful out there! Wave when you're ready!"

He gave her the wave and closed the faceplate again, carrying his looped line back into the oversize air lock. Minmei said, "Here we go!" to herself and strained against a wagon wheel dial. Rick did his best to keep calm as the inner hatch came down with a finality that made the deck jump and the air bled away. Next to him were a pair of heavy tanks of some kind; he clutched them close. He felt the ship's artificial gravity easing off him.

When the air was gone and the outer hatch was open, he took careful bearing and pushed himself off, trailing the long rope behind. His suit was already becoming a steam-bath.

The tuna was obliging in that it didn't move much, but his aim was off. He threw one of the tanks from him in one direction, Newton's third law driving him off in the other.

There'd be no time for fumbling; if he missed, he'd have to go back in and refill his suit with air, get more ballast, and try again. Exhausted and depleted, he didn't know if he had the strength for that and didn't want to find out. He tucked the second tank into the looser cloth windings.

He pinwheeled, unused to zero gravity, forcing down the appalling thought of how he'd die if he lost control of his stomach now and gave in to zero-g nausea.

Then he was drifting toward a lifeless eye the diameter of a dinner platter. He spread his arms and bulldogged the tuna. The big fish spun slowly as Rick clung to the left side of its head. He belayed a loop around a pectoral fin as insurance.

He tried heaving the second tank to get the tuna moving toward the lock, but without much luck; the thing was weightless, but its mass hadn't changed, and its mass seemed immovable.

The line he'd played out behind him reached its end, stretching just a bit, an extensive composite made for deep-space work, stronger than steel. Rick was jolted, realizing that if he hadn't looped the fin, he'd have been snapped loose from the fish like a paddleball.

The line's elasticity absorbed the fish's movement and contracted, starting the tuna moving back for the lock. Rick felt his air getting short and fought the urge to use the fish as a launching platform—to kick off for the air lock and hope he could recover it later. He and Minmei could survive for a while longer without food, but not forever, and the fish would probably be the difference between life and death for them both.

He held on, straining at the line to speed things up. The air lock seemed a long way away, and his air very, very thin, making him groggy, while the fish moved as slowly as a glacier.

He shook his head to clear it, concentrating. Everything was blurry. Wasn't there some book about an old fisherman who hung on somehow? Rick was pretty sure his father had made him read it, but he couldn't recall it.

The hatch was before him. Had he been napping? He didn't have time to get out of the way, and the tuna trapped him against the deck, plowing him along. He felt some tiny seam give, and the air pressure in his suit began dropping.

He shoved hysterically, fighting his way out against the impossible mass, kicking off and fetching up against the miles-high inner hatch. He slammed it with his fists, breath and consciousness slipping away—forever, he knew, if he didn't get air soon.

The hiss got louder, and he located the stressed spot just as it began to go, holding it together with his hand, hooking one foot on some kind of cross member, hammering and hammering with his free fist. He didn't notice the jarring of the outer hatch.

Nor did he notice the return of gravity until it flipped him off the inner hatch. He sagged against the armored door, now only able to thump it feebly, the world going red in his vision, then increasingly dark.

18

That suppressed longing of the Flower of Life, which desire generates the incalculable power of Protoculture, has its human equivalent. The interlude of the castaways is rich in insights as to those Greater Forces, so much more powerful than mere guns or missiles, that manifested themselves in the Robotech War.

Jan Morris, *Solar Seeds, Galactic Guardians*

RICK ALMOST FELL TO THE DECK ON HIS FACE. THE INNER HATCH had risen without his noticing it, and there was air all around him. Unfortunately, his helmet was still sealed.

Minmei raced for him, screaming something he couldn't hear. He reeled and staggered. At last, between them, they got the helmet off; he devoured air, his chest straining against the flight suit, sobbing on the exhale, but alive.

Minmei got a shoulder under his arm, steadying him as he sank to all fours. "I was so worried! I thought—" She didn't finish it.

"At least… I got the tuna back in," he labored. Catching his breath a bit, he straightened up and looked back over his shoulder into the lock, at his catch.

The fish had been thrust back when he kicked off from it and had been completely severed by the outer hatch; only the glassy-eyed head remained in the lock, and everything behind the gills was out drifting once more on some new vector.

"Or some of it, anyway," he amended. He wondered whether Minmei's aunt had taught her any recipes appropriate to the occasion.

"Hu-uuuh!" Rick observed, and sank to the cold deck.

...

Ushio jiru, a great delicacy, was more suited to the preparation of the porgy, exploiting the flavor and use of piscine parts Westerners usually discarded. The version Aunt Lena had taught Minmei, however, did *not* start "Take one fish head one and one-half yards long."

That didn't make Rick's mouth water any less as the hapless fish sat staring at them out of a big vat; *Mockingbird*'s jet fuel flamed through jury-rigged burners, and a delicious smell wafted out through the compartment.

"Why are you sitting there with such a sad look on your face?" Minmei prodded Rick. "You caught a fish in outer space! You were wonderful out there!"

Glumly, he sat with face cupped in hands. He'd underestimated her and had made a pact with himself to be honest with her from now on. "Thanks, but that little fishing trip ruined our chances of going out along the ship's hull." He showed her the rent that had appeared in his suit in the last instants before she had opened the inner hatch and saved him.

"We have no way to fix it. I don't know *what* we're gonna do." He hugged his knees, forehead sinking down against them.

"Maybe we could cut a hole in the roof and then climb right up," she proposed—anything to keep him from losing hope.

His head came up again. "I've already thought about that. I took some tools and climbed up to the ceiling yesterday. But it's like armor; I couldn't even make a dent in it."

Minmei gave the mountainous fish head a poke with her long sheet-metal fork. "What about an explosion?"

"What would we explode? That last of our fuel will run the camp stove a while longer, but it wouldn't even warm up this armor all around us."

Minmei prodded the fish head a little, trying to set it so it wouldn't topple. They'd lashed together some pitchforklike cooking tools, but those were pretty clumsy. They couldn't afford to spill the *ushio jiru* or waste any of the fish head; they might not have any other source of food for a long time.

She looked at the flame beneath the vat and wondered what would happen to them when the food, the fuel—perhaps even the air and water—finally gave out.

Minmei's tally of the days had grown: four verticals crosshatched with a fifth, and another group of five, and two more besides, for a total of twelve. Neither of them mentioned the count anymore.

They would leave the stove on, a tiny orange-yellow flame, for just a little while after the compartment lights went out each night. It was unwise from the standpoint of conservation, of course, but it helped their morale a lot, talking for a while in the peaceful quiet of their tent before going to sleep. Rick found himself looking forward to those moments all day as he dragged himself around the maze, his hopes dashed over and over by dead ends.

But he was already thinking about the moment when the stove would flicker out for the last time. There was always the wood from the many packing crates, of course, but Rick wasn't sure what danger an open fire might constitute to the air supply. He was already mapping steam and hot water lines, looking for the best and nearest place to do their cooking, and trying to interpret the utility markings in order to improvise a little light during the night cycles and recharge his flashlight once *Mockingbird*'s batteries were completely dead.

"And so I practiced as hard as I could—I didn't do much of anything else, I guess," he told Minmei. He was lying with his head pillowed on his arms, staring up at *Mockingbird*. Minmei lay across from him on her pallet, resting on one elbow. The soft light made her skin glow and her eyes liquid and deep.

"My dad grumbled a bit," he went on, "but he taught me everything he knew, and I came back to win that competition the next year. And I won it eight times in a row, even though I was only flying an old junker plane."

He stopped, wondering if it sounded like he was bragging. Then he dismissed the thought; Minmei knew him better than that. And he felt like he'd known her all his life—no, like he'd known her *always*.

She sighed, laying her head on her hands, watching him. "Rick?"

she said softly. "Do you think I'll ever get to fly with you again?"

He put all the conviction he could into his answer, trying to sound matter-of-fact. "Why, sure! Once we get rescued, I'll take you up whenever you want. That is, if you'll sing for me now and then."

She lay back, gazing up at the play of firelight on the inverted cockpit canopy. Their isolation had become their world, filling dreams as well as days.

Sometimes I dream of falling in love. She'd never dared mention it to him.

Minmei began singing, a song she'd written and never shared with anybody before. It took him a second to realize that he didn't recognize it.

"To be in love
My hero he must take me where no other can
Where silver suns have golden moons,
Each year has thirteen Junes,
That's what must be for me
To be
In love."

"You've got a beautiful voice." He'd said it before; though he tried to think of some flowery new way to tell her, it always came out the same way.

She looked over at him again; he couldn't tell if she was blushing or not. "Thank you, Rick." She averted her eyes for a second, then looked to him again. "If I could do one thing with my life, it would be to sing. I couldn't live without singing."

"It's always been planes for me," he answered, even though she already knew that. "All I ever wanted to do was fly." Then he felt awkward for repeating what he must have told her a hundred times already.

But Minmei sat up, embracing her knees, nodding gravely. "I know how you feel, Rick. Sometimes you can't be happy unless you do what you dream about."

"So you're sure that being an entertainer is what you want from life?"

"Yes, I guess." She added in a rush, "But what I really want is to be a bride."

He was suddenly alert and wary. "Ah. You mean, married?"

She nodded, the long hair shimmering in the stove's light. "In my family, there's so much love—well, I've told you that already, haven't I? You'll simply have to meet them! They're wonderful and—that's the kind of joy I want in my life."

"I guess you'll probably make somebody a terrific wife," he said noncommittally.

She was suddenly sad again. "Thanks, but now I'll never have the chance."

"Don't you even *think* that, Minmei! I *know* we're gonna get out of here somehow!"

"It's been twelve days. And I'm sure they must have given up searching for us by now." Her voice had shrunk to a whisper. "We'll never get out of here."

He didn't know what to say. Before he could decide, there were squeaks and chitters and a faint rattling.

"It's those mice again! I'll get them this time!" Relieved at a chance to work off his frustration, he grabbed an empty can and sprang to the opening of the tent.

He hurled the can, and it clunked and bounced in the darkness, scattering the mice.

She was standing next to him. "We're never going to make it out of here alive. We're going to be here forever."

Her hands were clasped, and she was gazing sadly into the darkness. She suddenly sounded bitter. "We've been here too long. They've all forgotten about us by now."

"Minmei, I don't want to hear that kind of talk!"

"It's true! We've just got to face it." She stood with her back to him, looking out into a void darker than deep space. "We'll live our entire lives right here in this ship. I'll never know what it's like to be a bride and start a whole new life."

She was weeping, unable to go on, her shoulders shaking. "Minmei," he said gently, "you will. I'll show you."

She sniffed. "How can you do that?"

"Um, we can have a ceremony right here. We can pretend."

She turned and came back to him, cheeks wet. "Oh, Rick, do you mean it?" He nodded slowly; Minmei wiped away her tears. "Then let me borrow your scarf?"

She unknotted it and drew it from around his neck, a long, white flier's scarf of fine silk, spreading it and carefully arranging it as a bridal veil.

"Minmei, you look beautiful. I—I guess I should be the groom, huh?" he said haltingly, then rolled his eyes at his own stupidity.

Minmei said nothing, holding her hand out. He took it. "Is that what we do next?"

She started to nod, then broke from her role, close to tears again. "Oh, Rick, why doesn't someone come and *find* us? *I want to go home!*"

"But you will, I promise you."

She squeezed his hand hard. "I'm just so scared." It sounded so small and forlorn in the huge, empty compartment.

"I know; so am I." He took her shoulders in his hands. "Come on, I'm telling you: We're gonna get out of here! There's got to be a way! We can't give up! I've never been a quitter, and you shouldn't be either!"

She pulled back out of his reach. "Stop it. That's all just silly talk! You know what's going to happen! We're going to die here!" She turned away, sobbing.

Rick stared at her, not knowing what to say. She was not quite sixteen, very much in love with life. "Minmei, it's not silly talk. I really believe it. You mustn't give up. I'm doing my best." He gestured vaguely. "I'm sorry."

She turned back to him. "No, Rick; I'm the one who should apologize. It's just that—" She threw herself into his arms. "I'm being so stupid—"

He held her close. "That's not true."

She turned her face up to his. "Kiss me, Rick."

"If you're sure…"

She closed her eyes, and they kissed.

It seemed to them that their lips had barely touched when there was a concussion that shook the deck, shook that whole part of the ship, like the crack of doomsday, nearly sending them sprawling.

The *Mockingbird* and their camp disappeared under tons of metal alloy. They barely kept their feet, holding each other in their arms.

Suddenly there was something—*the Leaning Tower of Robotech!* Rick thought wildly—canted to one side in its lodging place, having penetrated the deck above, the one totally immune to Rick's tools. Light shone down into the compartment.

Not just light; it looks like SUNLIGHT! Minmei thought, though she didn't understand how that could possibly be. Wasn't it night all over the ship?

Long shafts of artificial light—flashlights—probed down into the dust and smoke of the sealed-off compartment. There were voices.

"What was that? An enemy missile?"

"Looked to me like a bomb!" Human figures were gathering around the jagged entrance hole of the metal juggernaut that had struck daylight into Rick and Minmei's prison.

"Naw," somebody drawled. "New converter subunit from the ceiling level, according to Control. Mounting gave way."

The beams played this way and that while the castaways watched, too astounded to speak. Then one light found them, and another, and in a second four or five converged on them.

"Hey! There's somebody down there!"

"It looks like a coupla kids!"

They held each other close, not sure what might have happened to the rest of the universe in twelve long days and nights. The harsh flashlight beams sent shadows away from them in different directions.

Then a familiar voice said, "Why, that looks like Minmei down there!" It came from a squat, broad figure gazing down at the very edge of the abyss.

Minmei's grip on Rick tightened. "It's the mayor! Rick, Rick, we're saved!" She hugged him but then let go, moving into the center spotlight to wave.

Rick dropped his arms to his sides and wondered why he wasn't as ecstatic as he thought he'd be.

It took only a few minutes to get a crane rigged with a bucket to lift them out; there was construction equipment all over that part of

SDF-1. They were lifted up into more intense light than they'd seen in nearly two weeks. But that was hardly noticeable, insignificant against the shock of the new world in which they found themselves.

"Are we dreaming or something?" Minmei clung to the bucket's rail. "What in the world is going on here?"

They were looking around them at broad streets and tall buildings, signs, lamp posts, marquees, and throngs of people. They were looking at Macross City, except that far overhead was the expanse of a spacecraft's metal "ceiling." A far-reaching lighting system had already been set up to give Earth-normal illumination. The crowds were pointing at them and gabbling and yelling.

"I can't believe it," he muttered. "The whole city's here." The bucket set them down to one side of the hole in the deck.

Minmei was about to climb out when she gasped and pointed. "Oh, Rick, *look!*"

He remembered the corner well; he'd done enough crashing around on it in a Battloid he couldn't steer. Except these buildings all looked new, bright with fresh paint.

"The White Dragon and Aunt Lena's house are right here!" She was already clambering out of the bucket.

There's no place like home, Rick thought sourly, not remembering whether or not he'd clicked the heels of his ruby slippers.

He felt a little woozy, and there were a lot of confusing images, one on top of another, after that. A tiny dynamo came dodging out of the crowd. Jason threw himself into Minmei's arms, and the cousins hugged each other and cried.

Mayor Tommy Luan was slapping Rick on the back and saying things like "As you can see, m'boy, the entire city's been rebuilt! Now, we've got to get you rested up and hear what happened to you; you've been gone for almost two weeks!"

Minmei's Uncle Max had more to add, pumping Rick's hand with the powerful grip of a lifelong worker. "I appreciate the protection you provided our baby girl!"

"Uh, don't mention it," Rick said vaguely. He suddenly wanted very much to sit down. Then he caught other nearby voices.

People were gathered around Minmei, Macross City people

who knew her and regarded her as part of their extended family, not a castaway and a stranger—not as they would regard Rick.

"Oh, it was so frightening down there," she was telling her audience, wide-eyed. "You have no idea!"

"Oh, I can imagine," a woman said, while people nodded and murmured in agreement.

A godlike voice echoed through the strange, metal-boundaried world of the new Macross City, startling Rick. "Attention! Message from the bridge!"

He thought it was a voice he'd heard before somewhere, but he was too disoriented to place it. "The disturbance in Sector Seven-X was caused by a construction accident. There were no injuries. The damage will be cleared up very shortly. All divisions revert to normal status."

Where'd I hear that voice before? he wondered.

Minmei was regaling people now; she had the crowd in the palm of her hand. "Oh! And the *mice!*"

The onlookers laughed in anticipation, though they had no idea what the mice story was all about. Rick waited for her to catch his eye and draw him into the center of attention, but she was focused on her performance now.

A bad dream, he told himself, not sure if he meant the long wait below or coming back to a too-bright, too-loud, too-strange world.

"Well, m'boy, you must be one happy fella right now, by golly, huh?" Tommy Luan said, and slapped him on the back again in a man-to-man fashion. The mayor was built like a barrel weighted with cannonballs; the slap sent Rick teetering over to the deck.

It felt nice and comfortable there. He didn't have the strength to get up anyway and didn't think anybody would miss him if he just napped for a little while.

19

Heroism? Perseverance? When it comes to the story of Macross City and its citizens, we're talking about a whole lot of new superlatives for those concepts.

Mayor Tommy Luan, *The High Office*

IT FEELS SO MUCH LIKE HOME, MINMEI THOUGHT, WIPING DOWN the table, *even though it's not.*

There were little differences that let her know she wasn't really in the original White Dragon, but she could ignore them—ignore them happily—after her imprisonment in the deserted portion of SDF-1.

So, waiting for her uncle and aunt to return, she cleaned the place up the way she'd done back in Macross City. The furniture felt a little strange, lighter and far stronger than the wooden stuff she was used to, fabricated by Robotech equipment out of reprocessed wreckage; but it looked close enough to the original tables and chairs to make her feel like she was home again. She worked happily, humming, not realizing that the tune was the "Wedding March."

The front doors swept apart, just like the ones back on Macross Island, and her uncle and aunt came in. "We wasted half the day standing on line for this," Uncle Max was grousing, shaking a food ration package no bigger than a good-size book.

She thought again what a strange pair they made, her uncle broad and substantial as a boulder, barely coming shoulder high to his willowy, serene wife. And yet when Minmei thought about what it meant to be completely in love, she often thought about these two.

"We're lucky to have anything," Lena reminded him gently.

The SDF-1 had been equipped and supplied for a variety of missions, but not for feeding tens of thousands of refugees. Aeroponic and hydroponic farms and protein-growth vats were already in operation, but for the time being the dimensional fortress's stores, and the supplies salvaged from the shelters, were the extent of the food supply. Those were quite considerable, rumor had it, but rumor also had it that SDF-1 faced a very long trip back to Earth, and Captain Gloval was being careful.

"Hi, you two!" Minmei said brightly. "Welcome home! How'd it go?"

Aunt Lena tried to put on a cheerful expression. "About as well as could be expected, I guess."

"I'm feeling much better now," Minmei said, gesturing around to show them the progress she'd made toward putting the place in order. Uncle Max looked around despondently; it was so much like the White Dragon that was gone forever.

"I'm glad to hear that," Aunt Lena said. "And how's Rick? Is he up yet?"

When the medics released him, Aunt Lena and Uncle Max had insisted that Rick stay in a spare bedroom in the rebuilt restaurant until he was fully recovered. "I suppose he's still in bed," Minmei said. "I haven't heard him moving around up there."

"I'm not surprised." Lena smiled. "After watching over you for two weeks, he probably deserves a rest."

Minmei grinned. "I guess you're right about that. Oh, by the way, are you going to leave everything like this or will you reopen the restaurant?"

"What d'you mean reopen the restaurant?" Uncle Max exploded, though she could hear the sudden hope in his voice.

Minmei gestured around at the stacked chairs and boxed flatware and bundles of table linen. The White Dragon, which originally stood at the virtual center of Macross City, had served as a kind of field test for the engineers seeking to help the Macross City survivors rebuild their lives, an experiment to see if a piece of the city could be reproduced down to the last detail. There were working dishwashers and ovens and sinks and rest rooms, freezers and refrigerators, lighting and a sound system.

The only thing that was different was that there were no garbage pails or dumpsters. A system of oubliettes was being built into the new Macross City because everything—*everything*—would have to be recycled and reused. It made perfect sense to Minmei, who'd known thirst and hunger and other privations well in the past two weeks; anyone who couldn't see that was just being stupid.

"We have everything we need," she pointed out. "It'll be fun!"

She saw a rekindling in Uncle Max's eyes, but he said slowly, "Maybe so, but it'd be awfully difficult to run a restaurant when these are all the rations they give at one time." He shook the book-size box. "For four of us, for today."

"But you kept your place open all through the war!" Minmei cried.

Uncle Max ran his hand through the tight black curls on his head. Aunt Lena looked shocked, but happy. "*Whff!* That was much different," Max said. Then he reconsidered. "Well, the army *had* imposed rationing then too…"

"But—we're living inside a spaceship, Minmei," Lena said.

"But the main problem right now isn't shortages, right?" Minmei reminded her. "It's distribution and control. We've got thousands of people spending half the day on line! How's anybody gonna get anything *done*? That's the ultimate in stupidity!"

She saw that they were getting the point. "Aunt Lena, once the authorities know you're reopening the White Dragon, they'll give you all the supplies you want! And it wouldn't surprise me if they put us all on salary as food distribution specialists!

"And people can pay us with their ration cards; the army pays at least part of the overhead; there's room for a little markup, I would think; the tips are pure profit, whether they're in military script or in goods or service IOUs; and we'll get that new bookkeeping computer they're setting up to keep track of cost/profit margin!"

She was out of breath but triumphant. And she could see from their faces that she'd sold her aunt and uncle. "What d'you think?"

Uncle Max rubbed the back of his neck, wanting very badly to believe it. "I suppose it doesn't sound like a bad idea, after all."

"I guess so," Aunt Lena allowed. She drew in a great breath, looking at Minmei. "Doing business as usual is the answer to a lot of problems, right?"

Minmei nodded until her hair was rippling around her.

"Right!" barked Uncle Max. "Let's get cracking! Full steam ahead!" He laughed, full-throated, at the dark starburst of happiness in his wife's eyes and at Minmei's gasp.

"Wait just a second!" Minmei dashed off, hair whipping behind her. "I'll be right back! I'm just gonna change my clothes!" Mandarin dresses were no problem at all for computer-directed fabrication units that had produced alien technologies.

Uncle Max expanded his chest in pride. Aunt Lena put her arm around his broad shoulders and said, "I'm glad she's excited."

He nodded. "I only hope we're not making a mistake about this."

Lena kissed him tenderly. "We're not."

"Careful, that's it," Uncle Max instructed anxiously as he and Minmei carried the little stand out onto the sidewalk in front of the restaurant. "Now turn it around. Good!"

"Everybody'll see this!" Minmei said excitedly. The stand was covered with a bright red and yellow silk cloth announcing the restaurant's name in Chinese characters. Minmei's elegant mandarin dress was made of the same stuff. She'd arranged her hair in large buns with a braid to one side, weaving a rope of pearls into the coiffure.

She was so intent on her work that she almost collided with the mayor and his wife, who stared in surprise. "Well, well, what's this all about?"

Minmei replied, "A little surprise, Mr. Mayor. We're reopening our restaurant!"

Tommy Luau's eyebrows shot up. "Have you all gone completely crazy? Has it ever occurred to you that we're at the edge of the universe in the belly of a spaceship?"

"Why, no, we never thought of that," she said tartly. But then she gave him her sunniest smile. "But honestly, that doesn't mean we shouldn't make the best of things, does it? I think we can still have normal lives. After all, this is still our good old hometown, isn't it?"

She indicated the town. It was already an everyday thing for traffic to be moving around the streets—not just military vehicles but cars and trucks that had been salvaged after the spacefold jump as well.

One thing was for sure, the mayor knew: When the diversion of rebuilding the city was over, and that would be soon, the refugees would need something else to occupy them. And as she so often did, Minmei had seen to the heart of things.

"By gosh, you're right!" the mayor said excitedly. To get back to life as usual—how grand that would be! His head was suddenly swimming with ideas for restoring normality to refugee life, but he was distracted as a four-seater troop carrier pulled to the curb with a squeal of tires and a beep of its horn.

Three Veritech pilots sat there, gazing at the restaurant as if it were a three-headed dinosaur. "We saw it but we couldn't believe it!" the jeep's driver said. "Are you really open?"

"We certainly are!" Minmei said proudly.

They looked a little dazed as she led them inside, seated them, and brought glasses of ice water. "Welcome to the first Chinese restaurant in outer space," she beamed, distributing menus.

"Thanks; it's an honor to be here," the driver said. "Hey, you're that girl Minmei everybody's been talking about, huh? I'll bet you had some incredible adventures."

"Sometimes it was pretty scary," she admitted.

The biggest of the three, the one who'd been sitting in the back of the carrier, said in a sly tone, "I heard it was just you and whatshisname, that kid, alone for two weeks. What'd you do all that time?"

She blinked. "What do you mean?"

"Oh, I think you know," the big guy said.

"C'mon, it's obvious," the third one said.

"You make me sick!" she fumed, turning her back on them.

"You mean nothing happened?" the big one persisted. "Nothing at all?"

She whirled. "Yes, that's exactly right!"

"Speaking of whatshisname," the driver said, "is he still around? I mean, I heard he was living here or something."

Minmei answered carefully. "Yes, he's renting a room upstairs from my aunt and uncle. Why?"

The driver shrugged. "You're saying that with all you two went through together, nothing happened? You didn't fall in love or anything?"

"Don't be ridiculous! Rick is just a friend! Now, are you three gonna order or are you gonna leave?"

Rick, poised on the stairs, had heard enough. As the pilots hastened to order chow mein, he turned and went back up to his room.

He sat on his bed and stared glumly at the wall. *So, we're just friends, huh?* He remembered the feel of her in his arms, the electric thrill as they kissed.

After everything that happened, the next day we're just friends. He knew Minmei could be stubborn, but on this subject she was just going to have to change her mind.

The engineering section was a hive of activity where every tech, scientist, and specialist available was working twelve-, eighteen-, sometimes twenty-hour days.

Gloval, by his own order, was ignored as he entered, not wishing to break anyone's concentration even for a moment. "Doctor Lang, what do you think? Is the main gun usable or not?"

Lang gave Gloval a brisk salute from habit. The strange whiteless eyes were still mystical, dark. "Look at this schematic, sir."

Lang projected a diagram of SDF-1 on a big wall screen. "This is a first-level depiction of the primary reflex furnace, our power plant. And there you see the energy conversion unit for the main gun. Between the two is the energy conduit for the fold system."

He gave a bitter smile. *"Was,* I should say."

"Which means that after the fold system disappeared, the gun's power source was separated from it, correct?" Gloval asked. "What are you planning to do, since we haven't much spare conduit left?"

And, ironically, conduit was one of the very few things the fabricators couldn't reproduce with materials at hand. But the main gun was SDF-1's hope of survival; Gloval studied Lang, hoping the man had an answer.

Lang assumed the tone he'd used in his lectures back on Earth. "The SDF-1's construction is Robotech construction, sir. That is, the ship is modular, as our Veritech fighters are modular. Variable geometry, you see."

Lang ran a series of illustrations to show what he meant. "So, simplistically speaking, we should by all rights be able to reconfigure the ship, altering its structure in such a way as to bridge the gap that now exists between the main gun and its power source."

It was all a little breathtaking and bold; the proposed reconfiguration, with modules realigned in new shapes, was radically different from the SDF-1 as she now existed.

Gloval felt very uneasy. Lang went on, "The problem, very simply, is that until this modular transformation is completed, the main gun *cannot* be fired."

Lang gestured to the diagrams. "There are going to be major changes, both internally and externally. Of course, the rebuilding of the city and the other modifications made by and for the refugees were never planned for in the ship's construction. I anticipate considerable damage. It's going to be quite a mess for a while."

Gloval was staring at the diagrams, haunted by the awful scenes he'd been forced to witness out the SDF-1 bridge viewport after the spacefold. Mention of structural conversions and damage automatically made alarm bells go off in any seasoned spacer's head; despite Lang's cool calculations, the risk wasn't just of damage—it was of utter disaster.

"Don't we have any other way to fire the main gun, Doctor?"

"You mean besides a modular transformation, sir? No other way that I know of."

Gloval turned away from the screen angrily. "We just can't! The people are only now getting used to being here, trying to patch their lives back together. To subject them to such chaos and perhaps lose more lives—no, it would be just too much."

But a small part of him feared that the decision wasn't that simple; events could force his hand.

20

The Rick Hunter who crashed in that hold would never have listened
to Roy Fokker. The one who came out—
   Well, it's just funny how things happen sometimes, isn't it?

                                    The Collected Journals of Admiral Rick Hunter

"**C**AN I HAVE TWO MORE ORDERS OF EGG FOO YONG AND A MILK
shake, please?" the air crewman yelled over the din in the White
Dragon.

"*Milk* shake?" Minmei shivered at the thought, but she put the
order in anyway. Uncle Max didn't seem to mind in the least; he
was happier than she'd ever seen him, doing the work of three men
back in the kitchen, performing miracles with stove and wok.

And the place was packed; word had gotten around even faster
than Minmei had hoped. The SDF-1 liaison officers were overjoyed
at this solution to their food distribution headaches and provided
incentive packages to get the whole population to resume as
normal a life as was possible under the circumstances.

Minmei turned, then burst into a smile. "Oh, hi, Rick!"

But he gave no sign of having heard her, slouching toward the
door with hands in pockets. Minmei watched him go, her brows
knit, suddenly worried and confused.

The hangar bay was dark, quiet as a tomb. *Very appropriate*, Rick
thought.

He pulled the bright red-and-white striped chute off the dashed
remains of *Mockingbird* just enough to be able to gaze down at a

flattened section of engine. The racer was wreckage and would never be anything else again. He still couldn't bring himself to accept that, and so he forced himself to stare, to acknowledge.

He shook his head. "Boy, what a mess."

"Hey, Rick!" It was Roy, stepping into the little circle of light. "Now, show me this junk pile."

Rick came to his feet, fist balled. "Listen, buddy, this is the racer I won eight international championships in. You call it junk? I oughta knock your block off, Roy!"

Roy kneeled to take a better look at *Mockingbird*'s remains. "Actually, it's very *nice* junk. But—them's the breaks, kiddo."

Rick seemed about to explode.

"Hey, I've got an idea." Roy grinned. "Let's take a walk, okay?"

Rick looked startled. "I've never seen you so depressed in my life," Roy went on. "What you need is exercise!" He came over to put an arm around his friend's shoulders. "Try it! You'll like it!"

Roy's walk took them to the uppermost part of SDF-1 for an astonishing view.

From the lounge of the officers' club, Rick found himself looking down on the *Daedalus*. "Wow! An aircraft carrier connected to the Robotech ship?"

There was a long elbowlike housing holding the carrier fast. Rick could see that the ship had been patched and made airtight and was in service. All six bow and waist cats appeared to be in operation. As he watched, an elevator brought up two Veritechs for launch.

The Thor-class supercarrier, almost fifteen hundred feet long, had undergone a lot of other modifications. Most conspicuously, its "island"—the towerlike superstructure that had once dominated the flight deck and been the *Daedalus*'s bridge—had been removed to leave the deck perfectly flat. All flight operations had been combined in the SDF-1's command center, and the salvaged materials and equipment had been used in the design changes.

The Veritechs spread their wings, not for the sake of aerodynamics but rather because the wider placement of thrusters gave them better control. The hookup men and cat crews, not space-suited and still color-coded according to their jobs, went through the time-honored routine.

As Rick watched, a bow cat officer pointed to his "shooter," the man who actually gave the order to launch. The cat officer signaled the Veritech pilot with a wave of a flashlight, pointing toward the bow, dropping to one knee to avoid being accidentally hit by a wing.

The fighter was accelerated off the flatdeck's hurricane bow at almost 200 knots—not because airspeed was necessary in the airlessness of space but to get the Veritech launched and clear of the ship in a hurry, as it would have to be in combat, so as not to be a sitting duck for alien pilots.

The Veritech banked and soared away. Rick had to remind himself that it was flying in total vacuum; Robotech control systems made the operation of a fighter very much a matter of thought, and the Veritech pilots were used to thinking in terms of atmospheric flying. And so the Veritechs flew that way; it was wasteful of power, but power was something Robotech ships, with their reaction drives, had in great supply.

Rick watched longingly. "Terrific."

"How'd you like to fly one again?" Roy clapped Rick on the shoulder.

Rick spun on him. "What are you saying?"

"Join us, Rick. Become a Veritech pilot and stop all this moping around."

Rick's expression hardened. "I don't want to be a fighter pilot."

"Oh? You'd rather drag yourself around the SDF-1 like a lovesick idiot? Well?"

Rick broke loose of Roy's hand, turning away. "Roy?" he said over his shoulder.

"Yeah?"

"Roy, I think I'm—I mean, do you think it's possible for girls to change overnight? Completely?"

"How's that again?"

"Can a girl simply change from what she was the day before?"

"I don't think you have to worry about that. Minmei thought you were depressed, and it was *her* idea for me to bring you up here and have a little chat."

Roy slapped him on the back, knocking a little of the breath from him. "So just cheer up and go back to Minmei, kid; she's waiting for you."

He walked off, chuckling to himself, but paused to call back, "Oh, one more thing: Girls like her can be sort of flighty sometimes, know what I mean? You better be careful some guy in uniform doesn't catch her eye. See ya."

Across the solar system, maintaining position relative to Earth's nearby moon, the Zentraedi armada hung like a seaful of bloodthirsty fish.

Breetai returned to his command post in response to Exedore's request. "Trans-vid records of the aliens, you say?"

Exedore kowtowed to his lord. "Yes, they were just recovered from a disabled scout pod. And they confirm absolutely the eye-witness accounts of our warriors. If you would care to study them, Commander…"

A projecbeam drew an image in midair. The recorder's point of view was a fast-moving, almost bewildering sweep through the carnage and fury of the battle in the streets of Macross City. Explosions and fire were everywhere, but now and again there were split-second glimpses of the aliens, mostly fleeing or falling.

"I believe you'll find this intriguing," Exedore said. Then suddenly a pod loomed close by one of the inhabitants of the planet, and for the first time Breetai got a feeling of scale.

His voice reverberated in shock and anger, a guttural to shake the bulkheads. "*So!* It's true! *Micronians!*"

The trans-vid record cut to another shot that left no doubt: a human figure falling to its death from a high building, knocked off along with debris by the enormous foot of a pod.

"Precisely," Exedore said delicately.

"So the inhabitants here *are* Micronians, eh?" Breetai scowled. The conflicting emotions held by the Zentraedi toward normal-sized humanoids—"Micronians," as the giant warriors contemptuously referred to them—welled up in him. There was disdain and hatred but also something strangely close to fear.

"I brought the trans-vids to you as soon as I saw them," Exedore said. "They present us with a very unpleasant new situation. During my researches into the origins of the Micronians in our most ancient records, I encountered a decree from our dimmest histories.

"It directs us to shun contact with any unknown Micronian planet—and threatens disaster if we do not heed it."

Breetai's face looked like a graven image. "So I'm to keep my hands off this Earth, eh? *Bah!*"

"It is my considered opinion, m'lord," Exedore insisted, "that we must cease hostilities with this planet immediately. We now have a fix on the battle fortress; I consider it prudent counsel that we make its capture our priority." The pinpoint pupils bored into Breetai, unblinking.

Breetai knew that Exedore would drop his usual deference only for a matter of vital importance. Breetai, like all Zentraedi, had absorbed his race's legends and superstitions along with its lore and warrior code. Like them all, he felt a twinge of apprehension at the thought of defying his heritage.

It was in his mind to object—to say that Exedore's stricture came from the days when the Zentraedi's numbers were fewer, their ships less mighty, their weapons not as powerful. But he considered Exedore: the repository of most of the lore and learning of the Zentraedi race. In a way, the diminutive, physically weak Exedore *embodied* his people. And Exedore seemed to have no doubts about the correct course in this instance.

"Very well, then. We will execute a spacefold, immediately and pursue the dimensional fortress."

Exedore bowed. "It shall be done."

"And see to it that an appropriate reconnaissance vessel is sent out at once upon completion of the fold maneuver."

Exedore knew what "appropriate" meant; they had discussed Breetai's strategy for dealing with the SDF-1. Exedore bowed again. "Yes, m'lord."

"Oh, you're back, Rick! Anything special on your mind?" Rick paused with his knuckles poised to rap on Minmei's door.

It was a red door she'd chosen to decorate with a whimsical pink rabbit's head bearing her name. He'd wavered quite a bit before finally drawing a deep breath and preparing to knock on it. Only to find her standing in the hall behind him. "Uh, nothing, Minmei—really…"

She burst into one of those captivating laughs, eyes crinkling. "I'm sure! C'mon in, Rick." She opened the door and led the way. "Make yourself at home."

It was a bright little room, painted in shades of blue and yellow, easy on the eyes and not overfurnished. Bed, lamps, bookshelf, and a handmade throw rug; a few flowers very beautifully arranged— *thoughtfully* arranged—in a small antique vase. There were stuffed toys, too, and a favorite purse. It was a room of seeming clashes that somehow gave the impression of oneness—like its occupant.

Minmei sat on the bed. "Oh, could you open the window?"

"Right; glad to."

He slid the window aside, not that the air in the rest of the ship was very much different from that in Minmei's room. But here over the restaurant it was a little warmer than outside, and with the window opened more of the slight, never-ending breeze from the SDF-1's circulation system could be felt. It was as much like getting "fresh air" as people in the dimensional fortress could expect.

Minmei folded one leg under her. "So, what happened?"

"Not much. But it's nice to be back here." He looked around her place to avoid meeting her gaze and to give himself time to build up courage to say what he had to say.

His eyes lit on an envelope lying on her dresser. "Hey, don't tell me you got mail!" He picked it up and looked it over.

"That's what I went back for," she said, watching him. "That and my diary—when you rescued me." She shivered, remembering the concussions of the pod's titanic feet crashing down, nearer and nearer, behind her.

It had plainly been reread over and over. "A love letter, hmm?" The thought made him so depressed that he ignored the warmth in what she'd just said.

"Don't be silly! You can take a look at it if you like."

He did. It took him a minute to figure out what he was looking at. "What's this all ab—A *singing audition*? It says you, um, got to the preliminaries."

Her eyes were dancing. "That's right! I can hardly believe it!"

He read on. "This says you were accepted for the Miss Macross competition. *Miss Macross*?"

He wondered for a moment why she'd never told him about that in the long imprisonment they'd shared down in SDF-1's sealed nether regions. But then, he realized there were things he'd never shared with her, either.

"Uh huh!" Minmei was giggling.

Rick put the letter down slowly. "Well, I guess it's no surprise. Minmei, you really sing well."

"Thank you, Rick." But the joy abruptly changed to a faraway look, a sadness. She rose from the bed and went to the window to look out on Macross and the bulkheads and overheads that hung in the distance like the end of the world.

"But this isn't the Earth, and people there have forgotten about this contest, so it's all kind of pointless, isn't it? Who cares if I'm a star *here*?"

It was the first time he'd seen her great thirst to be famous and successful; in their imprisonment it had seemed such a distant, implausible thing. But now it was clear that it was what she lived for.

He looked at the letter again. "Minmei, don't be sad. You can always audition again when we get back to Earth."

"*If* we get back to Earth."

He had no ready comeback for that. They both knew how desperate the situation was, how terrible the enemy. As they gazed at each other a skycrane went by the window, floating a prefab condo module toward its destination. The illusion of home all around them only made them that much more homesick.

"Rick? Do you ever dream?"

He was surprised, answering hesitantly. "I used to have a dream. Now it's a pile of junk in a hangar bay up on the flight deck levels."

"*Mockingbird*."

"Yeah." *And I won't let my father down! I'm not going to be part of this war or any war! So—I guess I might as well get used to being a passenger.*

"I'm never gonna have another dream again, Minmei. They hurt too much when they die."

She hung her head. "Oh, Rick."

He wondered if it had occurred to her that he wasn't just talking about *Mockingbird*, wondered if she ever remembered that one kiss…

21

They still thought of mechamorphosis, of transformation and in fact transfiguration, as an unlooked-for last resort and a sort of desperate aberration. There was no point in my telling them that it was all in the nature of Robotechnology; they would come to understand that for themselves.

Dr. Emil Lang, *Technical Recordings and Notes*

"**W**E REGISTER A DEFOLD REACTION," REPORTED A VOICE FROM the monitor-lit cavern of the sensor operations center, "at the following coordinates."

Up on the bridge, Vanessa forced down her dismay as she relayed the information to Captain Gloval. "Radar reports unidentified object, bearing six-two-seven-seven, possibly of alien origin."

The information was pouring in quickly; Lisa correlated it at her duty station. "Enemy starships," she confirmed.

Gloval rose slowly and crossed to peer over her shoulder. "So, they've come at last." He stood looking down at the huge "paint," the wide splotch on the radar screen that indicated the enemy.

Claudia and the rest of the bridge gang took a moment to gaze too.

"All right, then," Gloval said. "Prepare to repel attack and launch an immediate counterattack."

"Aye-aye, Captain." Lisa moved with precision, sounding the alarms that were her province, speaking into a handset.

"Enemy attack. I say again, enemy attack. This is not a drill. Scramble all Veritechs. Scramble all Veritechs."

As general quarters sounded, the SDF-1 and its attached

supercarriers became scenes of frantic activity. Men charged to their planes, some of them to fly combat for the first time, as plane crews and launch crews, flight controllers and cat crews, all braced for the manic haste.

The hangar decks and flight decks were in a well-ordered turmoil. Elevators raised flight after flight of fighters to the flatdecks' waist and bow cats, and even more Veritechs blazed angrily from SDF-1's bays.

Roy Fokker pulled on his helmet, checking out his own ship's status and the rest of Skull Team's as well. It so happened that they were taking off from *Daedalus* after a familiarization mission; Skull's usual berth was in a bay on the dimensional fortress. But they were all experienced naval aviators. The hookup man had made the connections to the bow cat, and the blast deflector had been raised from the deck behind Roy's Veritech. The cat officer had her right hand up high, two fingers extended, waving it with a rapid motion.

This particular catapult officer, Roy knew, was a good one: Moira Flynn, who'd been reassigned to SDF-1 from the *Daedalus* and had thus been spared the horrible fate so many of her shipmates had suffered in the wake of the miscalculated spacefold. Moira and the other old hands had worked like coolies in the reorganization, training new crews for the fearsomely dangerous job of working a flight deck.

Troubleshooters made a last quick eyeball inspection of the fighter in a fast walkdown along either side and found no reason to abort launch. The cat officer registered their thumbs-up reports; some things hadn't changed much since the early days of carrier flying and visual signals were the communication of choice, even though the suit helmets had radios. Verbal communication among so many people would have made any communications net chaos. The hookup man was clear, and Moira Flynn pointed to Roy.

Fokker replied with a sharp salute to signal his readiness, cutting his hand away from the brow of his helmet smartly.

The cat officer turned to point at her shooter to alert the man for a launch, then turned as in some punctilious dance to make a last check that the deck was clear for launch. Roy felt his stomach get tight, as it always did.

The cat officer turned back to the fighter, kneeling in what looked like a genuflection so as to be clear of the launch in case of catapult or Veritech malfunction. Lieutenant Flynn gave final, ritual clearance, pointing along the track of the cat, with her flash light, into the void, in a pose like a javelin thrower who'd just released.

Her shooter hit the button, brought both hands together in signal, and ducked, as per procedure.

Roy felt himself shoved at 200 knots along *Daedalus*'s deck. All the catapults had had to be recalibrated because, while there was gravity on the flight decks now thanks to equipment from SDF-1, there was no air resistance.

Skull Leader's fighter shot forth over the ship's hurricane bow, going out straight as an arrow to avoid a collision with ships being launched from the waist cats. Another Veritech was about to be launched from the center bow cat, and it would bank starboard. A third was about to be guided into the slot of the third bow cat; a fourth was about to be guided into the slot Roy had just abandoned.

The Veritechs launched, one after another, all over the reconfigured SDF-1. The blue novas of their drives lit the darkness of the solar system's edge as they formed up and went to meet their enemies once again.

It promised to be a proper park someday, but now it wasn't much more than a patch of unproductive soil atop a castlelike upthrust of interior equipment overlooking Macross City. But somebody had planted trees and shrubbery, and somehow they were being kept alive. Rick suspected that it was the work of homesick Macross refugees rather than any official project. Up here, the gigantic city-compartment's overhead lights were close.

Minmei led the way to the low railing. "What a view!"

Rick grunted, shuffling along behind her with his hands in his pockets. He supposed that she was right; the city lay at their feet, and there probably wasn't a better vista of human-type scenery within a billion miles. He sank down on the wide railing, looking at the ground rather than at the city.

Minmei didn't notice his depression, too taken with the scene.

"It's so—" she started to say, just as the general quarters alarms cut loose and Lisa Hayes started making her announcements. Rick recognized the voice and decided he disliked it more than he'd thought possible.

"Will we be all right?" Minmei asked him as another voice started to yammer about air raid warnings.

He kicked a bit of dirt. "Don't worry. Roy'll take care of it. As usual."

She put her hands on hips. "How come you're always talking about Roy's flying? You're just as good a pilot as he is, any day!"

He looked away at that, up to the ceiling lights. Alarms wailed, and he wondered what Big Brother was doing.

Just then, Roy was leading Skull Team in the most furious dogfight he'd ever seen, as wave after wave of pods came in at the SDF-1. Zentraedi energy blasts and missiles flashed in all directions as the dimensional fortress's defensive batteries blazed away. The special Veritech autocannon ammo, designed to fire in airless space, was even more powerful and accurate there than in atmosphere.

There were explosions and more explosions, all in the eerie quiet of vacuum. Except the tac nets weren't quiet; if the explosions emitted no sound, the screams of dying men made up for that.

Every Veritech squadron rehearsal and drill went out the window; in the utter madness that swirled around the SDF-1, the pilots found that they could keep tight with their wingmen and engage the enemy only as the opportunity arose. It was a cloud of dogfighting like nothing that had ever gone before it in human history—fireballs created by exploding spacecraft, perhaps a half dozen of them at a time, and the relentless lancing of beam weapons and autocannon tracers.

"These aliens are a lot better up here than they were back on Earth," Roy told Skull Team, although they were all painfully aware of that already. "Looks like a real rat race this time."

He led his wingman onto a new vector and headed for a cluster of pods that threatened to break through SDF-1's defenses at a spot where two gun turrets had been knocked out.

Pods began erupting in flames as the VTs' shots rained on them;

the sally was turned back, but in the meantime three more cries for help came in. Roy told himself to ignore the big picture and just tend to his flying.

"Our special decoy vessel is now within their firing range," the report came to Breetai.

Exedore stood next to him, watching the same tactical display monitors. "I find it strange they haven't fired their main gun yet."

Breetai, arms folded across his immense chest, contemplated the screens. After a lifetime of soldiering, after uncountable contests in battle, he'd come to appreciate a shrewd enemy, and he'd begun to conclude that this enemy commander was either quite shrewd—or insane.

Still, a warrior fought to win. To meet a foe worthy of respect was a thing to be wished for but also a thing to ignite caution in any wise commander.

The metal and crystal of his headpiece caught the light. "What are you planning, my dear Micronian friend?" Breetai murmured.

"Perhaps we should offer them another enticement and see what they do," Exedore suggested.

"Mmmm." Breetai's metal-sheathed head inclined. "Very good idea. Tell the recon ship to open fire, but it is *not* to do serious damage to the battle fortress. Is that clear?"

Exedore bowed and hastened to obey.

Out in the lead of the armada's main body, the recon ship opened up with all batteries. At that distance, it was impossible to be sure an energy bolt wouldn't hit a dogfighting pod; the battling Robotech machines were in constant motion.

But the Zentraedi overlords cared little about that; their warrior code held that lives were expendable. Without warning, a terrible volley hit friend and foe alike and holed the battle fortress.

A pod was blown apart just before two converging VTs could make the kill themselves; another Veritech was singed along a wing surface by the barrage. Attempting to switch to Guardian mode so it could cope better with damage to itself, it was hit by another blast, flying to pieces in a bright globe. Secondary explosions blistered from the SDF-1's hull. Wreckage flew, and precious atmosphere puffed into space.

Lisa was thrown against her console by a direct hit to a reactor subcontrol unit several decks below the bridge. Gloval rose halfway from his chair. "Are you all right?"

She righted herself, nodding. "I'm okay, but what about the hull?"

He came to his feet, studying the damage reports pouring in all around him, gazing out the forward viewport at the eruptions of destroyed pods and VTs, and the blue hail of incoming cannon bolts.

"Just pray," Gloval said tightly.

A call came in from the engineering officer, the shouts of his men and the crackle of fire mixed with the hiss of fire-fighting foam in the background. "There's been some damage to the reactor subcontrol, Captain, but we'll manage."

"I'm counting on you," Gloval told him, wondering how long the ship could withstand the barrage.

Out in the savage killing ground of the dogfight, pod preyed on Veritech and Veritech upon pod. All was swirling combat, blazing weaponry, max thrust, and desperate maneuvers. The pods, like the VTs, often moved in a way that suggested atmospheric constraints, despite the fact that they were in deep space.

The Zentraedi recon ship continued to pour heavy fire into the SDF-1's general vicinity, though the dimensional fortress sustained less damage than it might have. The alien gunners weren't making it obvious, but Breetai's orders regarding the battle fortress's survival were being followed to the letter.

Still, carefully placed rounds seared through the ship's shields and armor, blowing apart a turret here, a radome there. A nearby hit shook the bridge gang around like dice in a cup and threw Gloval headlong out of his chair, his hat skittering across the deck.

"Thundering asteroids!"

Vanessa was back to her station before he got to his feet. "Captain, damage control reports that the second and fifth laser turrets have sustained heavy damage. They'll be out of action for seven hours minimum."

"Number four thruster is almost completely destroyed," Claudia declared grimly.

"Subcontrol systems report heavy damage and heavy casualties," Lisa added.

Another close hit jarred the ship, lifting a missile-launching tube away from it and scattering wreckage and pieces of human bodies.

Gloval reared up angrily. "That's the last straw! *We're firing the main gun!*"

Lisa heard herself gasp along with the rest of the bridge gang.

Gloval was stone-faced. "Stand by; upon my command, we will execute Dr. Lang's designated modular transformation!"

Kim couldn't keep herself from protesting. "But if we do that, it means the whole town might—"

"Yes, that's right, the damage—" Sammie agreed, breathless.

Gloval glared at them. "I either take this risk or see the SDF-1 completely destroyed. I have no choice! I have to do it."

Outside, the sinister festival of lights grew more intense. Another nearby hit shook the bridge again. Lisa whirled back to her duty station. "All systems attention, all systems attention! Begin preparations for firing the main gun!"

Her voice rang through the rest of the ship, through engineering compartments and fire control centers and living quarters alike. "Modular transformation will be initiated in three minutes, *mark!*"

An engine room tech looked to his squadmate. "They can't be doing that crazy transformation now."

"They're outta their minds," the other agreed.

"Two minutes, fifty seconds and counting," Lisa's steady voice echoed.

The two looked at each other for a moment, then dove for their emergency suits.

The traffic had halted in the city street below, but otherwise Macross looked the same. Rick and Minmei glanced up at the nearest PA speakers as the voice he'd come to so dislike said, "Attention, all citizens! This ship will be undergoing modular transformation in two minutes. This operation is dangerous; please take all safety precautions.

"Move outdoors at once. Beware of possible quake damage. If possible, evacuate to a designated safety area." There was a slight pause before the echoing voice added, in a softer tone, "And— good luck."

"Transformation? What's that?" Minmei wondered. She and Rick had stayed where they were once the fighting started because it seemed as safe a place as any.

"I dunno; maybe something they came up with while we were— while we were stranded."

"I guess that Roy must be out there in the middle of the fighting," she said sadly, looking out at the city.

"You mean—you think I should join the defense force?"

"No, I didn't mean that at all. It's just that airplanes are your dream, aren't they?"

He could see that the war didn't matter very much to her; that wasn't the way her mind worked. But she'd seen that he was sad and saw what she thought to be a remedy to that sadness.

"I guess so. But if I go and join the defense forces, Minmei, I won't be able to see very much of you anymore." Painful as seeing her under present circumstances was, he wasn't willing to give it up.

She was suddenly smiling. "Rick, we're on the same ship! On your days off or furlough or whatever it is, we can see each other whenever we want to."

"If I survive."

"Oh, how can you talk that way? All the soldiers who come to the restaurant are in exactly the same position!"

"The same position?" He smiled bitterly. "You'd be the one to know, now, wouldn't you?"

She started as if she'd been slapped. "What?"

Up on the bridge, Claudia watched her monitors. "Ten seconds to transformation."

22

And so, my preliminary conclusions lead me to believe these creatures harbor certain unpredictable impulses of a nature as yet unknown to us. It seems obvious that this irrational side to their nature will impede their warmaking ability and work in our favor, assuring us the ultimate victory.

Preliminary findings summary
transmitted by Breetai to Dolza

"**A**LL SECTIONS ON EXECUTION STANDBY?" GLOVAL DEMANDED.
"D and G blocks are running a bit late but they'll manage," Kim sang out.

"Good; continue," the captain said.

"Counting four seconds," Claudia resumed. "Three… two…"

"Commence full-ship transformation," Gloval ordered.

The bridge crew took up the quiet, critical exchanges of the transformation, listening to their headset earphones and speaking into their mikes. What would have been soft-spoken bedlam to an outsider was instantly intelligible to Gloval.

Sammie: "Commence full-ship transformation. J, K, and L blocks, stand to."

Kim: "Number seven reflex furnace, power up. Seven-eight section start engines. Not enough power, J block!"

Vanessa: "Activate main torque-sender units."

And the ghostly voices came back, complaining of trouble with substrata plasma warps, of injuries in a hundred different locations, of machinery that was being asked to do too much, of overtaxed components that simply could not do their jobs, and of civilians who, confused and disoriented, were not prepared for the upheaval that was about to take place. Through it all, the bridge gang worked selflessly, concentrating on their jobs and their responsibilities.

Gloval knew that no matter what was about to happen, he was proud of them, proud to serve with them.

"Full-ship transformation under way, sir," Claudia relayed.

With the ship trembling and vibrating all around him, Gloval drew on his reserves of inner calm, clasping his hands behind his back. Now, what would happen would happen; he'd done all he could, and the odds of numbers or the vagaries of engineering or happenstance or some higher power—or all of the above—would make the final judgment.

"Very good," he told Claudia.

Rick looked down at the city. People had streamed from the buildings, racing this way and that, with no clear destination or purpose. Some seemed to be headed for designated shelter areas, but others darted aimlessly, unable to bear another catastrophe so soon after the last.

Rick didn't particularly care, didn't feel any urge to find refuge. "Y'know, Minmei, sometimes I wish they'd never found us."

"I can't believe I'm hearing that from you! How can you be so spiteful? Oh, *I hate you!*"

He looked back at her. "The same goes for me. If it doesn't mean anything to you that you and I were—"

The vibration had reached a level that nearly knocked him off his feet as enormous pylons, each as wide as a city block, began descending from the gigantic compartment's ceiling. The grinding of the monster servomotors that moved them became deafening.

Rick and Minmei barely had time to get an inkling of what was going on, barely had time to begin to cry out, when the ground at their feet split apart, he on one side and she on the other.

The tower on which humans had so tentatively begun a garden had functions none of them had foreseen. In answer to the reconfiguration order, the tower halves swung away from each other.

Minmei lost her balance and fell, barely catching the brink of a metal ledge that jutted out a few inches below the soil level. The tower part to which she clung pivoted on its supports out over the roofs of the city; screaming, she kicked and scrabbled for purchase against a sheer cliff face of technical components, systemry, and equipment modules.

"*Minmei!*" Rick fought for balance as the tower segment on which he was standing shook, moving into place with a grinding of massive gears. The gap between the halves was growing wider. He took a running start and hurtled out over empty air, barely making the other side.

Rick knelt to where Minmei hung, legs kicking, hundreds of feet above the roofs of Macross. She'd lost one hand grip, and her fingers were slipping from the other.

He threw himself prone at the brink of the abyss and grabbed her wrist with both hands just as she let go. He gritted his teeth and pulled, but the leverage was difficult, and he hadn't had time to get a firm hold.

Minmei's wrist slipped through his grasp a fraction of an inch. She stared up into his eyes, terror consuming her. "Rick, help me!"

Again the monster cam devices rotated SDF-1's forward booms apart in preparation for the firing of the main gun. But other alterations were taking place, too; and the ship, particularly the stupendous hold where the refugees had rebuilt their city, was filled with devastation, injury, and death.

A hull structure the size of a billboard moved to one side like a sliding door to reinforce the new configuration; out through the gap in the ship's side poured a tidal wave of air, ripping up everything in its way, hurling cars and people and trees into space. An inner curtain of armor dropped to close the gap in moments, but not before part of the city had been sucked away to utter destruction.

Elsewhere, more pylons were in motion, this time rising from the floor, climbing up and up, crushing the buildings atop them flat against the hold's ceiling. Debris rained everywhere; the thousands who hadn't sought shelter or hadn't been able to find it were crushed or injured. Falling signs, toppling light poles, vehicles careening out of control, ruptured power lines, and tons of plummeting concrete and steel claimed as many lives as the Zentraedi had.

Roy bagged another kill, a pod that had very nearly bagged *him*, and brought his fighter around to locate Captain Kramer, his wingman, and get his bearings. Then he saw the SDF-1. *"What in the…"*

The *Daedalus* and the *Prometheus* were in motion, swinging on the giant elbow moorings that joined them to the dimensional fortress. In the blizzard of explosions and ordnance and fighter drives, the supercarriers swung from positions more or less alongside the SDF-1's stem, port and starboard, to a deployment that left them angled out from the hull.

Roy got a confused impression of movement along the hull, of realignment, of major structural features disengaging and then re shaping themselves. The entire midships area was turning. The great forward booms that constituted the main gun were on the move, and the bridge itself was shifting position. And the overall effect was— Roy stared, trying to believe it—the overall effect was of a *human figure*, a giant armored warrior something like a stylized Battloid.

The flattops resembled pincer-equipped arms, the tremendous aft thrusters were like legs and feet, and the bridge and the structures around it were the blank-visored helmet. And standing high above either shoulder, like uplifted wings, were the booms; with the shifting of the entire midships section, they were now in position to receive energy.

Somehow, Roy found himself accepting the strange apparition as a logical thing; Robotechnology seemed to have, as a primal component, a quality involving shape shifting, and anthropomorphic structures.

"So, that's the transformation," he breathed. *Now, if it only works!*

"Right wing section, modification percentage seventy-five," Kim relayed to Gloval.

"Left wing section, modification percentage at eighty-three. Main gun up," Sammie added. There was more booming and reverberating as the last components were mated and the final connections made.

"Modular transformation completed, sir," Lisa announced. "SDF-1 is now in Attack mode."

"Captain, another enemy assault wave is approaching from one-zero-niner-three."

"Disregard," Gloval ordered. "Fire main gun at designated targets."

"Yes, sir." Claudia thumbed the safety cover off a red trigger button and pressed it with her forefinger. There was a fateful little acknowledging click.

Out between and around the forward booms, the red flash flood of energy began building again, just as it had that day on Macross Island. A wash of energy a quarter mile in diameter sprang across space, instantly destroying all the alien pods in its path as well as pods on the periphery of the beam, out to a radius of a mile and more. They lit up, superheated by the eddy currents, their shields overpowered in seconds, armor heated to cherry-red and then white-hot before the occupants could take any evasive action or retreat.

They simply blazed in the stream of the main gun's volley for an instant, giving off trails like meteors, then disappeared.

The beam hit the decoy reconnaissance vessel and its escort ships, making them pop open like chestnuts in an arc furnace, then run like quicksilver and vaporize.

The glare of it lit Breetai's command post. "What's happening?"

Exedore looked out on the carnage, thinking of the strictures from the Zentraedi ancients. Try as he might, he couldn't fathom the workings or the strategies of these Micronians. He was intrigued, as he always was when he found something new to study, but he was also beset by doubts and misgivings.

Somewhere, somehow, Micronians had evidently given the Zentraedi good reason to shun them. But why?

"I wonder…" he said aloud, only partly in reply to Breetai's question.

"Enemy ships disintegrated!" Vanessa cried. The bridge was in a joyous uproar.

What those people at NASA used to call a "whoopee," Gloval reflected, recovering his hat from where it lay on the deck.

He cleared his throat, and the "whoopee" was over. "Get me a full damage report on all sections immediately," he said. As after-action reports started coming in, the thought of the losses the people in the Macross hold had suffered seriously dampened the festive mood.

In the shattered ruins of Macross, people were moving around again. Ambulances and stretchers and rescue teams swarmed through the aftermath of the latest disaster.

A voice on the PA was saying, "We have suffered grave losses both in the military combat squadrons and within SDF-1. However, we fired our main gun and completely destroyed the enemy attack force that was attempting to obliterate us. We thank and salute the residents of Macross City for their gallantry and courage."

There was more, about where to bring casualties and how the clean-up would proceed. And the rebuilding, of course. Rick Hunter, looking down from the tower, knew that rebuilding had become a part of the people of Macross. Whatever didn't kill them made them stronger and more determined to overcome any adversity.

Minmei stood beside him. Her brush with death had left her in a strange state—flushed with life and yet remote somehow. Rick knew the feeling, knew that all he could do was wait for her to come out of it before they started the long descent to Macross.

"Well, Rick," she said softly. "You said once that you wouldn't mind if the whole town were wiped out of existence, remember? How d'you like it?"

He stared down at the ocean of human suffering before him. "I didn't actually want anything to happen! I never wanted this."

She tried to identify city blocks from the fallen remains of buildings. "I wonder if the White Dragon is still there."

He turned to her. "Minmei, I'm gonna do it." He drew a deep breath. "I'm gonna join the defense forces."

"What?"

"You're right. It's no good, my moping around, especially when we're in the middle of a thing like this. I don't know if my father would understand; I think he would, though. I'm gonna enlist."

They turned to take a last look at the shattered city before going down to be of what help they could. Minmei took Rick's hand.

Roy had Skull Team back in some order, and the other surviving VT teams were forming up too. Instruments indicated that the aliens were withdrawing. Roy didn't blame them a bit, after that shot from the main gun.

Human losses had been considerable, though, and that was from an attack that could have involved no more than a tiny fraction of a percentage of the enemy forces. It was a sobering thought, and he tried not to think too hard about what the next set-to would be like.

No time to sound doubtful now, though. "Awright, boys," he drawled over the tac net, "let's head for home."

Yessir, mosey along. But as the other Veritechs formed up on his ship and their drives lit the eternal night on the solar system's edge— as they returned triumphantly to a ship that was now an armored techno-knight dominating its part of space—Roy couldn't help wondering how many more miracles were left in the magic hat.

Luck doesn't hold out forever; it never does. There were too many gaps now in the elite ranks of the Veritechs. Too many; filling them must be top priority, starting today. The very best of the best *had* to be in those seats.

Roy knew who it was that must be persuaded to join the Robotech warriors. *Even if I have to ram his head against a wall!*

The surviving VTs sped home; the Zentraedi paused for cold calculation. Decisions were made, and all eyes looked to the over whelming distance SDF-1 would have to cross in its journey back to Earth.

Unknowns... the situation was filled with unknowns. And the only good thing about unknowns was that they allowed marginal room for hope.

VOLUME 02
BATTLE CRY

FOR CARMEN, CARLOS, AND DIMITRI

MAMARONECK'S ROBOTECH DEFENSE FORCE

01

If there was any one thing that typified the initial stages of the First Robotech War, it was the unspoken interplay that developed between Captain Henry Gloval and the Zentraedi commander, Breetai. In effect, both men had been created for warfare—Gloval by the Soviet GRU, and Breetai, of course, by the Robotech Masters. When one examines the early ship's log entries of the two commanders, it is evident that each man spent a good deal of time trying to analyze the personality of his opponent by way of the strategies each employed. Breetai was perhaps at an advantage here, having at his disposal volumes of Zentraedi documents devoted to legends regarding the origin of Micronian societies. But it must be pointed out that Breetai was severely limited by his prior conditioning in his attempts to interpret these: even Exedore, who had been bred to serve as transcultural adviser, would fail him on this front. Gloval, on the other hand, with little knowledge of his ship and even less of his opponent, had the combined strengths of a loyal and intelligent crew to draw upon and the instincts of one who had learned to function best in situations where disinformation and speculation were the norm. One could point to many examples of this, but perhaps none is so representative of the group mind at work inboard the SDF-1 than the Battle at Saturn: Rings.

"Genesis," *History of the First Robotech War*, Vol. XVII

ZOR'S SHIP, THE SDF-1, MOVED THROUGH DEEP SPACE LIKE SOME creature loosed from an ancient sea fable. The structural transformation the fortress had undergone at the hands of its new commanders had rendered it monsterlike—an appearance reinforced by those oceangoing vessels grafted on to it like arms and the main gun towers that rose now from the body like twin heads, horned and threatening.

What would the Robotech Masters make of this new design? Breetai asked himself. Even prior to the transformation, Zor's ship was vastly different from his own—indeed, different from any vessel of the Zentraedi fleet. Protoculture factory that it was, it had always lacked the amorphous *organic* feel Breetai preferred. But then, it had not been designed as a warship. Until now.

The Zentraedi commander was on the bridge of his vessel, where an image of the SDF-1 played across the silent field of a projecbeam. Breetai's massive arms were folded across the brown tunic of his uniform, and the monocular enchancer set in the plate that covered half his face was trained on the free-floating screen.

Long-range scopes had captured this image of the ship for his inspection and analysis. But what those same scopes and scanners failed to reveal was the makeup of the creatures who possessed it. The bridge was an observation bubble overlooking the astrogational center of the flagship, a vast gallery of screens, projecbeam fields, and holo-schematics that gave Breetai access to information gathered by any cruiser or destroyer in his command. He could communicate with any of his many officers or any of the numerous Cyclops recon ships. But none of these could furnish him with the data he now desired—some explanation of Micronian behavior. For that, Breetai counted on Exedore, his dwarfish adviser, who at the moment seemed equally at a loss.

"Commander," the misshapen man was saying, "I have analyzed this most recent strategy from every possible angle, and I *still* cannot understand why they found it necessary to change to this format. A structural modification of this nature will most assuredly diminish, possibly even negate, the effectiveness of the ship's gravity control centers."

"And their weapons?"

"Fully operational. Unless they are diverting energy to one of the shield systems."

Breetai wondered whether he was being overly cautious. It

was true that he had been caught off guard by the Micronians' unpredictable tactics but unlikely that he had underestimated their capabilities. That they had chosen to execute an intra-atmospheric spacefold, heedless of the effects of their island population center, was somewhat disturbing, as was their most recent use of the powerful main gun of the SDF-1. But these were surely acts of desperation, those of an enemy running scared, not one in full possession of the situation.

In any straightforward military exercise, this unpredictability would have posed no threat. It had been Breetai's experience that superior firepower invariably won out over desperate acts or clever tactics. And there were few in the known universe who could rival the Zentraedi in firepower. The Micronians would ultimately be defeated; of this he was certain. Defeat, however, was of secondary importance. His prime directive was to recapture Zor's ship undamaged, and given the Micronian penchant for self-destruction, a successful outcome could not be guaranteed.

With this in mind Breetai had adopted a policy of watchful waiting. For more than two months by Micronian reckoning, the Zentraedi fleet had followed the SDF-1 without launching an attack. During that time, he and Exedore had monitored the ship's movements and audiovisual transmissions; they had analyzed the changes and modifications Zor's ship had undergone; they had screened trans-vids of their initial confrontations with the enemy. And most important, they had studied the Zentraedi legends regarding Micronian societies. There were warnings in those legends—warnings Breetai had chosen to ignore.

The SDF-1 was approaching an outer planet of this yellow-star system, a ringed world, large and gaseous, with numerous small moons. A secondary screen on the flagship bridge showed it to be the system's sixth planet. Exedore, who had already made great progress in deciphering the Micronian language, had its name: Saturn.

"My lord, I suspect that the spacefold generators aboard Zor's ship may have been damaged during the hyperspace jump from Earth to the outer planets. My belief is that the Micronians will attempt to use the gravity of this planet to sling themselves toward their homeworld."

"Interesting," Breetai replied.

"Furthermore, they will probably activate ECM as they near the planetary rings. It may become difficult for us to lock in on their course."

"It is certainly the logical choice, Exedore. And that is precisely what concerns me. They have yet to demonstrate any knowledge of logic."

"Your decision, my lord?"

"They have more than an escape plan in mind. The firepower of the main gun has given them confidence in their ability to engage us." Breetai stroked his chin as he watched the screen. "I'll let them attempt their clever little plan, if only to gain a clearer understanding of their tactics. I'm curious to see if they are in full possession of the power that ship holds."

Henry Gloval, formerly of the supercarriers *Kenosha* and *Prometheus* and now captain of the super dimensional fortress, the SDF-1, was a practical man of few words and even fewer expectations. When it came to asking himself how he had ended up in command of an alien spaceship, 1,500,000,000 kilometers from home base and carrying almost 60,000 civilians in its belly, he refused to let the question surface more than twice a day.

And yet here was the planet Saturn filling the forward bays of the SDF-1's bridge, and here was Henry Gloval in the command chair treating it like just one more Pacific current he'd have to navigate. Well, not quite: No one he'd encountered during his long career as a naval officer had ever used an ocean current the way he planned to use Saturn's gravitational fields.

The SDF-1; spacefold generators, which two months ago had allowed the ship to travel through hyperspace from Earth to Pluto in a matter of minutes, had vanished. Perhaps "allowed" was the wrong word, since Gloval had had his sights on the moon at the time. But no matter—the disappearance remained a mystery for Dr. Lang and his Robotechs to unravel; it had fallen on Gloval's shoulders to figure a way back home without the generators.

Even by the year 2010 the book on interplanetary travel was far from complete; in fact, Lang, Gloval, and a few others were still writing it. Each situation faced was a new one, each new maneuver potentially the last. There had been any number of unmanned outer-planet probes, and of course the Armor Series orbital stations and the lunar and Martian bases, but travel beyond the asteroid belt had never been undertaken by a human crew. Who was to say how it might have been if the Global Civil War hadn't put an end to the human experiment in space? But that was the way the cards had been dealt, and in truth, humankind had the SDF-1 to thank for getting things started again, even if the ship was now more weapon than spacecraft. All this, however, would be for the historians to figure out. Gloval had more pressing concerns.

Relatively speaking, the Earth was on the far side of the sun. The Fortress's reflex engines would get them home, but not quickly, and even then they were going to need a healthy send-off from Saturn. Engineering's plan was for the ship to orbit the planet and make use of centrifugal force to sling her on her way. It was not an entirely untested plan but a dangerous one nonetheless. And there was one more factor Gloval had to figure into the calculations: the enemy.

Unseen in full force, unnamed, unknown. Save that they were thought to be sixty-foot-tall humanoids of seemingly limitless supply. They had appeared in Earthspace a little more than two months ago and declared war on the planet. There was no way of knowing what fate had befallen Earth after the SDF-1's hyperspace jump, but some of the enemy fleet—or, for all Gloval knew, a splinter group—had pursued the ship clear across the solar system to press the attack. The SDF-1's main gun had saved them once, but firing it had required a modular transformation which had not only wreaked havoc with many of the ship's secondary systems but had nearly destroyed the city that had grown up within it.

For two months now the enemy had left the ship alone. They allowed themselves to be picked up by radar and scanners but were careful not to reveal the size of their fleet. Sometimes it appeared that Battlepods made up the bulk of their offensive strength—those oddly shaped, one-pilot mecha the VT teams called "headless ostriches." At other times there was evidence of scout ships and recon vessels, cruisers and destroyers. But if the enemy's numbers were a source for speculation, their motives seemed to be clear: They had come for their ship, the SDF-1.

Gloval was not about to let them have it without a fight. Perhaps if they'd come calling and *asked* for the ship, something could have been arranged. But that, too, was history.

There was only one way to guarantee a safe return to Earth: They had to either shake the enemy from their tail or destroy them. Gloval had been leaning toward the former approach until Dr. Lang had surprised him with the latest of his daily discoveries.

Lang was Gloval's interface with the SDF-1; more than anyone else onboard, the German scientist had returned his thinking to that of the technicians who had originally built the ship. He had accomplished on a grand scale what the Veritech fighter pilots were expected to do on each mission: meld their minds to the mecha controls. There was suspicion among the crew that Lang had plugged himself into one of the SDF-1's stock computers and taken some sort of mind boost which had put him in touch with the ship's builders, leaving him a stranger to those who hadn't. Gloval often felt like he was dealing with an alien entity when speaking to Lang—he couldn't bring himself to make contact with the marblelike eyes. It was as if the passionate side of the man's nature had been drained away and replaced with some of the strange fluids that coursed through many of the ship's living systems. You didn't exchange pleasantries with a man like Lang; you went directly to the point and linked memory banks with him. So when Lang told him that it might be possible to create a protective envelope for the SDF-1, Gloval merely asked how long it would take to develop.

The two men met in the chamber that until recently had housed the spacefold generators. Lang wanted Gloval to see for himself the free-floating mesmerizing energy that had spontaneously appeared there with the disappearance of the generators. Later they moved to Lang's quarters, the only section of the unreconstructed fortress sized to human proportions. There the scientist explained that the energy had something to do with local distortion in the spacetime continuum. Gloval couldn't follow all the details of the theories involved, but he stayed with it long enough to understand that this same energy could be utilized in the fabrication of a shield system for the SDF-1.

Since his conversation with Dr. Lang, Gloval had become preoccupied with the idea of taking the enemy by surprise with an offensive maneuver. With the main guns now operational and the potential of a protective barrier, Gloval and the SDF-1 would be able to secure an unobstructed route back to Earth. And Saturn, with its many moons and rings, was ideally suited to such a purpose.

Rick Hunter, Veritech cadet, admired his reflection in the shop windows along Macross City's main street. He stopped once or twice to straighten the pleats in his trousers, adjust the belt that cinched his colorful jacket, or give his long black hair just the right look of stylish disarray. It was his first day of leave after eight weeks of rigorous training, and he had never felt better. Or looked better, to judge from the attention he was getting from passersby, especially the young women of the transplanted city.

Rick was always reasonably fit—years of stunt flying had necessitated that—but the drill sergeants had turned his thin frame wiry and tough. "Nothing extraneous, in mind or body." Rick had adopted their motto as his own. He had even learned a few new flying tricks (and taught the instructors a few himself). Planes had been his life for nineteen years, and even the weightlessness of deep space felt like his element. He wasn't as comfortable with weapons, though, and the idea of killing a living creature was still as alien to him as it had been two months ago. But Roy Fokker, Rick's "older brother," was helping him through this rough period. Roy had talked about his own early misgivings, about how you had to think of the Battlepods as mecha, about how *real* the enemy threat was to all of them inboard the SDF-1. "'The price of liberty is eternal vigilance'," Roy said, quoting an American president. "There's no more flying for fun. This time you'll be flying for your home and the safety of your loved ones." Of course Roy had been through the Global Civil War; he had experience in death and destruction. He'd even come through it a decorated soldier. Although why anyone would have sought that out remained a mystery to Rick. Roy had left Pop Hunter's flying circus for that circus of global madness, and it wasn't something Rick liked to think about. Besides, as true as it might be that the war was right outside any hatch of the ship, it was surely a long way off for a cadet whose battle experience thus far had been purely accidental.

Rick was strolling down Macross Boulevard at a leisurely pace; he still had a few minutes to kill before meeting Minmei at the market. The city had managed to completely rebuild what the modular transformation had left in ruins. Taking into account the SDF-1's ability to mechamorphose, the revised city plan relied on a vertical axis of orientation. The attempt to recreate the horizontal openness of Macross Island was abandoned. The new city rose in three tiers toward the ceiling of the massive hold. Ornate bridges spanned structural troughs; environmental control units and the vast recycling system had been integrated into the high-tech design of the buildings; EVE engineers—specialists in enhanced video emulation—were experimenting with sky and horizon effects; hydroponics had supplied trees and shrubs; and a monorail was under construction. The city planners had also worked out many of the problems that had plagued the city early on. Shelters and yellow and black safety areas were well marked in the event of modular transformation. Each resident now had a bed to sleep in, a job to perform. Food and water rationing was accepted as part of the routine. The system of waivers, ration coupons, and military scrip had proved manageable. Most people had navigated the psychological crossings successfully. There would soon be a television station, and a lottery was in the works. In general the city was not unlike a turn-of-the-century shopping mall, except in size and population. Remarkably, the residents of Macross had made the adjustment—they were a special lot from the start— and the general feeling there was a cross between that found in an experimental prototype community and that found in any of the wartime cities of the last era.

Nearing the market now, Rick began to focus his thoughts on Minmei and how the day as he imagined it would unfold. She would be knocked out by the sight of him in uniform; she wouldn't be able to keep her hands off him; he would suggest the park, and she would eagerly agree—

"Rick!"

Minmei was running toward him, a full shopping bag cradled in one arm, her free hand waving like mad. She was wearing a tight sleeveless sweater over a white blouse, and a skirt that revealed too much. Her hair was down, lustrous even in the city's artificial light; her blue eyes were bright, fixed on his as she kissed him once and stepped back to give him the once-over.

Inside the cool and crisp cadet Rick was projecting, his heart was running wild. She was already talking a blue streak, filling him in on her eight weeks, asking questions about "spacic training," complimenting him, the uniform, the Defense Force, and everyone else connected with the war effort. Rick, however, was so drawn to her beauty that he scarcely heard the news or compliments; he was suddenly quiet and worried. Minmei drew stares from everyone they passed, and she appeared to know half of Macross personally. What had she been doing these past eight weeks—introducing herself on street corners? And what was all this about singing lessons, dance lessons, and an upcoming beauty pageant? Rick wanted to tell her about the hardships of training, the new friends he'd made, his unvoiced fears; he wanted to hold her and tell her how much he had missed her, tell her how their two-week ordeal together had been one of the most precious times in his life. But she wasn't letting him get a word in.

A short distance down the block, Minmei stopped in midsentence and dragged Rick over to one of the storefronts. In the window was a salmon-colored belted dress that had suddenly become the most important thing in the world to her.

"Come on, Rick, just for a minute, okay?"

"Minmei," he resisted, "I'm not going to spend my leave shopping."

"I promise I'll only be a second."

"It always starts out that way and, and…"

Minmei already had her hand on the doorknob. "Just what else did you have in mind for today, Rick?"

She disappeared into the woman's shop, leaving him standing on the sidewalk, feeling somehow guilty for even *thinking* about going to the park.

By the time he entered, Minmei had the hangered dress draped over one arm and was going through the racks, pulling out belts, blouses, patterned stockings, skirts, sweaters, and lingerie. Rick checked his watch and calculated that he'd be AWOL long before she finished trying everything on. She had entered the dressing room and was throwing the curtain closed.

"And no peeking, Rick," she called out.

Fortunately, there were no other customers in the store at the time, but the saleswoman standing silently behind Rick had found Minmei's warning just about the funniest thing she had heard all week. Her squeal of delight took Rick completely by surprise. He thought an early-warning signal had just gone off—and in the middle of squatting down for cover, he managed to lose some of the items from the top of the shopping bag. In stooping over to recover these, he tipped the bag, spilling half the contents across the floor.

The woman was laughing like a maniac now, the door buzzer was signaling the entry of three additional shoppers, and Minmei was peeking over the top of the dressing room curtain asking what had happened. Rick, meanwhile, was down on his hands and knees crawling under tables in search of the goods—bottles of shampoo, crème rinse, body lotion, baby oil, lipsticks, and sundry makeup containers—all of which had become covered in some sort of slippery wash from a container of liquid face soap that had partially opened. Each time Rick grabbed hold of one of the items, it would jump from his hand like a wet fish. But he soon got the hang of it and had almost everything rebagged in a short time. Only one thing left to retrieve: a tube of tricolored toothpaste just out of reach, bathing in a puddle of the face soap. Rick gave it a shot, stretching out and making a grab for it. Sure enough, the tube propelled itself and ended up under another table.

It was time to get serious. Rick set the bag aside and crawled stealthily after his prey, as though the tube had taken on a will of its own and was on the verge of scurrying off, like some of Macross

City's robo-dispenser units. He squinted, held the tube in his gaze, and when he was near enough, pounced.

The tube seemed to scream in his hands and immediately worked itself into a vertical launch. But Rick had prepared himself for this; he lifted his head, eyes fixed on the tube's ascent. The one thing he hadn't taken into account was the height of the table. His head connected hard with the underside, the tube made its escape, and Rick collapsed back to the floor, rolling over onto his back and holding his head.

When he opened his eyes, he was staring up at a rain of brassieres and three pairs of silken female legs. The women owners of these were backing away from the table, high heels clicking against the floor, hands tugging at the hems of their skirts as though they'd just seen a rodent on the loose.

Rick pushed himself out and got to his feet, facing the three women from across the table. They were still backing away from the tabletop lingerie display with looks of indignation on their faces. Rick was stammering apologies to them as they exited the shop, the saleswoman was once again laughing hysterically, and Minmei was suddenly behind him, tapping him on the shoulder, soliciting his opinion of the dress she was trying on. He stood shell-shocked for a minute, laughter in one ear, Minmei's questions in the other, and left the store without a word.

Minmei remained inside for well over an hour. She had two additional shopping bags with her when she came out. Undaunted, Rick once again tried to suggest a walk in the park, but she had already made other plans for the two of them. Her surrogate family, who ran Macross City's most popular Chinese restaurant, the White Dragon, had been asking for Rick, and this would be a perfect time to visit—he looked so "gallant and dashing" in his uniform.

Rick could hardly refuse. Minmei's aunt and uncle were almost like family to him; in fact, he had lived with them above the restaurant before joining the Defense Forces.

They were an odd couple—Max, short and portly, and Lena, Minmei's tall and gracious inspiration. They had a son back on Earth, Lynn-Kyle, whom Lena missed and Max preferred not to think about, for reasons Rick hadn't learned. Although there was little else that either kept from him. As Rick entered the restaurant they pretended surprise, but within minutes they had his favorite meal spread out before him. While wolfing down the stir-fried shrimp, he regaled them with the barracks stories he had been saving for Minmei. They wanted to know all about the Veritech fighters—how they handled in deep space, how they were able to switch from Fighter to Guardian or Battloid mode. And they asked about the war: Had Gloval managed to contact Earth headquarters? Did his commanders believe that the enemy would continue their attacks? Was Rick worried about his first mission? How long would it be before the SDF-1 returned to Earth?

Rick did his best to answer them, sidestepping issues he was not permitted to discuss and at other times exaggerating his importance to the Defense Forces. It concerned him that the residents of Macross City were not being given the same reports issued to the Veritech squadrons. After all, Macross was as much a part of the ship and the war as the rest of those onboard.

He was about to allay their fears for his safety by telling them that a combat assignment was far off, when he saw Roy Fokker enter the restaurant. The lieutenant's six-six frame looked gargantuan in the low-ceilinged room, but there was something about Roy's unruly blond hair and innocent grin that put people at ease immediately. He greeted everyone individually, made a show of kissing Minmei's hand, and took a seat next to Rick, snatching up the last of the shrimp as he did so.

"Figured I'd find you here," Roy said with his mouth full. "Gotta get you back to the base on the double, Little Brother."

"Why, what's up?" Rick asked.

"We're on alert."

Rick was suddenly concerned. "Yeah, but what's that have to do with me?"

Roy licked his fingers. "Guess who's been assigned to my squadron?"

Rick was speechless.

Aunt Lena and Uncle Max stood together, worried looks behind the faint smiles. Minmei, however, was ecstatic.

"Oh, Rick, that's wonderful!"

Like he'd just been awarded a prize.

Roy stood up and smiled. "Up and at 'em, partner."

Rick tried valiantly to return a smile that wasn't there.

The war had caught up with him again.

02

From the start it was inevitable that a cult should develop around the Veritech fighters. Like the World War I aces, jet fighter jocks, astronauts, and computer linguists before them, the men who were chosen to interact with the first by-product of Robotechnology considered themselves to be at the cutting edge of human progress. And in a sense they were. For who before them had interfaced with machines on such an intimate level? It was only fitting that they should form their own club and speak their own language—call themselves "mechamorphs." They were continually borrowing and applying mystic phrases from their Zen masters—those actually responsible for teaching the pilots the essentials of meditative technique... You'd be walking around Macross in those days and hear phrases like "dropping trou" and "standing upright" being tossed about—referring to reconfiguration to Guardian mode and Battloid mode, respectively. Pilots would talk to you about your "thinking caps," the sensor-studded helmets worn, or about the thrill of "haloing" (fixing an enemy on target in the mind's eye) or "alpha bets" (gambling with yourself that you were deep enough in trance for the mecha to understand you) or "facing mecha" (going into battle) or "azending"...

Zachary Foxx, Jr., VT: *The Men and the Mecha*

GLOVAL MET FREQUENTLY WITH DR. LANG DURING THE Development phase of what was being called the pinpoint barrier system. The lambent energy that once filled the spacefold generators' chamber had been harnessed and redirected. Such was the nature of this antielectron energy, however, that a photon shield for the entire fortress would have further destabilized an already weakened gravity control system. The best that Lang and his Robotechnicians had been able to come up with was a cluster of movable barriers capable of deflecting incoming bolts. An area aft of the ship's bridge had been retrofitted with three manually operated universal gyros, each tied to one of the cluster's photon discs.

With the barrier system now operational, Captain Gloval was confident that his "Blitzkrieg" attack plan would prove viable. The strategy was simple enough: When the SDF-1 was in close proximity to Saturn's rings, electronic countermeasures would be activated to jam the enemy's radar scanners. The fortress would hide within the rings to take full advantage of their intrinsic radio "noise," while at the same time, squadrons of Veritech fighters would be deployed in a simulated attack mission to act as decoys. When the enemy moved in to engage the VTs, the SDF-1's main gun would take them out. Orbital dynamics would make the timing critical: If the fortress reentered orbit too early, it would be catapulted back toward the outer planets; too late, and the launch window to Mars and the inner planets would be closed.

The VT fighter pilots would receive most of this information at the scheduled briefing, and it was to this briefing that Rick and Roy were headed after they left the restaurant.

Roy had been doing his best to cheer up the newly graduated cadet. Rick was one of five cadets chosen; it was really an honor, an endorsement of his flying skills. He would be able to move out of the dormitory barracks into his own room. There would be more free time, special privileges.

They were walking along the tall chain-link fence that surrounded the barracks compound now. Fifty-foot-tall Battloid sentries patrolled the perimeter, their gatlings shouldered like proper soldiers. Defense Force personnel were moving quickly in response to new orders which had been delivered to each unit.

But Rick's morale was low; his hands were in his pockets, and his shoulders drooped. Roy, however, succeeded in bringing him around with a sharp, "Ten-shun!"

Rick responded expertly to his conditioning: His head came up, he squared his shoulders, brought his back straight, hand at his forehead. His eyes searched for a superior's uniform, but the only people in his field of vision were four young women in civilian dress. The oldest among them, not more than twenty-three or twenty-four herself, was the one who returned his salute. She had thick brown hair coiled at her shoulders, small, attractive features, and an athletic body even her conservative outfit couldn't conceal. There was an air of cool command about her.

The other three were suddenly laughing and pointing at him; the tall, dark-haired one—Kim, Rick understood—was whispering something to the one with glasses—Vanessa. Rick was resisting an urge to check his fly buttons, when the short blonde among them yelled, "Mr. Lingerie!"

He decided to risk a full look and recognized three of the women from this morning's incident in the dress shop. One of them was saying, "Hold your skirts down, ladies," and Roy was elbowing him in the ribs.

"What gives, Little Brother?"

"Don't ask," Rick said out of the corner of his mouth.

The oldest had stepped forward; she gave Rick a look and turned to Roy.

"Commander Fokker, don't tell me this is the brilliant new pilot you were raving about?"

"One and the same. Corporal Rick Hunter, this is the Flight Officer Lisa Hayes. You'll be hearing a lot from her from now on."

Rick saluted again. The women were still needling him with comments.

"Rick Hunter…" Lisa Hayes was repeating. "Why does that name sound familiar? Have we met—uh, before this morning, I mean?"

"No, sir, I don't think so, sir."

Lisa tapped her lower lip with her forefinger. She knew that name from somewhere… and all at once she had it: Hunter was the civilian pilot who had shown up at Macross on Launching Day. The same one who had made unauthorized use of a Veritech, the same one who had rescued that Chinese girl, the same one who had called her—

"You're that loudmouthed pilot, aren't you?"

Rick stared at her. Yes, unbelievable as it was, she was the one he had seen on the Veritech commo screen months ago.

"Then you must be—"

"Go ahead, Corporal Hunter, say it: I must be…"

"Y-you must be… my superior officer, sir!"

Lisa smirked and nodded her head knowingly. She motioned to her group, and they started off down the sidewalk. But Lisa turned to Rick as she passed him and added, "By the way, I don't know what your particular problem is, but it's hardly appropriate behavior for a VT pilot to be hanging around lingerie shops looking for a cheap thrill."

Rick groaned. Roy scratched his head. The blonde said: "Creep."

Later, at the briefing, Rick was still replaying the incident; but in light of what was being said, embarrassment placed last on his list of concerns. A decoy mission—the VTs were actually going to pretend to launch a counter-offensive against the aliens! Judging by the murmurs in the crowd, Rick was not the only pilot to be floored by this directive. But like it or not, they had their orders.

"I want you to be thinking of one thing and one thing only," the general was saying. "Robotech! And I want you to know that we're all counting on you."

If the general had let it go at that, Rick would have been all right—afraid but not desperate. The general, however, had then added: "If there's anyone you want to see, you'd better do it tonight."

Rick was in a panic. What did he mean by that-that they were being sent out on some kind of suicide mission? And *do* what tonight—say good-bye, say wish me well, say please remember me always?

He stood on line to use the phone and managed to reach Minmei's aunt Lena. Minmei was at ballet school, but yes, Lena would relay Rick's message: Macross Central Park, their bench at nine P.M.

Rick rode back into the city with a few of the other pilots. He kicked around the market area for a while and was in the park by eight o'clock keeping their bench warm. Starlight poured in from the huge bay in the hull; lovers held one another; life went on as though filled with limitless tomorrows. But Rick couldn't see past the mission, and he was frightened.

By ten o'clock she still hadn't showed; the park was quiet, and he was about to move on. But just then she came running in, face flushed and out of breath.

"Rick, I'm sorry I'm so late."

He smiled at her. "At least you made it."

She pushed her bangs back. Her forehead was beaded with sweat. "What's the big emergency, anyway?"

"They're sending us out on a mission tomorrow."

He didn't need to add any dramatic accents to it; the words just fell out that way. But her reaction was unexpected. She was practically clapping for him.

"Oh, Rick, that's great! Really, I'm so happy for you!"

And for a moment her enthusiasm almost won him over. *Hey,* Rick told himself, *maybe this is how I'm supposed to feel, like I'm lucky or something.* The park fountain was even gushing in his honor! It didn't last, though, despite her continued exclamations.

"Your first mission! I can't believe it! I'm so proud of you!"

Obviously this was what supporting the war effort was all about, he decided. And she was very good at it.

Then Minmei was suddenly on her toes, twirling around in front of him. "Do you like it? Don't you just love it?" she kept asking. He was puzzled but caught on fast. The dress! The salmon-colored dress she'd picked up that afternoon.

"You look beautiful, Minmei."

She moved in close and made him repeat it.

"Do you mean it, Rick? Am I really beautiful?"

An idea came to him and he signaled to a robo-camera that was making rounds through the park. The stupid thing kept moving in circles, trying to home in on Rick's call, and he finally had to throw a stone at it to get its attention. The cam approached them, asking for money.

"We'll have a picture taken. You'll see how beautiful you are."

Minmei protested some, and the cam uttered some stock phrases to get them in the proper mood, but eventually they had the print and Minmei was pleased. A smile and a look of concern; Minmei clinging to his arm; the fountain behind them.

Afterward, she talked dance for half an hour; she read him the lyrics of a song she'd composed. Then she had to be going.

"Uncle Max gets mad when I stay out too late. But I'll see you when you get back, Rick. Have a good mission, and remember, I'm very proud of you."

And with that she was gone, leaving him wondering about tomorrow all over again.

He power-walked and jogged for an hour hoping he would exhaust himself and fall into a deep sleep back in the barracks. But sleep didn't seem to be on tonight's agenda; in fact, he couldn't even keep his eyes closed. It was too hot in his bunk, then too cold, there were too many noises in the room, the pillow just wasn't right... Finally he sat up and switched on the reading light. He took the park photo and brought it close to his face. Perhaps he could reach her by concentrating on her image; spoken words weren't doing much good.

Minmei was proud of him; earlier that day she'd been upset with him for carrying her shopping bag because the package hid too much of the uniform. Besides, it was wrong for a Veritech fighter pilot to involve himself in such mundane activities. Well, that much was encouraging to Rick because she had really been his motivation for joining up. During the weeks that followed their shared ordeal in that remote part of the ship, he realized that Minmei could never accept an ordinary man as her lover; he would have to be someone who participated in life to the fullest. Someone romantic, adventurous, full of grand dreams and positive hopes for the future—an all-day-long hero who would never fear, never say die. *A special man, a dearest man, someone to share his life with you alone,* as Minmei had herself written it... She was like someone who had gone from childhood to maturity without any of the intervening periods of longing or confusion. And even though Rick had saved her life on two occasions and spent two long lost weeks with her, he had yet to prove himself in her eyes. Without joining up there would have been no way for him to display the heroics she craved, no way to individualize himself, no way to accept himself as her equal.

And yet, even having taken those steps, he felt no closer to her than before. Her love had no fixed center; it was spread across the board and parceled out in equal packets for one and all to enjoy. A hero wouldn't even be enough for her because she belonged to everyone. She was more spirit than woman, more dream than reality.

Rick slipped into fitful sleep for a short while, only to have Roy wake him out of it. Fokker was just checking in, reminding him that they had to be up early tomorrow.

"Your first combat mission is always the worst, kid. I sympathize with you. Now, get some sleep—count fanjets or something."

Everyone had such encouraging words: At the briefing they'd been told to wrap up their personal business, and now Roy tells him that tomorrow is going to be *the worst*. Minmei had behaved like a cheerleader, his commanding officer thought him a lecher… It had been quite a day.

So Rick actually took Roy's suggestion—he began counting fanjets—although it wasn't sleep he found in the high numbers but an uncomfortable half state where Commander Hayes and the three bridge bunnies mocked him, and the giant enemy soldier he had confronted on Macross Island was reborn to stalk him.

The reveille call came too quickly. Rick felt like one of the walking dead as he gathered up his gear and zombied his way through morning rituals with the other VT pilots. There was a second preflight briefing, more detailed than the first. Then the men were loaded into personnel carriers and conveyed to the *Prometheus*. Roy and Rick's group drove through Macross City, past the park where he and Minmei had been together only hours before. The city was asleep, peacefully, blessedly unaware.

Even before the transport vehicle had come to a halt in the hangar of the supercarrier, pilots were hopping out and rushing toward their propped Veritechs. The Thor-class *Prometheus*—one of two ships that had been caught up in the spacefold and had since been grafted on to the main body of the SDF-1 was like an active hive, and every drone aboard save Rick seemed certain of his or her duty. He lost Roy in the crowds and stood by the transport scanning for a familiar face among those now rushing by him. He recognized Commander Hayes's voice coming through the PA system.

...

"All Veritechs report for roll call at *Prometheus*... All Veritechs report immediately for roll call at *Prometheus*... Orange, Blue, and Red squadrons will commence flight preparations on second-level afterdeck... All remaining squadrons prepare for takeoff from preassigned locations... Reactor control, bridge requests status report on first and third plasma shields..."

Suddenly Fokker had him by the arm and was propelling him through the hangar, filling his ears with last-minute instructions and words of advice. He gave Rick a quick embrace when they were alongside Skull Team's twenty-three and was soon swallowed up in the crowds again.

Rick was assisted into the pilot's crane sling by two techs, who also issued him boots, gloves, and a "thinking cap"—a sensor-studded helmet that was in some ways an outgrowth of the Global Civil War "virtual cockpits" and essential for rapport with the mecha. Rick regarded the plane as he was being lowered into the cockpit module. In Fighter mode, the mecha was similar in appearance to the supersonic jets of the late twentieth century. But in actuality, the Veritechs were as different from those as cars were to horse-drawn wagons. The aliens who had engineered the super dimensional fortress had found a way to *animate* technological creations, and working from examples found onboard the SDF-1, Dr. Lang and his Robotechnicians had been able to fabricate the Veritechs in much the same way—"chips off the old block," as the scientist called the VTs.

Once inside the cockpit, Rick strapped in and donned the helmet; from this point on he was mind-linked to the fighter. There were still plenty of manual tasks to perform, but the central defense capabilities that set the planes apart from their predecessors were directly tied in to the pilots' mecha-will.

The Veritech was fired up now, reflex engines humming, and cat officers were motioning Rick forward. He adjusted the helmet and seat straps and goosed the throttle to position the fighter onto one of the carrier elevators. A second Skull Team VT joined him there.

As the two crafts were lifted to the flight deck, Rick could see the disc of the sun far off to his left. At the end of the hurricane bow was Saturn, impossibly huge. Commander Hayes was once again on the PA and tac net.

"This operation will be directed toward the Cassini Quadrant. All squadrons will wait in the ice fields of the rings for further instructions."

The ice fields of Saturn's rings, Rick repeated to himself.

And he had thought *yesterday* was bad.

03

The so-called Daedalus Maneuver was the first demonstration of what I have termed "mecha-consciousness"—levels beyond the somewhat primitive, almost instinctual modular transformation. The officers of the bridge, along with the engineering section, did little more than offer a prompt to the SDF-1: The dynamics of the maneuver were carried out by the fortress herself, despite claims to the contrary. I, alone, recognized this for what it was—an attempt on the part of the ship to interface with the living units she carried within her... Later I would overhear someone in the corridor say that "the Daedalus Maneuver (would) go down in the annals of space warfare as a lucky break for an incompetent crew." In point of fact, however, the SDF-1 was able to repeat this "accident" on four separate occasions.

Dr. Emil Lang, Technical Recordings and Notes

"IT IS AS YOU PREDICTED, COMMANDER," EXEDORE SAID AS he entered the flagship's command center.

Without a word, Breetai rose from his seat; a wave of his hand and the projecbeam field began to assemble itself. Here was Zor's ship, still in that bizarre configuration, a speck of gleaming metals caught in starlight and silhouetted against the milky white bands and icy rings of the system's sixth planet. Breetai called for full magnification.

"The Micronians have activated electronic counter-measures and are about to enter the rings," Exedore continued. "They are endangering the ship."

"We cannot permit that."

"I have taken the liberty of contacting Commander Zeril."

"Excellent."

A second wave brought Zeril to the screen. He offered a salute.

"My Lord Breetai, we await your instructions."

"The Micronians are laying a trap for us, Commander Zeril. It would suit me to humor them a bit, but I'm concerned about the security of the dimensional fortress. As your scanners will indicate, the enemy has deployed several squadrons of mecha in the hope of luring you to your doom. Send out enough Battlepods to deal with them.

"The Micronian commander will bring his ship from the rings when you are within range of the main gun. I expect you to cripple the fortress before the gun is armed."

"Sir!" said Zeril.

"You understand that the ship is to be disabled, not destroyed. As we speak, relevant data concerning the ship's vulnerable points is being transmitted to your inboard targeting computers. Success, Commander."

"May you win all your battles, sir!"

Zeril's face faded from the field, replaced now by a wide-angle view of the SDF-1 at the perimeter of the ring system. Breetai and his adviser turned their attention to a second monitor where radar scanners depicted the exiting mecha as flashing color-enhanced motes.

"Attacking with such a weak force is completely illogical," Exedore commented. "They seem to have little knowledge of space warfare."

"They have been a planetbound race for too long, Exedore. Caught up in their own petty squabbles with one another."

"Absolutely and totally illogical."

Breetai moved in close to the scanner screen, as if there were some secret message that could be discerned in those flashing lights.

"I don't believe they realize that we are holding back nearly all our forces... But this is an excellent opportunity for us to demonstrate just what they're up against."

No sooner had Rick Hunter executed a full roll to avoid colliding with a chunk of ring ice than Commander Lisa Hayes opened the net, her angry face on the comma screen lighting up the Veritech cockpit.

"Skull twenty-three! What in blazes are you doing? Just where were you at the briefing—asleep? I'm getting sick and tired of repeating myself: That kind of stunt flying will give away your position to the enemy! This isn't the time or place for aerobatics, do you copy?!"

"It was just a roll," Rick said in defense of his actions. "I'm not the only one—"

"That'll be enough, Corporal. Follow Skull Leader's instructions, do you copy?"

"All right," he answered sullenly. "I gotcha."

But Hayes wasn't finished, not by a long shot.

"Is that the way you address superiors, Hunter? Look around you, bright boy. Everyone else here flies by the rules."

"Roger, roger, Commander, I copy."

"And get your RAS back where it belongs—why are you dropping behind?"

"Hey, you're not flying around up here—" He caught himself and made a new start. "Uh, Skull twenty-three increasing relative airspeed, Commander."

Hayes signed off, and Rick breathed a sigh of relief. This was going to be even more difficult than he had imagined. His first mission, and already he was being razzed by some know-it-all bridge bunny. Just his luck! What did she think, it was easy out here? *Oh, to be back in the* Mockingbird, Rick thought.

They were flying blind in Saturn's shadow, far from the surface of the rapidly spinning planet and deep in the ice fields of its outermost rings. Rick's eyes were glued to the cockpit screen and displays, and yet even with all this sophisticated instrumentation he had already had several close calls with debris too insignificant to register on the short-range scanners but large enough to inflict damage. He knew that the rest of Skull Team was out there somewhere, but visual contact would have been reassuring right about now—a glimpse of thruster fire, a glint of sunlight on a wingtip, anything at all. Soon enough there would be an added element of danger—the arrival of the enemy Battlepods.

Just then, Roy Fokker appeared on the port commo screen.

"Get ready, fellas, here they come."

There's no more flying for fun.

...

Claudia Grant, the black Flight Officer on the SDF-1's bridge, was monitoring Lisa Hayes's conversation with the young VT pilot when radar informed her of the enemy's counterattack.

Claudia and Lisa had adjacent stations along the curved forward hull of the bridge, beneath the main wraparound bays which now afforded views of the rocks and ice chunks that made up Saturn's rings. Each woman had two overhead monitors and a console screen at her disposal. Elevated behind Lisa's post was the command chair, and behind the captain along the rear bulkheads on either side of the hatch sat Sammie and Kim, each duty station equipped with nine individual screens that formed a grand square. Vanessa was off to starboard, positioned in front of the ten-foot-high threat board.

Claudia's station was linked to those of the three junior officers by radio, but such was her proximity to Lisa's that scarcely a word the commander uttered escaped her hearing. Not that there would have been anything left unshared between them in any case. They had forged a close friendship; Claudia, four years Lisa's senior, often playing the role of older sister, especially in matters of the heart. But for all of her desirable traits, her natural attractiveness and keen intelligence, Lisa was emotionally inexperienced. She projected an image of cool and capable efficiency, rationalizing her detached stance in the name of "commitment to duty." But buried in her past was an emotional wound that had not yet healed. Claudia knew this much, and she hoped to help Lisa exorcise that demon some day. This new VT pilot, Hunter, had touched something deep inside Lisa by calling her just as he had seen her— "that old sourpuss"—and Claudia wanted to press her friend for details. But this was hardly the time or the place.

"Enemy Battlepods now engaging our Veritechs in the Cassini Quadrant, Captain," Claudia relayed.

"Enemy destroyer approaching the target zone," Vanessa added. Gloval rubbed his hands together and rose from his chair. "Excellent. If we can get a visual on the destroyer, I want it on the forward screen. Let's see what these ships look like."

Sammie punched it up, and soon the entire bridge crew was

staring at the enemy vessel. It was surely as large as if not larger than the SDF-1, perhaps two and a half kilometers in length, but in no other way similar to it. Broad and somewhat flat, the warship had a vaguely organic look, enhanced by the dark green color of its dorsal armored shells and the light gray of its seemingly more vulnerable underbelly. Oddly enough, it also appeared to be quilled; but there was good reason to suspect that many of those spines were weapons.

"Not a pretty sight, is she?" said Gloval.

"Sir," said Vanessa, "the destroyer is within range."

"All right. Bring the ship around to the predesignated coordinates. Make certain there are no fluctuations in the barrier system readings and prepare to fire the main gun on my command."

Claudia tapped in the coordinates. She could feel the huge reflex-powered thrusters kick in to propel the ship away from Saturn's gravitational grasp. The pinpoint barrier system checked out, and the main gun was charging.

Free of the rings now, the SDF-1 was repositioning itself. The twin main gun towers were leveling out from the shoulders of the ship, taking aim at a target hundreds of kilometers away.

Main gun locked on target, sir."

Gloval's fist slammed into his open hand. "Fire!"

Claudia pushed down a series of crossbar switches, threw open a red safety cover, and pressed home the firing device.

Illumination on the bridge failed momentarily. The gun did not fire.

Again Claudia tapped in a series of commands; there was no response.

"Quickly!" Gloval shouted. "Get me Lang."

"On the line," Kim said.

Lang's thickly accented voice resounded through the bridge comlink speakers.

"Captain, the pin-point barrier is apparently interfering with the main gun energy transformers. We're doing a vibrational analysis now, but I don't think we'll have use of the gun unless we scrap the shield power."

"*Bozhe moy!*" said Gloval in his best Russian.

Sammie swiveled from her console to face the captain, "Sir—particle-beam trackers are locked on our ship. The enemy is preparing to fire!"

Eight weeks of special training had failed to prepare him for the silent insanity of space warfare. Disintegration and silent death, the pinpoints of distant light that were laser beams locked on to his ship, the stormy marriage of antiparticles, the grotesque beauty of short-lived spherical explosions—bolts of launched lightning, blue and white, igniting the proper combination of gases...

Rick Hunter fired the VT's thrusters as two Battlepods closed in on him from above—the relative "above" at any rate, for there was no actual up or down out here, no real way to gauge acceleration except by the constant force that kept him pinned to the back of his seat, or pushed him forward when the retros were kicked in, no way to judge velocity except in relation to other Veritech fighters or the SDF-1 herself. Just that unvarying starfield, those cool and remote fires that were the backdrop of war.

It was said that the best VT pilots were those who simply allowed themselves to forget: about yesterday, today, or tomorrow. *"Nothing extraneous, in mind or body."* Warfare in deep space was a silent Zen video game where victory was not the immediate goal; success to any degree depended on a clear mind, free of expectations, and a body conditioned for thoughtless reaction. Stop to think about where to place your shot, how to move or mode your mecha, and you were space debris. Fight the fear and you'd soon be sucking vacuum. Rather, you had to embrace the terror, pull it down into your guts and let it free your spirit. It was like forcing yourself through the climax of a nightmare, confronting there all the worst things that could happen, then piercing through the envelope into undreamed-of worlds. And the dreamstate was the key, because you had to believe you had complete control of each detail, every element. The silence of space was the perfect medium for this manipulated madness. Out here, content was more important than form; wings were superfluous, banking and breaks unnecessary, thoughts dangerous.

Rick knew when he was trying too hard: He would feel the alpha vibe abandon him and the mecha follow suit. *You are the mecha, the mecha is you.* Left empty, the fear would rush in to fill him up, like air rushing into a vacuum, and the fear would trigger a further retreat from the vibe. It was a vicious circle. But he was beginning to recognize the early stages of it, the waverings and oscillations, and that in itself represented an all-important first step.

He stayed at Fokker's wing, learning from him. The pods were not as maneuverable as the Veritechs and nowhere near as complex. They also had far more vulnerable points. It was just that there were so damned many of them. One Battlepod, one enemy pilot. How strong was their number? How long could they keep this up?

Rick came to Roy's aid whenever he could, using heat-seekers and gatling, saving the undercarriage lasers for close-in fighting.

The assault group had fought its way out of the rings and shadow zone, but not without devastating losses to the Red and Green teams. And the SDF-1 had still not fired the main gun. It was difficult to tell just what was going on back at the fortress. Rick could see that it was taking heavy fire from the enemy destroyer, a bizarre-looking ship if ever he'd seen one: a cross between a manta ray and a mutant cucumber. But for some reason the enemy was using rather conventional ordnance, easily thwarted by the fortress's movable shields. It would only be a matter of time before the destroyer upped the ante.

Rick guessed Command's new orders for Skull Team long before Roy appeared on the screen with them: The VTs were to attack the destroyer.

Fokker led them in, searching for soft spots in the forest-green hull. Battlepods continued to exit the ship through semicircular topside portals, so the Skull Leader directed the attack along the underside of the destroyer, using everything his fighter was prepared to deliver.

Rick had completed one pass, discharging half his remaining Stilettos. He was preparing for a second run now, coming in across the nose of the destroyer this time, zeroing in on two massive cannons set close to the central ridge. Suddenly a Battlepod streaked in front of him with a VT in close pursuit; the mecha let loose a flock of heat-seekers which caught up with the pod directly over Rick's fighter. He dropped the VT into a nose dive, expecting concussion where there was none, then executed two rollovers but still couldn't manage to pull the mecha out of its collision course with the destroyer. Desperately, he reached out for the mode levers and reconfigured to Guardian. This would at least enable him to extend the "legs" of the mecha and utilize the foot thrusters to brake his speed. But the angle of his approach was too critical. With the nose beginning to dip and the energized foot thrusters threatening to throw him into a roll, Rick again switched modes, this time to Battloid configuration. Regardless, he was committed to completing the front flip, and the Battloid came down with a silent crash, face first on the armored hull.

As on the SDF-1's shell, there was artificial gravity here, but Rick had no time to be impressed: two Battlepods were on him, coming in fast now for strafing runs. He thought the mecha to a kneeling position and brought the gatling cannon out front. Blue bolts from the pods were striking the hull around him, fusing metals and blowing slag into the void. It didn't seem to bother the enemy pilots any that they were firing on their own ship; they were intent on finishing him off, homing in now, bipedal legs dangling and plastron cannons firing like spheroid kamikazes.

Rick was backing away from blue lightning, returning continuous fire. The big gun was dangerously close to overheating in the Battloid's hands.

Then, suddenly, the hull seemed to give way under him. Instantly Rick realized that he had stumbled the Battloid through one of the topside semicircular ports.

The mecha landed on its butt, twenty-five meters below the action on the floor of a loading bay. Rick worked the foot pedals frantically, raising the Battloid to its feet in time to see the overhead hatch close—a shot from one of the pods had probably activated the external control circuitry. There was a second hatch in the bay which undoubtedly led to the innards of the destroyer.

Rick began to approach this second hatch cautiously, studying the air lock entry controls and feeling strangely secure in the sealed chamber. Just then the air lock door slid open. On the other side of the threshold stood an enemy soldier who had apparently heard Rick's fall to the floor. He was easily as tall as the Battloid and massively built; but although he was armored, his head was bare and he was weaponless.

The alien goliath and the small human in the cockpit of the mecha had taken each other by surprise. As dissimilar as these potential combatants were, their frightened reactions were the same. The defenseless soldier's eyes darted left and right, desperately seeking an escape route as Rick's did the same. The alien warrior then stepped back, body language betraying his thoughts.

It was all that was needed to break the stalemate: Rick raised the muzzle of the Battloid's gatling, metal-shod fingers poised on the trigger.

The enemy destroyer was bearing down on the SDF-1, peppering her with hundreds of missiles. Radar scanners located throughout the body of the fortress relayed course headings of the incoming projectiles to inboard computers, which in turn translated the data into colored graphics. These displays were flashed to monitors in the barrier control room, where three young female techs worked feverishly to bring photon disc cover to projected impact points, the spherical gyros of the pin-point barrier system spinning wildly under the palms of their hands.

On the bridge Captain Gloval feared the worst. The main gun was still inoperable, and despite the effectiveness of the shields, the ship was sustaining damage on all sides. Skull Team was counterattacking the destroyer, but it was unlikely they'd be able to inflict enough damage to incapacitate it. Was there ever in Earth's history a commander who had more than 50,000 civilian lives at stake in one battle? For all these long months Gloval had never once contemplated surrender. Now, however, he found that possibility edging into his thoughts, draining him of strength and will.

As if reading Gloval's thoughts, Lisa suddenly came up with an inspired plan. But first she needed to know if it was possible to concentrate and direct the pin-point barrier energy to the front of the *Daedalu*—the super-carrier that formed the right arm of the SDF-1.

Gloval immediately contacted Dr. Lang, and the reply came swiftly: Yes, it could be done.

Gloval ordered him to begin the energy transfer at once and quickly set in motion phase two of the plan. This required that all available Destroids, Spartans, and Gladiators—the "ground" support weapons mecha—be gathered together at the bow of the *Daedalus*. The final phase would be handled by the Captain himself; he reassumed the command chair, his strength and confidence renewed.

"Ramming speed," he ordered. "We're going to push the *Daedalus* right down their throat!"

Members of the Skull Team who took part in Operation Blitzkrieg would later report on the spectacle they witnessed that day in Saturn space. How the SDF-1, gleaming blue, red, and white, engulfed in explosions and locked on a collision course with the enemy, had executed a backward body twist, followed by a full-forward thrust of its right arm that brought the bow of the *Daedalus* like a battering ram squarely into the forward section of the destroyer.

One can not imagine the scene from Commander Zeril's point of view: the impact; the sight of the front of his ship being splintered apart, cables and conduits rupturing as the destroyer impaled itself on the arm of the fortress; stressed metal groaning and giving way, cross-ties and girders ripped from their lodgings; the mad rush of precious air being sucked from the ship.

Perhaps Zeril and his second were alive long enough to see the forward ramp of the *Daedalus* drop open, revealing row after row of deadly Destroids, thick with guns, missile tubes, and cannons. Perhaps the two Zentraedi even saw the initial launch of the five thousand projectiles fired into the heart of the destroyer, the first series of explosions against the hull and bulkheads of the bridge.

Rick couldn't bring himself to waste the enemy soldier. His mind and trigger finger were paralyzed, not out of fear but forgiveness. This was no Battlepod he was face to face with in the air lock but a living, breathing creature, caught up just as Rick in the madness of war. *Remember what they did to us at Macross Island,* Roy had drilled into him. *Remember! Remember!* …humankind's war cry for how many millennia now? And when would it end—with this war? the next? the one after that?

Suddenly the soldier turned his head sharply to the right, as though he had heard something unreported by the Battloid's sensors. Rick saw the soldier's face drain of color, his eyes go wide with even greater fear.

In the next instant a conflagration swept through the corridor. The soldier was vaporized before Rick's eyes, and the Battloid was thrown back into the loading bay by the explosive force of the firestorm. The air lock was sealed, but the chamber walls were already beginning to melt.

Rick brought the Battloid's top-mounted lasers into action to melt through the overhead latch controls, and soon enough the semicircular hatch slid open. Foot thrusters blazing, the mecha rose from the floor and clambered out onto the destroyer's outer skin.

The ship was convulsing beneath Rick, disgorging a death rattle roar from its holds. Forward, he could see the SDF-1 propelling itself away from the crippled enemy, its pectoral boosters blow-torching and its *Daedalus* right arm flayed of metal and superstructure.

Rick returned the mecha to Guardian for his takeoff, then well into the launch he reconfigured to Fighter mode, kicking in the afterburners to carry him away from the destroyer.

A series of enormous blisters was forming along the outer shell of the ship as explosive fire launched by the Destroids was funneled front to stern. But the hull could contain it for only so long; the pustules began to burst, loosing coronas and prominences of radiant energy into the void. A violent interior explosion then blasted the destroyer's skin from its framework. At last there was nothing left but a self-consuming glowing cloud, a war of gases bent on mutual annihilation. The energy flourished wildly and dispersed, leaving in the end no trace of itself nor its brief struggle.

04

Several historians of the Robotech Wars—Rawlins, Daily, Gordon, and Turno, to name but a few—have advanced the claim that it was Breetai's decision [to call up Khyron's troops as reinforcements] that placed the Zentraedi squarely on the road to defeat. Rawlins, in his two-volume study, *Zentraedi Triumvirate: Dolza, Breetai, Khyron*, states: "It was more than a tactical blunder... Khyron's use of the dried leaves of the Invid Flower of Life had drastically affected his Zentraedi conditioning. Subsequent research clearly demonstrated that alkaloids present in the leaves had a direct effect on the limbic system of the brain. The Flower had the power to stimulate a resurgence of archaic patterns of behavior. In the case of the Zentraedi, ironically enough, those behavior patterns were the ones which most clearly defined the human condition... So in this sense it may be said that Khyron was the most human of them all."

History of the First Robotech War, Vol. XXXIV

BREETAI WAS NOW BEGINNING TO ENJOY THIS MICRONIAN battle game.

"'Cat and mouse' did you call it?"

"Yes, my lord. Apparently it refers to a game the stronger animal plays with the weaker before the final kill."

"Excellent. You must teach me their language, Exedore."

"Of course, sir. It is most primitive, easy to absorb. Our three operatives from surveillance are making rapid progress."

"Yes... I may want to talk to these Micronians soon."

The flagship and several of the fleet's scout and recon ships had made a hyperspace jump along the projected course of the SDF-1.

Breetai had left behind several cruisers and destroyers, along with plenty of Battlepods, to keep the Micronians busy while he plotted his next move in the game.

The Zentraedi commander smiled wryly as he viewed the trans-vids of Zeril's destruction. Enhanced-motion playback had captured the giant ship's final few moments splendidly. He had to credit the Micronians for the unorthodox nature of their counter-attack. Instead of further depleting their power by firing the main gun, they had used one of their oceangoing vessels to ram Zeril's destroyer headlong. Once inside, a sufficient amount of firepower must have been unleashed to destroy it. The ship blistered, glowed, became a veritable tunnel of trapped photon energy, and exploded.

Yes, Breetai was amused by the challenge of illogical behavior; it forced him to step outside his own conditioning and search for novel approaches to destruction.

His thoughts were now interrupted by a communiqué from astrogation. Exedore relayed the message.

"Sir, emerging from hyperspace-fold."

The composite projecbeam disassembled itself. Exedore called for an exterior view of local space. Cameras panned across the unbroken blackness and locked on a small red planet, arid and angry-looking. For Breetai it brought to mind memories of Fantoma, and the mining worlds he had worked and patrolled long ago. A schematic appeared on one of the side screens of the command bowl showing the planetary system of this yellow star the Micronians referred to as their "sun."

"Mars," said Exedore, "the fourth planet."

Breetai turned to his adviser.

"Has the recon vessel been deployed?"

"As you ordered, sir. The Cyclops transmissions are coming in now."

The projecbeam revealed an abandoned Micronian base that showed signs of an earlier battle: craters from explosions covered with the fine red swirling dust of the planet's deserts, a shuttlecraft disabled and still in its launch bay, the shells of buildings and fractured domes.

"Our scanners reveal no life readings, no energy levels of any

form save minimal low-level background radiation, Commander."
Breetai put his massive hand to his head and unconsciously
stroked the metal plate there. The plate concealed scar tissue that
had overgrown the wounds received while protecting Zor from
the Invid; now, it seemed, each time he came close to fulfilling his
imperative—to capture the fortress—the original pain returned.

"It would appear that the Earth people abandoned this installation."

Exedore studied the data screen. "Long-range surface scanners
indicate that a military conflict took place here at a neighboring
installation. Nevertheless, the Micronians' reflex power furnaces
are still operative, and we've managed to tap into their computer
banks and access some of the information. It seems that most of
the inhabitants, sir, were destroyed in a battle with their allied
forces, and the few that survived were unable to escape the
harshness of the planet itself."

Breetai continued to stroke his faceplate. "Hmmm... see to
it that one of the computers is activated and the contents of its
memory transmitted on a hailing frequency."

One of Exedore's eyebrow's arched. "Certainly, my lord, but why?"

"Because this abandoned post will make a perfect trap. I have
ordered the Seventh Mechanized Division of the Botoru Battalion
to assemble here immediately."

The Seventh had a reputation for ground-based savagery and more.

"Impossible," said Exedore with alarm. "Surely, sir, this cannot
be; you haven't ordered up *Khyron's* division?"

Breetai smiled bemusedly at his companion. "Indeed I have, and
why not?"

"You're familiar with his battle record, his reputation."

"What of it?"

"During the Mona Operation, he was intoxicated and ended
up killing some of his own men." Exedore pressed his point. "And
in the Isyris battle zone he almost wiped out two divisions of
friendly forces—"

"While successfully destroying the enemy."

"True, sir, but because of that his own troops have named him
the 'Backstabber.'"

Breetai was about to respond, when without warning the bridge went on alert. Lights began to flash, and warning klaxons were sounding general quarters. Exedore had already positioned himself at the control pads of one of the monitors, trying to ascertain the cause. Breetai stood over him now as data began to flash across the screens.

"What is it?" the commander demanded.

"Armed ships emerging from hyperspace in the midst of our battle group. A collision appears imminent!"

Breetai turned to the forward projecbeam. "Some of the Micronians' unorthodoxy!"

A card player at a show of hands, Breetai readied himself, fully expecting the materialization of a squadron of Micronian mecha. But what appeared instead were the ragtag ships of the Botoru Battalion.

Visual distortions in local space preceded their crazed arrival, shimmerings and oscillations in the fabric of real time. Several vessels of Khyron's battle group collided with ships of the main fleet, spreading shock waves throughout the field. Even the flagship itself was rocked by debris, the force of the impact strong enough to knock Exedore off his feet. Damage reports were pouring in to the bridge; debris appeared in the projecbeam field.

Exedore picked himself up; his voice was full of anger when he spoke.

"This is happening just as I expected! Khyron, sir, is totally without discipline!"

Was this an oversight, Breetai asked himself, *or just a demonstration of Khyron's recklessness?*

The Backstabber's face suddenly appeared on the forward screen. Khyron, long steel-blue hair falling over the collar of a uniform of his own design, saluted. His face was a curious mixture of boyish innocence and brooding anger, Prince Valiant's devilish shadow with a fire in his eyes that was not quite Zentraedi.

"Commander of the Seventh Mechanized Space Division reporting as ordered." His lowered salute turned into a mock wave. "Good to see you again, Commander Breetai." He finished off with a laugh.

"The sheer audacity—" Exedore started to say.

A square-jawed battle-scarred warrior had appeared by Khyron's side in the projecbeam field, sharing some sort of joke with him. "Ha! Just as I thought, Khyron. We crashed into four ships total."

Khyron tried to silence him, but it was too late.

"You thought it would be three at best. I win the bet."

"Be quiet, you fool," ordered Khyron finally. "Our conversation is being broadcast."

Breetai fixed him with his one eye. "Khyron, don't trifle with me if you value your command. I'm willing to give you a chance to make up for your past mistakes, but I have no time for your games. Is that understood?"

Khyron straightened his smile, but the laughter remained in his eyes. "Yes, Commander, what is it you want me to do?"

"There's an abandoned base on the fourth planet of this star system. We intend to lure Zor's ship there, and I want you to see to it that it doesn't leave. Trap it with gravity mines if you have to, but understand this: Your Seventh will blockade the ship without damaging it unduly. You will then await my further instructions. Is that clear? You are to await my instructions before engaging the enemy."

"Perfectly clear, Breetai. I would naturally prefer you to have the honor and glory of the capture. Commander-in-Chief Dolza expects nothing less of you, I'm sure."

"That will be enough, Khyron," said Exedore.

Breetai gestured to his adviser. "Send out a recall order to our Battlepods. Let's give the Micronians enough breathing room to take the bait we're going to lay out for them."

Khyron signed off. Exedore continued to plead the case against using him, but Breetai was already looking forward to the plan. The prospect of a trap excited him. Furthermore, real sport required the unexpected, and in this contest for Zor's ship and the precious cargo it held, Khyron would play the Zentraedi's wild card.

Two Battlepods were right on his tail, pouring fire into the mecha. Rick didn't need gauges to feel the lock of those lasers; they might as well have been burning into his skull. He opened up the gap somewhat by hitting his afterburners, then tacked toward relative-twelve and waited for the pods to split up. He knew they'd attempt to pinch him, but he had plans of his own.

Rick took his mind off the pod below him. He had number one haloed in his rear sights. Firing the forward retros to cut his velocity, he loosed a cluster of heat-seekers. The missiles tore from beneath the right wing of the mecha and accelerated into a vertical climb, homing in on the enemy ship. Rick used the port thrusters to angle himself free of the debris and risked a brief look up and over his shoulder. The rockets caught the Battlepod in the belly, blowing off both legs and cracking the spherical hull.

Scratch one.

Number two was still below him, trying to roast the underside of Rick's mecha with continuous heat. A little more of this and he'd be cooked. Lateral swings were getting him nowhere, so he thought the fighter into a rapid dive, rolling over as he fell. The enemy lasers were now tickling the back of the Veritech, and Rick had to act fast: He returned fire with its own top-mounted guns, training them on the hinge straps of the pod's chestplate.

The enemy pilot understood Rick's move and arced his guns toward the more vulnerable cockpit of the mecha. But he was too late; the hinges of the chestplate slagged out, and the pod opened up like a newly hatched egg. Rick caught a glimpse of the giant flailing around in his cockpit before he completed his roll and engaged the boosters.

Scratch two.

He was headed away from the fortress now. The scene before him had to have been lifted from some nightmare: Space was alive with swarms of Battlepods… photon beams laced through the blackness, and silent explosions brought the colors of death and destruction to an indifferent universe.

For three days now the pods had pressed their attack. There had been little sleep for the Robotech forces, even less for the SDF-1 flight crews. After the *Daedalus* Maneuver and their success in the rings of Saturn, there was some hope that the enemy had for once suffered a setback. And for almost a month, while the fortress

crossed the Jovian orbit and the asteroid belt, there were no attacks.
But that period of calm was behind them.

Captain Gloval and Dr. Lang had reversed the modular transformation and disassembled the pin-point barrier system in an
attempt to arm the main gun once again, but their efforts had
proved futile. For the rest, the still slightly shell-shocked masses
of displaced persons of Macross city, catapulted like himself from
the southern Pacific to the icy regions of deep space, there was
nothing to do but adjust to the reality of the situation, continue
to rebuild lives and the city itself. Every now and again, they could
marvel at the wonders of space travel, the stark and silent beauty
of it, and forget for a moment that they were not tourists out here
but unwilling players in a nonstop game of death, pursued by the
seemingly limitless forces of a race of giant warrior beings who
had dropped out of the skies and turned the world upside down.

Only a month before, Rick had been face to face with one of
those titans in an air lock on one of the alien ships. He recalled
staring out of the cockpit of the transformed Veritech at the giant,
who at first had openly feared him, then cursed and ridiculed him
for not having the will to blast him away. The laughter of that alien
still rang in his ears followed by his guilt and confusion. But most
of all the memory of the giant's fiery death.

How could one ever forget?

Two Battlepods were suddenly behind him, looking for laser lock.
Rick executed a double rollover and dive to lose them. Peripherally,
he saw the Blue Team leader swoop in and take them out.

"Way to go Blue Leader!" Rick shouted into the tac net.

"Just do the same for me sometime, buddy," came the reply.

"You got it."

Rick and the Blue Leader, wing to wing, led a frontal assault on
yet another enemy wave. They launched themselves into the thick
of it, dispatching several of the enemy. Lateral thrusters took them
out of the arena momentarily, and the SDF-1 came into view, her
main batteries, Phalanx guns, and Gladiator mecha issuing steady
fire. The fortress, enveloped by a swarm of pods, looked as though
it had somehow wandered into a fireworks display.

Commander Hayes was calling for an assist in Fifth Quadrant, and Skull and Blue Teams were ordered to respond. Rick and Blue Leader were initiating course corrections when five pods appeared on Rick's radar screen. Three of them were quickly dispatched by Roy Fokker in Skull One, but the remaining two were hounding Blue Leader's VT with a vengeance. The enemy unleashed a massive volley of rockets that caught the mecha broadside. For a moment Blue Leader seemed to hang in space; then the fighter exploded and disintegrated, its parts scattered, its pilot a memory.

Rick turned his face away from the wreckage. *I could be next,* he thought.

How could one ever forget?

The pods continued to press their attack.

Death had a free hand.

Then, as suddenly as they had appeared they were gone. The fighting was over and recall orders came in from the bridge.

Rick followed Roy Fokker's lead into the docking bays of the *Prometheus.*

Roy caught up with him in the hangar and slapped him on the shoulder.

"You looked good up there, Rick. Keep it up."

Rick grunted, removed his helmet, and kept walking, increasing his pace.

Roy caught up with him again. "You can't let it get you down, kid. We sent them home, didn't we?"

Rick turned and confronted his friend. "If you believe that, you're a bigger idiot than I am, Roy."

Roy draped his arm around Rick's shoulders and leaned in. "Listen to me. You're beat. We all are. Get yourself into town after the debriefing. I'm sure Minmei would like to see you."

"That would be a surprise," Rick said, and stormed off.

Monorail lines now ran from the *Prometheus* and *Daedalus* arms into Macross. A central monorail line ran through the body of the fortress, through enormous interior holds originally meant for creatures ten times human scale—a vast forbidden zone only a portion of which was understood by Dr. Lang's teams of scientists—and through that area where Rick and Minmei had passed two weeks together deep beneath the present streets of the city.

Each passing day brought changes here. There was even talk of using EVE, enhanced video emulation, to bring sunrise and sunset, blue skies and clouds, to the place. Already there was a grid of streets, carefully arranged according to the dictates of the modular transformation schematic, multiple-storied dwellings, shops and restaurants, a central marketplace, even a few banks and a post office.

The city went on living through the war, almost oblivious to it except when energy drains through diversion led to power shortages or when the enemy fighters and Battlepods scored direct hits. Even the ubiquitous uniforms didn't signal war— uniforms were worn by everyone to denote job and detail, a carryover from the island where most of these same people had been connected in one way or another to the reconstruction of the SDF-1. A public address system kept the residents of the city informed about the ship's course through the solar system but was seldom used to report accurate battle results. In fact, it was speaking to the population now, as Rick meandered in vague fashion toward the Chinese restaurant, hoping for an *accidental* encounter with Minmei. Passersby paid the message little mind, but it caught him off guard. "News from the bridge: We have been attacked by one hundred twenty enemy pods, but our first, fourth, and seventh fighter squadrons have succeeded in completely destroying them. Our casualties have been light, and our astrogational system has not been affected. That is all."

Incredible! Rick thought. He was looking around for someone to talk to, someone he could grab by the lapels and awaken with the truth, when an arm caught hold of his. He turned and found himself looking into Minmei's blue eyes.

"Hello, stranger," she said. "I've been worried about you."

She embraced him like a brother.

He had rehearsed how he was going to play this, but standing here with her now, the half-truths from the bridge echoing inside him, he just wanted to hold and protect her. But he managed to keep some distance, and she caught his mood.

He explained about the announcement. "It wasn't true, Minmei. They're misleading everyone. We didn't hit half of them, and our losses were—"

She put a finger to his lips and looked around. "I don't think it's a good idea to talk about this here, Rick."

He broke from her hold. "Listen, Minmei—"

"Besides, everyone's doing all they can for the war effort, and I don't think you'll accomplish anything by getting them—or me—depressed. Especially with my birthday right around the corner."

He could only stare at her and wonder where her mind was, but she was way ahead of him already. She smiled and took hold of his arm.

"Come on, Rick. Let's get something to eat. Please?"

He gave in. How could he make her understand how it was out there? In here she was doing what they all were: going on with life as if nothing had happened, as if this were home, as if there were a wonderfully blue ocean just over that rise. As if there were no war out there.

On the bridge of the SDF-1 there was little else but war to talk or think about.

Captain Gloval removed his cap and ran a hand through his salt-and-pepper hair. What were the aliens planning now? Obviously their constant attacks were not meant to turn the tide but to wear him down, perhaps in the hope that the SDF-1 would be surrendered. The attacks were like sparring matches; it was as if the enemy was feeling him out, trying to gain some insight into his tactics. Psychological warfare conducted with an inexhaustible supply of ships and no regard for the pilots who flew them. Gloval wondered what his counterpart might look like, what kind of being he was. He recalled the video warning the fortress had broadcast to his small band of explorers some ten years ago… One thing was becoming clear: The aliens did not want to damage the SDF-1. They hoped to recapture it intact.

The attacks had thrown them drastically off course, and although closing in on Earth's orbit, they had months of travel ahead of them.

Gloval asked for information about the aliens' retreat. The only thing Claudia and Lisa could be certain of was that there were no longer any traces of enemy pods on the radar screens. Gloval was pondering this when Kim Young announced that incoming data was being received on one of the open frequencies.

Gloval stepped down from his chair and walked over to take a look at the transmissions.

"…'If mice could swim,'" he read, "'they would float with the tide and play with the fish. Down by the seaside, the cats on the shore would quickly agree…' What is this nonsense? Where is it coming from?"

Vanessa Leeds tapped in a set of requests and swiveled in her seat to study a secondary monitor. In a moment she had the answer. "A transmitter located sixteen degrees off our current course."

"That would put it at Sara Base on Mars!" said Claudia.

Lisa Hayes turned from her post in a start. "What?! That's impossible! Are you certain of those readings?"

"Sara Base is deserted," said Gloval. "All life there was wiped out during the war. It just can't be."

Lisa and Claudia exchanged a conspiratorial look. "No, Lisa," said Claudia. "Don't get your hopes up."

"Why couldn't there be survivors?" Lisa said excitedly. She turned to Gloval. "Isn't it possible, sir?"

Gloval crossed his arms, "I don't see how, but it was a pretty big base, and I suppose anything is possible. We've all seen enough lately to convince me of that."

"We have secondary confirmation on the origin of the transmissions, sir. The origin is definitely Sara."

Claudia said, "Perhaps we should check it out, Captain. It would only mean a minor deviation in our course." Again she and Lisa exchanged looks.

Gloval returned to his chair. He thought it unlikely that there were survivors on the base. And the possibility of an enemy trap had to be considered. But there were no radar indications of activity in the area, and the risk presented by a landing would certainly be justified if they could manage to replenish their rapidly diminishing supplies. It would be the last chance until Earthspace, and who knew when that might be. *If* that would he…

Gloval turned to his crew. "How badly hurt are we?"

Vanessa responded, "Astrogation and engineering sections report limited damage only, sir."

"All right," said Gloval. "Change course and head for Mars."

05

The destruction of Sara Base on Mars was in some ways typical of the setbacks experienced by the newly formed World Unification Alliance, the unfortunate result of suspicion, misinformation, and manipulation by an unnamed collective of separatist factions. That Northeast Asian Co-Prosperity Sphere could be so easily duped into believing the base a military installation was all the more cause for concern. But more than that, the attack upon the base marked the first instance that humankind had taken warfare off the planet and brought it to the stars.

Malachi Cain, *Prelude to Doomsday:*
A History of the Global Civil War

*M*ARS!
Lisa stared at the barren world as it came into view through the forward bays. Arid, lifeless, named for the ancient god of war, it was like an angry red wound in her heart. Eight years earlier her love had died here, on this world that she was destined to visit, one that had visited her so often in tear-filled dreams. But even so she couldn't suppress the belief, the hope, that one of the many survival scenarios she had played endlessly through these lost years would run to completion. The last time she had seen and held Karl Riber was the evening he had told her of his assignment to Mars Base Sara.

"The Visitor" had crash landed on Macross Island three years earlier, and the Internationalists—men like her father, Admiral Hayes, Senator Russo, Gloval, and the rest—were doing their best to bring about world unity, centered on the restoration of the SDF-1 and the potential threat to Earth posed by the arrival of that ship built

by an advanced race of intellectual and physical giants. But peace
and unity were not so easily secured. Factionalism was rampant and
borders changed overnight, sides were drawn and redrawn, bombs
were dropped, and the killing continued unabated.

She had known Karl only a short time but had loved him from
the start. He had been assigned to her father as an aide and was
doing his best to be the soldier Admiral Hayes expected at his side.
But through and through Karl was a peace-loving man, a sensitive
scholar who, like others of his type, was looking forward to a day
when the bloodshed would end and humankind would begin to
focus itself on its destiny, its true place among the stars. The arrival
of the SDF-1 had further inflamed his passion for peace; but when
even that event failed to put an end to the reigning madness, there
was nothing left for him but cynicism and the need to escape.

That farewell night found Karl and Lisa together at the Hayes
estate in upstate New York. They sat together under a grand old tree
under star-filled skies, and Karl told her that he had been reassigned
to Base Sara, a scientific observation post on Mars. He had pointed
out the planet and confessed how torn he was to be leaving her. But
there was no place on Earth for him any longer; even the Robotech
project had been co-opted by the militaristic power wing of the
Alliance. Instead of profiting from the miraculous find, they were
merely gearing up for an anticipated war, a *projected* war.

She knew it was the right move for him, even if it was the wrong
move for *them*. But that night her young mind had seized on a
plan she hoped would keep them together: She would enlist in the
Defense Force and would apply for an assignment to Sara Base.

She had confessed her love for Karl.

And lost him to the stars.

But she made good her promise, and with her father's assistance
had received a security clearance and an assignment to Macross
Island to work under Dr. Lang aboard the SDF-1.

She and Karl never saw each other again. But there were letters
and tapes and the occasional transworld calls. Karl was in his
element there, and all signs had pointed to her being able to join
him soon. Until war had reached out its long arm and seized on

the one place humankind had yet to spill blood. Sara Base became a graveyard overnight, almost a symbol of humankind's need to take war with it wherever it set foot in the universe.

The SDF-1 became her future from that moment on. She had thrown herself into the project with a fever born of forgetting that meant for rapid advancement but left little time for personal growth. Vanessa and Claudia chided her for her attachment to the ship, and sometimes she knew that she did come across as cold and distant.

The old sourpuss!

It was left unfinished between her and Karl, as if emotional time had been frozen on the night she learned about Base Sara's destruction.

This planetary touchdown then was more than a mere landing to her; it was an emotional pilgrimage. Karl Riber was alive in her heart, moment to moment; to her it meant that he could really be alive, one of a group of survivors here. He had said to her, *We'll be together again someday, when the Earth is at peace.* Love was simply not meant to perish in angry flames; love couldn't be extinguished by war!

Gloval was shouting her name; she turned a confused face toward him, caught between past and future in a present that was of her own making.

"Lisa, what's wrong? Are you sure you're feeling all right?"

She composed herself and awaited his command.

"Send out a Cat's-Eye recon unit. Order them to report any anomalies in their findings—any at all."

Lisa turned to her task. *Let him be alive,* she prayed to herself.

The Cat's-Eye recon scanned the deserted base and radioed its findings to the bridge of the SDF-1: no sign of the enemy, no sign of life of any kind. And yet, inexplicably, data continued to pour into the onboard computers. Somehow one of the Sara Base computers had gone online. Captain Gloval was convinced of this much. Still, wary of a possible enemy trap, he convened a special meeting with colonels Maistroff and Caruthers and high-ranking officials of Macross City to discuss the prospect of setting the giant space fortress down on the surface of Mars.

There were two reasons for attempting such a landing, as opposed to holding the fortress in low orbit and using cargo ships and drones to ferry up the much-needed supplies. The primary reason was that a setdown would enable ground crews to repair damage sustained during four months of space warfare. Most of these repairs could not be effected in deep space or even in low orbit without the constant threat of enemy sneak attacks and the overwhelming logistical problems that extended extravehicular activity would entail. The second advantage, although less clear-cut, was of greater concern to Gloval and Lang than to the Macross City leaders, for whom replenished supplies was reason enough. The fact was that the SDF-1 *had never been landed;* the closest it had come was more a controlled drop than an actual landing, months ago when the antigravity devices had torn through the hull of the ship and it had fallen back to its docking bay supports on Macross Island. The lower gravity on Mars would allow engineering to stage a dress rehearsal of the landing they would have to perform once the fortress reached Earth.

Recalling that first day of attack, Gloval resisted an urge to dwell on how defenseless he had felt with the ship grounded. There was no assurance that this wouldn't be the case again, but he had to convince himself that the advantages outweighed the risks.

It took two days to bring the SDF-1 down.

Astrogation held her in stationary orbit for what seemed an eternity, and then the fortress was allowed to begin its slow nerve-racking descent to the surface of Mars. Gloval sat at the helm wondering what surprise Lang's half grasp on Robotechnology might result in this time, but to his relief and to the delight of everyone onboard, the SDF-1 was set down without incident. After months in space it was difficult to believe they were down on solid ground once again. It made no difference that this wasn't their homeworld; after all, humankind had once occupied this planet, and that was reason enough to call it home for the moment.

Half of Macross City jammed itself onto the observation deck after the all-clear was sounded and the ship had docked. At least half that number would have gladly disembarked then and there to begin new lives for themselves; but there would be no liberty for civilians at this port.

Gloval continued to have misgivings—he felt as if he was standing on solid ground with nothing beneath his feet. For this reason he ordered the ship down at a point several kilometers from Sara Base. Destroids were then deployed to secure a supply route, with squadrons of Veritech fighters launched to provide cover. The Cat's-Eye recon plane continued its sweeps over the area, and long-range radar watched the skies. When Gloval was convinced that there was no threat to their position or operation, he ordered that the ship be moved closer to the base, employing the auxiliary lifters and gravity control system, something they wouldn't have been able to do on Earth.

Now the base complex, what remained of it, lay spread out below the ship. From the bridge, the crew could observe the destruction that had been visited upon it, a grim reminder of the days when humankind was at war with itself. It was a forlorn-looking place covered with debris swept in by the continuous Martian winds.

The supply routes secure, Battloids began their patrol, gatling weapons ready. A long line of wheeled and treaded transport vehicles now stretched from the loading bays of the *Daedalus* and the *Prometheus* to the heart of Sara.

Lisa was waiting for the right moment; if she didn't act quickly, though, there wouldn't be another chance. Data from the base was still coming in, and Gloval had yet to organize a recon team to investigate the source of the transmissions. Finally she gathered up enough nerve and turned to the captain.

"Requesting your permission to leave the ship, sir, and recon the interior of the base."

The captain regarded her with concern. "But Lisa—"

She interrupted him. "I'd like to check out the source of those signals, sir. There could be survivors here!" Only when she caught the look of protective paternalism in his eyes did she break down. "Please, sir. It's important to me." She had no idea whether Gloval knew anything about her past; but he knew her as a crewmember, knew when she needed his attention.

Claudia offered an unsolicited assist. "I'll cover her duties here," she told the captain.

Gloval thought it over. Anyone who was within 500 kilometers of the base would have already come running. But there was something so personal in her insistence that he decided to allow her to go.

"But I want you to take two security personnel with you!" he called out as she hurried from the bridge.

Lisa ignored the captain's command; after all, it hadn't been issued as a direct order. She outfitted herself with helmet and environment suit, radio, and laser sidearm and took charge of a small personnel carrier from supply.

Had she been thinking about it, she might have compared her short ride across the Martian wastes to the driving training she'd undergone on the moon years ago, but her thoughts were elsewhere. She had to find Karl and renew their life together or discover for herself that he was dead.

The base had the familiar look and feel of the countless war torn cities she'd experienced on Earth—not voluntarily abandoned but simply cut down in its prime. All life had been sucked from the place in an instant, and that sort of ending always left ghosts lingering about. She could sense their presence all around her, almost as if they were still confused by what had occurred here and were now demanding an explanation from this stranger who was visiting their resting place. Yes, it was like those ravaged cities but more so: The howling of the winds was louder and angrier, the soil appeared more blood-stained, and there was never a blue sky here.

She used the homing device to direct her to the source of the transmissions received by the SDF-1. They emanated from a large building, central to the complex, that had served as the communications center. She entered this through the blown front hatchway and made her way through deserted halls to the computer room, the sound of her own breathing heavy in her ears. Everywhere she looked there was evidence of the disaster. The scientists who were stationed here must have had some sort of warning, though, because there were no bodies lying about—

how she had feared that!—just general disarray, as if there had been a last-minute effort to collect what they could and leave this place before the sky fell.

At last she reached computer control. She stood motionless in the doorway and peered into the deserted room: chairs tipped over, papers strewn about, a carpet of glass shards from blown monitor screens wall-to-wall. But at the far end of the room there were flashing console lights, greens and reds, and an on-line computer frantically emptying its memory banks across a monitor screen no eyes were meant to read, like an infant left crying in a crib. Lisa walked over to the machine and shut it down. She turned and took another look around the room, puzzling over its emptiness.

So there was no half-starved band of survivors huddled in one sealed room using the computer as shipwrecked sailors would a signal fire. Just a machine that had somehow activated itself.

The way memories did.

Hidden in a deep chasm fifteen kilometers from Sara Base, Khyron and his attack force of 200 Battlepods waited. The Backstabber himself occupied his Officer's Pod, a mecha different from the rest, with lasers protruding like whiskers from its elongated snout and two arms that were deadly cannons. He ingested the dried and intoxicating leaves of the Invid Flower while monitoring reports from his squad leaders who were holding at other points along the perimeter.

A Micronian recon ship had already overflown the canyon and failed to detect the presence of his troops. The abandoned base was surrounded, the gravity mines were in place, and the fortress had set down just where he had predicted it would. The foolish Micronians had taken the bait—an on-line computer—and the trap was almost ready to be sprung. Soon he would capture Zor's ship, *for the glory of the Zentraedi!* And for the honor of Khyron. It would be a shame if he was forced to take on the fortress himself. He did *so* want the credit to go to Breetai. If only things weren't going so slowly. The leaves always made him somewhat impatient.

"Gerao, aren't those gravity mines ready yet?" he shouted into his comlink mike.

The Battlepod speaker crackled with static and the monitor erupted into patternless noise bars before Gerao's face appeared on the screen. His droid team was operating at almost three kilometers below the surface. Gerao may have won the collision bet, but it didn't pay to best one's commander. Khyron laughed to himself.

"The energy accumulation is up to seventy percent, my lord. Not much longer."

"Blast it, this waiting is irritating me! Drive those droids harder, Gerao, or I'll leave you buried on this godforsaken world. You have my word on it!"

Gerao's emphatic salute signaled that he understood Khyron's threat completely. He signed off. Khyron began to drum his fingers on the console. *Zor's ship*, he thought to himself. Why was Commander in Chief Dolza wasting his time with this one when there were countless worlds left to conquer? Since when were the Zentraedi errand boys? If the Robotech Masters were so desperate about getting Zor's Protoculture matrix back, they could go retrieve it themselves. What did Khyron care about Protoculture? It was the Invid Flowers that were important to him… He picked up one of the dried petals and regarded it lovingly: Here was the true power.

As Khyron was placing the petal in his mouth, the face of one of his troops surfaced on the Officer's Pod commo screen.

"We've waited long enough, Commander," the soldier said. "I'm going in now. Any longer and we will jeopardize our mission."

To Khyron's amazement, the soldier's Battlepod fired its thrusters and began to lift off from the chasm floor. Was he seeing things or had this fool actually decided to use his own initiative? Khyron was as fond of insolence as anyone, but this was pushing things too far. He allowed the pod to climb almost to the rim of the chasm before bringing up one of the cannon arms of his mecha and firing. The Battlepod took a direct hit, turned end over end, and plummeted and crashed on the chasm floor.

The pilots of two other pods hopped their crafts over to their fallen comrade and checked his status.

"He's still alive, my lord."

"So much the worse for him, then," yelled Khyron. "If I can wait here patiently, so can the rest of you. The next one who disobeys my orders will meet a worse fate. I promise you that!"

Khyron was imagining his underlings stiffening into postures of salute inside the pods when the voice of Gerao entered the head-set.

"My lord, I fear that use of the cannon may have compromised our position. The Micronian recon plane is circling back in this direction."

"The recon plane! Gerao, are you ready with the mines?"

"Just ten percent more to go."

Khyron slapped his hands down on the pod console. "Ninety percent will have to be good enough. You have my permission to attack!"

Claudia was worried: There had been no word from Lisa for almost an hour now. The incoming data from the base had terminated, but the seismic sensors were picking up something new. Captain Gloval and Vanessa were trying to make sense of the readings.

"Nearby in the mountains, I think—a disturbance or explosion," said Vanessa.

"A landslide, perhaps."

"No, there's too much sonic attached to it. It must have been an explosion."

Gloval turned to Claudia. "Instruct the Cat's-Eye to make another pass over the eleven o'clock zone at the fifteen-kilometer perimeter. And see to it that recon readings are patched into the main screen here."

Claudia contacted the Cat's-Eye, and within minutes new data was filling the screen: The sensors indicated hundreds of individual mecha units moving in from the cavernous mountains that surrounded Sara Base.

"Battlepods!" said Gloval. He ordered Claudia to sound general quarters. "Recall all transport vehicles immediately and scramble the Veritech fighters! They won't catch us napping this time!" Gloval paced the bridge, then threw himself into the command chair. "Activate the gravity control system and prepare the ship for takeoff."

Claudia swung around from her terminal. "But Captain, Lisa's still out there. She'll never make it back in time."

Gloval waved his hand in a gesture of dismissal. "I told her I didn't want her to enter that base. Now she'll have to come up in one of the VTs."

Claudia hid a look of concern from Gloval and carried out her orders. But something was wrong: The ship wasn't lifting off. The gravity control system wasn't damaged, there were correct readings on all the sensors, but the SDF-1 would not rise. It bellowed and shuddered like some captured beast.

"Captain," Vanessa managed to shout above the noise, "the seismic sensor indicates an intense gravity field underlying the base!"

Gloval leaped from his seat to study the threat board. "Gravity mines! So this is what the enemy has in mind—they mean to pin us down like a trapped insect. Shut down all engines before she comes apart at the seams!"

"Battlepods!" said Claudia.

Gloval and the bridge crew turned to face the front bays: The Martian sky was filled with enemy mecha.

06

It's become my routine these past two months to wander over to the observation dome and spend hours at the scope watching our beautiful blue and white world transit the Martian night. How bright, how incredibly alive and tranquil, Earth appears from afar! And how misleading that impression is... I often think about our last night together. It was more difficult for me to leave you than to leave our planet, the global madness, the small minds at work who have robbed us of our dreams. But I don't want to get started on all this again; I want to talk about this place, and how happy I know you will be here. The stars seem close enough to touch, our distant sun no less warm, and even these incessant winds do not disturb... Base Sara is a new experiment in peace, a new experiment in the future...

Karl Riber, *Collected Letters*

THE BATTLEPODS AND CARAPACE FIGHTERS OF THE BOTORU Seventh left the cover of the mountain chasms and descended on Sara Base. Khyron led the assault, screaming into his communicator, "Kill them, kill them all!"

The Robotech forces threw everything they had into the Martian sky. Battloids and Spartan defenders took up positions on the base, while squadrons of Veritechs went up to meet the enemy one on one. The main batteries and CIWS Phalanx guns of the grounded space fortress rotated into position and filled the thin air with orange tracers, armor-piercing discarding sabot rounds, and deadly thunder.

In an attempt to cut off the supply line to SDF-1, Khyron and his forces went after the transports first. The pods fell from the Martian sky unleashing a torrent of energy bolts and missiles. The all-terrain trucks bounded off the gravel highway to evade fire, but scarcely a dozen made it to the fortress intact. Explosions tossed the vehicles off the ground like toys, and soon there was only a pathway of fire where the vehicles had once traveled.

The Destroids were next on Khyron's list; then he turned his attention to the Battloids and Guardians.

The Battloids of the Skull Team were positioned along the SDF-1's defensive perimeter when they received launch orders. Roy and Rick transformed their mecha to Guardian mode and lifted off from blasting carpets to engage the enemy.

Rick retracted the legs and threw the fighter into a long vertical climb, exchanging fire with three pods on the way up. The three gave chase while he banked at the crest of his ascent and dropped off into a fusillade fall, weapons blazing as he came back down on them. Heat-seekers ripped from his mecha, scoring hits against two pods. Rick and the remaining enemy raced above the rough terrain, trading shots. At the foot of the mountains they split apart, only to encounter each other at the craggy summits. It was a game of aerial chicken, pod and fighter on a collision course, Zentraedi and Terran pilots emptying their guns.

Rick yo-yoed and took the fight deeper into the mountains. The enemy pursued him, launching rockets which Rick's mecha successfully evaded with breaks and jinks and high barrel rolls.

Skull twenty-three banked sharply now and fell away into a narrow valley, luring its opponent toward a forest of wind-eroded rock spires. Rick used two of his rockets to blast an opening for himself and dove in. The pod stayed with him but was having trouble negotiating the forest's tight groupings of columns. Too late, the enemy pilot attempted to pull out; one of the pod's clawlike legs snagged on a spire, and the pod suddenly became a high-speed pinball, careening from tower to tower. Flames and debris from the resounding explosion tore past Rick's mecha as he climbed from the canyon.

This was more like it, he told himself, rejoining his battle group on the Martian plain. Sky above, ground below. Sound and light, explosions of finality. No clouds for cover, but it seemed as though you could see forever through the thin air.

Just then Roy's face appeared on the left screen of his cockpit. "What d' ya think, Little Brother? It's a little like the old days, isn't it?"

"The 'old' days, yeah, *four months ago!*"

Roy laughed. "Let's get 'em, tiger!"

Rick watched his friend's fighter face down two of the pods and dispatch both of them. He quickly scanned the busy sky: If each Veritech could take out two pods, the enemy would only have them outnumbered four to one.

From the bridge of the SDF-1, Gloval and his crew had a clear view of the ongoing massacre. Brilliant strobe-like flashes of explosive light spilled in through the forward and side bays as the enemy continued to pour fire at the ship. The fortress rocked and vibrated to the staccato beat of battle. The Martian landscape had become an inferno.

"The sixth and eighth Spartan divisions have been wiped out, Captain," Claudia reported. "Veritech squadrons are sustaining heavy casualties."

Gloval paced the deck, fingers of one hand tugging at his thick mustache. "There must be a way out of this..." He turned to Vanessa. "Put the seismic schematic on the screen again."

Gloval studied the computer graphic display as it came up. The source of the induced gravitation that held the ship captive was located some three kilometers beneath the surface. Gloval now had Kim project a schematic of the underground power center that fueled Sara Base. He stepped back to take in both screens, folded his arms across his chest, and nodded.

"It's just as I thought. There is a reflex furnace beneath Sara." Reflex power was one of Robotechnology's first by-products—back in more peaceful times. "If we were to overload it, the explosion that would result might take out the enemy's gravity mines as well."

Gloval instructed Vanessa to run a computer simulation based on the available data. Then he turned to Claudia: "Contact Lisa, immediately."

...

Lisa was trying to figure a way out of Sara Base when Gloval's call came through. With what she recalled from her engineering courses and the technical assists the SDF-1 onboard computers would provide, there was a good chance that she'd be able to shut down the reflex furnace as Gloval requested. He instructed her to keep her radio tuned in to the bridge frequency so that they could monitor her location and position.

The first step would be to get herself safely from the communications center to the main power station, which meant an unescorted trip through the thick of the fighting. There was one other option, though, and it would require her to be out in the open only for a short time. The power center was linked to the barracks building through a system of underground tunnels and access corridors. And the barracks was just a short hop through hell.

Lisa poised herself on the threshold of the communication building's blown hatch. Ground-shaking explosions were going off all around her. Alien pods, hopping nimbly through the devastation, were leveling everything in sight. Hundreds of missiles corkscrewed overhead, converging on what was left of the supply line and the fortress itself. Lisa's dream was finished, and Sara Base was finished with it. She pushed herself from the front entry like a parachutist leaving an old-style aircraft and flung herself into the firestorm. She ran a slalom course, jagging left and right through fields of fire, and made it to the safety of the barracks just short of a violent blast that took out the area she'd left behind. The concussion threw her off her feet, but she was unhurt.

Inside, she accessed information from the SDF-1 to locate the main shaft elevators. There was auxiliary power here, so she would be able to ride down to the underground room.

The descent was a long one. It felt as though she were traveling into the very bowels of the fiery planet. Each level lessened the effects of the overhead bombardment until the world seemed silent once again.

Stepping out at Sublevel Fifteen, she made her way to the control room. There was an uncommon, low-level vibration down here, and she was forced to move with more exertion, almost as though she'd been returned to Earth gravity. She reasoned that the enemy gravity mines were responsible for this.

It took Lisa several minutes to locate the furnace controls, a confusing array of switches, dials, and meters, antiquated and needlessly complex. There were redundant systems and far too many command switches and manually operated crossovers. But instructions from the onboard computer simplified her task. Finally she had the reflex computers programmed for overload. The control systems that allowed excess charge buildup to be safely shunted into runoffs were now damped down, and all backup outlets were similarly closed. Next she instructed the CPUs that operated the furnace to bring the power up to maximum, canceling out the safety programs with override commands.

Warning lights were starting to flash on the console, and she thought she could detect the sound of warning sirens and klaxons going off somewhere. The sequence, however, had kicked in several other built-in safety systems that were unanticipated: Hatchways were beginning to lower throughout the room. According to an overhead digital clock, she had less than fifteen minutes to get off the base.

Lisa returned to the main elevator and rode the car back to ground level. The sounds of battle had increased. She tried to retrace her path to the entrance, but the barracks had taken several hits, and debris now blocked the corridor. There was an unobstructed second corridor that led to the officers' quarters; a hatchway there would allow her to exit on the other side of the building. She entered this and was making for the hatch, when the corridor suddenly sealed itself off. Iron doors dropped from overhead vaults at both ends, trapping her inside.

Hatchways to individual quarters lined both sides of the corridor, and while she was opening each of these looking for some way out, a terrible thought occurred to her: What if one of these rooms had belonged to Karl?

In the dim light, Lisa's fingers traced the letters of raised name tags on the doors, and it wasn't long before she found RIBER, KARL.

Slowly the will to survive began to abandon her. All she could feel now was a terrible sadness and a pain from long ago, as though her body was recalling the hurt and bringing it up to the surface.

She hit the button that opened the hatchway to Karl's quarters and stood at the threshold, afraid to enter, supporting herself against the doorjamb. "Oh, Karl," she said to whatever ghosts were lurking there.

Lisa entered, mindless of the countdown to self-destruction.

"The destruct sequence has been initiated, Captain," Claudia said. "T minus ten minutes and counting."

Gloval nodded his head in approval. "Good. I knew Lisa could do it. Now, issue a recall order to our remaining Destroids and Valkyries. But I want them to pull back slowly. With a little luck we'll catch the enemy in *our* trap this time."

"Nine minutes and counting, Captain."

"Contact Lisa; let's see how she's making out."

Claudia tried, but there was no response. The radio transmitter was still on, but Lisa wasn't answering the call.

"Lisa, come in, please," Claudia said. "She's not responding, Captain."

Gloval rose from his chair. "If she's still on-line, we should be able to get a fix on her position."

Kim already had it up on the screen.

"She's in Barracks C. But she's not moving."

"She could be hurt, or trapped," said Gloval. "Claudia, quickly, contact the Skull Leader."

Rick released two rockets and dove under the Battlepods. White-hot shrapnel impacted against his fighter, and the shock wave threw him into an involuntary sink.

He narrowly missed buying it at the hands of an enemy Officer's Pod that leaped into view out of nowhere. It was the same one he had seen on and off throughout the battle. And whoever piloted it was someone to fear. Rick had seen the pod take out three Veritechs in one pass, and later he had seen that same pilot blow away two of his own men to get to one of the Robotech Valkyries.

Roy pulled alongside Rick, gesturing to the enemy mecha. His face was on twenty-three's left screen.

"You wanna watch that one, Rick. He means business."

"Let's gang up on him, buddy."

"Negative, Rick. We've got new orders. Seems that Commander Hayes has gotten herself stranded on the base and it's up to us to rescue her."

"Hey, like we don't have more pressing matters at hand?"

"Come on, I thought that damsels in distress were your stock 'n' trade, Little Brother."

"One damsel at a time, Roy. One at a time."

Roy's face became serious. "Patch your system into the SDF-1 mainboard and home in on the signal they transmit. I'll be covering you."

"Roger," Rick said. "One rescue coming up."

He pushed the fighter into a shallow dive that brought him into and through a group of alien pods. Those that didn't take each other out in an effort to bring him down, Rick dispatched with close-in laser fire directed at the pods' fuel lines. Roy was running interference up ahead, diverting some of the pods positioned between Rick and the base.

Rick dropped the fighter to ground level, relaxed back into his seat, lowering his mind into transitional alpha and directing the Veritech's transformation to Guardian mode. The fighter was soon tearing along the ground in a sort of combat crouch, gatling cannon held out front by the huge grappling hands of the mecha. Rick rode out a cluster of explosions in this form, then hit his thrusters and brought the mecha into full Battloid mode to deal with several pods along his projected course.

Upright, the Battloid swung the cannon in an arc and trap-shot two of the pods. A half twist and Rick beat another to the draw. Rick let Roy deal out injustice to the rest and shifted his attention to the homing signal. Info from the SDF-1 bridge told him precisely where the commander was located: inside the barracks building, just on the other side of the wall in front of him.

In four minutes the entire base was going to be a memory. And that didn't leave him enough time to use the doorway. He retransformed to Guardian mode and readied the massive metalshod fists of the mecha.

Now it was Lisa's turn to play the ghost.

She had walked through Riber's quarters, insulated from the harsh atmosphere by her suit, arms extended, gloved fingers reaching out and touching everything in the small room, expectant, in search of something she couldn't identify or name. What was it she hoped to find here? she asked herself. It was as if Karl's clothes, still in the wardrobe closet, his bed, reading light, and phone held clues to some mystery she hoped to unravel.

And now as she sat at his desk, paging through his notebooks and reading the titles of the books stacked there—*The Martian Chronicles, Mankind Evolving, Gandhi's Truth*—Lisa realized that she would never get over his loss; she would never be able to leave this place. Her life, along with Riber's, had ended here six years ago.

She fell forward onto the open notebooks and began to weep. Claudia was desperately calling to her through the headset, but Lisa already felt disconnected from that present. She switched off the radio transmitter. She was about to raise the faceshield of her helmet when she heard her name called out through a speaker phone of some sort.

On the other side of the room's thick translucent window, she could discern the shape of a Veritech fighter—a veiled Guardian behind a Permaglass gate.

"Commander Hayes," the voice called out. "Please stand back. I'm going to crash my way in."

Quickly, she switched her radio back on.

"Whoever you are, stay away from here. Return to the ship. That's an order."

The fighter pilot paid her no mind.

"Stand back. My orders are to get you out of here."

Before she could speak again, the Guardian's huge hand had smashed through the window and the pilot—Rick Hunter!—was staring at her from the cockpit.

"Climb aboard-quickly! We don't have much time left!"

"I'm not leaving this room!"

"One minute and counting, Commander."

"I don't care! Go on, do you hear me, save yourself!" She saw him shake his head.

"I don't know what's going on here, but you're coming with me."

And in an instant Lisa was held fast in the grip of the Guardian's hand. It was useless to struggle; the Veritech was already backing away from the barracks building and preparing for takeoff.

She found herself reaching out toward Riber's room nevertheless, clinging to it with all the strength she could summon, screaming out his name as the fighter launched itself and sped from the burning base.

Khyron pressed the attack, urging his forces onward with calls to glory and promises of promotion; when those failed, he resorted to simple threats and imprecations. Several times during the exercise he had decided to deal out punishments on the spot, and occasionally he had been forced to sacrifice the innocent. But this was all part of the warrior's life, not regrettable but expected behavior.

It had been a glorious battle—up until now.

The Micronians had begun to retreat toward Zor's ship, a retreat with at least three-quarters of their original forces still occupying the arena. He was confused and angered. Were the Micronians such spineless creatures that they would choose surrender over death in battle? Zor's ship, held fast by the gravity mines, wasn't going anywhere, so what did these fools expect to gain by a retreat? It would only mean a nastier mop-up operation for Khyron's troops. The space fortress would have to be stormed, or perhaps he would decide to starve them out; but in either case the end result would be death, so why not go out fighting?

Gerao was reporting certain anomalies in the gravity mine field—some sort of pressure buildup the sensors had yet to identify—but with the Micronians on the run, this was hardly the moment for caution or indecisiveness. Khyron would have the enemy captain's head before nightfall!

The Zentraedi forces had routed the enemy from the base, and their commander was about to join them there, when the surface of the planet began to quake with unnatural force. Some massive explosion deep below ground level was working its way upward. And when it broke the planet's skin, it was greater than anyone— Zentraedi or Earthling—might have expected.

In an instant, the base and most of Khyron's occupying army were obliterated as a tower of raw unleashed energy shot from within the planet. Through the blinding glow of the initial explosion, Khyron could see Zor's ship lifting off, just moments before a second explosion of equivalent force atomized what was left of the area.

Khyron's Officer's Pod was far enough away to withstand the blast, heat, and follow-up shock waves and firestorms.

Madness, Khyron thought. *Madness!*

He raised the cockpit shield of the Battlepod and sat for a moment in stunned silence. Thick clouds of rust-colored dust were being sucked into the area. Zor's ship was just a preternatural shimmer in the Martian sky. The Micronians had surprised him.

Unpredictability was something to fear and respect in an opponent. But failure in battle was something that could not be tolerated.

He vented his anger by smashing his fists into the console of the Battlepod, then collapsed back into the seat, spent. He reached out for the dried leaves of the Flower of Life, ingesting several of these and urging their narcotic effect to wash over him. Ultimately Khyron smiled maliciously. He gazed up at the dwindling space fortress and said aloud:

"We'll meet again, Micronians. And next time I will give you no quarter."

07

I admit it: In those early days I had trouble playing by the rules. Of course, ultimately I learned to return salutes, use the proper phrases, demonstrate respect for my superior officers, and generally behave like a model Robotech soldier. But I continued to have real problems with the system of promotion. If it had been up to me, medals would have been handed out to everyone who went out there. There wasn't one among us who wasn't deserving; not one among us who wasn't qualified to lead.

The Collected Journals of Admiral Rick Hunter

THERE WAS A SPECIAL DATA CHAMBER IN BREETAI'S FLAGSHIP THAT was off limits to all but the highest-ranking officers of the Zentraedi elite. In here were stored the historical records of the Zentraedi race: documentation of past victories, military campaigns, great moments in the lives of great warrior leaders. In addition to these were banks of information relating to the Invid and several dozen other sentient life forms that inhabited the Fourth Quadrant of the galactic local group. As chief science officer and transcultural adviser on all issues dealing with interracial contact (more frequently, conquest), it was Exedore's duty to commit to memory a vast amount of this accumulated lore and knowledge. Indeed, this room belonged more to the misshapen Zentraedi than to any other. And the more he delved into data pertaining to the Micronians, the more apprehensive he became. The pursuit of Zor's ship, and this continued contact with the ship's Micronian warriors, was destined to end in unprecedented failure—an undoing of all that had been carefully laid down and preserved for millennia. Try as he might, Exedore could not put this thought from his mind. If the Zentraedi were defeated, what then could stand in the way of the dreaded *Invid?*

He had mentioned these misgivings to Breetai, careful to couch his phrases in such a way that no fear or cowardice could be inferred; he had even gone so far as to quote some of the documents to the commander, pointing out the specific warnings about contact with the Micronians. Legends which spoke of a Micronian secret weapon that would be used against any invading race. But his words fell on deaf ears. Breetai was, after all, a military tactician; like most of his race he lived and breathed for battle and warfare—the Zentraedi were born to this. Moreover there was some unspoken fascination at work here, as if in some half-understood way Breetai too was aware of Exedore's thoughts about destiny and undoing.

Just now the two Zentraedi were standing together in the observation bubble of the bridge. The SDF-1, in high relief against a starlit crescent of this system's fourth planet, filled the forward screen. Khyron's forces, though unsuccessful in capturing the ship when it had been lured into Breetai's trap, had nonetheless prevented the Micronians from gaining any distance to their homeworld.

"It amazes me that they have managed to come this far," said Breetai.

"Yes, Commander, and they will fight more fiercely as they near their planet. I fear that the ship itself may be destroyed long before we can enforce a surrender."

Breetai became agitated. "That must not be allowed to happen, Exedore. My orders have been most specific: I want the fortress captured intact and undamaged. The *ship* is our primary concern, not the people in it."

"Sir, I fear that Khyron understands destruction only. 'Capture' is too subtle a strategy for him to comprehend."

Breetai shot his adviser a look. "Khyron is a Zentraedi. He'll do as he's ordered or face the consequences."

Exedore bowed slightly. "Certainly, my lord."

Would that it were so, he thought. And did the Micronian

commander in charge of Zor's ship have similar issues to deal with, or were orders carried out without question at all times? Like the Zentraedi, the Micronians were a warlike race; but had they too arrived at that evolutionary point where individual initiative was willingly relinquished for the greater glory of the whole? The data documents were not clear on this point.

Exedore stared at the fortress, as if attempting to project himself onboard. What were the Micronians planning? he wondered. What would any *one* member of that race be thinking at this very moment?

She loves clothes. Her favorite colors are shades of pink and purple. She lacquers each fingernail with a different color polish. She likes to wear dangling, outrageous earrings, shoes that give her more height and match her mood, bright belts with large buckles… "It's no use!" Rick said out loud. He got up off the bed and began to pace the scant distance it took to cover his new quarters wall to wall.

The invitation to Minmei's birthday party lay unopened on his bed, the envelope sealed with a paste-on red velvet heart. *Cute*. There was no need to read it—half of his division had received invitations, and everyone was flashing them in front of his face with knowing smiles. He wasn't sure that he was even interested in going to the party under the circumstances. When it was just the two of them, everything was fine. But in a large group, Minmei wanted center stage and Rick often felt like just another nobody in the audience. Just another faceless member of Minmei's adoring public. *Neglected*. Yeah, that was how he felt. And jealous, he had to admit it. Angry, confused, depressed… the list went on and on. It was almost as long as the list of possible gifts he'd formulated. But none of the items seemed quite right, not one of them was *perfect*, and that was what he was shooting for. Something that would say what he couldn't confess.

And just what was that? he asked himself. He wanted to tell her how special she was—how beautiful, and sexy, and charming. How flirtatious and conceited and spoiled and—

All this was getting him nowhere—fast. He collapsed onto the bed, put his hands under his head, and stared at the ceiling. When he closed his eyes and tried to think things through once more, something unexpected happened: The face of Lisa Hayes filled his mind. This wasn't something new, but it continued to take him by surprise. The truth was, it had been happening a lot since Sara Base.

Was he really such an idiot that he was going to invite yet another woman to run roughshod over him? An older woman at that, a superior officer who gave every indication of despising him in spite of his rescue efforts on her behalf? A cold and distant plain-looking woman who seemed more a part of the SDF-1 than a part of the crew? So why was he suddenly feeling that she too needed protection and affection?—*his* protection, *his* affection. But Lisa occupied a different place in his heart than Minmei, someplace he couldn't reach with thoughts alone.

Rick was rescued from this by a call announced through the intrabarracks comm system.

"Attention the following personnel: report to headquarters: third lieutenants Justin Black and James Ralton; second lieutenants Xian Lu, Carroll James, and Marcus Miller; first lieutenants Thomas Lawson and Adam Olsen…"

Rick listened for a moment, lost interest, and was about to rehash his dilemma, when he heard his own name called.

He made himself presentable and left the barracks, walking listlessly toward headquarters and wondering what he might have done to get himself called on the carpet this time. He ran through a mental list of the possibilities as he rode the elevator to the command level of the ship.

It was a day for lists, that was for sure.

A female lieutenant led him into a briefing room where the others whose names had been called were already gathered. Rick fell into an end position and looked down the line: Black, Ralton, Olsen… these guys were all square shooters. No one needed to read them the riot act, and not one of them seemed the slightest bit concerned; just the opposite, in fact: confidence and pride radiated from each face.

When a captain called attention, Rick squared his shoulders and feigned unconcern. Colonel Maistroff and some of the top brass entered the room. The colonel seated himself at a long table and glanced through the files piled in front of him; then he cleared his throat and addressed the line.

"Since the battle for Sara Base on Mars, the men assembled here have established for themselves records of bravery under fire. Therefore, I am pleased to award them the titanium Medal of Valor for their distinguished service. Gentlemen: We proudly acknowledge your achievements!"

The female lieutenant had carried over a flat unlidded box, and from this Maistroff lifted out the medals, pinning one to each breast in the line and offering his hand in congratulations. Rick wanted to pinch himself to make certain he wasn't dreaming. He craned his neck to try to get a good look at the medal after Maistroff had decorated him.

When the brief ceremony ended, Rick left the room. He found Roy Fokker waiting for him, all smiles and beaming like a proud older brother.

"Nice going, Rick."

They shook hands and embraced. Rick said, "I still can't believe it."

"Amateur civilian ace for eight years running and you're not used to awards by now?" Roy laughed. "Come on down to my office for a minute."

They caught up on the events of the past few days as they walked. At the office, Roy motioned Rick to a chair and positioned himself behind the desk opposite him. He opened a drawer, retrieved something, and tossed it to Rick.

It was a small, flat leather case. Rick hefted it and asked, "What is it?"

Roy's smile was enigmatic. "Go on, open it."

Rick snapped open the lid: Lieutenant's bars rested on a green velvet bed.

"You've been promoted, Rick."

Lieutenant Rick Hunter.

Rick asked Roy to say it so he could get used to the sound of it.

"Lieutenant Rick Hunter."

Rick signaled his approval with a nod. It sounded fine. Next he

turned his attention to the information contained in the dossiers
Roy had given him.

I'm assigning two subordinates to your command.

Some of the dossier material flashed across the monitor
screen on Roy's desk: CORPORAL BEN DIXON; 378 HOURS IN FLIGHT
SIMULATION AND 66 ACTUAL HOURS. CLASS A. MAXIMILLIAN
STERLING; 320 HOURS IN FLIGHT SIMULATION AND 50 ACTUAL HOURS.
CLASS A.

While he listened, Rick absently fingered the medal of valor
pinned to his jacket.

"These guys are novices, Roy."

Roy stuck out his jaw. "You're the old veteran now?"

"Well, I've flown more missions than these two."

"To me you're not a lot different from them, Little Brother.
You've flown more than some but a lot less than most of us. It's too
early for you to get cocky."

Rick considered this sullenly. He removed the medal and
regarded it. *What is it really? Just something to make me feel better about
going out as cannon fodder again.*

Roy had gotten up to answer a knock at the door, and when Rick
looked up, he found his two new subordinates stepping forward in
formal salute to introduce themselves.

Dixon, the larger of the two by almost a foot, was muscular and
aggressive. He had a crop of undisciplined brown hair that rose from
his head like flames caught in freeze frame. There was a note of
arrogance about him, but this was softened somewhat by his husky
self-mocking laughter. Sterling, in contrast, was mild-mannered and
soft by voice. And yet there was something almost false about his
humility. He wore his hair long, with uneven bangs that kept falling
in front of his aviator glasses. It was unusual to meet a pilot with
impaired vision, and Rick reasoned that Sterling's talents had to
outweigh the disadvantages presented by less-than-perfect eyesight.

Rick acknowledged their salutes, and Roy made the informal
introductions. But after a few minutes of pleasantries, Rick was
beginning to feel uncomfortable with his two new dependents and
took advantage of a lapse in the conversation to excuse himself.

Minmei's party would be kicking off soon, and he wanted to catch her alone for at least a few minutes. However, when Ben and Max suddenly expressed an interest in accompanying him, Rick reconsidered his options: Showing up at Minmei's with new lieutenant's bars *and* two subordinates in tow would surely gain him some points. At least it would show her that his superiors viewed him as responsible and serious, even if she chose not to.

So the three of them left Fokker's together, already exchanging stories and searching out common ground. They tubed into Macross City, hitting a few spots on the way, and it wasn't long before they were fast friends.

Macross was a different experience each time Rick visited it. Resident old-timers—people born back in the 'forties and 'fifties—claimed that it would have taken generations to construct what Robotech engineers and crews managed in a week. All of this was due to technological advances brought about with the arrival of the SDF-1. Some of the city had been "created" through the use of Enhanced Video Emulation—the people were fed illusions as in some turn-of-the century film—but most of it was a real, pulsing metropolis now. Certainly no city on Earth could boast of a park with views to match those from Macross Central. You were not just staring up at the stars from the benches there; you were among them.

The three VT pilots were a few blocks from the White Dragon, when several "death-beds" rumbled by—huge flatbed vehicles carting off the battle-damaged remains of Veritech fighters to recycling. Without raw material, the SDF-1 techs had to reuse everything.

Rick looked over at his new comrades and studied their reaction to the passing wrecks. His jubilant mood had vanished. Fighter pilots were similarly recycled, he told himself.

"There's the whole truth about war," Rick said, gesturing to the death-beds.

"I don't want to end up like that," said Max.

Ben bellowed his laugh. "While I'm around you've got nothing to worry about."

Lieutenant Rick had an impromptu speech on the tip of his tongue, but he decided to let Dixon's remark slide. Ben would find out for himself soon enough.

The war machine would chew them up and spit them out. You could only give it your best shot and hope the odds were in your favor.

"Luck" was a term the Zentraedi were unfamiliar with; their language contained no words for it, and their psychological makeup embraced no such concept.

Khyron had suffered a setback. It had nothing to do with chance or odds. He had failed because he had listened to Breetai and disregarded his own instincts. This would not happen again. This enemy was unpredictable. Where it would be advantageous to press an attack, they would retreat; where it would have been wise to use the massive firepower of Zor's ship, they instead relied on small fighters. And the worst of it was that they seemed to value life above all else. Sooner or later Khyron would have to play on that fear of death they carried around.

He had appointed a new second-in-command to replace Gerao, who was now in solitary confinement for having failed to detect the Micronians' countermeasures at the abandoned base. The blank faceplated visage of this second was currently on the monitor screen in Kyron's quarters.

"But, my lord," the second was saying, "what about Commander Breetai's reaction to our continued attacks? He has made it clear—"

"Forget about him! Do you dare question my authority?"

"My Lord!" The second saluted.

"We'll deal with that ship in our own way. Now pay close attention: Breetai has prescribed war games for us. This is his way of humiliating me for our failures. But we're going to turn this opportunity to our advantage. We're going to take that ship, if it takes every last piece of mecha in the Zentraedi armada!"

Things were quiet on the bridge of the SDF-1, a little too quiet to suit Claudia Grant. The ship had been in a deep-space orbit around Mars for scarcely a week, but that week felt like an eternity. And it had been that long since Lisa had exchanged more than three words with Claudia or any of the others on the bridge. Something had happened to Lisa down there, but even Claudia couldn't pry any of the details from her. To be sure, it had something to do with Karl Riber. Claudia figured that he must have been quite a man to keep Lisa in limbo for eight years. For most of the ship's crew and the population of Macross City the red planet afforded some sense of stability and center, but for Lisa it was a constant reminder of loss, an orbit of pain.

The enemy had been hammering away at them for the past week, determined to keep them from making any progress toward Earth. But the launch window for a return to Earth was still two weeks away, so they would have remained here regardless. Conserving fuel, making repairs, and using Mars's gravity to throw them toward Earth when the right moment came. Nevertheless, they had attempted to keep the planet between themselves and the enemy; until yesterday, when long-range recon units had reported that a sizable contingent of enemy ships had dropped to an inner orbit near the Martian moon Phobos. The enemy was sandwiching the fortress between their forces. Claudia was worried, and Lisa's continued silence and sulking were not helping at all.

Claudia held something in her hand she thought might break her friend's distracted mood: It was a dispatch from Maistroff's office listing the new field promotions. Rick Hunter's name was on the list. Claudia tapped the dispatch against the palm of her left hand. Maybe anger was just what the doctor ordered.

She sidled over to Lisa, suppressing a grin as she handed over the dispatch.

Lisa accepted it disinterestedly and scanned the short column. Claudia watched her expression change as the name registered. Lisa crumpled up the paper and slammed both her palms down on the radar indicator board.

"I can't believe it! I just… I can't believe this! It's unbelievable!"

"What is it, Lisa?" Claudia was still playing dumb, and not very effectively.

"Don't be coy with me, Claudia. You've seen this list. How does Hunter rate a promotion to group leader?"

Claudia stroked her chin. "Uh, let's see, I think he was involved in some sort of rescue operation—"

"That's a matter of opinion, Claudia. Oh oh…"

Lisa was staring at the radar screen and fiddling with the control knobs. Claudia went over to her.

"What's up?"

She was working the dials, trying to tune something in. "I guess I shouldn't have slapped this thing so hard—it's all static."

"Try switching over to the backup overrides," Claudia suggested. She did, but the static remained.

"I'm going to run this through computer analysis," said Lisa. The two women waited for the system to display its diagnosis.

They sucked in their breath when it appeared: It was a jamming pattern.

"Put us on yellow alert," Lisa said with newfound enthusiasm. "Notify all VT teams to report to their fighters and stand by."

Things at Minmei's party had gone from bad to worse, and for Rick, the yellow alert siren blaring in the streets of Macross City felt like a reprieve.

By the time he and his new cohorts had arrived at the party, the restaurant was already packed. In addition to scores of Veritech defenders and a few of Minmei's show business friends, the mayor and his cronies were circulating around, pressing the flesh. At times it seemed to Rick that Mayor Luan harbored some secret plan for Minmei, as if she was some pet project or secret weapon he was going to unleash on the world. Minmei, dressed to kill in her purple mandarin tunic was at her butterfly best flitting from table to table, center stage no matter where she was in the room. She was hard on Rick for arriving late. Moreover, he had forgotten to pick up a present. She was duly impressed with the new lieutenant's bars but an instant later had taken an immediate shine to shy Max and was at that very moment singing harmony with him to guitar accompaniment. And the mayor hadn't helped matters any when he came over to Rick and in a conspiratorial whisper warned him about letting Minmei get too far out of sight—"She seems quite taken with your new corporal, Rick"—as if Rick could influence what she did and where she went.

Rick had quickly become withdrawn and moody, noncommunicative even when Minmei's orbit took her past his table or her wink from across the room was meant to single him out as some sort of accomplice in her performance. Rick stayed close to the mildly intoxicating punch and kept his eyes down for most of the afternoon.

But then the alert had been sounded.

And now all the flyboys were gulping down their drinks and racing for the door, leaving Minmei standing alone, her song left unfinished, center stage stolen from her by the war. And even though Rick couldn't approve of her petulance and spoiled behavior, he couldn't help being moved by her innocence and naiveté. He wanted to run to her and promise her that this war would go away soon and that all her dreams would come true. But the best he could promise was his return later with the gift he had for her. He gave her his kerchief to wipe the tears from her face, and she put her arms around his neck and thanked him with a hug.

"What would I do without you, Rick?"

He pulled away from her embrace; Max and Ben were calling to him from the hexagonal doorway, motioning for him to get himself in gear—after all, there was a battle to be fought, a war to be waged!

"Come on, Lieutenant, we don't want to keep the enemy waiting, do we?"

Rick looked at Ben and felt a sudden urge to strangle him. *No,* he thought, *we mustn't keep them waiting.*

08

One must now address the reasons for Khyron's failures. Was he
defeated on each occasion by the Earth forces, or was he in fact
defeated by his own commanders? So often recalled from the very
brink of success; so often within reach of victory. Why wasn't he
allowed full rein? Again, there is wide disagreement among the
commentators we have been discussing throughout. Gordon (along
with several of his psychohistorian disciples) wants to convince us
that Dolza and Breetai had so misread Gloval's tactics as to believe
that he would have destroyed the ship rather than allow it to fall in
Zentraedi hands. And yet, Exedore himself has stated that: "...rivalry
had completely splintered the Zentraedi high command. Continued
contact with Human self-initiative had by this time fostered
unrecognized and certainly in comprehensible competitive drives in
the commanders themselves. Dolza, Breetai, and even Azonia (who
had reasons of her own to behave otherwise) were unconsciously
mimicking an emotion they had never experienced. 'For the greater
glory of the Zentraedi' had already become an archaic phrase."

Rawlins, *Zentraedi Triumvirate: Dolza, Breetai, Khyron*

RICK, BEN, AND MAX—THE NEWLY FORMED BLACK TEAM—WERE
ordered to defensive positions in the Fourth Quadrant, close to
the fortress and too far from the main fighting to suit Dixon. He
was anxious to get into the thick of it.

Below them, between the SDF-1 and Mars, Skull, Red, and the
other squadrons were engaging enemy pods. From his vantage
point, Rick could make out a cat's cradle of interlacing laser light

punctuated by brief spherical flashes of death, but most of the battle information came to him via the aircom net. It was beginning to sound like the boys had the enemy on the run; indeed the explosive bursts seemed to indicate that the pods had fallen back to positions closer to the planetary rim.

As the exchanges continued to diminish in size and frequency, Rick began to worry that Gloval was permitting the VTs to fly right into a trap, or worse, that he had ordered offensive action against one of the mother ships. Dixon was ready to join them nevertheless.

"Can't we get into some of that?" he wanted to know.

"We have our orders," Rick told him sharply. "Now, stick close to me and stay alert."

On the bridge of the SDF-1, Gloval was studying the deployment of pods and Veritechs on the threat board. The enemy was trying something new. Instead of assaulting the fortress, as was their usual routine, they were keeping their distance, perhaps fearful that the main gun had been repaired. *Would that that were the case,* thought Gloval. But the more he studied the screen, the more suspicious he grew. The enemy wasn't turning tail to avoid battle. Gloval shook his head in amusement. Did they really think him such a fool? It was obvious that they were hoping to lure the VTs away from the fortress in order to open up a second front.

He was ready to issue a recall order when new data verified his hunch.

Vanessa announced, "We have an attack force of enemy pods at our stern."

Gloval ordered that the Gladiator force be called up, and Dr. Lang was requested to shunt sufficient energy from the shields to arm the main batteries aft. The second enemy wave was coming in from the relatively unguarded Fourth Quadrant, where Hunter's Black Team was on defensive patrol. As this sector was put up on the screen, the bridge crew readied themselves to render assistance.

Rick received the communiqué from the bridge and moments later had the enemy assault team on his cockpit radar display.

"Company's coming," he told Max and Ben. "Let's show them how we treat party crashers."

Locked into the bridge command center, the three Veritech pilots swung their fighters toward the advancing pods. They were still too distant for visuals, but Rick was soon facing those characteristic pinpoints of explosive light that signaled laser bombardment.

A nanosecond later the bolts reached them. Rick ordered his men to begin evasive maneuvers to lessen the staying power of the charge. Some of his own circuits were already fried, but it was nothing he needed to worry about.

And then they had a visual on the pods: There were only a dozen of them, including an Officer's Pod. They came into the quadrant, weapons blazing, the Black Team ready for them.

"I'm gonna fly rings around these guys, Lieutenant. Just watch me go," Rick heard Ben say.

Dixon fired off a cluster of heat-seekers and attempted to roll out. But the enemy had outguessed him, and two of the pods were following him through, positioning themselves on either side of his mecha well inside the lethal cone.

"Break across that seven o'clock bandit, Ben," Rick shouted into the net. "Don't get cute, they're going to catch you in their cross fire!"

Dixon realized he was in trouble and called for an assist. The two pods were practically on top of him, pouring particle-beam energy at his booster pack. A Veritech could stand only a few seconds of this; ultimately, structural molecules would be altered and the ship would come apart. Ben would be fried alive.

Rick kicked in his aft boosters, found one of the pods in his reticle, and loosed two missiles. They caught the pod at its weakest spot, just where the cockpit cover was hinged to the main body of the sphere. The hatch blew open, precious atmosphere was released and the pilot inside clawed frantically at his controls. Soon the lifeless thing was drifting aimlessly out of the arena.

The second pod was still throwing heat into Dixon's fighter, but the pilot, realizing that *he* was now outnumbered, began to drop away.

"I'm going to save your skin, Ben. Just retro when I give the word." Rick haloed the ostrich and shouted, "*Now!*"

His thumb came down hard on the Hotas trigger. Two missiles

dropped from their pylons and connected with the pod, blowing it to pieces.

While Ben was thanking him, Rick looked around for Max. There was a lot of activity going on off to his right; as Rick was soon to realize, Max was at the center of it.

The corporal had shifted to Battloid mode and was using the gatling cannon to take out pod after pod, executing evasive maneuvers the likes of which Rick had never seen. Max was pushing the Veritech into reverses Rick wouldn't have believed possible. He had heard about pilots who could totally surrender themselves to the alpha state, but he had never seen anything like this with his own eyes.

"Look at him go!" Dixon was yelling on the tac net.

Max had second sight, eyes behind his head, a sixth sense… the enemy mecha couldn't get near him. He was polishing off the last of the assault group, and Rick was on the horn congratulating him.

"I'm happy I was able to help out," came the humble reply. "Now I'll show you something I learned in flight school."

Rick was amazed: Max was literally about to *talk* Ben and him through a maneuver; it was difficult enough to control the complexities of the Veritech weapons system and answer to the demands of the mecha, but to have anything left over for movement, let alone human speech!… But here was Max, explaining every move as he went after two new entries. He drew the enemy in, then suddenly inverted himself, firing his thrusters so that he was coming right down their throats with his weapons blasting. The two pods were taken out, along with a third that had appeared at Rick's port side unannounced.

Rick's jaw went slack.

"It's called Fokker's Feint," said Max. "You have to confuse them. And while they're looking for you, you come up behind them and tap them on the back!"

Lisa Hayes was suddenly on the net at the same time, berating Rick for his poor response time. He offered as an excuse the two inexperienced pilots he had with him, listening to himself while watching Max execute a flourish of moves.

Maybe this was one of the advantages to being a superior

officer, he thought. Foul up and you could lay the blame on your men; succeed, and their victories were your own.

Khyron was observing the progress of the battle from his Officer's Pod. The diversionary strategy wasn't working out exactly as he had hoped, but it had opened up a few holes in the fortress's defensive perimeter. Most of the Micronian mecha had been successfully lured far from Zor's ship, and those few remaining fighters were rapidly being eliminated. The second assault team had taken the sting out of the main batteries of the SDF-1, and the mecha dispatched to slow their attack had been eliminated. Now it was time for the coup de grace: Khyron's special elite assault team would storm the fortress and put an end to this game.

It was almost too easy…

Through his headset, Rick heard the voice of Lisa Hayes:

"Enemy forces have broken through our defenses in the Third Quadrant. You're our only hope, Black Leader."

"We're on our way," Rick told her.

Ben was out front, making up for lost time with continuous fire, little of it effective. Rick warned him not to waste his ammo. Max, meanwhile, took two pods off Rick's tail and asked Rick if it was all right to fire when it *wasn't* a waste. Rick ignored the joke and ordered Max and Ben to split up, hoping they could drive a wedge into the attacking enemy units.

Only a few of the Phalanx and close-in guns on the SDF-1 were capable of giving them cover fire, and most of those had sustained some damage. Destroids and Gladiators floated above the ship, pieces of debris, sparking out as they drifted toward oblivion.

Rick, already reaching out for the B mode lever, ordered his team to switch over to Battloid. He watched as the tailerons of Max's fighter folded down and the wings swept fully back to lock into place. Next, the entire undercarriage, including the twin aft thrusters, swung down and forward, riding on massive pins located beneath the cockpit module. As rear thruster sheaths chevroned to become the Battloid's feet, the ventral fuselage halves split away from each other and spread outward to form the arms. Hands slid out from armored compartments. Inside the mecha Max's seat would now be riding upward along a shaft that would reposition the pilot inside the head—a minute ago the undercarriage laser-gun bubble. Rick's own fighter was going through the same changes. He could sometimes feel his own body react, as though unseen hands were at work on him.

Thus reconfigured, the three members of the Black Team touched down on the SDF-1's hull and brought their gatlings to bear on incoming enemy pods. Ben stood his ground, screaming curses at the ostriches as they made their approach. Initially he was positioned near one of the damaged phalanx guns, his cannon at high port, but he stepped out into the open to trap-shoot an incoming bandit just as a second flew in from behind and dropped him with a blast that caught the Battloid full in the back. Rick winced and tried to raise him on the net.

"Ben, are you alive in there?"

Dixon answered weakly; he was hurt but had somehow managed to survive the hit.

Rick was moving in to lend a hand, when several pods appeared over the horizon of the ship. High-density transuranic slugs from the galling brought two down. Two others loosed their rockets ineffectively and streaked overhead, but the Officer's Pod that led them seemed determined to go one on one with him. It was the second time that day that Rick was to witness incredible maneuvering.

The Officer's Pod—not spherical like the others but somewhat elongated and fishlike above its legs, with twin "hand-gun" arms and a top-mounted long-muzzled plastron cannon—toyed with him, dodging each of his shots as though the pilot inside could read Rick's mind. The pod leaped over a conning tower and came down behind him; Rick turned and fired, but the enemy was already spaceborne again and swooping in, clawed legs swinging back and forth, discharging rounds from its hand-guns.

Rick's mecha took several hits through the torso; then the glancing blow of a projectile sheared off the Battloid's left arm.

Rick thought the damaged vehicle down to one knee as the enemy pod came in to finish him. When it was within reach, he brought the Battloid to its feet and used the useless cannon to bat at the thing. He connected, driving the ostrich into a spin that brought it crashing down to the surface of the ship, minus one of its own cannon appendages.

The two mecha faced each other across a distance of about 200 meters—a showdown on a western street. Rick worked frantically at the controls, trying to divert power from the main mechamorphosis systems into the main gun, but all his efforts proved futile. He stared out of the cockpit faceplate of the Battloid as the enemy manning the Officer's Pod raised the muzzle of the one good arm and prepared to fire…

Onboard the Zentraedi flagship Breetai was informed of the battle being waged against the SDF-1, in direct violation of his orders. He rushed from his quarters to the command bubble, where Exedore was waiting for him, watching images play across the projecbeam field with growing disgust.

"It is as I feared, Commander. Khyron has taken matters into his own hands once again."

Breetai stood, arms akimbo, regarding the action as explosive flashes of light reflected in his faceplate.

"So this is Khyron's idea of war games?" Breetai snorted. "Again he has the temerity to disobey my orders!"

"I suggest that we recall him… before he succeeds in destroying the ship."

"The fool, I warned him." Breetai turned away. "Use the nebulizer to override the astrogational systems of his attack force. We'll pull this offensive out from under him."

Exedore moved to the nebulizer controls. "Ready to initiate on your command."

"Mark!" Breetai shouted to the screen.

Warning lights were flashing on the bridge of the SDF-1. Sensors were picking up energy readings of an extraordinary type. Astrogational and engineering were reporting dangerous fluctuations in the drive systems; it was as if all control had been lost.

Meanwhile, on the skin of the ship, Khyron was taking aim at Rick's Battloid.

The Zentraedi commander felt the pod suddenly surrender itself to a higher power and knew at once what had happened: Breetai was recalling them. On the very brink of victory, and the fool was recalling them! He could do nothing; the nebulizer had even neutralized the weapon system of the pod. This fortunate Micronian pilot would live to fight another day, Khyron said to himself as the Officer's Pod rose involuntarily from the skin of Zor's ship. He could see the Battloid lift its head in some gesture of wonder or amazement and could only guess how the pilot inside was reacting.

Rick would recall his feelings later, too stunned at the moment to analyze his reactions.

In the aftermission debriefing room they would all report the same thing: that the pods had suddenly abandoned their attack and lifted off, as though they had been given some sort of recall signal.

While Dr. Lang tried to postulate the cause of the strange readings he had received and Gloval asked himself why the enemy had called off its attack, Lieutenant Hunter had a private session with his two new charges in the mess hall of the *Prometheus*.

Ben's head was bandaged. On the positive side, it seemed that one of those blasts had finally gotten it through the corporal's thick skull that discretion was the better part of valor. Max, on the other hand, credited with at least nine kills, was basking in self-adulation, wondering only half in jest whether the brass might not end up promoting him from corporal to general overnight.

Still amazed by what he had seen Max accomplish during the battle, Rick found that his respect for his fellow pilot was marred by feelings of jealousy. But he was too exhausted to dwell on it; he had just enough residual energy to carry him to his quarters. He was already thinking about crawling into his bunk and courting sleep.

An hour later he was standing in the doorway to his room,

reaching in to hit the light switch. One step inside and his eyes fixed on the bed and the invitation laying there, paste-on red heart seal still unbroken. He groaned: Minmei's birthday present! It was like a bad dream, like being up in your Veritech and suddenly realizing you'd forgotten to ammo up.

Rick started pacing the room, trying to recall the mental list of gift possibilities he'd composed earlier. What was it—shoes, jewelry, clothes? He checked his watch: twenty-two thirty. He knew he didn't stand a chance, but he had to give it a go.

He rode an empty tube into Macross City and ran up and down the streets searching for an open store, cursing EVE with every step, because before these artificial sunrises and sunsets the city had rocked twenty-four hours a day. Now you were lucky if you stumbled on a place that served hamburgers past midnight. Then he spied a robo-vending machine on one corner and called to it; he would swear that the thing turned and looked at him before streaking away. Why did they do this? Rick asked himself as he gave chase. Human and animated robo-vendor ran for several blocks through the late-night deserted streets of Macross, Rick calling out to it, pleading with it, and ultimately cursing it. But the device managed to outrun him.

He caught his breath and began heading in the general direction of Minmei's apartment above the White Dragon. He was going to have to tell her *something*—*anything* but the truth: that he'd been too busy doing battle with the enemy to get her a gift. Of course, there was a chance that she was already asleep. Maybe he would just sort of lurk around underneath the balcony of her apartment, see if there were any lights on up there…

As if on cue, though, she came to the window, saw him out there under the streetlight, and threw open the balcony doors, calling to him.

"Rick, I knew you wouldn't forget." She was checking her wristwatch. "Five minutes to go. What did you bring me?"

He started to trip over his words. "Well, look, Minmei, about your present, you see, I was planning… er, that is, what I meant to tell you before…"

She laughed. "Come on, Rick, don't be a jerk. I don't care what you brought me. It's the thought that counts. Now, throw it up here. Come on."

Rick's arms fell to his sides in a gesture of complete helplessness. But his right hand had found the boxed Medal of Valor in his trousers pocket. He pulled it out and regarded it in the streetlight. The brass had given him this to single him out; it said: Listen, you are something special, you've been of extraordinary service to all of us in this war we're waging, wear this and be proud, wear this and be recognized by your fellow comrades.

So why couldn't it say the same thing to her: By giving it to her he was saying that *she* was really the special one, that his bravery and valor were in her honor, that she was his inspiration, the person he returned *to—the reason he returned.*

He snapped the lid closed and gave the box an underhand toss toward her outstretched hands. He couldn't see her face well enough to judge her reaction, and for a moment the silence unnerved him. But when she spoke, he was certain there was no insincerity in her voice.

"Rick, I don't know if I can accept this. Really…"

"I want you to have it, Minmei. It—it says what I can't say to you. Please, keep it."

She held the box to her cheek. "It's beautiful, and I love it."

Rick smiled. "Happy birthday."

She blew him a kiss and waved good night.

Rick waited until the lights went out, then walked the quiet streets of Macross City. It was peaceful and pleasant. Dogs barked in the distance and laughter filtered out of open doorways. It was almost like real life.

09

There are so many wonderful things going on in my life, it's sometimes hard to believe it can continue like this. But what would the people of Macross City think of me if I announced to them that getting stuck in the fold and landing out here in deep space was one of the greatest things that ever happened to me? Aunt Lena and Uncle Max's restaurant is really happening; even the mayor comes to eat there. I have three complete songs written: "My Boyfriend's a Pilot," "Stagefright," and "To Love." My dance instructor and my voice coach tell me that I'm making excellent progress, and I'm actually even thinking of sending in an application for the Miss Macross pageant. But I know that I could never be accepted! That is just too wild a dream to come true—even for me!... The only rough spot in my life right now is Rick; and I can't figure out what to do about him. I owe him my life, for real; but he wants me to be something I can never be: a loyal girlfriend, maybe someone who would be content to live in his shadow. But I have shadows of my own to cast!

From the diary of Lynn-Minmei

As THE MAYOR OF MACROSS CITY, TOMMY LUAN HAD A LOT TO deal with. For a long time after the spacefold he harbored a fear that the population was one day going to wake from the collective shock of the experience and he'd have a mass riot on his hands. But that never came about. It was probably an indication of how inured the human race had become to tragedy; ten years of global war had started it, and the arrival of the SDF-1 from deep space, carrying with it evidence of extraterrestrial life forms, had sealed it. But in any case the residents of Macross City were a breed apart from the start.

Tommy Luan had been part of the second wave of newcomers to arrive on Macross Island. The first consisted mainly of scientific and military representatives from the newly formed World Unification Alliance, Dr. Lang and his group, Gloval, Fokker, Colonel Edwards, and others from the supercarrier *Kenosha*. Then there followed the decision to attempt a construction of the ship— "the Visitor," as it was called—and this brought in the numerous tech teams who were really Macross City's founding fathers. Luan was one of these. His background was construction—immense projects: bridges, skyscrapers, hospitals—no job was too large. But the Global Civil War had put an end to an unprecedented period of growth in the building trades, and like far too many others Luan was on the skids and looking for a job. He applied for a position on the Macross project and was accepted. He received a security clearance and once on the island found himself placed in charge of housing construction for the tech and support groups.

As the SDF-1 began to take shape, so did Macross City. The ongoing project to decipher and apply the principles of Robotechnology became the one to try for; Macross Island became a haven for scientists from every discipline, pacifists and idealists disheartened by continued warfare, Senator Russo's military teams, and the support network that grew up to house, feed, and entertain these various groups.

Tommy Luan built Macross City, no one would have taken issue with that; so when it came time to call Macross City what it was and elect officials, Tommy Luan won hands down. And four years later, when the city had grown to a population of over 100,000, Tommy Luan would still be on top.

And now, months after the fold, here was Tommy Luan still in charge. The fact that the city and most of its inhabitants had been rescued was miraculous; what had been done to the city since was equally so. For a time it had been like living in a giant's cellar; enormous conduits and pipes overhead, bulkheads for horizons, the eerie sounds of the ship permeating the city. There was room enough for the 50,000 survivors, but a kind of collective claustrophobia prevailed.

Then there was the disaster that befell them during the first modular transformation and the continued attacks on the SDF-1 by their unseen enemy. But Macross City had weathered it all, and the new city was a marvel to behold. Constructed on three levels that ascended to the massive starport dome, the city had everything it had had on Earth—and then some. There were streets (even hills), shopping malls, electric cars and trucks, a monorail, tube and lift systems, several movie theaters, arcades, an amphitheater, even a radio station. The engineers who had come up with EVE— Enhanced Video Emulation—were experimenting with the blue skies, sunrises, and sunsets. And soon the Macross Broadcasting System would be inaugurated.

But there was an important something missing: There was no news.

Except, of course, what they were *permitted* to broadcast to the population concerning the war. Births and deaths; no crime to speak of; no traffic accidents; no corruption. There was no real life sense to the place; some fear and paranoia, but no real fun or excitement.

Which is precisely why Mayor Tommy Luan had jumped at the idea of running a Miss Macross pageant when Jan Morris's people had approached him.

Jan Morris's people—her agent, her manager, her publicity agent, the whole lot of them along with the noted Hollywood star—had become overnight residents of Macross City since the spacefold. She had been part of a variety show organized in the States and newly arrived on Macross Island to take part in the Launching Day celebration. Now Macross City had the whole show on a permanent basis; in addition to Jan Morris, there was an entire show band, two rock groups, two stand-up comics, and three singers. The Morris group presented the idea of the beauty pageant with real humanitarian zeal: Macross City needed a little excitement, and what better way to inaugurate the new television station than with a knock-'em-dead show with plenty of beautiful women and production numbers. Macross Island had been gearing up for just such an event, but what Morris's people were proposing was not a beauty pageant in the traditional sense of the term—Jan's people knew better than to put their star up against seventeen-year-olds in a swimsuit competition—but more of a Miss Popularity contest based on each individual's contributions to the spirit and growth of the transplanted city. The way they had it figured, Jan would be crowned with the title at the end of the show and everyone would walk away happy.

The mayor had listened patiently to their plan, all the while formulating some thoughts of his own. It was a terrific idea—Macross City could use the boost, any excuse to gather behind an issue that wasn't war-related—but he saw through their motives: It was true that Jan, like so many others, had done her share to keep up the morale in the city, but as an actress (and only a fair one at that) in a world without movies, what else *could* she do but play on her past? But now with the SDF-1 through the launch window and the actual final leg of the ship's homeward journey a real possibility, it was time to think about the future of Jan Morris as a marketable property. After all, her audiences on Earth had surely regretted her loss, and just as surely they had moved on by now. So unless Jan Morris could return to Earth singled out by a title like Miss Macross from the other 50,000 returnees, her future as a star would be bleak. She would have missed her personal launch window.

With the right publicity, Jan Morris would certainly be a shoe-in for the title. But Mayor Tommy Luan didn't want to see that happen. Jan Morris was deserving enough, but her image was all wrong; she represented the past, and moreover, she was not really a *voluntary* resident of the city. No, what Macross City needed was someone whom they could call their own; not just a figurehead but some young woman who would embody the spirit of adventure and survival, of victory and hope.

The Morris group continued to lay out their plans, but unknown to them, the mayor had already chosen the winner. *She would be perfect!* he told himself. Not only was she of mixed background and ancestry, lovely to look at, personable, and talented, but she was already a minor celebrity in her own right.

For two weeks she and her young lieutenant friend had faced an ordeal in the bowels of the ship; it was her family that had reopened the first restaurant in the resurrected city, the White Dragon; and the flyboys all adored her. Yes, she would be perfect, the mayor decided:

Lynn-Minmei, Miss Macross!

Rick was having lunch with Minmei at Variations, a popular eatery on the upper tier of Macross City, when she told him about her entry in the Miss Macross pageant. They had been seeing each other frequently during the past two months. The enemy had pulled back for some reason, and the ship was on a course that would return them to Earth in six months or so. In general, things had been going well, but this was the first definite news Rick heard of the resuscitated contest, and he was speechless; it was hard enough sharing her with half the Robotech Defense Force, and now she was on the brink of becoming the communal property of the entire SDF-1!

"Rick, please don't get like that," she responded to his silence. "The mayor went ahead and entered me without even asking. And besides, you know how much this means to me."

"What are you, his secret weapon or something? I mean, what about *us*, Minmei? I mean… oh, forget it, I don't know what I mean."

She reached across the table for his hand. "Listen, Rick, will you be there for me—you and Roy and the guys? I'm going to need all the help I can get."

He looked into her blue eyes and began to feel the anger leaving him. His smile brought one to her face.

"Of course we'll be there. We're on standby patrol that night, but Roy will be able to pull some strings. Anyway, you're going to win that contest hands down."

"You really think I have a chance?"

"You're a sure thing," he told her. "You *are* our secret weapon, don't you know that?"

After Rick left the restaurant, Minmei ordered more tea for herself and stared out at Macross City's experimental blue skies. *A sure thing,* she mused. If only that were true, if only she could have the confidence that others had in her. The mayor, for one; he was treating her like she'd already *won* the contest, building up her chances, seeing to it that she had enough money for a new outfit. But what chance did she stand against girls like Hilary Rockwell and Shawn Blackstone? Let alone Jan Morris! Hey, Jan Morris was her *idol*!

Minmei's hands fell to her lap. She looked down at her plaid school skirt, the blazer and tie. She thought she saw herself as she really was: just a kid with big dreams. A kid who needed constant attention and encouragement, even when she hated herself for bringing that about. At war with herself: one half weak and scared and full of self-doubts, against a constantly charming, vivacious, confident other half. The former could not for an instant sustain the dream that she would win, while the latter self seemed to embrace that dream as if it was something *meant to be*—destined.

Well, wasn't it enough, she asked herself, just to be a part of the pageant, among those others she looked up to?

The answer was a resounding *no*!

The Macross amphitheater (the Star Bowl, as it was affectionately known) was located at the extreme edge of the enormous hold that housed the city. When planning the amphitheater, Robotech architects and engineers had taken full advantage of a preexisting bowl-shaped depression in the ship's floor and a large spacelight in the ceiling above the building site. The result was about as close to an open-air theater as one could hope for aboard a spaceship. The Star Bowl could seat 30,000, and there wasn't an empty place to be found on the night of the pageant.

The Macross Broadcasting System had labored long and hard to position their cameras for maximum coverage of the event. If all went as planned, the other 20,000 residents would be able to view the pageant from their shops, homes, or any of the curbside monitors that had recently been installed throughout the city.

The host for the show was Ron Trance, a veteran of countless benefit and rear-line shows for the troops during the Global Civil War. Trance had been slated to run the SDF-1 launch celebration and had been caught up in the fold. The seven judges included Colonel Maistroff and Captain Gloval, the editor of the newspaper, a former advertising executive, and three officials from the mayor's office; but these seven were a mere formality—they would handle the contestants' questions and choose the semifinalists but would cast no final votes. That voting would be left to the people of Macross City. Each seat in the arena had been equipped with a sensor that would transmit a vote during balloting, and those in the city could cast their votes by phone or at any of several dozen voting booths.

Minmei's cheering section was seated to the left of the central runway, along the midsection of the amphitheater. Roy and his Skull Team were there, along with the members of Rick's newly formed Vermilion. Other squads were scattered throughout the area. The young lieutenant himself had yet to arrive.

The mayor opened the show, and after a few technical glitches the pageant got under way. The orchestra performed a piece written especially for the pageant, lasers crisscrossed overhead through colored smoke, spotlights played across the stage, and a series of holoprojected letters assembled themselves above to spell out "Miss Macross!" To thunderous applause Ron Trance made his entry, hoofing and singing. The curtains parted, and the twenty-eight contestants strutted on stage in a simple choreographed parade. The grand prizes were announced: a recording contract, a screen test, and a new fanliner, "the latest thing in sports mecha… featuring the powerful new VA hydro-turbine engine, designed by Ikkii Takemi himself…"

Minmei was comfortable with this part of the show. She hadn't realized that the bright lights at the front of the stage would make it impossible for her to see the audience, but it was probably just as well: It was more dreamlike this way, and she felt that she possessed more control over fantasy than real life. But backstage later on, the frights began to take hold of her. All week long she had been coached by her chaperons and support group on how to act during the next portions of the event, but just now she couldn't recall one bit of their advice. So she relied instead on Uncle Max's words: "Just be yourself."

It was while everyone was running around making costume changes for the upcoming poise and question portions of the show that she spotted Jan Morris.

Minmei had been trying to meet her all week long, but Jan's agents had kept her inaccessible. She was the real star of the show, Minmei supposed, and here she was, just one of the contestants, a few seats away talking to her manager. She certainly was pretty, though—blond curls piled by a black and white striped headband, long legs, gorgeous blue dress with red horizontal bands, and that million-dollar smile. But as Minmei overcame her shyness and drew nearer, pen and memo book in hand, to ask for an autograph, she couldn't help but notice that Jan was a lot older than most of the girls and a lot shorter than she appeared to be in her films.

She was also upset about something.

Jan's manager was saying, "I guess they put you at the head of the list because you're the only star. But I've talked them into calling you last."

"Oh, thanks a bunch, Mary." Jan's voice dripped sarcasm.

"Listen, Jan, it's only right that you—"

"Will you stop it, please!" the actress snapped. "This isn't Hollywood. I didn't ask to go to the… planets! Or get stuck in this oversized sardine can."

"So why are we doing this? We don't have to participate in this thing, Jan."

Jan just stared at her. "It goes with the territory, sweetheart. You should know that. I mean, someday we're going to get back home, and I'm not about to play the forgotten star—"

She glanced up at that moment and saw Minmei standing there.

"Now what?" Jan muttered.

"Excuse me, Miss Morris, I'm really one of your biggest fans, and so I was wondering if you'd be kind enough to give me your autograph." Minmei pushed the memo book forward. "I'm afraid this is all I have to write on, though. Would it be all right?"

Jan Morris gave her a cold once-over and, suddenly on the verge of tears, declined. Mary interceded before Minmei could apologize. "If you want an autograph from a *real* star, get yourself a real autograph book." Jan Morris stood up, and the two of them walked away.

Minmei was stunned by the encounter, but she didn't have a moment to think about it: Center stage was calling.

Rick arrived at the amphitheater just in time to catch Minmei's grand entrance. Macross City's mass transit system was so jammed, he'd had to bicycle over from his quarters. He took a seat in the balcony, his binoculars zeroed in on the runway.

Minmei wore a hand-woven lavender mandarin gown of clinging silk, a dress that had belonged to her grandmother and had been altered to suit the girl's slim figure and long legs. The tunic had a simple round collar, flawless embroidery over the left shoulder, and revealing slits. She wore matching pumps and had strands of pink cultured pearls in her braided and bunned hair. Rick thought she looked fantastic as she stepped forward into the bright spot to wait for the judges' questions.

"Could we have your thoughts about the war and the needs of Macross City, your hopes for the future, your ambitions…"

Rick was simply too taken with the sight of her to pay much attention to Minmei's responses, but just then Captain Gloval asked a relevant question: "Do you have a steady boyfriend among all the fighter pilots you count as your friends?"

Rick hung on her every word.

"I don't believe I'm ready for that at this point. I mean, I think it's best to have a lot of different friends."

Colonel Maistroff followed up: "Do you find it difficult having male friends?"

Minmei laughed. "Not at all! In fact, I have one really good friend who's just like a brother to me."

Rick slapped himself in the forehead with the heel of his head. *A brother?! A BROTHER?!!* And just then, while Minmei was taking in the applause, his pager went off. He raised his eyes to the starlight, wondering who was calling him out this time.

10

"Rome wasn't built in a day—Macross City was!"

Mayor Tommy Luan

Had it not been for the Miss Macross pageant, I might never have
undertaken the journey which led me to enlightenment—a journey I
hope to guide you through in the pages that follow. It was only after
I had opened my heart to the First Truth—that beauty and fame were
not only transitory but illusory—that my soul was sufficiently prepared
to accept the profound wisdom of the heavens: the knowledge that we
are but seeds in the cosmic garden, potential given form and the will
to evolve, true children of the stars beings of noble light!

Jan Morris, *Solar Seeds, Galactic Guardians*

WHEN ACCOUNTS OF THE FIRST ROBOTECH WAR WERE FINALLY
written, not one of that war's many chroniclers failed to point
out the curious turn of events precipitated by the Miss Macross
pageant. The word "irony" appears often in those accounts, but
irony is a judgment rendered after the fact and, in the case of Lynn-
Minmei and the part she would come to play in the hostilities,
much too simple and soft a term.

Exedore could no longer allow his growing concerns about the
Micronians to go unspoken. The Tritani pattern was being woven
again, and although it was not the Zentraedi way to look back, the
application of lessons from the past was now essential. Otherwise

the quadrant would surely fall to the vengeful *Invid!*

Just when events had calmed somewhat—Khyron was temporarily reined in and Dolza had issued an order allowing the SDF-1 a brief stay of execution—the Earthlings had once again demonstrated their penchant for the unpredictable.

Strange, incomprehensible telecommunications were being broadcast from the dimensional fortress. Exedore had requested that Commander Breetai meet with him on the bridge.

The audio and visual signals were being broadcast on a relatively low-frequency wavelength; reception was intermittent at best. But even strong and continuous, they would have remained equally baffling to the Zentraedi commander and his adviser. What they saw were images of female Micronians undergoing what appeared to be an unusual metamorphosis, complete with bizarre changes in chroma and an alarming lack of any cause-and-effect sequencing. Breetai and Exedore stared at the screen and turned to each other with confused looks.

"'Miss… Macross… pageant'… What does it mean, Exedore?"

"I understand the individual words, Commander, but the meaning of it escapes me."

"A call for reinforcements, perhaps."

"No, Commander. The signal is far too weak for that."

Breetai experienced a moment of disquiet. Had he overlooked something important in the legends—something about a secret weapon the Micronians possessed, an innate ability to conquer all who threatened them?

"We must decipher this code, whatever it is. Have you been successful in your efforts to teach our agents the Micronian tongue?"

"As successful as can be expected, Commander. They aren't—"

"Ready one of the Cyclops recon ships. Tell your operatives to stand by."

"M'lord," said Exedore, and backed away.

While his adviser was left to carry out the orders, Breetai studied the screen; there was something disturbing about those partially clothed and strangely colored females, a power about them that pierced him like an ancient arrow.

...

As regimented as the Zentraedi were, there were still individual personality types, and the three agents chosen to man the Cyclops recon were to prove as pivotal in the unfolding of events as the Miss Macross pageant itself. At the helm of the arachnidlike vessel was Rico, a wiry, effectively one-eyed warrior with a thin, sunken face, prominent cheekbones, and chiseled features. Bron, a beefy, powerful man with greasy red hair, was the navigator, and in charge of communications was Konda, a nondescript second lieutenant with shaggy, lavender hair well suited to current Earth fashions.

They'd been given a dangerous assignment: The Cyclops had to be brought in close enough to Zor's ship to monitor and record the curious Micronian broadcasts while at the same time evading detection. But Rico was an experienced surveillance pilot, and he soon had the Cyclops well situated for reception. He was not, however, prepared for what greeted his eyes (nor would he be for quite some time to come): Here was a Micronian male wearing some sort of strange devices in front of his eyes, holding in his hand an equally unusual device which he seemed to be directing toward... *a female!* An unclothed female at that! A-and the two of them were actually *together*—in the same space!

"This is unthinkable!" he cried.

Bron and Konda were similarly appalled.

Rico adjusted the recording controls to enhance the monitor image. "She must be wearing some new type of armor."

Bron disagreed: The armor covered the female's hips and breasts only; it didn't make sense.

"Perhaps those are the only vulnerable parts of a Micronian female," Rico offered.

"It's not armor at all," said Konda. "It's a formal uniform."

Bron shook his head. "You're both wrong. It's not even a female. It must be a secret weapon designed to *look* like one!"

Rick Hunter was missing the swimsuit competition.

He cursed his luck and muttered to himself while he strapped into the cockpit module of the armored Battloid. Why did

Hendricks have to pick tonight to get sick, and why did Rick's name have to appear on the top of the patrol list?

He had already gotten into an argument with Commander Hayes—"As primary patrol backup, you should have remained on the base, Lieutenant Hunter, not run off to some foolish beauty pageant!"—and now Minmei was going to be disappointed that he'd missed her big moment. "This sucks!" he yelled to the techs who were operating the module cranes and servos. They had one eye fixed on getting Rick's module into position and the other glued to monitors tuned in to the Miss Macross broadcast. No doubt Lisa Hayes and the SDF-1 bridge crew were doing the same. Meanwhile, Rick Hunter gets to go out into space and search for some enemy ship picked up on the long-range scanners.

Alone!

But if that was the way it had to be, he was going to recon in style, and the armored Battloid was just the ticket.

Still classified as experimental, it was the latest innovation from the Robotech Weapons Division. In addition to the standard armaments and defensive systems of the phase one design, the Battloid was equipped with new generation boosters and retros—the so-called deep-space augmentation pack—multiple-warhead "pectoral" launchers, and ejectable Bohrium-plated armor on those areas previously considered to be "vulnerable to penetration" by the boys in the RWD.

Rick spent a few moments familiarizing himself with the new controls. Fewer foot pedals, that was a plus. A new Hotas design—the hands on throttle and stick—improved ADF and ADI, totally useless before in deep space; a horizontal situation indicator—*ha!*; and a triple-screened TED, stocked with an up-to-date library of alien craft signatures. Rick donned the "thinking cap" and thought the mecha through some simple maneuvers. He then walked it cautiously to the *Prometheus* bay and launched himself from the fortress.

This was deep-space patrol once again, Mars just a memory. But there was some security to be gained from the sight of Sol, blazing bright in the heavens. It was almost beginning to feel like home turf out here.

Rick engaged the power pack boosters and relaxed back into the padded seat, locking onto the coordinates furnished him by the bridge. The enemy ship was thought to be a recon ship patrolling the outer limits of the SDF-1's sensor range.

The comtone sounded through his headset, and the face of Lisa Hayes appeared on the left commo screen. By the look of her, she was disturbed about something. In fact, she was livid.

"Lieutenant Hunter, who issued you permission to take out the armored Battloid? You are supposed to be flying ghost support, not confrontational."

Rick winced as the commander's words rushed out. "Excuse me, sir, but I'm out here on my lonesome, up against some—"

"We'll discuss this later, Lieutenant! Prepare to receive new coordinates."

Rick switched ADF from lock to standby, but the data transfer was incomplete. The displays shut down, and the monitor was suddenly nothing but static lines and snow. Even audio was getting shaky. Rick heard something about "Zenny's fast food." He flipped the toggle to automatic fine-tuning.

"Some sort… -ust interference," Lisa was saying. "I'm…-witch… laser induction. Stand by."

Lisa's face faded and disappeared, replaced by the curvaceous form of Sally Forester walking the Star Bowl runway in a yellow two-piece.

Well, well, thought Rick, relaxing again, *the latest in diversion technique for the battle-weary fighter pilot.* Then Lisa was back on-line for an instant, instructing him to switch over to channel D-3. He tried that, but video reception seemed to be locked on the MBS transmissions. *Tough luck,* Rick said to himself, rubbing his hands together and grinning. It was Hilary Rockwell now, looking choice in her blue suit. Rough decision ahead; *almost easier to be up here,* Rick thought.

And then Minmei was on stage.

It was certainly one of the oddest feelings Rick had experienced in a while: Here he was in deep space, and there was Minmei in her teal bathing suit. As his spirits began to improve, the mecha responded; the Battloid was practically doing pirouettes in space! But the mood was to be short-lived: The console displays were flashing wildly, not out of contagious joy but because heat-seeking missiles had locked onto his tail!

Quickly, Rick commenced evasive action and instructed the stealth systems to launch ghosts. The rear cameras gave him a glimpse of his deadly pursuers—a flock of A/As—and sure enough, the scanners had picked up, registered, and catalogued the enemy vessel. A schematic formed on the port commo screen, profiles, front and rear views, weapons systems, vulnerable spots, suggested response. recon vessel: cyclops type.

Rick fired the boosters and put the Battloid through its paces, pushing it for all it was worth while the heat-seekers continued to narrow the gap. So much for the ghosts. Concerned about their own survival, the warning systems were shouting out instructions, breaking his concentration. He shut down the interior audio supply and looked inside himself for the tone. A cold sweat broke out all over him. He thought the mecha left, right, up, down, and every which way but loose. The missiles were still with him.

And all the while, Minmei was parading across his three screens. They were flashing her measurements, for Pete's sake!

Rick was leading the missiles on a merry chase, but one that was going to have a most unfortunate ending unless he pulled something out of the hat—fast! Fratricide was his only hope. Desperately, he willed the Battloid to turn itself face to face with the heat-seekers and raised the gatling cannon; locking the targeting coordinator onto the leader of the pack, he fired!

Minmei stood in the wings, trembling. But when her name and contestant number were announced, all the anxiety seemed to leave her, she threw her shoulders back, stood straight and tall, and strutted on stage. She knew she looked good—the teal-colored stretch suit fit her perfectly—and given the audience reaction to her previous appearances, she figured she at least had a shot at one of the runner-up positions. If she could only keep it together for the next few minutes...

Her legs were shaking. She felt very unsteady on the high heels; she understood the need for them—added height and their pleasing effect on body posture—but she was unaccustomed to them. Nevertheless, she made it down to the end of the runway without incident. She had made her turn and was starting back, when it happened.

In thinking about it later, she would recall that the heel of her left shoe didn't so much let go as completely disappear as if it had been blown out from under her. But at the moment all she could think about was the embarrassment and the agony of defeat. Two pageant officials came to her aid and helped her up. There was some laughter from the audience, but mostly concern. And she did her best to alleviate that by demonstrating she was a trooper: She put on her best smile and hobbled her way back to center stage. The applause didn't end until long after she reached the wings.

Shawn Blackstone, who had become her close friend during the pageant, was at her side in a flash. She made light of the incident and said that it would have no effect on the judging.

"It shows them you're human, Minmei. Not like you-know-who."

You-know-who was Jan Morris, now making her walk down the runway to cheers and applause as Minmei watched from the wings. Jan was completely self-possessed; she'd been there a hundred times already. She wore a bold, striped suit with a halter top, more daring and revealing than the suits worn by the rest of the contestants— revealing enough to show some stretch marks, Minmei noticed.

Jan stood at the end of the runway taking it in; she had them eating out of her hand. Minmei couldn't watch. She turned aside, the contest over.

Time to wake up.

"You haven't beaten me yet, chumps!" Rick shouted to the stars.

The detonation of the heat-seekers had shaken him up and fried some of the Battloid's circuitry, but he was intact. Fortunately (and puzzlingly), the enemy had not followed up their initial attack. And now it was Rick's turn. He had a fix on the ship and launched enough missiles to wipe out a fleet.

Inside the Cyclops recon ship, the three Zentraedi operatives were so transfixed by the swimsuit competition that they almost failed to react to the counterattack. On the monitors were all those Micronian females, scantily clad (in armor or uniform, depending on whom you listened to), parading themselves in front of an enormous audience. It just had to be weapons demonstration; why else would so many people gather in one place?

And one of the females had fallen. Uncertain if this was part of the ceremony or not, the three began to focus on the fallen one to the exclusion of all else. Something was stirring in each of them—a novel feeling, confused as though half remembered from a previous life, disturbing but strangely appealing.

In fact, it took Rick's missiles to bring them to their senses. The Cyclops took the full force of the explosions and sustained heavy damage, but the weapons system had not been affected. Rico ordered visuals on the source of the missiles and returned fire. He watched the Micronian pilot throw the Battloid into a series of successful evasive maneuvers. Then, without warning, the pilot blew the armor from the ship and swung the Battloid toward them, gatling cannon blasting away.

Rico recognized the no-win situation when he saw one; sacrificing the ship for the crew was not something normally allowed by the Zentraedi command, but this was an important mission, and Rico thought it prudent to do so. With the Battloid still on the approach, he initiated the self-destruct sequence, then ordered his men to the escape pod.

Inside the Battloid cockpit, Rick engaged the foot thrusters and willed the mecha's legs forward; he was hurtling toward the enemy ship now, bent at the waist, feet stretched out in front of him. Upon contact with the recon ship, he grappled on and used the feet to batter his way through the forward bays and into the ship's control station. He was actually seated on the instrument console when he brought up the cannon once again, but by then the crew had already abandoned ship. He raised the Battloid and walked it forward cautiously. A hatchway slammed shut somewhere, and all at once, off to his right, a bank of porthole monitors lit up, Minmei's face on each of the dozen screens.

She was the last image in Rick's mind when the ship exploded.

From the twenty-eight contestants the judges chose five finalists; Minmei was among them. They were seated in the center of the stage now, Shawn and Hilary on Minmei's right, Sally and Jan Morris on her left. Vertical light bars computer-linked to the voting processor rose behind each of them. Ron Trance was speaking. The big moment had arrived.

"And now, ladies and gentlemen…" Ron milked it a bit, playing on the suspense, walking to and fro, cordless mike in hand. "It is time for *you* to decide who will be crowned *Miss Macross!* So get ready to cast your vote."

There was a moment of undiluted silence before Trance gave the word. Then the orchestra began a soft and slow build that quieted the murmurings from the audience and kept time with the ascending columns of light. Minmei wanted desperately to turn around, but she felt glued to her chair. The orchestra continued to pour out an atonal modulation which strained for a crescendo, the audience began to cheer and scream, the light rose higher and higher…

Some of those who were fortunate enough to have been there recall that Jan Morris was rising from her chair when Ron Trance made the final announcement. But it was Lynn-Minmei's chair that he approached, her hand that he took, her song he sang.

Minmei's recollection of the events was poorer than most; try as she might when viewing the tapes afterward, she could not recall her thoughts. All she remembered was the cape that had been draped over her shoulders, the crown placed upon her head, and the fact that when she looked up toward the starlight, it had seemed to her that unseen eyes were upon her, as though the stars themselves had ceased their motion to pay tribute to her moment.

Rick was semiconscious in the cockpit of the drifting disabled Battloid. The damaged instrument panels were flashing out, filling the small space with stroboscopic light. Shafts of pain radiated through him as he fought to reach the surface. Once there, a beatific creature appeared to him, and he felt a glimmer of hope. It wore a beautiful smile, a crown, and resplendent robe of many colors; it carried a scepter and stood proud and tall...

Rick Hunter, however, had strong survival instincts. He managed to reach forward through his stupor and activate the mecha's distress and self-guidance systems. Performing that act brought him around to full consciousness, and at once he realized that the Battloid was still receiving transmissions from the SDF-1. The angel who had visited his vision was none other than Minmei.

Lynn-Minmei, now Queen of Macross.

Rick watched as she surrendered herself to the audience. He reached toward the monitor as though he might touch her one last time before she passed beyond him forever, a part of something that would always be bigger than both of them.

Rick let his head loll forward.

What good was it to wake up in a world he could never enter?

11

"You have to look at things from our perspective: An alien armada appears in lunar orbit and launches an attack on Macross Island, the site of the SDF-1 reconstruction project; Captain Gloval, the fortress, and the entire island disappear. The aliens give chase to the ship and leave us alone. Then a year goes by and Gloval makes contact, informing us all of a sudden that he's returning the fortress to Earth, along with 50,000 people who were supposed to have perished during a volcanic eruption. What else were we supposed to tell the planet—that giant aliens had attacked and might or might not be back? And in addition to this, Gloval still had the armada on his tail, and he's leading the enemy back to Earth! I put it to you, who in their right mind would grant him permission to land? You might just as well invite catastrophe…"

Admiral Hayes, as quoted in Lapstein's *Interviews*

RICO, BRON, AND KONDA WERE BROUGHT BEFORE BREETAI AND Exedore for debriefing. They had escaped death at the hands of the Micronian ace but had failed to return to the Zentraedi mother ship with any substantial information regarding the unusual transmissions from the SDF-1. As a consequence, their lives were once again in jeopardy.

Breetai regarded the three operatives from his lofty position above the floor of the interrogation chamber. The debriefing was going nowhere fast, and he was tempted to put an end to it, but he decided to give it one last chance.

"We will review this again. What did you see?"

Once more the three commenced their explanations simultaneously.

"They were wearing military costumes—"

"It was armor—"

"Just looking at them gave me the strangest feeling—"

"Silence!" yelled Breetai. "It's apparent that none of you know what you saw."

In response to their salute, Breetai folded his arms across his chest and turned to his adviser. Exedore concurred with his plan to send out a second recon unit but went further in suggesting that it might be advantageous at this point to capture one or two of the Micronians alive.

"To what end?" Breetai wanted to know.

"To examine them, my lord. To determine for ourselves if they possess any knowledge of *Protoculture*."

Exedore whispered the word.

Breetai considered it. He was directing his thoughts toward Commander-in-Chief Dolza's possible reactions, when another argument broke out below him. Each of the pilots was certain of what he had seen. It was most curious: armor, military costume, a secret weapon disguised as a partially clad Micronian female…

Breetai allowed the bickering to escalate somewhat, but put a stop to it when physical blows were exchanged. Then he brought his massive fist down on the curved railing of the balcony.

"Enough of this! You were given an assignment, and you bungled it." He made a dismissive gesture. "Return to your quarters and await my judgment."

The pilots bowed and exited, leaving Breetai and his adviser alone in the chamber. Exedore had adopted a pensive pose.

"Of late I have witnessed this same scene all too frequently, Commander. Continued contact with these Micronians has threatened the integrity of your command. Our forces are confused and demoralized."

"Your point is well taken, Exedore. They are accustomed to decisive victories."

"I fear that this game of 'cat-and-mouse' will undermine us, my lord."

"Then perhaps the time has come to talk to them."

"I agree, Commander."

"All right then, consider it done." Breetai grinned. "But we must be persuasive. I doubt they will surrender one of their kind just for our asking."

A planet was centered in the main extravehicular monitor screen of the SDF-1. Even under full magnification it was impossible to discern any surface details; but that made no difference to the men and women on the bridge, who had long ago committed to memory those oceans and continents and distinctive cloud patterns. *Earth!* Darker than they knew it was due to the filters used on the giant reflector scopes, but their homeworld nonetheless. From their vantage, the planet was scarcely ten degrees from the solar disc itself, still on the far side of the sun, but there it was: visible, almost palpable.

Save for the ever-present whirls, hums, and beeps Robotechnology contributed to life on the bridge, you could have heard the proverbial pin drop. Lisa Hayes, Claudia Grant, Sammie, Vanessa, Kim, and Captain Gloval—all of them were transfixed by the sight. But their silence was purposeful as well as ceremonious. They had just directed a radio beam transmission to the United Earth Defense Council headquarters and were now awaiting the response.

All at once static crackled through the overhead speakers; all eyes fixed on these now, the forward screen forgotten.

"Captain Gloval," the voice began, "due to the possibility that our security may be breached and this transmission intercepted by the enemy, we cannot give you the information you requested about our present support systems… Fortunately for us, the enemy forces were more interested in following the SDF-1, and consequently, you are requested to continue to keep them at bay and *not* return to Earth. Repeat: Do not attempt a return at this time. That is all."

This time the bridge crew was just too stunned to speak.

Finally, Vanessa deadpanned, "Welcome home."

· · ·

"I can't believe this," said Claudia. "We're expected to stay out here and be sitting ducks while they, they—Oh, forgive me, sir, I've spoken out of turn."

Captain Gloval said nothing. Was it possible, he was wondering, that after more than a year in space the SDF-1 could simply be turned away, that the council had decided to offer them up as sacrifices? Gloval pressed the palms of his hands to his face as if to wipe away what his expression might betray. It was more than possible, it was probable.

Eleven years ago, when initial exploration of the recently arrived SDF-1 had revealed the remains of alien giants, the World Unification Alliance had decided to reconstruct the ship and to develop new weaponry designed for defense against this potential enemy. It was a ruse, but it had succeeded to some degree in reuniting the planet. Confrontations during the past year had made it plain to Gloval that the enemy had traveled to Earth to reclaim their ship. Just what was so important about this particular vessel remained a mystery, but it was obvious that the aliens wanted it back undamaged. The spacefold undertaken on that fateful day had inadvertently rescued Earth from any further devastation. In this way, the Robotechnicians had done their job: An alien attack had been averted.

Gloval was now forced to take a long hard look at the present situation through the eyes of the Earth leaders. And through the eyes of the enemy. Several possibilities presented themselves. The fate of the Earth might still hang in the balance regardless of whether or not the SDF-1 was captured, destroyed, or surrendered. If the Council was thinking along those lines, then perhaps work was under way on some unimaginable weapons defense system, and time was what they needed most—time that the SDF-1 could buy for them. But if the ship was the enemy's central concern, it would occur to the aliens sooner or later to use their superior firepower to hold the Earth hostage. And how could one compare the loss of 50,000 lives to the annihilation of an entire planet?

Sadly, there was something about the short message that led Gloval to believe that Earth had already written them off.

When the Captain looked up, he realized that Lisa, Claudia, and the others were staring at him, waiting for his reaction.

Full of false confidence, he stood up and said:

"We're changing course."

The Zentraedi had grown so accustomed to the Micronians' erratic behavior and unpredictability that it hardly surprised them when the SDF-1 repositioned itself. Where at one time they would have puzzled over the situation and analyzed its strategic implications, they now simply altered their plans accordingly. And it just so happened in this instance that the course change was easy to accommodate.

Breetai and Exedore communicated their attack plan to Grel, acting liaison officer for the Bortoru's Seventh Division—Breetai refused to have any further direct dealings with Khyron. Grel relayed the information to his commander.

Khyron received him in his quarters onboard the battle cruiser. He had been using the dried leaves again, a habit he turned to in tranquil times, and ingested one as Grel spoke.

"They've changed course?"

"Yes, my lord. Already they have recrossed the orbit of the fourth planet, and our course projections show them closing on the system's planetoid belt."

"Hmm, yes, they seem to fear deep space. Go on."

"While the Noshiran and Harmesta assault groups are engaging the enemy, we are to choose a planetoid of suitable makeup and sufficient size and destroy it. It is Commander Breetai's belief that the Micronians will raise their shields against the resultant debris—"

"Shunting power for the shields from their main battery weapons system."

"Such is Breetai's belief. With their main gun inoperable and their Battloids engaged, Zor's ship will be rendered helpless."

Khyron slapped the table. "Then we move in for the kill!"

"No, Commander."

"What then?"

"Warning shots across the bow of the ship.."

"What!—without hitting them?"

"Commander Breetai will then demand a surrender."

A look of disbelief flashed across the Khyron's face. He threw back his head and laughed. "This reeks of Exedore's hand. What can he be thinking of? We've chased these Micronians through this entire star system. They know we won't destroy the ship, so why expect a surrender now?" Khyron's gestures punctuated his words. "A demand must be backed up with the threat of annihilation."

"I agree, Commander. The Micronians have demonstrated a remarkable tenacity. They will continue to fight."

Khyron thought for a moment. "Suppose they had to fight blindfolded, Grel. Say, without their radar…"

"But Commander, our orders—"

"To hell with our *orders!* I'm not afraid of Breetai."

Khyron stood up and approached his underling conspiratorially.

"What we need now is someone to toss to Central Command. Someone willing to admit to a tactical blunder—a misdirected laser bolt."

"I understand, my lord."

"Good. If no one volunteers, then use your discretion and choose one… We must take care to cover our tracks, my dear Grel."

Had Lieutenant Rick Hunter been privy to Captain Gloval's decision to alter the SDF-1's course (or had he been able to read the stars), he might not have been feeling so desperate, sitting there on a bench in Macross Central Park waiting for Minmei to show. But the way Rick had figured it, Earth was only a few months away, and he had to win Minmei before they arrived. For all its 50,000 inhabitants, Macross still felt like a small town; he stood a chance here. Once they were home it would be a different story.

Rick was not in the best of moods in any case. He was still burning from his most recent confrontation with Flight Officer Lisa Hayes, and now Minmei had kept him waiting for over an hour. He checked his wristwatch against Macross City's new midday sun. A little more magic from the EVE engineers and no one was going to care about returning to Earth, he said to himself.

Since the Miss Macross pageant, Minmei had been all but

inaccessible; seeing her practically required a formal appointment, and on those rare occasions when Rick managed to cut through the red tape, their time together had been brief and awkward. She hadn't even bothered to visit him in sick bay after the recon encounter. Still, the field was clear; she wasn't dating anyone. Her picture adorned the radomes of many of the Veritechs, but only Rick Hunter had access to the real thing.

He checked his watch again and looked around the park. The three bridge bunnies were approaching him. Kim, Vanessa, and... he couldn't remember the young one's name. He didn't feel up to making small talk with them, but there was nowhere to hide.

They started right in on him:

"Well, hello there, Lieutenant Hunter."

"Who are you waiting for?"

"Do you have a date?"

"Been waiting long?"

"Is she really beautiful?"

"Prettier than we are?" the young one asked.

Rick took a good look at them as they struck mock poses for his benefit. They were all attractive, especially the brunette in shorts. But in his eyes Minmei had them beat. He gracefully sidestepped their further questions and a moment later was rescued by a robo-phone that was cruising around the park paging him. The persistent machine was arguing with someone on a neighboring bench when Rick called out to it. Once, then again and again, adding volume to each shout.

Finally the phone homed in on him, insulting some innocent as it left the nearby bench. Rick deposited a coin; Minmei's face appeared in the viewscreen. The three women moved behind him to get a better look. Rick didn't hear their surprised reactions at seeing Miss Macross on the screen and barely acknowledged their good-byes when they wandered off.

Minmei was apologizing. "...It's just that my singing lesson was set back an hour and I'm afraid I'm not going to make it now."

"That's great, Minmei. The one afternoon I'm not on flight duty and you've got singing lessons."

"Listen, Rick, they've decided to do a recording session—"

"Another new career for the 'Queen'?"

Minmei's response was interrupted. She turned away from the camera to respond to someone seated at a piano. The guy was summoning her back to practice.

Minmei said, "Rick, I've got to go," and broke the line.

The robophone moved off. Rick took a walk through the park, not sure if he was feeling anger or self-pity. He was standing by the central fountain when the city's warning sirens sounded. A general alert, but conditional, not confrontational—an environmental threat as opposed to an enemy attack. People were heading toward shelters, but with such unconcern that Rick was tempted to ride it out where he stood.

But just then the fortress was struck.

Rick was knocked off his feet and thrown into the fountain— that fountain that figured all too frequently in his thoughts of fond moments and better times. But he had no time to bathe in waves of memory or irony. The ship was sustaining impact after impact, shaking Macross City to its foundation, and the mood was now one of panic. The "sun" disappeared, and through the overhead starlight, Rick could see an enormous hunk of planetary debris on a collision course with the ship.

"Sound general quarters!" ordered Gloval as he stooped to retrieve his cap. "Give me course correction options based on the current data, and alert—"

The bridge quaked with such force that Gloval was thrown from his chair. Fragments of the exploded asteroid Pamir continued their rain of death against the ship. Klaxons blared, and damage reports poured in.

"Our port side is taking the brunt of it, sir," said Lisa. "Macross is being badly shaken."

"All right," Gloval said, picking himself up. "Concentrate the shield energy there. Divert weapons power to the pin-point barrier system. And get me the air wing commander."

"I have Skull Leader on the horn," said Claudia. "He reports heavy fighting in the Third Quadrant. He's requesting backup, Commander."

"Negative. Give him the situation here. Tell him to stand by for recall. In a minute we're going to be defenseless."

Vanessa, Sammie, and Kim stumbled onto the bridge as Gloval was issuing course correction coordinates. The three women strapped in and began to monitor ship systems status.

It was Vanessa's threat board that revealed the enemy ships.

"Enemy destroyers! They're moving into firing position."

"Those bastards!" yelled Gloval. "Reroute power to the main gun."

"Sir, Macross City will be destroyed if we lower the shields," said Sammie.

"You have your orders," Claudia reminded the young tech. "Without defenses there won't *be* any Macross City!"

"Confirm enemy fire—laser-bolt signatures!"

"Brace yourselves!" said Gloval.

But no shock came. The SDF-1 was fenced in by blue lightning but left unstruck. And Gloval didn't know what to make of it. All at once, however, it became a moot point: The ship sustained a terrible direct hit. All systems failed on the bridge. Presently auxiliary power brought some of them back to life. Gloval requested damage assessment from all stations.

Lisa reported the worse news: The conning tower had been hit. The entire radar control crew had been wiped out.

Gloval ordered all engines stopped.

The dimensional fortress shut down. The enemy had ceased their fire, but chunks of rock continued to impact against it. Debris from the conning tower drifted by the front and side bays. Lisa averted her gaze from the sight of a human body hanging lifeless in the void, a red-trimmed Battloid...

"Can we raise Skull Leader?"

"Negative, sir," said Claudia.

"Do we have any radar functioning—wide-range, perhaps?"

"The report from the technical repair unit is coming in now," said Lisa. She listened a moment. "Estimates of ten hours to effect minimal repairs."

Incoming data to Sammie's station broke the stalemate. It registered a code, but unlike any encrypted transmissions they were familiar with. Gloval ordered her to patch it through the speakers. The ever-present static of deep space infiltrated the bridge; then, a voice: deep, resonant, menacing.

"In the name of the Zentraedi forces, I order you to surrender. The last attack on your ship was a warning of what we will do. You cannot escape. If you wish to save the lives of your crew, you must surrender at once."

"My God," said Claudia. "It's the aliens!"

"We repeat," the voice continued, "in the name of the Zentraedi forces, I order you to surrender. The last attack on your ship…"

Gloval listened carefully to the message. *The Zentraedi,* he said to himself.

Now at least he knew what to call them.

12

It was only during the final stages of the [Global] War that women were assigned to active military operations. Up until that time most women held rear-echelon positions; but as casualties increased among the men unilaterally, these positions came to be of paramount importance. Indeed, by the time of the First Robotech War those positions could only he filled by women. True, there were no women on the United Earth Council, but the entire bridge crew of the super dimensional fortress, the SDF-1, was female. One recalls the postfeminist claims that women were now not only victimized by male aggressive instincts but instrumental in carrying them out, that women (especially in the case of the SDF-1) had exchanged the traditional pots and pans for the keyboards and consoles of the bridge. But those claims not only simplify the issue but malign those women who contributed their unique skills to the war effort. What is most disconcerting is the fact that although women had finally achieved their long-sought-after goal of equality, the Global War had introduced a new set of polarizing issues which now had to be taken into account—there was mutual respect between the sexes but a continued sense of the same old bugaboo about knowing and adhering to "one's place in the world." In terms of male–female relationships, the attitudes of twenty-first-century society suggested those prevalent in the middle of the previous century.

Betty Greer, *Post-Feminism and the Global War*

THE CAT'S-EYE RECON UNIT, ESCORTED BY RICK HUNTER'S Vermilion Team, was launched from the flight deck of the

Prometheus. Fragments of the exploded planetoid littered local space.

Where only hours before they had been ordered to buy time for the United Earth Defense Council, Captain Gloval was now buying time for the SDF-1. The enemy's offensive strength had to be ascertained—the *Zentraedi's* strength—and with the ship's radar down this could be achieved only by deploying the recon vessel.

Lisa Hayes had the stick—the unit's former pilot had been a casualty in the latest Zentraedi offensive. Her copilot was an inexperienced second lieutenant on loan from the Gladiator Defense Force. Most of the air wing strike teams had been deployed to guard the badly damaged SDF-1, looking crippled and deathly still now on the Cat's-Eye's rear commo screen.

Lieutenant Hunter was on the forward screen.

"Ironic, isn't it, Commander," he was saying, "that I should end up your wingman?"

Lisa knew what he was referring to; less than twenty-four hours ago they had gotten into yet another tiff.

One of Vermilion squadron's VTs had taken a hit, and Hunter had informed the bridge that he was taking his group home. The pilot of the stricken VT maintained that the damage was only slight, and scanners showed continued fighting in Hunter's quadrant, with only the Skull Team left to take up the slack; so Lisa had denied him permission to come in.

"I'll be the judge of that," Hunter had said. "I'm group leader, and I'm responsible for the safety of my men!" Then he went on to lecture her about the dynamics of space dogfighting, how seemingly insignificant damage could quickly prove fatal, how she was safe and sound on the bridge while the big brave men of the VT strike force were constantly in jeopardy... On and on.

She dismissed it as battle fatigue. But instead of letting it go, she had vented her own anger and frustration. After all, she *was* his superior.

Then Roy Fokker, guitar-strumming darling of the Defense Force, had stepped in on Hunter's side. They went right into their big brother-little brother act, and the next thing Lisa knew, Fokker was ordering the Vermilion Team home. He did, however, scold Hunter for talking too much.

If the incident had ended there, she would have forgotten it by now. But among the space debris that had floated past the bridge bays following the Zentraedi attack there was a disabled Battloid she had been certain was Hunter's red-trimmed own. She had even imagined (or, more likely, hallucinated) that she saw Rick's lifeless form drift from the shattered cockpit module...

Even now the image was too painful to recall.

Hunter had rescued her on Mars. But so what? He'd been *ordered* to do it. Any of the VT pilots would have done so; it certainly didn't mean that she had to feel anything special for the guy. Of course, it might have been different if she felt something coming from him, but—

"I show four bogies at four o'clock relative," her copilot informed her.

"I see them," Lisa heard Rick say.

"There going to try a surprise attack," said Ben Dixon. "Let me at 'em."

"Negative, Ben," Hunter countered. "Do not give pursuit. We're going to stick to the Eye."

Here he goes, thought Lisa. He was doing it again, making her feel like she couldn't take care of herself. He infuriated her with his unsolicited protection. She went on the tac net.

"I can protect myself, Lieutenant Hunter. Give pursuit. That's a direct order, do you copy?"

Hunter was silent for a moment, then said, "All right, boys, you heard the little woman. Let's go get 'em."

The three VTs of Vermilion Team broke formation and went after the Battlepods. The Cat's-Eye was relaying positional data to them, but the enemy bandits were still too far off for visual contact. Rick called up full magnification on his port and starboard screens, and suddenly there they were: guns bristling, extended claw thrusters radiant in the perpetual night.

"I see them," said Max Sterling. "Going in..."

Max and Ben, both of them anxious to post a few more pod decals on their fighters, hit their afterburners and passed Rick by. Rick found himself holding back, thinking about Lisa's safety.

Damn her, he thought. *Let her go ahead and get herself atomized.* What did he care? He shook his head as if to clear it and threw his VT into the fight.

A Battlepod had swooped in and fixed him in its lasers. Rick in turn engaged his starboard thrusters, then cut his forward speed and fell away from the laser lock. At the same time, he loosed aft heat-seekers, which caught the pod where the legs met the spherical body. The pods were highly vulnerable there, and this one went into an uncontrolled accelerated spin as the legs blew away. Rick saw two quick flashes ahead of him, and soon his fighter was sailing through more pod debris.

It was easy if you let yourself think of the pods themselves as the enemy. Remind yourself that there was a fifty-foot humanoid giant in each of them though, and your brain began to short-circuit. In Battloid mode, Rick had been face to face with Zentraedi warriors on two occasions. And each time he had been paralyzed with fear. The Robotech Defenders who had trained on Earth before the invasion had been shown the skeletons and had been conditioned to *accept* the reality, but Rick had to learn it the hard way. Rick, however, was one of the few men who had actually met a live Zentraedi and lived to tell about it.

Battloids were the perfect mating of mind and mecha and were ideally suited to a war with giants. But what would it be like to confront a Zentraedi without the mecha? What could you do against something ten times your size? There was a seventy-year-old film on videotape in the ship's library about a giant ape who had been found on a remote Pacific Island. The ape had terrorized New York City the way later mutants and giants would wreak havoc on Tokyo. But there was something about that old film… it had somehow managed to communicate the mixture of awe and terror Rick felt where he faced the giants. There had been a woman in that film, he recalled…

The Battlepods destroyed, he switched on the tac net and tried to raise the Cat's-Eye. But there was no response.

The recon ship was in trouble.

In pursuit of their surveillance mission, Lisa and her copilot had entered into an area filled with massive chunks of what had once been the planetoid Pamir. They had their hands full dodging these while at the same time reporting on enemy locations.

"We have multiple radar contacts, picking up four, five, six, eight, and twelve heavy," the copilot said.

Lisa watched the radar hand sweep across the color-enhanced screen. There was something enormous ahead of them. It would have to measure more than fifteen kilometers in length. Possibly a piece of Pamir, but the shape was all wrong. This thing was like an elongated ellipse, a zero stretched at its poles. It had to be an enemy ship!

She began maneuvering the Cat's-Eye in for a closer look, her attention fixed on the radar screen.

She didn't see the island of space rock they collided with.

The radar disc was torn from the ship, and one by one the life support systems began to fail. The forward portion of the canopy was damaged but intact. But the copilot had not been as fortunate; his limp form hung in space, still tethered to the ship by an untorn length of seat strap. *There's no atmosphere in space,* Hunter's words came back to her before she slipped from consciousness.

The smallest damage could prove fatal.

Exedore watched his commander pace the bridge.

Continuous setbacks and defeats at the hands of the Micronians were beginning to take their toll.

When the projecbeam field formed itself for viewing, the now crippled SDF-1 could be discerned amid the asteroid field. Scanners indicated that Micronian fighters had taken up defensive positions in all quadrants in anticipation of a second offensive.

"Look at that ship," said Breetai. "We're fortunate that it survived the attack."

"No thanks to Khyron. This time he has gone too far."

"Too far, indeed. And do you see how the Micronians react to our demands for surrender, Exedore? They ignore us."

"Yes, Commander. I fear that they have seen through our strategy. There is in fact a word for it in their language—bluff. It means to mislead or intimidate through pretense."

The comlink tone sounded on the bridge, followed by the voice of the duty officer.

"Commander Breetai, we have Commander Khyron standing by."

Breetai dissolved the projecbeam and hit the communicator switch. "Patch him through—immediately!"

Khyron wore his familiar expression of slight bemusement. Exedore had heard rumors to the effect that he was addicted to the Invid Flower; if this was true, Khyron was even more dangerous than Breetai realized.

"You will be pleased to learn that the matter has already been settled," the Backstabber was saying.

A frightened junior officer was then shoved forward into the screen's field of view. His shackled hands managed a two-handed breast salute as Khyron ordered him to speak.

"Commander Breetai, I take full responsibility for the misplaced laser bolt which destroyed the radar tower off Zor's ship. My aim was untrue, and I humbly await your judgment."

The officer hung his head in shame.

Breetai stared at the screen with a look of disbelief that quickly refocused as anger.

"Khyron, do you take me for a complete fool?!"

Khyron smirked, "Not complete, Breetai."

Exedore's commander was enraged; he shouted, "You have not heard the end of this!" and shut down the comlink. He resumed his pacing as a second message was fed to the bridge: An enemy recon vessel disabled by a collision with an asteroid had been captured and was being brought to the flagship.

So something had been salvaged from this operation, after all, Breetai told himself. He heard Exedore give the order that all survivors were to be left unharmed.

"Well, Exedore, it looks like you have the specimens you wanted."

"So it would appear, Commander," Exedore replied guardedly. These would-be minor triumphs had a vexing way of reversing themselves.

Nevertheless, Exedore and Breetai rushed from the bridge and made for the docking bays. They were halfway along the main corridor to the elevators when an announcement from ship security brought them to a halt.

"Three Micronian ships in pursuit of the captured recon craft have broken into the lower deck holding area. Commander Breetai, contact the bridge."

Breetai growled, "They *dare* to enter my ship?! Now I will deal with them *personally!*"

The Zentraedi commander broke into a run; Exedore was behind him, throwing caution to the wind.

The Vermilion Team had pursued the captured Cat's-Eye into the lower hold of the huge ship, reconfiguring to Guardian mode when they cleared the hatchway. After-burners were now accelerating them along the kilometers of floor in the enormous chamber.

Rick took out the enemy tow which had ensnared Lisa's craft and ordered the team into Battloid configuration. The two Zentraedi pilots who jumped from the flaming wreck were easily chased off by gatling fire loosed by Max and Ben.

The two corporals were speechless. Those were living, breathing *giants* who had clambered out of the tow. All that training—the photos, the videos, the skeletal remains—hadn't prepared them for this moment of actual confrontation. They couldn't help but notice, however, that the place was a wreck all on its own: Spare parts from Battlepods and other mecha littered the area, overhead gantries and hull hatchways were in desperate need of attention, and an atmosphere of ultimate neglect and disrepair hung over the area like the stench of decay.

Rick, meanwhile, was bringing the Battloid down on one knee to inspect the Cat's-Eye. He could see Lisa begin to stir inside the smashed cockpit. Seeing the Battloid, she switched on the external speakers.

"Lieutenant Hunter, take your men and get out of here. You've got no time to spare."

Her voice was weak.

"Time enough to bring you with us."

Max came on the line: "Lieutenant, the Zentraedi are taking up positions at the end of the corridor. We better blow this place."

"Just give me a few minutes of cover fire, Max. Then we're outta here."

"That'll just about deplete my cannon charge."

"Mine, too," Ben added.

"Cut the chatter. Open fire."

Rick returned his attention to the Cat's-Eye while his teammates laid down a deafening barrage of fire.

"Can you operate the manual eject mechanism, Commander?"

"Negative," Lisa answered him. "The controls are jammed. Move out, Lieutenant. I'm giving you an order."

"This is no time to stand on protocol, Commander. Cover yourself; I'm going to break into the cockpit."

Lisa saw the Battloid's enormous hand come down on the shield and screamed. "Keep your hand off me, Hunter! I'm not kidding, don't touch me with that thing!"

The Battloid's fingers pinched the shield, shattering it. Cursing Rick the entire while, Lisa pulled herself up and free of the wreckage.

"I'll have your stripes for this, Hunter. I swear it."

Rick heard Ben's gatling sputter out; Max flashed him a signal that he, too, was out of ammo. Lisa had moved away from the Cat's-Eye. Rick was offering her the outstretched open hand of the Battloid when he caught her startled reaction to something that had appeared on the overhead catwalk.

Halfway to standing, that something landed *hard* on the Battloid's back, driving the mecha to the floor of the hold with a force not to be believed.

13

Few of us were fortunate enough to have seen the interior of the SDF-1 before Dr. Lang's teams of Robotechnicians had retrofit the fortress with bulkheads, partitions, lowered ceilings, and doorways and hatches proportioned to human scale; so our entry into the enormous lower hold of [Breetai's] flagship proved to be a veritable assault on the senses. Although I learned much later that human-size enclosures did in fact exist aboard the SDF-1 prior to reconstruction, here were all the things Sterling, Dixon, and I had been hearing about from members of the early exploratory teams: the three-hundred-foot-high ceilings, thirty-foot-wide hatchways, miles of corridors... It was not surprising, then, that our minds refused to grapple with these new dimensions. We didn't experience the hold as human beings entering giant-sized spaces; it was instead as if we had been reduced in size!

The Collected Journals of Admiral Rick Hunter

EVEN BY ZENTRAEDI STANDARDS, THE SOLDIER WHO LEAPT from the hold gantry and decked Rick Hunter's Battloid was enormous.

Max calculated the giant's height at sixty-plus feet. He wore knee-high utility boots and a blue uniform trimmed in yellow at the collar and sleeves; over this was a long, sleeveless brown tunic adorned with one bold vertical blue band. At breast level was some sort of insignia or badge of rank—almost a black musical note in a yellow field. But the most memorable thing about him was the gleaming plate that covered one side of his head, inset with what appeared to be a lusterless cabochon. He had jumped more than

200 feet from the catwalk, yet here he stood glaring at them, ready to take on the entire Robotech Defense Force single-handed.

Max didn't have to be told that he'd met one of the Zentraedi elite.

Sterling allowed these diverse emotional reactions to wash through him; he then relaxed and began to attune his thoughts to the Battloid's capabilities. Quickly positioning his mecha behind the giant, he swung the depleted gatling cannon across the warrior's chest and held it fast with both hands, pinioning the giant's arms at his sides. Displays in the Battloid cockpit module ran wild as the Zentraedi struggled to free himself. Max could sense the extent of the enemy's will reaching into his own mind and grappling with it on some newly opened front in this war, a psycho-battleground.

The Battloid's arms were stressed to the limit, threatening to dislocate with each of the giant's chest expansions. The Zentraedi was growling like a trapped animal, twisting his head around, each deliberate move calculated to bring that gleaming faceplate into violent contact with the canopy of the mecha. Max knew that something was going to give out soon unless he changed tactics.

The Battloid's environmental sensors indicated that the hold was indeed an air lock; it could therefore be depressurized. Max wasn't certain what size hole would be necessary to achieve the effect he was after, but he had to take a chance. He raised Ben on the tac net, all the while struggling with foot pedals and random thoughts, and ordered him to fire his warheads at the ship's hull directly overhead.

Ben triggered release of the missiles; the explosion tore a gaping hole in the ship. But something unexpected was happening even before the smoke was sucked clear: The hull was actually repairing itself! Max couldn't believe his sensors; the process was almost organic, as though the ship was... alive.

But he lost no time thinking about it. He fired the mecha's foot thrusters, launching himself, along with the Zentraedi, toward the ceiling. Just short of the healing rend, he released his grip on the cannon. Momentum carried the giant out into space seconds before the hull patch completed itself.

Back on the floor of the hold, Rick had picked himself up. He had snatched Lisa from midair during the depressurization and was holding her in the Battloid's metal-shod hand now, ignoring her protestations. Max brought his Battloid down beside him.

"Nice work, Max. Guess we won't be seeing that character again."

"Not unless he can survive deep space without an extravehicular suit."

"Now what do we do?" Ben asked.

The three men panned their Battloid video cameras across the hold, searching for a way out.

Breetai, meanwhile, who was made of much sterner stuff than any of the Earthlings realized, was not only alive but was at that moment pulling his way along the outer skin of the flagship, using as handholds the numerous sensor bristles and antennae that covered the ship. The gaping hole had of course closed itself too quickly to permit reentry into the hold, but he had managed to recollect his strength by latching on to a jagged piece of the ruptured hull before beginning his trek across the exterior armor plating.

His genetic makeup allowed him to withstand the vacuum of deep space for a limited period only, but he had nothing less than complete confidence in his ability to survive. Thoughts of vengeance drove him on: That Micronian was going to pay dearly for this.

Inside the ship, the diminutive Lisa Hayes had resumed command of the three pilots in their Battloids. She spoke into her helmet communicator from the open hand of Rick Hunter's mecha, instructing Max and Ben to use their top-mounted lasers to burn through the port hatch.

"You'll have to do it quickly," she advised them. "They're going to be on us any second now." She then swung herself around to face Rick. "And Lieutenant, would you mind putting me down now? I know how you enjoy holding me, but you'll have to learn to admire me from a distance."

Rick mumbled something into his headset and set his commander back on the floor of the hold. Max and Ben were taking alternate turns on the air lock to keep their lasers from overheating.

Rick stepped forward to join them. He was motioning Ben's

Battloid aside when he heard what sounded like a war cry—not through his headset but shattering the air of the hold itself. He spun the Battloid around in time to see the returned Zentraedi leap from an open hatchway overhead. The giant attacked like a samurai warrior; he held aloft a thick, pipelike tool that he brought down with gargantuan strength on the head of Ben's Battloid, dropping the mecha to the floor with a resounding crash.

The Zentraedi stood victorious over his fallen enemy, then turned his attention to Max and Rick. Issuing a guttural sound, he gripped the tool with both hands and thrust it in front of him.

Max and Rick separated some and raised their useless cannons, gripping them palms down like battle staffs. The Zentraedi was moving in slowly, each step calculated and deliberate.

"He's getting ready to charge," said Max.

Rick risked a step forward, motioning Max to fall in behind him. He brought the cannon up over his head and stood his ground, waiting for the charge.

The Zentraedi launched himself with a basso yell. Rick planted himself and brought the cannon down like a sledge, putting every ounce of strength he could summon into the blow. Metal met metal with fusion force.

Breetai swung his weapon like a bat, sending the gatling flying from the Battloid's hands. It hit the floor nose first, almost flattening Lisa Hayes.

Now six more Zentraedi soldiers in helmets and full-body armor arrived on the scene. One of them rushed forward with some sort of satchel and sacked the dazed Micronian pilot.

Max witnessed it, but three soldiers now stood between him and the commander. Regardless, he moved in to engage one of them. The Zentraedi tried to wrestle the gatling from his grip, so Max turned the sallow-faced man's strength to his own advantage, relaxing his own hold on the cannon for a moment, then using the soldier's uncontrolled momentum to heave him to the floor. But he was hardly in the clear: A cluster of five more were opening fire on him with shock guns. Max tossed aside the cannon and leaped up, firing the Battloid foot thrusters as he did so. Halfway to the ceiling of the hold he reached for the mode levers, reconfigured the Guardian, and began returning fire, dodging blue bolts of energy that shot past him and impacted on the inner skin of the ship.

Rick had been knocked flat on his back by the Zentraedi commander. The giant stood over him now, preparing to pile-drive the tool through the Battloid's abdomen. Rick brought the mecha's right leg up, bent at the knee, and fired the foot thruster full into the face of his assailant. As the Zentraedi went back, clutching his face and losing his grip on the weapon, Rick pulled his thruster lever home and went in for the kill, catching the giant's midsection and somersaulting him into a midair front flip. But the giant somehow managed to reverse the throw. Although Rick landed on top of him, he found himself facing the Zentraedi's feet. And the next thing he knew, he was being pressed into the air by the standing Zentraedi and launched across the hold.

Rick engaged the shoulder retros to cut his airspeed. He executed a neat front flip with a half twist that left him standing face to face with the Zentraedi, but he was unfortunately off balance and stunned. A right cross followed by a front kick sent him down to the floor again. This time his opponent was playing for keeps.

Breetai grabbed the mecha by its right aim, spun it into a three-sixty, and hurled it against a set of bulkhead cargo spikes; these perforated the Battloid's arms, chest, and shoulders and left it hanging there, pinned to the wall.

Identifying with the mecha, Rick felt like the victim of a careless circus knife thrower. The Battloid was immobilized, half its systems disabled, and now this giant with the faceplate was coming in to finish him off. Valiantly, Rick fired the top-mounted lasers, but the Zentraedi dropped himself out of range in the nick of time.

Rick was suddenly looking at foot-long life and love lines—the giant had brought his hand up over the canopy and was beginning to crush it. One by one the life support systems began to fail. And now the giant was working on the chestplates, literally tearing the Battloid apart! He ripped the armor from the mecha and tossed it aside as though it weighed nothing.

Grinning, the Zentraedi peered in at him now through the torn cockpit module, taking obvious delight in Rick's fearful situation. Rick armed the mecha's still-functioning self-destruct warhead and in desperation, reached down under the seat for the manual eject ring and gave it a wholehearted tug. The head of the Battloid lolled forward, its explosive charges crippled, but the cockpit seat managed to launch itself.

The Zentraedi, too, launched himself with a powerful jump. He snatched Rick from the air, crushing him in his fist, bringing on blessed relief from further fear…

Witnessing the giant's catch, Max, his Guardian still moving through the hold dodging laser bolts, was certain that the lieutenant had been killed. Hunter's murderer was going to pay in kind, Max decided. He nose-dived the VT, preparing to loose all the firepower he had left.

But all at once the remains of Rick's Battloid exploded. The Zentraedi was thrown off his feet, a breach was blown in the hull, and Max's Veritech was sucked from the air lock.

The hull quickly sealed itself, and the Zentraedi soldiers gathered around their fallen commander. Breetai was flat out on his back, his tunic and uniform torn and tattered. But he was made of sterner stuff than even *they* realized. He said as much as he got up.

His right hand was still clenched. Carefully he relaxed his grip to regard the small creature held there, strapped to its ejection seat, unmoving and as quiet as death.

14

As I have elsewhere stated, preliminary tests on the three Micronian
subjects indicate that their anatomical makeup and physiological
systems are very similar to those of the Zentraedi; I hasten to
add, however, that I am here referring to "wet-state" subjects
rather than mature and viable ones. [Editor's note: There is as
yet no adequate Panglish equivalent of the Zentraedi term. Some
linguistic camps favor "pretransformed," while others have
pushed for "neocast" or "neocloned." See Kazinsky, Chapters
Seven and Eight, for a lively overview of the continuing controversy.]
Subsequent psychoscanning, in any case, brought to light the
dissimilarities which are the focus of this report. These include: (1)
significant anomalies throughout the neocortical regions and topical
convolutionary conduits, (2) structural anomalies in the vascular and
neural networks of the infundibulum, the pyramidal tracts, and the
hippocampus, (3) pineal insufficiency, and (4) reticular imbalance of
the pons and attendant cerebellar pathways.

Exedore, from his Military Intelligence Analysis Reports to
the Zentraedi High Command

Micronians think too much!

Khyron

PREVIOUS DEALINGS WITH MICRONIANS HAD LARGELY BEEN A
matter of eradication. But now Exedore actually had three
live specimens to analyze and examine. And the results of tests

thus far conducted were as surprising as they were baffling and discomforting. Genetically, anatomically, and physiologically, the Micronians appeared to be almost identical to the Zentraedi. They were of course culturally and behavioristically worlds apart, but the physical similarities suggested a point of common origin lost to time and history.

Exedore studied the prisoners from his sealed-off operating station inside the ship's laboratory—who knew what contagious diseases these beings harbored? The scanner umbrella which in effect kept them isolated and confined to the specimen table was probably sufficient in itself for this, but Exedore was taking no chances.

Breetai, however, wanted no part of the laboratory or the operating station. Exedore brought him up to date on the findings in the command center, illustrating facts and speculations with data readouts, x-rays, scans of various sorts, and relevant historical documents, all of which flowed freely across the center's many monitor screens.

Breetai took particular interest in the female of the group. He shifted his attention from one screen's anatomical depictions and turned to the specimen table monitor. The Micronian female appeared to be unconscious or asleep, the other two as well.

"Is it wise to keep the female and males together?"

Exedore had the camera close on the table. "It is apparently their practice, Commander. It will certainly benefit us to observe their interactions."

A look of surprise came over Breetai's face, and Exedore now turned his attention to the monitor. The Micronians were beginning to stir.

The two Zentraedi watched intently.

The black-haired one was first to rise—the tough little pilot who had manned the mecha Breetai had destroyed. The female recon pilot was next, but together they couldn't seem to rouse the third and largest member of their party.

"This one has a very slow metabolic rate and is less intelligent than the others," Exedore said by way of explanation.

Something curious began to happen just then: The female and

the male were arguing. Breetai signaled his adviser to activate the audio monitors. The words came fast and furious and were for the most part unfamiliar to Breetai, but he understood enough to get the gist: They were blaming each other for the failure of their mission and their eventual capture.

Breetai was amused.

"They fight with words as aggressively as they fight with mecha."

"A result of the commingling of males and females, sir—an ancient practice long ago abandoned by the Zentraedi."

"I see... anger without discipline."

"Precisely that, Commander."

As Breetai continued to observe the argument, however, he was overcome by a feeling of sickness; he felt debilitated and phobic. He ordered Exedore to deactivate the monitor and collapsed down into his chair.

"My head is spinning. I can no longer stand to watch them."

"I feel the same," said Exedore. "However, we must not allow any of our personal reactions to interfere with the mission at hand."

Breetai lifted up his head. "Well, suppose you tell me how I should proceed with these creatures."

"The Micronians should be brought to Dolza himself. There they should be subjected to the most rigorous interrogation possible."

"That will require a fold operation and the expenditure of substantial quantities of energy."

"It will be justified, Commander. The Micronians' own words will doom them to defeat."

Lisa couldn't believe her ears: Who in the known universe did Hunter think he was talking to?

She and Hunter and dead-to-the-world Dixon were on some sort of alien grid platform, curtained and contained by a nebulous rain of electrical energy directed from an overhead generator. But through this translucent umbrella could be glimpsed the enormous machines, scopes, scanners, and data analyzers that constituted the laboratory beyond. One portion of the energy canopy afforded them visual access to an exterior bay of the ship.

And somewhere out among that starfield was the SDF-1 and a world the three of them might never see again.

Hunter, nevertheless, seemed less interested in establishing where they were than in establishing who was to blame for their being there.

"Are you telling me that you wouldn't have been captured if a *man* had been piloting the Cat's-Eye? Because if you are—"

"I'm not saying that. I'm just saying there are some jobs that are better left to experienced pilots. You don't find VT pilots muscling onto the bridge, do you?"

Lisa glared at him. "I'm your superior, Lieutenant Hunter!"

"Only in rank, *Commander* Hayes."

"In rank and military experience!"

Rick made a dismissive gesture. "Don't give me that Robotech Academy superiority. I'm talking about *combat* experience."

Lisa crossed her arms to keep him from noticing that she was shaking with anger. Her foot tapped reflexively.

"Do you need to be reminded of the *conversation* we had yesterday— the one where you complained about my always being 'safe and sound on the bridge'? Now I'm out here with you, and I still can't do anything right in your eyes. It's a no-win situation with you, mister."

Rick softened somewhat. "Look, it's just that I feel more... I don't know, *vulnerable*, with you around. You're always getting yourself in a fix, just like on Sara Base—"

"Hunter!" she screamed. "You're an idiot! Just who appointed you my personal guardian?"

"Someone's gotta protect you from yourself."

She looked around for something to throw at him, but Dixon would be too heavy and there was nothing else on the grid.

"Who had to be towed in after completely destroying the armored Battloid, Lieutenant?"

Rick's face went red with rage and embarrassment.

"You think fighting those Zentraedi is some kind of cakewalk. Maybe you didn't see that guy tear my mecha apart with his bare hands, huh?"

"No, I didn't see it. *I* was in the sack, remember?"

"Yeah, well..."

"Yeah, well," she mimicked him, and turned away.

Ben Dixon was coming to, stretching and yawning as though he'd just taken a terrific nap.

He looked around and asked if he had missed anything.

Rick shot Lisa a cruel look and stepped over to his corporal. "Uh, nothing much, Ben. The *Commander* and I were just discussing an escape plan."

Lisa smirked and looked out the bay.

"Great," Ben said. "When do we get started?"

Rick said something Lisa didn't catch; she was too mesmerized by what was occurring outside the ship: The stars were becoming tentative, strung out, as if trailing threads of light behind them.

My God! She realized what she was seeing. The Zentraedi were beginning a fold operation!

Back onboard the SDF-1 the period of anxious waiting had ended an hour ago with the restoration of wide-range radar. But a new period of apprehension had just begun. The bridge had lost communication with the Cat's-Eye recon and the VTs of the Vermilion Team, and now there was evidence of fluctuations in the timespace continuum of that area. Most of the massive enemy ships had disappeared from the scanner screen, but numerous small ships and battle mecha were still swirling around the fortress. Gloval was certain that half the fleet had executed a spacefold.

In all his long years of military command, Gloval had never faced a more unpredictable foe. They had crippled his ship, threatened him with extinction, demanded surrender, and suddenly disappeared off the scopes. Gloval was perplexed.

He instructed Sammie to try to raise Commander Hayes again.

"Negative response, sir. I can't raise anyone at all in that Veritech group."

Have we lost them? Gloval wondered. *Please, not Lisa!*

"Sir, we can't just give up on them," said Sammie.

"It could be radio trouble," Claudia said.

"I'm not about to give up on them," Gloval said at last. "But we can't afford to sit here and wait for the enemy to return and make good their threats." He hung his head. "We'll give them twelve hours. Claudia, if we've had no contact with them by then, I want the ship out of this quadrant by oh-six-hundred hours. Is that clear?"

"Yes, Captain. And about Commander Hayes… and Lieutenant Hunter and his men?"

"Enter their names on the list," Gloval responded flatly. "Missing in action and presumed dead."

Roy Fokker seldom visited Macross City, and when he did it was usually at Claudia's insistence—dinner somewhere, a movie, or the Miss Macross pageant a while back. It wasn't that he didn't like the place, just that he had little use for it. Its presence onboard the SDF-1 had all but undermined the ship's original purpose. The SDF-1 was to be Earth's guardian and defender, not surrogate or microcosm, and certainly not *decoy*. As one of the men (along with Dr. Lang and Colonel Edwards) who had first explored the ship shortly after its arrival on Earth, Fokker had a profound attachment to her. But the spacefold accident and this resulting city had devitalized that attachment, and for the past year Fokker had come to feel more the hopeless prisoner than anything else.

His motivations for visiting the city today, however, had nothing to do with entertainment or a lover's obligation; he was here because duty demanded it of him. Rick had been MIA for almost two weeks now, and there were people who had to be told.

Two weeks missing in action, Roy told himself. Was it still too early to grieve, or was it too late? Wouldn't he be able to feel the truth one way or another in his heart? Their friendship went so far back… Pop Hunter's flying circus, the fateful day Rick had turned up on Macross Island, their first mission together—

What was the use of tormenting himself? When he did search his heart for feelings, he found his "Little Brother" alive—this was a certainty. And yet, his mind would ask, what were the odds they would ever see each other again? The SDF-1 was a million miles from that area in space where Rick and the others had last been heard from, way beyond the range of any VT. And did it ease the pain any to think of him as a prisoner? The Zentraedi weren't likely to hold him hostage, not when they had an entire planet at their disposal. So maybe it *was* better to believe the worst, accept his death and get the grief behind him. Then he could at least remove himself from this timeless agony and begin to court the future once again.

It might have been the need for partnership in grief that led Roy to seek out Minmei. He, too, had been attracted to the blue-eyed Chinese girl from the start, and he liked to think that there was some special bond there, even though Minmei rarely acknowledged it by words or actions. But that wasn't her style, anyway. Especially now that she was on the brink of stardom. In fact, the "Queen of Macross" was going to be headlining a concert at the Star Bowl on Monday night.

Soon she was coming down the sidewalk toward him, flanked by two of her woman friends and looking the starlet part in some sort of green military-chic shorts outfit, complete with epaulets and rank stripes. Roy recognized it as the piece she'd worn for the Defense Force enlistment posters that had begun to show up all over the city.

Roy had been waiting for her outside the White Dragon. As she approached, he straightened up to his full height, tugged down on his belted jacket, and waved to her.

She came at him with a big smile, increasing her pace and excusing herself from her friends. Right off, she wanted to know if Rick was with him.

He returned the smile, strained though it was, and suggested they take a walk together. She looked at him questioningly.

"Why, Roy? What's happened?"

"Come on, walk with me a minute."

She pulled back when he tried to take her arm.

"I don't want to take a walk, Roy! What's happened? Where's Rick? Has something happened to Rick?"

Roy faced her, placing both hands on her shoulders, towering over her. He met her eyes and held them as he explained.

Halfway through the explanation she was shaking her head, refusing to believe him. "He's dead!"

"Minmei, listen, please don't think he's dead—we don't know that for sure."

Roy was doing just what he had promised himself he wouldn't do. And she was inconsolable. She twisted free of his hold.

"I don't want to hear anymore! You're a liar, and I hate you!"

She glared at him, turned, and ran off.

Her friends offered him sympathetic smiles. Roy stood with them, feeling utterly helpless. He sucked in breath and tears and clenched his teeth.

Minmei ran to *their* bench in the park.

It was a special bench, set apart from the others in Macross Central, tucked away on a small subtier of its own overhung by the full branches of an oak tree and surrounded by flowering plants and thick bushes. It was almost a secret place, curiously unfrequented by park users, with an incredible view of the city spread out below and the closest view possible through the enormous starlight in the ship's hull. Rick used to say that it was their balcony "with a view of forever."

They spent many long hours here—after their two-week ordeal together, before Rick had joined the Defense Force, and before Minmei had been crowned "Queen"… She had listened to Rick talk about the horrors of space battle, his victories and defeats, his fears and dreams. And he had listened to her fears, her plans for the future, her song lyrics, her dreams.

And now—

Why did this have to happen? Why, when everything in her life was so wonderful, did tragedy have to visit? Why did this collision of dream and reality always have to occur?—as if no good fortune was possible without a balancing amount of evil. What sort of god would have set such a mechanism in motion?

Face to face with that portion of the universe revealed by the starlight, Minmei began to cry. Later she would bang her fists against the rail of the balcony and curse those stars, then sink back against the wooden slats of the bench and surrender to her sorrow. And ultimately she would retrieve from her handbag a penlight she carried there, and, aiming it toward the ship's bay, she would click it on and off, again and again, a light signal into "forever" of her undying affection for him.

15

Spirit does not willingly abdicate its throne. The Big Bang was Spirit's first rebellion against form—its imprisonment in matter. Subsequently it fought humankind's acceptance of fire; it battled against steam; it contested electricity and nuclear power; it raged against Protoculture . . . War is Spirit's attempt to attain freedom from matter, its effort to remain autonomous. Wars are waged to prevent matter from becoming too comfortable or complacent. For it is Spirit's divine purpose to someday abandon its vehicle and transcend, to reunite with the Godhead and suck the universe back into itself.

Reverend Houston, from the foreword to
Jan Morris's *Solar Seeds, Galactic Guardians*

Protoculture is technology's royal jelly.

Dr. Emil Lang

UNKNOWN TO BREETAI OR HIS CREW, THERE WAS A STOWAWAY aboard the Zentraedi flagship—a Micronian Veritech ace named Max Sterling.

Sucked into space through the hole in the hull created by Rick Hunter's self-destructed Battloid, Max had unknowingly duplicated the walk Breetai had undertaken along the outer surface of the ship sometime earlier. Breetai, however, was familiar with the manual air lock mechanisms, so he merely had to let himself in; Max had to discover a way in. Fortunately he had stumbled upon an unclosed breach in the hull—the fried bristle sensors surrounding the hole gave evidence of a previous exploration—flown himself into an empty bay, and, returned to Battloid mode, made his way into the ship through an unlocked hatchway. His gatling cannon had been left in the hold, his lasers were burned out, and he had scarcely half a dozen rockets left. Max was operating on willpower, driven by the hope of rescuing his friends.

The interior of the flagship was a labyrinth of corridors and serviceways, some well lighted and maintained, others dark, damp, and in varying states of disrepair. But luckily, all of them had been deserted.

Until now.

Max was at the intersection of two corridors—curved ceilings, large overhead light banks—peering around the corner when he saw the alien enter. A private, Max guessed: standard-issue drab highrise-collared uniform, a round cap with an insignia. He moved the Battloid back a step and scanned the area. A short distance down the corridor behind him was what appeared to be a utility closet with a curved-top hatch. He made his way to this as quickly and quietly as he could manage, threw the bolt, and secreted the mecha inside. Shut off from the corridor, Max had no way of knowing which route the Zentraedi had taken, so the look of surprise on the alien's face upon discovering a Battloid in the utility closet was no greater than the startled look on Max's own.

For what seemed like an eternity they both stood there marveling at each other, until Max's training brought a decisive end to it. He executed a sidekick with the Battloid's right foot that caught the Zentraedi's midsection, instantly doubling him over. Gathering up the unconscious private in the Battloid's right arm, Max stretched out the left, grabbed the door bolt, and slammed the hatch shut.

He was puzzling over what to do with the guy, when all at once the cockpit indicators began crying out for attention. He checked the readouts but still couldn't make sense of anything: All systems were functioning, and there didn't seem to be any immediate threats to the mecha, environmentally or otherwise. So what was going on?

Then Max glanced at the astrogation displays. The temporal sensors were spinning wildly—the flagship was *folding!*

Max watched as hours and days began to accrue on the gauge. He slumped into his seat and waited...

The emergency spacefold which had catapulted the SDF-1 and Macross City clear across the solar system had been Lisa's first; and, as such, there hadn't been time to... well, *look around.* It had also been a relatively short jump through space and therefore a brief one through time. But for this, her second trip through the continuum, the temporal indicator built into her suit registered the equivalent of fourteen Earth-days. Wherever the Zentraedi were going, it was a long way from home.

Lisa had plenty of time to look around.

It was nothing like she had expected, nothing, in fact, like she had been *trained* to expect. The stars did not so much disappear as come and go. She couldn't be certain, however, that it was the *same* stars that were rematerializing each time. The heavens seemed altered with each fade, as though someone had snipped frames from a strip of film, editing out the transitions from event to event. The energy umbrella that kept her and the others confined to the grid prevented her from observing flux details in the laboratory, but when she looked at Rick or Ben, she noticed a slight shimmering effect that blurred the boundaries of objects; occasionally, this effect intensified so that there was a sense of double focus to everything: the form of the past, the form of the future, distinct, discrete, unable to unite.

In real time, one Earth-day elapsed; and as the flagship began to decelerate from hyperspace, the past twenty-four hours took on a dreamlike quality. Had she slept through most of it, dreamed a good part of it? Or was this some new condition of consciousness yet to be named?

Lisa, Rick, and Ben stood at the edge of their small world, watching the stars assume lasting form once again. These were alien configurations to their eyes; brilliant constellations of suns, dwarfs and giants, three planets or moons of some unknown system, all against the backdrop of a gauzy multihued nebulosity. And something else—something their unadjusted vision labeled an asteroid field, so numerous were the dark objects in that corner of space.

"What are those things?" asked Ben.

"Space debris," Rick suggested. "We might be near their home base."

Lisa squinted; then her eyes opened wide in amazement.

Not asteroids, not space debris, but ships: amorphous ships as far as the eye could see, ships bristling with guns, too numerous to count, too numerous to catalogue—scouts, recons, destroyers, cruisers, battle wagons, flagships. Thousands of ships, *millions* of them!

"The enemy fleet!"

It was too much to take in, but Lisa used the microvideo recorder the aliens had overlooked to capture what she could.

More than a year would pass before they learned the exact count; a day of reckoning…

The flagship was now closing on a dazzling cluster of lights, a kind of force field that housed an immeasurable asymmetrical fortress their senses refused to comprehend.

But they soon had other issues to confront. Without warning, the energy umbrella had been deactivated and the circumstances of their world redefined. They had wondered how their captors had been able to provide them with food and drink served on human-size plates, with cups and utensils in proper proportions. But there would be no such comfort for them from this moment on.

Two giants now stood on either side of the grid, which turned out to be some sort of specimen table. Could anything have prepared them for the assault of sensations that followed—the deafening basso rumble of the giants' voices, the sonorous roar of their mecha and machines, the intensity of the corridor lights, the overpowering smells of hyperoxygenated air, stale breath, sweat, and decay?

They were transferred to a second platform—a hover-table directed through the corridors by their jailers—and ultimately to a gleaming conference table as large as a football field. There were banks of overhead lights and several chairs positioned around the table. Lisa noticed that amplifiers had been strategically positioned here and *there—the better to hear you with, my dear!* And one by one their interrogators entered the room and sat down.

The first to arrive was a male scarcely half the size of those Zentraedi they'd seen. A slightly hunched back was evident beneath his blue cowl; swollen joints and outsize hands and feet suggested some sort of birth defect. He had an inverted bowl of henna hair thick as straw concealing a deformed cranium, uneven bangs bisecting a high forehead above a drawn face, a bulging, seemingly lidless eyes with pinpoint pupils. He was carrying notebooks, which he placed on the table next to a light-board device; this he activated as he sat down, bending forward to regard his three prisoners analytically.

Next to enter the chamber was the immense soldier Rick had battled in the hold; there was no forgetting that faceplate, no forgetting that malicious grin. Trailing behind him were three more males of differing heights, wearing identical red uniforms, not one of them as short as the disabled Zentraedi or as tall as their commander. They took seats at the far end of the table.

Lisa was wondering who or what was going to fill the empty seat between the commander and his adviser; when the answer to her whispered question arrived, she was at once sorry she had asked.

"How many sizes do these guys come in?" said Ben in amazement.

The grand inquisitor stood well over eighty feet tall and wore a solemn gray robe with a high upturned collar that all but enclosed his massive, hairless head. The heavy brow ridge, pockmarked sullen face, and wide mouth gave him a fearful aspect, and when he spoke there was no mistaking his meaning.

"I am Dolza," he began. "Commander-in-Chief of the Zentraedi. You will submit to my interrogation. Should you choose not to, you will die. Do you understand me?"

Rick, Ben, and Lisa looked at one another, realizing suddenly that they had failed to elect a spokesperson—for the simple reason that they hadn't expected an actual session with the enemy. The fact that they would be able to communicate with the Zentraedi gave them new hope.

Lisa secretly activated the audio receiver of the microrecorder, while Rick stepped forward to speak for his group.

"We understand you. What do you want from us?"

Dolza turned to the dwarf. "Congratulations, Exedore, you have done well in teaching me their primitive language."

Exedore inclined his head slightly.

"Why do you continue to resist us, Micronians?" Dolza gestured to the male on his right. "Surely Breetai has already demonstrated our superiority."

Rick pointed his finger at the one called Breetai. "You launched the attack on *us!* We've only been trying to defend ourselves for the past year—"

"Immaterial," Breetai interrupted. "Return to us what is rightfully ours—Zor's ship."

"'Zor's ship'? If you mean the SDF-1, that's our property. It crashed on our planet, and we rebuilt it. You—"

Dolza cut Rick off. "It is as I feared," he said to Exedore.

"Tell us what you know of Protoculture. You—the fat one."

Ben gestured to himself questioningly. "Me? Forget it, high rise. I don't know anything about it."

"Tell us what you know about Protoculture!" Dolza demanded.

"You deny that you've developed a new weapons system utilizing Protoculture?" Exedore wanted to know.

Rick turned to his companions and shrugged. The questions kept up, increasing in volume, until Lisa decided she'd had enough. She stepped forward boldly and held up her hand.

"That's enough! I will no longer submit my men to your questioning!"

Dolza raised what he had of eyebrows. "So the female is in charge here." He sat back in his chair, steepling his fingers as he did so. "You underestimate the seriousness of your predicament, Micronian."

And with a wave of his hand the room was transformed.

Lisa, Rick, and Ben were suddenly in deep… *space!* At least it appeared that way: Here were the stars, planets, and tens of thousands of ships they had seen upon defold into Zentraedi territory. And yet they had not moved from the table, and Dolza's voice could still be heard narrating the phenomenal events occurring in that unreal space.

Photon charges were beginning to build up in several of the fleet ships; they were taking aim at a planet not unlike Earth in appearance...

"We are in possession of sufficient power to destroy your world in the blink of an eye," Dolza was saying. "And if you need proof of that, behold..."

As lethal rays from the battle wagons and cruisers converged on the living surface of the planet, a glow of death began to spread and encompass it; and when that fatal light faded, a lifeless, cratered sphere was all that remained.

Lisa hung her head; the Zentraedi had just destroyed a planet merely to make a point. Is this what they had planned for Earth? But then, why were they holding back? What had Exedore said about "a new weapons system utilizing *Protoculture*"? She made up her mind to try a bluff.

"You don't have enough power to destroy the SDF-1, Dolza."

"Impertinence!" their interrogator yelled.

Ignoring Rick's plea for caution, she continued: "The SDF-1 has powers you've never dreamed of."

Dolza brought his fists down on the table, throwing the Terrans off their feet. He then reached out and grabbed Lisa in his right hand. He brought her close to his face, warning Rick and Ben to stay put.

"Now, my feisty female, I want to know by what process you become Micronians," He tightened his grip around Lisa, demanding an immediate answer.

"Stop squeezing her!" said Rick. "We're born this way. We're born... *Micronian!*"

"Born from *what* is the question," said Exedore.

"Huh? Well... from our mothers. What else?"

"What is this thing you call 'mother'?" one of the Zentraedi behind Rick asked.

Ben swung around to face the red-uniformed trio.

"Mother. You know, like the parent that's female." Ben turned to Rick, twirling his forefinger against his temple.

Exedore was startled. "You mean that you are actually *born* from the females of your kind?" Breetai was incredulous.

"Hey," Ben continued. "It happens, you know. You put a man and a woman together and… well, it just happens." He laughed. "It's love."

Breetai looked over at Dolza, then fixed his gaze on Ben. "'Love,' yes, I have heard that word mentioned in some of your transmissions. But what is it? How do you express it?"

"Oh, brother," Ben said under his breath. "You field this one, Commander."

Rick shot him a look and chuckled, in spite of himself, in spite of the gravity of the situation. "It can start with a kiss, I guess."

Dolza wasn't buying it: If Micronians could be produced by kissing, then he wanted living proof of it. He ordered Rick and Ben to demonstrate.

"Demonstrate this kissing or I will crush all of you!"

Rick was stammering an explanation of the facts, when he heard Lisa agree to volunteer. Released from Dolza's grip, she staggered weakly over to Rick, leaning against him as though regaining her strength and taking advantage of their proximity to explain her plan: She wanted Rick to kiss her… so she could record the aliens' reaction on her microcamera.

Rick stepped away from her. "Do it with Ben, Commander."

She turned and looked over at the corporal briefly. "Listen, Rick, I'd rather do it with you, all right?"

"You'll have to make it a command, sir."

"Proceed at once!" said Dolza.

Lisa held Rick's gaze, softening his anger somewhat by the hurt look he thought he saw in her eyes.

"I'm giving you a direct order, Lieutenant Hunter: Kiss me."

Rick made a silent appeal for Minmei's forgiveness and stepped into Lisa's arms. They kissed each other full on the mouth, and for several seconds the two of them were far away from it all. It was, however, difficult to sustain that romantic mood while six giants were making sick sounds behind their backs. They broke their embrace and stepped apart.

"What is happening to us?" said Dolza. "This results from Protoculture?"

"It is their weapons system at work," said Exedore.

Dolza was on his feet, glaring at the Terrans. "Take them out of here at once! Get these Micronians out of my sight!"

Rick turned to Lisa as the three of them were being herded onto the hover-table once again. "Are we *that* bad at it?"

She looked at him and said, "I guess we are."

16

"Ya gotta picture it, gang: I mean, here's Rick, Lisa, and Ben, surrounded by these six giants. Hunter and Hayes step into each other's arms, liplock, and these big, bad hombres begin to freak! I mean... [laughs shortly] 'magine if Lisa's microcamera had been set up to show X-rated movies? The war woulda been over on the spot!"

Unnamed VT pilot, as quoted by Rick Hunter

"What's love got to do with it?"

Late twentieth-century song lyric

DOLZA AND HIS ADVISORY GROUP REMAINED IN THE interrogation room after the Micronian prisoners had been taken away. The Zentraedi commander in chief was disturbed by the reactions he had experienced when the female and male had kissed each other. Breetai stated that he had felt weakened after witnessing a verbal argument between these same two Micronians; and apparently, similar feelings had plagued the three operatives of the surveillance team that had been dispatched to monitor transmissions from Zor's ship. Now, as Dolza listened to the recon team's report, he asked himself whether Exedore's suspicions about the Micronian use of Protoculture might not be justified, after all. Perhaps he should have killed Zor when he had had the chance, or simply destroyed the dimensional fortress, instead of seeing in it a road to freedom for himself and the rest of his warrior race.

"...and Konda here had the same reaction when he saw the unclothed female," Rico, the commander of the team, was saying.

"It's true, sir," Konda affirmed. "Although I didn't agree at the time."

"This could only be done with Protoculture," said Dolza. He folded his arms and addressed the group. "What I'm about to tell you must never leave this room. Is that understood?"

Breetai and Exedore nodded their assent. In unison, Rico, Konda, and Bron said, "Yes, sir!"

"Protoculture, as Breetai and Exedore are aware, is the essence of Robotechnology developed by our ancestors. Yes, *ancestors*," he emphasized for the sake of the recon team. "In the beginning, members of the Zentraedi race were the same size as these Micronians. And at one time we, too, lived together, male and female, in something that was called a 'society.' But through the use of Protoculture we were able to evolve to our present size, strength, and superiority. However, a series of events that must even now be kept secret from you led to a loss of our understanding of Protoculture."

Dolza put his open hands on the table and leaned forward.

"I have every reason to believe that those lost secrets are to be found aboard Zor's ship." He allowed this to sink in for a moment. "This is why the Micronians present such a potential threat. And this is precisely why we must take that ship back undamaged."

"We have not been able to determine to what extent the Micronians have applied their understanding of Protoculture," Breetai added. "But it is obvious to me that they know enough to effect repairs on Robotech equipment and perhaps enough to be experimenting with a new weapons system."

"Sir," said Rico. "We have demonstrated our power to them. Why not hold their planet hostage for the return of the ship?"

It was a generally unheard of notion, but Dolza was willing to entertain it. He stroked his chin and turned to Exedore.

"You have made a thorough study of this race. You appear to have an understanding of their language and culture. Would such a threat be effective?"

Exedore weighed his words carefully. "Sir, it is not the Zentraedi way to speak of past defeats, but may I be permitted to remind this table that these Micronians have already demonstrated an uncommon determination to survive. In response to our initial attacks on their homeworld, the commander of the ship, with no regard for the lives of tens of thousands of his fellow creatures, executed an intraatmospheric spacefold to escape us. This same commander detonated a reflex furnace on the fourth planet in their system, endangering the ship and the lives of all aboard rather than surrender to Commander Khyron's mechanized division. Even though crippled in space and without radar, they simply ignored our most recent demands for surrender... In response then to your query, my lord: No, I do not think that such a plan would work."

"We cannot risk losing those secrets," said Dolza. "We must infiltrate the ship and determine what the Micronians know about Protoculture."

Breetai, who knew Zor's ship inside and out, had a plan he began to relate to Dolza. Rico, Konda, and Bron, meanwhile, hatched a plan of their own: They made a joint decision to volunteer to go through the cellular transformation process which enabled a Zentraedi to assume Micronian dimensions.

Dolza and Breetai would find the trio's proposal acceptable, and later, even commendable. And fortunately for Rico and the others, they were never called up to give reasons for their sudden dedication to the cause. Because if the truth were known, all this talk about Robotechnology and Protoculture was way beyond them. They were simply anxious to have another look at those partially clothed Micronian females and experience again those curious feelings that were the result.

In a holding cell elsewhere on Breetai's ship, Lisa, Rick, and Ben, sitting in a patch of corridor light which poured through cellular windows in the chamber's double doors, were comparing their own reactions to the Zentraedi interrogation. It was a little like being locked in an empty airliner hangar, but at least there were no giants on the scene.

"It was the weirdest thing I've seen in a while," Ben was saying. "You two kiss, and the big guys go nuts. I don't get it."

"They have enough power to atomize the Earth, but simple contact is too much for them to handle," said Rick.

Lisa was deep in thought.

"And what about this 'Protoculture' business? What do you think, Commander?"

Lisa looked at Ben. "Do you realize that we haven't seen any female Zentraedi? No children, no civilians, not even any techs or maintenance crews. Only soldiers."

"We haven't exactly been given the grand tour," Rick reminded her.

"I realize that, Lieutenant. But it could be that there *are* no females of their kind."

"No, that can't be. They know you're female. They had some kind of knowledge about mothers and birth."

"Lieutenant, we gotta get outta here," Ben said, looking around.

"I know. I've been giving it some thought. We might be able to use our new weapon on them."

"What new weapon? What are you talking about?"

Rick smacked his lips. "The kiss. Don't you get it? We wait till the guard comes with our food, we confuse him with our, uh, weapon, and we make a break for it."

Ben was already on his feet. "Great! Any place'll be better than this."

Lisa looked at the two of them. "Are you joking? You mean that every time a Zentraedi shows his face we're going to put on a show for him? Forget it, Lieutenant. I've heard some lines in my day, but that one beats them all."

Rick's mouth dropped open. "Just hold it a minute, *Commander*. Whose idea was it in the first place? Besides, if you think I'm doing this because I want to, you've got another—"

"That'll be enough, mister! I only kissed you to get their reaction on tape." She patted the camera. "We've got it now; we don't need to do another take."

Ben stepped forward, "Hey, listen, I'm perfectly willing to volunteer to be your partner, Commander Hayes."

"At ease, Corporal," Lisa told him.

She turned her back on the two of them, angry but wondering: Was there anything about strategic osculation in the officers' manual?

Help was on the way.

In what was certainly the most complicated set of mecha-motions executed to date, Max Sterling had managed to clothe his Battloid in the uniform he had taken from the Zentraedi private. That he had succeeded so completely in wedding his mind to the mecha controls was justification enough for the many articles later devoted to the feat, but the fact that he had accomplished this within the confines of the utility closet was what ultimately led to his legendary status as a VT hero.

Making certain the Zentraedi was neatly tied up and stowed away, Max checked the corridor, eased out of the closet, and began to follow his instincts. The Zentraedi uniform was well suited to the Battloid's purpose, the high-collared jacket especially so. And even with the round cap pulled low, the cockpit wide-angle and long-range cameras and scanners had enough clearance for operation.

Not ten paces down the hallway, Max encountered one of the massively built, armored shock troopers, who luckily paid him little notice. Now having passed the test, he began to move with increased confidence, and not long after he spotted two of the enemy guiding a hover-table through the ship. Max upped the magnification on his cameras, locked in on the table, and found Lisa, Ben, and Rick, looking none the worse for wear but in no condition to do battle with their giant captors.

Max trailed the guards at a discreet distance and watched as Lieutenant Hunter and the others were deposited in some sort of double-doored holding cell. A single sentry was posted outside.

Max was not inclined to wait much longer; besides, the sentry was already betraying his boredom with yawns and general inattentiveness. Max primed the Battloid for action and moved in.

When Lisa heard the commotion in the corridor outside the cell, she had a change in heart: Maybe Hunter's plan would work. There wasn't much to lose at this point, so she convinced herself that kissing him was just part of the mission. She told him so, and the two of them readied their "secret weapon" while Ben waited by the door.

Though Max's reaction to throwing open the cell door and finding his commanders locked in a loving embrace was more pure surprise than anything else, his temporary paralysis convinced the prisoners that they had made the right move. The three were ready to bolt for the corridor when Max opened the external com net and called out to them.

"It's me—Max!"

They stopped in midstride and stared up at him. "M-Max?" Rick said tentatively.

"Yeah, I'm in here all right."

"God, Max, we thought you were dead," said Lisa.

"Yeah, well, long story."

Ben wanted to know where the uniform had come from.

"Later. We better get a move on." He lowered the Battloid's gloved left hand. Rick and Lisa climbed in, and Max raised it up, leaving Ben on the floor.

"Hey, man!"

"Hang on, Ben, I want you in the other hand."

Ben climbed into the lowered right. Now Max brought both the Battloid's hands level with the uniform's breast pockets. Lisa and Rick grabbed hold of the insignia-pocket and pulled themselves in; Ben did likewise on the other side of the jacket.

"I don't want you to interrupt the lovebirds, Ben."

"Now wait a minute, Corporal," Lisa protested. "We only did that to escape."

"Kissing each other to escape, huh? I understand."

"Listen up, Max—"

"Save it, Lieutenant. You've got my word that I won't spread this around Macross City. Although I must say you had me fooled. I thought you preferred younger women."

"Max!"

"Get yourselves down in there. We're moving out."

Rick held in his anger and slid down into the pocket alongside

Lisa. The Battloid parted the double hatches of the holding cell and began to take long, stiff strides down the corridor.

It wasn't long before they heard Max utter a sound of alert. A Zentraedi soldier, armored and armed with a hip blaster, was approaching them. Soldier and disguised Battloid passed each other seemingly without incident, and inside the pocket Rick and Lisa breathed a premature sigh of relief.

But the soldier had stopped and was calling for Max to halt. Max was in no position to defend himself or his passengers; launching his few remaining rockets would have fried Rick and Lisa. So he took the only course available: He ran—straight into two more shock troopers who were coming down the corridor. Max tackled one of them, lifting him and swinging him into the other as he continued on his way, but by now the first soldier was chasing him and opening fire. He was quickly joined by his comrades.

The Battloid sustained blasterbolt after blasterbolt to the back as it flew through the ship, pieces of burned and tattered cloth flying in its wake. At Rick's urging, Max reconfigured the VT to Guardian mode, ripping open the uniform jacket as he hit the aft thrusters. In that hail of lethal fire, the Guardian looked like some sort of caped bird of prey fighting its way to freedom.

Corridor length, however, was suddenly in short supply, and Max knew the VT wouldn't be able to pull off a ninety-degree turn in such limited space. Set in the bulkhead at the top of the corridor T, however, was a control panel which could probably be pierced without undue damage to the fighter. Max opted for it and pulled the thruster lever home.

The bulkhead surrendered too easily, and by the time Max realized that the VT had broken through a large circular viewing screen in a control room, the Guardian was way beyond it, tearing through a series of projecbeam astrogational charts free-floating in an immense central chamber of the ship. An open rectangular port at the far end of the room delivered them into another serviceway, at the end of which was a sealed elevator. They were still taking rear fire when the elevator doors parted. A surprised Zentraedi soldier saw them coming and leaped out into the corridor, narrowly escaping impalement on the radome of the VT.

Once inside the cubicle, Max blew the canopy and clambered out onto the arm of the craft, clutching his laser rifle.

"The circuits are fried! This thing's gonna blow!"

Rick left the pocket and catwalked the extended arm of the Guardian to the elevator closure lever. He jumped up and grabbed hold of it, riding it down as the doors closed. The fighter was temporarily sealed off from enemy fire, and the elevator began to descend.

One, two, three, four, five levels and they were still going down, the Guardian giving off predestruct noises and smoke now, Max and the others offering up silent prayers for the doors to open.

At level six the elevator stopped. The doors parted, and the four defenders were off and running. But out of nowhere a Zentraedi shock trooper made an airborne grab for them, landing facedown and miraculously empty-handed in front of the elevator. The soldier got to his feet, his quarry long gone, and stared at the smoldering uniformed thing inside.

He had perhaps a second to contemplate its crouched birdlike form before the ensuing explosion blew him away.

If the soldier's last grasp failed to capture the four, it had at least succeeded in dividing them.

Rick and Lisa ran for quite a while before realizing that Ben and Max were no longer with them. They searched for a while, but the explosion of the VT had drawn more Zentraedi to the scene, and it seemed a wiser move to push on.

They entered an area where several corridors converged. It was a vast, domed chamber crowded with generators, computer terminals, conduits, and ductwork. There was an overpowering smell to the place, as alien as anything their senses had yet encountered, and a sonic roar that reminded them of pressure-cooker sounds, amplified and low-frequency-enhanced. They secreted themselves behind a long console covered with switches and control knobs. Then, cautiously, they peered over the top.

What they saw was a cluster of thirty-meter-high vessels, like medicinal capsules stood on end, transparent and filled with a purple viscous, churning fluid. In at least six of these vessels were half-formed, featureless Zentraedi. Rick was totally bewildered and vaguely upset by the sight, but Lisa's sharp intake of breath told him that she recognized something here.

"So *that's* why so many of the Zentraedi soldiers look alike—they're all clones!"

Lisa risked a better view: Now she could see a second cluster of human-size capsules positioned in front of the larger ones, also churning, also containing some half-formed shape. It took her a moment to make sense of this, and when she turned to Rick with an explanation, she scarcely believed her own words: The Zentraedi were reducing their soldiers to human size.

Rick looked at her like she was crazy, and she didn't blame him. But there it was, happening right before their eyes, and no other explanation was forthcoming.

They pulled back as more soldiers entered the chamber searching for them and resumed their conversation some distance away in a dimly lit weapons room.

"You remember how Dolza kept asking us how we became Micronians?"

"Yeah, so?"

"They're wondering if we have similar clone chambers and reduction devices. That's why they can't understand any closeness between the sexes, because, well, love and sex wouldn't be necessary in a society of clones."

"Incredible."

"You're not kidding, incredible. And it wouldn't surprise me to learn that Zentraedi and humans are genetically related. In the beginning they were probably the same size as us!"

"So what are they, human giants or giant humans?"

She looked at him blankly. "I guess it's too early to say. Maybe after we analyze the videos we'll know. But right now, I'd say they can go either way. They've found some way of rearranging their molecular structure—big for hostile environments, small for..." Lisa shrugged.

"Yeah," said Rick. "Small for what? Why are they *reducing* some of their troops? And how are they doing it?"

"Protoculture," Lisa said evenly.

The word had scarcely left her lips when Rick heard the growl. Suddenly a giant hand reached into the room and took hold of Lisa. She screamed. Rick yelled and gave chase, mindless of the consequences.

The giant had straightened from his crouch by the time Rick hit the corridor; he was holding Lisa near his face, growling at her. As Rick ran into view, the Zentraedi soldier simply extended his foot—not a kick, really, but more than enough to lift Rick off the floor and send him careening into a rack of upright laser rifles. Why every bone in his body wasn't broken, he had no idea (*adrenaline,* he'd tell himself later), but at the moment all he knew was that he was buried under the weapons, stunned and crushed but alive and angrier than ever.

Rick allowed the fear and anger to get hold of him; he positioned himself on one knee and heaved one of the rifles over his shoulder like a bazooka—a five-meter-long bazooka. Putting all his meager weight to the trigger, he managed to yank off three rapid blasts. The Zentraedi caught all of them—one through the fish eye faceshield and two through the pectoral armor—and went down like an oak. Rick dropped the weapon and rushed in to find Lisa still in the soldier's hand, crying.

He stopped in his tracks, then moved in slowly, afraid to touch or move her.

"Jeez, Lisa… how bad are you hurt?"

"I dropped the camera, I—I… it shattered."

"Forget the camera! You mean you're not hurt?"

"No, I don't think so. But the mission…"

"Unbelievable," Rick muttered as he helped her from the slack hand. "Sometimes women just don't make any sense, even when they're officers."

It wasn't in any way meant to bring her around, but it surely did: She threw him off and ran a hand over her wet eyes. "Don't start with me, Hunter."

Rick felt the footsteps coming. He grabbed her hand, and the chase was on again. *This has got to be the way mice feel,* he told himself while they were running.

The Zentraedi soldiers were right on top of them, forcing them into left and right turns indiscriminately. Ultimately they found themselves in a dark and deteriorated corridor, with stress fissures in the walls and great gaping holes in the floor. Explosive bolts of energy threw light and short-lived shadows all around them as they ran. And suddenly the world dropped out from under them, light and sound beginning to fade as they plunged toward emptiness together...

17

The list of players was still incomplete when Miriya took to the stage; but was there ever a harder act to follow?

The Collected Journals of Admiral Rick Hunter

THE BEST THEY COULD DO WAS CLEAN UP THE MESS.

Breetai looked on as two lower-echelon soldiers carted fragments of the broken viewscreen from the bridge. The front shield of the observation bubble was also in ruin. Much as Breetai's career.

Dolza, Breetai, and Exedore had been on the bridge when the Micronians' mecha had punched through the wall. Only seconds before, they had been informed of the prisoners' escape, and Breetai was promising their speedy recapture. Then, suddenly, the transformed Battloid had exploded into their midst and soared belligerently out across the astrogation hold. Breetai had glimpsed the look on Dolza's face then, and now that look was being leveled against him.

"So, Breetai, have the Micronians been recaptured?"

"I'm sorry to report that they haven't. Their size presents difficulties."

The Zentraedi commander-in-chief cocked his head to one side. "Indeed. And further difficulties are the last thing we need at the moment. Do you understand?"

"M'lord."

"The responsibility was yours, and this failure will have to be entered into the record." Dolza turned his back to Breetai. "I am relieving you of active duty for the time being, Commander."

He turned around and motioned to the shattered observation bubble. "You can hardly continue to operate in this… *condition*, in any case."

It was even worse than Breetai had expected. But he thought there might still be a way out. Exedore stepped forward to speak for him.

"But sir, the infiltration—who will assume responsibility for the operation?"

Dolza considered this. "Breetai's knowledge of Zor's ship has been an invaluable aid to us in this matter. It will be duly noted. However, Azonia will now be in charge of our three agents."

"Azonia?!" Breetai and Exedore exclaimed.

"But Azonia isn't briefed—"

Dolza held up his hand to silence Exedore. "Commander Azonia is a loyal subject who has never failed me. Once more, I am assigning our finest pilot to her charge."

Just then two soldiers requested entry and conveyed the hover-table onto the bridge. Grouped together on the tabletop and clothed in the only suitable garments available—sleeveless sackcloths cinched at the waist by rough cords—were the three now "micronized" operatives, Rico, Konda, and Bron.

Dolza looked down on them soberly.

"You understand the gravity of your mission?"

"Sir!" three small voices shouted in unison.

"Miriya will oversee your insertion into the dimensional fortress." The agents exchanged looks and expressions of excitement.

"Succeed and you will each have a cruiser to command upon your return."

Three arms were raised in salute: "For the glory of the Zentraedi!"

Dolza returned the salute and turned to Breetai as the hover-table was taken from the bridge.

"This time we will not fail."

Ben remembered having hurdled the giant alien's spread fingers, but Max assured him that he'd done nothing of the sort. They'd both taken a dive off to one side of the corridor when the Zentraedi pounced and found cover behind an open hatch just as the VT exploded. They saw Rick and the Commander make their escape, but neither Max nor Ben was able to pick up the trail. While enemy soldiers poured into the area, the two corporals had moved swiftly through a serviceway that ran parallel to the ship's central corridor. They had made good progress for several hours, until Max had inadvertently tripped a scanner alarm reset to detect movement along the floor of the passageway.

They had three shock troopers on their tail now and a deadly flock of projectiles overhead. The soldiers were herding them toward a waiting elevator, hoping to corner them inside. But perhaps the enemy hadn't identified the weapon one of the Micronians carried, or perhaps they hadn't even seen it. In any case, no sooner did the two enter the car than Max swung himself about face, trained his laser rifle on the elevator controls, and fired. The intense beam soldered the proper circuits; the doors slid closed, and the car began to descend...

In that liquid dream, Minmei was leaving him and Rick was calling out to her, over and over again...

Then Lisa's face floated into focus, and the dream faded. She helped him sit up and asked if he was all right.

He began to take stock of himself and these new dark and wet surroundings. They were in an area of huge pipes, containment chambers, baffles, valves, and regulating devices, seated near the edge of a system of channels and reservoirs that stretched out into the darkness. Shafts of light filtered down from far above them, and the thick air was filled with the sounds of mechanized pumps and filtration units, running water, and the clank and hiss of fluid control conduits.

They were both soaked to the skin; Lisa's uncoiled long brown hair hung in wet waves halfway down her back.

She said, "We must be in the water-recycling chamber. It's in terrible disrepair." She laughed at her words. "Great time to be judgmental, huh? This pool saved our lives. We must have fallen a hundred feet."

With effort, Rick got to his feet. "Maybe the water broke our fall, but something else saved me from drowning."

Lisa averted his gaze. "I wasn't about to have you die on me, Hunter." Then she looked directly at him. "Let's just call it even."

Rick's vision was adapting itself to the dark; he began to take notice of the refuse and debris all around them. Nearby there were hatchways and elevator platforms, and somewhere in the distance, faint light.

"They do let things get run-down, don't they?"

"I've been thinking about it, Lieutenant. Even with all their technical knowledge, maybe they only know how to *use* the equipment but not how to repair it. No techs, no maintenance personnel. Just soldier clones, every last one of them."

"All this destructive power… I wonder how many worlds they've ended, how many lives they've taken. It's sickening to think about: an entire civilization dedicated to war."

"I guess I should feel right at home."

"What d'ya mean?"

"My father had a favorite saying: 'Only where there is battle being waged is there life being lived.'" She sighed. "My family has been connected with the military for the past century… The only life I've ever known is the Defense Forces. 'The mission,' that's all I can think about." She gestured. "You heard me up there."

"Yeah, but that's why you're an officer. You're a leader. Head of the class and all that."

Lisa's eyebrows knitted. "How did you find that out?"

"It's common knowledge." Rick laughed. "Some of the VT pilots call you Supergirl."

"Wonderful…" She looked hard at Rick. "You know, I don't mean to intimidate anyone. It's just that…" A sly smile replaced her grim expression. "Forget it. But I'll bet Miss Macross isn't a bit intimidating, is she?"

Rick was taken off guard. "Minmei? What makes you think—"

"You were calling her name: 'Minmei! Minmei!'" Lisa playfully mocked him.

"All right, all right. What of it?"

"You tell me."

"Nothing to tell. We're friends, that's all. You know how it is.

She's a celebrity. Public property. We don't have time for each other anymore."

"A major talent, I'm sure."

Rick gave her a look that signaled she'd gone too far.

"Listen, Lieutenant, I'm only kidding. At least you *have* someone to return to. All I have is another mission to look forward to."

"There's no one in your life?"

"Just call me Miss SDF-1."

"That's just a matter of time. You're a beautiful woman. Most guys would give…"

"Yeah?"

"What I mean is, you're a brilliant officer, and…"

Lisa didn't say anything for a minute; then she cleared her throat and stood up. "Well, I'm not going to meet anyone sitting around here, am I?"

She took hold of Rick's hand. "Let's get out of here, Lieutenant."

They walked toward the light.

Engine rooms, storage rooms, empty holds, a second recycling plant, more storage areas—all in the same shabby, unwashed, and unmaintained state. But something had changed: The air had begun to lose that overpoweringly dank smell and thickness. A slight breeze played through Lisa's long hair.

They moved toward the source of the wind.

At the far end of the supply room filled with Battlepods and ordnance of every conceivable type, they found their exit: a rectangular port in the hull of the ship. They ran toward this, the wind no longer gentle but chilled and full of sound, and stopped short of the edge, awestruck.

So wrapped up in finding a way out, they had forgotten that they were actually onboard a ship within a ship!

If you could call it a ship.

Beyond the portal was a sight their senses were unprepared for: hundreds of Zentraedi ships anchored weightless in the seemingly sky-blue docking chamber of the command center. Overcome by a sudden wave of vertigo, Lisa took a step back. Was it possible? Dolza's ship would have to be the best kept secret in the universe—a thousand miles long—to accommodate all these vessels! Her mind wrestled with it, her thoughts spinning out of control.

Rick had taken hold of her arm. "Someone's coming!" he told her.

They concealed themselves behind some crates near the portal. Rick tuned in to the sounds he had heard and realized at once that no Zentraedi was capable of making so little noise. It had to be…

"Ben! Max!" Lisa yelled.

The four of them reunited in a group embrace, and capsule summaries of their respective adventures and ordeals were rapidly exchanged. Max complimented Lisa on how lovely she looked with her hair down, and she congratulated him on having been able to hang on to his "thinking cap" all this time. Ben was in his usual good humor.

"So what's next on the agenda, friends?"

The intrusion of reality cooled their warm reunion somewhat; what was next, indeed? From the edges of the portal they could see a cruiser taking on supplies through a transfer tube at a neighboring port in the flagship.

"We could get aboard easy enough," said Max, "but where do you think she's bound?"

"Does it matter?" Ben asked. "Let's go."

"Hold on a minute, Ben," said Lisa. "We were brought here on this ship. I think we'd stand a better chance of getting back to the SDF-1 by remaining aboard."

Max didn't like the idea. "Not if the Zentraedi capture us. We've seen too much by now. They won't take any chances with us."

"He's right," Rick agreed. "You're in charge, Lisa, but I vote for the cruiser."

Lisa crossed her arms, then relaxed and smiled at them.

"All right, let's do it."

They set off at once.

Finding their way to the adjacent port was more difficult than they'd imagined, but once there it was a simple matter to conceal themselves from the guards and at the right moment jump aboard the cargo conveyer. Rick thought about mice and rats again as the team was carried out of Breetai's flagship and into the purple-armored cruiser.

...

Azonia was the commander of the cruiser and her all-female crew. Highly skilled, respected, and powerful, she had earned a reputation for succeeding where others had failed. Her attractiveness and magnetism had helped secure a brilliant career, but her soft eyes and small features belied the arrogant, self-absorbed megalomaniac many knew her to be. Here was one who would sacrifice half her fleet to fulfill that all-consuming passion for victory-a fact that had endeared her to the Zentraedi Command but one that instilled fear in the hearts of anyone of lesser station. In fact, among all the Zentraedi there was only one who would have defended her to the finish and whose respect for her some said was tainted by an atavistic lust for sensual experience. That one was Khyron, the so-called Backstabber.

Azonia was joined on the bridge of the cruiser by the ace pilot Dolza had promised her to carry out the infiltration—Miriya Parino of the Quadrono Battalion.

If Miriya was not as ambitious as her superior, she was certainly as respected. Where Azonia lived for self-glorification, Miriya fought for personal perfection: to rank first in this game called war the Zentraedi had been born into. Ever on the alert for new challenges, new tasks to master, new worlds to conquer, she was possessed of an intensely curious nature well suited to the extraordinary level of her talents, a trait that set her apart from the other pilots. But she was loyal to a fault and never failed to carry out her orders to the fullest. In this way she was much like her commander, but where Azonia would seek out ways to promote herself, only Miriya could rightfully judge Miriya. She had earned her own command a dozen times over but had rejected it on each occasion. Promotion would have placed her too far from the action, and it was hands-on action that she craved—contest, confrontation, challenge. She had little patience for the relative ease of a commander's life, having always to be ready to accept blame or praise based on how well the troops had carried out their mission. No, it was far easier to accept the orders of those unskilled superiors and bask in the freedom that a secondary position allowed.

She was eager to mix it up with these Micronians. They were making fools of the pilots under Breetai's command. And even the great Khyron had not fared well with this new enemy.

It was time to let the female Zentraedi take over.

Anyone unaware of the motivational differences between Azonia and Miriya might have been inclined to read rivalry into their relationship, and in fact many of the female soldiers on the bridge did just that, even though no such condition existed.

Azonia swirled the gray commander's cloak over her crimson uniform as she turned to face the female ace. Her close-cropped bluestone-colored hair gave her an air of efficiency, unlike Miriya's long thick fall of forest green and large emerald eyes that radiated sensual fire.

"I take it you have already been briefed on your mission."

"I have, Commander Azonia. But may I speak freely?"

"Say what's on your mind."

"Delivering spies into the SDF-1 hardly seems a mission worthy of my talents."

"Yes, I thought it might be something like that."

"After all, I'm a combat pilot, not some delivery drone."

"This mission happens to be of utmost importance. It has been authorized by Commander-in-Chief Dolza himself."

"Of course, sir, but still—"

"Have you considered that these Micronians might prove to be more dangerous than you have been led to believe?"

"That is something to be hoped for, Commander."

"Need I remind you that my reputation rides on this mission?"

Miriya bowed and saluted. "I will not fail you, my lord."

Azonia narrowed her eyes.

"The three micronized operatives are presently aboard our sister ship. They have been placed inside a capsule-craft that you will retrieve once we are within range of the dimensional fortress. Now, how will you get the spies aboard?"

"I am not at liberty to discuss that aspect of the operation with anyone."

The commander stiffened somewhat. "I see."

"Commander, it will be good to best Breetai in this matter. And Khyron, of course."

"*Commander* Khyron to you, Miriya—now and always. Is that clear?"

"My apologies, sir."

"You are dismissed. Return to your quarters and prepare for hyperspace-fold."

The fold operation was the first note of encouragement struck for the four Micronian escapees who had sequestered themselves in a supply hangar elsewhere in Azonia's cruiser. The Zentraedi guards had left the hold when the spacefold began, leaving them alone in a room full of armaments and Battlepods. But they remained cautiously optimistic. Especially Ben.

"I know a way we can pass the time—we can count the number of different places we might end up after this fold."

Lisa's attention had been riveted on the real-time indicator, but Ben's comment intruded on her concentration.

"Lieutenant Hunter, you didn't tell me you had such a comedian on your team." Lisa gestured to Ben. "We've gone from the frying pan to the fire, and all he can do is make jokes."

"All right Ben, can it," said Rick.

"How are we going to get outta here, anyway?" said Max. "Even if we do defold back in Earthspace?"

"We're going to commandeer one of these Battlepods."

Lisa said it so matter-of-factly that the three men did delayed double takes.

"Just climb into the Battlepod and fly it out of here, huh? Who's going to teach us how to operate it? You think they left an operating manual inside, in the glove compartment maybe?"

Lisa put her hands on her hips. "Have you been playing hooky, Lieutenant?"

"Wait a minute!" Rick said defensively. "Sure, I've studied the insides of these things just like everybody else. But those were wrecks. Nobody's actually piloted one of them."

"Listen, Rick, you said yourself that their systems are complex but not impossible to understand. It shouldn't be a problem for three ace pilots like you boys."

"Come on, Commander…"

Lisa checked her watch. "It took us twenty-four real hours to make the hyperspace jump from Earthspace to Dolza's command center. Assuming we're headed back to the SDF-1, we've got twenty hours left to learn."

"And suppose we're not headed back to Earthspace? Suppose we defold at some other Zentraedi front or base or I don't know what?"

"Then it won't matter whether we learn how to operate it or not."

Rick stood up and cracked his knuckles. "All right, gang, let's get crackin'."

Aft in the special weapons hold, Miriya strapped herself into the Quadrono scout ship—a combination thruster unit and multiple-missile launcher developed by the Invid, and designed for infiltration or solo penetration operations. Defold was complete, and the time had come to retrieve the three micronized agents from the cruiser's sister ship.

Miriya lowered the canopy of the extravehicular pack and stepped forward to the edge of the port. In the distance she could see the object of her mission: the SDF-1. It was under attack by the remnants of Breetai's tattered fleet.

Azonia came on-screen in the mecha's cockpit:

"We'll draw the enemy's attention away from you. May you win all your battles!"

"As always!"

Miriya launched herself into space, a darting dragonfly among the stars…

Max had his arms stretched out deep into the pod's waldolike gun controls. Ben was scratching his head, puzzling over the firing mechanism for the missiles. Lisa wondered how she was going to be able to activate those huge radio toggles. And Rick tried to figure out how he was going to fly the thing.

The interior of the Battlepod was not entirely dissimilar to human-made Robotech mecha. In fact, the design of the cockpit went a long way toward verifying Lisa's theory about a point of common origin; the layout and placement of the controls had the logic of human construction, albeit on a grand scale.

Lisa, her arms overhead hugging a toggle switch, glanced at her watch and dropped to the sphere's seat. She looked hard at her companions, calculating the present level of visual distortion against the indicator's display. Satisfied with the results of her scan, she announced:

"We're coming out of defold right on schedule. It's got to be Earthspace or an incredible coincidence."

The four regarded one another and took a collective breath; they all knew what had to be done next.

Rick readied himself at the controls. "Let's see if we can start this thing up."

He engaged the drive lever and activated the sensor and scanner systems. The mecha began to hum and come to life, and the first thing that greeted their eyes on the forward screen was the sight of two Zentraedi soldiers just returned to the hangar.

The soldiers spun around at the sound of the activated pod.

"They're on to us!" yelled Rick.

"Blast 'em!"

Max shouted, "Here goes nothing!" as laser bolts shot from the arm cannons and dropped the guards to the deck.

Lisa and Ben cheered. Rick told Max to keep firing.

"Keep it up; let's open up this can of worms and get out of here." Meanwhile, he nudged the stick forward and the Battlepod lifted away from its still silent companions.

Max continued to pour particle heat into the hull, until all at once the lasers burned through, and air and mecha were being sucked in a rush toward the breach.

"We're gonna have to be fast," Max warned them. "These things heal themselves."

Ben said, "Not while I'm around!" and loosed two rockets at the hull.

Rick let out a rousing yell. Simultaneously with the explosions, he sent the thruster stick home; the pod soared across the hangar and through the breach.

Miriya had retrieved the ejected canister which contained the micronized agents. Battlepods were swarming around Zor's ship like angry insects and engaging enemy mecha throughout the field. It would have been a simple matter to insert the canister and be done with it, but she couldn't resist testing these waters.

She flew straight into their midst, executing a series of teasing maneuvers meant to draw the enemy out; but not one of them succeeded in getting a fix on her. She made up her mind that these Micronians were nothing to worry about and grew even more daring, positioning herself in the center of an entire squadron of enemy fighters. And again their heat-seekers could not find the mark. She laughed aloud and stung back.

Roy Fokker, Skull Team leader, would later recall the strange sight he witnessed that day: how a Zentraedi mecha, not much larger than a giant with a jet pack, had taken out five VTs at once.

Through the breach, the commandeered Battlepod rolled into a near front gainer and was almost taken out by Zentraedi crossfire. But the occupants of that pod were filled with such vigor and élan that they scarcely took notice of their predicament. Ahead of them enveloped in a cloud of metal anger, was their ship. And beyond that, their planet and its silver satellite.

"Can you raise anything on the radio?"

"I'm trying," said Lisa. Ben came to her aid; together they put their strength to the knob and managed to give it a fraction of a turn.

Rick heard singing: a familiar voice, a familiar song.

"That's Minmei! That's her song—'My Boyfriend's a Pilot'!"

"As long as it's not *was* a pilot," said Ben.

Miriya easily avoided the Phalanx and Valkyrie fire from the SDF-1 and came alongside the fortress at a point where Breetai claimed the hull could be easily breached. She summoned Protoculture strength to the outsize grappler hands of the mecha and tore away some new hatchway the Micronians had installed. She deposited the cylinder inside an air lock in the mecha, then opened and resealed.

"Insertion successful," Miriya said aloud. "Returning to base."

Status reports, enemy trajectories, battle coordinates...

"We've got the military frequency," said Rick excitedly.

Lisa leaned into the mike. "Please respond, SDF-1, we are in your air space. This is Commander Hayes and the Vermilion Team attempting to make contact with our home base. Do you read me? Over. Rick, do you think they heard us?"

"I hope so, Lisa. I'd hate to be taken out by one of our own VTs."

Three Battloids were closing on the pod in attack formation, gatling cannons in hand. Rick and Lisa, Ben and Max, turned to each other with undisguised looks of concern.

"Did they hear us, Rick? Did they hear us?!"

Rick closed his eyes as the Battloids moved in for the kill.

With home so close you could almost touch it...

HOMECOMING

FOR RISA KESSLER,
WITH THANKS AND HIGH REGARD

01

The enemy armada, so vastly superior to us in numbers of fighting mecha and aggregate firepower, continues to harry and harass us. But time and again the Zentraedi stop short of all-out attack. They impede our long voyage back to Earth, but they cannot stop us. I am still uncertain as to what good fortune is working in the SDF-1's favor.

I do not point out any of this to the crew or refugees, however. It does no good to tell grieving friends and loved ones that casualties could have been far worse.

From the log of Captain Henry Gloval

BLUE LINES OF ENEMY CANNON FIRE STREAKED BY ROY FOKKER'S cockpit, scorching one of his Veritech fighter's tail stabilizers, ranging in for a final volley.

"Flying sense" the aviators called it, jargon that came from the twentieth-century term "air sense": honed and superior high-speed piloting instincts. It was something a raw beginner took a while to develop, something that separated the novices from the vets.

And it was something Lieutenant Commander Roy Fokker, Skull Team leader and Veritech squadron commander, had in abundance, even in the airlessness of a deep-space dogfight.

Responding to his deft touch at the controls and his very will—passed along to it by Robotech sensors in his flight helmet—Roy's Veritech fighter did a wingover and veered onto a new vector with tooth-snapping force. Thrusters blaring full-bore, the maneuver forces pressed him into his seat, just as the enemy was concentrating more on his aim than on his flying.

The Zentraedi in the Battlepod on Roy's tail, trying so diligently to kill him and destroy his Robotech fighter, was a good pilot, steady and cool like all of them, but he lacked Roy's flying abilities.

While the giant alien gaped, astounded, at his suddenly empty gunsight reticle, the Skull Team leader was already coming around behind the pod into the kill position.

Around that fragment of the battle, an enormous dogfight raged as Zentraedi pods and their Cyclops recon ships mixed it up ferociously with the grimly determined human defenders in their Veritechs. The bright spherical explosions characteristic of zero-g battle blossomed all around, dozens at a time. Blue Zentraedi radiation blasts were matched by the Veritechs' autocannons, which flung torrents of high-density armor-piercers at the enemy.

Roy was relieved to see that the SDF-1 was unharmed. Most of the fighting seemed to be going on at some distance from it, although it was clear that the enemy fleet had all the odds on its side. The Zentraedi armada easily numbered over a million warships.

Roy located his wingman, Captain Kramer, in the furious engagement; forming up for mutual security, he looked around again for the fantastic Zentraedi mecha that had done so much damage a few minutes before. It had flown rings around the Veritechs that had gone after it, taking Roy and the Skulls by surprise and smashing their formation after cutting a swath through Vermilion Team.

Whatever it was, it was unlike any Zentraedi weapon the humans had seen so far. Unlike the pods, which resembled towering metal ostriches bristling with guns, the newcomer was more human-shaped—a bigger, more hulking, and heavily armed and armored version of the Veritechs' own Battloid mode. And fast—frightfully fast and impossible to stop, eluding even the SDF-1's massive defensive barrages.

Roy had expected to see the battle fortress under intense attack; instead, the super dimensional fortress was cruising along unbothered and alone. Moreover, transmissions over the tac net indicated that the Zentraedi pods and Cyclopses were withdrawing. Roy couldn't figure that out.

He switched from the tac net to SDF-1's command net. There

was word of the new Zentraedi mecha. The thing had made it as far as SDF-1—getting in beneath the fields of fire of most of the ship's batteries—then had suddenly withdrawn at blinding speed, outmaneuvering gunfire and outracing pursuit. The ship had suffered only minor damage, and the operations and intelligence people had concluded that the whole thing had been a probing attack of some kind, a test of a new machine and new tactics.

Roy didn't care as long as the battle fortress was still safe. He gathered the Veritechs, ready to head home.

"Enemy pod," Skull Five called over the tac net. "Bearing one-niner-four-seven."

Roy already had the computer reference on one of his situation screens. A pod, all right, but evidently damaged and drifting, none of its weapons firing; it was leaking atmosphere.

"Could be a trick," Skull Seven said. "What d' ya think, skipper? Do we blast it out of the sky?"

"Negative; somebody may still be alive in there, and a live captive is what the intelligence staff's been praying for." The incredible savagery of deep-space war was such that few survived as casualties. Alien or human, a fighter almost always either triumphed or died, a simple formula. The humans had never recovered a living enemy.

Besides, for very personal reasons, Roy was especially eager to see a Zentraedi undergo interrogation.

"We're getting signals from it, nothing we can unscramble," a communications officer reported over the command net.

Whatever was going on, none of the Zentraedi forces seemed to be turning back for a rescue. Veritech fly-bys drew no fire; eyeball inspection and instruments indicated that the damaged pod's main power source had been knocked out but that some of its weapons were still functioning. Nevertheless, it passed up several opportunities to blast away at nearby VTs.

"This is too good an opportunity to pass up," Gloval finally announced over the main command net. "If there is a survivor aboard, we must get him into the SDF-1 immediately."

"That thing could be booby-trapped—or its occupant could be!" a security staff officer protested from one of Roy's display screens.

Gloval replied, "That is why we will push the pod closer to SDF-1—but not too close—and connect a boarding tube to it. An EVA team will make a thorough examination before we permit it any closer."

"But—" the officer began.

Roy cut in over the command net, "You heard the captain, so put a sock in it, mac!" Roy was elated with Gloval's decision; it was only a slim hope, but now there *was* hope of finding out what had happened to Roy's closest friend in the world, Rick Hunter and Lisa Hayes and the others who'd disappeared on their desperate mission to guide the SDF-1 through danger.

Roy began swinging into place, shifting his ship to Battloid mode. "Okay, Skull Team; time to play a little bumper cars."

Two more Skulls went to Battloid, their Robotech ships transforming and reconfiguring. When the shift was complete, the war machines looked like enormous armored ultramech knights.

They joined Roy in pushing the inert pod back toward the battle fortress.

The men and women of the EVA—Extra Vehicular Activity—crews were efficient and careful. *They're also gutsy as hell*, Roy reflected, his Battloid towering over them in the boarding tube lock. But of course, everybody knew and honored the legendary dedication and tenacity of the EVA crews.

Crowded into the boarding tube lock with two other Battloids behind him, Roy watched expectantly. The huge lock, extending from the SDF-1 at the end of nearly a mile of large-diameter tube, was a yawning dome on a heavy base, equipped with every sort of contingency gear imaginable. The captured pod and EVA crew and Roy's security detail took up only a small part of its floor space.

"Not beat up too bad," the EVA crew chief observed over the com net. "But I dunno how much air it lost. What d' ya say, Fokker? Do we open 'er up?" She was holding a thermotorch ready. She'd turned to gaze up at Roy's cockpit.

As ranking officer on the scene, Lt. Comdr. Roy Fokker had the responsibility of advising Gloval. Tampering with the pod was very risky; they could trigger some kind of booby trap humans couldn't even imagine, destroying everyone there and perhaps even damaging the SDF-1.

But we can't go on fighting war this way! Roy thought. *Knowing next to nothing about these creatures we're up against or even why we're fighting— we can't go on like this much longer!*

"Cap'n Gloval, sir, I say we take a shot."

"Very well. Good luck to you," Gloval answered. "Proceed."

Roy reached down and put a giant hand in front of the EVA crew chief, blocking her way as she approached the enemy mecha. "Sorry, Pietra; this is my party."

His Battloid stood upright again and walked to the pod, shouldering its autocannon, its footsteps shaking the deck. "Cover me," he told his teammates, and they fanned out, muzzles leveled, for clear fields of fire. The Battloid's forearms extruded metal tentacles, complicated waldos and manipulators, and thermotorches.

"Just try not to break anything unnecessarily," Pietra warned, and led her crew to the shelter of a blast shield.

Roy looked the pod over, trying a few external controls tentatively. Nothing happened. He moved closer still, examining the pressure seals that ran around the great hatch at the rear top of the pod's bulbous torso. Being this close to a pod's guns had him sweating under his VT helmet.

"Careful, Roy," Kramer said quietly.

He didn't want to use the torch for fear of fire or explosion. He decided to try simply pulling the pod's hatch open with the Battloid's huge, strong hands. He ran his ship's fingers along the seams, feeling for a place to grab hold…

The pod shook, rattled, and began to open.

Roy's Battloid leapt back, weapon aimed, as the hatch lifted up. Battloid forefingers tightened on triggers, but there was no occupant immediately to be seen.

However, the Battloids' external sound sensors relayed a remarkable exchange, muffled and a little resonant, coming from the pod.

"Well, finally! Thank goodness! When you start bragging to your fighter pilot buddies about *this* mission, boys, don't forget it took you just about forever to get a simple hatch open!"

That voice was womanly and very pleasant, if a little arch and teasing. Another, a young male's, sounding highly insulted, answered, "You weren't so hot at getting in touch with your precious bridge, I noticed!"

If this is some kind of trick, we're up against the zaniest enemies in the universe, Roy thought.

"I thought you both did very well," another male voice said calmly, humbly—placatingly.

"Ah, look out, Max," the first male voice said. "And let's get outta here."

There was a certain amount of grunting and straining then, and at one point the female voice yelled, "Ben, if you don't get your big foot out of my face, I'm going to break it off!" A vociferous argument broke out.

"Everybody shut up!" the first male voice screamed. "Ben, Max: Gimme a boost up, here."

Moments later, two flight-gloved, human-size hands gripped the edge of the hatch. A dark mop of black hair rose into view.

Rick Hunter, standing on the head of the husky Ben Dixon, hauled himself up triumphantly.

"Hold your fire! We're back! Roy, we escaped from the Zentraedi—um…"

Three Battloids stood there looking at them, hands resting casually on the upturned muzzles of their grounded autocannons, heads cocked to one side or the other. Their attitude seemed to be one of resigned disgust.

"We escaped!" Rick repeated, thinking perhaps they hadn't heard him. "Man, have we got stories to tell! We were in an enemy ship! We met their leaders! We shot our way out in this pod! We… we… What's wrong?"

Roy couldn't tell Rick how overjoyed and relieved he was; it would have spoiled their friendship.

"We were *hoping* for a POW," he said. "Boy, is Captain Gloval gonna be sore at you for not being a Zentraedi."

02

The Zentraedi version of psychology could only be termed primitive, of course, except as it applied to such things as maintaining military discipline and motivating warriors. And even there, it was brutal and straightforward.

No surprise, then, that when those particular three Zentraedi were quick to accept their spying mission, Breetai scarcely thought twice about it.

But of course, he hadn't spent as much time watching transmissions of the swimsuit portion of the Miss Macross contest.

Zeitgeist, *Alien Psychology*

THE SDF-1'S SURVIVAL OF THE LATEST ZENTRAEDI ATTACK HAD buoyed morale all through the ship—at least in most cases; there were those whom the lessons of war had made too wary to quickly believe in good fortune. Even with Earth looming large before it and the long, dark billions of miles safely crossed, the battle fortress was dogged by the enemy—now more than ever. Continued vigilance was imperative.

One of those acutely aware of the continuing danger was Claudia Grant, who was acting as the vessel's First Officer in Lisa Hayes's absence. Though Claudia and Lisa were friends, Claudia had always felt a little put off by Lisa's single-minded devotion to duty, her severity. But now, elevated to the responsibilities of her position—especially at this moment, with Gloval off the bridge—Claudia was seeing things in a different light.

The members of her usual watch, the female enlisted-rating techs,

Sammie, Kim, and Vanessa, were off duty for a long-postponed pass into Macross City. Lisa, Claudia, and the other three had formed something very much like a family, with Gloval as patriarch; they had become a highly efficient team both under everyday stresses and demands and under fire.

The turmoil of the war had brought an assortment of other techs to the bridge on relief watches, and Claudia didn't trust any of them to really know what they were doing, just as Lisa hadn't. So even though she was almost out on her feet with fatigue, Claudia had refused to be relieved of her duties as long as Gloval was away.

There was no telling how long that would be. The glorious news of the rescue of Lisa and the others was tarnished by the fact that the SDF-1 was still surrounded by the enemy armada. Debriefings and command conferences might go on for a very long while.

Claudia looked up wearily from her instruments as she heard one of the relief-watch techs say wistfully, "Boy, is that beautiful! D' you think we'll ever set foot on Earth again?"

The tech had brought up a long-range image of their blue-white homeworld on the screen before her.

Claudia was a tall woman in her late twenties, with exotic good looks and glowing honey-brown skin. Her dark eyes twinkled and shone when she was happy, and flashed when she was angry. Right now, they were flashing like warning beacons.

"Why don't you go ask the commander of that Zentraedi fleet? Go ahead, take a look at them! Maybe they've gone away!"

The tech, a teenage girl who wore her auburn hair in a pageboy and still didn't look quite comfortable in uniform, swallowed and went a little pale. Claudia Grant's temper was well known, and she had the size and speed to back it up when she needed to.

The tech worked her controls obediently, bringing up a visual of the Zentraedi fleet. They were all around the battle fortress, standing out of range of the ship's secondary batteries and lesser weapons. They were like a seaful of predatory fish—cruisers and destroyers and smaller craft in swarms, blocking out the stars. And farther away, the instruments registered their flagship: *nine miles* of armor and heavy weapons.

The tech gasped, eyes big and round.

"Still there, huh?" Claudia nodded, knowing full well they were. "All right, then, let's not hear any more about wanting to go home; not until our job's done. Understood?"

The tech hastened to say, "Aye aye!" as did the rest of the watch.

Claudia eased off a bit, looking around at the watch members. "There are a lot of folks depending on us. And I guarantee you, you *don't* want to know what it feels like to let people down in a situation like this."

In a far-off compartment of the SDF-1, three strange beings skulked and crept around. They were not Zentraedi, at least not any longer; they were of human scale. But neither could they fairly be called human, though that was the appearance they gave; until a few hours before they had been members of the giant warrior race.

The devastatingly fast and ferocious enemy mecha that had wreaked such havoc among the VT—the one the humans hadn't seen before—had put this threesome aboard. The one thing they *could* accurately be called was "spies."

They had hastily retreated from the metal canister in which they'd arrived. The mighty Quadrono Battalion mecha that had, in its lightning raid, torn open a section of the SDF-1's hull to toss them inside had also (understandably enough) attracted a certain amount of attention. If the canister was found before it quietly dissolved, it might set off a massive search.

The smallest of the three, Rico, said, "Okay, let's start spying!" He was dark-haired and wiry.

The sturdy Bron, a head taller, said sourly, "But we can't spy in these clothes; they'll know who we are!"

Even though the Zentraedi military had little experience in espionage—out-and-out battle was what the warrior race preferred—it was obvious that Bron was right. The Zentraedi fleet carried no wardrobe in human size, of course, and so the three wore improvised, shapeless knee-length robes of coarsely woven blue sackcloth. The sleeveless robes were gathered at the waist with a turn or two of Zentraedi string, more or less the thickness of clothesline. Not surprisingly, the spies were barefoot.

It all had them a bit shaken, this matter of dress. The Zentraedi drew much of their sense of self from their uniforms. The best the trio had been able to do was agree to maintain the attitude that they were wearing the special attire of an elite unit. A very *small* elite unit.

Konda, nearly Bron's height but lean and angular, shook his hair back out of his eyes. His hair was purple, but intelligence reported that the color wouldn't stand out much in light of current human fads. "Then, let's find some other clothes," Konda proposed.

They'd been given some briefings and rather broad guidelines by Zentraedi intelligence officers, but to a great extent they were improvising as they went along. Still, Konda's idea made a lot of sense. The spies leapt from hiding and set off down a passageway, slipping among the shadows and peering around corners, much more conspicuous than if they'd simply strolled along chatting.

Naturally, SDF-1 had no internal security measures against Zentraedi spies, since it was generally assumed that a fifty-foot-high armored warrior wouldn't be difficult to spot in the average crowd.

There followed a period of ducking and darting, of peeping into various compartments and avoiding any contact with the occasional passerby. The spies knew the general location of the battle fortress's bridge and worked their way in that direction, since the ship's nerve center was something the Zentraedi wanted very much to know about.

As the motley trio peeked out from concealment, they heard a very strange and appealing sound, something none of them had ever heard before. It was human; Konda wondered if it was some alien form of singing, even if it didn't sound very military.

The sound was coming in their direction. They yanked themselves back out of sight. The oddly interesting sound stopped, and the spies heard human female voices.

"Where d'you want to go tonight, Sammie?"

There was the sound of slender shoe heels clicking along the deck. The human females were coming their way, so the spies drew back even deeper into darkness.

"Oh, I really don't care, as long as I can get out of this uniform," Sammie answered.

"Mine feels like it'll be glad to get off me!" Vanessa said.

The Terrible Trio giggled together again; they'd been laughing with delight ever since the relief watch had shown up on the bridge to give them a brief taste of freedom. The hatch to a complex of enlisted ratings' quarters compartments slid open for them and they entered. The hatch closed, shutting off the giggles.

The accelerated course in human language the three spies had been given let them understand the words perfectly, but the content was another question entirely. "What did all that mean?" Konda wondered, rubbing feet that had been made very, very cold by the deck plates.

Little Rico was thinking of a uniform wanting to get off somebody. *Can these creatures have sentient clothing? Perhaps with artificial enhancements? That would indicate a supreme control of Protoculture!* "It seems these Micronians have some great powers."

"Micronians" had always been a derogatory Zentraedi term for small humanoid beings such as *Homo sapiens*. Now the spies weren't so sure that the condescension was justified.

Bron nodded. "Well, let's keep watch and see what else we can find out."

It seemed like a very long time before the hatch reopened. The Terrible Trio emerged, each dressed for a night on the town in a different, fetching outfit. They laughed and joked, going off in the opposite direction, leaving the very faint but heady fragrance of three perfumes in the passageway.

"Different clothes!" Rico exclaimed softly. *With different powers, perhaps, specialized for a particular mission?*

"I *know*!" Bron said with a certain surprising emphasis.

"Do these people change uniforms every time they do something?" Konda posed a tactical question.

But why, then, did the clothes all look different? The spies somehow knew what they'd just seen weren't uniforms. But how could the Micronians bear to lose their identity by not wearing their uniforms? It was all too unsettling for words.

Not to mention the fact that the three Micronian females looked and sounded, well, somehow delightful. Beguiling. It was very puzzling. The three looked at one another.

"Incredible," Bron summarized.

"Uh, but what does it all mean?" Rico said with troubled brow.

Konda rubbed his jaw in thought. "They changed their clothes in that compartment down there. So that means... *we can get disguises!*"

"Good thinking!" Bron cried. "Let's go!" Rico exploded.

They dashed down the passageway, bare feet slapping the deck. After first making sure nobody was still inside, they piled through the hatch together, anxious to blend in with the Micronians. And though none of them admitted it to the others, they were all thinking of those three intriguing Micronian females but trying not to.

They'd had a previous close encounter with the human enemy, monitoring SDF-1 transmissions that were confusing and puzzling but ever so fascinating. What they'd seen was the swimsuit competition of the ship's Miss Macross pageant. Though they hadn't been able to make head or tail of it, and neither had Zentraedi intelligence analysts, the experience had made Rico, Bron, and Konda eager to sign up for the spying mission.

Inside, various small subcompartments opened off a narrow central passageway. The spies began searching through them, looking for garments that might fit.

They approached the clothes tentatively, timidly. The human fabric constructions *seemed* unthreatening enough, hanging there docilely; but if they somehow incorporated Protoculture forces, there might be no limit to what they could do. The threesome moved as carefully as if they were in the midst of a pack of sleeping Dobermans.

When at last they worked up the nerve to actually touch a dangling cuff and nothing catastrophic happened, the Zentraedi proceeded with more confidence.

A pattern emerged: The lockers in those quarters on the forward side of the passageway tended to have rather recognizable clothing suited to normal activities, even if the cut was a little strange. The ones on the aft side, however, had frilly things, as well as trousers and the skirt-type uniforms the females had worn, as well as more elaborate designs of the same undivided lower garments.

After a lot of rummaging and trying on, Konda and Rico, now in human attire, stepped back into the main passageway. Konda wore dark slacks and a yellow turtleneck, settling the collar uncomfortably. Rico had found blue trousers and a red pullover.

"Hey, Bron, let's get moving!" Rico called.

"This uniform is very unusual," Bron said, lumbering to catch up. "But it's all I can find that fits me. I dressed to conform with a two-dimensional image I saw in that compartment. What d' you think?"

Bron held out the hem of his pleated skirt, standing awkwardly in the large pumps he'd found. His white silk blouse was arranged correctly, its fluffy bow tie and the tasteful string of pearls exactly corresponding to the fashion photo he'd seen.

"Y' look fine, Bron! Now, let's get started," Rico snapped. Bron looked wounded.

Rico was edgy; he and the others had come aboard unarmed, since all Zentraedi weapons were now far too big for them to handle or hide. They'd found no Micronian weapons at all in the humans' personal quarters except those of a makeshift and unsuitable sort. How could these creatures feel any peace of mind without at least a few small arms close at hand? It all made less and less sense.

Bron glowered, and Rico subsided; it was unwise to get the big fellow irritated. Bron gave his skirt a final hitch and said, "Ready."

They fell in together and trooped off in the direction the Terrible Trio had gone, ready to bring triumph and glory to the mighty Zentraedi race.

03

We had met the enemy, and he wasn't us. Then we wound up in front of some of "us," and they were the enemy.

Lisa Hayes, *Recollections*

"**P**LEASE CONTINUE YOUR REPORT, COMMANDER HAYES," THE captain bade her.

They sat in high-back chairs along the gleaming conference room table, all in a row. A short time ago they'd been greeted as heroes, but now—despite Captain Gloval's comforting presence—Lisa felt very much as if she were sitting before a board of inquiry.

Lisa, Rick, Ben, and Max looked across the long, wide table at the row of four member officers of the evaluation team. Only one of them held rank in one of the combat arms, Colonel Maistroff, an Air Group officer with a reputation as a martinet and stuffed shirt.

The others were intelligence and operations staffers, though the bearded and balding Major Aldershot was supposed to be something of a mainstay over at G3 Operations and had earned a Combat Infantry Star in his youth. The team studied the escapees as if they were something on a microscope slide.

Gloval, presiding at the head of the table, was encouraging Lisa. "You are certain that what you've made is a fair estimate? At this Zentraedi central base there are *really* that many more ships than we've already seen?" The comlink handset next to him began beeping softly; he ignored it.

Lisa thought carefully. So many things about their captivity in the planetoid-size enemy base, a spacefold jump away—somewhere else in the universe—were astounding and unnerving that she rechecked her recollections again, minutely.

Rick looked over to her, and their eyes met. He didn't nod; that might have tainted her testimony. But she saw that he was ready to back her up.

"Yes, sir, at least that many. And quite possibly millions more. I made a conservative estimate."

Gloval, hand on the phone, looked to Rick. "Truly?"

Rick nodded. "Yes, sir. That many."

Gloval listened to the handset for a moment, then replaced it in its cradle without responding. "Based on all combined reports," he resumed, "our computers place the total enemy resources at somewhere between four and five million ships."

"Sir, forgive me, but that's ridiculous," one team member said. From the security branch, he was the officer who'd been all for destroying the escapees' pod. "Our projections are based on the most accurate data and statistical techniques known.

"No species could accumulate that sort of power! And even if they could, they couldn't possibly remain at the primitive social and psychological level of these aliens!"

"Now, granted, we're seeing a great deal of military display here," the intel man, a portly fellow in his early thirties, added. "But how many of those ships have actually proved themselves to be combat-ready? A comparative handful! No, Captain; I think what we're seeing is just a bluff. And I think your people here have been taken in by it. My analysis is that Commander Hayes and her party were *permitted* to escape so that they could bring us this… hysterical report and demoralize us."

"*Permitted?*" Ben Dixon was halfway out of his chair, the big hands clenched into fists, about to leap across the table and pummel the intel officer. "D' you know how many times we almost got killed? How close we came to not making it? When was the last time *you* saw any action, you—"

"Captain!" the intelligence officer burst out to Gloval by way of complaint.

"That will do!" Gloval thundered, and there was sudden silence as Max Sterling and Rick Hunter pulled Ben back.

Having shown his Jovian side for an instant, Gloval lapsed back into a reasonable voice. "Gentlemen, let's hear the entire report before discussing it." It wasn't a suggestion, and everybody understood that. The debriefing team subsided.

Lisa had thought her words out carefully. "In the course of our captivity, we observed that the aliens have absolutely no concept of human emotions. They've been groomed entirely for war. And their society is organized along purely military lines.

"It appears that they've increased their physical size and strength artificially through genetic manipulation and that they also have the ability to reverse the process."

The others present were studying the few video records she'd managed to make surreptitiously during captivity, but Lisa's memory, with Rick's, Ben's, and Max's, provided vivid and chilling recollections. They'd witnessed Zentraedi trans-vid records of the destruction of an entire planet, seen the gigantic Protoculture sizing chambers the aliens used to manipulate their size and structure, felt the deathly squeeze of Commander-in-Chief Dolza's fist around them.

And something else had happened, something Lisa could only bring herself to refer to obliquely. The enemy leaders had been repulsed, but fascinated, by the human custom of kissing. At their demand, and to ascertain what effect it would have on them, Lisa and Rick had kissed, long and deeply, on an enemy conference table as big as a playing field.

None of the four escapees had mentioned the kiss. Lisa still wasn't sure exactly what it was she'd felt afterward. She suspected that Rick was also a little confused, in spite of his love affair with the girl called Minmei. Max and Ben had kept silent. Rick's friends as well as his wingmates.

Lisa finished, "And I think this last part is very important: While they examined and interrogated us, they constantly made reference to something they called 'Protoculture.'"

The intel officer who had almost been attacked by Ben Dixon tilted his chair back arrogantly. "That's pure fantasy."

His security buddy added, "And were there any little green men?"

Major Aldershot glanced around at him stiffly, the ends of his waxed mustache seeming to bristle. "I will point out that the commander is a much-decorated soldier. This insulting levity is unbecoming from someone who has yet to prove himself under fire." It was the most he'd said all morning.

"What is this 'Protoculture'?" Gloval put things back on track. Lisa hesitated before answering. "It's apparently something that relates to their use of Robotech. I'm not sure, but they think that Protoculture is the highest science in the universe and that somehow *we* possess some of its deepest secrets."

Colonel Maistroff said with a sly grin to the other evaluation team officers, "Too deep for me!" and guffawed at his own joke.

The intel and security officers roared spitefully along with him as Lisa's cheeks colored and Rick felt himself flush in anger.

"Silence!" Gloval barked. It was instantly quiet. "This is a very grave moment. This alien armada has pursued and harried us across the solar system for almost a year and yet has never made an all-out attempt to destroy us; perhaps we *do* possess a power in the SDF-1 that we don't fully understand."

That was a good bet, the way Rick saw it. Even the brilliant Dr. Lang understood only a fraction of the alien ship's secrets, and he was the one who had masterminded its reconstruction from a burned and battered wreck.

Maistroff fixed Lisa with a gimlet stare, red-faced at being rebuked in front of junior officers. "Commander Hayes, is that all?"

Lisa met his glare. "Yes, sir, that's all."

Ben whispered to Rick, "I don't think they believe us." Ben wasn't exactly point man on the genius roster, and the idea that such a thing could happen had never occurred to him until the debriefing was well along.

"It's probably the dishonest expression on your face," Rick whispered back absently.

Maistroff placed both hands flat on the table and turned to Gloval. "Do you really believe this wild tale? It's enemy trickery! Hallucinations!"

Gloval began stoking up his evil-smelling briar, tamping the tobacco slowly with his thumb, pondering, "This information must be correlated and reported to Earth immediately, whether I believe it or not—"

Maistroff interrupted him, saying tightly and too quickly, "I'll send a coded message right away—"

"—Colonel Maistroff." It was Gloval's turn to interrupt. "No, you won't." He lit his briar while they all gaped at him.

Gloval said, "We've got to break through the enemy elements that stand between the SDF-1 and our homeworld."

The evaluation team was aghast, Maistroff shouting, "We can't make it!"

Rick looked around and saw that everybody on his side of the table thought it was a magnificent idea. Gloval rose. "At our current speed, we are only two days from Earth, and they must have this information." He started for the hatch.

Maistroff scowled at Gloval's back. "And then what?"

The captain answered over his shoulder. "And then nothing. We just await orders while we relax, Colonel Maistroff."

He cut through all their protests. "That will be all, gentlemen."

Gloval turned to the escapees. "And as for you four…" They all shot to their feet at rigid attention.

"At least for the time being, you'll be relieved of duty. You've earned a little R and R. You're dismissed."

The four saluted him happily. "Enjoy yourselves," Gloval said gruffly, puffing his pipe. They did a precise right-face and marched out of the conference room in style. But at the last moment, Gloval removed his pipe from his mouth and called, "One moment, Lisa."

The others continued on. Lisa paused at the hatch and turned back to him. "Yes, Captain?"

"Personally, I am inclined to believe that your report is accurate. However…"

"Certainly," she said. "Thank you, Captain. I know you believe in us, and I appreciate that."

"I'm glad you understand."

The door slid open again, and she turned and left. Gloval, looking back to the debriefing team, saw that the fact that he'd chosen to tell Lisa what he did, where he did, wasn't lost on them.

"I'd rather face the aliens again than *that* bunch of brass," Max Sterling told Rick as they walked down the passageway. They were walking side by side, with Ben behind. They could hear Lisa's quick footsteps as she fell in at the rear.

"Gloval wasn't so bad, and that Major Aldershot," Ben said.

"They're only doing their job," Rick maintained. "I'd feel the same way in their place."

"Sure you would," Lisa put it, a little surprised that Rick Hunter had been so transformed from a headstrong discipline problem to a trained military man who understood why and how the service functioned. "And they'd feel exactly the same way we do in ours."

"That's right; why not look on the bright side," Ben said. Rick looked back to Ben but found himself making eye contact with Lisa. He looked ahead again quickly, in turmoil, not sure what he felt.

"After all, all of us were promoted, weren't we?" Ben went on, noticing nothing, very jolly. "And we're going home to a big hero's welcome! So why not relax and enjoy the rest and recreation Captain Gloval gave us?" He clapped Rick on the shoulder, staggering him.

Rick looked back at him sourly. "*You* could probably relax in the dentist's chair, Ben."

"Are you sure this is the right way?" Konda asked nervously, watching the elevator's floor-indicator lights count down toward One.

"We're headed for the area of greatest activity in this battle fortress," Rico said confidently. "Surely the most important concentration of military secrets will be there."

"I still think we should be trying to reach the bridge," Bron grumbled.

The elevator stopped, and the doors parted. A brilliant ray of light broke on them. The three spies stood rooted, making astounded, strangled sounds.

Before them was Macross City in all its glory. The streets were jammed with traffic; the sidewalks were crowded with busy, hurrying people. Streetlights and signs and headlights shone, as did the starlight projected by the Enhanced Video Emulation system. Display windows were filled with clothing and appliances, books, furniture, and an astonishing variety of other goods.

Rico gulped and found his voice. "There's so much to spy on! Where should we start?"

Konda drew a deep breath. "Perhaps we should just mingle with the Micronians and observe their habits."

They gathered their courage and stepped out. Humans were everywhere, alone and in pairs and bigger groups, all going every which way. Some were in military uniforms, but in general everybody was dressed differently. Reassured that he and his companions wouldn't be noticed, Bron pulled up his knee socks and smoothed the pleats in his skirt.

It took all their self-control not to shout upon seeing male and female Micronians mingling freely. No officers or overseers were in immediate evidence, although it was just as plain as could be to the Zentraedi that such hivelike activity would be totally impossible without some strong central control. Still, there were humans who strode along purposefully while others stood idly conversing and still others browsed along, glancing through the gleaming store windows.

And nobody, *nobody*, was in step with anybody else.

They started off, observing carefully. Bron said, "Well, I think there's a good chance we're going to be observing them for a very long time before we figure them out."

They came to a window-shopper, a young man staring longingly at a display in a music store, eyes fixed on a red crystal electric guitar that had three necks and a set of speakers bigger than public comcircuit booths.

"What d'you suppose he's doing?" Bron whispered.

Rico considered, then smiled in sudden realization. "Taking inventory!"

Bron and Konda murmured, "Ahh!" and nodded knowingly.

04

THE TRIO OF MICRONIZED ZENTRAEDI CAME TO AN INTERSECTION.
Before them, crosswalk signals blazed and traffic lights changed
colors. The movement of vehicles and people was orchestrated
somehow, but the logic behind it was difficult to grasp. Everything
was so disorderly, so unmilitary.

And all around them was the barrage of lighted signs and
flashing neon of Macross City's "downtown." They could read
the signs—at least when the logos and print styles weren't *too*
fanciful—but couldn't make any sense of them. And there was so
little uniformity! *Surely,* they thought, *these Micronians must be mad.*

And none of the three dared admit to the others how oddly
appealing he found it all.

Rico threw his hands in the air. "What military purpose could
all those indicators possibly serve?"

Konda glanced around at lovers strolling with arms about each
other's waists, at parents leading their children by the hand, at old
people enjoying coffee at an outdoor café. It was just as horrible as
the intelligence reports had indicated. "You can be sure some kind

of sinister force is at work here."

He started off, the other two falling in with him. "There's something strange at the root of all this, something that makes these creatures so completely unlike us. But I haven't been able to put my finger on it."

"I noticed it, too!" Rico said excitedly. "Like something's out of balance—something weird that affects all of them."

They heard laughter and shouting coming their way, and the hiss of small wheels against the sidewalk. Bron pointed. "Warriors!"

A young male and a young female sped with easy, athletic grace along the sidewalk on small wheeled contrivances barely big enough to stand on.

Their hair streamed behind them, and they whooped and laughed, tilting and swaying to steer. From their merry demeanor, the spies could see that the young Micronians enjoyed their drill and the prospect of combat.

"Gangwaaaay!" called the boy.

"Yahooooo!" sang the girl.

Trying to hide his dismay at their bloodthirsty war cries, Bron dodged, then faked the other way. The skateboarders, unaware that they were part of an interspecies skirmish, effortlessly avoided him. Bron mistook their evasive maneuvers for an attack, reversed field too quickly in the unfamiliar low-heeled pumps, and ended up on his backside.

Konda and Rico hurried to kneel at either side. "Bron, are you wounded?"

"No, Konda, but I think they suspect something."

The spies looked around apprehensively. Passersby were gazing at them curiously, sometimes murmuring to one another but not stopping or making aggressive moves.

"Perhaps that was only a probing attack," Rico speculated. His voice betrayed an unusual lack of self-confidence. If the Micronians were playing such a sadistic cat-and-mouse game, they must be masters of psychological warfare.

More and more people were noticing them now, laughing outright before moving along, passing comments among themselves. Their attention seemed to be focused on Bron and his attire.

"It could be that there's something wrong with our uniforms," Rico hissed.

"I don't see any difference between our uniforms and theirs, do you?" Konda demanded as he and Rico each took one of Bron's arms and hauled the bulky warrior to his feet.

Bron pulled up his white knee socks and rearranged his string of pearls. "I don't see any difference, either. But just the same, I wish I'd chosen something a little less breezy down around my legs." He flapped the hem of his skirt in the air.

People were stopping now, staring at them, laughing and slapping each other on the arm. The female Micronians seemed inclined to look, avert their eyes, then look again, blushing and shaking with laughter.

Rico caught a few words here and there—"women's clothes," for example—and made a brief, horrified comparison study of the garments he saw all around him and their wearers.

"That's it! It's a *female's* uniform you're wearing!"

So, they hadn't been spotted by the Micronians' secret police. Bron had his eyes closed, almost collapsing back into Konda's arms with the mortification of it.

Konda shoved him upright. "Come on! Let's get out of here *now*!"

Nobody appeared inclined to stop them, and most were laughing too hard, anyway. They dashed off in a line, Konda leading, around a corner and down a street, around another corner and across to a park, making sure not to bump into anybody.

"Frat initiation," someone said sagely.

"Another bunch of drunken performance artists!" an old man yelled, waving his cane at them vengefully.

But other than that, they drew a few puzzled glances and nothing more. Konda had spotted an illuminated symbol whose meaning they'd learned on their earliest explorations, the little stick-figure Micronian near the lighted sign, MEN.

The attendant was standing outside, whiling away the time and watching the people go by. He watched as Konda and Rico dashed into the men's room, not terribly interested; he'd seen guys in a bigger hurry in his time. Then he heard the pounding of heavy footsteps and did a classic double take as Bron brought up the rear.

The picture of offended righteousness, the attendant held up his hand. "Just a second, madam! Nothin' doin'! Ladies' room to th' left!"

"Okayokayokay!" Bron veered off and ran into the ladies' room.

There were a few relatively quiet moments, during which the attendant looked up at the evening sky synthesized by the EVE system—tonight they were recreating a northern hemisphere summer sky—and reflected on the sorry state of the human race. Women in the men's room! Boy, if you weren't on your toes every minute...

Distracted, wandering to the corner of the little building to look up and philosophize, he failed to notice the dim cries of "A man!" "Get out!" and "Pervert!" that came from the ladies' room along with shrieks and howls of outrage.

Bron emerged from the ladies' room a moment later in a low crawl, the shoulder of his blouse ripped, hair askew, and face scratched in parallel furrows, several spots on his shins promising remarkable bruises.

Panting, he took a moment to catch his breath, slumped against a partition, preparing to move on quickly before he was attacked again.

"These... Micronians certainly have a warlike culture!"

Elsewhere in the park, in the Star Bowl—the open-air amphitheater where Minmei had been crowned Miss Macross—a different sort of ceremony was about to take place.

None of it fazed Max Sterling very much—few things seemed to—but Ben wasn't happy. "Hey, Max, I thought we were supposed to be resting and relaxing."

Max adjusted his large aviator-style eyeglasses, smiling his serene, mischievous smile. "Aw, what's the matter? Don't you want to be a hero? Didn't you say you were looking forward to it?"

Ben considered Max sourly. Now, here was this little guy—not even twenty yet—who wouldn't even be *flying* in one of the old-time wars. In prewar days, pilot candidates who needed corrective lenses were as sought after as those with untreatable airsickness.

And then there was Max's self-effacing style, his quiet, somehow *Zen* humility, which wouldn't have been noticeable except that he was the hottest pilot who'd ever climbed into a Veritech, and everybody knew it. Not Rick Hunter, not even Roy Fokker himself, was Max's equal, but Max just went along like a good-natured kid who was rather surprised at where fate had brought him, bashful and loyal and given to blushing. Even if he did follow the fad of dying his hair—blue, in this case.

"Aw, pipe down," Ben growled at him, but in fact Ben wasn't that unhappy. Who gets tired of being cheered? Pity them, whoever they are.

Banks of lights came up all around them, until they were standing in a lighted area brighter than brightest day. Triumphant music soared from the sound system as curtains swept aside, and the applause and cheering and whistling began, like waves hitting a shore.

Rick and Lisa, who'd been conversing haltingly and enjoying a kind of mutual attraction they couldn't seem to resist, looked relieved that the extravaganza had started. The four escapees, in full-dress uniform, stood in a line on the stage; from all around the packed Star Bowl the outpouring of joy and admiration came.

There'd been good war news and bad, and virtually everyone in the amphitheater had lost friends and relatives; besides, many in the audience were military. But *these* were four who'd gone into the very heart of the enemy stronghold and come back, and returning—coming *back home*—was something very much in the minds of the people of Macross City these days.

The master of ceremonies, a man in a loud suit with an oily voice, held the microphone right up against his capped teeth.

Rick sighed and made up his mind to put up with the show as best he could. The music was still all trumpets and drums, and the ovation was growing louder and louder. A tech somewhere turned up the gain on the mike so that the emcee could be heard.

"And here are the four young champions who have miraculously escaped the clutches of our enemy: Commander Lisa Hayes, our number one space heroine—"

Lisa was breathing quickly, eyes on the floor, Rick saw; by an iron application of will, she forced herself not to bolt from the stage; there was bravery and there was bravery, and facing a crowd took a great deal of hers.

"And Lieutenant Rick Hunter, whose flying exploits are already legendary!"

Rick *was* used to crowds, was used to taking bows and waving and soaking up the glory, from his days in his father's air circus. He could easily have played to the crowd, knew just what it was they wanted and just how to make them like him even more: the little tricks of eye contact, of perhaps singling out a child to kiss or an elderly sort to shake hands with or a good-looking woman to hug.

But he did none of that. The mission that had landed him in the Zentraedi ship and in the heart of the mad Zentraedi empire hadn't been undertaken to win cheers. Playing to the crowd was a thing that was behind him now, something out of a different life. Rick Hunter acknowledged the ovation with a bow of his head and remained more or less at attention.

He looked aside only once, to see what Lisa was doing. She was watching him.

"And here are their intrepid companions," the emcee went on in a voice so ebullient that the listeners might have thought he'd been along on the mission. "Max Sterling and Ben Dixon! To these four, we express our deepest gratitude."

The crowd did. Earth was so close now, and there was a holiday spirit in the air. A homecoming; a victory; the sight of four humans who'd gone up against the relentless enemy and come back covered with glory—these things all had the Macross City inhabitants at a fever pitch.

The emcee was holding his hands up. The uproar died a little. "There's more to come! To properly demonstrate our high regard for these young heroes, we present that singing sensation, Miss Macross herself, Lynn-Minmei!"

"Miss Macross? Minmei!" Rick had almost forgotten about the Miss Macross contest Minmei had so recently won when he'd gone out on this last mission. It felt like a century before, but it was really only a few days.

She emerged from the wings, most of the spotlights going to her—followed by an escort, a fellow in white tie and tails who carried bouquets of red roses, as if she were royalty. And she was, of a sort; the audience went wild, shouting her name and whistling, clapping.

Rick could see a cluster of people waiting in the wings—Minmei's entourage, apparently—men in expensive suits who wore sunglasses at night and stylish women with calculating looks in their eyes.

But Minmei… She was gorgeous in a frilly dress whose hem was gathered up high on one side to show off long, graceful legs. Her jet-black hair swayed behind her, and her eyes were alight. She seemed used to the spotlight, used to the devotion of the crowd. She was the same young woman who had shared so many adventures and so much privation with Rick and—at the same time—a new *persona*, a darling of the mass media.

She blew kisses to the crowd, and it went even wilder; guards at the edge of the stage, who hadn't been too hard-pressed to keep people away from the military heroes, had all they could do to keep rabid fans from getting out of control. Young girls especially were reaching out in a hopeless effort to touch Minmei, many of them crying.

"I don't know about you," Ben's voice grated. "But I'm embarrassed, being put on a display like this. And just look, will you?" He held up a limp lapel that had been stiffly starched at the beginning of the evening. "My uniform's starting to wilt."

Lisa was watching Rick watching Minmei. Lisa didn't feel very much like a heroine, didn't feel strong or brave. Instead, she found herself resenting the sideshow atmosphere. What did civilians know about military achievements, anyway? Show them some beautiful contest winner and they forgot all about the people who put their lives on the line to safeguard the SDF-1.

"I think I'd rather be trapped back in that Zentraedi headquarters station," she blurted before she herself could quite analyze what she meant by it. Rick gave her a quick, troubled glance, then looked back at Minmei.

It was Max Sterling, calm and unflappable, who answered good-naturedly. "Well, it might never happen again, so let's sit back and enjoy this, huh?"

Minmei held up her hands for silence, and the ovation became relative silence. She took the first of the bouquets of red roses from the man in the tuxedo and gave it to Lisa.

"Congratulations on your safe return!" Minmei's winsome smile and enthusiastic manner were difficult to resist. She had a way of putting something extra into the words, of breaking through resistance, so that whomever she was talking to virtually *had* to respond in kind.

Lisa simply couldn't think badly of Minmei—found herself saying, "Thank you very much," and meaning it, and even returning the bright smile. Minmei surprised her by shaking her hand warmly, then went on to Rick, taking another bouquet.

Lisa closed the hand into a tight fist. In those seconds Minmei had made her feel like a *friend*, as if she was all-important to Minmei. Lisa had to admit that that would be a very hard thing for anybody to resist—especially a man.

05

As veteran Zentraedi warriors, you will, of course, even in your micronized state, find it necessary to hide your natural superiority. Be sure to conceal your immunity to the degenerate behavioral impulses of the humans.

> Breetai, from his instructions to the spies
> Rico, Bron, and Konda

MINMEI HAD GONE ON TO RICK, TAKING ANOTHER BOUQUET AND presenting it to him. "And congratulations on *your* safe return, you handsome devil!"

She handed him the flowers with a wink and a laugh. He stood for a second looking as though he'd just touched a live wire. Then he blurted out, "Well! Um, thank you!"

Minmei put one slender hand to his right cheek and held him steady while she kissed his left. Fire and ice coursed through him; he remembered the moment, months before, when, trapped together in a distant compartment of the SDF-1, they'd shared a deeper, more lasting kiss.

The crowd had suddenly gone ugly. Minmei was everybody's favorite, and there was a strange current of jealousy at seeing her single out a nobody lieutenant, hero that he might be, for special treatment. She was the dream girl, the idol, the fantasy figure; an undertone of hostility ran through the crowd.

She turned to the audience without losing her merry persona. "Now, now!" she chided, shaking a finger at them in mock chastisement. Amazingly, the sounds of resentment died away as quickly as that, and people were applauding her again. To make her point, Minmei kissed Max's cheek, and Ben's, as she gave them their roses. "Congratulations… congratulations…"

The crowd loved it; the crowd loved *her*.

Down among the people near the stage were the three spies. At first they'd merely drifted along with the people assembling in the amphitheater, to make sure they'd eluded any Micronian pursuit. Then it had become apparent that a major gathering was taking place, and they'd set out to infiltrate it. That had proved amazingly easy.

Bron had gotten rid of his pleated skirt and knee socks and white silk blouse and even the tasteful string of pearls. He was wearing a blue turtleneck and dark slacks, although it had taken a little doing to get new clothes.

On a quiet side street, they had stumbled across a metal bin stenciled CONTRIBUTIONS FOR THE NEEDY. With some effort, the portly warrior had hauled himself into it and found Micronian male garments that fit.

The three spies concluded that keeping contributions for the needy in the difficult-to-enter metal housing served as a kind of minimum qualification test in the savage Micronian culture; any needy individual who wasn't fairly spry would be out of luck. It was a stern way to run things, the trio agreed, but no doubt very efficient.

Now, though, they looked around themselves worriedly. These Micronians were obsessed with the creature Minmei. At first the spies had thought that they'd stumbled onto a simple propaganda rally and that they'd get insights on the humans' attitudes toward the Zentraedi, but the Zentraedi had hardly been mentioned.

Instead, there was a lot of strange business with passing plants *around*—*flowers*, to be precise—and a very confusing level of noise and emotion, virtually all of the outpouring directed at Minmei.

Konda in particular felt that they were close to uncovering some important military secret. There was no question but that the enemy was highly motivated; perhaps some new sort of mind control technique would be revealed.

They recognized Minmei from transmissions of her that they'd intercepted on their original signal-intelligence mission, of course. She'd abandoned the bizarre armor the Micronians called a bathing suit, and wore a slightly less revealing but even flimsier cover. The trio had as yet seen no demonstration of Protoculture powers from the humans' garments, but they were still very edgy.

The crowd was still carrying on over Minmei. "Hey, what's going on? A riot?" Bron yelled over the uproar.

They were packed in together tightly by the massed crowd, but Konda got his hands onto Bron's shoulders. "Don't panic! I don't *think* it's a riot; it seems to be something else…"

Rico was nearly at the end of his rope, sweating and shuddering a bit; a good old fashioned anti-enemy hate rally was something anybody could understand, but this was utter chaos! He covered his ears with his hands, squeezing his eyes shut. "Oh, my head!"

He began to slump in a near faint. His companions managed to catch him somehow in the press of the crowd. Just then, Minmei came to the edge of the stage in a convergence of spotlights and the gathered residents of Macross began applauding and cheering all over again.

"Now what's the matter?" Bron asked, referring to Rico as well as the Minmei situation.

Chairs had appeared from somewhere, and Rick, Lisa, Max, and Ben were sitting uncomfortably. Minmei, angelic in the spotlights, indicated them with a sweeping gesture. "To celebrate their return, my first song this evening is dedicated to these four heroes and all the others who guard and defend us!"

She threw kisses to the crowd as the band came up, uptempo. Streamers and confetti rained down, and light effects blazed. As she threw her arms wide, she seemed to be a creature of pure light, of spirit, of magic. The streamers and confetti rained down on the crowd, too, and many joined in, joyously, knowing the words, arms around each others' shoulders.

"Stage lights flashing,
The feeling's smashing,
My heart and soul belong to you
And I'm here now, singing,
All bells are ringing,
My dream has finally come true!"

In a time when the most adored performers were unapproachable and inaccessible, she was somehow the exact opposite of the media sirens who reigned elsewhere. She was, after all, one of the citizenry, another Macross Island refugee like virtually everybody else aboard. Her success and stardom could as easily have been theirs—was theirs in a way.

She was one of them, and she gave herself to them totally, letting them share the moment. Her silver-bright voice soared, taking the high notes with complete confidence. Her slim, straight figure reflected the light back into their eyes, the joy back into their hearts.

They were a battered, war-weary community, and in a way nobody quite understood, she made them feel hope and experience a soaring elation. It had been said—and not discounted by Minmei herself—that she was a *reflection* of them, the military and civilian occupants of SDF-1.

Certainly there were precedents in history. Times of greatest danger and tribulation inevitably bring forth symbols.

In *human* societies...

The three spies couldn't quite understand it but couldn't resist it either. It had to be admitted, the gathering of humans might as easily be an assembly of Zentraedi in some ways—except that this spirit of undisguised joy was utterly weird. People swayed and laughed and forgot their problems, thinking about home, and there wasn't a single pro-war propaganda message to be seen anywhere.

Somebody threw an arm around Rico's shoulder from one side, somebody else hanging one around Bron's from the other, and they were caught up in the swaying of the throng. It so happened that the groups on either side were keeping separate time, one going one way while the other went counter.

"This must be some kind of tribal ceremony," Konda speculated, but he found himself enjoying it.

Still, somehow, as easily as if they'd been doing it all their lives, the Zentraedi sorted out the conflicts and in a moment were swaying along with the thousands upon thousands of others. It began to dawn on them what they were seeing.

As had happened before, a symbol had arisen, and Minmei was it, uniquely suited to the role. One tiny Micronian female, hoping to get home, possessed of a kind of deathless optimism; and all that was set off by remarkable singing skills and a personality that won over whomever she encountered. And none of it was calculated; people sensed that. She was wonderful and straightforward, and Macross City threw itself at her feet.

She's incredibly dangerous to the Zentraedi cause, Rico mused. *Why do I like her so much?*

"I feel incredibly primitive," Bron reported dubiously.

"But it has a pleasing effect on the senses," Rico was honest enough to admit.

"It's—*mass hypnosis!*" Bron burst out, even though he'd been trained to recognize mass hypnosis and knew this wasn't it.

"Yeah, but I kinda like it," Konda confessed. They swayed along with the music and laughed at the people who swayed and laughed with them...

"Stage fright, go 'way—
This is my big day,
This is my time to be a star!
And the thrill that I feel
Is really unreal:
I can't believe I've come this far..."

In the midst of the performance, people had forgotten about the four forlorn figures sitting on their chairs, very much in the background now but unable to make an escape. Only Max Sterling seemed unbothered and happy.

Rick shifted the bouquet on his lap despondently. He saw it all now: Minmei had been elevated to a different level of existence. What they had gone through together and felt for each other didn't matter anymore. He had lost her.

Lisa leaned toward him to ask, "What's the matter, Rick?"

He shook himself, drawing a deep breath. "Nothing. The light bothers my eyes, is all."

Lisa saw it wasn't true. She hadn't gotten to be a commander and the SDF-1's First Officer by being unobservant or slow to understand what was going on. But that didn't help her figure out what she was feeling as she looked at Rick and the now-unreachable Minmei: some complicated mixture of relief and foreboding.

Minmei's hands were high, and she had moved the crowd into a veritable transport of joy. White light blazed all around her, and it seemed that every hope and aspiration was embodied in her.

"I can't believe I've come this far,
This is my time to be a star!"

The hatch to the battle fortress's bridge slid aside; all heads turned. Gasps and yells sounded from all sides.

Lisa felt better already, there in the place that was most important to her. "Hi," she said shyly, not recognizing many of the faces and wishing only to get back to her station, get back to her work. She would have died before admitting that she wanted to drive all other thoughts out of her mind—to forget.

Claudia placed one hand to her chest in a "mercy me" sort of pose. "The prodigal returns!" The dark face creased in lines of real welcome, and Lisa began to feel better.

Gloval was absent from the bridge. The relief-watch tech at Lisa's usual station stepped away from it, glad to see Lisa but a little intimidated before the omnipotent superwoman. "Nice to see you again," the enlisted rating squeaked.

Lisa, nervous as a cat, managed to meet her eye for a moment. "Thank you very much," Lisa got out, essaying a smile and then hiding behind her thick curtain of brown hair again. "It's nice to be back."

She ran her fingertips across the console's controls, lost in thought. There had been so many times when she'd never expected to stand there again.

The women on the bridge were paying her a kind of attention that didn't really conform to any conventional military courtesy—happy for her and taking liberties with standard procedure.

"Congratulations on your promotion!"

"And you're a real hero!"

"We're all so proud of you, Lisa!" The tech who'd been watching over Lisa's station had her hands clasped, smiling beatifically.

These were all women who had served their time under fire, who had come to know what it was Lisa Hayes did so well and how much of a difference her actions had made in the fate of SDF-1. Their few words meant so much more to her than the spotlights and crowds—she felt her tension ease; she was home again.

Now that she was back in familiar surroundings, everything that had happened came back to her. A small part of her was preoccupied, shifting through her emotions, but Lisa just savored the contentment of being back where she belonged.

The things that had brought conflict to her—the kiss in the enemy stronghold, the sight of Rick and Minmei—were, perhaps, aberrations. Maybe it was just her destiny to be what those in her family had always been—members of a military dynasty, her destiny tied to that of the SDF-1.

Certainly, all things seemed clear there on the battle fortress's bridge. Doubts, misgivings—they fell away like dead flower petals.

Then Claudia was leaning an elbow on the console, too good a friend not to understand exactly how Lisa felt, too good a friend not to kid her out of it. "Well, how does it feel to be a heroine?" she purred.

Lisa's pale cheeks colored. "Oh, you!"

"Come on! Tell Aunt Claudia!" The dark eyes narrowed mischievously. "Or did this promotion give you a sudden sense of modesty?"

Lisa lowered her gaze to the deck, avoiding eye contact as she often did when she wasn't on duty. But she grinned at Claudia's jibe, the first time she'd grinned in a while. She gave her friend a bemused smile.

"That's it! My secret's compromised!" Lisa crossed her arms on her chest and made a severe face, imitating Captain Gloval at his sternest. She rolled her r's, so there'd be no mistake. "So let's have a little *respect* here!"

Somebody Lisa didn't recognize returned from a coffee run, and they all had some. "It's good to be here," Lisa said meditatively, letting the cup warm her palms. Then she made a puckish expression. "And lemme tell ya, the Zentraedi make lousy coffee."

Claudia realized something and set her cup down. "Hold on! Lisa, I thought you were supposed to be on special furlough."

Lisa lowered her cup, not wanting to think too hard about the ceremonies and the tangled feelings that had driven her back to the bridge. She bit her lower lip for a moment and said, "I wanted to come home."

Claudia was about to say something to that; Lisa was both shielding something and waiting for someone to draw her out of it. It seemed to Claudia Grant a good time to order the enlisted crew off the bridge for chow or whatever and get down to business.

But just then the hatch slid back again, and the Terrible Trio stood there. Sammie, Kim, and Vanessa spied Lisa and charged in, the dignity of rank forgotten. Lisa forgot it, too, swapping hugs with them and loving the calm and strength and serenity of the SDF-1's armored bridge.

Claudia filed the subject of Lisa's furlough and her strange new introspection away for discussion in the near future. She'd been protective of Lisa ever since they'd met and tried not to let that spill over into nosiness, but—

This girl needs a talking to, Claudia decided. *And I'm not even sure about what!*

06

As an insect seen through an enlarging imager may appear as a monster, so these Micronians, magnified by a few minor successes and by an unforgivable timidity among certain Zentraedi leaders, are permitted to resist us. This has led to a stalemate; what Zentraedi worthy of the name would permit this?

Khyron the Backstabber

THE JEEP ROARED DOWN THE EMPTY SDF-1 PASSAGEWAY, rounding corners on two wheels, tires shrieking. Ben Dixon enjoyed this kind of outing; he usually took a slightly longer route to the fighter bays than he had to because he so missed the open road.

Ben's dragster had been parked in an alley on Macross Island on the day of the fatal spacefold maneuver. So now it was either a floating relic in space back near Pluto's orbit or had been completely dismantled by the salvage and reclamation people. Either way, he didn't like to think about it.

But barreling around the roomier parts of the dimensional fortress helped ease his loss. The civilians had crowded-but-very-livable Macross City, but once in a while *some* people needed to hit the road, floor the accelerator, and let off a little steam. It was an open secret that some of the less traveled regions of the SDF-1 had become virtual racetracks.

Ben took a corner even more sharply than usual and waited for Rick, who was sitting in the seat next to him, to make a perfunctory objection. But, lost in thought, the Vermilion Team leader didn't say anything. Sprawled in the back, Max Sterling looked supremely unworried. Ben was a little bit offended by that; Max was a good friend, but Ben expected passengers to be a little *intimidated* when he drove. Yet nothing seemed to ruffle Max or dim the boyish cheerfulness for which he'd become famous.

In fact, a few guys had decided that Max's good-naturedness meant that he was a wimp despite his ferocious flying skills. There'd been a few fights, and Max had insisted that Rick keep Ben from interfering on his friend's behalf.

Help wasn't necessary, anyway; Max's astonishing reflexes and hand-eye coordination more than sufficed. Max always helped his opponents to their feet afterward, still with that boyish smile; he even performed first aid in one extreme case. After a while, interest in bothering Max Sterling waned.

Max gave his blue hair a toss and resettled his glasses, turning at the sound of another jeep engine. He leaned forward to tap Rick and point; at the wheel, Roy Fokker was catching up to them accompanied by three of his Skull Team fliers.

"Hey, Rick!"

"Hi, Roy."

"Uh oh." Roy came up *very* close alongside, and Ben had to cut the wheel to avoid an accident.

"Where d' you three think you're going?" Roy demanded.

They were on one of the longest straightaways in the ship, but they were moving fast. Ben knew he was being tested; he sweated a bit but kept on a steady course. But they were approaching the far bulkhead at an alarmingly rapid speed, and there was room for only one jeep in its hatchway.

The Skulls in Roy's jeep didn't seemed very thrilled about the encounter either, but they knew better than to say anything to their hotheaded leader.

"What'd you say?" Rick asked mildly.

Roy hollered, "I said, where d' you think you're going?"

Max leaned forward. "The PA system said for all military personnel to report for duty!" he said. Ben Dixon began sweating bullets as the far bulkhead got closer and close.

"You had orders to stay behind, you nitwit! That announcement doesn't apply to you guys!" Roy was shaking his fists in the air; the guy riding shotgun grabbed the wheel while one of the others in the back seat began crossing himself and the other spun a tiny prayer wheel. Roy ignored them, keeping the accelerator floored.

"But that wasn't an order... specifically," Rick pointed out.

Roy had his hands back on the wheel. "Well, I'm *making* it an order! Specifically! Return to quarters, and make it fast!"

Ben eased back, breathing a sigh of relief. Roy's jeep took the lead as Rick yelled, "Gonna take on the enemy alone, huh?"

Roy turned and rose, his front seat passenger diving for the wheel again. Roy shook his fists at the heroic escapees. "Maybe you'd rather report to the brig for insubordination?"

Ben began braking. He and his friends chanted in perfect unison, "Not really, sir! No thank you, sir!" a bootcamp response used here to mock Roy by implying that he was as dumb as a drill sergeant.

Roy cracked an unwilling smile, then turned to take the wheel back from his ashen-faced front seat passenger. "I'm glad you understand," he called back, voice growing fainter. "Nobody likes a smart aleck!"

Ben stopped just short of the bulkhead, and Roy's jeep shot through the hatch, speeding toward the fighter bays.

"There goes a wonderful guy," Ben said, letting out his breath.

The Zentraedi had a saying that in Earthly terms would translate to: "Even wolves may be prey to the tiger."

So the huge armada kept its distance from SDF-1, pacing it on its homing journey. Ironclad orders stated clearly that Zor's fortress was to be captured with all its Protoculture secrets intact. From the perspective of the fleet's commanders, the more important point at the moment was that the SDF-1's main gun had proved itself operational, even though the Micronians had used it very sparingly.

The Zentraedi couldn't figure out why—one of the mysteries that prompted the placement of Bron, Rico, and Konda aboard SDF-1. What the Zentraedi *didn't* know was how little the human race understood about the giant ship and how vulnerable the SDF-1 really was.

All the Zentraedi knew for certain was that the ship contained enough power to destroy whole star systems and rip the very fabric of space and time. So the armada paced the battle fortress, watching and waiting.

A report was being delivered by a technician in a fleet command vessel. "Commander Azonia, the super dimensional fortress has started to increase its velocity."

Azonia looked up sharply at her intelligence analyst. Azonia sat in the control seat amid a vast array of machinery and consoles and holographic data displays that stretched away in every direction.

"What are your orders?" the analyst asked. Azonia glanced at the various maps, readouts, and tactical projections.

"Dolza has given me no authority to destroy it," the armada's commander replied, running a hand through her close-cropped blue-black hair. "So we'll just follow it and see what happens." Azonia had replaced the legendary Breetai as commander when he'd made one mistake too many, and she had no intention of suffering similar humiliation.

The analyst bowed obediently, and withdrew from the command center. Azonia pulled her campaign cloak tighter around her and adjusted the high collar; she was having doubts she would never betray to a subordinate.

The Micronians' homeworld was close; what would happen there? The original Zentraedi invasion force had smashed all terran opposition until it encountered those thrice-damned Robotech mecha—the Veritechs. And after all these months, who knew what *new* defenses the perversely ingenious humans might have developed?

Allowing the super dimensional fortress to reach its destination was a risky game at best; a disastrous one, perhaps. Yet Azonia couldn't see any new orders coming from her superiors, nor could she come up with an alternative course of action to offer them that didn't risk the loss of the all-important secrets of Protoculture.

Azonia forced down those thoughts. There was still time to win, and victory in *this* campaign would bring the most precious prize in all the universe.

...

The SDF-1 was in its cruiser mode, which meant that the great main gun couldn't be fired. This was unavoidable, however, since the giant weapon would function only in Attack mode—a formation that rendered Macross City virtually uninhabitable.

In its present configuration it looked like a conventional spacecraft or even a naval vessel. The Thor-class supercarriers *Daedalus* and *Prometheus* were swung back flush against it, and the two great booms of the main gun were mated together to form a prow. The bridge and its attendant structures rose above the main deck but still sat rather low.

As its gargantuan thrusters flared blue fire, the ultimate warcraft approached the orbit of pockmarked Luna.

Claudia studied Earth's moon in her displays. "We are proceeding at maximum speed, Captain," she reported. "Beginning Earth-approach maneuver... *now!*"

Gloval appeared to be asleep: The polished visor of his cap was pulled low down on the bridge of his nose, and his arms were folded across his chest. But he said quite clearly, "Vanessa, how has the enemy fleet reacted?"

Vanessa pushed her glasses up, made a final sweep of her instruments to be sure, and then turned to Gloval. "They're still all around us, Captain, but they're maintaining distance. It's strange—they're still matching our speed exactly."

Gloval rubbed his cheek and realized he needed a shave. He didn't even want to *think* about how tired he was. "It would appear they still don't want to risk firing on the SDF-1. This would seem to bear out your theory, Lisa."

Lisa broke her intense concentration on her instruments to say, "I certainly hope so, sir." If she was wrong, the battle fortress wouldn't last another hour.

"We are approaching the orbit of Luna, Captain," Vanessa said tensely.

"Keep monitoring the enemy closely."

"Yes, sir."

Lisa chimed in, "Fighter ops reports Vermilion and Ghost teams ready to takeoff, Captain." She did her best to sound businesslike and not think about one of those Vermilion Team Veritechs. Especially its pilot…

Gloval nodded and hoped he wouldn't be forced to use them. They were some of his very best pilots, but they'd been chewed up badly in the latest installment of the running battle the SDF-1 had been fighting for months in the remote, dark places of the solar system.

Earth was so close. Gloval would have given his own life without an instant's hesitation if it would have meant repatriating all the refugees who'd survived the brutal voyage. But that wasn't how things worked.

In a Zentraedi command center, a finger the size of a log stabbed at a tactical display screen representation of the SDF-1 and the armada around it.

Khyron could barely keep his voice from breaking in rage. "The Micronian ship is *here*, and the ships under my command are *here*, behind it. Now, at maximum speed, their vessel stands a good chance of penetrating the net around it and escaping!"

He stared angrily at his second in command, Grel, and his trusted subordinate, Gerao. "Are we to sit here with our arms folded while these creatures get away and not raise a finger to stop it?"

"But Azonia has forbidden us to act," Grel pointed out. "What can we do?"

Khyron slammed his palms down on the display console. "We will crush them!"

Khyron, handsome and fiendish commander of the Zentraedi Seventh Fleet and its mecha strike arm, the Botoru Battalion, had a reputation that gave even the giant warriors pause. He had *earned* the nickname "Backstabber": He had a reputation for savage ferocity, a total lack of feeling for his own men, and an unquenchable thirst for bloodshed and triumph.

Grel knew better than to contradict his superior when the killing rage was upon him. There was a persistent rumor that Khyron's secret vice was the essence of the Flower of Life, a forbidden addiction; if that were so, he used it in some form that made it a flower of death. In this mood, he was capable of anything.

"Order the lead ships in the squadron to increase speed and attack!" he roared, holding his hand high in a salute and gesture of command. "For the glory of the Zentraedi... and of *Khyron*!"

Vanessa stared intently at her screens, calling out, "A squadron of enemy battle cruisers has broken away from the rest of the fleet and is moving in on us, Captain. Approximately ten of them."

Gloval stared out the forward viewport morosely. "Scramble fighters."

"Yes, sir." Lisa drew a deep breath, opening the PA mike. "Vermilion and Ghost Teams, scramble, *scramble*!"

Down in the hangar decks of the supercarrier *Daedalus*, there was the controlled chaos of a "hot" scramble, one that everybody knew was no drill. The huge elevators began raising the Veritechs to the flight deck port and starboard, two to a lift.

Roy Fokker pulled on his flight helmet and checked his controls as his ship was moved out for lift by a tow driver. Roy was Skull Leader, but experienced pilots were in such terribly short supply and Rick and the others were on enforced R&R, so he had to help fill the ranks of the depleted Vermilions, especially at a critical time like this.

The Veritechs' stabilizers and wings began sliding into flight position. Cat crews rushed to hook up and launch the fighters; The Veritechs went into a vigilant holding pattern, ready to fend off any attack against the VTs that were still vulnerable, awaiting launch.

The cats slung the fighters out into space; the blue Robotech drives flared, and the Vermilions and Ghosts formed up to do battle yet again.

Gloval had hoped to avoid it, but he gave the order nevertheless. "Engage SDF-1 transformation and activate pin-point defensive barrier. We are breaking through the alien fleet!"

"Macross City evacuation is nearly complete, Captain," Sammie told him.

The voices of the others kept up a constant, quiet flow of orders and report. "All sectors begin transformation." "All section chiefs please report to the bridge." "Damage crews stand by." "Emergency medical and rescue personnel ready, Captain."

Banks of screens showed interior and exterior scenes, the frantic haste to brace for attack and reconfiguration.

Once again the awesome, incredible, and perilous Robotech transformation of SDF-1 was about to take place.

It had been hard to get used to the bustle and activity of Macross City, but this sudden abandonment of it was even stranger.

The three Zentraedi spies still had no idea what was happening. The PA announcements were bewildering, impossible to understand. The trio was hesitant to show ignorance at first, but by the time they'd worked up the nerve to start asking questions, everybody was scurrying in a different direction and answers were impossible to get.

Now they found themselves standing at the center of a deserted intersection as traffic lights and crosswalk signals blinked through their accustomed sequences. The EVE system was shut down, the artificial sky gone, leaving only cold, distant metal high overhead. "Everyone's vanished," Rico said slowly, pivoting through a 360-degree turn. It felt very spooky to be standing in the middle of an empty city.

"What d' you think that announcement was?" Konda asked. "What could it be—this 'transformation' they're talking about?" Bron was about to add something when the street began to quake beneath them, tossing them around like water droplets on a griddle. As deep grinding noises began, they were thrown to the surface, so they tried to cling to the pavement. They could feel the vibrations through the ground.

Then the street parted beneath them and an enormous sawtooth opening widened rapidly. Despite his hysterical scrambling, Rico disappeared into it.

07

What they never asked themselves was whether Khyron would have behaved as he did if it hadn't been for the accursed Micronians! I hated Micronians, too; we all did. It was just that Khyron was better at it.

Grel, aide to Khyron

REACTING FASTER THAN BRON, KONDA JUST MANAGED TO GRAB Rico's sleeve and keep him from falling beyond reach. Then Bron was there to help pull his companion back out of the abyss.

It was a long drop, into a type of machinery they hadn't seen in the battle fortress before. Rico lay puffing and gasping, white-faced. "What kind of insane place is this?"

Elsewhere, the titanic booms that were the battle fortress's bow were rotated to either side by monster camlike devices. Whole sections of hull moved and slid, opening the ship's interior to the vacuum of space as precious atmosphere escaped. Giant armor curtains slid into place to seal the gaps, but not before there was grievous loss of the very breath of life. The SDF-1's life support systems would eventually replace it, but the inhabitants of Macross would be living under the same atmospheric conditions as Andean Indians for a while—if they survived.

Enormous pylons the dimensions of a city block rose from the floor and descended from the ceiling, crushing the buildings in their way. The grinding of servomotors shook every bolt and rivet in the ship.

Scraps of buildings, torn loose by the outpouring of air, were whirled around like leaves in a cyclone. Macross City was being leveled.

The three spies went dashing down the middle of a broad, empty street, dodging a falling sign here, a broken cornice there. Utility poles toppled, whipping live power lines around like snapping, spitting snakes. Konda puffed, "I think it would be advisable for us to take cover as soon as—"

He never got to finish. Just then, the ship's internal gravity fields shifted from the effect of the massive power drains of the transformation.

The three went floating into the air among drifting automobiles, scraps of roofing material, uprooted trees, and spinning trash barrels.

All through the great fortress, modules shifted, and billboard-size hatches closed here, opened there.

The full-ship transformation had the two Thor-class flattops, *Daedalus* and *Prometheus*, swinging out from the SDF-1's sides by the elbowlike housings that joined them to the ship. The midships structure that housed the bridge and so many other critical areas rotated, coming end for end into the center like a spinning torso.

Inside, cyclopean power columns met and latched as cables snaked out to connect with them and complete the new configuration.

Gloval fought to stifle his impatience; the ship was nearly helpless while undergoing transformation, but there was absolutely no way of hurrying it. And there was no alternative: The SDF-1's main gun *couldn't* be fired in any other configuration because the ship spacefold apparatus had simply vanished after that first disastrous jump from Earth to Pluto. The transformation was a kind of glorified hot-wiring, bringing together components that would otherwise be out of each other's reach.

"Starboard wing section transformation seventy-five percent complete," Vanessa said.

"Port wing section transformation complete," Kim added. "Now connecting to defensive power system."

"Enemy vessels approaching in attack formation," Lisa said, her face lit by her screens. "Estimated intercept in fifty-three seconds. Ghost and Vermilion teams on station to engage."

The battle fortress had become a tremendous armored ultratech warrior standing, straddle-legged, in space, awaiting its enemies. They swooped at it eagerly.

"The enemy's within range of our main gun, sir," Kim said.

From Vanessa: "Fighter ops reports all Veritechs clear of the line of fire."

"Transformation complete, Captain," Sammie told Gloval.

"Fire!" Gloval growled.

The safety shield had been retracted from the main gun's trigger. Lisa pressed the red button hard.

Tongues of starflame began shooting back and forth between the booms that constituted the gargantuan main gun, whirling and crackling like living serpents of energy.

The blizzard of energy grew thicker, more intense. Then it leapt away, straight out from the booms, merging and growing brighter until suddenly there was a virtual river of orange-white annihilation, as broad and high as the ship itself.

The hell-beam tore through space. The first ten heavyweight warships from Khyron's contingent flared briefly, like matches in the middle of a Veritech's afterblast. In a split second their shields failed, their armor vaporized, and they were gone.

Khyron's handsome face was distorted like a maniac's. "We must press the attack! Move the next wave in!" The Zentraedi warrior's code could forgive audacity—even direct disobedience—from an officer who *won*. But defeat might very well be unforgivable and earn him the death penalty.

More heavy ships-of-the-line moved up, firing plasma cannon and annihilation discs. The SDF-1 shook and resounded from the first hits. There were a few gasps on the bridge, but Gloval and the bridge crew concentrated on their jobs.

The enemy dreadnoughts' blue-fire cannon volleys rained on the SDF-1 as Khyron's second attack wave bored in.

The three green-white discs of the dimensional fortress's pinpoint barrier system, each bigger than a baseball infield, slid along the ship's surface like spotlight circles. The disaster of the spacefold equipment's disappearance had left the vessel unable to protect itself completely; the pin-point system was the stopgap defense developed by the resident Robotech genius, Dr. Lang.

Now, the female enlisted-rating techs who operated the pin-points sweated and flickered their eyes from ship's schematics to threat-display screens to readouts from the prioritization computers. In a frantic effort to block enemy beams they spun and twirled the spherical controls that moved the pin-point barrier shield loci across the ship's hull.

The circles of light slid and flashed across the battle fortress's superalloy skin. Enemy beams that hit them simply dissipated, changing the locicircles into a series of concentric, rippling rings for a split second. Then the circles came back to full strength, racing off to intercept another shot.

No one had ever done that kind of work before, and the three young women were good at what they did—experts by necessity. But sometimes, unavoidably, they missed…

The SDF-1 shuddered at another impact. "Starboard engine has been hit," Claudia informed Gloval without looking up from her console.

Gloval said nothing but worried much. Even now, a decade and more after the SDF-1's original appearance and crash landing on Earth, nobody understood very much about its enigmatic, sealed power plants—not even the brilliant Lang. What would happen if an engine were broached? Gloval didn't spare time to worry about it.

The bad news was coming fast. "Industrial section hit." "Sector twenty-seven completely nonfunctioning."

Claudia looked to Gloval. "The pin-point barrier is losing power."

Gloval didn't permit himself to show his dismay. *Now what?* he thought. *We've fought so hard, endured so much, come close.* "Keep firing the main battery!" he said, aloud.

Lisa knew how to read him so well after all these years. *Look at him,* she thought. *It's hopeless! I know it!*

"Lisa, didn't you hear the order?" Claudia was yelling, a little desperately.

"Yes," Lisa said resolutely. She pressed the trigger again. Another unimaginable flood of utter destruction leapt out to devour the second Zentraedi wave.

In her command center, Azonia watched a dozen proud Zentraedi warships vanish from the tactical display screens.

"That imbecile Khyron! What does he think he's doing? He has no authority whatsoever for this attack!"

Yaita, her aide, said laconically, "No, Commander." Then, "Therefore, what are your orders?"

In an event of this magnitude there was opportunity for the right junior officer to get herself noticed, perhaps even mentioned in dispatches to Dolza's headquarters. Interfering with the unstable battle lord risked a confrontation, perhaps even combat, but by nature Yaita was a risk taker.

Azonia, even more so. "I shall have to force Khyron to break off his attack myself."

Yaita said, "You mean to divert part of the fleet blockade? But the enemy vessel might find a way to break through!"

"It can't be avoided," Azonia said coldly. "That ship must not be destroyed. Its Protoculture secrets are the key to the Zentraedi's ultimate victory."

Vanessa relayed the information, "The aliens are bringing up reinforcements, Captain; nearly two hundred heavy warships." She looked up from her console. "Analysis indicates that's too many for us to handle."

"The barrier's weakening rapidly," Sammie said.

"We're losing power," Kim added.

Vanessa watched her tactical screens, ready to give the grim details as the enemy closed in for the kill. But she suddenly had trouble believing what she was seeing. "What's going on? The reinforcements are breaking formation—spreading out and closing in on the other enemy ships!"

. . .

Khyron watched his trans-vid displays furiously as Azonia's fleet swept in to close with his own reduced forces. "What is that woman up to now?"

The Micronian vessel was nearly his; he could feel it. *I will not be thwarted again!*

A projecbeam created an image of Azonia in midair over his head. "Khyron, *you fool!* Dolza has given you no authority whatsoever to destroy the Earth ship!"

Khyron felt that insane wrath welling up in him once again, a fury so boundless that his vision began to blur. He growled like an animal through locked teeth.

Azonia was saying, "As commander of this force, I am ordering you to cease this attack at once and withdraw to your assigned position—or you will find *yourself* facing Zentraedi guns!"

Studying the tactical readouts, Grel said, "Captain, her entire arsenal is already being aimed at us."

Khyron crashed his fist on the map console. "That blasted meddling idiot of a woman!"

He may have been called Khyron the Backstabber by some, but he'd never been called Khyron the Suicide or Khyron the Fool. Azonia had the rest of the armada to back her in this confrontation.

Khyron had no choice. With Azonia's ships blocking their way, his vessels reduced speed, and the SDF-1 began to put distance between itself and its enemies.

"They're escaping!" Khyron's voice was a harsh croak. "And so Azonia robs me of my triumph. But I swear: I shall not forget this!"

Grel had heard that tone in his commander's voice before. He smiled humorlessly.

If Azonia was wise, she would begin guarding her back at all times.

The immense Robotech knight that was the SDF-1 descended to Earth's atmosphere, toward the swirling white clouds and the blue ocean.

"I don't understand it," Claudia said. "They screened us from their own attack."

"I know, but we'll worry about that after we get back to Earth, Claudia," Gloval answered.

"Reentry in ten seconds," she told him.

"Steady as she goes, Lisa," Gloval ordered calmly. All the equations and theories about how the reconfigured SDF-1 would take its first grounding in Earth-normal gravity were just that: theories. Any one of an almost infinite number of things might go wrong, but there was no alternative. Soon the ship's crew and inhabitants would find out the truth.

"Atmospheric contact," Claudia reported.

The giant warrior ship descended on long pillars of blue-white fire that gushed from its thruster legs and from the thrusters built into the bows of *Daedalus* and *Prometheus*. "Order all hands to secure for landing," Gloval directed.

Elsewhere, the strain was beginning to tell. Power surges and outages, overloads and explosions, were lighting up warning indicators all over the bridge.

"Starboard engines have suffered major damage from the reentry, sir," Claudia said. "And gravity control's becoming erratic."

"The explosions have caused some hull breaches, Captain, and we're losing power quickly," Lisa put in.

"This is going to be some splashdown," Gloval muttered to himself. At least the loss of atmosphere didn't matter anymore; in moments they'd either have all the sweet atmosphere of Earth to breathe or they wouldn't need air ever again.

Claudia counted off the last few yards of descent. Vast clouds of steam rose from the ocean as the waters boiled from the heat of the drive thrusters. Then the ship hit the water.

At first, the ocean parted around it, bubbling and vaporizing. Then it came rushing back in again, overwhelming even that tremendous heat and blast. SDF-1 sank, sank, the waves crashing against its armor, then racing away from it, until at last it disappeared from sight beneath the churning water.

Moments passed, and the sea began to calm itself again. Suddenly, a spear of metal broke the surface; then three more: the long tines at the tips of the booms of the ship's main gun. The booms rose, shedding water, and then the bridge. The SDF-1's shoulder structures came up, and then the elbow housings, until at last *Daedalus* and *Prometheus* were up, their flight decks shedding millions of gallons of water.

The calculations were right; SDF-1 was an immense machine, but it was quite buoyant and seaworthy. It gleamed brightly as the seawater streamed down its hull.

08

"There's no excuse for sloppy discipline—not even victory," Colonel Maistroff was fond of lecturing us. Maybe so, but I never saw a haircut win a battle.

The Collected Journals of Admiral Rick Hunter

GLOVAL AND HIS BRIDGE CREW GAZED OUT AT THE SERENE ocean. The Terrible Trio was intoxicated with joy.

"Home again—after so *long*!"

"It's just beautiful!"

"Home—"

Sammie, Vanessa, and Kim, arms around one another, turned to the others. *"Welcome back!"*

Claudia was brushing tears away, and Lisa just stared at the sea, not knowing exactly what she felt.

Gloval lit his pipe; regulations be hanged. "Now, how about a little fresh air?"

Major access hatches began cranking open all around the Macross City area; light and wonderful sea breezes flooded in. Blinking and gaping, the inhabitants of the city began to congregate in the air locks and on the outer decks.

When they finally believed what their senses were telling them, the cheering began—the backslapping and hugging and kissing and laughter. People stood in the sunlight and cried or prayed, shook hands solemnly or jumped up and down, sank to their knees or just stood, staring.

Kim's voice came over the PA. "We've touched down in the Pacific Ocean. The captain and crew extend their gratitude to the citizens of Macross for your splendid cooperation during a difficult and dangerous voyage. It's good to be home."

A big hatch dropped open just below the bridge. Ben Dixon was the first one out onto the open deck, laughing and turning somersaults, leaping into the air ecstatically.

More Veritech pilots and crew people rushed after him. Rick and Max stood watching Ben carrying on. "He'd make a pretty good acrobat, wouldn't he?" Max commented.

Rick smiled. "Probably, but—look at that blue sky. That's no EVE projection! I can't say I blame Ben a bit."

Ben was pointing into the sky. "Look! They're giving us a fighter fly-by to welcome us!"

So it seemed; twenty or more ships that resembled VTs, bearing the familiar delta markings of Earth's Robotech Defense Forces, came zooming in in tight formation to pass over the SDF-1.

But the three pilots felt their joy ebb as they were struck by the same thought: The Zentraedi were still out there, millions of ships strong.

An endless series of details kept Gloval busy for the next few hours, including the recovery of the Vermilion and Ghost fighters who'd flown escort during the SDF-1's final bolt to safety.

But at last he put aside other duties, satisfied that subordinates could take care of the remaining details, and repaired to his cabin to complete his compilation of log excerpts.

The Earth authorities would soon have all the facts as he knew them. Gloval wondered if the leaders of the United Earth Government would believe all that had happened to the SDF-1 in the months since it had disappeared. Sometimes Gloval himself had trouble.

He reviewed the long tape he'd compiled to amplify the other materials. Starting with the initial Zentraedi attack, when so much of Earth's military force had been obliterated and the dimensional fortress had activated itself, the log covered all the important incidents of the running battle with the aliens.

There'd been the ghastly aftermath of the spacefold jump and the almost insurmountable problems of getting tens of thousands of Macross refugees settled in the ship. The *Daedalus* Maneuver, Lisa Hayes's inspiration, had allowed the humans to win their first resounding victory amid the icy rings of Saturn.

Lisa saved the day again, this time on Mars, by destroying the alien gravity mines that had been holding SDF-1 on the Red Planet's surface. The ship's most recent crisis began when radar was disabled by enemy fire, leading to a foray by a Cat's-Eye recon ship—piloted by Lisa Hayes, of course.

Gloval didn't like to think too hard about the fate his command would have suffered if he hadn't been lucky enough to have had Lisa with him. Certainly there were skilled and courageous men and women throughout the SDF-1; examples of extreme bravery and ingenuity were too many to mention. But it seemed that Lisa's devotion, valor, and special loyalty to the SDF-1 and to Gloval made her the pivotal figure in almost every action the ship fought. It made it that much more difficult for Gloval to see how few real friends Lisa had, how empty her life was of anything but service and duty. Of course, he had no right to interfere with her personal life, but he couldn't help being worried about her.

The most important thing Gloval had to present to the United Earth Government was an enigma: the molecular and genetic structure of the Zentraedi was so formidable that some of them could even survive unprotected in the vacuum of space for short periods of time; their sheer physical strength was a match for that of Battloids and other human Robotech mecha—yet they had nearly collapsed at the sight of two relatively tiny humans sharing a kiss.

Moreover, the Zentraedi didn't seem to know anything about *repairing* their equipment. It was as though they were a servant race using the machinery given them by some higher power, yet they boasted of being the mightiest warriors in the known universe.

Gloval shook his head, hoping the Earth authorities would have additional information or analyses that would shed some light on the mysteries surrounding the war.

He worked for hours, inserting updates and clarifying things that warranted it, condensing wherever he could. Twice he dozed briefly, then got back to work, making an occasional status-check call to the bridge. The relief officer on duty, Lieutenant Claudia Grant, assured him all was well.

A quarantine area had been established around the battle fortress—not surprising, Gloval supposed—and a communication blackout had been imposed for the time being. The crewpeople took that fairly well—they were used to military discipline—and even the civilians had been too delirious with joy to be very upset by it so far. Gloval could see why his superiors might want to maintain radio silence until he'd appeared to give his full report, but he hoped the need for it wouldn't last much longer.

The civilians were still celebrating, but they wouldn't be satisfied with that indefinitely.

He brought the tape to a close, puffing on his briar as he dictated. "I am convinced the Zentraedi have more firepower than we can even imagine. The situation is extremely critical, and I believe that a central issue in this war they've forced on us is this mysterious 'Protoculture' they keep mentioning. I therefore suggest that— what? Come in!"

The rapping had been gentle. Lisa entered with a pot of fresh coffee. "I thought you could use some about now, sir."

"Thank you; it smells wonderful." She came in, and the coffee's aroma filled the cabin, cutting the aroma of the pipe tobacco.

She poured while he glanced up at an ancient brass ship's clock on his wall. "I did not realize what time it was."

He put the pipe aside. The ashtray lay next to a detailed analysis and history of living arrangements and social organization in Macross City and the SDF-1 during the voyage. The SDF-1 held far and away the largest human population ever to travel in space, and that on a voyage of very long duration. The data on how people had coped with their living conditions and somehow managed to make things work would be very important, Gloval suspected. There would have to be a lot more humans in space for long periods of time, sooner than anyone expected.

Gloval threw back the curtains, looking out the high, wide curve of viewport at a Pacific dawn. He'd forgotten how many seemingly impossible colors there could be in such a sunrise—the purples and reds and pinks. He'd forgotten how the water broke the light into a million pieces and the sky ignited.

"Here you are, sir," Lisa said, handing him his cup, prepared just the way he liked it. They gazed out at the peace and powerful beauty of the dawn.

"I never thought I'd see anything as beautiful as this ever again," Lisa said. It was a moment of such tranquility, such oneness with the planet that had been their goal for so long, such satisfaction with a protracted, seemingly hopeless mission accomplished at last, that she did her best to lock it in her heart and senses and memory—a treasure that she could relive occasionally. Sparingly.

"You're right," Gloval said at length. "I feel the same way. You know, I have a confession to make."

Lisa sipped her coffee, watching the sea, saying nothing. Gloval went on. "I had a premonition when I took command of this ship, the feeling that something terrible would happen. It's difficult to explain, but it was a conviction that something would happen to us that would change us forever."

She studied his face. "And it seems that you were right."

He was staring at the sea and the rising sun, though she doubted he was really seeing them. "This ship still has its secrets, Lisa, but *what are they?* We must find out; I can't escape the feeling that *everything* depends on it."

It was strange to see the flight deck crews working in conventional coveralls and safety helmets again after months in vacuum suits, strange to think that most planes would *need* a catapult launch from the SDF-1 and the flatdecks now in order to get up airspeed.

Theoretically, the transport that was waiting for Gloval and Lisa didn't need a launch; it was a VTOL job, capable of lifting off like a helo. Still, it had the reinforced nose and landing gear of a naval aircraft, and SOP recommended that fixed-wing aircraft receive cat launch.

Gloval walked toward it with Lisa at his side, his attaché case weighted with documents, tapes, photographs, reports, and evaluation reports on *those* reports. His feet scuffed against areas of missing nonskid surface on the flight deck, flaps of it having been peeled loose by the violence of SDF-1's homecoming.

Scores of crewmen were just completing an FOD walkdown of the flight deck, pacing its length in a line abreast running from port to starboard. Foreign Object Damage was a thing much to be feared on a carrier; no scrap of debris could be left to be sucked into a jetcraft's air intake.

The weather remained fair, but now a thick odor rose from the sea. The superheated steam and hard radiation produced by the dimensional fortress's touchdown had resulted in a considerable fish kill, even so far out at sea; the sun was warming the foul-smelling soup that lapped around the hulls of the carriers and the approximate hip level of the SDF-1's "torso." Still, the stench came from far below and was easy to endure, mixed as it was with the trade winds that carried Earth's inimitable air to people who had been breathing reprocessed gases for months now.

Gloval was tight-lipped and silent, feeling strange premonitions like the one he'd mentioned to Lisa. The United Earth Government's replies to his messages had been terse, noncommittal. It seemed he had another desperate job of convincing to do.

Lisa emulated her captain, saying nothing and betraying nothing by her expression as she followed him up the boarding ladder into the transport. A crew member closed the hatch, and the transport's turbines increased their howl.

The plane had already been boxed—aligned on the catapult and fitted with an appropriate breakaway holdback link that was color-coded for this particular job. The transport's downswept wings bobbed minutely as the catapult crew got ready to launch.

When the cat crew had gone through their ritual, the transport shot away, taking lift from the sudden flare at the bow, off the angled flight deck, in a cloud of catapult steam.

Kim stretched, arms behind her head, gazing down at the carrier deck from the SDF-1's bridge. She sighed. "Well, there they go; at least they got a clean launch."

She was standing at the vast sweep of the bridge's forward viewport with Sammie, Vanessa, and Claudia, following the transport's climb.

Little Sammie shook her long, straight locks of blond hair back from her face. "I wish I were going, too," she said forlornly, resting her chin on the viewport ledge.

Claudia unwillingly told herself that it was time to scold a little, not sympathize; these last few hours or days before the SDF-1 crew was relieved might be the most demanding of all where discipline was concerned.

So she chided, "What're you talking about, Sammie? D' you know how *cold* Alaska is this time of year? Or any time of year? You should be glad you're staying where it's warm."

"Well, I'm not," Sammie said bravely.

"At least we'd be off the ship," Vanessa pointed out, adjusting her glasses self-consciously. She and Kim nodded supportively and made low "uh huh!" sounds.

Claudia was suddenly stern. "All right, that's enough of that! First off, the captain and Lisa are on a classified mission, which means we don't talk about it any more than we have to for duty purposes. And we *don't* mention it at all outside this bridge, *do you roger that transmission?*"

The Terrible Trio nodded quickly, gulping, in unison.

The hatch slid aside as a voice startled them. "*Good* morning, ladies! I'd like—"

The greeting was cut off by a sharp *whap*! of impact. The bridge crew turned in surprise, Sammie letting out a small cry. Claudia maintained her composure, but it wasn't easy.

"Oh! Ouch! Uhhhh!" Colonel Maistroff was in the hatchway, rubbing his forehead, his cap knocked back cockeyed on his head by the impact, holding himself up with one hand against the frame.

Everyone there knew Maistroff, and not for any cordial reason; one didn't make allies of the bridge crew by crossing Captain Gloval.

Claudia fluttered her eyelashes and said disingenuously, "Colonel, are you all right? The hatchway's *terribly* low! I recommend you duck down when coming onto the bridge, sir. Captain Gloval always does."

There was something in the expressions of the bridge crew

that said that they resented Maistroff's taking this liberty; it was his right to act as if he were Gloval, but they were not required to play along with the pretense.

Maistroff rubbed a growing knot over one eye, making a low grating sound so that subordinates wouldn't hear him groan in pain. "Thank you for that warning, Lieutenant Grant; you're only about ten seconds too late."

He stopped rubbing his forehead and squared his cap's visor away. The Terrible Trio trooped past him, in step, on their way to their duty stations. "I just came up to officially take over command of this vessel in Captain Gloval's absence."

Claudia held all her personal feelings in check; she'd had a taste of what command was now and was willing to give even Maistroff the benefit of the doubt. "Yes, sir; I'd heard that you would. I'm sure you'll enjoy the experience."

He glowered at her. "Mmm. I don't think that 'enjoy' is quite the appropriate word, miss. But I do expect to run a tight ship." He moved past her, going to the forward viewport.

Claudia tried to get a grip on herself. *Tight ship!* She'd had the feeling he'd say that. *As though Captain Gloval runs a loose ship! As if Captain Gloval isn't the best skipper in—*

"No more slipping around the rules," Maistroff was saying. "What this bridge needs is a good dose of discipline." Gazing grandly out the forward viewport, he drew a long cigar from the breast pocket of his uniform jacket.

It was plain that he was savoring the moment. Perhaps he had saved the stogie all this time since the SDF-1's accidental departure so that he could smoke it on the bridge as master. Maistroff made a production of biting off the end, rolling the cigar between his fingers, and moistening it front and back between his lips.

His indescribable pleasure in the moment was broken by a high-pitched voice. *"There's no smoking on the bridge, sir!"*

"*What?*" Maistroff whirled on Sammie, who was out of her chair and didn't look in the least daunted by his scowl.

"It's on page two of the ship's SOP rule book—standard operating procedure, isn't it, sir?"

Claudia couldn't for the life of her figure out whether Sammie was serious or was having her little snipe at the colonel. Apparently, neither could Maistroff.

He turned back to the viewport, holding the cigar as if somebody else had put it in his fingers, not willing to throw it away but unable to do much of anything else with it. His back was ramrod straight, and his cheeks flushed a bright red.

"Ah, of course. I was only holding it. I had no intention of lighting it." He gritted his teeth but refused to take official recognition when he heard female giggling and tittering behind him.

"Excuse me, Colonel," Claudia said. "Will there be anything else, sir?"

He turned to her, trying to put down his anger, cold cigar clenched in his teeth, hands clasped behind him. "What? What?" She said gently, "I was officer on the last watch, sir. Am I relieved?" She saluted.

He was doubly red-faced to have forgotten so simple a thing as relieving her of the command. "Oh!" He answered her salute. "Sure, you go right along, Lieutenant Grant. I'm sure we'll be able to operate just fine until you get back." He smiled indulgently.

As Claudia gathered her things, Maistroff went to inspect the rest of the bridge and incidentally try Gloval's chair to see how it felt. Making sure that he wouldn't hear, Vanessa whispered to Claudia, "Y' better check in later to make sure the bridge is still *here!*"

The Terrible Trio stifled their laughter. Claudia smiled. "You hang in there, girls."

Reflecting that Maistroff didn't know what *real* opposition was like but would find out if he crossed the Terribles, Claudia left the bridge.

09

Hey, I was managin' a couple of other class acts when I signed Minmei, y' know? I mean, I wasn't just chopped liver, kapish? I mean, I had the Acnes, who had a big, fat bullet: "I'll Bee a Goo-goo for You."

Anyway, Minmei-doll hits the scene, and I can't even get my other acts arrested! "Minmei! Minmei!" People don't wanna hear anything else.

The public—go figure.

Vance Hasslewood, Minmei's personal manager,
interviewed on Jan Morris's on-ship
TV show, "Good Morning, SDF!"

THE CITY OF MACROSS HADN'T SEEN FIREWORKS SINCE THAT fateful day when the Zentraedi first appeared in the solar system. There had been plenty of explosions, all right, but not simple skyrockets and colored bursts.

Now, fireworks flashed high over *Prometheus*'s flight deck. Canopies and marquees were set up, and an old-fashioned town festival was in progress.

Strings of firecrackers banged and snapped on the nonskid, and streamers and confetti flew in squalls, carried by the sea breezes. Many had chosen to wear costumes, and some wore fantastic, gruesome giant masks that covered them from head to foot. There was dancing and laughter, a sort of communal drunkenness with joy.

On an improvised speaker's platform, Mayor Tommy Luan held his hands high. "Our troubles are finally over! Let's make this party last all week!"

The stocky little mayor's good friend, Vern Havers, a lean, mournful-looking man with a receding hairline, clung to the side of the platform to call up anxiously, "But what about packing? Shouldn't we be getting ready to *leave*?"

"Vern, this isn't a day for packing! We have plenty of time for that! Don't you think that the Macross survivors deserve a celebration after all we've been through?"

The mayor looked up at the looming SDF-1, its silent guns throwing long shadows across the deck. "Besides, once we leave this ship, we'll probably never see it again."

Vern hadn't even thought about that, but it made sense; SDF-1 would have to take up its job of guarding Earth; the rebuilt Macross City would of course be dismantled.

Like many others, Vern had dreamed of returning to Earth, had lived for it, all these months; but now, like many others, he felt strangely sad that a unique time in his life was ending. He hoped there could be some kind of open house or something so people could see what the citizens of Macross had accomplished before all their handiwork was swept away.

"Well," he said, "if you put it that way, I suppose you may be right."

The major was literally hopping up and down, from his own swelling emotions. "Of *course* I'm right! Now, let's party!"

Vern resigned himself to the inevitable. It *was* good to be back on Earth, but he was beginning to realize how difficult it would be to get used to uneventful peacetime life.

Elsewhere in the milling, boisterous crowd, the three Zentraedi spies were trying to absorb what they were seeing around them.

Gaiety like this was unknown among their people; certainly the frivolous consumption of food and drink, scandalous mingling of males and females, and pointless merrymaking would be a court-martial offense among the warrior race.

Konda was absorbing something else—his third cup of an intriguing purple liquid with ice cubs floating in it—when Bron, gawking at all the goings-on, jostled his elbow.

Konda, vexed when some of his drink spilled, gave the bigger spy a shove. "Clumsy! Can't you be more careful?"

Bron looked hurt. Konda said, "I'm sampling something called 'punch,' and you interrupted my experimentation."

Bron looked at the beverage dubiously. "It seems to me you've imbibed more than is necessary for a mere effects test, Konda."

Konda pushed the cup into Bron's hands. "Here! You try it! I know where to get more, and the requisitioning procedure is puzzlingly informal." He hiccupped.

Bron sniffed the stuff suspiciously; then, after a final glance at Konda to make sure he showed no sign of toxic reaction, he downed the punch in two big swallows. It was cold but somehow had a warming effect. He gagged a little but felt a pleasant sensation course through him.

"I don't know what's in this stuff," Konda said with a foolish grin, "but it sure is getting *me* charged up!"

Oh my goodness! thought Bron. "You… you mean it's got some kind of Protoculture in it?"

Exasperated, Konda was considering clouting Bron in the head for being such a dummy, when Rico rushed up to them angrily. "Why aren't you two making noise like the rest of these people? You want them to notice us? Well then, pretend you're having fun!"

Rico, too, held a cup of the punch; it was all but empty, and he looked a little bleary-eyed. He threw one fist up and yelled, "Yayyyy!" so loudly that he quite startled his companions. "We finally made it back! We're home again!"

"Hurrah! We beat the enemy!" Konda added helpfully. "Hurrah for us! Hurrah for Earth!"

"Down with the Zentraedi!" Bron burst out, doing a little jigging dance step. That punch beverage, whatever it was, had him feeling rather, well, *happy*. "Up with the Micronians! Down…"

He realized the other two were staring at him. Bron covered his mouth with his hand in anguish. "Oh, my! I didn't know what I was saying! Konda, Rico—please don't report me!"

Just then a young woman dressed as a medieval princess and carrying two cups of punch swept by. She saw the three standing together, one without a cup. She put her extra one into Konda's hand and clinked glasses with them, grinning behind her silvery domino mask. "To home and friendship!" Then she was gone in the crowd.

The three spies looked at one another for a moment, then echoed, "To home and friendship," and clinked cups as the celebration swirled around them.

With most of the off-duty crew and virtually all the civilians up at the party, SDF-1's passageways were empty, giving the ship a haunted feel. Making her way toward the VT pilots' living quarters section, Claudia Grant tried to put that fool Maistroff out of her mind and concentrate on enjoying her brief time off watch.

For the first time in months, the Veritech pilots weren't flying constant patrols or combat missions, and SDF-1 was being manned by a virtual skeleton crew. So her free time meshed with Roy's for the first time in a long time.

The love affair between Claudia Grant and Lieutenant Commander Roy Fokker, as passionate as it was romantic, had been terribly strained by the demands of the SDF-1's desperate voyage. But now there would be time to be together—the very best thing about the dimensional fortress's return, as far as Claudia was concerned.

She signaled at the hatch to his quarters but got no response. Rapping on it with her knuckles was no more effective.

Claudia wasn't about to miss her chance to see him. Perhaps he'd left her a note. She tapped the hatch release and entered as the hatch slid aside.

Roy Fokker—leader of the Veritech Skull Team, heroic ace of the Robotech War—lay snoring softly, dead to the world, his long blond hair fanned out on the pillow. At six foot six, he hadn't yet found a military-issue bunk that fit him; his feet and the covers stuck off the end of the bed.

It had been said of Roy that "he doesn't *fly* a jet; he *wears* it." But right now Roy looked like nothing so much as a sleepy kid.

For months we never have the chance to be alone, and when the opportunity finally arrives, he sleeps through it! But she couldn't be mad at him. He'd been on duty, usually in the cockpit of a fighter, just about every waking hour since the spacefold jump.

Poor dear; he must be exhausted. "Oh, well…" She pulled the covers up over his shoulders, then turned to go.

"Hey, hold up!" She turned to see Roy sitting up in bed, blinking the sleep away, smiling. "You just gonna run off?"

She grinned at him. "I figured the Skull Leader needs all the beauty sleep he can get."

"You were wrong. C'mere."

He grabbed her wrists, his big hands engulfing hers, and pulled. Claudia gave a laughing yelp as he dragged her down next to him, then relaxed against him in a kiss that took away all the pain and sorrow and weariness of the long voyage home.

Back in the midst of the festivities on *Prometheus*'s flight deck, Rick Hunter stood waiting next to an aircraft. He was wearing his old flying circus outfit of orange and white trimmed with black, and his silken scarf. The plane was the fanliner sport ship won by Lynn-Minmei when she'd taken the Miss Macross title. This was to be its maiden voyage in the atmosphere of Earth.

It was a sleek, beautiful propfan design by the illustrious Ikkii Takemi himself, with powerful, pinwheel-like propellers in a big cowling behind the cockpit. It reminded Rick very much of his own *Mockingbird*, which depressed him because that in turn reminded him of the time he'd spent with Minmei, stranded together in a remote part of the SDF-1. During that time she'd come to mean so much to him, but now…

"You're a lucky guy, Rick, to be flying Minmei home," a ground crewman was saying. "You not only get to leave the ship, but you spend time with a beautiful—huh?"

Rick heard it, too, and looked around. The roar of the crowd had increased, and there was cheering and applause.

"Like I said," the ground crewman went on, "you get to spend time with a beautiful celebrity."

Minmei's entrance was worthy of her star status—her *superstar* status, as far as the crew and passengers of the SDF-1 were concerned. She was being chauffeured across the flight deck in a glittering new Macross City-manufactured limo, the crowd parting before her. They held up signs with hearts and fond sentiments on them or waved autograph books somewhat hopelessly.

Flower petals and confetti and streamers rained down on her car; people pressed up against the glass to smile, wave, and call out her name—to feel close to her, if only for a moment.

"Y' know, she's the only one who's been given permission to leave the ship so far, even for a short time," the crewman continued. "Hope you enjoy the ride."

Minmei sat quietly in the exact middle of the limo's rear seat, hands folded in her lap, watching the people throng around her car and pay homage. She wore her old school uniform: white blouse and necktie, brown plaid blazer, plaid skirt. Audience research indicated that her public liked to see her in attire that emphasized her youth.

Her manager, Vance Hasslewood, sat next to the chauffeur, happily surveying the crowd. "Well, this is quite a turnout for you, Minmei."

Minmei gave a little sigh. "Yes, I suppose these mobs are the price one must pay for fame."

Hasslewood and the uniformed chauffeur exchanged a wry, secret look.

"Could we go a little faster? I'm late as it is," Minmei added.

The driver sped up a bit, honking his horn, and Minmei's adoring public had to move out of the way quickly.

I wonder if she's changed much, Rick thought as the limo screeched up beside the little sport plane. Minmei had promised that she and Rick could still see a lot of each other once he joined the Robotech Defense Forces, but between his duties and her sky-rocketing career as the SDF-1's homegrown media idol, that promise had been forgotten.

The chauffeur held the rear door open for Minmei while Vance Hasslewood went to confer with a liaison officer from the SDF-1 Air Group.

"Hello, Minmei." Rick smiled. "It looked like you had a lot of trouble, getting through that crowd back there."

She giggled, her eyes shining in the way he remembered. "Those are my loyal fans. They follow me everywhere. I just *love* them!"

She turned to wave to the people being held back by a cordon of security guards. "Hello, hello! Thank you for coming down to see me off! I love you all very much!"

Apparently she was unaware that a lot of the people, the majority of them perhaps, were simply there for the party; maybe she didn't even realize that there *was* a celebration going on. Rick shook his head, laughing; Minmei was sweet and charming, but she still lived very much in a world of her own.

The fans were clapping, stamping, and whistling for her, waving their signs and banners. Vance Hasslewood looked on approvingly, eyes hidden behind tinted glasses.

"Thank you!" she called, throwing kisses.

"Boy, they really like you," Rick remarked.

"I know," she said matter-of-factly. "Rick, when can we take off? I'm really anxious to see my parents."

"Well, I guess we can take off any time; the engines are all warmed up."

He led her to the boarding ladder. "Just climb into the rear seat—careful, now—and sit down, strap yourself in."

She got into the fanliner and settled her shoulder purse next to her, taking up the safety harness. "Thanks, Rick. It seems like you've become a lot nicer now than when we first met."

Huh? Minmei *was* still living in her own world, he saw—revising her memories of the past according to her preferences, forgetting whatever was inconvenient or troubling or replacing it with something that freed her from introspection.

So now she'd decided that Rick had been unkind to her. Perhaps she'd forgotten that he'd saved her life several times... forgotten that they'd held a mock wedding ceremony and she'd worn the very white silk scarf that he now had around his neck as a bridal veil.

Perhaps she'd forgotten their kiss, there in the remotest part of the ship. Certainly she was now surrounded by people who would go along with almost anything she said or chose to think, people not eager to remind her of her past life and ties. She was free to be completely self-absorbed.

As he stood on the boarding ladder looking down into the cockpit at her, he saw her in a new light. "Maybe I've grown up, Minmei."

Her brows met, and she was about to ask what he meant; but just then Vance Hasslewood, standing at the foot of the boarding ladder, thrust his face up into Rick's. "Young man! Your name; what is it, hah?"

Rick threw him a sarcastic salute. "Lieutenant Rick Hunter, sir."

"Well, Lieutenant Rick Hunter, I expect you to take good care of Minmei! She's a very busy person, and she must get back to the ship on time."

Minmei surprised both men by jumping in on Rick's side. "Don't worry, Vance! I feel perfectly safe! Rick's a *very* good pilot!"

Hasslewood backed off a bit. "Er, yes, I'm sure he is, but he's so *young*, I, uh—"

Rick wondered just who and what Hasslewood really was. Certainly, Minmei's astounding popularity had been very lucrative for the man, and he was very proprietary about her. But what else was there to the manager-client relationship?

Nothing romantic, Rick was pretty sure of that; even at her most career-hungry, Minmei wouldn't have fallen for an abrasive hustler like Hasslewood. But *how* had Minmei gotten permission for even a brief visit to her parents when the SDF-1 was virtually quarantined?

To be sure, Rick's confidential orders were specific enough: Make sure that Minmei had no access to outside media interviews. Just the family visit, and then right back to the SDF-1, *whatever that took.*

Rick had thought about Minmei's brief liberty privilege and could only come up with one explanation: her talents and appeal had been a major factor in keeping up morale and fighting spirit during the long return voyage to Earth. And no matter what the public information people were saying, the war wasn't over and there was still a threat of invasion. If Minmei could do for the general population of Earth what she'd done for the people on SDF-1, she would be a tremendously important resource. That gave her and, in turn, Hasslewood, an awful lot of leverage.

Right now, though, Rick wasn't worrying about influence or power. He stuck his face into Hasslewood's, cutting him off. "How about standing back? We're taking off now."

Hasslewood just about fell over his own feet, retreating. "Sure, kid; don't get touchy! Have a good trip, Minmei! Hurry back!"

Rick pulled on his goggles and headset, lowering the cockpit's front and rear canopies.

Vance Hasslewood mopped his forehead with his handkerchief, watching as Rick increased the propfan RPMs. The manager prayed silently for a quick, uneventful flight; all his personal marbles were riding in that rear seat.

Rick turned the fanliner's nose and taxied. The sport plane wasn't equipped for cat launch, but it was so little and light and there was more than enough runway for a takeoff. With *Daedalus*'s bow turned into the wind, the little ship fairly leapt up off the deck.

Minmei sighed happily, looking down at the SDF-1, savoring the freedom of the flight. "Ahhh! It's been a long time!"

"It sure has," Rick murmured, bringing the plane onto its course for Japan. A vivid, seductive fantasy had begun running in the back of his mind, of being forced to land with Minmei—marooned on some idyllic desert island, perhaps; of things being the way they once were.

"I forgot how I felt about her."

"What?" Minmei asked, leaning forward to peer around his seat.

He hadn't meant to say it aloud. Flustered, he hastened. "Oh, nothing, nothing!" But his face was reddening, and she looked at him oddly.

He tried to concentrate on his flying as she settled back in her seat. But that little fantasy just wouldn't let him alone.

10

We weren't deaf to the innuendo, of course. Claudia and the
Terrible Trio and I heard all the sniping about "Gloval's Harem,"
though people were very careful not to say anything around Claudia
after she decked a cat crewman.

There is a loneliness to command, it's no myth. But there's also an
area around the commander—where you're not in charge but not part
of the rest of the ship's complement, either—that's often a difficult
place to be, too.

Lisa Hayes, *Recollections*

THE UNITED EARTH GOVERNMENT'S COMMAND COMPLEX WAS
like a landlocked iceberg—only a fraction of it was visible
aboveground. In fact, the communications towers, observation
and surveillance structures, defensive emplacements, landing
pads, and aircraft-handling facilities constituted less than half a
percent of the cubic area of the enormous base.

It was still a highly classified installation. The fighters escorting
the transport plane bearing Gloval and Lisa wouldn't have hesitated
for a moment to open fire on any unauthorized aircraft that entered
its restricted airspace and failed to respond to their challenges.

Changing the angle of its engine blast, the transport eased in for
a vertical landing. Lisa, glancing out her viewport, saw Battloids
pacing on guard duty.

Once the plane's authenticity and clearance were verified, its
landing pad became an elevator, lowering it deep beneath the
bleak, subarctic landscape.

Lisa and Gloval released their seat belts and gathered their things.

"I hope they're prepared to listen," Lisa said. "Captain, we've *got* to convince them! Surely they'll listen to reason!"

"That would be nice for a change," Gloval growled.

The Ikkii Takemi-designed fanliner rolled and soared, glinting in the sun.

"Woo-hoo-ooo!" Rick exulted. Piloting a Veritech through deepspace had its appeal, but there was nothing like feeling control surfaces bite the air and making a light stunt plane do exactly what you wanted it to.

"Having fun, Minmei?" He laughed again, and she joined in. He adored the sound of her laugh.

Maybe, he thought, he could just set down on some little island and say he wanted to check out the engine. Then he'd have a chance to talk to her, would have her full attention for a while.

While he was turning the idea over in his mind, a familiar voice came over his headset. "Veritech patrol to Minmei Special. Hey, Lieutenant! It's Ben and Max!"

"Huh?" Rick saw them now, back at five o'clock. The fighters had their variable-sweep wings extended all the way for the extremely low speed needed to keep pace with the sport plane. He was a little embarrassed that they'd managed to sneak up on him.

"We understand you have a VIP aboard," Ben went on.

"Some guys have all the luck," Max added suggestively.

"We're returning to base; have a nice date," Ben finished, laughing. The Veritechs waggled their wings in salute, then peeled off onto a new course. Their wings swept back to an extreme angle as they picked up speed, punching through the sound barrier.

They were doing better than Mach 2 and still accelerating when Rick lost sight of them. "So long, wise guys," he called over their tac net. "See you later."

"Ben and Max are silly, but it *does* sort of feel like a date."

He felt his pulse race. "Yep."

She inhaled the cold, clear air, watching the glitter of the sun on the canopy. "It's great to get away for a while, but when I get back, I have a whole lot of work to make up. You should *see* all the things they want me to do!"

Show biz again!

"I suppose it fills your time," Rick snapped, vexed.

She hadn't noticed his tone, ticking off her projects on her fingers. "Oh, yes! I've got to do a television show, and then I'm cast in a play. Why, I'm even supposed to do a movie!"

"Mmm," Rick tried to sound elaborately bored. She still didn't notice.

"That's going to be really great," Minmei gushed. "I expect to work really hard. This *is* my first movie, y' know. Say! If I speak to the director, I might be able to get you a small part, hmm?"

That made him smile. Maybe she did think about others after all, notwithstanding the fact that he thought movies were a rather brainless occupation and definitely inferior to flying a fighter.

"Maybe some other time, Minmei. But, hey, where d' you get all your energy? Flying heel-and-toe patrols is one thing, but I'd be exhausted trying to keep up with a schedule like that one. Minmei?"

He hiked himself around to look over his seat at her. "Minmei, are you all right? Speak to me!"

For a moment he was afraid the cockpit had lost pressure and looked to his instruments frantically. Then he saw what had happened. "Well how d'you like that? She's asleep."

Her chin was resting on her chest, and she was breathing softly. Again, Rick felt a wave of that fierce protectiveness he'd felt toward her when they were stranded. And tremendous affection rose up in him as well.

He turned back to his piloting with a fond smirk. *I hope she wakes up long enough to say hello to her parents.*

The streamlined tramcar, mounted on twin magnetic-lift rails, plunged deeper and deeper into the gigantic headquarters installation.

Aboard, Captain Gloval sat with arms folded across his chest and cap visor pulled down over his eyes, as if asleep. He would have loved a meditative pipe but knew how unpleasant that would have been for Lisa.

Lisa shifted nervously on the padded passenger bench. "Will it take long to reach the Council chambers?"

Gloval lifted his visor. "Just a little longer. The shaft goes down almost six miles." He didn't remark on his disdain for all this burrowing and hiding—Earth's governing body skulking at the bottom of a hole in the ground like frightened rabbits! When the Zentraedi were capable of blowing an entire planet to *particles!*

"By the way, that reminds me," he went on. "Have you heard anything about this Grand Cannon?"

Lisa's face clouded; the words sounded so ominous. "No, what is it?"

"It is a huge Robotech weapon that's been under construction here for almost a decade now."

Gloval gestured to the illuminated schematic of the base that was displayed by the tramcar's access doors. The elaborate details of the sprawling underground complex were mostly represented in coded symbols for security's sake; but the essential layout was in the shape of a gargantuan Y. The blinking light representing the tramcar was moving down one arm of the Y, heading for the vertical shaft.

"The Grand Cannon uses Earth's gravitational field as its main energy source," he told her. "In fact, the shaft we're traveling in at this moment is the barrel of the weapon."

Lisa looked around uncomfortably. "You mean, if this base were attacked right now and Command decided to fire the cannon, we'd be blown away?"

Gloval chortled. "Well, I'd like to think they'd clear the barrel first."

He knew she was astute enough to see the major disadvantage of the great gun: Even with the Y arrangement and the titanic rotating gear, the Grand Cannon's field of fire was very limited—and even United Earth Command hadn't come up with a way to tilt and traverse the planet Earth to bring the weapon to bear on inconvenient targets. Arrangements to overcome the problem were part of the plan, of course, but...

Gloval had been one of the loudest voices against the project; wars, he maintained (with history on his side), aren't won by defense but rather by offense—by an SDF-1 that could go out and confront the enemy, not by a Grand Cannon in a hole in the ground.

He had gone head to head with Lisa's own father during that argument, taking the opposite side from a man who had been a valued friend and a comrade in arms until then. It had been the beginning of a rift that had only widened and deepened in the years since.

It made him sad to reflect on those days gone by—they had saved each others' lives... they were bonded by more than mere blood. Yet Admiral Hayes had become an opponent, almost an enemy.

Henry Gloval knew the way of the world and of highest-echelon politics; he was as shrewd as anyone who played the game. But there was still something in him, something bred in the bone, that found it bewildering and saddening that there could be such a falling out between men who'd served together in war.

I suppose it's just as they say, he thought. *I'm a peasant at heart, and there's no changing that.*

He shook off his brief distraction. There was an Isaac Singer story he'd taken to heart—"The Spinoza of Market Street"? Perhaps; in any case, the point was that the virtue lay in *behaving* in accordance with one's ideal, not necessarily in *being* it.

And one of Henry Gloval's ideals was steadfastness in friendship. So he asked Lisa pleasantly, "Your father never brought you down here before?"

"A few times," Lisa answered, "but I was never allowed to come down the main shaft. Now I understand why."

"Yes, this Robotech project was top secret. Only a few outside officers had access. It made the old-time Los Alamos reservation look like open house!" He chuckled; there were fond memories of those days among the bitter.

"And no civilian visitors," he finished, "not even an admiral's daughter."

Lisa wore a puzzled look. "But then, why did they let Father in?"

Gloval said staunchly, "Who else was there? He was the visionary. He pushed for the creation of this complex when no one else thought it was necessary."

She looked around again, looked to the vast schematic on the wall. "My father was responsible for all this? I didn't know that!"

Gloval drew a deep breath. "Your father was always decisive." How could he talk to her of friction and resentment? He couldn't.

"When I was serving under him in the Global Civil War, a problem came up about inadequate rations for the troops. When Admiral Hayes didn't get satisfactory action from headquarters, he led our entire Combined Action Group in a raid on the logistical depot. Camo face paint; real *guerrilla* stuff!

"He personally sat on the log-command three-star general while we got something to eat. There were a lot of brave and deserving men and women who had their first real meal in a long time that night."

Lisa was laughing heartily, one hand at the base of her throat. "My father got away with *that*?"

Gloval was laughing again. "It's true. The general thought sappers had infiltrated the base, kept sending down orders for us to find them. There wasn't a woman or a man in that entire unit who wouldn't have done anything, *anything*, for your father, Lisa. Would've followed him to hell if he'd given us the word."

Lisa was still laughing, shoulders shaking. But her laughter no longer had anything to do with the story about her father. The sudden freedom from the SDF-1, the astonishing size of headquarters base, the very emphatic and yet somehow empty joy of being home again had cast a certain familiar pall over her. It was strangely overwhelming; there was nothing she could do but laugh.

Lisa Hayes had realized a long time before that a life in the military didn't exactly make for happily-ever-after, particularly for a woman. Nevertheless, there was a warmth of that moment, something between people who'd served together, something no outsider could have ever shared.

"It's good to hear you laugh again, Commander." Gloval smiled slowly. "I think this is the first time I have heard you laugh since you escaped from the enemy, no?"

Lisa said, "Ahh," and "Umm," trying not to think of a particular VT pilot, trying to keep the warmth and the laughter alive, doing her best not to be vulnerable to desires and attractions and yet be open to Gloval's confessions. A small part of her wondered if male subordinates of *female* flag-rank officers went through this.

"But I wonder if we'll feel much like laughing after this meeting with the governing council," Gloval went on. "It's crucial that they be made to understand that the aliens are *only* interested in the battle fortress and its secrets, *not* in our world."

Gloval tilted his cap forward on his brow again. "I hope you've thoroughly prepared your arguments, Commander Hayes."

Her chin came up; her eyes shone. "Ready to go, Captain," Lisa said, managing a smile as she was reminded of the loneliness she felt.

All her life, it had been so difficult for her to establish a relationship with men her own age, even men in the military. But it was not surprising, really; she had been surrounded by men like Gloval, men like her father. How many men like that could there possibly be? One in a hundred thousand? In a million?

Hard to match, in any case.

Gloval was saying, "Mm-hmm, that's good."

Lisa replied, "I'm sure we'll be able to convince them. After all, *we're* the only ones who've had close contact with the aliens!"

Yes, Gloval reflected, it would seem so cut and dried to her; Lisa's father was one of the most powerful people on Earth, but despite that—perhaps *because* of that—Lisa herself was completely naive about political machinations.

He knocked a bit of ash out of the bowl of his pipe and tamped down some new tobacco, as was his habit when he was thinking. Just as he struck one of the old-fashioned kitchen matches he so loved, a surveillance eye in the wall lit up and a feminine computer voice said, "ATTENTION! SMOKING IN THIS CAPSULE IS FORBIDDEN! PLEASE EXTINGUISH ALL SMOKING MATERIALS IMMEDIATELY!"

Gloval yanked his briar from his mouth guiltily. "Ah? Can't I smoke *anywhere*? If it's not my bridge crew warning me, it's these machines!"

Lisa was clearing her throat meaningfully. "Captain, are you worried about the SDF-1? Sir, *is something going to happen to us?*" Gloval's aching conscience made him leap on the question, "Why do you ask?"

Lisa only smiled and said, "When something's bothering you, I've noticed, you always pull out your pipe and make a big production about lighting it."

Gloval lowered the pipe slowly and, not caring who might be listening on some bugging device, said, "Hmmph! I must confess I'm very worried about this meeting. I'm not sure these—" he made a gesture with his head to indicate his disdain for anyone who would protect themselves underground while ordering brave men and women to die "—not sure these men will listen to us with open minds. And Lisa, *it's vital to our future that they do so, do you understand?*" Gloval spread his broad, brown peasant's hands on his knees and looked down at them.

Lisa nodded slowly. She was Admiral Hayes's daughter, used to having people view her as an access road to the highest levels of decision; *that* was one of the things that set Lisa Hayes so far apart from her contemporaries.

She'd seen power politics *in excelsis* all her life, had sickened of them and the unspeakable people drawn to them.

After Karl Riber had died she felt she would never heal from that hurt. But surely there were others out there, people who were kind and patient and true? The image of Rick Hunter suddenly came to her. Though she refused to admit it to herself, Rick Hunter had come to mean very much to her.

"What will happen if we can't convince the Council?" she asked Gloval.

He answered in a grim, level voice. "Then the Earth will go to war against the aliens."

Before, he had always spoken of triumph and the need to win; this time, with only Lisa to hear his confession, Gloval mentioned nothing about that. Lisa knew him well enough to know what that meant: Captain Gloval's estimation of the human race's chances against the Zentraedi were very bleak indeed.

The tramcar came to the bottom of the Y's arm and began the vertical descent to the innermost chambers of the United Earth Defense Council.

11

Did You Ever See a Dream Walking?

Early twentieth-century song title

"**M**INMEI? MINMEI, WAKE UP; YOU'RE ALMOST HOME."

She stirred a little; it was a voice she liked, she knew, and it was a message that was wonderful beyond compare. Minmei yawned charmingly against the back of one hand, trying to stretch but restrained by something. Her head was filled with the marvelous images and memories that the word "home" conjured up.

Minmei opened her eyes, recalling that the restraint was the fanliner's seat belt. Behind her, the steady vibration of the propfan engine drove them along. "Look!" Rick said, pointing.

"Mount Fuji!" she shrilled, happy beyond words. The mountain wore a crown of snow despite the fact that it was midsummer—something that happened very rarely. Minmei took it as a good omen and a welcome home.

Rick cruised slowly past Fuji, giving Minmei a chance to look. Air traffic was being rerouted to give him an unobstructed course; he wondered again what secret deals had been struck just so Minmei could see her relatives and wondered too how soon the Macross City survivors would lose patience with their confinement.

He banked the little aircraft, heading for Yokohama. Though he was happy that Minmei would soon have the joy of reunion, he was despondent that their time alone together was nearly half over. He tried to picture her family and how they would react to their daughter's status as SDF-1 superstar.

He trimmed the ship and shook his head. *There are billions of people on this planet. Why did I have to fall in love with public property?*

He took on a bit of altitude; the island chain lay beneath them like so many gemstones.

In the deepest vaults of the Alaskan base, Lisa Hayes and Henry Gloval sat at a simple, unadorned desk in the middle of a vast hearing chamber. The walls of the chamber were several dozen yards thick; though the pressures of the Earth itself were enormous down there, the room itself was as comfortable, in terms of temperature and air pressure, as any surface garden.

There was a multimedia console, perhaps ten yards away, at the base of the wall before them, and all around were display screens as big as billboards. Lisa and Gloval were still arranging documents and papers on the table, preparing to give their testimony.

Though he said nothing about it and gave no outward sign, Lisa knew that Captain Gloval was absolutely furious. He and his First Officer had been denied the courtesy of a face-to-face meeting with Earth's governing body and had been shown, instead, to this interrogation chamber.

Lisa knew he didn't blame her, but she couldn't meet his eye. She knew that her own father was one of those responsible for this shameful, cowardly treatment.

Suddenly all the screens came to life. There were a half dozen extremely magnified faces glaring down Lisa and her captain. All the faces were male, middle-aged to elderly, and all but two were in military uniform.

It confirmed Gloval's worst misgivings. Lisa had to remind herself to breathe. *Military running the government? This wasn't what we were fighting for!*

Before her, on the center screen, was the towering face of her father.

"Welcome home, Captain Gloval," said Admiral Hayes. "It's been a long time since you reported in person."

Gloval snapped his hand to his forehead in salute, and Lisa followed suit. Others might forget their vows, their obligations; but the one thing that sustained Gloval was the certainty that while he still lived he would never renege on his sworn word. Even if it meant rendering military courtesies to men he no longer respected.

It was a code of conduct few outsiders could have understood; a samurai maybe. Gloval had understood and willingly accepted his oath of allegiance to the new United Earth Government, back when the alternative was racial annihilation. He meant to live up to that oath just as long as he was able.

So he rendered military courtesy crisply.

"Yes, sir," replied Henry Gloval.

The huge eyes of the projected image, as blue as Lisa's, turned to her. "You too, Commander."

"Yes, Admiral," she said quietly. She gave no outward sign that her heart was breaking.

After her mother's death, her father had been her only emotional mainstay, until Karl Riber and, later, Claudia, Captain Gloval, and a very few others. And now, Admiral Hayes didn't even deign to break formality. An embrace and a few tears weren't military, perhaps, but she'd hoped for them; and, to be sure, she'd come prepared with some of her own.

But instead, the screen face said, "Good. Now, why don't you both have a seat and we'll hear your report?"

"Yes, sir." Lisa and Gloval cut their salutes away smartly, precise and correct. They both sat while Lisa gathered her briefing data, then she stood again. Gloval felt a sudden burn, since she would have to bear the brunt of their inquiry. But the structure of the meeting was traditional and dictated by custom: The First Officer made the presentation because the Captain was sacrosanct and not subject to cross-examination outside of a court-martial.

"We must know everything from the beginning," said a white-haired man with a snowy handlebar moustache. He was a former political hack who had oiled his way into a direct commission in the Judge Advocate General's office and made his rise from there. Lisa took one look at the ribbons on his tunic and knew he had never seen a single moment of combat.

She had two decorations for courage under fire as well as

numerous other campaign ribbons and medals, but she bit her lip and said, "Of course, sir."

Lisa arranged the papers in her hands and looked straight into the image of her father's face. He didn't look away. All around her were august visages; it was like being in an observatory with televisor screens running from floor to ceiling apex.

Lisa gazed at her father coldly.

"This report presumes that everyone present is familiar with the details of the situation up to the time of the Zentraedi's appearance in the solar system. Supplementary reports will be made available to you."

She glared at her father for a second, then went back to her report, happy that Gloval was at her side but ashamed of her own family. She turned instead to a commissioner whose face was displayed to her right, a man who looked like Clark Kent in those ancient *Superman* comics.

She cleared her throat, looked at the overbearing faces around her, and suddenly felt strong; strong as only people with simple truth and dedication to duty on their side can feel. She could stand up to any of them.

"The following are the abbreviated details of the miscalculated spacefold jump undertaken by the Super Dimensional Fortress One while under unprecedentedly intense attack from hostile alien forces and its consequent actions in returning to Terra."

That was quite a mouthful, but Lisa took pride in how fascinated and *intimidated* those enormous, concave faces looked.

These were men who had used the emergency of the Zentraedi's appearance to take control of Earth. Along the way they had evidently forgotten how terrible and overwhelming the enemy was that currently prowled the dark beyond their tiny planet.

Lisa let herself feel a little vindictive; she figured they had it coming. "At that time, the strength of the alien fleet was estimated at nearly one million ships of a size three or more times larger than our Terran Armor class," she said with a certain relish.

And before anybody could say anything, Lisa Hayes added, as she stared her father in the eye, "That number has since increased and our best intelligence evaluations indicate the Zentraedi commitment to this war to be in excess of two and a half million ships-of-the-line."

Nobody said anything, but there was clearly a mental echo running around the sad little rabbit hole of the United Earth rulers: *TWO AND A HALF MILLION SHIPS???!*

Chew on that! Lisa thought to herself as she went on to the next page, watching out of one eye as the great and the mighty of Earth squirmed in their seats.

Yokohama was picture-postcard perfect under a blue sky dotted by slender wisps of white cloud.

Minmei tugged Rick along by the hand as they headed for her parents' restaurant. She stopped in the middle of the esplanade, looking out at the glittering ocean.

"Just smell that beautiful sea air!" She drew in a great breath of it. "*Nothing* smells as good as Yokohama!"

She took her hands from the guardrail, went on demi-point, pirouetted, and then did a few jetés. "It makes me want to sing, and dance, and *carry on!*"

Rick, trying not to feel like a secret agent but aware of his responsibility, caught her by the upper arm. "Minmei, would you please stop acting like this? Everybody's looking at you."

Shaking off his grip, she spun on him, putting her face up to his furiously. "Listen, I'm happy to be home, and if I feel like singing and dancing, *I will! Hmmph!*"

Rick was about to mention their obligation to the SDF-1 and the secrecy to which they'd *both* been sworn for this mission, when Minmei spied a tall, slender structure nearby.

"Look! There's the New Yokohama Marine Tower!" she squealed, pointing down the esplanade. She took on the reserved voice of the tour guides she'd heard so often while she was growing up.

"'When it was built, the New Marine Tower, which replaced the first, was the tallest structure in the world; over twenty-eight hundred feet high! It's an engineering masterpiece.'"

She did another jeté. "It's the same age as me!"

Rick's patience was fading. He doubted that the tower had very much longer to live if its life expectancy was tied in to Minmei's.

"It looks it," he commented.

She thumped him hard on the chest with her fist. "Doesn't anything impress you, Rick Hunter? I want you to *like* my city!"

It was another one of Minmei's masterful emotional flip-flops: She won him over again in a single moment, as he stared into those enormous blue eyes while she tossed her head, sending ripples of light through her jet-dark hair.

Does she know she has this effect, or is it all unconscious? he wondered. He'd never dared ask the question.

She had her hand in his. "I just *know* you're going to like my mother! She's the nicest, friendliest woman in the whole world! Rick, I'm not kidding!"

She tugged him along. "Come on!"

Who am I to resist? he thought, yielding to the inevitable.

A few minutes later, they came to a *torii* that spanned the street, inscribed with ideographs. "Hey, this is the local Chinatown!" Rick remarked.

Minmei shook her head in dismay; how could such a brilliant pilot be so dumb about other things? "I know, silly. *I'm* Chinese; this is where I live. Come on; let's go!"

She grabbed his hand again and dragged him along, under the *torii* and into Chinatown.

People stared at them a bit, curious about the trim young man in the circus flier's outfit and the enchanting young woman who seemed to radiate life and exuberance. "Now, the grocery store is right over there," Minmei was saying, "right next to the gift shop. And the bakery is still—Rick, have you ever tasted mandarin root? Oh, and I'm *so* glad they haven't changed the street signs!"

The signs were in the shape of smaller *torii*. "You haven't been gone *that* long," he reminded her. What did she expect? Funeral bunting on every corner?

"Right," she said, barely having heard him. "I hope my house is still the same. Just a minute now…"

He'd stopped as she slowed to a halt.

"*Look!*" She was pointing to a building facade covered with ideographs and intertwined symbols, gold on scarlet, with a very conspicuous dragon in the midst of it. "We're here!"

She turned to Rick excitedly, and he found himself returning her smile in spite of himself. "It's the Golden Dragon, our restaurant, see? Just like the White Dragon is Aunt Lena's in Macross!"

"It's very nice," was all Rick could find to say.

Minmei was close to tears of joy. "I hope everybody remembers my face."

Rick sighed. "I keep trying to tell you, you haven't been gone that long!"

"So? Maybe I've changed a lot." She struck a pose; he recognized it from her glamour photos and feared the worst.

Minmei gave a carefree laugh and went dashing into the Golden Dragon. With no alternative, Rick followed after.

"Chang! Chang!" she was shouting into the face of a startled and rather nervous-looking Chinese gentleman dressed in a white waiter's tunic and matching Nehru hat. "D' you recognize me? Look! Who am I?" She twirled before him.

Chang, his eyes the size of poker chips, said something in a language Rick didn't recognize and charged off into the kitchen, crying, "Look! Come look, come look!"

He was back in a moment, dragging a brown-haired, kind-faced woman whose features bore a resemblance to Minmei's. "Chang, why are you shoving me? What in the world—stop pushing—*oh!*"

"Don't *you* recognize me, Mother?"

She had spied Minmei and stopped, wordless—perhaps close to cardiac arrest.

"Does that mean you do?" Minmei smiled.

"Minmei… we were sure you'd been killed!"

"No; I'm home," she said brightly.

Minmei's mother rushed over to throw her arms around her daughter, nearly knocking her down. "I can't believe it! My darling little girl is home! She wasn't taken from us!" She was racked with sobs.

"Well, I *was*, really," Minmei said, pulled a little off balance by her mother's tight embrace around her neck. "But they brought me back."

Her mother suddenly had her at arm's length again. "Back from where? And who's this?"

"This is Rick Hunter, Mother. He's the boy who saved my life."

Minmei's mother suddenly clasped Rick's hand, bowing over it solemnly, again and again. "Thank you; thank you, son!"

Rick scratched his head with his free hand, not knowing what to say. Among other things, he wasn't at all sure he liked being referred to as a "boy"—especially by the young woman he cared for so much.

"Minmei! We thought you were dead!" A thick-bodied, angry-looking man had appeared from the kitchen. He had dark eyes and hair as black as his daughter's.

"How could you not contact us and let us know you were alive?" But even though he was scowling, her father touched her face tenderly.

Meanwhile, Rick was having some very troubling thoughts of his own. The G2 Security officers who had briefed him for this oddball mission had been very emphatic that he not discuss any details of the situation on the SDF-1; even Minmei had agreed to be circumspect about revealing any information about the vessel or its mission.

But these people behaved as if the ship had been lost with all hands even though it had been back for over twenty-four hours now.

Rick took the briefing officers' instructions to heart, deciding to say as little as possible—and to see that Minmei did the same, though that promised to be a chore—until he had a clearer idea of just what was going on here on Earth.

12

Gloval's ship and crew had been tested in the flame and come through. The Robotechnology and the civilian refugees, likewise, had undergone a make-or-break trial.

No one had foreseen that an even more severe strain was to be put on Gloval's own oath of allegiance.

"The Second Front," *History of the First Robotech War*,
Vol. LXVI.

THE GIANT FACE OF A COUNCIL MEMBER LOOKED DOWN AT LISA AS she set down her briefing book, her summary complete.

"That was a very comprehensive report, Commander Hayes," the Council member, General Herbert, said. "But come now, don't you think you've overestimated the enemy's strength by quite a lot?"

Herbert disappeared, and the image of Marshal Zukav, silver-haired and silver-mustached, took its place. "Yes, I can't help but wonder why these aliens didn't destroy the battle fortress if they had such overwhelmingly superior numbers."

Lisa, who'd seated herself, came to her feet again. Gloval said nothing, glaring up at the magnified faces around him, content to let his First Officer draw out the Council's attitudes and arguments before he made his stand.

"I've already stated what we believe to be their motives in my report."

Herbert was back. "You expect us to accept that report as the truth?"

Lisa growled, gritting her teeth, her hands bunching into fists, trying to keep her temper.

Then her father, Admiral Hayes, was staring down at her "That will be all, Commander; we've heard quite enough. You may resume your seat."

"Admiral, I—"

But Gloval was on his feet now, with a calming hand on her shoulder. She held her peace.

"Gentlemen," he addressed the Council, "what about the authorization for the requests that were attached to that report?"

Now Zukav glared down at him again. "The proposal to negotiate with the enemy and the plans to relocate the Macross City survivors?"

Herbert broke in, "We will discuss your requests in private session. You and your First will stand by!" There was a loud comtone, and all screens went blank, leaving Lisa and Gloval in a sudden silence in the dim, domed chamber.

Lisa's fists were trembling. "Ohhhh! I can't *believe* they treated us like this!"

Gloval lowered himself into his chair, head thrown back, eyes closed. "I do. I think we've lost the fight."

"But—how can you know that already?"

"There's something going on here that we don't know about, Lisa. Their minds are made up."

She gazed around at the darkened screens. "I wonder what they're planning to do with us?"

Minmei's father slammed his fist on the table, making the teacups jump. "No! You're *not* going!"

"That's right!" her mother added. "After more than a year we finally discover that you're not dead; how can you think we'd let you leave?"

"To go entertain troops on some warship." Her father sneered.

Minmei was on her feet, hands on hips. "Hah! Is that what you think I'm doing?" She stamped one little foot. "I'm not just some run-of-the-mill USO singer, you know! I'm an important person back there!"

Her father shouted, "Well, you're *not* back there! You're *here*, and I'm not letting you return, and that's that!"

She threw her head back, eyes squeezed shut, shaking her fists.

"*No-o-o-o!*" Then she went on. "I've *got* to go back! I'm doing a TV show, I've got a record coming out, and I'm going to be starring in a film! Isn't that right, Rick?"

Rick was completely taken by surprise at the sudden shift of focus to him. "Uh, um—"

"Ridiculous! Your family comes first!" her father barked.

Rick was wondering about that, too. When he and Minmei were stranded, she had talked at length about all the love and mutual support there was in her family. It looked like a little celebrity could change a *lot* of things.

"I want to be a movie star!" she pouted, stamping both feet this time, just as her cousin Jason did when he threw a tantrum.

Her mother was weeping into a snow-white napkin. "How could you hurt us like this? You know we've always counted on you to get married and take over the Golden Dragon and run it with your husband."

Married? Run the restaurant? *Those* were new wrinkles! Rick suddenly felt a little queasy at the very thought of giving up flying, even for Minmei. Maybe they weren't destined for each other, after all.

"What about you, young man?" her father snapped. "What d' you think about all this hogwash, eh?"

"Huh? That is—well—"

Minmei was furious. "I don't see why you're asking him! His opinion doesn't count here! I'm the one making the decision! It's my life, and I'm going back to the ship; I can't turn my back on thousands of loyal fans and all the people I work with!"

Her mother sniffed and said, "But you're turning your back on us."

Score one for Mom, Rick thought; that shot had hit home, stopping Minmei in her tracks, at least for the moment.

But just when she might have yielded, a new voice interrupted. "Hey, what's all the screaming about down here? I can't even concentrate on my studies—hey! Minmei!"

He was about Rick's age or a little older, tall, with straight hair as black as Minmei's that fell past his shoulders. He'd stepped down out of the stairway—a slim, athletic-looking fellow, handsome but somehow sullen. Still, his face lit up when he saw her.

She flew to him, hugging herself to him. "Kyle! Oh, I can't believe it! You're *here!* I thought I'd never see you again!"

He laughed and held her close.

She spoke in a flurry. "We thought you died on Macross! We never found you in the shelters, or later on the SDF-1, so your parents and I assumed—"

He shrugged. "After my father kicked me out of the house for being in the peace movement, I figured it wasn't such a good idea to stick around a military town. So I left the day before Launching Day."

Rick was looking at him jealously. Kyle had a sort of inner balance, a calmness—unflappable and very self-possessed.

"When I tried to get in touch with you," he was telling Minmei, "they told me that everything on the island had been destroyed and that it was off limits for good. Radioactive or something." His face clouded with the memory, a sensitive and strong face.

"It was terrible." She nodded sadly.

He took her shoulders. "Well, I'm glad *you're* here; I'm glad *somebody* survived."

"Oh, but your mom and dad are doing just fine, running the White Dragon!"

"*What?*" His grip tightened on her shoulders for a moment, powerful fingers digging in until he realized what he was doing and eased off. "They're alive?"

She gave him a smile warm as a hearth fire. "Sure, silly; they're on the ship."

"Ship? What're you talking about?"

She tched and explained, "The *space*ship."

"You mean you didn't know?" Rick asked, wondering just how much covering up he was going to have to do.

Kyle was shaking his head happily, baffled but laughing. "No."

"Most of us survived, even though we lost a lot of people." Minmei told him. "This is Lieutenant Rick Hunter; he's one of the fighter pilots from the ship."

Kyle said, "Oh. Hello." It sounded like he was greeting the lowest known life form.

Rick rose anyway, trying to be polite. "Hi."

"Rick," Minmei gushed, "this is my cousin Lynn-Kyle; he's been like a brother to me. Kyle, Rick is the one who saved my life."

"It was a privilege." Rick shrugged.

Kyle's expression was full of anger and resentment. "I thought soldiers were *expected* to aid civilians in times of emergency."

Rick cocked his head to one side, trying to figure out what Kyle's beef was. "Hmmm."

"But we appreciate your efforts, anyway," Kyle told him with a frown.

Minmei slipped an arm through Kyle's elbow. "No, no: When Rick saved my life, he hadn't *become* a soldier yet."

Kyle was looking him up and down with narrowed eyes. "So you decided to join up later, eh?"

Minmei's mother and father were watching the whole exchange without interfering; Rick wondered just what he'd gotten into the middle of. "That's right."

Kyle held his chin high, gazing down his nose at Rick. "What d' you think's so good about the military?"

Rick showed his teeth in a snarling smile. "Free bullets, free food... and it sure beats *working* for a living."

"It's getting late," Gloval said grimly just as a comtone sounded.

Hours had gone by. In the interview chamber at the bottom of the Alaskan base, the screens flashed to life again. Gloval and Lisa looked up expectantly, wondering what the result of the deliberation was. The wall clock read nearly midnight.

General Herbert gazed down at them. "Captain, Commander— sorry to keep you waiting." He didn't sound sorry at all. "The Council has been going over your report, and we have found most of it to be accurate."

"And what about my requests?"

"Captain Gloval, all negotiations with the aliens for an end to hostilities are flatly rejected."

Gloval spat, "You think we can win against a force like that?"

"We don't know whether we can win or not. The point is, we

don't understand the invaders' thinking. We scarcely understand their Robotechnology. How can we begin peace talks with them?"

Gloval was about to interrupt, but Herbert pushed on. "We have no way of knowing if they would participate in good faith or simply ignore any treaty commitments and attack again when it suited them."

"But—you must realize—" Gloval began.

Then Admiral Hayes's image was front and center. "Captain, we think our Grand Cannon will protect us as long as we stay prepared and alert. We will *not* negotiate away that advantage."

"Very well," Gloval snapped. "I understand, sir. But what about resettling the fifty thousand or so Macross survivors?"

Herbert fielded that one, seeming irked that he would even ask the question. "They've all been declared dead, so having them leave the SDF-1 is out of the question, Gloval."

Gloval shook his head slowly. "I don't understand."

Lisa shot to her feet. "Just what is it you're saying?"

Herbert's answer was acid. "Do you think we made an official announcement that we're at war with *aliens?* Why, there would have been worldwide panic and probable insurrection by the peace factions!"

"They'd have been screaming for immediate unconditional surrender," another Council member, Commissioner Blaine of US-Western, added.

Admiral Hayes's image held the center spot again. "We invoked a strict media blackout from the day the SDF-1 disappeared, using the excuse that a guerrilla force of antiunification terrorists had attacked Macross Island and destroyed it after the ship left on its maiden test flight. Now, how could we let the tens of thousands of Macross inhabitants who *know* what a tremendous threat we face return to Earth?"

"It's impossible!" Zukav threw in. "The government would be overthrown!"

Are they crazy or am I? Gloval asked himself.

For ten years, throughout the rebuilding of SDF-1, the world government had used the threat of alien invasion to justify their staggering defense budgets and its own ever-expanding influence.

But when the Zentraedi finally appeared with power so far beyond anything humans had envisioned (except for a few hard-headed realists like Gloval), the Council had, in effect, become completely paranoid: They lied to the populace, hid in a hole in the ground, and simply prayed the menace would go away.

All for the sake of their political power base, all so that they could rule a little longer.

Gloval's voice rose a few decibels. "We're going to have a riot on our hands if we don't allow those people to get off the ship! They've been through a lot and endured it gallantly, but now they're safely back home and their patience is wearing thin!"

Herbert answered that. "Keeping them under control is your responsibility. And anyway, if, as you stated in your report, the aliens are so curious about our customs, then carrying an entire city within the SDF-1 should ensure that their attention is focused on it, don't you think?"

"It's crucial that you draw the enemy forces away from this planet!" Kinsolving, a bloodless-looking man with eyes like glass pellets, and from one side.

"At what price?" Gloval roared.

He felt very close to surrendering to his rage—perhaps going back to the SDF-1 and launching a little revolution of his *own*.

But he knew he wouldn't, knew he couldn't fire on innocent men and women who believed the Council's lies and who would rise to oppose him—knew he couldn't break the oath of allegiance he'd sworn.

He'd seen enough civil war; he knew he couldn't start another.

Admiral Hayes was saying, "Captain, we're not insensitive to your situation, but we must have time to strengthen our defenses and increase our knowledge of Robotechnology. And you're the only one who can give it to us."

Lisa cried, "Father, this is too much to ask of all those civilians!"

Hayes's huge projected face glared down at her icily. "Commander Hayes, we may be father and daughter, but during these proceedings I expect to be addressed by my rank, is that understood?"

"Yes, sir," she spit out the words.

"And what if the aliens decide not to follow the battle fortress?" Gloval posed the question. "What if they attack the Earth instead? You can fire your Grand Cannon until you broil away the planet's atmosphere and make the surrounding land mass run molten, but you *still* won't be able to destroy all those ships!"

Hayes answered, "Your own analysis indicates that that's highly unlikely; the invaders are interested in your ship. You will receive your sailing orders in the morning. That is all."

Again the screens went blank.

Gloval picked up his hat tiredly. *I guess that's the end of that.*

"Captain, how are we ever going to be able to explain this to the people on the ship? Not just the survivors; the crew—they've been in constant combat for more than a year!"

Gloval had no answer. In the corridor outside, he asked, "Lisa, wouldn't you like to spend some time with your father while you're here? As family, I mean? I can authorize a brief leave…"

They came to an elevator to begin the long trip back to the surface. Lisa kept her eyes lowered to the floor. "No, sir. I have no particular interest in seeing him right now."

"I understand, my dear," said Gloval as the elevator doors closed.

13

The patterns of behavior observed so far indicate that either all these humans are demented or else the three of us suffered head injuries upon first landing here.

Preliminary observation of the
Zentraedi spies Rico, Bron, and Konda

"I REALLY DON'T THINK THIS IS GETTING US ANYWHERE," LYNN-KYLE said in his soft, reasonable voice.

Hours of argument had gone by, but the five—Minmei and her parents, Rick, and Lynn-Kyle—were still gathered around the table. "Minmei's made her decision," Kyle went on, "so why don't you let her go?"

Minmei clapped her hands, eyes dancing. "Oh, Kyle, you're wonderful! I knew you'd say that!"

"Just a minute!" Minmei's father said angrily.

His wife was quick to head off the brewing confrontation with Kyle and keep the debate on track. "You're the last one we'd expect to send Minmei away from her home, Kyle."

"Especially with no one to watch over her," the father added. Rick almost said something about that: *Listen, I saved her from fifty-foot-tall aliens and death by starvation and thirst! What d' ya call that, a passing interest?* But it didn't seem like the time.

"I thought I would go with her," Kyle said casually, "and live with my folks."

Minmei was ecstatic. "Hurray, Lynn-Kyle! I knew you'd find some way to come to my rescue!"

Rick made a bored sound.

"Well, I guess that's all right," Lynn-Jan said slowly, deciding it might be for the best to let his daughter get this foolishness out of her system. His wife, Lynn-Xian, looked relieved, saying, "It would make me feel a lot better."

"No problem," Kyle said with a charming smile. "It's just temporary, anyway."

The transport hurtled through the frigid night air, bound for the SDF-1. A full squadron of fighters was flying escort around it.

Gloval knew now that it was no longer a matter of honor; he wouldn't be given the chance to divert or disobey orders now that the Council had made its decision.

Lisa, sitting in the window seat, opened an envelope that one of her father's aides had given to her. She read:

> *My dearest Lisa,*
>
> *I know that you're angry about my decision regarding the SDF-1, but it was unavoidable under the circumstances. I want you to try to understand and realize I'm concerned about your welfare. The battle fortress is a very dangerous place, and I'm working on getting you reassigned to another ship, or possibly here to headquarters, before it's ordered to move out into space once more—*

Without finishing the note, she tore it into tiny little pieces.

From another direction, the speedy little fanliner cut the sky, bound for the ship. It was handling a little less nimbly than before; Lynn-Kyle was seated in the back with Minmei in his lap.

"You mean to say you don't have *any* girlfriends?" she was asking him coquettishly, batting those big blue eyes.

He looked at her fondly, but he seemed to be one of the few people immune to her manipulation. "Well, I've been traveling around so much, I haven't had time."

"If you *did* have a girlfriend, I'd probably be jealous."

He chuckled. "What d' you have in mind? You want me to stay single forever?"

"Well, not exactly," she said slyly.

It sounded like a game they'd played often, Rick thought.

"Then what *do* you want?" Kyle coaxed.

She knuckled his shoulders, giggling. "Oh, nothing; I'm just teasing."

Rick lost patience with all the cuteness; he couldn't take any more of it. "Hey! It's hard enough to fly this crate, overloaded like this, without all that jabbering back there! How about buttoning up until we land?"

He was also bothered by the idea that he might have exceeded orders. There were no provisions for him to bring an outsider aboard the SDF-1; but, on the other hand, the briefing officers were very emphatic that Minmei was important to the war effort and must be returned, and Minmei couldn't come back without Kyle, so…

Minmei was giggling again. "That boy's always kidding," she confided to Kyle.

That tears it! "Guess again," he told her. "It's no joke!"

He banked sharply; Minmei let out a squeal and clung closer to Kyle. Rick poured on the speed, impatient to be rid of the two of them.

Lynn-Kyle held his cousin close and smiled triumphantly.

"That's not fair!" Kim Young cried, hearing Gloval's heartbreaking news.

"It's like we're prisoners here!" Sammie added.

Gloval stood his ground, unmoving, betraying no emotion. He'd thought it best to let his trusted bridge crew in on the news first, in the privacy of the bridge; they were the ones who would form the core of what he was coming to think of as his crisis-management team, helping him ensure that things didn't fall apart aboard SDF-1. They had to be given time to get over the shock before they could help the entire ship's population cope with it.

Claudia was the first one to get things in perspective. "Orders are orders, even if there are a lot of idiots at central headquarters who have no idea what they're doing!"

Lisa nodded to herself; she *knew* that was the kind of woman and officer Claudia was.

Still, Sammie insisted, "But there must be *something* you can do, Captain. Please tell us you're not going to accept this quietly. You will change their minds, won't you?"

"Won't you, Captain?" Kim added pleadingly.

Gloval cleared his throat in the way he did when he'd heard enough and expected to be obeyed. "Your lack of discipline is only compounding the problem, so get back to your duty stations immediately. I appreciate your concern, but right now I have to begin deciding how to break the news to the Macross survivors and the rest of the crew."

He stood up from his chair, brushing past them. "You will excuse me."

Shifting her glasses nervously, Vanessa couldn't help calling a last desperate objection after him. "Captain, can't you—"

Gloval cut her off stiffly. "That will be all, Vanessa."

"Yes, sir," she said contritely.

"Try to understand," Gloval said softly over his shoulder to them just before the hatch closed.

Vanessa removed her glasses to wipe away a tear of anger. "But—it's not fair!"

"That's absolutely true," Lisa said, speaking up for the first time. "But you can't blame the captain for something headquarters did. Everybody has a right to gripe, but you should at least be mad at the right people."

"Okay, okay—the captain needs our support, right?" Claudia said soberly.

"Yes. He knows he can't possibly succeed without it," Lisa answered.

The bridge hatch opened, and the relief watch started filing in. Kim let her breath go with a rasp. "All this talk isn't going to change anything, and I'm hungry," she declared, careful to mention nothing specific in the outsiders' presence.

Sammie took the cue. "Let's go into town and eat lunch!"

Vanessa nodded energetically. "Yeah, let's go down to the White Dragon; I'm starving."

. . .

At the White Dragon, the front doors slid aside. Minmei's aunt Lena quickly went to greet the first customers of the lunch rush, bowing hospitably. The restaurant was braced for a busy day; people were boisterous, in a mood to continue their celebrating even though a lot of them were getting restless and edgy with the delay in disembarkation.

It didn't disturb her husband Max very much; "People will always have to eat," was his motto. But Lena knew a certain sadness. In spite of the dreadful things the SDF-1 and Macross had gone through, the rebuilt restaurant held a wealth of happy memories.

"Welcome," she said, "welc—*oh!*"

A ghost had come through the door, surrounded by a cloud of brilliance from the brighter EVE "sunlight." Her hands flew to her mouth. "Oh, Kyle, is it really you?"

He took a step closer. In the well-remembered, soft, clear voice, he said gently, "Yes, Mother; I'm home. And I've missed you very much."

Dimly, she was aware of the traffic passing by on the street outside and of Minmei and Rick Hunter waiting a few paces back. Minmei was barely keeping herself from weeping. Rick was straightfaced, showing no emotion; but he envied the Lynn family their connectedness and their warmth, Minmei's tantrums notwithstanding.

When he thought about *it*, Rick realized that the closest thing he had to family was Roy Fokker and—to a slightly lesser extent—his wingmen, Max and Ben. So Rick endeavored not to think of it.

Lena walked haltingly to her son. "Kyle, is this a dream? I can hardly believe my eyes! Oh, my baby!" She cupped his face in her hands.

"No, it's not a dream, Mother; it's me."

Tears rolled down her cheeks. "I've missed you so." Lena threw herself into his arms.

"Gee," Minmei said, wiping away moisture from her eyes. "I'm so happy, I'm gonna cry."

Lena truly noticed Rick and her niece for the first time. "Oh, dear! This is no way to welcome you two home!"

Minmei was snuffling and sobbing openly now. "Aw, don't worry about us," Rick said.

Lena said, "Now, now; come in!" She kept her hold on her son's shoulders as he took another step into the White Dragon. Minmei had assured him that in virtually every detail it was an exact duplicate of the old place, the one that had been destroyed on Macross Island. But this was astounding!

There was a clatter of bowls and a rattle of chopsticks over by the pickup counter. Lynn-Kyle essayed another of his gentle smiles. "Father. I've missed you, too. You're looking well."

Max snorted gruffly, looking the boy over. Gathering the last of the bowls with an irritated grunt, he vanished back into the kitchen.

Lena went to plead with him. "Now, dear! *Please* don't be so—"

But Kyle had caught her wrist, pulling her back. "Mother, don't get upset, I beg you. Father's always been that way around me, you know that."

Washing up the last of the dishes, Max scarcely knew what he was doing; his mind was far away, on the years and the rift between himself and his son. "I always knew he'd come back," he muttered to himself, words drowned out by the jetting water and the other sounds of the kitchen. "No alien sneak attack could've killed *him*."

He had to stop, to dry his eyes and blow his nose. "What else could I think? He *is* my son."

And he couldn't help but surrender to the proud smile he'd kept hidden.

The three Zentraedi spies crouched before the display window of a sushi and tempura shop not far away, gazing hungrily at the appetizing dishes there. Their mouths watered, and their jaws ached with hunger. Rico's face and hands were pressed flat against the glass.

"So d' you suppose that stuff is food?" Konda asked aloud.

Bron had a hypnotized grin on his face, eyes never leaving the display. "Mmm, well, *something* sure smells good here, and I'm getting pretty hungry."

The tiny supply of concentrate capsules they'd brought with them was long gone, and they hadn't eaten since the free food at the party on *Daedalus*'s flight deck the day before.

The other two made ravenous sounds of agreement. Thus far, they hadn't been able to figure out how to requisition food on the SDF-1; Macross City was filled with an astounding variety of things, all of which seemed to change hands through a system based on pieces of paper. But how to get the paper? The humans' system of distribution and ration allocation seemed the maddest thing of all about their society.

The three took a few steps back to stare in fascination at the window and consider their problem. "So who's goin' in to get our rations?" Konda posed the question.

"That's easy," replied Bron, hitching his belt up. "I'll go."

"No, *I'll* go!" Rico insisted. Before the other two could raise the question of tactics, the smallest spy backed up a few steps and, with a running start, slammed his shoulder into the plate glass.

The glass heaved and shattered, pieces of it raining down inside the display case and out on the sidewalk. By some chance, Rico wasn't hurt at all.

The owner, a sturdy-looking woman in her forties wearing flat slippers and an apron over her working clothes, came charging out onto the sidewalk. She held a heavy, long-handled ladle in one formidable-looking fist.

"Hey, what's going on out here— Oh!" She watched dumbfounded as Rico, squatting on his haunches, claimed his right as winner of the food and had the first portion. Konda and Bron were looking on avidly.

But Rico spit out the stuff that was in his mouth and spit again, making horrible faces. "Inedible! *Plaugh!*"

She shook her ladle at him. "What's wrong with you? Of *course* it's not food. Don't you know the difference between real food and a plastic window display?"

She took a step toward him, and Rico fell over backward on the seat of his pants, intimidated by the implement she held—from the confidence she showed, it was obviously a lethal weapon, perhaps a Robotech device. Konda and Bron skipped back, ready to do battle but more inclined to run from such a fearsome opponent.

She set her hands on her hips, looking down at Rico, who

waited miserably to be set upon and wounded or killed. But she said, "If you're trying to eat that, I guess you really *must* be hungry."

She'd thought that arrangements for feeding everyone in the SDF-1 had missed nothing, but perhaps these three loonies were a special case—incapable of coping with even the least contact with bureaucracy. There were always going to be those who fell through the social safety net, she decided, even on the SDF-1.

She wasn't the kind to let people go hungry, and what's more, she was filled with the joy of the return to Earth and the promised end to her hardships. She pointed to the door of her restaurant.

"C'mon inside, you three, and I'll fix you something to eat. And I mean *real* food!"

She went inside, and the three spies looked at one another. "She's going to give us food? Just like that?" Bron said blankly. "Just because she sees we're hungry?"

"How can a chaotic system like this possibly function?" Konda wondered, rubbing his jaw.

"I don't care, just as long as it functions for another half hour or so!" proclaimed Rico, scrambling to his feet.

It was insane, against all logic. And yet, knowing how it felt to be very, very hungry and have someone act toward them in this absurd but *very* welcome manner, they had to admit that there was something about it—something admirable. Something that struck a chord deep within them.

It was completely unlike the Zentraedi; it even smacked of a kind of weakness. But it stirred up new and confusing response patterns.

"Hey, wait for us!" Rico yelped, scuttling along after her. Konda and Bron crowded each other for second place.

14

In recent years, Karl Riber hadn't come so often to mind—not more than once or twice a day, sometimes.

Occasionally, I wonder why I stayed in the service, since it was war that took us apart, war that had made peace-loving Karl volunteer for duty on the Mars Sara Base, that got him killed in that raid.

I was only a teenager, and a rather young one, when he left. When he died, I thought someday the pain would go away, the years would wear it out. I know better now.

Lisa Hayes, *Recollections*

LISA AND HER WATCHMATES SHOWED UP AT THE WHITE DRAGON with Max Sterling bringing up the rear. Max knew that Rick claimed to dislike them, especially Commander Hayes; but Max didn't share his feelings.

He even suspected that Rick protested too much, was too loud in his denunciation of Lisa; Max had seen them together and knew there was more there than met the eye, more than either of them was willing to admit. But far be it from the self-effacing Max Sterling to make any comment.

As for Kim, Sammie, and Vanessa—the ones Rick had dubbed the "bridge bunnies"—Max was delighted to have their company. He thought it good luck to have run into them and been invited along and figured any VT jock who wouldn't jump at the chance to have four good-looking women for company ought to report immediately for a long talk with the flight surgeon.

"Looks kind of crowded, doesn't it?" Kim was saying, just as they realized someone was signaling them. He had a big roundtop all to himself, the only unoccupied table in the place. The bridge bunnies thought it was a sign from providence, and Lisa made no objection to joining him.

"Talk about a case of perfect timing," Rick said as Max ran around trying to hold all the women's chairs at once. "Minmei's long-lost cousin Kyle was in Yokohama. And she wouldn't come back without him."

Lisa's face clouded with disapproval. She knew Rick's orders, and bringing an outsider was tantamount to disobedience. Still, if that was the only way Miss Macross would rejoin the ship, Rick had probably done the right thing, she admitted, even though she couldn't see why the staff people—especially the civilian affairs and morale officers—were so determined that the girl be catered to.

Besides, she knew from her visit to the Alaskan base that there would be no leak of information about the SDF-1's return or Minmei's visit, not even from Minmei's parents. The damned Council gestapo would apply pressure to make sure of that.

"So it's a big reunion," Rick was grousing. "Everybody in the neighborhood came in to see him."

"Gee! What a *hunk!*" Sammie gushed.

Her two cohorts were quick to agree, sounding as if they were about to swoon. Lisa looked over to where Kyle stood with Minmei and his mother, greeting people and exchanging pleasantries with that gentle reserve of his.

Lisa gasped. *He—he reminds me so of Karl!*

Gentle, peace-loving Karl, her one and only love, gone forever.

The Terrible Trio were into their act. "Kim, you shouldn't stare; not so hard!" Sammie giggled.

Kim sniggered back, "Oh, sure! And I suppose *you* saw him *first?*" Sammie dissolved in laughter.

Max seated himself, tossing a forelock of long blue hair out of his eyes, and polished his glasses on his napkin. Vanessa asked Rick, "What did you say her cousin's name was again?"

"I think I said Kyle," Rick grunted.

The Terrible Trio had practiced enough to say it as one, so that everybody in the place could hear: "OH! WELL, HE'S SURE GOOD-LOOKING, ISN'T HE?"

Maybe "bridge bunnies" isn't such a bad name for them, after all, Max mused, putting his glasses back on and taking another look at this Lynn-Kyle.

"Gee, Minmei looks so happy," Kim sighed.

Rick had something sour to say on the subject, but at that moment Mayor Tommy Luan sauntered up to the table, his usual effervescent self.

"Well, well, well, Rick, m'boy! So these are some of your friends, eh? Why don't you introduce me to the ladies, hmm?"

Rick wondered if there was ever a time when Tommy Luan *wasn't* campaigning. But before he could comply, Minmei's cousin was there, with Minmei trailing behind like a faithful pet.

"Hello, Mr. Mayor; glad to have you back on Earth. I'd like to introduce myself: My name is Lynn-Kyle. Welcome to my family's restaurant."

Minmei, clinging to his arm, added, "Hi!"

Rick heard a little sound escape Lisa and saw that something about Kyle made her very distraught. The Terrible Trio fell all over one another greeting Kyle, and Max mumbled some adequate response.

The mayor said heartily, "Well, Kyle, even if you don't like the army, you'll have to admit there are some lovely ladies in the military!"

Lisa gasped. He even had the same convictions as Karl!

"Oh, uh, did I say something perhaps I shouldn't have?" Tommy Luan asked with elaborate innocence. "Well, young people should get to know one another." He sauntered off. "'Scuse me."

Max had the distinct impression that the mayor was wearing a satisfied smirk—as though he'd succeeded at something. But what?

"Was the mayor implying you have something against the service?" Sammie piped up.

Kyle shook his head, the long, straight midnight hair shimmering. "It's not just the military. I don't like fighting of any kind."

Sammie rested her chin on her hands and batted her eyelashes at him. "Oh, really?" For a guy this dreamy, she'd have sat happily listening to him do Zentraedi halftime cheers. Minmei gave Sammie a suspicious scowl.

"Fighting produces nothing!" Kyle declared. "It only results in devastation and destruction!"

Max was studying Kyle with an unusual directness. "Are you saying that everyone in the service enjoys destroying things?"

Rick couldn't help jumping in, even if it offended Minmei. Maybe even because it would. "Well, I didn't join the Robotech Defense Forces because I like devastation and destruction."

Divine as Lynn-Kyle might be, even the Terrible Trio had to nod and murmur their agreement with that. Minmei intervened, afraid that things were about to get out of control.

"Hey, relax, everybody! We're celebrating Kyle's return, after all. I've got it: They're broadcasting that show I taped yesterday. What about turning on the television?"

That met with general acclaim; if Minmei was the darling and idol of the SDF-1, she was an empress among her friends and neighbors. In another moment the six-foot screen showed her in the center of the spotlights, microphone in hand—not that the sound crew couldn't have used directionals, but she preferred it as a prop. She wore a stunning new Kirstin Hammersjald creation.

The crowd in the White Dragon was cheering and stomping and whistling, as was the crowd in the taping studio. Rick strained to catch a little of the song:

I spend the days alone,
Chasing a dream—

All at once the entertainment special disappeared in an avalanche of zigzag, to be replaced by Colton Van Fortespiel.

Everyone in the SDF-1 knew Van Fortespiel, the SDF Broadcasting System's supervising announcer and the only TV anchorman on record to wear dark wraparound sunglasses on camera. His appearance sent a signal of fear through the room;

unscheduled announcements of this sort usually spelled trouble for the dimensional fortress.

For this reason, *and* the sunglasses, Van Fortespiel was sometimes called the Boogieman. The Boogieman was wearing earphones today, too, and speaking into a jumble of mikes that took his voice over the various sound-only circuits, intership comlines, and alternative TV channels.

"We interrupt our regular programming for this very important news bulletin."

The White Dragon resounded with angry resentment. The crowd had felt at home, safe, and had been eagerly watching Minmei; the people wanted no part of any more disaster reports. They were yelling for Minmei's show to be resumed.

"At a news conference moments ago," the Boogieman continued, "Captain Henry Gloval disclosed to the press that permission for any survivors to leave Macross has been denied."

There was a moment of stunned silence as Van Fortespiel shifted his sheets of copy, until a grandmotherly woman howled, "What does he *mean*, 'denied'? Does that mean we're stuck here? For how long?"

Others were raising objections, too, but most were shushing them to hear what else the Boogieman had to say.

"Rumors circulating throughout the ship's upper echelons today indicate that this prohibition may only be temporary."

A man in a brown sport coat shook his fist at the screen and hollered, "We finally make it back to Earth and now they're telling us we have to stay aboard this junk heap?"

A redhaired woman, holding a frightened little girl who wore an RDF insignia on her rompers, wailed, "How much more do they think we can endure? When will all this ever come to an end?"

There were plenty of angry voices to second that. "Yeah; we demand an explanation!" bellowed a guy in a black T-shirt.

But the Boogieman was already returning them to their normally scheduled programming. In another second, Minmei, smiling winsomely in the spotlights, was finishing.

—here by my side!

...and taking a bow. The crowd in the restaurant didn't spare her a clap or a whistle.

Kim murmured, "They spent all that time and *this* was the best announcement they could come up with to break the news?"

Max and Rick traded puzzled, worried looks: *What's she talking about?*

Sammie gulped. "Look, they're not taking it very well. I sure hope this doesn't turn into an all-out rebellion!"

The man in the brown coat said, "Hey, look; we've got those military officers right over there! I say let's get some kind of explanation out of 'em!"

A number of the men there went along with the idea, and in a moment the five RDF members seated at the table found themselves surrounded.

The brown sport coat shook a fist in Rick's face. "C'mon, Lieutenant! Tell us what's goin' on!"

Rick spluttered and stammered, as surprised as anyone. "Well, uh, I guess I don't really know..."

"Stop this!" Lisa snapped. "Stop it right now! How dare you treat us this way? We risked our lives—and plenty of us died!—to get you back here safely!"

Some of the crowd paused at that, but the man in the brown sport coat and a number of others weren't buying it.

"What d' ya want, gratitude?" He sneered. "When we lost everything we had because of your SDF-1? And now you're making us prisoners here?"

He slammed his fist on the table; the Terrible Trio jumped, startled and frightened. "Well? I want a straight answer!"

Lisa tried again, more calmly. "Please, it's just a temporary measure. Just give us—"

He cut her off. "For what, more of the same old promises? We're tired of lies! We're tired of being held here like convicts! Now we take matters into our *own hands*!"

Whoever the brown sport coat was, he was a rabble-rouser of considerable talent. He had almost all the men and quite a few of the women with him, talking about justice and fighting for their rights.

And for Lisa the agonizing thing was that she knew that there was a lot to justify their reaction and that her father had been one of those chiefly responsible for doing this to the Macross survivors.

Some loudmouth was yelling, "Why don't we show 'em we mean business? Let's take these punks *and force* 'em to get us off this ship!"

Lisa stood, gathering the others in by eye. "Let's go."

A broken-toothed man clapped a big paw on her shoulder. "Hold it!"

She tried to stare him down. "You'd better let me go."

He shook her. "Siddown!"

But a hand closed on *his* shoulder. "Okay, that's enough."

It was Max Sterling. Rick, halfway out of his chair to help Lisa, did a bit of a double take. Max had been sitting beside him a moment before. *What'd he do,* teleport *over there?*

Max's voice was still mild, but his face showed a certain intensity Rick had seen only during combat. *Look out, tough guy!* Rick thought to the broken-toothed man.

"Take your hand off her. Now."

Max had barely gotten it out when the man threw a punch, screaming, "Shut up!"

Max ducked, but not far. Rick had seen him do this before; Max's incredible reflex time and psychomotor responses let him deal with such things by split seconds and fractions of an inch.

Max avoided the clumsy haymaker and delivered a jolting left, snapping the other's head around, stepping back neatly as he began to collapse.

Other members of what had now become a mob saw what had happened and began to converge on Max, snarling and getting ready to fight.

Max glared at them, unruffled. "You'd better get back."

Somebody shrieked, "Let's get 'em!" and Rick found that he couldn't get to Max because the mob was closing in on *him,* too. A man in a green turtleneck threw a wild left. Rick bobbed under, came up, and planted a solid uppercut, sending him staggering back. Two more men closed in, swinging hastily and inaccurately. He avoided them, backpedaling.

Max was taking on a very muscular young man who had plenty of power but not much style. Max warded off a roundhouse with an inside block, getting a quick hold on that arm. Max's fist went ballistic under the guy's chin, lifting him right off his feet. It was the brawler's good fortune that his tongue was well back in his mouth, or his teeth would have snipped it off.

The muscular one landed sprawling across a table; it crashed down, slamming him on the back of the head as he landed on his butt on the floor.

Lynn-Kyle had neither advanced to help his cousin's friends nor withdrawn from the scene. Rick got one brief look at him: Kyle was standing as rigid and indifferent as a stone idol.

Rick stopped another vigilante with a short, hard shot to the sternum, then rocked him back with a left cross.

Things had gone very well for the two VT pilots up to now, but more and more men were getting ready to wade into the melee as soon as an opening occurred. On the outskirts of things, Lisa and the Terrible Trio were doing what they could. Quite a number of self-appointed public prosecutors never got to mix it up with the pilots because a chop across the neck or a kick to the kneecap put them out of the fight for good.

But the odds against them kept growing. With no chance for a breather and no escape route, Rick and Max knew things would probably swing the other way shortly. There was no helping that, and the brawl had gone too far to be stopped now; they fought on. Rick was accomplished in hand to hand, quick, well trained, and in good shape, but Max Sterling was simply unleashed lightning.

It was then that Max, blocking a punch so that he had his foe's arm in a firm lock, threw the man through the air. Only this fellow, thrashing and kicking madly, was lofted straight at Lynn-Kyle, who had been watching the fight impassively. Behind Kyle, Minmei let out a kind of squeak and ducked for cover.

Kyle never even moved his feet; he simply bent aside and struck, sending the unfortunate man flying through the air again, away from his cousin and himself.

The vigilante crashed into the table the muscular fellow had overturned, shattering it on impact as a result of the amazing force Lynn-Kyle's move had imparted to him and somehow contriving to land on his face.

Two of the brawler's friends were at his side instantly. "You all right?" one of them asked idiotically when it was obvious the man was not all right.

The brawler looked up woozily. "Who *is* that guy? He's an incredible fighter!"

"His name's Kyle," said the other buddy, "and that was nothin' but luck!" He straightened. "But I'm gonna fix him."

15

"I'll tell ya somethin' about your Lynn-Kyle," Max said. "He might be anti-military, but he's no pacifist. What'd ya think, Gandhi could do spin kicks?"

The Collected Journals of Admiral Rick Hunter

KYLE WAITED, SERENE AND UNMOVING.

"No! *No!*" Lisa breathed, seeing them close in on him. It would be too much like having gentle Karl Riber beaten up. But there was nothing she could do; it was all she and the Terrible Trio could do to hold their own against the peripheral crowd members.

Rick wondered later if Max Sterling knew all along—or had at least guessed—what was to happen next and had deliberately thrown that first opponent Kyle's way. Max, in his supremely humble way, assured Rick that such a thing was preposterous. Rick might have believed him more if he hadn't seen the things Max could do in combat.

The first two were a pair of stumblebums; barely moving at all, Kyle disposed of them contemptuously with foot sweeps, evasions, leg trips, and beginner's-class shoulder throws.

That drew the attention of the men waiting for another crack at Max and Rick; more and more of them came at Kyle.

Minmei's cousin seemed to have chosen a particular spot on the floor and decided to defend it—not from preference but rather as an exercise of will and proficiency. Certainly, the fight didn't seem like much of a challenge—at least at first.

There was a lot of *aikido* in his style, plus *bando*, some *judo*, *uichi-*

ryu, and a lot of stuff Rick couldn't identify. It wasn't until he was pressed very hard that Kyle used his feet, and after that there were teeth and blood on his area of the White Dragon's floor.

Defending himself on several fronts, Kyle didn't seem to notice the roughhouser closing in behind him. Lisa happened to see it, and she had the weird impression that he knew what was coming and chose to undergo it as a sort of test, as if he *wanted* to be hurt.

Be that as it may, the big bruiser got Kyle in a full nelson, and somebody else tagged him good and hard on the mouth. Kyle didn't seem to feel it much; he shrugged down out of the hold with some fluid move, sidekicking the man who'd done the punching so that he went down and stayed down.

Then Kyle whirled and brought the flat of his hand in an unsweeping blow along the face of the one who'd held him. The man reeled back, face leaking crimson but not as badly as he would have been if Lynn-Kyle had been truly angry.

Kyle had taken just enough of the pressure off Rick and Max so that they were doing okay again. They'd both taken more than a few shots and at one time or another had, between them, squared off with just about everybody on the other side of what had become a minor war. The opponents were bouncing back more slowly now, and many of them were out of it for good.

As for Lynn-Kyle, he was a whirlwind, leaping over and ducking under, spin kicking but never surrendering the spot he'd chosen to defend in the middle of the White Dragon. He jumped impossibly high, out of the way of a powerful kick, got his opponent in a wristlock, and rammed him headfirst into a man who was attacking from the opposite side.

It was an amazing demonstration, like some martial-arts fantasy, marking the beginning of Lynn-Kyle's legend on the SDF-1. But it should be remembered that for the most part he was facing antagonists who'd already been around the dance floor once or even twice—and in some more insistent cases three times—with Rick and Max.

At one point, Rick put away a shaven-headed tough who'd been trying to gouge his eyes, working fast, jabbing combinations with knuckles that were long since lacerated and bleeding. He turned and saw Kyle, leaping high, lash out with the sword edge of his left foot and down another opponent.

Rick wiped blood from his face. "Hey, Kyle! Why don'tcha hand him a *pamphlet*?"

Rick went back to his own fight. Kyle made no response but wondered if the VT pilot knew how deeply that jape—and the dissonance of this violence—upset Kyle's inner harmonies.

The fight didn't so much end as slow to a halt; at last there was no one to come at them again. Rick was left sitting on the floor, huffing and puffing, bone-weary and sore all over. Max was panting, too, leaning against a wall, blood seeping from a swollen, split lip, his ribs starting to ache where somebody's knee had gotten a piece of him.

Lisa and the Terrible Trio were standing by the line of brawlers they'd taken out of the action, having neatly composed some of them as if for sleep. Lynn-Kyle stood squarely on the spot he'd chosen to defend in the middle of his family's restaurant.

"You okay, Rick?" Max panted.

Rick was too tired to do anything but nod slowly, tonguing a tooth that felt like it had been loosened. He felt a certain dread: There were some inflexible laws aboard the SDF-1, mandated by the insanely unlikely circumstances of so many civilians and service people thrown together in such close quarters for such a long time.

Many of those laws had to do with *"No Fighting with the Townies!"* Rick figured Gloval was going to be mildly crazy about all of this. Then it occurred to Lieutenant Hunter to think about the bigger picture, about what was happening all over the super dimensional fortress in the wake of the Boogieman's announcement.

We'll be lucky if there is an SDF-1 by tonight! he realized.

Lisa and the Terrible Trio were dusting their hands off, making a few first-aid suggestions to the people they'd taken out of the action. It occurred to Rick that without them, he and Max and even Kyle would have gone down, martial arts notwithstanding. Minmei was gazing at Kyle with stars and hearts and flowers in her eyes.

"Oh, Kyle, I'm so proud of you! Are you okay?" She threw her arms around his neck.

Lynn-Kyle only nodded and made a soft, "Mm hmm."

"'Okay'?" Rick sniggered tiredly, and spit out a gobbet of blood.

Max had come upright, staring at Kyle strangely. "They barely laid a hand on you." Kyle only looked down at the floor like some demure maiden.

Men who had been in the fight were helping each other to their feet, staunching blood flows, helping hobbling friends. One tucked an injured hand into his shirtfront with much pain, wiped the blood from his broken nose, and said grudgingly, "He's the best I've seen or fought against. That's the truth."

"Yeah," said Max Sterling reflectively. "He's got moves I never saw before. Doesn't make sense." He went over toward Kyle, and Rick hauled his aching body to its feet, prepared to back up his friend if the ultimate slugfest were to begin.

There was a sudden, particular something in Max's manner now: an acuity, an unveiled dangerousness, that the aw-shucks everyday Sterling demeanor usually shrouded.

But Max only stood looking at Kyle, and Kyle back at Max. Max said after a moment, "You're a pretty well-trained fighter for someone who doesn't like to fight."

They stood measuring each other. On the one hand was quiet, bespectacled Max, with his natural gifts, miraculous coordination, and speed so superior that he could afford to be humble in all things—already a Robotech legend. Unassuming and kind unless some evil threatened. Max the placid and benign, truer to what Kyle aspired to be, in a way, than Kyle himself.

On the other hand was Kyle, seemingly apart from any worldly consideration or motivation, his incredible martial-arts skills just a reflection of things that relentlessly drove him for spiritual transcendence. People sought him, virtually courted him, sensing that he'd passed beyond everything that was superficial, and wanting—what? His attention and approval? His friendship? He didn't have them to give.

But people wanted it more than anything. Kyle's gift was a kind of cold invulnerability that brought him close to being superhuman for the most dire and yet formidable reasons, reasons that combined the very best and the very worst in him.

Those who knew certain spiritual and fighting systems could see the symptoms in him: all things lay within his grasp, excepting only that which he wanted most. So his innermost passions had been brought under control by an act of will, the dark side of his nature subdued in a battle that made lesser contests, mere physical duels, seem childishly easy.

And that made for a powerful fighter who was without fear and who would give obeisance to the very best conventional values— while his inner being fought an endless war.

Some of the people who were in the White Dragon that day later swore that the very air between Max and Kyle crackled like a kind of summer lightning or perhaps the terrifying glow between two segments of a critical mass being brought too close together.

But Kyle lowered his eyes to the floor and said softly, "It was just something that had to be done, I guess." His head came up, and he looked about at the men he'd bested. "I'm sorry." A trickle of blood ran from the corner of his mouth down to his chin.

Minmei was deciding how best to show her concern for Kyle, when Lisa stepped up to him, holding a scented, daintily folded little handkerchief in her hand. This was the woman who'd kept a rioter from pouncing on Kyle two minutes earlier by bringing down a chair on his head.

"You're bleeding! Maybe this'll help."

He drew away from it as if it carried plague, but his voice was still soft and measured. "Please don't bother. I'd rather not have help from any of you people. But thank you, anyway."

She was shattered. "I see."

Minmei was quick to see her opening and use it, snatching the handkerchief from Lisa's upturned palm. "That's right; Kyle dislikes servicemen."

Lisa stared at the floor and hoped the hot red flush of anger in her cheeks didn't show too much. Service*men*?

"Let *me* help," Minmei said, dabbing at the wound on his cheek.

Kyle hissed in pain. "It hurts if you press too hard."

She drew a quick breath. "Oh, Kyle, please forgive me!"

Punches and kicks hadn't seemed to bother him that much. "Is he for real or am I crazy?" Max muttered. Rick shrugged; if he hadn't just seen Kyle take care of some of the more hard-core rowdies aboard the SDF-1, he would have said Minmei's cousin was a complete wimp.

If it was an act, it was brilliant. The bridge bunnies were oozing sympathy for Kyle, and somebody was going to have to stick a stretcher under Commander Hayes if she got any more emotional over his well-being, while Minmei glared at all the other women jealously and shielded Kyle from them as much as she could. Miss Macross stroked her cousin's arm with a proprietary air.

Rick turned to Max, feeling the swelling on his own forehead and the throbbing of assorted contusions suffered in the riot. "Max, if you're asking me, the answer is *yes*!" Rick told him.

Azonia, mistress and overlord of the Zentraedi, surveyed the strategic situation from the command post of her nine-mile-long flagship.

Matters were coming to a head. She was determined that *this* would be the proof of her abilities. A stellar chance! Once she defeated these Micronian upstarts, the universe would be hers. Supreme commander? That would lie well within her grasp, and farewell, Dolza!

Or perhaps she would become the *new* Robotech Mistress. Others had played that dangerous game, only to lose. But none played it as well as she, Azonia was confident.

She was less than happy at the moment, however, having just been informed that Khyron, the mad genius of war, had again disobeyed her orders.

Azonia rose to her feet from the thronelike command chair on the bridge of her own vaunted, combat-tested battleship, fury striking from her like lightning as though she were a goddess who could smash worlds.

And, in fact, Azonia was.

"What? Are you saying Khyron left the fleet's holding formation in violation of *my orders*?"

The communications officer knew that tone of voice and was quick to genuflect before her, then touch her forehead in abasement. "Yes, Commander."

She was tall even for a Zentraedi woman, some fifty-five feet and more. Her mannishly short hair had been dyed blue, not because she cared for meaningless fads but rather so she would not be thought *unaware*.

She had exotic, oblique eyes that were piercing beam weapons of intellect that had served Azonia's rise beyond her contemporaries to the very pinnacle of Zentraedi command. "That is all," she said coldly.

"Yes, Commander." The messenger withdrew quickly and very gratefully; beheading the bearer of bad news was a not-uncommon Zentraedi custom, which among other things served to keep the lower orders in their place. She was glad—and lucky—to have her life.

But Azonia had dismissed the messenger from her mind completely; her concentration was all for the problem at hand. Technical readouts and displays told her all the details she needed to know: The Backstabber, with a strike force from his infamous Seventh Mechanized Division had, by Robotech fission, detached a major vessel-form from his own flagship and was proceeding at flank speed toward the spot where the Micronians had landed their stolen starship.

Azonia touched a control almost languidly. Close-up details showed streamers of fire and ionization trailing from Khyron's craft, its outermost skin glowing red-hot; he was making his entry into the Earth's atmosphere at a madly acute angle, risking severe friction damage.

Azonia had sufficient experience to know that Khyron and his attack troops were sitting out a roller coaster ride in an oven, all in the name of a possible extra few minutes of surprise.

It was so audacious. It was so willful, so disdainful of anyone's criticism or interference. So Zentraedi. Azonia resumed her throne, chin on fist. "Khyron, what have you come up with this time, eh?"

She was in some small part envious, sorry that she wouldn't be there for the fight. With Khyron in charge, there was sure to be a splendid battle, bloodshed—that highest glory that was *conquest*.

On a previous venture, Khyron had been yanked from his objective at the last moment by Breetai's manual-override return command, which had caused the Backstabber's war machines to return to the fleet despite his countermanding orders. Khyron had apparently taken steps to ensure that it couldn't happen to him again.

By now the Earthlings would be hearing the peal of Khyron's thunder. Azonia, eyes slitted like a cat's, savored the moment, knowing she couldn't lose either way. If the Backstabber won, the credit would go to her as armada commander, she would make sure of that; if he lost and was unfortunate or unwise enough to return to the fleet, she would have the pleasure of executing him herself.

Azonia savored the thought. Violence and death and a certain sensual cruelty were things to command any Zentraedi's emotions. Khyron was becoming quite intriguing.

Azonia watched the displays with feline glee. Decorate him, kill him; she was equally eager to do either one.

16

There before him were the Micronians, doing everything that was anathema to the Zentraedi. But the lure of the forbidden was always strong in Khyron, and so there were certain things about Micronian behavior that, I think, he found tremendously seductive—not the weakling things, of course, but rather the sensual.

Is it any wonder he loathed and hated them, could not bear to have them even exist?

Grel, aide to Khyron

S HE'D BEEN THROUGH THIS DRILL BEFORE, BUT IT DIDN'T MAKE IT any easier. Donna Wilhelm, an enlisted-rating tech who was relief-watch fill-in for Sammie, tried not to lose her composure and let her voice quaver.

Her fingers clenched at the edges of the console, so hard that it felt like she might crease it. "Captain Gloval, unidentified cruiser-class spacecraft closing on our position at Mach seven."

She was the one Claudia had chewed out for daydreaming; Donna was exacting now, more practiced. She'd learned the lessons anybody under Gloval learned, and as a result she was capable of manning her station through hell's own flames. Which looked like it was about to become a job requirement.

Donna hadn't heard footsteps, but Gloval was suddenly at her shoulder, massive and calm, whacking his briar pipe against the heel of his shoe to knock out a bit of dottle. "Punch it up, please."

"Yes, sir. Altitude twelve thousand." Donna lit up her part of the bridge with tactical displays. It was a given that this could be the minute in which every soul aboard died.

But that couldn't excuse sloppiness in the discharge of one's obligations. There was a pure, white-hot kind of *bushido*, an ultimate calmness in matters of overwhelming importance, a very privileged eye-of-the-storm serenity, that the people on the bridge of SDF-1 were expected to have.

Once you'd been a part of it, it was just impossible to settle for anything less. Donna had learned it in a school that permitted very few errors and *no* inattention, under Gloval, Lisa Hayes, Claudia Grant, and the others.

So now Donna did her duty, up to SDF-1 standards, which is to say without flaw and with the guts of a cat burglar. "Eleven thousand," she updated. "If it maintains present course, it'll touch down approx ten miles from the SDF-1 magnetic bearing three-two-five."

It couldn't be anything but trouble; the war was on again, and if peace had seemed too good to be true, that was because it *was*. But Gloval's broad hand patted Donna's shoulder for a moment, transferring what felt like an infinite calm even while he was calling orders to other bridge personnel.

"Order up a B status encrypted comline to headquarters immediately! And one of you find Commander Hayes and get her up here on the double! Somebody else tell Ghost and Skull teams to get ready for a hot scramble!"

People were doing all of that, and still the bridge was as quiet as a well-run switchboard. Gloval told Donna Wilhelm, "Well done. Give me updates every fifteen seconds, understood? And if you see I'm not listening, come stand on my foot."

Then he was gone, and the SDF-1 bridge was quietly chaotic with a general-quarters combat alert. Arm Hammerhead missiles and Deca missiles and Scorpion missiles; power up to main gun batteries; secondaries; to all firing positions. Hot scrambles, ready on go, aye.

Donna looked at her screens and got ready to relay the first update to Gloval. Over a year ago, her family had been one of those that were simply vacuumed up in the catastrophic first encounter between Zentraedi and human. Now her father was an emergency team specialist, her mother supervised an elite EVA squad, and her younger brother was dead, one of Ghost Team's KIAs back in that big blitzkrieg in Saturn's rings.

So Donna did her duty. The aliens had followed SDF-1 to Earth; the aliens would follow the SDF-1 everywhere, hound the ship and hound those within it until this fight was settled one way or the other. Only, there was one thing that the aliens didn't seem to understand: The SDF-1's crew would never surrender now.

No matter; it was war again. And the Zentraedi didn't know that they themselves were refining, like precious metals in some torturous crucible, a counterforce within the human race that was their match—in willpower if not in firepower—and more.

Much more.

In the vast command center under the Alaskan wilderness, an operator called out over his headset, "Confirmed enemy craft continues descent, sir. Will touch down at point K-32, R-56 Bravo."

The duty officer, Brigadier General Theroux, leaned forward, staring up at the immense display screen. "Are you certain? Are you positive that this craft is confirmed as the enemy?"

"That's affirmative, sir."

Theroux got to his feet, squaring away his cap. This was Command's worst fear made real. The Grand Cannon wasn't yet ready to fire, and even if it had been, the approaching alien warship wasn't in its range. Until the planned network of unique dish satellites was in place to redirect the Grand Cannon's superbolts as needed, it was virtually useless.

Theroux opened an emergency com channel, sure that the ruling council would want to reconsider standing instructions under the circumstances. But he could reach only General Herbert and Marshal Zukav.

"And the enemy is headed straight for the SDF-1," Theroux finished his brief situation report.

General Herbert's face blinked at him out of the screen. "And? You mean you haven't carried out Special Order Seventy-three yet?"

Theroux said desperately, "But sir, that will only—"

"Carry out your duty!" Zukav screamed, florid-faced, from another screen. "Do it this instant or I'll personally see you hanged for mutiny!" The screens blanked.

That will only goad them into attacking the SDF-1, and the SDF-1 is a sitting duck, Theroux had been about to say. But Herbert and Zukav knew that as well as he. It was as if they *wanted* the battle fortress obliterated—

Brigadier General Theroux forced his thoughts away from that line of contemplation. He had his orders.

He addressed his launch control officer. "Very well, then: execute Special Order Seventy-three. Launch missiles immediately." And as techs were acknowledging and carrying out the command, he murmured, "And heaven help us."

"We are now monitoring all base com signals and telemetry," Claudia reported.

"Very good," Gloval said. While he had no direct orders *not* to eavesdrop on his superiors, it went against all operating procedure. But he had so few things working to his advantage in this crisis; if a man with cloven hooves, smelling of brimstone, had appeared on the bridge at that moment, it's very likely that the captain would have struck a bargain with him.

Claudia looked over to Lisa, who seemed lost in thought even though her boards appeared to be registering a lot of activity. "Lisa?" Claudia called softly. "Lisa! Girl, what seems to be the problem? You've been in some kind of daydream ever since you got back. Tell me, is it Kyle?"

For a moment Lisa looked like a startled deer. Then she became very defensive, even though she should have been used to her best friend's teasing by then. "Claudia, you know that's just not true!"

"Ahem," Gloval said softly, materializing behind them. "Ladies…"

They both got back to work, but Claudia was chuckling and an angry red spot appeared on each of Lisa's cheeks.

Kim shattered the gentle, joking atmosphere for good. "Captain, headquarters has just launched defense missiles. Our instruments show approximately fifteen seconds to impact."

Gloval settled into his chair. "Fifteen seconds, understood." *What in blazes can those fools be hoping to accomplish? Conventional weapons are totally useless against the Zentraedi.*

"Prepare to send in the Veritechs," he said.

With the disappearance of Dr. Lang and the SDF-1 and the destruction of its orbital force in the wake of the initial Zentraedi attack, Earth's defense command had been forced to fall back on older technologies, at least until their Grand Cannon was completed.

Even the production of VTs was impossible, since most of the necessary fabricating and power-plant replicating devices were on the battle fortress; the earthly RDF fighters who'd greeted the ship on its return were just that, ordinary fighters, even though they *looked* like VTs. The only real Robotech weapons now in the Council's possession were the handful of Battloids that had, predictably, been preempted to guard the Council's own Alaskan warren.

The huge, silvery missiles that rose up from the planet's surface now, recently manufactured and bearing the kite-like delta insignia of the Robotech Defense Forces, were nevertheless primitive in comparison with Robotechnology. But the order to fire was in place, and the workings of command structure spun and reacted automatically.

Khyron's great cruiser moved more slowly in the thick lower atmosphere. He didn't even bother trying to evade the missiles or shoot them down; he relished the shudder and thunder of their harmless detonations against his vessel's massive armor. He loved toying with his prey, loved to pretend that slaughter was battle.

Hellish fire washed across the ship's armor and swirled away behind it, like foam off a killer whale, having no effect.

Behind the big transparent bubble of his command post, Khyron looked down contentedly at the activity on his warship's bridge. Grel, his second in command, growled in a fierce, deep Zentraedi guttural, "Khyron, what about a counterattack?"

It was Khyron's pleasure to speak differently from his fellows, to be unique in all things. His accent was over-refined, almost foppish, though the Zentraedi lacked such a concept except in his case. But few people had ever dared call the Backstabber on it, and all of those had met with grief.

"A brilliant idea, Grel! But just what are we counterattacking?"

Grel's thick brows met as he pondered the question. "You mean," he said slowly, "that this planet is not the actual main objective."

Khyron's handsome, sinister face lit with a predatory smile. "You're beginning to see the light." Another glorious victory for Khyron! And oblivion for the hated SDF-1; things were going perfectly.

"Veritechs, you have permission to engage the enemy," Lisa said. "Fire at will."

A swarm of angry VTs swooped in on the descending alien, lances of bright blue energy stabbing from their pulsed laser-array cannon, another of Lang's developments.

"SDF-1 to United Earth Command," Lisa transmitted. "Our fighter squadron has initiated contact." *Chew on that, you burrowing moles!*

The VTs were in close, flown by veterans who knew where to aim and how to avoid the bigger ship's clumsy cannon volleys. They did only minor damage on the first few passes; but there were dozens of them, so more serious damage would be inflicted if they were allowed to have their way.

Gloval was counting on something he'd noticed before: There were definitely differing factions among the enemy, sometimes working at cross-purposes. One faction seemed to be commanded by an injudicious hothead, and this attack smacked of him—or her.

Gloval was right. Even as the enemy cruiser closed on the dimensional fortress, fighter bays opened and alien mecha poured forth to battle for the skies. For this engagement, Khyron had elected to use a mix of his best fighting machines; the VTs swooped in to find themselves facing stubby triple-engine fighters with fuselages like narrow eggs: tri-thrusters—Botoru pursuit ships, agile and spoiling for a fight.

But no more so than the RDF fliers, who were now on their home planet, their backs literally to the sea. There was nowhere to run, no thought of surrender, and no battle plan needed except to make the aliens pay very, very dearly for each moment they spent in Earth's atmosphere.

"I'm getting heavy contact reports and increased readings of enemy activity, sir," Claudia relayed.

Out where war mecha jousted with spears of pure ruin for the fate of the SDF-1 and the human race, lines of fire and counterfire crisscrossed ferociously, taking a heavy toll on both sides.

Despite a steady rain of blasts from the SDF-1's primary and secondary batteries, Khyron's cruiser swung in a low pass toward the battle fortress. Gloval wasted no time wishing that the all-powerful main gun could be fired. That wasn't possible; damage to the main gun mechanism suffered on reentry hadn't been repaired yet. So the battle would have to be won another way.

More VTs were ordered to the flight decks, Rick's Vermilions among them, and every weapon on the ship concentrated fire on the invader. Gloval spoke quickly to engineering, preparing for other, desperate measures.

The SDF-1's fire was punishing Khyron's ship as even the VTs couldn't, but that didn't matter to the Backstabber; he needed only a little longer. His cruiser passed overhead, all batteries firing, the two heavyweight ships hammering away at each other with all they had, inflicting appalling damage.

At the same time the cruiser released more mecha, a virtual hail of Battlepods that dropped down toward the SDF-1. The pods and the tri-thruster pursuit ships kept up a heavy fusillade. The VTs did their best to turn back the assault drop, but they were simply outnumbered; there would be many empty bunks down in the squadron quarters that night, if indeed the SDF-1 lasted at all.

Leading his troops in his own tremendously powerful officer's Battlepod, Khyron saw the carnage and grinned like a lunatic.

"Keep firing and don't stop until we've destroyed every last one of the miserable Micronian vermin!"

17

And so the stage was set by the eternal mandala, the yin and the yang—the good that is in evil, and the evil that is in good. Human betrayal, Zentraedi disobedience of several kinds, and yes, that fanatic courage of the aliens—these all played their part that day.

Jan Morris, *Solar Seeds, Galactic Guardians*

CLAUDIA TURNED TO CALL TO GLOVAL. "A MIXED GROUP OF fighting vehicles is approaching our decks, sir. The Veritechs couldn't hold them."

"I want Vermilion ready for immediate launch," Gloval snapped.

Lisa found herself seeing Rick's face and shook her head to regain her concentration. "Yes, sir."

As his ship and Max Sterling's were raised to the flight deck, Rick thought, *Well, here we go again. And how many will die this time? Damn all Zentraedi! You want death? Come on, then; we'll give you death!*

Claudia updated, "Enemy breakthrough heaviest now at blocks three, seven, niner, and sixteen."

Gloval turned and called, "Get the tactical corps mecha out on deck. Double-check to make sure all civil defense mecha are in position and have them stand by for possible redeployment!"

Everybody knew what that meant: Gloval was practically admitting that the aliens might penetrate to the very interior of the ship itself—perhaps to Macross City.

Lisa shuddered, but she kept on at her work, seemingly calm

and self-possessed. "Vermilion Team, stand by at block number three for protection and await further orders." From that position a number of the dimensional fortress's functioning gun turrets and missile tubes could provide some cover for them until Gloval decided where to commit them.

"Roger," Rick acknowledged.

Almost all the other VT teams were either in the air or waiting to be lifted to the flight deck, but that didn't seem to be daunting the enemy. More and more alien mecha were dropping, an unbelievable assault force. *That cruiser must have been packed cheek by jowl with them!* Lisa thought.

She saw Vermilion forming up on an outboard pickup. Enemy fire was sizzling down all around them, blue-white beams that vaporized the nonskid and scored the armor deeply.

Rick's voice came on again. "Hey there, Commander Hayes! How many of these things do we have to shoot down before they stop coming at us? Ten thousand or twenty thousand? Or two million, or what? Just checking, you understand."

A sudden volley hit right near his VT and almost got it; she could hear the shock and adrenaline in his voice as he cried out, "God damn you!" at the aliens.

Lisa looked stunned. "Hold position," she said slowly, feeling her skin go cold and her heart pounding so hard she could feel it all through her. She watched her screen, hypnotized, waiting for the next salvo to claim him.

"Await… further orders…" she managed. She saw Rick's face before her, in a cockpit, but then suddenly Karl Riber's—or no, it was Lynn-Kyle's, wasn't it? What was happening to her?

There was such a thing as personal initiative, and junior officers—especially team leaders—were expected to recognize a time when it was their duty to exercise it.

"Well, I'm getting these fighters out of here before it's too late!" Rick snapped, as much to himself as to Commander Hayes. "All right, Vermilion; follow me!"

There was no time for a catapult launch, even if the cat crews had been able to function in that firestorm. None could, and many of the brave crews were down for good.

The VTs rolled behind Rick, engines shrilling; only Robotechnology gave them power to reach sufficient airspeed in the short space available. Rick's VT howled out into the air, followed by Max, Ben, and the rest.

Even so, they hadn't gotten away fast enough. The fifth VT took a direct hit while lifting, crashed to the deck again, burning out of control because overworked damage and firefighting crews were fully occupied elsewhere. From the explosion, it was clear that the pilot had died instantly.

But the deck would have to be cleared for more launches and for eventual landings, assuming any Veritechs came back this day. A courageous cat crew officer named Moira Flynn climbed into a cargo mover. Braving the flames, the exploding VT ordnance, and the withering enemy fire, she began bulldozing the wreckage to the edge of the deck, to dump it into the sea.

Lisa could barely spare an instant in which to watch the launch of Vermilion; there were a thousand other things that demanded her attention. But she shut her eyes for an instant. *Please let him be all right!* But Rick's face was superimposed in her mind with Karl's, with Kyle's...

Out on the flight deck, a bulky Gladiator attack mecha from the tactical corps—a smaller, cruder version of the Battloids—fired its chest cannon, missile racks, and straight-lasers. It suddenly found itself confronted by a quintet of Battlepods that dropped to the deck almost simultaneously, blowing the Gladiator away; both human crewmembers were dead practically before they knew what was happening.

More pods landed, firing the heavy guns mounted on their plastrons and, in some special cases, missile launchers, particle cannon, and other offensive armaments.

Two more Gladiators came forward to seal the hole in the defensive lines, braving the enemy rounds to throw out a wall of fire of their own. The crewmembers loved life as much as anybody, but they were unswerving in the defense of their ship and their planet. They opened up with gatlings and missiles and lasers. The Battlepods kept coming until the mecha were at point-blank range.

Another Gladiator went down. Amid the smoke and confusion, the third found itself out of ammunition and standing toe to toe with a pod.

The Gladiator crew reacted at once; as the pod sprang at it, their war machine swung an armored fist, caving in the lower half of the Zentraedi's plastron. The Gladiator ducked, and the pod crashed to the deck a little beyond.

Unarmed, the RDF mecha turned to grapple with the next pod, but it leapt high in the air like an immense grasshopper, all guns firing. The Gladiator collapsed in on itself, becoming a fireball.

Rick lined up another bogey, one of the small, fiendishly fast Botoru pursuit ships. The enemy fired a poorly aimed stream of the annihilating energy discs that were one of its armaments, then flared like a meteor before the Vermilion Leader's volley.

The battle was the biggest fighter ratrace yet, an the more frantic and hysterical because it swirled through the relatively small area around the battle fortress. Speeds were therefore much lower than usual, but distances were so short and maneuvering room so limited that everything happened in split seconds.

One dogfight got mixed up with another. Pilots from both sides collided, shot friend instead of foe, lost sight of their prey only to find a bandit on their tail.

Lisa's voice sounded in Rick's headphones. "Proceed to enemy penetration at block number seven."

Only Max and Ben were left now. They managed to make it over to the designated defensive block, where they were witnesses to something out of an old-time Western movie.

Civil Defense mecha had been rushed up to serve as reinforcements for the tacticals. The thickset war machines, like walking dreadnoughts, stood straddle-legged on the deck, blasting away at the massed enemy.

Excalibur Mark VIs and Gladiators, drum-armed Spartans with

their huge circular canisters of missile launchers, and multibarreled Raider Xs swinging their beam cannon this way and that—they all stood shoulder to shoulder against the main Zentraedi onslaught as enemy fire took them out of the line one by one.

The pods were closing in fast; the enormous losses they'd suffered seemed to have no effect on the size of the fleet. They had advanced to a point where none of the SDF-1's primary batteries— and only a few of the remaining secondaries—had a line of fire on them; the batteries were primarily for air defense.

The RDF mecha were standing their ground, laying down fire with everything they had. They knew that if their line collapsed, there would be nothing to stop the aliens from getting into the ship—and winning the war.

It was truly the hour of the attack mecha, with even the VTs taking a back seat. They made their stand as the Zentraedi closed the distance by leaps and bounds. The killing in the skies had numbed him, yet Rick thought this was one of the most savage scenes ever seen during the war.

As Vermilion came in to see what they could do to help, two foremost Raider Xs went up like cans of firecrackers. The pods bounded past the wreckage to close in on the last of the defenders. Khyron was gleeful, nearly mad with the joy of war, as he led the final charge, addressing the cannon of his Officer's Pod to a new target. In minutes, the ship would be his; and with it, the universe.

In the meantime, three of the accursed VTs made a close strafing run, destroying the leading line of pods. But other pods would soon be there to deal with them; even Veritechs couldn't keep Zor's ultimate creation away from Khyron now!

Khyron was distracted by two lumbering Excaliburs that were closing in on him, their power low, missile racks exhausted. He blew them both away in the same moment with the tremendous derringerlike cannon that were arms of the Officer's Pod.

The VTs were making another pass, and the enemy mecha were being outrageously stubborn—but the final conclusion should only take another minute or so.

But just then Khyron heard an alarm signal on his instrument panel. He read his indicators, turned, and craned to look up into the distant sky. "What's this? *No! Impossible!*"

Grimly, without looking up from her data displays, Claudia said, "Captain, a second enemy attack force is on the way down now, from another ship. They appear to be a new type of mecha."

Leading her combat drop, Miriya looked approvingly at the bitter struggle raging all around the dimensional fortress. Behind her came a full battalion of her Quadrono Battalion's powered armor mecha.

Azonia was still reiterating instructions over the com net, a rather offensive bit of interference, Miriya thought. "Miriya, the purpose of your operation is to thwart Khyron's plan. Therefore, do not fire at the enemy or damage the dimensional fortress."

Azonia had done some thinking in the interim and had consulted several of her personal informants. It seemed Khyron was playing a game truly his own; everything pointed to his intention to take the SDF-1 for himself.

And Azonia would win no approval from her superiors or the Robotech Masters if that were to happen; quite the opposite, in fact. Thus: Miriya and her Quadrono Battalion were launched to stop him.

So a Zentraedi warrior is expected not to fire at the enemy, eh? Miriya smiled to herself maliciously. "Well now, it's too bad I never heard that order because my communications gear is malfunctioning, Azonia!"

Her own personal mecha-suit was the one that had so dazzled the RDF during her insertion of the three spies. It was super-charged, more maneuverable and powerful than any other in the Zentraedi fleet. Now she zoomed down like a lightning bolt, blowing an unsuspecting VT out of the air with a double stream of the annihilation discs, destroying another a split second later.

"I love it when a good plan works out well," she said languidly. And the good plan in this case was her own—the one that had gotten her another crack at the enemy and, if she was lucky, a little scuffle with Khyron's incompetents as well.

The Quadrono armor hit thrusters, rocketing for the deck.

Azonia ranted at the com pickup in her flagship bridge command center. "Khyron, come in immediately! Can you hear me? You are in violation of your orders! Therefore, stop this attack at once!"

Perhaps he would claim that his equipment wasn't working properly. That was the damnable thing about the Zentraedi armada, and for that matter their whole instrumentality. With a few exceptions like that bitch Miriya's, Zentraedi war machinery had a far from flawless operational record.

It was only right that warriors care only for war; maintenance and mechanics were work for slaves. But there never seemed to be nearly enough of those, at least ones of any use.

Azonia swore under her breath and waited to see what would happen.

But Khyron wasn't opposed to answering her. He was merely completing his latest maneuver, having leapt his pod high to come down directly over two of the last enemy attack mecha, a pair of Raider Xs, blowing them to bits with the derringer cannon.

"Violation of my orders?" he mocked her. "But I haven't done anything to these despicable Micronians, at least not yet!" He was firing to all sides. "But in the centuries to come, if any of them are left alive, they will speak the name of Khyron with terror!"

"Don't play games with me!" Azonia shouted. "Turn back at once or I'll have you shot!"

The last of the enemy mecha were down, and Khyron was about to lead his forces to the ultimate plunder, when the odds suddenly changed. Aircraft elevator platforms ground up into view to either side despite the fact that the last of the SDF-1 combat aircraft had long since taken off.

They were loaded, instead, with every MAC II Destroid cannon the desperate defenders had managed to get to the trouble spot, arriving in time only because of the attack mecha's courageous last stand and Vermilion's skillful flying. Six of the stumpy, waddling gun turrets were on either elevator, port and starboard.

Mounting six pulsed laser-array cannon and four supervelocity electromagnetic rail-guns apiece, the MACs had the pods in a perfect cross fire—and opened up. What had been imminent victory for the pods became instead a disastrous firestorm.

The rail-guns fired solid slugs at a velocity that delivered incredible kinetic energy on impact, velocities so high that making the slugs explosive would have been redundant. Zentraedi combat armor was no protection, and Battlepods collapsed in on themselves like crushed eggs or came apart in fragments, only to explode instants later.

The MAC's pulsed lasers swept back and forth at the massed alien war mecha, quartering the sky with grazing fire that raked the flight deck, and caught them as they leapt or while still on their feet. Pods went up like exploding oil-well rigs or expanding spheres of shrapnel and flame.

Khyron had instantly leapt his pod away to comparative safety upon seeing the MACs appear. He would have gone truly berserk with frustration and wrath at that point, but his own life was now at stake.

There would be no quick taking of the objective, and SDF-1's deck was being swept clear of his troops. More, Miriya's hated Quadronos were hovering above, out of range but capable of intervening at any moment. But on whose side? In some ways she was as capable of duplicity as Khyron himself.

And then, of course, there was Azonia's promise to have a shot.

He gave a low, bestial growl as he landed his Battlepod on a safer area of the deck, opening his command channel. "All right, men! Cease firing! We're returning to the fleet!"

His mission exec, Gerao, came up over the net, sounding shocked. "Ex-excuse me, mighty Khyron; would you please repeat that? We're going back *now*?"

Khyron could see from his instruments that Gerao was fairly well in the clear and could reach the cruiser quickly. The cruiser was exactly where he'd directed that it be: submerged in the ocean not far from SDF-1.

"Yes." Khyron sneered. "I have just received a direct order from Commander Azonia. "But—don't forget to get your *souvenir*, my friend."

"My *souvenir*?" Gerao's tone said he'd understood Khyron's hidden meaning. "Why, no, sir. I certainly won't forget that!"

Khyron began regrouping his forces for the shameful withdrawal. But part of him burned fusion-bright.

If Khyron couldn't have his victory, he would at least have his revenge!

18

No one, gunner or VT jock or attack mecha crewmember, could recall a more intense fight. Certainly they all earned their pay that day, and a lot more than money besides. Many paid the final price of freedom.

It is interesting to note, however, that although everyone on the VT teams had seen intense combat, it was the men and women of the air-sea rescue teams [whose units had also suffered heavy casualties] who, upon entering the various pilots' hangouts, found that they would not be allowed to pay for their own drinks, period.

Zachary Foxx, Jr., VT: *The Men and the Mecha*

GIANT SAUCER SHAPES THAT WERE ZENTRAEDI AMPHIBIOUS-assault ships dropped from Miriya's cruiser to retrieve Khyron's surviving Battlepods.

At Khyron's order, the first of his retreating units kangaroo-hopped from the SDF-1's deck into the sea to get well clear of the fortress's guns and fighters before making their rendezvous. He'd lost enough of his vaunted strike force without having them and their pickup ships shot out of the sky.

Now it was Zentraedi mecha that fought the holding action as RDF attack machines and VTs pressed them ever harder and turned the kill ratios around. Battlepods bobbed and churned through the waves as the great saucers descended for the rendezvous point.

Overhead, the fighters were still going at it with the Botoru tri-thruster pursuit ships while the SDF-1's gun batteries took more and more enemy ships out of the fight as the tactical and civil defense attack mecha took over mop-up operations on deck.

Elsewhere, Gerao reached Khyron's cruiser as it rose from its submerged position. He gave quick orders as his pod was being brought aboard, preparing to take command and wreak Khyron's vengeance on the Micronians.

Vanessa called out, "Captain, that first enemy cruiser has reappeared! It's on a collision course with us!"

Gloval thumbed the bowl of his empty pipe absentmindedly. "It looks like a suicide maneuver. Lisa, Claudia! Prepare the *Daedalus* for its Attack mode, immediately!"

Up on deck, Vermilion Team had its Veritechs in Battloid mode.

Rick concentrated on control, letting his helmet's receptors pick up his thought-commands and translate them into the Battloid's instant, fluid movements. The Battloid traversed its autocannon from one target to the next, firing depleted transuranic slugs that had awesome, armor-piercing capabilities. The powered gatling consumed ammunition at an amazing rate, and the Battloid had to transfer fresh boxed belts of rounds to it frequently from integral reserve modules built into various parts of its body.

The reloading took only moments, but in the middle of a firefight that could be a long time. Rick found himself on empty as a pod dashed at him. He hit the thrusters built into the Battloid's feet and launched himself at it, just as its cannonade blew up the deck where he'd been standing.

He had no choice but to attack it hand to hand before it could get a bead on him. All around him, Battloids were locked in similar close-quarters fighting against the pods, up and down the SDF-1's decks.

But the alien Battlepod crewman was shrewd and quick. The pod lashed out with one foot and sent Rick's Battloid flying backward with a tooth-rattling jolt. The Battloid crashed to the deck, its pilot dazed.

He shook his head clear just in time to send the Battloid rolling to the side. He avoided the pod's next fusillade, rolled again, and brought the Battloid to its feet dexterously. And now, the chain gun was reloaded.

Rick fired a long burst, taking the pod dead center; he watched it dissolve and fly into pieces, an expanding, blazing sphere. But out of the ballooning explosion zoomed a new enemy, one of those strange alien mecha that had been mostly staying out of the fight up until now.

Whoever was flying it was either a masterful pilot or crazy or both. The battle-armored figure came through the fireball in one piece, though, and nearly bowled Rick over. Its weapons came close to downing Max on one side and Ben on the other as the two Vermilion wingmen dove for cover.

The lightning-fast attacker was gone before they could fire at it, since the SDF-1's surviving batteries were hopelessly slow in tracking it. The three Vermilion fliers got their Battloids to their feet, shaken but unharmed.

"Let's finish this thing!" Rick said in clipped tones. At his command, Vermilion went into Veritech mode, skimming the deck, turning pods into expanding balls of incandescent gas with intense autocannon fire.

The last few pods leapt high, thrusters cutting in, trying for a slim-chance vertical escape while the remaining Botoru pursuit ships dove to try to cover them. The lower battle and the upper became one as the mecha swirled and fought. Rick peeled off to go after two escaping pods.

"So they think they have won, eh?" Khyron mused, his pod standing in the shelter of a superstructural feature of the dimensional fortress's flight deck, hidden and waiting.

Rick bagged the pods, and Ben and Max went back down to take care of an insistent pursuit ship that was still strafing the SDF-1. They returned to Battloid mode, blasting it into ten thousand pieces.

Meanwhile, Rick had picked up two more tri-thrusters on his tail. He led them down to deck level, and Max and Ben bagged them from behind with streams of high-density slugs.

"Nice shooting!" Rick said, relieved. Then he saw what was coming up fast behind him. "No!"

It was the strange alien attack mecha, the one that had nearly nailed him moments before. He braced himself to be hit, perhaps killed, then and there. But it zoomed past, gaining altitude rapidly, pulling away as if the VT were standing still.

Rick realized that it matched the description of that souped-up Zentraedi who had done so much damage to Roy Fokker's Skull Team just before the Skulls recovered the stolen pod in which Lisa, Rick, Ben, and Max had made their escape from the aliens.

Rick cut in auxiliary power, going ballistic, determined to end the warped cat-and-mouse game.

In her special suit of Quadrono powered armor, Miriya laughed scornfully.

Khyron's cruiser was close enough to the SDF-1 that the ship's turret guns were making serious hits on it now. The remaining Battloids on the deck were also keeping up a steady volume of fire at the suicide ship. But that was of no matter; in moments, the battle would be over.

In his massively reinforced command center, Gerao braced for collision.

"Veritechs, be ready to get clear on my command," Claudia said, having taken over some direction of fighter ops while Lisa readied the *Daedalus* Maneuver.

Miriya swept by, only a few feet off the deck. Rick was right on her tail, chasing her high and low, around and around.

She went into another climb, but the irritating Micronian stayed with her in the six o'clock position, chopping away at her with autocannon fire.

Not that it concerned her very much; Miriya was sure she could turn on him and kill him whenever she chose. But she monitored the coming impact of the enormous ships closely. "Khyron, do not fail!"

"*Daedalus* attack in five seconds," Claudia marked. "Four..."

The Terrible Trio braced for collision; the enemy cruiser blocked the sky, growing larger every instant.

In one horrifying moment, Claudia realized that Lisa was paralyzed.

Lisa saw Rick's face, saw poor dead Karl's, saw Kyle's. Over and over, so obsessively that she failed to see the cruiser's bow filling the bridge's forward viewbowl.

"LISA!"

Claudia's shout brought her back at the very last moment. Her hands were reacting even before she could order her thoughts, flying across the controls. She heard herself responding calmly, "Executing *Daedalus* attack now." It was as if someone else were speaking.

They felt the SDF-1 shift, its buoyancy radically altered, as the supercarrier *Daedalus* was lifted clear of the water—a battering ram the size of a hundred-fifty story building. There was the rumble of the dimensional fortress's foot thrusters firing to keep balance. The sea boiled all around them.

The astoundingly powerful Robotech servos lifted the huge flatdeck clear of the sea, thrusting it at the incoming enemy like a titanic warrior throwing a slow-motion punch.

Gerao saw the carrier's prow coming; it was far too late to do anything about it. He triggered his personal ejection mechanism, to flee the ship while he still could, leaving the rest of his crew to perish.

The *Daedalus*'s hurricane bow and can-opener prow had been reinforced by Lang and his technicians to the point where they were all but invulnerable, even against Zentraedi armor. *Daedalus* punched through the cruiser's hull, keelside and forward, as if skewering it. The carrier burst through armor, structural members, bulkheads, and systemry, smashing everything that was in its path as if it were passing through rotted wood and plasterboard.

The cruiser's velocity carried it into the blow, and the SDF-1's incomparable power lifted *Daedalus* and the enemy vessel high. The supercarrier's prow emerged from the cruiser's upper side, protruding more than fifty yards beyond.

Lisa, still monitoring the attack and shaken by her near failure, hadn't noticed that protrusion. She was alarmed that the cruiser's residual momentum was grinding it forward toward the SDF-1 like a wild boar coming up a hunter's spear to deal death before it died.

"Emergency missiles: Fire!" she said, hitting the switch.

High above, the carrier's bow swung open and a thousand missiles screamed out of their launchers. But instead of seeking targets within the enemy vessel, as they were programmed to do and as they had done in the Battle at Saturn's Rings, they boiled out into the open sky.

Here and there they found a damaged, limping Battlepod or a disabled Botoru tri-thruster, obliterating them; but the majority climbed, searching for targets and rose up at—a Veritech.

He juked and hit his countermeasures and jamming gear, giving his ship everything he had while simultaneously screaming over the command net.

"Lisa, this is Rick! I'm in direct line of our missiles! Abort firing! Destruct! Destroy them!"

She'd barely begun when he was yelling, "Mayday! Mayday, I'm hit!"

The jolt to his wing and another to the rear stabilizers, as well as the sudden, uncontrollable spin, let him know that there was no hope of keeping his VT in the air. He was preparing to eject when another missile hit the fuselage forward of the wing—just below the cockpit.

Above the VT that pursued her and slightly farther away from the missile barrage, Azonia gave her powered armor suit maximum emergency power, dodging and diving. The explosions of the missiles that had hit Rick's ship had set off fratricide explosions in other missiles, causing them to destroy one another and upsetting the guidance systems of many more.

She turned, dove, shook off the last of the missiles chasing her, and came back past the SDF-1 in a low pass that clipped the tops off the ocean swells heated by the dimensional fortress's thrusters. Her jamming equipment, the surface clutter, and her own speed and maneuverability had somehow saved her. Unscathed, she flashed into the sky once more as the missile barrage died away.

Khyron's cruiser was beginning to glow and tremble from massive interior damage and ruptured power systems. Claudia and the others moved fast to pull the *Daedalus* free and back away. They were barely clear when the cruiser's engines overloaded and it became a globe of blinding light, rocking the SDF-1 in the water.

"The follow-up missile attack on the enemy was a complete success!" Claudia crowed. "Captain, the enemy ship has been totally destroyed!"

Looking down from his hovering Battlepod, far out of the radius of battle, missile attack, and explosion, Khyron pounded his metalshod fist against the arm of his seat over and over.

"No! My plans can't have failed! Not again! I won't have it!"

Azonia's image appeared on one of his screens. "Well, Khyron, it looks as though your perfect plan was slightly less than perfect. In fact, if it had been any *less* perfect, you'd be dead too!" Her jeering laugh let him know that such an event wouldn't have been so imperfect to her.

The remaining enemy forces withdrew in their big saucer-like amphibious ships. Gloval vetoed any idea of pursuit. "Let's not push our luck *or* theirs, eh? The battle is over." He rose to go. "Just maintain present position."

"Yes, Captain," Claudia responded, when Lisa didn't.

He paused to look back at Lisa. "Oh, and Commander Hayes: I want to commend you on the excellent job you did this afternoon."

They all saw her shoulders shaking as she bent over her console, heard the sobs in her voice as she replied, "Thank you, sir."

Later, as she sat in her cabin, her head whirled with bits and pieces of the things that were tearing at her: Rick. Karl. Kyle. Her father. Gloval. And the fate of all the innocent people on the SDF-1... The cruel faces of the UEDC councilors.

And, more than anything, what she should *do* about it all, because Lisa Hayes wasn't anybody's crybaby.

But she spent most of the time thinking about Rick's frightened voice as the missiles closed in. There's been no word yet of any sightings by the air-sea rescue teams.

In the end it was Rick's voice she heard over and over, Rick's face she saw. Then for a while she did cry, wondering if she would go insane.

"I didn't know! I just didn't know," she wept. Didn't know she would be putting him in danger with the missiles, didn't know how deeply it would affect her and how much she felt for him.

Didn't know if she could go on, if he were dead.

She gazed up to where the bulkhead met the overhead. "Please, *please* don't let him die!"

The Barracuda helo swept in low. The pilot radioed back to the search plane, "Uh, roger, two-niner-niner. I have the dye marker in sight and now have the chute in sight. But I have no movement, I say again, no movement."

The helo descended, churning up the water with the backwash of the rotors. The buoyant VT parachute was below it, lying like a dead sea nettle amid the yellow stain of the dye marker that had automatically been released by the wearer's safety harness on impact with the water.

There was a figure in a flight suit, buoyed by automatic floatation pockets that had expanded when he'd hit, his helmet having sealed itself to keep him from drowning. But all the automatic gear was worthless if he'd been shot while in his ship or coming down.

Big, sinuous shapes were circling; large dorsal fins cut the water. The rescue teams got ready for a pickup while the door gunners did a bit of shark hunting.

Back at the hospital in Macross City, Rick was taken into the ER, priority. The medical personnel continued fighting their *own* battle long after the killing had stopped.

19

It was very strange. It took such an awful mishap to crystallize
something that had been so murky up until then. I'm not much for
romantic fiction or tell-all autobiographies, but from what I'd read,
it's usually something grand and poetic that brings on a realization
like this, not just almost causing somebody's death.

Lisa Hayes, *Recollections*

HE LAY COVERED BY A PROTECTIVE MED-BUBBLE, ATTACHED TO
banks of intensive care machinery.

The monitor-robot overseeing his millisecond-to-millisecond
care recorded:

"Lieutenant Rick Hunter. Multiple lacerations, concussion
and minor skull fractures causing temporary encephalographic
irregularities. No internal damage. This unit will continue to
monitor. Probable symptoms of delirium."

Somewhere deep in his thoughts the word registered, echoing.
Delirium… delirium…

He was off on a midnight roller coaster ride, composed of the
various wonderful and dreadful experiences he had had in wild
juxtaposition throughout the Robotech War.

*He was watching Minmei sing at the Star Bowl, staring at her wistfully. Then
an enormous blue-gray hand reached out of infinite distance and grabbed her
away. Breetai laughed against a field of stars. "You'll never get away!"*

*Rick went after them in his VT, through battle and dogfight, only to be
chided by Lisa Hayes, only to crash in Macross again. He relived episodes of*

his time aboard the SDF-1, while Minmei cried out for rescue. Basic training, friction with Lisa, ratracing against pods and a maelstrom of emotions.

He and Max and Lisa and Ben were on Breetai's ship again. And at last he flew his VT to where Breetai sat in the rubble of Macross City, holding Minmei in the palm of his hand like a trained nightingale.

But she spurned Rick's rescue, because, "Lynn-Kyle told me I can't go out with soldiers." And then it wasn't Breetai holding her but a Lynn-Kyle big as Breetai and wearing the Zentraedi's uniform and metal skullplate and crystal eyepiece.

But Kyle self-destructed, and Rick was saving Minmei again in the fist of his Guardian, as he had the first day they'd met.

"Observation hour ten," the monitoring robby recorded. "Lieutenant Hunter still unconscious. Low-grade fever. Encephalogram remains disturbed."

Rick and Minmei were stranded inside the SDF-1 once more. They stood looking out at the endless Zentraedi fleet, and suddenly it was Lisa standing next to him, then Minmei again. The time stretched out to years.

The Miss Macross pageant and photographers were all mixed into their solitary time together somehow.

"Patient progressing steadily," the robby told itself. "Prognosis good. Anticipated return to consciousness in approximately one hour."

Rick and Minmei went through their pretend wedding once more. But as he kissed her, Dolza came crashing through the bulkhead, and suddenly Rick was standing beside Lisa on the football field-size table in Zentraedi HQ.

"You shall never have Minmei!" Dolza promised.

"You belong to my world now, Rick; you belong to the service," Lisa told him gently, with love in her eyes.

Then it all dissolved into white light for what seemed like a half second. But when he opened his eyes, he was lying in a hospital bed.

Rick sat up, groaning and dizzy. "What a terrible dream that was," he slurred.

Terrible, yes, in parts, it occurred to him, as the dream fragments blurred even as he sat trying to gather them into memory. But some were wonderful, sending emotional surges through him.

And some had just plain shocked him.

The nurse was taking his pulse to verify what the instruments had told her, which made Rick wonder why they bothered with the instruments.

He groaned, bored stiff, and wondered when they would let him get back on active duty; he had the *flight surgeons* to worry about in addition to the attending physicians.

That was assuming, of course, that fighter ops and Gloval would entrust another VT to a pilot who'd managed to stumble into a barrage of his own side's missiles and get shot down by them.

"Oh, brother; what an *ace*," he muttered, thinking that a slightly different pronunciation of the word might be more appropriate.

"Hmm?" asked the nurse. She was young and attractive, with nice legs displayed by the daring hemline of her uniform.

But somehow he wasn't interested. "Nothing. Will I live?"

She dropped his hand and checked his chart. "Basically, you've got a bad bump on the canopy, flyboy. I think you'd better plan on being our guest for a while, Lieutenant, at least until we get the results of your tests back from the lab."

"How come?"

She made a wry face. "So the doctors can find out if it's really true that pilots' heads are made out of granite."

"Why aren't you telling jokes for the USO?"

She patted his shoulder. "Cheer up, Lieutenant. You'll be out of here before you know it."

She turned to go, and he looked out the window at Macross's beautiful EVE sky. "I've got rounds to do," she said. She opened the door. "See you later."

He didn't hear the door close. It took him a moment to realize that he wasn't alone. "Well, look who's here."

Lisa stood in the open door, looking down at her feet. Then she looked up at him miserably.

"Hey, why the long face? Didja come to bury Caesar?"

"Hello, Rick." She walked to his bedside, a small bouquet dangling from her hand. He had a flashback of her face from his delirium but pushed it out of his mind. "I came to apolo—to say I'm sorry," she confessed.

"Apologize? Apologize for *what*, for Pete's sake?"

She turned to put the flowers in a little vase, arranging them so that she wouldn't have to meet his stare. "For your being here. We both know it's my fault that your VT was downed and you were injured."

He couldn't believe what he'd just heard from the ever-in-control Commander Hayes. "Lisa, I have nobody to blame but myself. I made a mistake in judgment and that's *it*, see?"

She brought the flowers to his nightstand. "Thanks for your generosity."

He snorted, "What's happened to that old command confidence? This isn't like you at all."

He still sees me as just a martinet, an old lifer! She went to crumple up the wrapping paper angrily and toss it out. "No, Lieutenant, I don't suppose it is, at that! Anyway—I've said what I came to say, and now I have to get back to my duties on the bridge. Get well."

"Thanks, Lisa. Drop by again?"

As she closed the door: "I don't think so, Lieutenant. I'll be too busy."

On the bridge, Claudia stopped trying to pretend she was taking care of minor duties and turned to where Lisa stood with head bowed over her console, lost in thought.

"How *is* Lieutenant Hunter, Lisa?" Lisa turned around, startled and downcast. Claudia sympathized. "Come on, baby; it can't be as bad as all that."

"You're wrong."

Claudia held folded hands to her bosom. "'And now the sting of Cupid's arrow strikes home!'"

Lisa's mouth dropped open. *"What?"*

"You needn't be ashamed to talk about it, Lisa. I know what it's like to be in love, y' know. Roy and I started out the same way."

"But you two love each other!"

Claudia put her hands on hips. "Of course, silly. So what's the difference?"

Lisa was practically gnawing her fingertips. "I don't think Rick cares."

Claudia leaned close, towering over her. "It's very simple, Lisa. If you're in love with him, go after him! You're in love with Rick Hunter, isn't that true?"

She sighed, nodding slightly. "What should I do, Claudia?"

"Be a woman! Stop moping and—" She gave Lisa a light cuff on the shoulder. "Smile more often!"

The hatch had slid open, and Gloval was on the bridge. "Let me know as soon as logistics has loaded all supplies."

The two women saluted. "It's already been ordered, Captain," Claudia replied.

He studied the two women, so vital to the survival of the SDF-1. "Is there anything else I should know?"

"No, sir," Claudia said blithely. "I was updating Commander Hayes on other military procedures just now."

"Umm." Gloval stroked his dark mustache. "Well, it's unlikely we'll need much hand-to-hand combat expertise up here on the bridge, but carry on."

He turned to go, and Claudia slipped Lisa a wink.

Rick was listening to Minmei singing on the radio, alternatively recalling shards of his dreams and putting them out of his mind, when the door opened and uniforms started pouring through.

"Hi there, buddy. How goes it?"

Roy Fokker grinned, Max and Ben bringing up the rear. "Big Brother!" Rick said happily, sitting up in bed.

"Y' just can't keep outta trouble, can you? Here." He tossed Rick a gift-wrapped package that was just about the right size for a new robe he had no use for.

Ben cocked an ear to the little radio. "Hey, it's Minmei! That's great!" He fiddled with the volume control.

"Aw, can it, Dixon." Rick slapped the thing off.

Ben stood looking bewildered and hurt. "Whatsa matter?"

"I just like it quiet, all right?"

Ben wore his bemused, goodnatured look, scratching a hairstyle that resembled a fuzzy brown turnip. "Absolutely! Anything you say, skipper! You're the boss!"

"So tell me something, y' big loafer," Roy intervened. "When're you gonna quit playing invalid?"

"'Playing' isn't the right word, Roy."

Max grinned. "What you need is a visit from someone like Minmei, to come over and give you a command performance right here."

Rick turned on him so angrily that Max clapped a hand over his own mouth. Then Rick leaned back on his mound of pillows, head resting on hands. "I don't imagine Minmei's very interested in a washout like me."

Ben sounded his heartiest. "Well, then maybe you oughta introduce her to a certified flying ace like myself, Lieutenant." He laughed loudly.

Rick sat up again, fist clenched. "How about a punch in the nose?"

Roy was on his feet, one hand on Ben's shoulder. To Rick, he said, "Easy, tiger; Ben didn't mean anything."

Big as Ben was, Roy lifted him onto tiptoes without much trouble. "Let's go, ace, before you make his condition any worse."

As he dragged Ben off, Roy threw back, "Glad to see you're okay, kid!"

Max asked Rick, "*Has* Minmei been here? I thought the flowers—"

"No; they're from Commander Hayes."

As Roy paused to open the door, Ben got out, "So what's wrong with that?"

Roy caught his arm. "I said c'mon!"

Ben got off a salute and a "See ya later!" before Roy yanked him out of sight.

"Well, it was nice of *her* to bring flowers, wasn't it?" Max persisted. "Uh, skipper?" Rick wasn't listening, arms folded and chin sunk on chest.

Max saluted uncertainly. "Well, get well soon, sir. Be seein' ya."

Out in the street, Roy told Ben and Max, "At this rate he'll be laid up for months. Guess I'll have to do something to get Little Brother out of this depression."

Ben wore an even more baffled look than usual. "But how, Commander?"

Roy wore a rakish smile. "There's only one kind of medicine that I can think of that'll cheer him up."

Variations, his favorite coffee shop, was fairly busy for that time of day, and so Claudia had a little trouble finding him.

She gave him her bright, winsome smile as she joined him at a window table for two. "Hi, hon; what's the urgent summons all about?" She leaned closer to breathe, "Official business or personal?"

He showed a roguish smile. "A little of both."

She looked him over. "This Minmei business you mentioned *better* be the official part."

"Yep. I have a friend who could use some cheering up; I need to talk to her."

She considered that. "Easy enough; she's making a motion picture. You'll find her on the set every day. *Now*, could we get to the personal part, Commander Fokker?"

He leered at her fondly. "How personal d' you wanna get?"

"Dinner tonight?"

He was corning to his feet. "You got it, kid, but only if you make your famous pineapple salad. But I've gotta get going. See you about seven, okay?"

She watched him rush off again. The SDF-1's new predicament—the work to reequip and rearm combat units, train replacements, restock all supplies, do all maintenance and repair work possible—still left them little time together.

Sure, Commander Fokker, she thought calculatingly. *Dinner tonight and, although you may not know it yet, breakfast tomorrow.*

20

So Sammie gave me this puzzled look and said, "But we know perfectly well how bad things look, Claudia. But that's exactly the time when we should go into town and have fun! Didn't you know that?"

All I could do was explain that us old folks are often forgetful and send the Terrible Trio on their way. Whatever they have, there're times when I could sure use some.

Lt. Claudia Grant, in a letter to Lt. Commdr. Roy Fokker

BRON, KONDA, AND RICO LOOKED DOWN AT THE STREET CORNER huckster's portable table, transfixed by fear, awe, and the deeper impulses that their sojourns among the Micronians had awakened.

"Not available in any store!" the huckster ran through his spiel. "Dancing and singing just like the real thing! Batteries not included. Wouldn't you love to have a Minmei doll of your very own?"

Bron, hands clasped reverently, nodded furiously, proclaiming, "I'd *love* to have one of my very own!"

He was squatting now, eyes level with the table, as were his companions. The little mechanical dolls in their bright crimson and gold mandarin robes, black hair bunned and braided like Miss Macross's, didn't actually dance; their movements were more like penguins'. But that didn't stop the gathered children and adolescents from scooping them up.

The huckster, a black-bearded, bald-headed, burly fellow, was doing a land-office business. Nobody even wanted to *look* at bare-chested swordsman dolls or lovable stuffed cutsies anymore. The girls wanted Minmei, the boys wanted mecha—although sometimes it was just the opposite.

"It must be Robotechnology!" Rico muttered to his companions. And a secret weapon, too, he suspected, from its hypnotic effect on him.

The spies had a hopeless long-distance crush on Minmei and an all-consuming yearning to have one of the dolls. But money was still a problem, as it had been since the beginning of their mission.

"We must seize one of them," Konda decided. "On my signal—now!"

They came surging up, upsetting the table and knocking the huckster back off balance as he squawked, "Hey, watch it! Ahh!"

The crowd milled, and shoved; Minmei dolls slid or were lofted all over the place as the huckster landed on his rear.

"Grab it!" Konda yelled, and Rico got his hands on one, taking it quickly but lovingly. The fearless espionage agents made their escape in the confusion, clutching their crucial item of enemy technology. They could hear the huckster swearing that somebody would be made to pay.

They didn't return directly to the hideout they'd established, of course; that would have been poor tactics. They had to make sure they weren't being pursued.

They couldn't risk having their refuge compromised; it was filled with critical pieces of human instrumentation, things that would give Commander-in-Chief Dolza and the other Zentraedi lords vital intelligence data and perhaps the key to overcoming the Micronians. There was a piano, an assortment of movie posters, a box of kitchen utensils, radios, TVs and personal computers, a food processor, a bicycle wheel, several street signs, a Miss Macross jigsaw puzzle, and a jumble of broken toys from the city's charity discard bins that the spies so loved.

Every time they thought about their plunder, the spies' chests swelled with pride. But this! A Minmei doll! A crowning achievement!

The Terrible Trio paced through the streets of Macross City in the throes of a real crisis.

Kim groused, "Will you *look* at us? Walking around town with a day off and nothing to do? No place to go? Ugh, how *boring!*"

"*Ew,*" Vannessa agreed.

"*Yuck,*" Sammie concurred.

To top it all off, they were dressed for a real good time: Vanessa wore white slacks and a Gigiwear sport coat with the sleeves shot back, Sammie was in a prim but cute outfit that looked like she belonged in the Easter parade, and Kim wore a revealing citypants outfit set off by saddle shoes and knee socks.

"And not a man in sight!" Sammie piped up. "It's a lot worse than just *boring!*"

An abrupt commotion off to one side drew their attention. With pounding feet, three figures came dashing, just about *tumbling*, around the corner. There were three guys, a big husky one and a tall lean one and a small, wiry one, panting and frantic. They crowded on top of one another as they hid around the corner, looking back the way they'd come.

The three spies had recently plugged the special Protoculture chip given them by Breetai into an unguarded portion of the SDF-1's systemry. The towering commander had made it clear that the chip was valuable, irreplaceable, one of a very limited number remaining from the research of Zor himself. The chip would slowly draw on surrounding components and the ship's power to create a pod for their escape. Exedore had been loath to spend the irreplaceable chip even on so important a mission, but Breetai had decided that the spies' return must be assured. And so, they must be sure they weren't pursued.

"Anyone following us, Bron?" the little one said between gulps of air.

"What's the merchant doing?" the tall, lean one panted.

Gasping for breath, the husky one said, "He seems to be sitting there, trying to get the other dolls back."

Rico turned, gloating over their prize, holding the little toy up to inspect it gleefully. "Look: *Minmei!*" The other two bent near, feasting their eyes on it. "Ah!" exclaimed Rico. "Robotech—Robo—uhhh."

He'd noticed something; when Bron and Konda looked up, they

too saw three young Micronian females standing nearby, studying them strangely.

Rico was the one among them with a certain presence of mind. He stood up at once, whisking the doll behind his back, sweating profusely. "Um, hello! W-w-we're *strolling*!" The other two nodded diligently in agreement, showing their teeth in unconvincing smiles.

Sammie pointed at them and declared. "Yeah? It looks to me like you're playing with a Minmei doll!"

"D-d-dunno what you mean!" Rico insisted. But the three spies were terrified that their valiant mission had run its course, defeated by the malevolent Micronian genius for war and intrigue.

Sammie shrugged. "It's just that I've never seen a grown man playing with a doll before."

"Adults don't do it?" Bron burst out, trading astounded looks with his cohorts.

Sammie sniggered. "Silly man! Only kids play with dolls."

The spies reflected on the perversely complicated, often contradictory behavioral code the Micronians maintained—no doubt as a safeguard against infiltration by outsiders. A matter of warped genius, and now it had worked; they had blundered and come to the attention of what appeared to be three patrolling secret police.

Vanessa resettled her glasses and took a closer look at the three nerds she and her friends had stumbled across. "What planet d' you come from, anyway?"

Bron went, "Duh," and almost fainted. Konda blurted, "We come from right around here!" and Rico did the best he could, although he was sure they were about to be apprehended and tortured. "Yeah, we work right across the street." He'd heard somebody say it a day or two before, and it seemed to be some kind of verification or identity-establishing phrase.

The spies had learned about "work," a noncombat function considered demeaning and suitable only for slaves among the Zentraedi yet somehow desirable and even *admirable* among the deviate Micronians.

The Terrible Trio looked where he was pointing. It was one of the loudest, most garish spots in Macross City, ablaze with lights and raucous music. The sign over it said, DISCO BAMBOO HOUSE.

Kim clapped her hands. "You mean you work at the disco? We go to the Bamboo House all the time!"

Sammie gave them an even closer look. "I wonder why we've never seen any of you there?"

Bron began, "Uh, what is a dis—" before Rico got an elbow into his middle and he subsided.

Sammie grabbed Rico's wrist. These three guys might be slightly strange, but what the heck? Weird as they were, they worked at the disco, and that would at least mean that they could dance.

"I've got an idea," she said, batting her eyelashes. "Why don't we all check it out together?"

"What a wonderful idea!" Kim threw a fist in the air in elation.

Vanessa figured it was better than another few hours of trudging around town. "I want the big, handsome one," she said, winking at Bron. All the color left his face, and his knees knocked.

Sammie was towing Rico into the street; he didn't dare to resist too much or put up a fight.

"Come with me," she pouted.

"Can't we talk this over?" Rico bleated.

Was this as innocent as the females were making it out to be, or were they superlatively well trained counterespionage agents with a clever plan to drive the Zentraedi spies into paranoid madness and thus make them easier to interrogate?

Bron whispered to Konda, "D' you suppose this disco thing is some Micronian method of torture?"

Kim and Vanessa were looking at them expectantly. Konda hissed, "We must perform our duty as Zentraedi!"

Their chins came up, and their mouths became ruled lines; they advanced bravely to endure whatever sadistic, ultimate torment the experience called "disco" might hold in store.

The cruiser that had been completely destroyed was only a minor part of Khyron's titanic flagship, a part that was now slowly being replaced by the organic growth characteristics of Protoculture.

In the command post bubble overlooking the flagship's bridge,

Khyron stood alone, raging at the figure on the projecbeam screen. He'd driven out all his subordinates, even the faithful Grel, determined that they would not witness his helpless fury before the mockery of the woman warrior Miriya.

"How *dare* you question my leadership abilities?" he railed at her. "Just who do you think you are?"

She stood projected before him, erect and lithe, a tall woman with a flowing mane of green-black hair. She drew herself up even taller. "I am the backbone of the Quadrono Battalion, and the finest combat pilot in all the Zentraedi forces."

Khyron snarled, "Your ego will one day cause your destruction, Miriya."

One corner of her mouth tugged upward. "Just as *yours* caused you to be defeated by the Micronians yet again and made you an object of ridicule to all those whom you command, Backstabber?"

He pointed a finger at her. "Because you have never faced a capable opponent, you believe you're something special. But take care, little Miriya! For there is one aboard the alien ship whom you cannot best!"

She heard the would-be taunt with calm interest. "So! A superior pilot, a super-ace, aboard the SDF-1? Interesting!"

She smiled just the slightest bit, dimples appearing at the sides of her mouth, giving her a beautifully hungry, dangerously feline look. "I'd like to meet him!"

Huh! Everything's phony! Roy thought, looking around the movie set. Somehow he'd never believed it even though that was what people had always said. But the little *Shao-lin* temple and its shrine and the trees, plants, and grass were all a variety of cunningly fabricated plastic and other synthetics from the ship's protean Robotech minifactories.

People were running around yelling, mostly being rude to one another. You could tell who was more important, because the other person would just have to stand there and take it. Roy heard things that would have started major fistfights in a barracks, differences in rank notwithstanding.

A man he recognized as Vance Hasslewood, Minmei's personal

manager and now codirector of her movie, was running around being important. "Let's set up for the next shot!" "Minmei, Kyle: Relax for a few minutes!" "Wardrobe? Listen, sweetie, those blouses are awful!"

Roy tuned him out, strolling around a phony corner and glancing up a phony staircase. "Well, hey!"

Minmei squealed. "Commander Fokker!" and came racing down the steps to him. She wore a Chinese peasant-style tunic and trousers combination, her hair gathered tightly and done up in a long braid in back.

He looked down on her fondly from his rangy height. "How's everybody's favorite recording star?"

She gestured around at the lights and all the other equipment. "Trying to be an actress. I get to play the cute little heroine."

"Sounds like fun," Roy lied; it looked like appalling drudgery, but then, it was probably tolerable to people who couldn't fly.

"Oh, it is!" she enthused. "But—where's Rick? Is he hiding?" She glanced around.

"'Fraid Rick couldn't make it this time."

Her hand flew to her mouth. "He's not hurt, is he?"

"Not seriously, but he's gonna have to spend some time in the hospital, and I thought you might like to stop in and see him."

Roy's voice took on a slightly harder edge. "That is, if you can spare time from all this." He indicated the overturned anthill confusion of the movie set with a disdainful toss of his shaggy blond head. "I'm convinced a visit from you would be worth more than all the medicine in the world."

Minmei had discovered that life on a movie set was a lot less exciting than she'd pictured it—tedious and time-consuming and endlessly repetitive, just the opposite of what she'd envisioned. She still aspired to super-stardom, but the movies' hold over her was less now.

Besides, even though she was flighty, she wasn't blind to the things she owed Rick Hunter. The news that he had been wounded brought out the very best in her—so winning that few people could resist it—and perhaps a sense of *real* drama.

"Of *course* I will! If it weren't for Rick Hunter, I wouldn't even be alive!"

Roy gave her a broad conspiratorial smile. "Atta girl!"

"Commander!"

Roy and Minmei turned together to see Lynn-Kyle striding their way. He glowered at them, an angry young man in a black, white-trimmed jacket and trouser costume. "If you're through wasting Minmei's time, I wonder if we could get back to work?"

Roy took his time staring down his nose at Kyle. He'd heard all the stories about the fight at the White Dragon. He wondered if Kyle had heard the adage that a good big man will beat a good little man every time...

But Roy knew even more about women than he knew about martial arts and, it is a verifiable fact, preferred the former. Kyle was playing the heavy without even being coaxed; let it be so.

"Of course." He smiled blandly at Lynn-Kyle.

A little frown had crossed Minmei's face at her cousin's boorishness. Then Vance Hasslewood was yelling for his stars— the first team, as he called them.

Minmei's mood appeared to brighten; but Roy wasn't sure, and neither was Kyle. She went running toward the set; Kyle spared Roy a steely look and turned to follow.

Roy left the sound stage whistling happily. He was still feeling pretty smug when the com unit in his jeep toned for his attention. "What is it?"

It was Lisa's voice. "Commander Fokker, one enemy ship has broken out of the fleet and is heading this way, closing fast. Two Vermilion Veritechs are on scramble, and Captain Gloval directs you to take command of the flight and intercept."

"Who's on?"

"Sterling and Dixon," Lisa answered. "Captain Kramer will have your Skull Team standing by for backup as needed."

"Good," Roy told her. "If things begin to boil, I always like those Jolly Rogers around."

The EVE system was off, and the distant reaches of the stupendous hold were above him. Roy Fokker roared his jeep down through a quiet Macross, wondering what the fight was going to be like *this* time.

21

There are few more indicative incidents in the Robotech War, from my viewpoint, than this sudden transference of impulse and disobedience from Khyron to Miriya. The evidence of what was happening was all around them, but still the Zentraedi High Command was, in any meaningful sense, blind to it.

Zeitgeist, *Alien Psychology*

"SOUND GENERAL QUARTERS," GLOVAL SAID, HIS CALM, LEVEL voice enveloping the bridge. "Prepare pin-point defense shields. Tell fighter ops to scramble Vermilions."

The new attack had come, as Gloval had feared, right in the middle of his own *political* offensive—his effort to make an end run around the Council.

If anybody aboard the dimensional fortress was curious about his encrypted "back-channel" calls to unnamed addressees since his return from the Alaskan fiasco and his silence on the issue of the Council's insane mandates, they'd kept it to themselves. Good crew! No one could ask for better.

The single enemy ship was drawing nearer. The exhausted and heroic logistics people, straining to do an impossible job of taking on the endless rations, ordnance, equipment, life support consumables, and the rest, had secured themselves; the ship was battening down.

The turnaround time for a supercarrier in pre-Global Civil War days, included shipyard overhaul and the rest, ran as much as six months; the United States Navy was doing well if it had *half* its carrier groups at sea at any one time. The SDF-1 had had less than a week to lick its wounds, and unless Gloval's plan worked, it would get no more, but be driven out into space once again.

In the Disco Bamboo House, the three spies, sweating and exhausted from a brave effort to keep up with the torturous convolutions the Micronian females called "dancing," were shocked and worried by the sudden alarms but also relieved. The Terrible Trio's endurance on the dance floor was simply not to be believed.

The women dove for their things, about to head for the door. Sammie stopped to pat Rico's cheek. "You have the strangest style I ever saw, but it was fun!"

Vanessa gave Bron a quick hug. "Let's do it again soon, boys!" And Kim, blowing a kiss to Konda as she and the others hurried to go, yelled, "We really had a good time!"

Standing there and watching them go, Konda said wonderingly, "You know—I did, too."

The other two looked at him for a moment but then nodded in agreement.

Khyron's words had not seared long at Miriya's pride before she'd taken action.

Now, her own attack cruiser threw off the heat of atmospheric entry unfeelingly, and she and her Quadrono stalwarts poised for the moment when they could go hunting.

Indicators signaled GO. Encased in their top-heavy-looking powered armor, the Quadronos stepped one after another into the drop bays.

They were released seemingly at random but all in a plan to assume a combat-drop formation, backpack thrusters blaring, forming up for the assault on the SDF-1.

Inside the green-tinted face bowl of her interior suit, the light gave Miriya's complexion a verdant tinge. "I am looking for one particular enemy fighter," she told the massed assault mecha behind her. "He will show himself by superior performance. When he has been identified, you will maintain distance and leave his execution to me, personally! Am I understood?"

That was confirmed all through her mingled force of Quadrono mecha and tri-thrusters. Miriya monitored her powered armor and contemplated her kill.

There were so many things that made this violation of standing orders so irresistible! There was the chance to show up that posturing fool Khyron; the opportunity to meet an enemy worthy of her mettle (for in his taunt, the Backstabber had been right on target—she'd never met an antagonist she regarded as her equal); a way to defy Azonia; a chance to have the Robotech Masters *sing* the name of Miriya; a crack at ending this war once and for all, to her own personal glory; and of course that ultimate thrill, flirting with complete disaster.

Because if she failed—and Miriya never had—then all would probably be taken from her, her life included. But what was any of it for, if not for the risking? She lived for combat and victory. It was as easy to keep bleeding prey from the jaws of a lioness, as it was to protect the foe from Miriya's attack.

This time, the SDF-1 was ready.

Cat crews nosed up VTs in the launch boxes; the flight decks of the dimensional fortress and *Daedalus* and *Prometheus* were cluttered with combat aircraft, looking like toys under a Christmas tree from the lofty height of the bridge. The VTs' wings were at minimum sweep, ready for launch.

Lisa Hayes had already given Ben and Max the go. Lt. Moira Flynn, cat crew officer, pointed to her shooter. A moment later, Max Sterling rode a rocket off a bow catapult at 200 knots, while Ben Dixon "*Yahoooed*" off a waist cat a moment later.

Lisa asked over the intercom, "Is Commander Fokker's ship ready for takeoff?"

Claudia left her station—left it entirely!—and strode over to Lisa. "Is *Roy* leading that intercept flight?"

Lisa bit back what she'd been about to say: *You mean he didn't tell you?* "Yes, Claudia."

Roy pulled on his VT helmet—the "thinking cap," as some liked to call it—as his own trusty Skull fighter's forward landing gear was boxed up by the cat crew.

"Good hunting, Commander," Lisa said, her face on his display screen looking as worried and self-contained as ever.

"I'm more interested in hunting for a pineapple salad," he radioed back.

Lisa couldn't quite believe her ears. She tried to get a confirmation on the pineapple salad transmission as Claudia laughed behind her hand and Gloval marveled at the resilience of young people.

Roy, Max, and Ben joined another flight of VTs off *Prometheus*. In command, Roy took them up and up, going ballistic, all of them eager for the dogfight that had been forced upon them. Roy looked at them, a bit dismayed. None of the VTs had fought with Quadronos on an even footing yet, except for Rick, who hadn't come out of it so well.

But Roy remembered the souped-up Zentraedi better than anyone, and if the SDF-1 was facing a division of them, that was all she wrote. Endgame.

"Dogfight?" muttered Ben. "You Zentraedi ain't hardly been bit yet! Now, it's *lockjaw* time!"

Wow, where is this great enemy ace that Khyron fears so? mused Miriya as she and the first few of her armored Quadrono deployed under power to engage a slightly lesser number of enemy aircraft.

She howled a Zentraedi word, a Quadrono battle cry that translated as "Smite them from the sky!"

Immediately the Quadrono battle suits began pouring forth a cascade of fire. The Veritechs dove up into it eagerly, dodging and jamming missiles, betting their reflexes against the enemy's.

Roy did a wingover and banked as a Quadrono's red-hot beams ranged past him. Skull leader did a loop that would have torn the wings off any other fighter ever built, then centered the bulky, top-heavy-looking Quadrono in his gunsight reticle, and thumbed the trigger.

He had a lot of bad-tasting memories in his mouth of how an armored bogey just like this one had rousted him and cost him men in the attack near Luna's orbit. A lot of that pain went away as he watched the Quadrono's head module cave in, then be plowed to nothingness by high-density rounds.

The alien mecha fell, leaving a long, curlicuing trail of oily, red-black smoke.

"Scratch one," whispered Roy Fokker to himself, and went looking for scratch two.

They fought their way up above the cloud cover. One Quadrono burst through, pursuing Ben's banking VT; a second followed, folding into some sort of bizarre fetal configuration, only to bring forth a hornet's nest of missiles.

The missiles moved faster than the eye could follow, detectable only by their flaming wakes and corkscrewing trails of smoke. Somehow, though, they weren't fast enough to get Max Sterling; he twisted and rolled his VT through seemingly impossible maneuvers, jamming some of the missiles' guidance systems, getting others to commit fratricide, and just plain outflying the rest.

He was putting his Veritech through mechamorphosis even before the last of them had gone by. Changing to Battloid mode, he leapt down at his attacker like a cross between a sleek, superswift gunship and Sir Lancelot.

Max fired his autocannon, riddling the Quadrono and blowing it to burning shreds that fell almost lazily. He turned just in time to catch a Quadrono that was trying to sneak up on him. The Robotech chain-gun made its howling, buzzsaw sound again, and the alien became nosediving wreckage.

Miriya had seen it all, the blue-trimmed VT's latest victory in its rampage across the sky. No Zentraedi had been able to stand against it; who else could this be but Khyron's vaunted Micronian champion?

She cut in full power, diving at him like a rocket-powered hawk. "Now you die!"

Except dying wasn't on Max Sterling's agenda today. He dodged her first volley and got a few rounds into her armor as she zigzagged past.

Miriya turned and loosed a flight of missiles that arced and looped at the Battloid, leaving ribbons of trail as graceful as the streamers on a maypole. He dodged those, too, while he charged straight at her, firing all the time. An unbelievable piece of flying.

"You devil!" Miriya grated softly, almost fondly, knowing now what a pleasure it was going to be to kill him. The powered armor and the Battloid whirled and pounced, the upper hand changing sides a dozen times in a few seconds. Miriya was astounded; could this Micronian have artificially enhanced reflexes and telepathic powers? That was certainly the way he flew his aircraft.

She went into a ballistic climb, and Max got a sustained burst into the Quadrono's backpack thruster-power unit. Miriya's mecha trailed sparks and flame as it tumbled back down but suddenly straightened out again; she played hurt and turned the tables once more.

Her particle cannon pounded away at the Battloid, knocking it back as several rounds hit home. Max regained stability by shifting back to Veritech mode and taking evasive action to get a little elbow room before going at it again.

Miriya laughed like some wild huntress and pursued him down through the clouds, crying, "You can't dodge forever!"

"That's very odd," Lisa murmured. "Those alien mecha aren't attacking us. In fact, they seem to be holding off, covering the one that engaged Max Sterling."

Claudia nodded. "It seems like the leader, or whoever it is, has a personal vendetta against Max."

"Who can understand the mind of a combat pilot?" Gloval shrugged. "Especially an alien one?"

"There must be *some* reason Max has been singled out:'

She was right. "Order the lieutenant to retreat. If they continue to pursue him, it will mean that the target isn't SDF-1."

Max received Roy's order with a good deal of bewilderment. "Retreat? Wa-wait, I don't get it!"

It would not be exactly true to say that he was having a good time, but he was doing what he did best—did better than anyone else alive. Bashful, unassuming Max Sterling could afford to be deferential and mild-mannered on the ground. It was a kind of wide-eyed but honest noblesse oblige, because in aerial combat he lived life at lightspeed and ruled the sky.

"That bandit on your tail is trying too hard," Roy explained. "They want to find out what his game is."

"You got it," Max said amicably. He *thought* there was something different about this one. At any rate, whoever this alien was, he was one hot pilot.

Max shoved his stick into the corner for a pushover and dove for the surface of the ocean. The Quadrono powered armor streaked after.

Watching the instruments on the dimensional fortress's bridge, Gloval came to his feet. "So, now we know."

Roy's gift box hadn't contained a bathrobe at all but rather his treasured and superb collection of miniature aircraft.

Rick's favorite was also Roy's: a fragile yellow World War I fighter, a German Fokker triplane with black Iron Cross markings, made at the time of that conflict and nearly a century old. "Fokker, Little Brother, that's me!" as Roy liked to say.

The door opened, and Rick looked to it uninterestedly. Then, abruptly, he was sitting bolt upright in bed. "Minmei!"

She was looking very stylish in a long, red suede coat with white fur collar and cuffs and a pair of yellow tinted aviator glasses. "I hope you don't mind; you didn't look like you were sleeping, so…"

He hastily put the toys aside as she came over to him. Whatever subtle things the movie makeup and hairstyle people were doing to her looked great. "Nice big room," she said brightly, glancing around. Her eyes fell on the flowers for a moment.

"It's wonderful to see you."

"I must look an absolute mess," she fished a little, "but I came right over from the studio when I heard you were hurt."

"How'd you find out? Not many people know." Casualty figures and many details of the war were still classified.

"Commander Fokker told me. He came by the set this afternoon to visit me." She patted the bed. "D' you mind if I sit down?"

That's another one I owe you, Big Brother! thought Rick.

"Mm, this is nice," Minmei said, stretching out at the foot of the bed. Her eyes fluttered, and she yawned charmingly, then laid her head on her arm.

"You look tired."

"I'm exhausted, Rick. There just doesn't seem to be enough time in the day to do the things I'm supposed to do now."

"Would you like to just lie there and get some sleep for a little while, Minmei?"

Her eyes were already closed. "That would be wonderful! If I could just stay here... for a little while..."

She was asleep in seconds. Watching her, he mused, *I don't understand what's happening to our world, Minmei, or what's going to become of us. But your safety and well-being makes everything worthwhile to me.*

He sat with his knees drawn up under the sheet, arms folded across them and chin resting on his arms, watching her sleep. He couldn't remember the last time he'd felt so happy.

"Let's get on with it!" howled Roy Fokker, putting a final burst into a damaged Quadrono mecha and sending another Zentraedi flier to the great beyond. The skull-and-crossbones VT banked and dove, looking for new quarry in a sky crowded with missile tracks, alien beams and annihilation discs, gatling tracers and explosions.

The enemy leader and Max were still battling it out for the championship, but Roy and the other VT pilots weren't about to let the rest of the invaders hang around like wallflowers. The RDF fliers were ready and willing to fill their dance card.

The Quadronos didn't hesitate, either. And so: the dance of death.

Captain Kramer, Roy's Skull Team second in command, had shown up with reinforcements when it became clear that the single combat between Max and the enemy leader wasn't simply a diversionary tactic.

Now, Roy pulled out of an Immelmann, split S and zapped another Quadrono just as he saw Kramer zoom past with a Zentraedi on his tail. Roy went after to help, but he was too late; the captain's ship was already in flames.

"Kramer, punch out, damn it!" Roy yelled, waxing the one who'd hit Kramer. "You're clear, boy! Punch out!"

Kramer ejected as another Skull pilot called the SDF-1 air-sea rescue. The captain should have left his chute undeployed until he had fallen well out of the dogfight, but it opened for some reason. Roy figured that meant that Kramer had been hit and his ejection seat's automatic systems had taken over.

Roy circled anxiously, determined to make sure none of the invaders took advantage of Kramer's vulnerability. The grizzled captain had been with Skull Team for years, had flown off the old flatdeck *Kenosha* with him in the Global Civil War. Kramer was the oldest VT pilot on the roster, and Roy meant to see that he got older.

The Skull Leader was so intent on watching over his friend that for once he was careless. He didn't realize it until bolts from a Quadrono chest-cannon blew pieces from his plane.

"Ahh," he groaned, with pain like white hot pokers being thrust through him. Ben Dixon came to his rescue and engaged the Zentraedi before it could make another pass, but Roy's VT began losing altitude, trailing smoke.

The dogfight raged away from him like a tornado of combat ships and weapons fire as Kramer's limp form glided peacefully toward the sea.

22

There quite simply had never been anything like it, and veteran fighter pilots who witnessed it shook their heads and did quite a bit less boasting for a while.

Zachary Foxx, Jr., VT: *The Men and the Mecha*

MAX AND MIRIYA STILL FOUGHT THEIR INCREDIBLE DUEL ACROSS the sky.

Max had gone back to Battloid mode, and the two darted and zigzagged like maddened dragonflies. Max released another flight of missiles that she avoided, then nearly clipped her with a tracer-bright stream of gatling rounds.

But she evaded him again. It was the most difficult, dangerous, exhilarating contest Max had ever been in; his sense of time had slipped away, and he didn't think of victory so much as excelling, of outperforming his foe.

For Miriya it was different. Not only had she *not* destroyed the Micronian, she'd come very close to being killed herself. He was as good as Khyron had said and better. For the first time, she was beginning to know what her *own* opponents, her long list of kills, had felt.

Perhaps, as the ancient wisdom goes, there is always someone better than oneself. The thought repelled her and filled her with an angry dread.

She came tearing through a small white puff of cloud to see that the SDF-1 was close by. "His ship!"

She made straight for it at maximum speed. Perhaps in tight quarters with his own unprotected fellow beings all around, he would know a hesitation to shoot, would lose concentration.

It was a deliciously audacious, risky plan; she adored it.

"I won't be able to catch him in time!" Max hollered over the command net, seeing what this brilliant, devious enemy had in mind.

"They're heading this way, Captain—straight for us!" Lisa reported.

"Tell the AA batteries not to fire!" Gloval barked. "Sterling is too close to the enemy! Make sure all hatches are sealed! Double-check that all civilians are in shelters!"

The banshee song of sirens echoed through the stupendous hold that housed Macross City.

Rick looked up from his peaceful contemplation of the sleeping Minmei. He got to his feet, then staggered for a moment as his bandaged head pounded like a bass drum. He had no idea what the procedure was for patients and visitors during an alert.

Minmei hadn't even stirred. Rick found the corridor empty; he didn't know it, but doctors, nurses, and other staff members were busy helping priority patients—newborns, intensive care, and other nonambulatories. He could hear internal hatches booming shut.

Rick looked at Minmei; for the moment she was as safe where she was as anywhere he could think of. He had to find out what was going on. Rick trotted off to find someone, his head punishing him with every step.

Most of the exterior hatches on the SDF-1 were sealed, of course, the ship being at general quarters. But one wasn't: the one through which the air-sea rescue helo had just left to make the pickup on Captain Kramer.

The enormous hatch couldn't be closed quickly, but it was more than half closed already. Miriya saw it and dove through it, into the dimensional fortress.

"This is it!" Max steeled himself and followed grimly, his ship in Fighter mode. His rear stabilizers barely cleared the descending upper half of the hatch; the VT's gleaming belly nearly scraped the lower.

He chased the giant powered armor suit through a long curve of enormous passageway usually used to shuttle large machinery, components, and vehicles to and from the fabrication complex situated near Macross City.

"Run, little man, run," Miriya beckoned, watching him, approaching in her rearview screen while simultaneously flying at hair-raising speed through the relatively tight passageway. "And when you catch me, you die."

Rick was gazing out through a permaglass window in the solarium, watching the last few civilians scuttle into shelters, when outside debris began falling from overhead.

An enormous figure dropped to the streets of Macross, making the ship tremble. Rick found himself staring at the back of the Quadrono's head.

They're inside the ship! We're finished! The Quadrono's back thrusters flared, and it went racing down the street, taller than some of the buildings, its backwash nearly knocking out the solarium windows.

Rick had barely regained his balance when another cyclopean form dropped from above. Rick recognized the Battloids's markings as Max Sterling's.

Maybe we're not finished, after all! "Go get 'im Max! Yeah!"

Standing erect like the Quadrono, the Battloid flashed off into the streets of Macross in search of its antagonist.

Miriya wasn't used to such close quarters; though she handled her Quadrono mecha well, she bashed through walls and ripped out overhead signs and fixtures. None of that mattered to her, and it didn't affect the mecha at all.

But Max had the advantage of knowing the streets of the city. Miriya came around a turn to see the Battloid, feet gushing thruster fire, skid to a halt before her.

Several blocks separated them. Max whipped up the long, cigar-shaped gray chain-gun and opened fire from the hip. The hail of massive bullets spattered the Quadrono, holing it in places where its armor was thinnest, driving it back off balance. Do what she might, Miriya couldn't prevent her mecha from being knocked over backward.

The Quadrono heaved itself to its feet again, Miriya caught in a red haze of rage. "You think to do combat with *me*?" she screamed, though he couldn't hear her. "You impudent *fool*!"

No radio reply or translation from Max was needed. The Battloid said it all as it stood waiting, poised, with autocannon ready, allowing her the option. The clearest challenge imaginable.

Her words couldn't dispel the thought that assailed Miriya. *Khyron was right! This Micronian is a* demon *of war!*

"Open the overhead hatch that's nearest to them!" Gloval snapped. "We have to force the alien out of the ship!"

The Quadrono's exterior pickups caught the sound of grinding brute servomotors, and Miriya detected the opening of the hatch above her as she shouldered aside a building, crumbling it to pieces like a plaster model, to get some fighting room.

Her Quadrono fired with the energy weapons built into its giant hands—particle beams and annihilation discs. The Battloid ducked one volley, leapt high on thrusters to elude another.

Then Max started slowly walking his Battloid toward the enemy, still holding his fire until he had a perfect shot, determined that his next burst would end the duel. He was sure the other was enough of a warrior to know just what was happening, a test of nerve and backbone.

How close do we come before we open fire? Who gets rattled and shoots first, afraid to go toe to toe? Afraid to shoot it out point-blank?

It was all so bizarre, so impossibly unlikely, a unique moment in the Robotech War. Max couldn't help feeling like one of the good guys in the Westerns he'd loved so much as a kid. If the Duke could only see this!

The Battloid's footsteps resounded, the autocannon cradled at its side like the Ringo Kid's Winchester. Max was a little too busy to whistle "Do Not Forsake Me, Oh My Darlin'," but he heard it in his head.

Miriya almost fired a dozen times in those moments, but pride kept her from it. If the Micronian had the nerve to close the distance to point-blank—to a distance where they'd almost certainly *both* be killed when the shooting started—then so did Miriya, leader of the Quadrono.

On this, our weddin' day-ayy, went the tune in Max's head.

The Battloid's feet measured off ten yards at a stride; the city blocks between the huge mecha disappeared quickly.

It's not good enough simply to die killing him! Miriya's mind yammered. *He must die knowing that I live!*

Before she could reconsider, the Quadrono's thrusters novaed, and the powered armor rocketed up through the open hatch. She loosed a flock of sizzling missiles, but the pursuing Battloid avoided them and kept coming.

Max mechamorphosed to Veritech mode, chasing her in a ballistic climb. "Turnin' tail, are yuh, pilgrim?"

Then Lisa was saying in his ear, "Return to base, Vermilion Three. You've beaten him."

Not decisively, Max told himself, turning for home. He knew that, and the Zentraedi surely did, too.

Seething, Miriya guided her Quadrono back into the stratosphere. "Miriya will not forget this day, Micronian—and you will pay for it. So I vow!"

Elsewhere, the rest of the VTs were chasing the last of the surviving pursuit ships and Quadronos. Roy, fighting down the pain in his chest, managed to drawl, "Awright. Looks like they've had enough."

"Commander Fokker," Lisa said, "you're losing altitude. Are you all right?"

He smiled into the visual pickup and did his best to sound amused. "Yeah, I'm great. But how 'bout Max?"

"He's fine, Commander."

"And my old buddy Kramer? Any word?"

Lisa's face on the display screen was sphinxlike, unrevealing. "He's in intensive care now, Roy. Come on home."

"Roger, SDF-1; we're comin' in."

"Godspeed."

The dreams had been lovely, but the waking was not.

"Ah, so *here* you are! I been lookin' all over for ya! *C'mon*, Minmei! Wake up! Wake up!"

She didn't want to; she'd always loved to sleep. It was so wonderful and cozy, and her dreams were her very best friends.

Now, though, waking up was easier than being shaken so rudely—almost roughly.

She rubbed her eyes, blinking, and looked up at Vance Hasslewood. "What's the matter?"

He made a big production of his exasperation. "*Sweetie, honey*, you're holding up production, that's what's the matter! You're the star! Without you, they can't finish the picture!"

She yawned, looking around, then stopped suddenly. "Wasn't there a young man in here when you came in the room?"

"Hey! Toots! Are you nuts?" He was yelling now; time was money, and when it came to money, Vance Hasslewood could be very unpleasant. His contract said that he got a percentage of every dollar saved if the picture came in under budget.

"You got a *career* to think about, sweetie! Ya don't have time for this kid stuff anymore, *comprende*?" He looked at the bed. It wasn't at all messed up, barely looked slept in. He breathed a sigh of relief; it looked like there'd be nothing to hush up, nobody to bribe, no favors to call in or promise.

"We have five more setups today!" he snapped. "C'mon, babe; let's go." He grabbed her wrist and dragged her off the bed.

Minmei surrendered and trotted along dutifully. She'd discovered that being a star meant that she had to put up with being herded around. She loved the glamour, but she had never counted on having to be so *passive*. Still, it was worth it, she guessed—wasn't it?

"My dad was right," Vance Hasslewood steamed. "I shoulda been a CPA!"

In the Veritech hangar bays, the maintenance crews were getting to work on the parked aircraft. There had been plenty of damage in the dustup with the Quadronos; nobody on the crews was going to be sleeping very much for the next few days.

Two enlisted ratings had deployed the boarding ladder of Skull Leader's ship, ready to climb up to the cockpit. "Whew! This time he *really* got himself clobbered," one said. "I don't believe he could *taxi* this thing, let alone fly it."

He followed his sectionmate up the ladder, bumping into him when the other stopped short. "Hey, what—"

He swung around and came up the side of the ladder with angled feet, a common practice. And he, too, stopped short when he got a look at the cockpit.

There were bulges in the pilot seat's chickenplate armor and several holes in the back of it. And the seat was red with blood that was now seeping through, running to the floor.

Roy Fokker sat in triage with the others who had been injured. The boys who were really bad had been taken to the ERs first.

Roy had lost a lot of blood, making him light-headed; but the wounds had been closed easily enough, and he was hooked up to a plasma bottle.

"Hey," he asked a passing nurse, "is all this really necessary?" He held up his shunted arm, the plasma tube dangling from it.

"Just shut up and sit there or I'll get Big Bruno the odorly orderly to come sit on that pretty blond head," she said sweetly. She was the same nurse who had looked after Rick, having been mobilized as soon as the alert sounded as part of the special shock-trauma-burn military medical team.

"Doctor Hassan wants a few pictures of your gorgeous insides, dreamboat, to make sure there's no internal hemorrhaging."

Beside being a top-notch RN, she was handsome and leggy and had a way of getting men, even headstrong fighter jocks, to do what she told them. She was an esteemed member of the MM team.

Roy smiled and relaxed, leaning back. She blew him a kiss and went on her way. He felt a little floaty from blood loss, but he'd refused a shot for the pain, so he was lucid.

Then he remembered Kramer. He reached out almost blindly for the nearest institutional-green uniform. "Hey, nurse—"

But he'd grabbed the trouser leg of Dr. Hassan, the stocky heart and soul of the MM unit. Hassan, a surgical mask around his neck, stopped and looked Roy over.

The doctor and the Skull Team leader knew each other somewhat; Roy had had plenty of his men racked up, had been in that same room quite a few times before.

"Kramer?" Roy asked hopefully.

Hassan had almost been out of the medical profession, maintaining a limited practice, doing some consulting and a bit of teaching, for years up until the SDF-1 spacefolded. Time and events had thrust him back into the center of things, and there was no more dedicated individual on the ship. He had originally started easing out of medicine because of moments like this, and these days such moments were all too common.

"I'm sorry, Roy. He was dead before the rescue people even got to him."

Roy squeezed his eyes shut tightly, tears finding their way out the sides, nodding. He forced his fingers to open, to release the leg of the doctor's trousers. But how do you let go of the pain of a close friend's death?

Hassan patted his shoulder. "Take it easy; I want to take a better look at you. Be back in a minute."

Hassan hadn't gone ten feet when an orderly came rushing up to drag him away for an emergency. The nurse was busy with a stat case that had just come in, another downed flier, this one brought in alive by air-sea rescue.

Unnoticed, Roy disconnected the plasma tube, closing the shunt. His flying suit had been mostly cut off him by the medics, but his robe would do until he could get a uniform. All he wanted now was to be with Claudia—to hold her and tell her he loved her and hear that she loved him.

23

These mecha that they're always talking about—those are a perfect symbol of the warmakers. Our lives and the life of our planet are too precious to be entrusted to the military machines!

All they care about are their battles, their glory, their victories. The only thing they love is their endless killing. They want to control us all to make sure that their war goes on and on until they've destroyed the universe.

And I say, we're not going to let them run our lives anymore. Peace, no matter what the price! Peace now!

From Lynn-Kyle's pamphlet, *Let the People Make the Peace!*

CLAUDIA ADORED ROY WITH ALL HER HEART, BUT HONESTLY, sometimes she had difficulty dealing with their love affair—dealing with *him*.

Like now. There he sat on her couch, silent and lost in thought, strumming her guitar softly, his long fingers sure and gentle on the strings. As if he were mute. She made final preparations, the pineapple salad looking magazine-cover perfect.

"All right," she said. "I blew up at Lisa for not telling me you were leading the Vermilions today, but that's squared away between her and me. But what about *you* and me, Roy? It's just not fair to blame me for worrying about you!"

Roy didn't say anything, sitting and strumming. He looked pale and a bit dazed. She made up her mind that he *was* having breakfast with her, and dinner again tomorrow night. She was going to get him to rest even if she had to strong-arm the flight surgeons into taking him off the duty roster!

She turned to look at him from the tiny kitchenette. "I don't think you realize how terrified I get every time you fly off on a combat mission. It's almost as if you pilots think it's all some kind of wonderful game that you're playing when you go up in those Veritechs!"

The music stopped. "It has never been a game, Claudia," he said quietly. "You know that." He wanted to resume his song, to feel connected to the music and to feel connected to Claudia and to feel connected to life.

But his vision was going dim, and he couldn't recall what he'd been playing. He felt cold, unutterably cold.

"Anyway, I said what I had on my mind, and I promise that I'll keep my mouth shut about it in the future," she said, putting a few final flourishes on the halved pineapple.

Claudia told herself to let it drop. They were together, and they would be together that night. She thought of his touch, how tender and caring he could be, how he had always been there whenever she really needed him. And all the other problems vanished; their love had a way of making that happen.

Claudia turned, holding up the salad plate triumphantly. "Well! Don't tell me I put you to sleep!"

His head lay bent back at an awkward angle, the blond hair hanging from it. His hands had fallen from the guitar, and his eyes were closed. He moaned very faintly.

Something about it filled her with a fear worse than anything she'd ever felt on the SDF-1's bridge. "Roy?"

He moaned again, louder, tried to stand up but instead fell, to stretch out facedown on her carpet. The back of his uniform jacket was sodden with blood.

Roy heard Claudia, far away, and wanted to answer but couldn't. He didn't know how he'd forgotten, but there was a mission he had to fly.

There was Kramer now, with the ships waiting to go. Strangest fightercraft Roy had ever seen: far sleeker and more dazzling than Veritechs, and they seemed to shine with an inner light.

But—how had Pop Hunter, Rick's dad and Roy's old mentor, gotten tapped for this mission?

It didn't matter. There were plenty of good men on this one, many of the best Roy had ever flown with. Why hadn't he seen them lately? Not important. Pop Hunter handed Roy his helmet, and Kramer slapped his back in welcome.

Then they were airborne, going ballistic into the blue, free and proud as eagles. What was the mission, again? Oh, yeah; the big one! How could *that* have slipped his mind?

They were going to ride forth and rid the universe of war itself, so that there would be peace, nothing but peace, forever. Then, after this last mission, he could go home and turn in his helmet and never fly another.

He could hold Claudia to him and never let her go.

The fighters climbed, and the sky became lighter instead of darker, and then impossibly bright. With his squadron arrayed behind him, Roy Fokker zoomed straight into the center of the white light.

"I'm terribly sorry, Lieutenant Grant," Doctor Hassan was saying. "We did everything we could for him. But there was massive internal hemorrhaging, and-he had just lost too much blood."

Claudia was shaking her head slowly; she heard the words, understood what they meant, but they made no sense to her. She was looking down at Roy's unmoving body, not believing he was dead.

Hassan and the nurse looked at each other. The doctor had seen this before; he tried to get through to Claudia again.

"It's a terrible tragedy." He gave the nurse a look; she understood the signal, and they turned to leave Claudia for a while so that she could begin the long, painful healing.

"Commander Fokker will be sorely missed," Hassan said, closing the door gently behind him.

Claudia stared down at Roy's face until the tears blinded her, then threw herself to her knees, burying her face in the sheet that covered his chest.

She wept until she thought her heart would burst, unable to

believe he was gone. It seemed that the entire world had simply vanished, leaving nothing but a cold, silent void.

Rick was sitting up in bed, playing with the triplane again, fairly happy, although he didn't realize it. Even worry, lovesickness, and depression couldn't be on the job all day and all night, so his natural resilience had surfaced. He looked up as the door opened.

"Well, hi, Lisa! What's got you out around town on this fine morning?"

Then he saw something in her expression, and all the ebullience went out of him.

Lisa had never been good at this sort of thing; she still didn't understand why she had agreed to be the one to tell Rick.

"Commander Fokker's dead. From wounds suffered during the air battle yesterday."

The little yellow airplane with the Iron Cross markings fell from his limp grasp. "Fokker, Little Brother, that's me!" It hit the floor and broke into a dozen pieces.

"My Big Brother's dead?" He whispered it without tone, with barely the inflection to make it a question, staring at the wall.

When he began weeping into the bunched sheet that he gripped in his fists, racked by sobs that it seemed would tear him apart, Lisa turned to go. But she reconsidered, her guardedness and reserve and the hurt of what she'd taken earlier as his rebuff dropping from her. She went to sit by his side, her arm around him, as he cried inconsolably.

Gloval showed no emotion when he read the casualty report. But he was distant and distracted, remembering the gangling, blond-haired teenager who had flown for him off the *Kenosha*, who had helped him explore the just-crashed SDF-1 when it first came to Earth... who had believed so much that war must end that he was willing to fight for it.

Let him be the last! Gloval thought wrathfully. *They're not sending us out for more killing and dying! If I have to end the Robotech War here on Earth, then I will!*

For more fantastic fiction, author events, exclusive
excerpts, competitions, limited editions and more

VISIT OUR WEBSITE
titanbooks.com

LIKE US ON FACEBOOK
facebook.com/titanbooks

FOLLOW US ON TWITTER
@TitanBooks

EMAIL US
readerfeedback@titanemail.com